AMERICAN
Terrorist

Cover Illustration and Logo: Andy MacDonald
Book and Production Design: Pete Carlsson

Tyler Chin-Tanner: Co-Publisher
Wendy Chin-Tanner: Co-Publisher
Justin Zimmerman: Director of Operations and Media
Pete Carlsson: Production Designer
Erin Beasley: Sales Manager
Jesse Post: Book Publicist
Hazel Newlevant: Social Media Coordinator

American Terrorist, November 2020. Published by A Wave Blue World, Inc. American Terrorist is copyright ©2020 Tyler & Wendy Chin-Tanner. A Wave Blue World and its logos are trademarks of A Wave Blue World, Inc. No part of this publication may be reproduced or transmitted, in any form (except short excerpts for review purposes) without the express written permission of A Wave Blue World. All names, characters, events and locales in this publication are entirely fictional. Any resemblance to actual persons (living or dead), events or places, without satirical intent, is coincidence.

ISBN: 978-1-949518-08-5   Printed in Canada   AWBW.com

Publisher's Cataloging-In-Publication Data
(Prepared by The Donohue Group, Inc.)

Names: Chin-Tanner, Tyler, author. | Chin-Tanner, Wendy, author. | MacDonald, Andy (Artist), illustrator. | Wilson, Matthew, 1981- colorist. | Wiggam, Michael E., colorist. | Carlsson, Pete, letterer.
Title: American terrorist / [script by Tyler & Wendy Chin-Tanner ; art and cover by Andy MacDonald ; colors by Matt Wilson & Michael Wiggam ; lettering by Pete Carlsson].
Description: [Rhinebeck, New York] : A Wave Blue World, 2020.
Identifiers: ISBN 9781949518085
Subjects: LCSH: Political activists--United States--Comic books, strips, etc. | Journalists--United States--Comic books, strips, etc. | Protest movements--United States--Comic books, strips, etc. | LCGFT: Graphic novels. | Political fiction.
Classification: LCC PN6727 .A44 2020 | DDC 741.5973--dc23

Script by Tyler & Wendy Chin-Tanner
Art and Cover by Andy MacDonald
Colors by Matt Wilson & Michael Wiggam
Lettering by Pete Carlsson

Foreword

I hope the world will be in a better place by the time this introduction sees print.

That seems like a taller order than usual today—April 5, 2020—when everyone in the world is rightly consumed with the coronavirus, which continues to spread and leave countless dead in its wake.

The disease would be terrifying by itself, but its socioeconomic impact is just as frightening. The gap between the haves and the have nots seems starker than ever and it emerges from every angle of news coverage. Public schools closing means depriving many children of needed breakfasts and lunches. Shelter in place orders are fine for people whose jobs allowed them to work from home but what about the many who cannot? Celebrity culture has also taken a beating, thanks to some tone-deaf millionaires who seem bored waiting in mansions for the curve to flatten.

There is plenty about the haves and have nots in AMERICAN TERRORIST, which I first wrote about in 2011 in The New York Times. The questions it raised then are as relevant today: What is the dividing line between civil liberties and national security? When does a protest go too far in making its point? Does corporate ownership influence what is presented on the news?

I read a ton of comics every week, trying to keep up with my favorite characters and looking for potential story ideas. Many of the plot lines are of the moment. In rereading AMERICAN TERRORIST for this introduction, I was impressed by how timely it still is nearly 10 years since it was first published. I have to tip my hat to Tyler and Wendy Chin-Tanner. The graphic novel made me feel sad and frustrated for the characters, which is a good sign as to how well they are written. There are a lot of ideologies represented, but the characters are well grounded and seem like people you could meet.

The art and design team deserve a shout out as well. Andy MacDonald is asked to draw a lot—classrooms, therapy sessions, standoffs against law enforcement, a violent protest in Times Square and much more—and enlivens all the scenes with rich details. The sequence in Chinatown felt especially real, down to its funky (and accurate) curved street. I was particularly enamored by the color work of Matt Wilson and Michael Wiggam. There is something lulling about the bookcases in the therapist's office and the cafe in which Hannah Bloom spills coffee on her laptop. A shout out also to the lettering and design work of Pete Carlsson, who provides elegant chapter breaks.

I've just now—this moment—decided to make a reread of AMERICAN TERRORIST an every decade event.

I hope the world will be in a better place when I read it again in 2030.

- George Gene Gustines

George Gene Gustines is a senior editor at The New York Times. He began writing about the comic book industry in 2002 and hopes to continue for many more years. He also wants to land a comic book story with his byline on the front page.

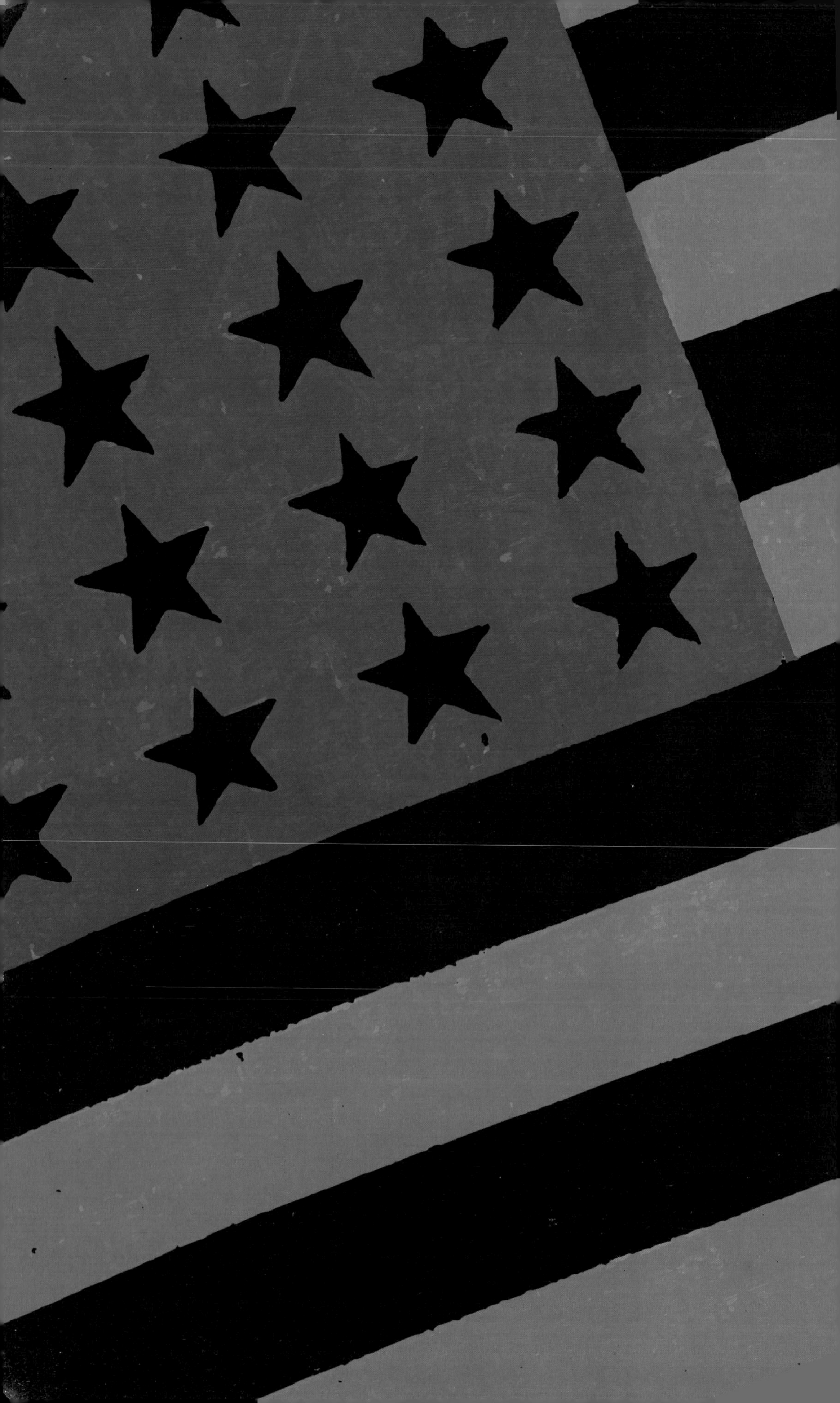

Chapter 1

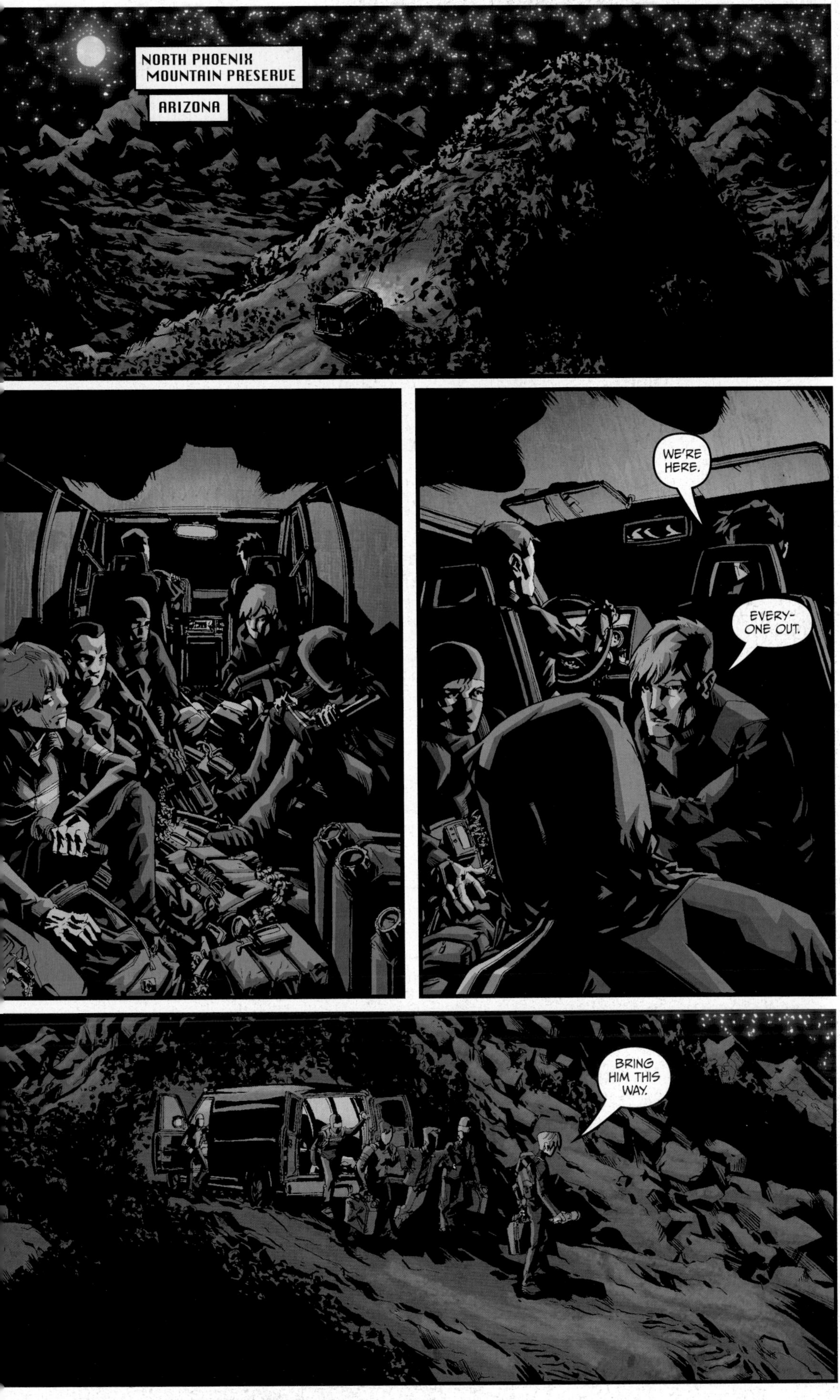
NORTH PHOENIX
MOUNTAIN PRESERVE
ARIZONA
WE'RE HERE.
EVERY-ONE OUT.
BRING HIM THIS WAY.

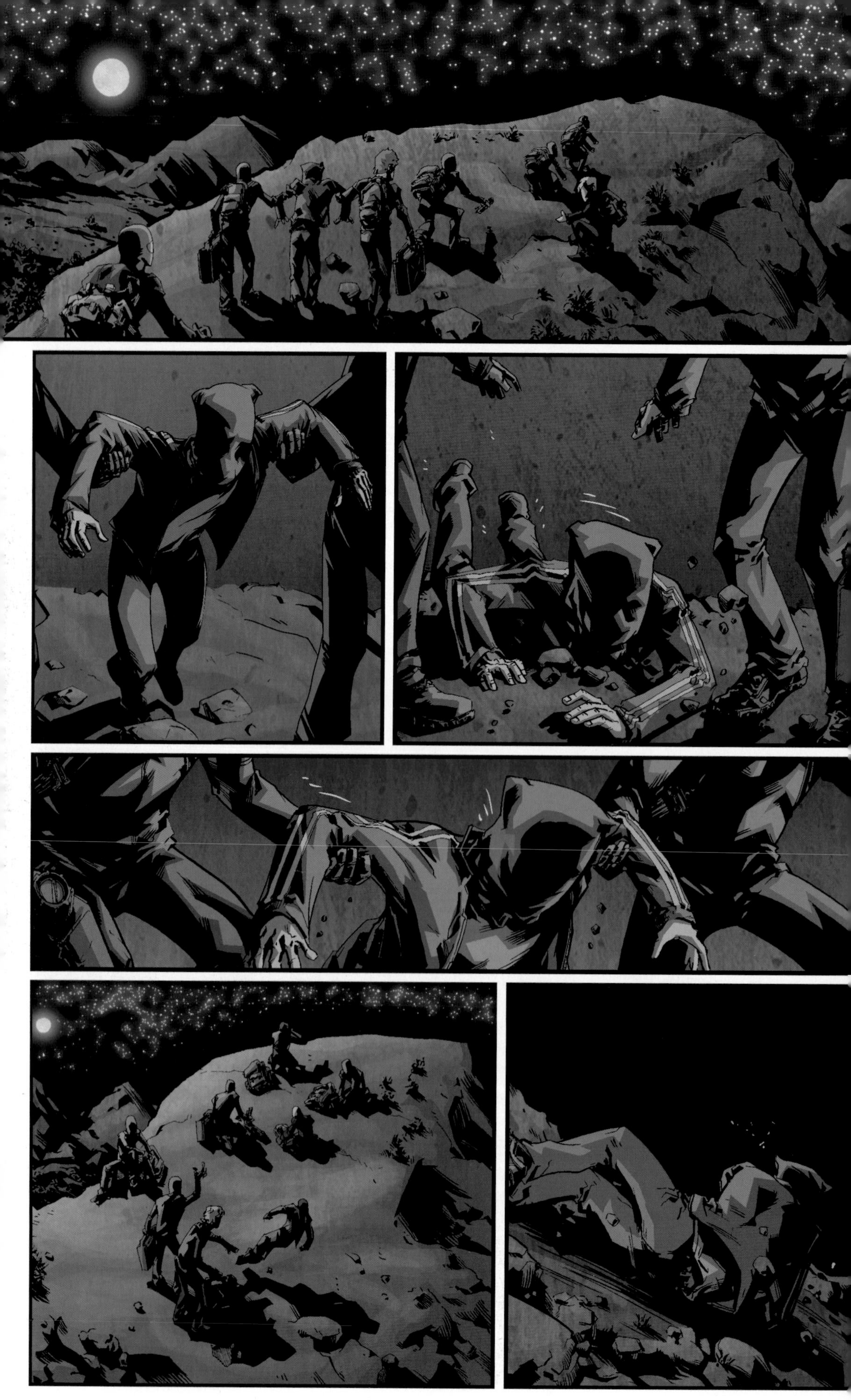

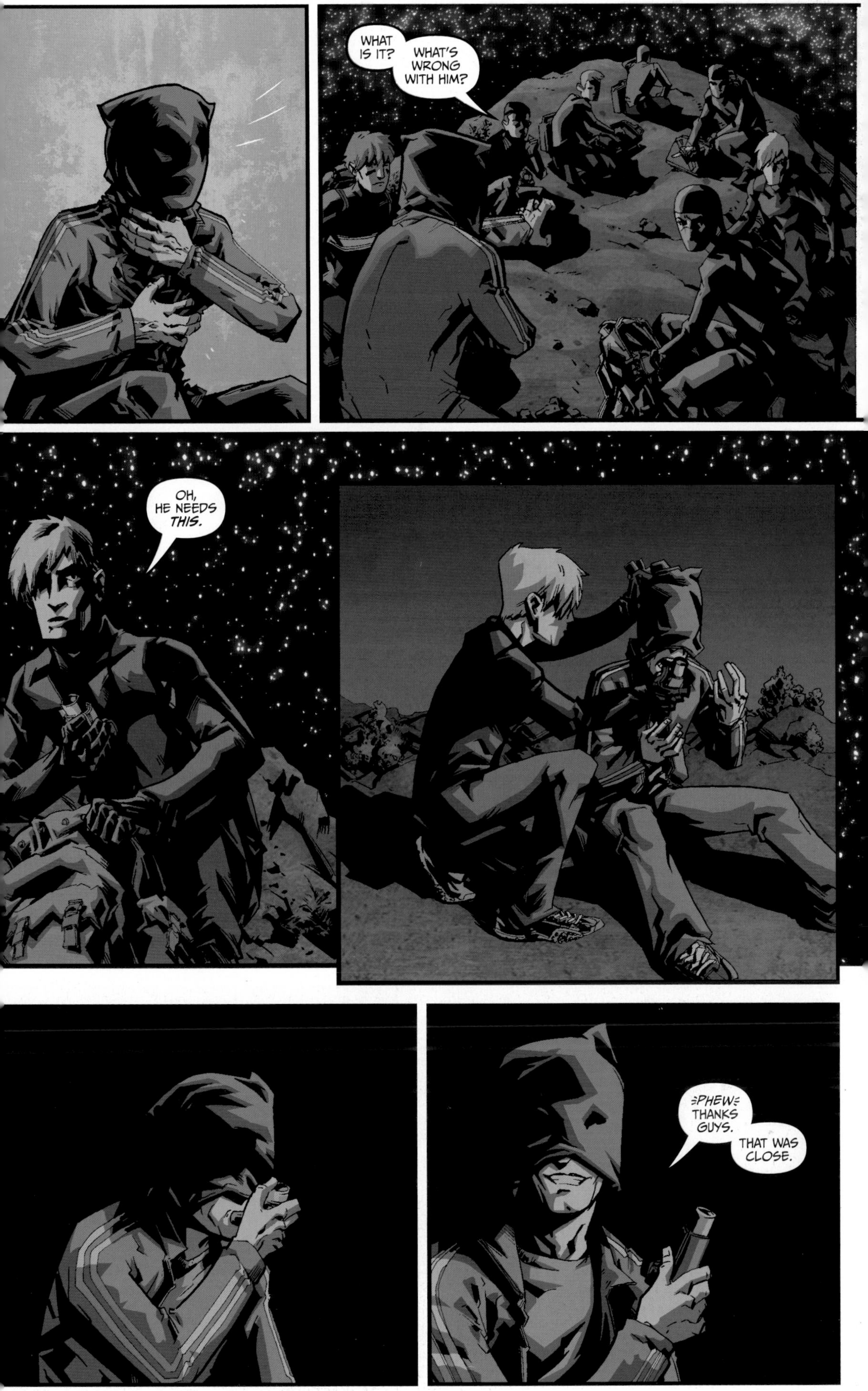
WHAT IS IT?
WHAT'S WRONG WITH HIM?
OH, HE NEEDS *THIS.*
=PHEW= THANKS GUYS.
THAT WAS CLOSE.

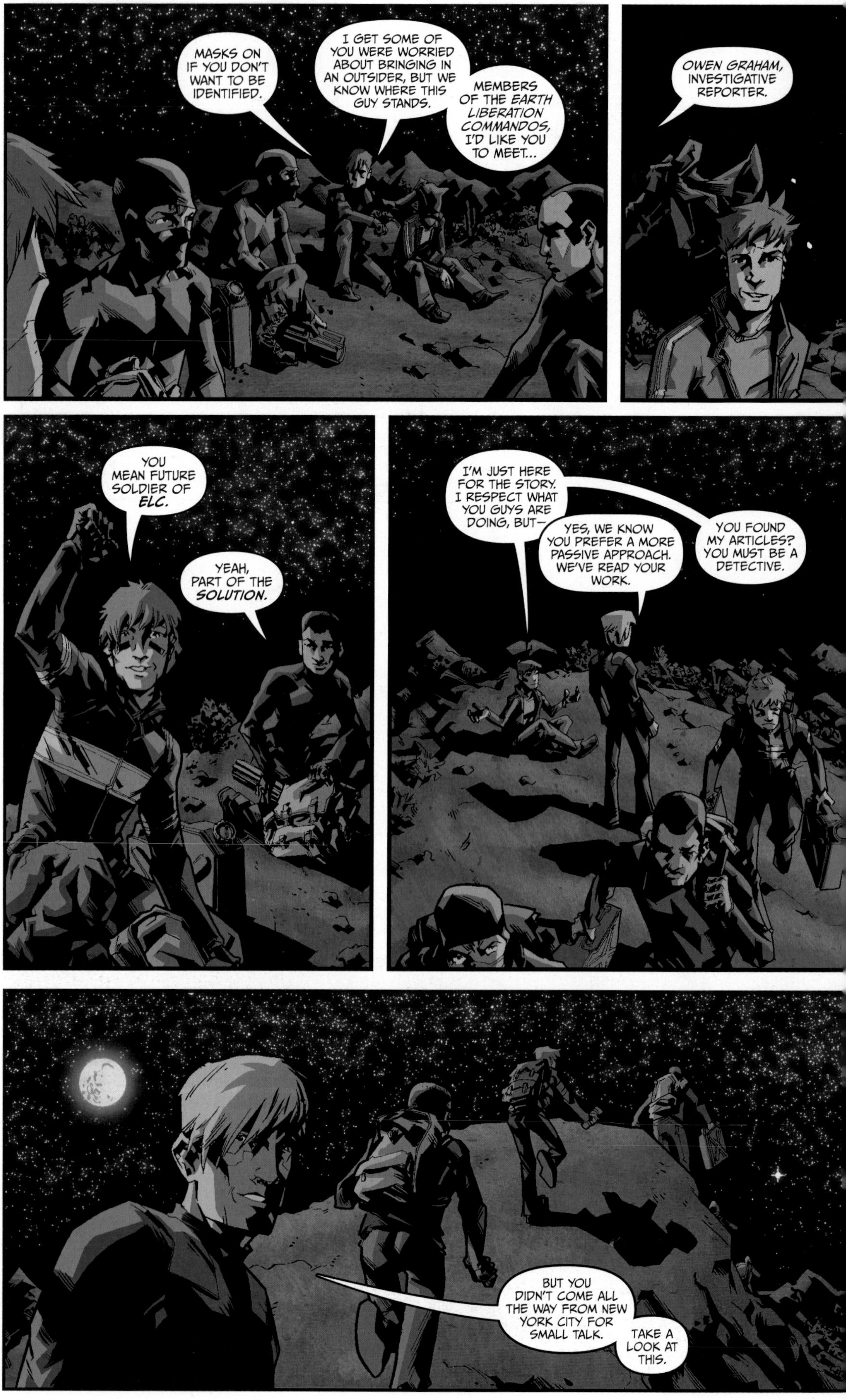
MASKS ON IF YOU DON'T WANT TO BE IDENTIFIED.
I GET SOME OF YOU WERE WORRIED ABOUT BRINGING IN AN OUTSIDER, BUT WE KNOW WHERE THIS GUY STANDS.
MEMBERS OF THE EARTH LIBERATION COMMANDOS, I'D LIKE YOU TO MEET...
OWEN GRAHAM, INVESTIGATIVE REPORTER.
YOU MEAN FUTURE SOLDIER OF ELC.
YEAH, PART OF THE SOLUTION.
I'M JUST HERE FOR THE STORY. I RESPECT WHAT YOU GUYS ARE DOING, BUT—
YOU FOUND MY ARTICLES? YOU MUST BE A DETECTIVE.
YES, WE KNOW YOU PREFER A MORE PASSIVE APPROACH. WE'VE READ YOUR WORK.
BUT YOU DIDN'T COME ALL THE WAY FROM NEW YORK CITY FOR SMALL TALK.
TAKE A LOOK AT THIS.

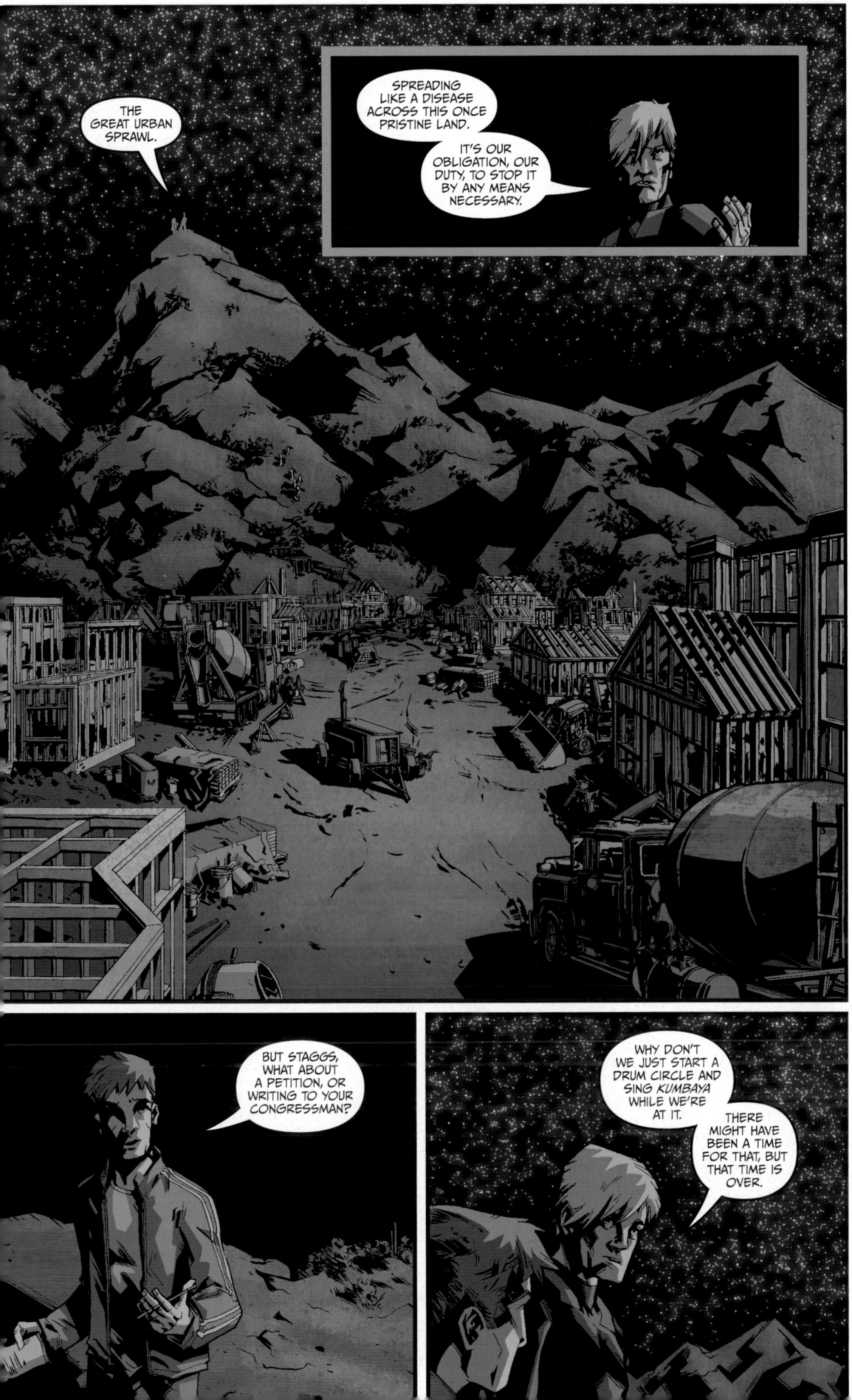
THE GREAT URBAN SPRAWL.
SPREADING LIKE A DISEASE ACROSS THIS ONCE PRISTINE LAND.
IT'S OUR OBLIGATION, OUR DUTY, TO STOP IT BY ANY MEANS NECESSARY.
BUT STAGGS, WHAT ABOUT A PETITION, OR WRITING TO YOUR CONGRESSMAN?
WHY DON'T WE JUST START A DRUM CIRCLE AND SING *KUMBAYA* WHILE WE'RE AT IT.
THERE MIGHT HAVE BEEN A TIME FOR THAT, BUT THAT TIME IS OVER.

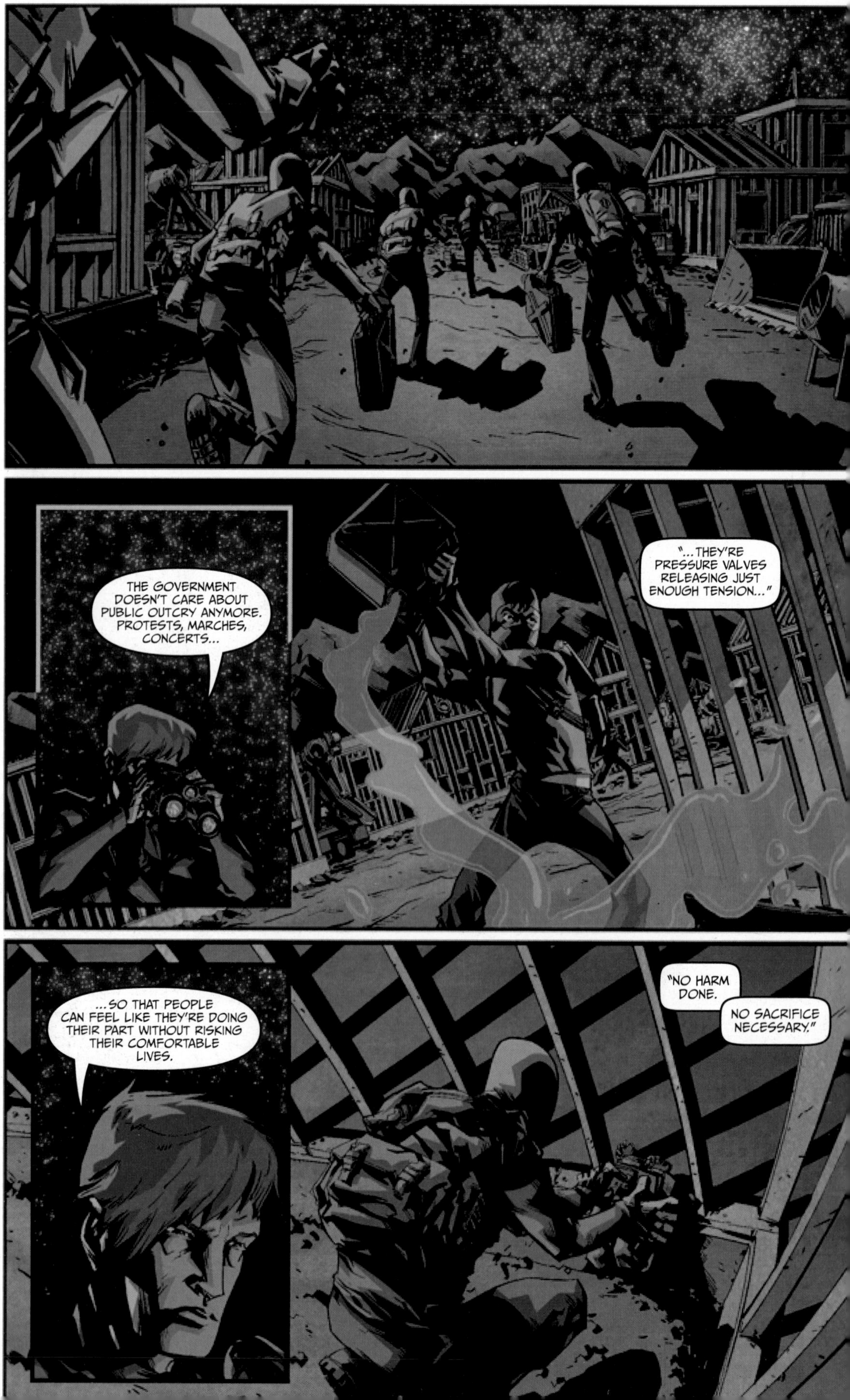
THE GOVERNMENT DOESN'T CARE ABOUT PUBLIC OUTCRY ANYMORE. PROTESTS, MARCHES, CONCERTS...
"...THEY'RE PRESSURE VALVES RELEASING JUST ENOUGH TENSION..."
...SO THAT PEOPLE CAN FEEL LIKE THEY'RE DOING THEIR PART WITHOUT RISKING THEIR COMFORTABLE LIVES.
"NO HARM DONE.
NO SACRIFICE NECESSARY."

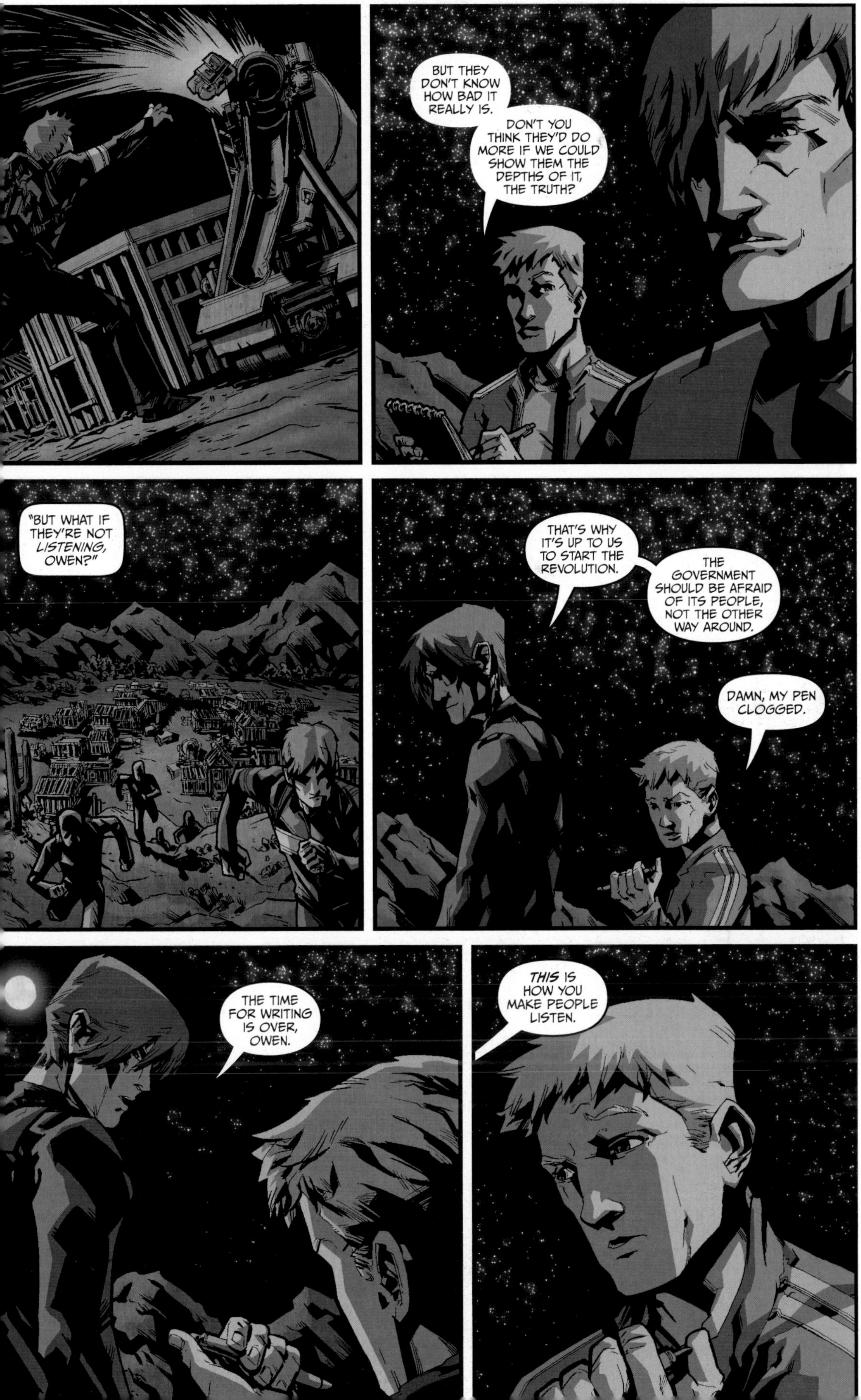
BUT THEY DON'T KNOW HOW BAD IT REALLY IS.
DON'T YOU THINK THEY'D DO MORE IF WE COULD SHOW THEM THE DEPTHS OF IT, THE TRUTH?
"BUT WHAT IF THEY'RE NOT *LISTENING*, OWEN?"
THAT'S WHY IT'S UP TO US TO START THE REVOLUTION.
THE GOVERNMENT SHOULD BE AFRAID OF ITS PEOPLE, NOT THE OTHER WAY AROUND.
DAMN, MY PEN CLOGGED.
THE TIME FOR WRITING IS OVER, OWEN.
THIS IS HOW YOU MAKE PEOPLE LISTEN.

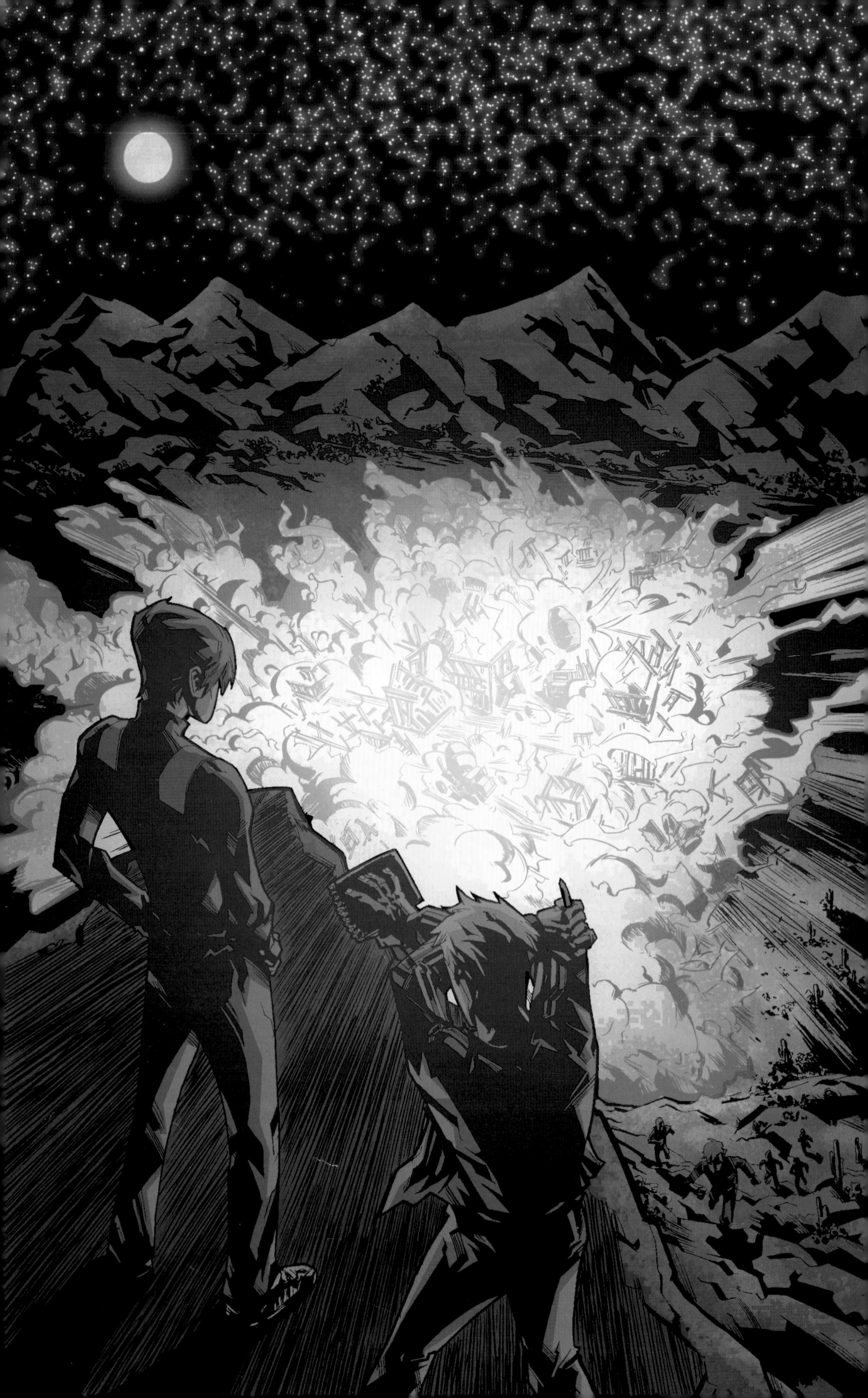

AMERICAN
Terrorist

Created by
Tyler and Wendy Chin-Tanner
& Andy Macdonald

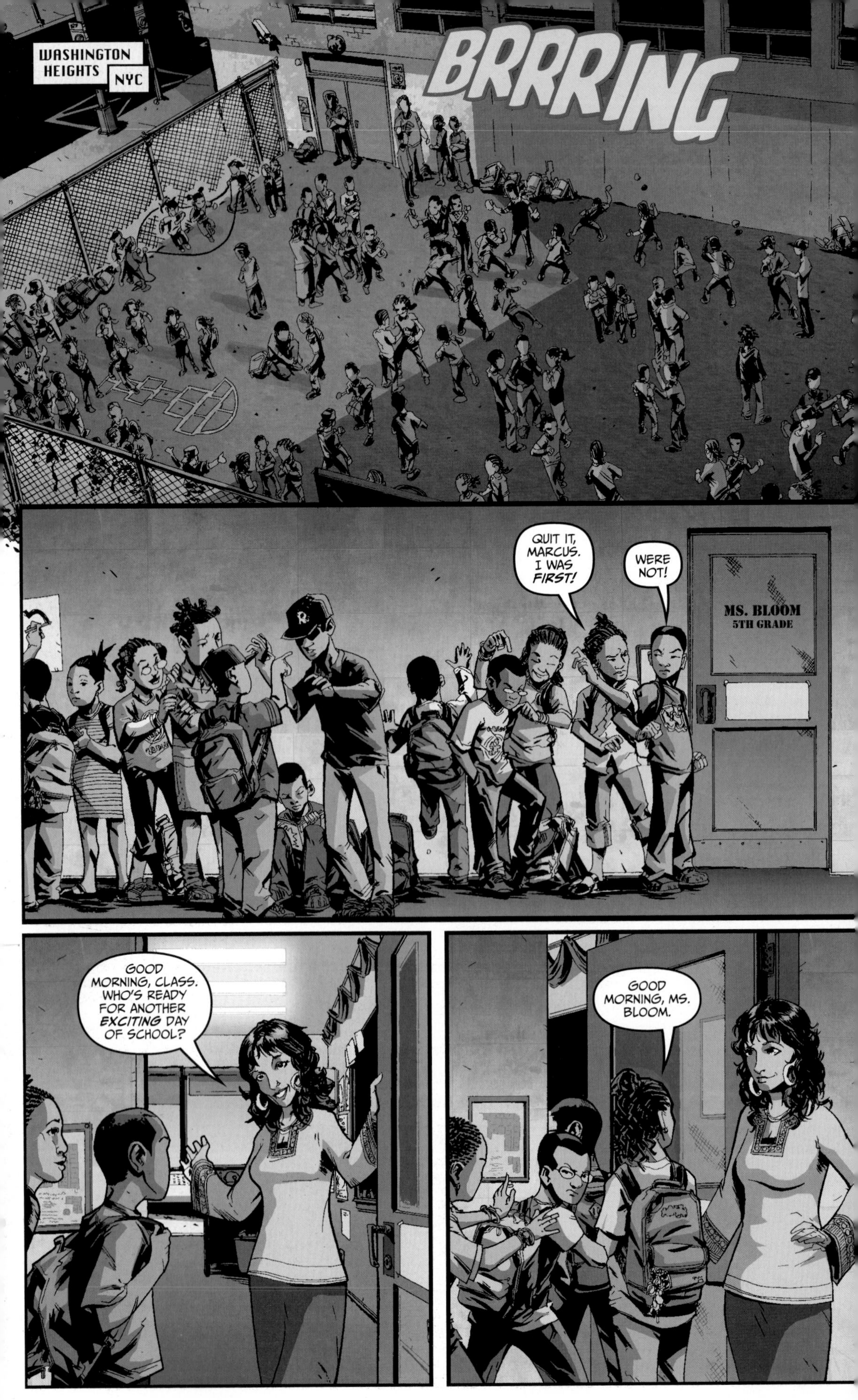
WASHINGTON HEIGHTS
NYC
BRRRING
QUIT IT, MARCUS. I WAS *FIRST!*
WERE NOT!
MS. BLOOM
5TH GRADE
GOOD MORNING, CLASS. WHO'S READY FOR ANOTHER *EXCITING* DAY OF SCHOOL?
GOOD MORNING, MS. BLOOM.

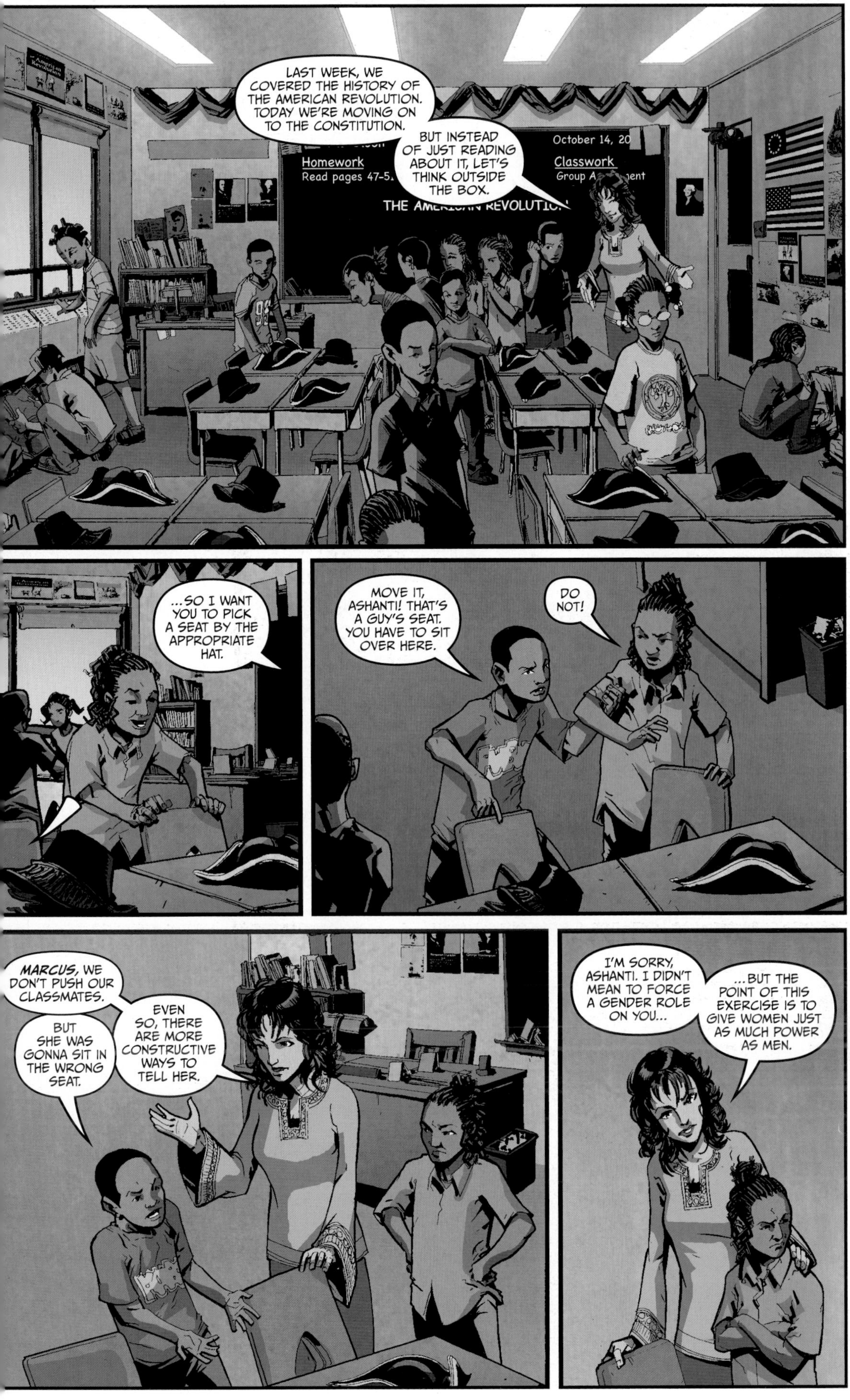

LAST WEEK, WE COVERED THE HISTORY OF THE AMERICAN REVOLUTION. TODAY WE'RE MOVING ON TO THE CONSTITUTION.
BUT INSTEAD OF JUST READING ABOUT IT, LET'S THINK OUTSIDE THE BOX.
October 14, 20
Homework
Classwork
...SO I WANT YOU TO PICK A SEAT BY THE APPROPRIATE HAT.
MOVE IT, ASHANTI! THAT'S A GUY'S SEAT. YOU HAVE TO SIT OVER HERE.
DO NOT!
MARCUS, WE DON'T PUSH OUR CLASSMATES.
BUT SHE WAS GONNA SIT IN THE WRONG SEAT.
EVEN SO, THERE ARE MORE CONSTRUCTIVE WAYS TO TELL HER.
I'M SORRY, ASHANTI. I DIDN'T MEAN TO FORCE A GENDER ROLE ON YOU...
...BUT THE POINT OF THIS EXERCISE IS TO GIVE WOMEN JUST AS MUCH POWER AS MEN.

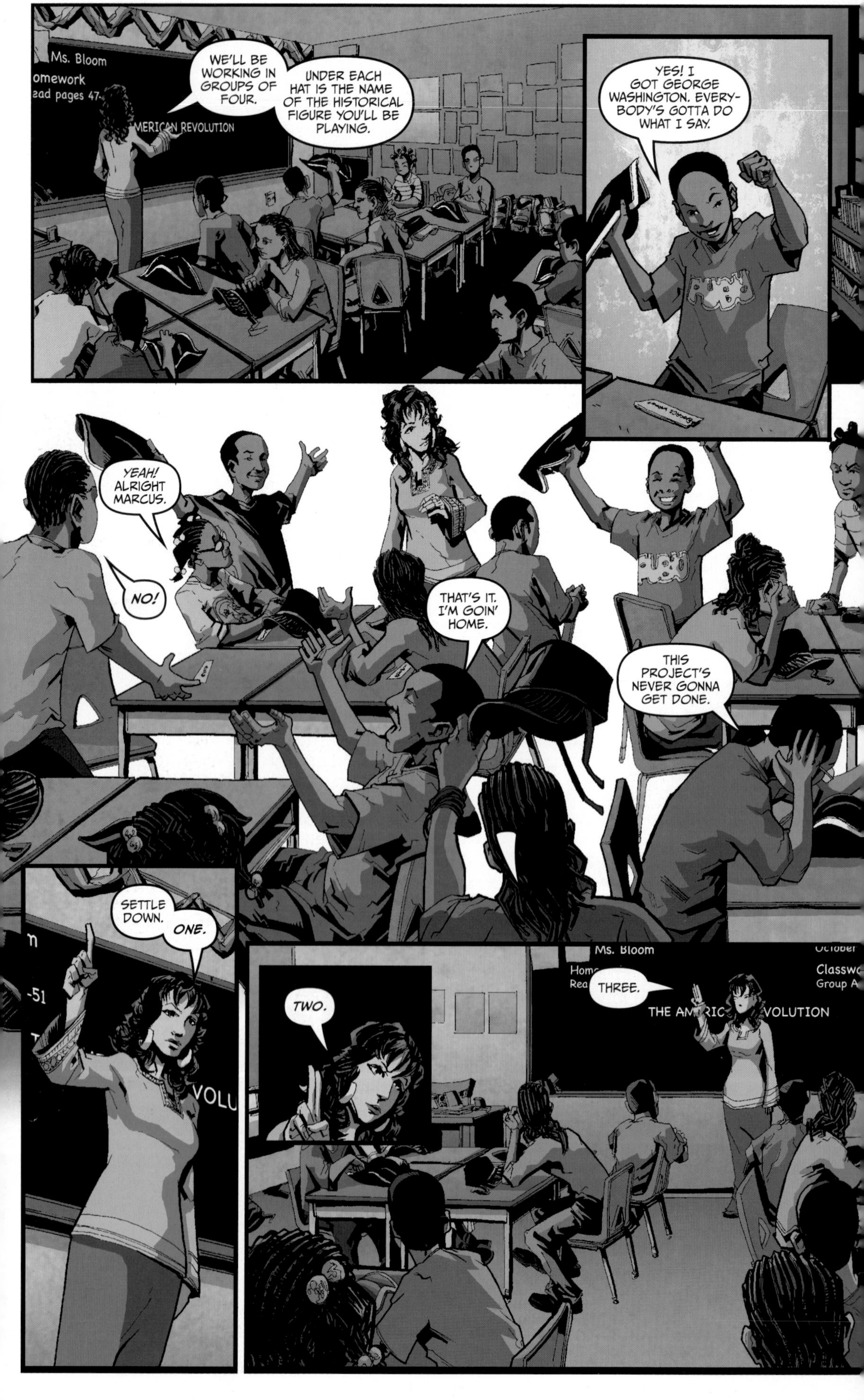
Ms. Bloom
omework
ead pages 47-
MERICAN REVOLUTION
WE'LL BE WORKING IN GROUPS OF FOUR.
UNDER EACH HAT IS THE NAME OF THE HISTORICAL FIGURE YOU'LL BE PLAYING.
YES! I GOT GEORGE WASHINGTON. EVERYBODY'S GOTTA DO WHAT I SAY.
YEAH! ALRIGHT MARCUS.
NO!
THAT'S IT. I'M GOIN' HOME.
THIS PROJECT'S NEVER GONNA GET DONE.
SETTLE DOWN.
ONE.
-51
VOLU
TWO.
Ms. Bloom
THREE.
THE AMERIC VOLUTION
Classw
Group A

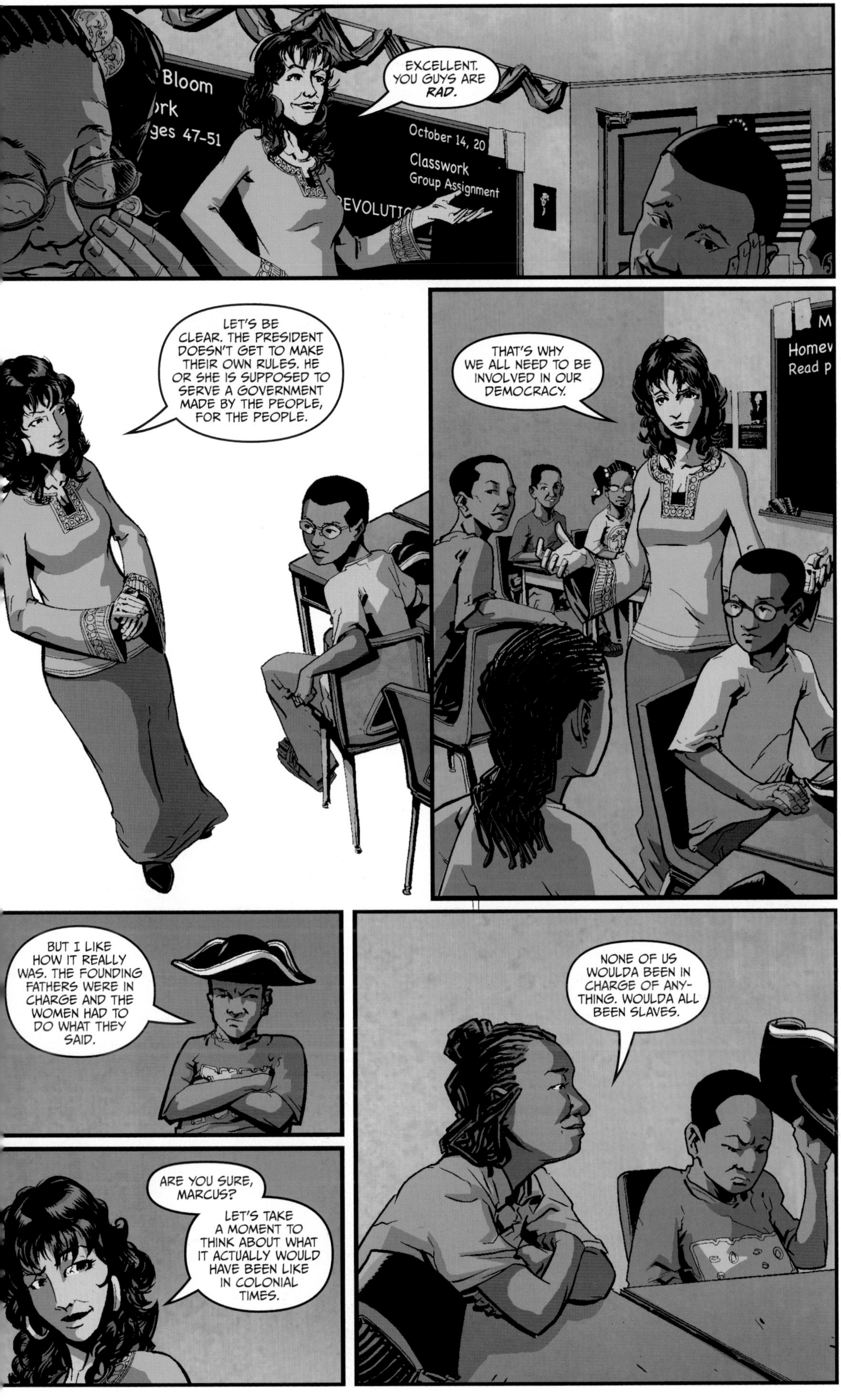
Bloom
rk
ges 47-51
October 14, 20
Classwork
Group Assignment
REVOLUTI
EXCELLENT. YOU GUYS ARE *RAD.*
LET'S BE CLEAR. THE PRESIDENT DOESN'T GET TO MAKE THEIR OWN RULES. HE OR SHE IS SUPPOSED TO SERVE A GOVERNMENT MADE BY THE PEOPLE, FOR THE PEOPLE.
THAT'S WHY WE ALL NEED TO BE INVOLVED IN OUR DEMOCRACY.
BUT I LIKE HOW IT REALLY WAS. THE FOUNDING FATHERS WERE IN CHARGE AND THE WOMEN HAD TO DO WHAT THEY SAID.
ARE YOU SURE, MARCUS?
LET'S TAKE A MOMENT TO THINK ABOUT WHAT IT ACTUALLY WOULD HAVE BEEN LIKE IN COLONIAL TIMES.
NONE OF US WOULDA BEEN IN CHARGE OF ANY-THING. WOULDA ALL BEEN SLAVES.

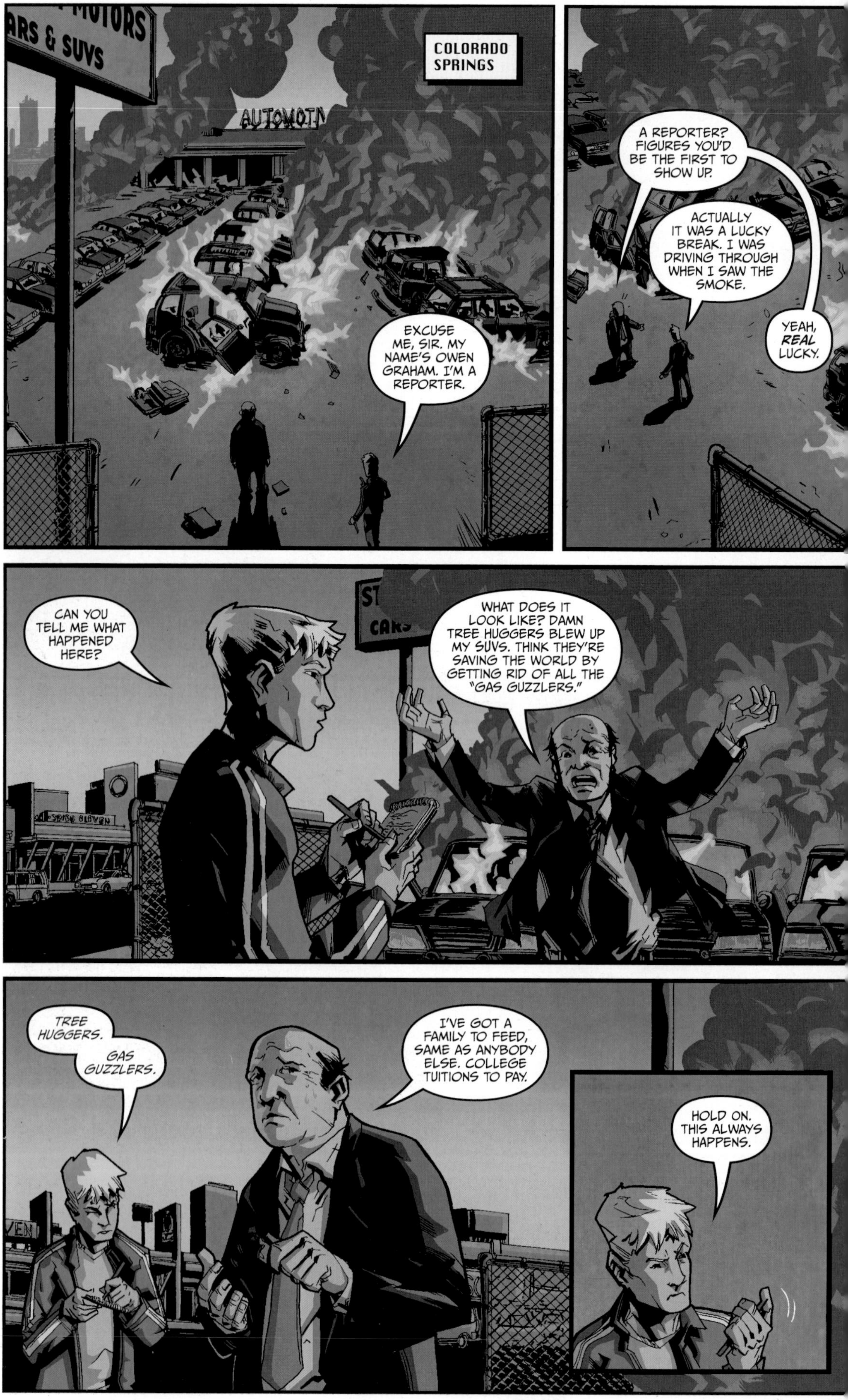

ARS & SUVS
COLORADO SPRINGS
AUTOMOTIV
EXCUSE ME, SIR. MY NAME'S OWEN GRAHAM. I'M A REPORTER.
A REPORTER? FIGURES YOU'D BE THE FIRST TO SHOW UP.
ACTUALLY IT WAS A LUCKY BREAK. I WAS DRIVING THROUGH WHEN I SAW THE SMOKE.
YEAH, *REAL* LUCKY.
CAN YOU TELL ME WHAT HAPPENED HERE?
WHAT DOES IT LOOK LIKE? DAMN TREE HUGGERS BLEW UP MY SUVS. THINK THEY'RE SAVING THE WORLD BY GETTING RID OF ALL THE "GAS GUZZLERS."
TREE HUGGERS.
GAS GUZZLERS.
I'VE GOT A FAMILY TO FEED, SAME AS ANYBODY ELSE. COLLEGE TUITIONS TO PAY.
HOLD ON. THIS ALWAYS HAPPENS.

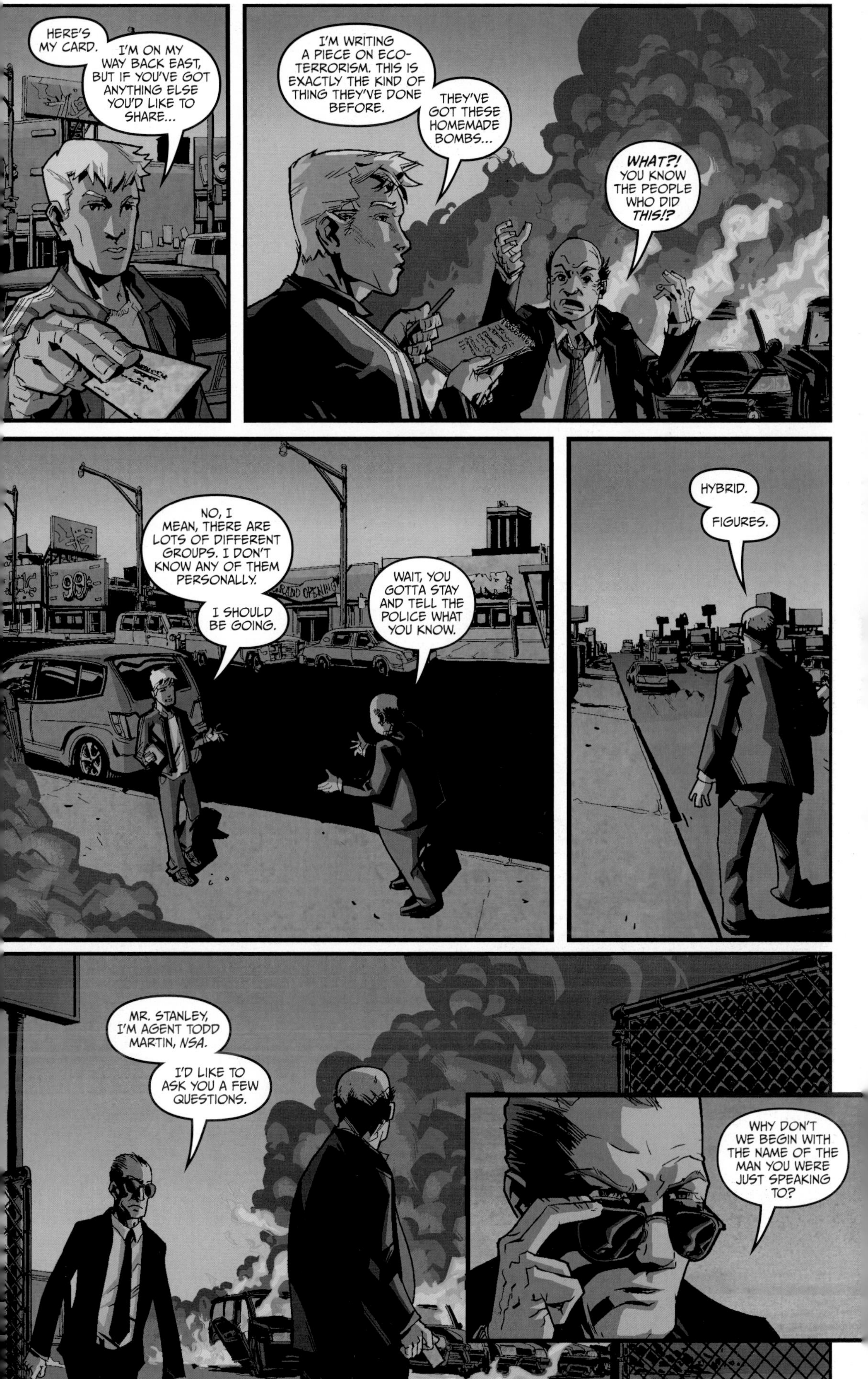
HERE'S MY CARD.
I'M ON MY WAY BACK EAST, BUT IF YOU'VE GOT ANYTHING ELSE YOU'D LIKE TO SHARE...
I'M WRITING A PIECE ON ECO-TERRORISM. THIS IS EXACTLY THE KIND OF THING THEY'VE DONE BEFORE.
THEY'VE GOT THESE HOMEMADE BOMBS...
WHAT?! YOU KNOW THE PEOPLE WHO DID THIS!?
NO, I MEAN, THERE ARE LOTS OF DIFFERENT GROUPS. I DON'T KNOW ANY OF THEM PERSONALLY.
I SHOULD BE GOING.
WAIT, YOU GOTTA STAY AND TELL THE POLICE WHAT YOU KNOW.
HYBRID.
FIGURES.
MR. STANLEY, I'M AGENT TODD MARTIN, NSA.
I'D LIKE TO ASK YOU A FEW QUESTIONS.
WHY DON'T WE BEGIN WITH THE NAME OF THE MAN YOU WERE JUST SPEAKING TO?

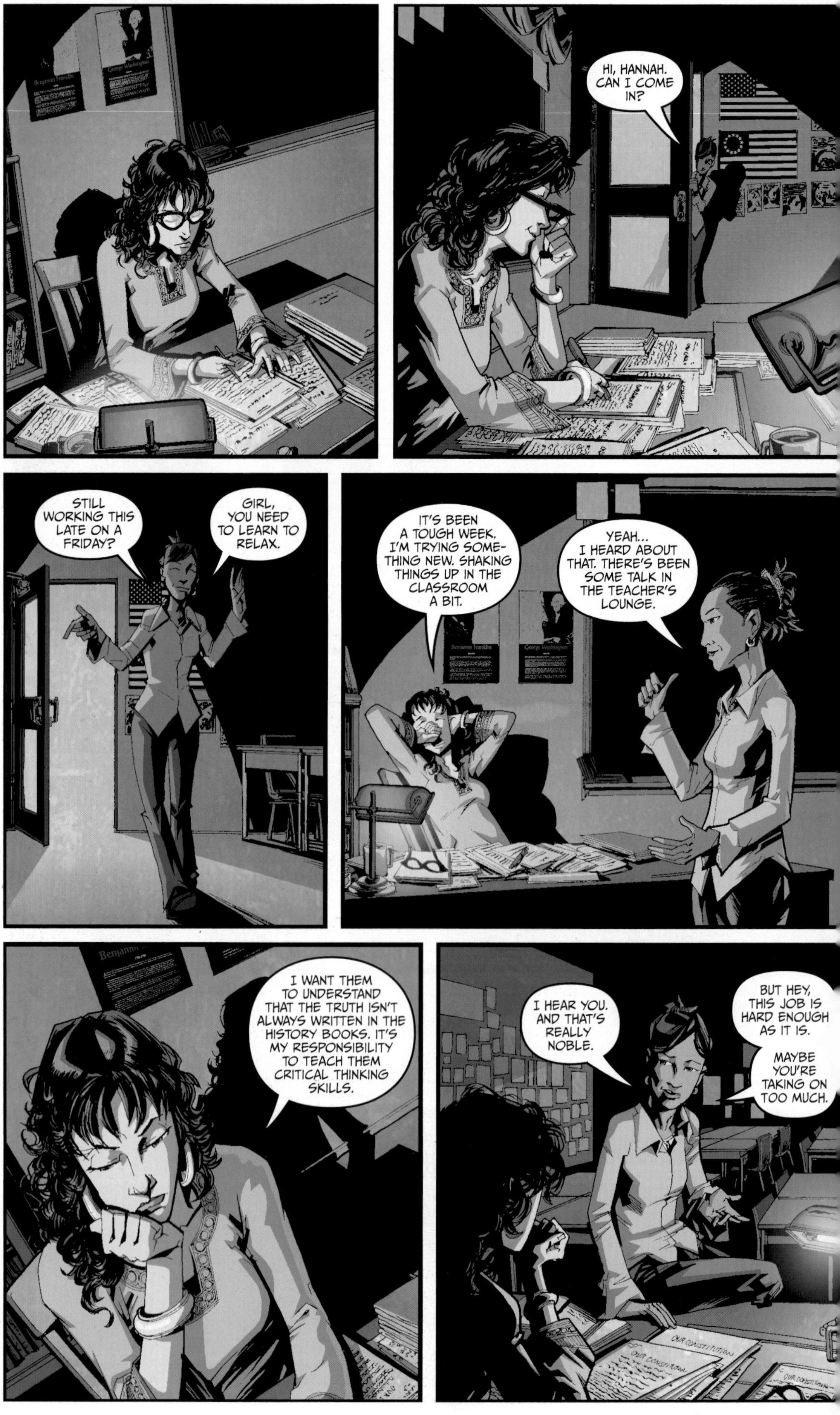
HI, HANNAH. CAN I COME IN?
STILL WORKING THIS LATE ON A FRIDAY?
GIRL, YOU NEED TO LEARN TO RELAX.
IT'S BEEN A TOUGH WEEK. I'M TRYING SOMETHING NEW. SHAKING THINGS UP IN THE CLASSROOM A BIT.
YEAH... I HEARD ABOUT THAT. THERE'S BEEN SOME TALK IN THE TEACHER'S LOUNGE.
I WANT THEM TO UNDERSTAND THAT THE TRUTH ISN'T ALWAYS WRITTEN IN THE HISTORY BOOKS. IT'S MY RESPONSIBILITY TO TEACH THEM CRITICAL THINKING SKILLS.
I HEAR YOU. AND THAT'S REALLY NOBLE.
BUT HEY, THIS JOB IS HARD ENOUGH AS IT IS.
MAYBE YOU'RE TAKING ON TOO MUCH.

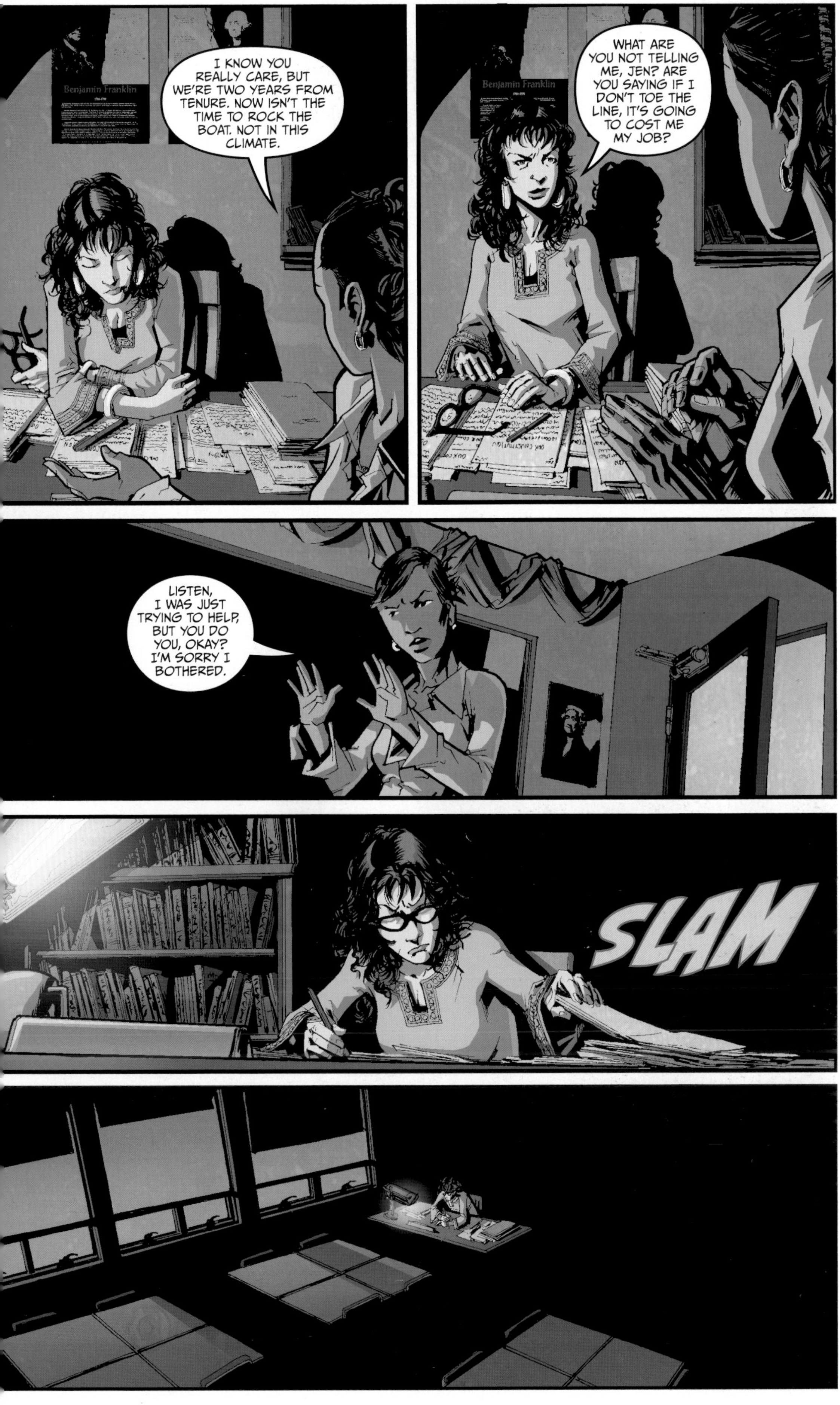
Benjamin Franklin
I KNOW YOU REALLY CARE, BUT WE'RE TWO YEARS FROM TENURE. NOW ISN'T THE TIME TO ROCK THE BOAT. NOT IN THIS CLIMATE.
WHAT ARE YOU NOT TELLING ME, JEN? ARE YOU SAYING IF I DON'T TOE THE LINE, IT'S GOING TO COST ME MY JOB?
LISTEN, I WAS JUST TRYING TO HELP, BUT YOU DO YOU, OKAY? I'M SORRY I BOTHERED.
SLAM

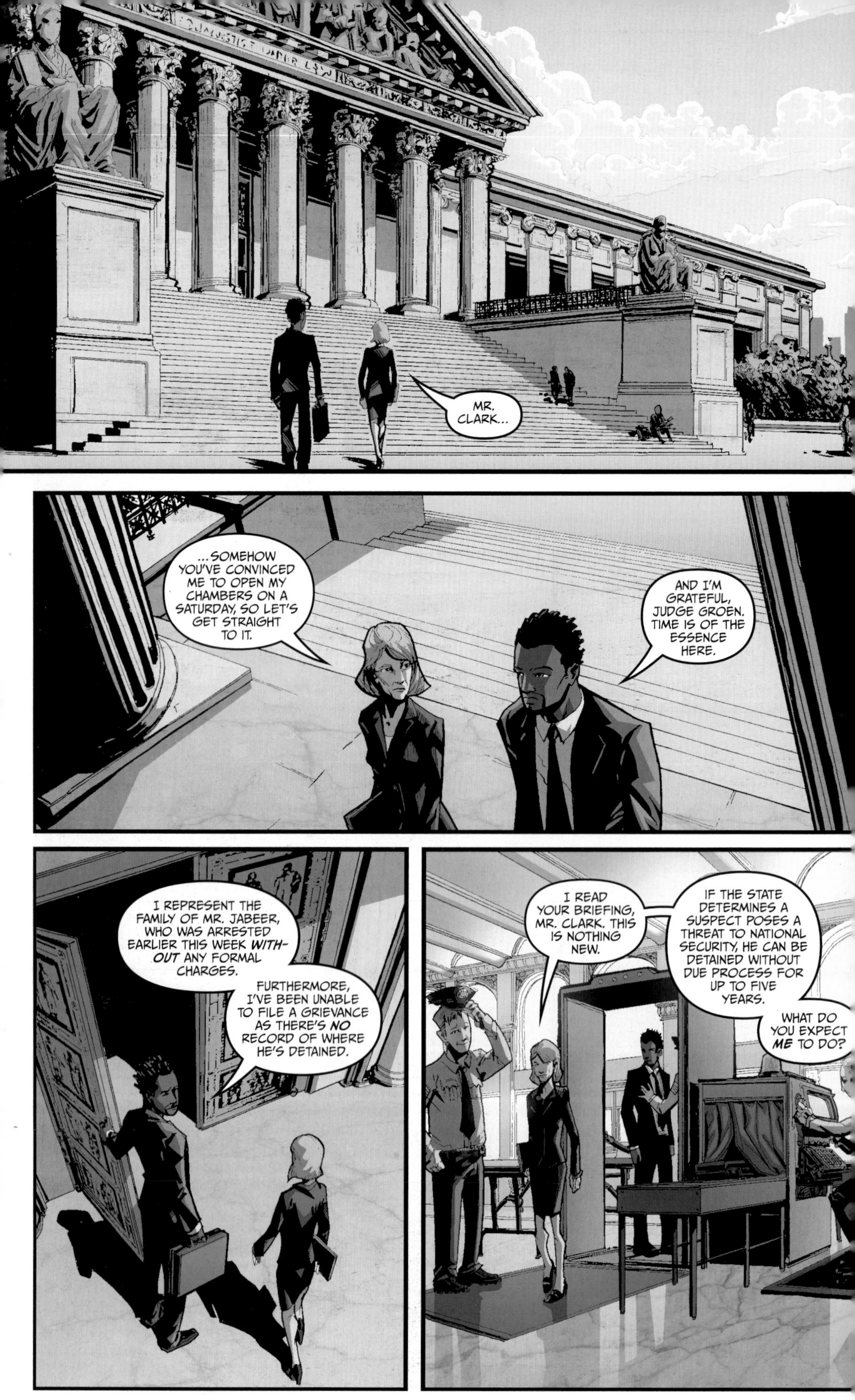
MR. CLARK...
...SOMEHOW YOU'VE CONVINCED ME TO OPEN MY CHAMBERS ON A SATURDAY, SO LET'S GET STRAIGHT TO IT.
AND I'M GRATEFUL, JUDGE GROEN. TIME IS OF THE ESSENCE HERE.
I REPRESENT THE FAMILY OF MR. JABEER, WHO WAS ARRESTED EARLIER THIS WEEK *WITH-OUT* ANY FORMAL CHARGES.
FURTHERMORE, I'VE BEEN UNABLE TO FILE A GRIEVANCE AS THERE'S *NO* RECORD OF WHERE HE'S DETAINED.
I READ YOUR BRIEFING, MR. CLARK. THIS IS NOTHING NEW.
IF THE STATE DETERMINES A SUSPECT POSES A THREAT TO NATIONAL SECURITY, HE CAN BE DETAINED WITHOUT DUE PROCESS FOR UP TO FIVE YEARS.
WHAT DO YOU EXPECT *ME* TO DO?

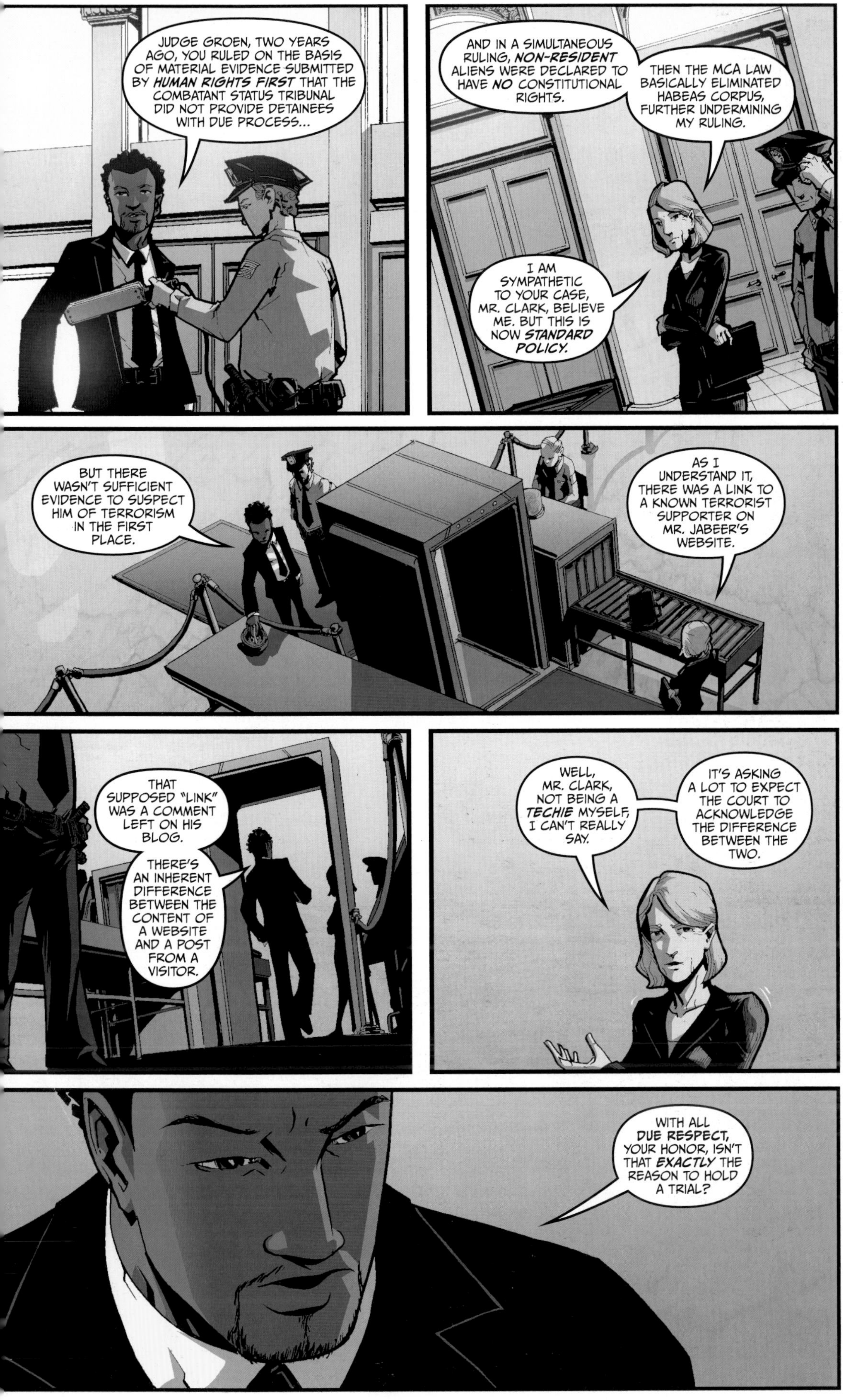
JUDGE GROEN, TWO YEARS AGO, YOU RULED ON THE BASIS OF MATERIAL EVIDENCE SUBMITTED BY HUMAN RIGHTS FIRST THAT THE COMBATANT STATUS TRIBUNAL DID NOT PROVIDE DETAINEES WITH DUE PROCESS...
AND IN A SIMULTANEOUS RULING, NON-RESIDENT ALIENS WERE DECLARED TO HAVE NO CONSTITUTIONAL RIGHTS.
THEN THE MCA LAW BASICALLY ELIMINATED HABEAS CORPUS, FURTHER UNDERMINING MY RULING.
I AM SYMPATHETIC TO YOUR CASE, MR. CLARK, BELIEVE ME. BUT THIS IS NOW STANDARD POLICY.
BUT THERE WASN'T SUFFICIENT EVIDENCE TO SUSPECT HIM OF TERRORISM IN THE FIRST PLACE.
AS I UNDERSTAND IT, THERE WAS A LINK TO A KNOWN TERRORIST SUPPORTER ON MR. JABEER'S WEBSITE.
THAT SUPPOSED "LINK" WAS A COMMENT LEFT ON HIS BLOG.
THERE'S AN INHERENT DIFFERENCE BETWEEN THE CONTENT OF A WEBSITE AND A POST FROM A VISITOR.
WELL, MR. CLARK, NOT BEING A TECHIE MYSELF, I CAN'T REALLY SAY.
IT'S ASKING A LOT TO EXPECT THE COURT TO ACKNOWLEDGE THE DIFFERENCE BETWEEN THE TWO.
WITH ALL DUE RESPECT, YOUR HONOR, ISN'T THAT EXACTLY THE REASON TO HOLD A TRIAL?

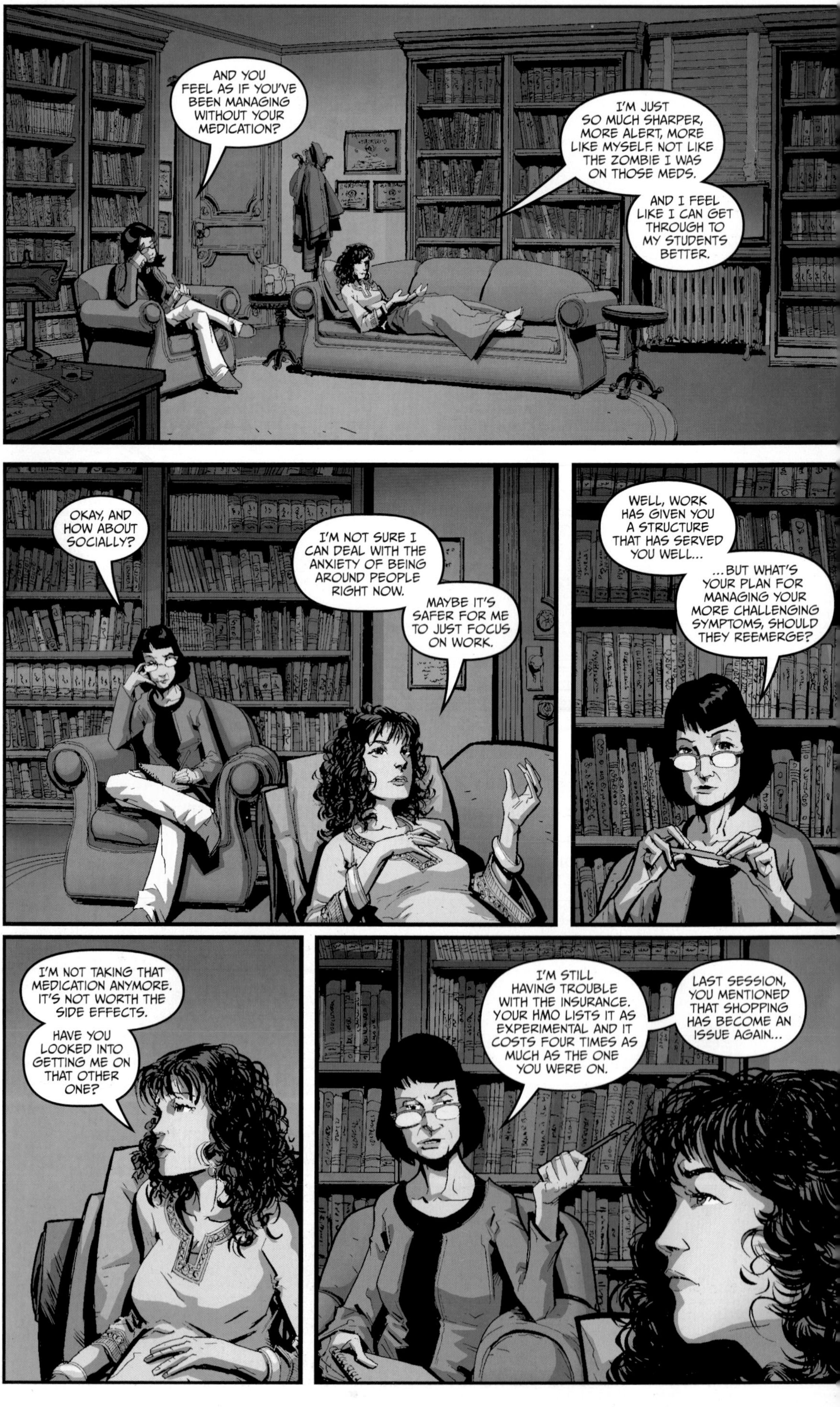
AND YOU FEEL AS IF YOU'VE BEEN MANAGING WITHOUT YOUR MEDICATION?
I'M JUST SO MUCH SHARPER, MORE ALERT, MORE LIKE MYSELF. NOT LIKE THE ZOMBIE I WAS ON THOSE MEDS.
AND I FEEL LIKE I CAN GET THROUGH TO MY STUDENTS BETTER.
OKAY, AND HOW ABOUT SOCIALLY?
I'M NOT SURE I CAN DEAL WITH THE ANXIETY OF BEING AROUND PEOPLE RIGHT NOW.
MAYBE IT'S SAFER FOR ME TO JUST FOCUS ON WORK.
WELL, WORK HAS GIVEN YOU A STRUCTURE THAT HAS SERVED YOU WELL...
...BUT WHAT'S YOUR PLAN FOR MANAGING YOUR MORE CHALLENGING SYMPTOMS, SHOULD THEY REEMERGE?
I'M NOT TAKING THAT MEDICATION ANYMORE. IT'S NOT WORTH THE SIDE EFFECTS.
HAVE YOU LOOKED INTO GETTING ME ON THAT OTHER ONE?
I'M STILL HAVING TROUBLE WITH THE INSURANCE. YOUR HMO LISTS IT AS EXPERIMENTAL AND IT COSTS FOUR TIMES AS MUCH AS THE ONE YOU WERE ON.
LAST SESSION, YOU MENTIONED THAT SHOPPING HAS BECOME AN ISSUE AGAIN...

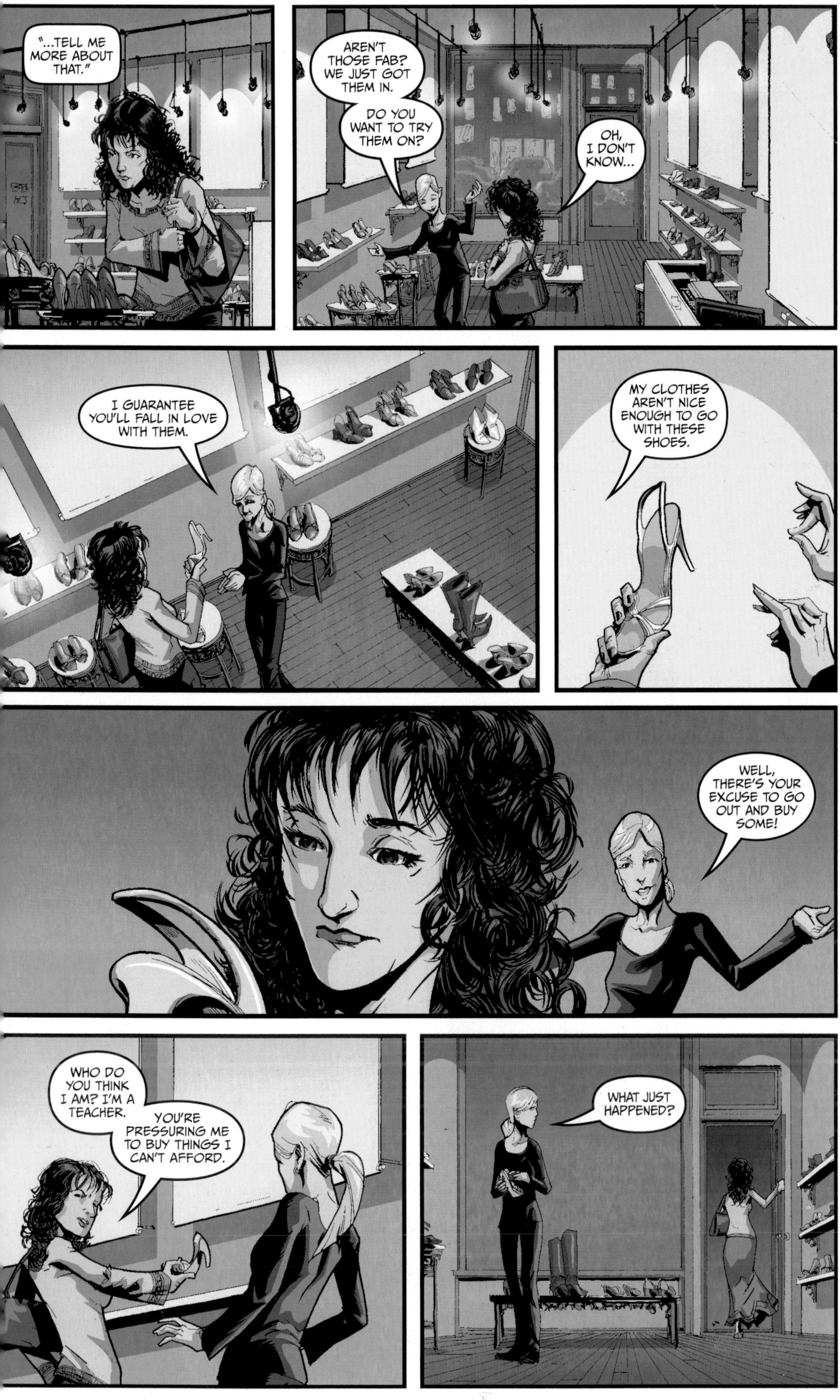
"...TELL ME MORE ABOUT THAT."
AREN'T THOSE FAB? WE JUST GOT THEM IN.
DO YOU WANT TO TRY THEM ON?
OH, I DON'T KNOW...
I GUARANTEE YOU'LL FALL IN LOVE WITH THEM.
MY CLOTHES AREN'T NICE ENOUGH TO GO WITH THESE SHOES.
WELL, THERE'S YOUR EXCUSE TO GO OUT AND BUY SOME!
WHO DO YOU THINK I AM? I'M A TEACHER.
YOU'RE PRESSURING ME TO BUY THINGS I CAN'T AFFORD.
WHAT JUST HAPPENED?

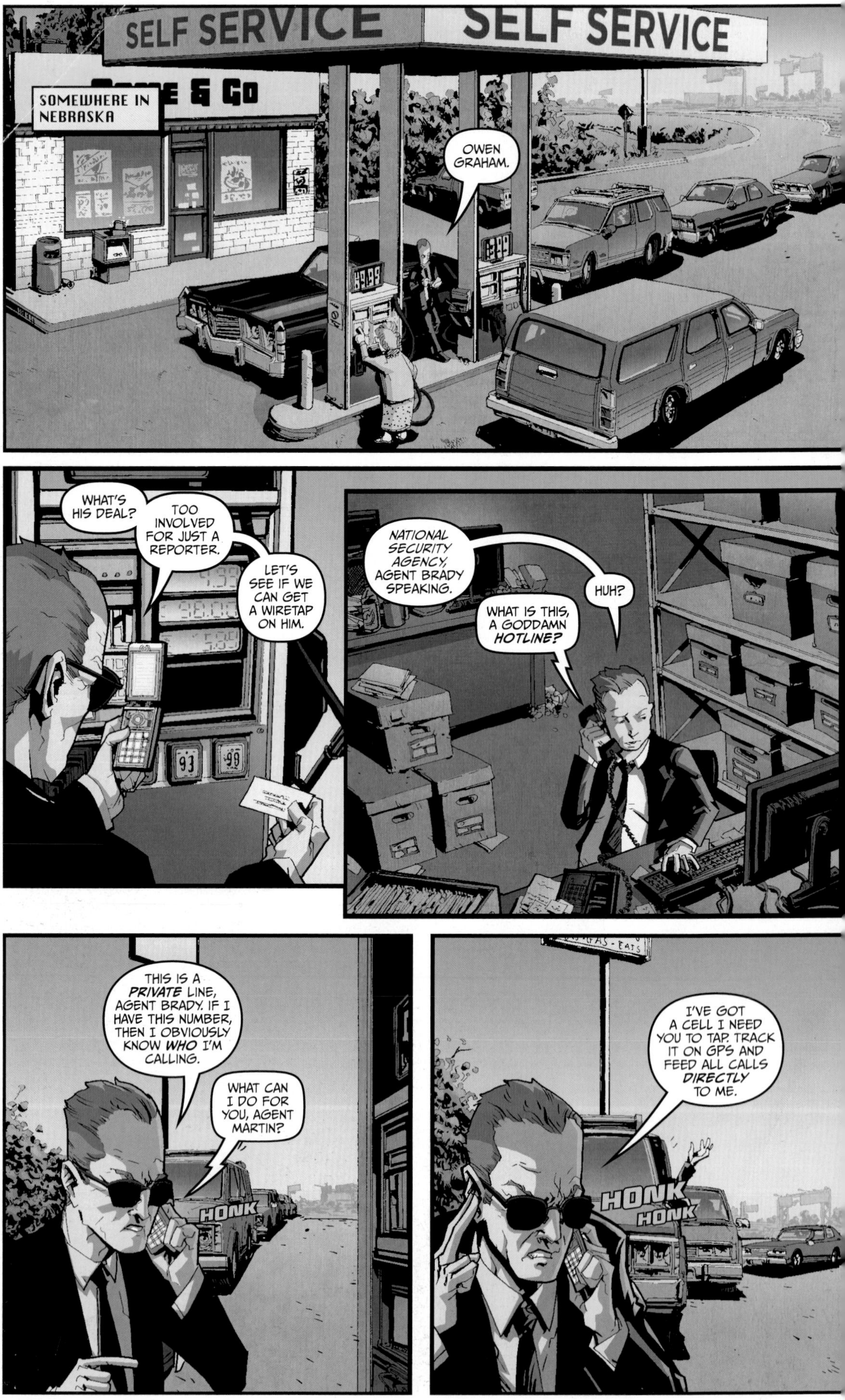
SELF SERVICE
SELF SERVICE
SOMEWHERE IN NEBRASKA
OWEN GRAHAM.
WHAT'S HIS DEAL?
TOO INVOLVED FOR JUST A REPORTER.
LET'S SEE IF WE CAN GET A WIRETAP ON HIM.
NATIONAL SECURITY AGENCY, AGENT BRADY SPEAKING.
HUH?
WHAT IS THIS, A GODDAMN HOTLINE?
THIS IS A PRIVATE LINE, AGENT BRADY. IF I HAVE THIS NUMBER, THEN I OBVIOUSLY KNOW WHO I'M CALLING.
WHAT CAN I DO FOR YOU, AGENT MARTIN?
HONK
I'VE GOT A CELL I NEED YOU TO TAP. TRACK IT ON GPS AND FEED ALL CALLS DIRECTLY TO ME.
HONK
HONK

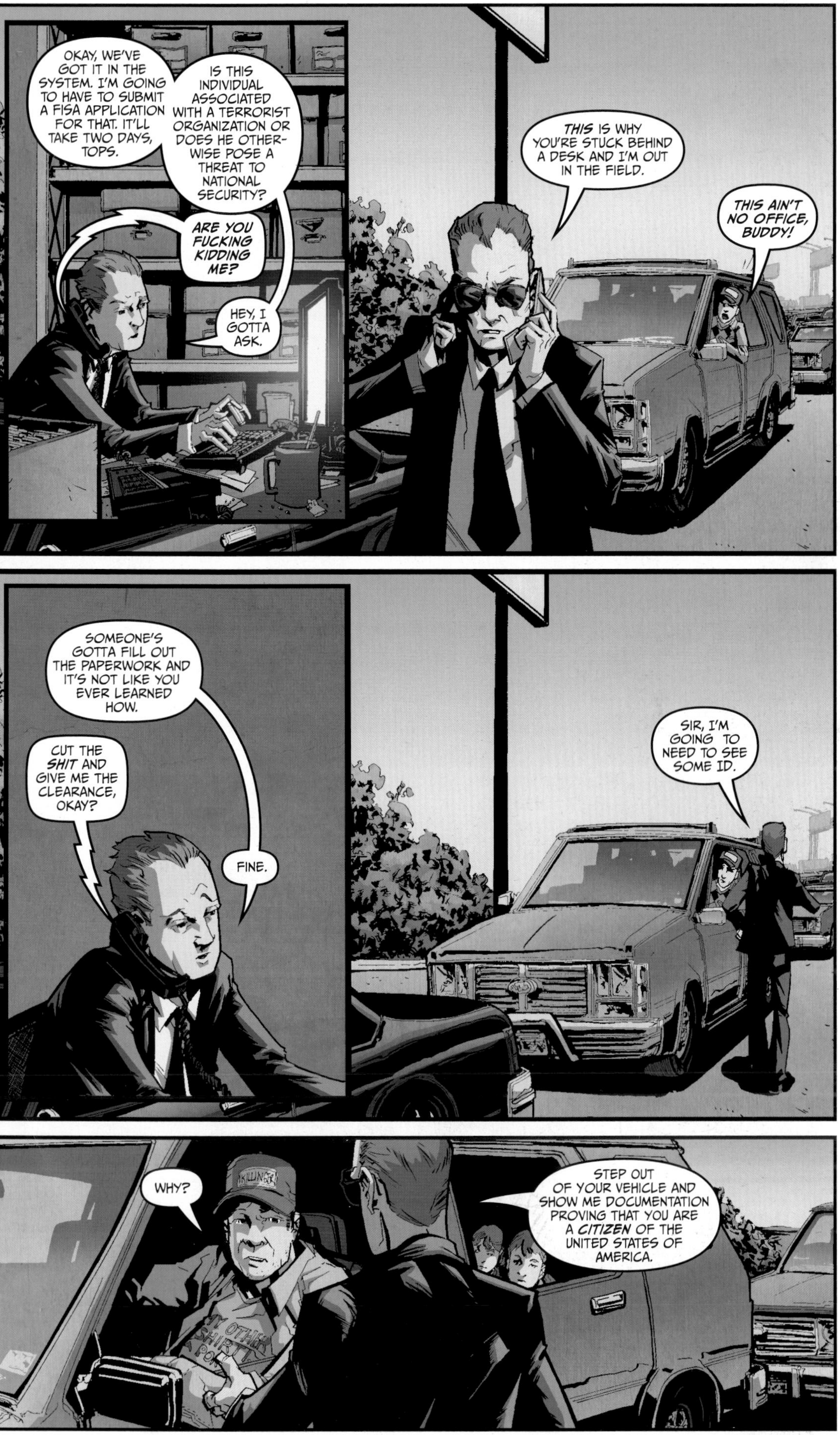
OKAY, WE'VE GOT IT IN THE SYSTEM. I'M GOING TO HAVE TO SUBMIT A FISA APPLICATION FOR THAT. IT'LL TAKE TWO DAYS, TOPS.
IS THIS INDIVIDUAL ASSOCIATED WITH A TERRORIST ORGANIZATION OR DOES HE OTHER-WISE POSE A THREAT TO NATIONAL SECURITY?
ARE YOU FUCKING KIDDING ME?
HEY, I GOTTA ASK.
THIS IS WHY YOU'RE STUCK BEHIND A DESK AND I'M OUT IN THE FIELD.
THIS AIN'T NO OFFICE, BUDDY!
SOMEONE'S GOTTA FILL OUT THE PAPERWORK AND IT'S NOT LIKE YOU EVER LEARNED HOW.
CUT THE SHIT AND GIVE ME THE CLEARANCE, OKAY?
FINE.
SIR, I'M GOING TO NEED TO SEE SOME ID.
WHY?
STEP OUT OF YOUR VEHICLE AND SHOW ME DOCUMENTATION PROVING THAT YOU ARE A CITIZEN OF THE UNITED STATES OF AMERICA.

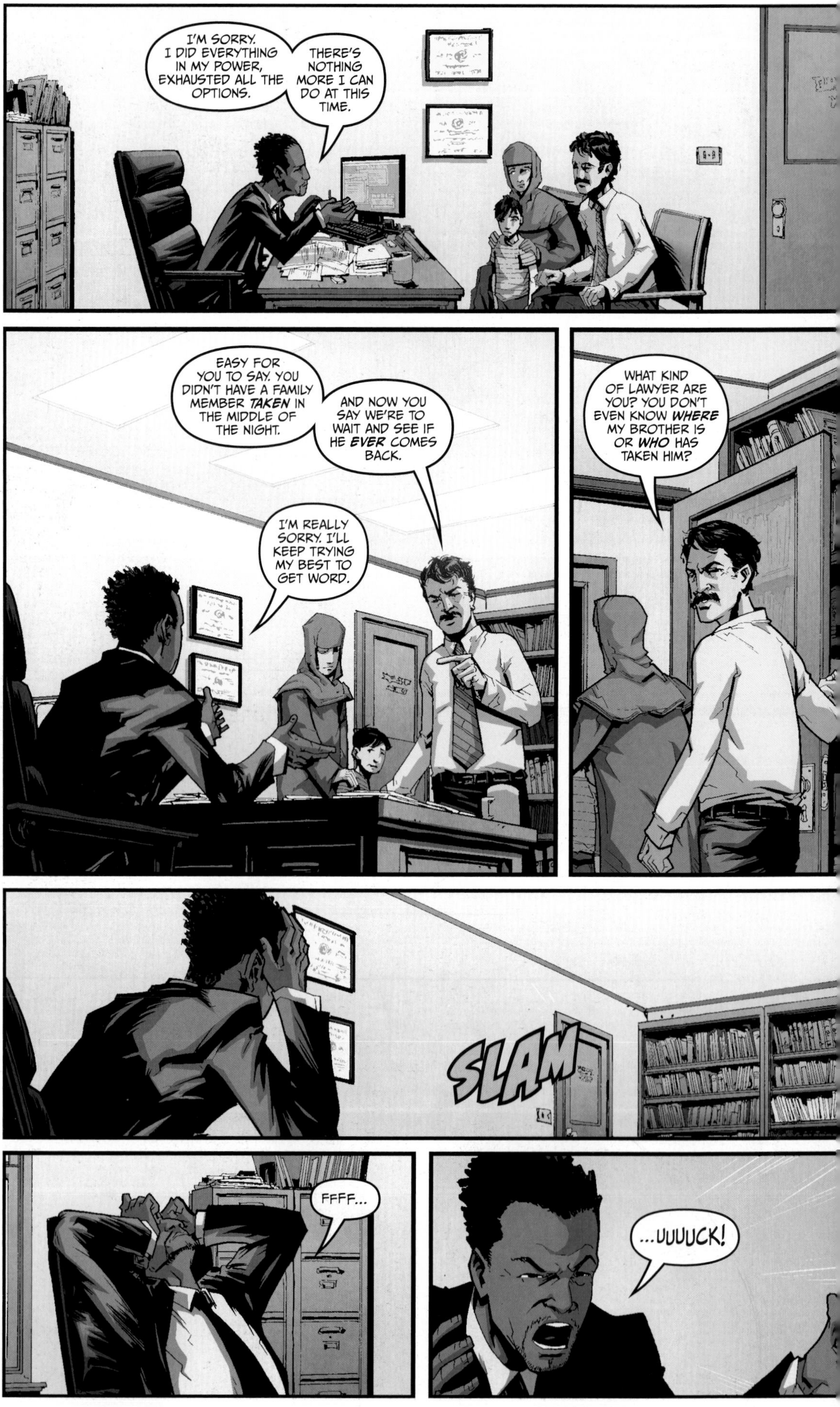

I'M SORRY. I DID EVERYTHING IN MY POWER, EXHAUSTED ALL THE OPTIONS.
THERE'S NOTHING MORE I CAN DO AT THIS TIME.
EASY FOR YOU TO SAY. YOU DIDN'T HAVE A FAMILY MEMBER *TAKEN* IN THE MIDDLE OF THE NIGHT.
AND NOW YOU SAY WE'RE TO WAIT AND SEE IF HE *EVER* COMES BACK.
I'M REALLY SORRY. I'LL KEEP TRYING MY BEST TO GET WORD.
WHAT KIND OF LAWYER ARE YOU? YOU DON'T EVEN KNOW *WHERE* MY BROTHER IS OR *WHO* HAS TAKEN HIM?
SLAM
FFFF...
...UUUUCK!

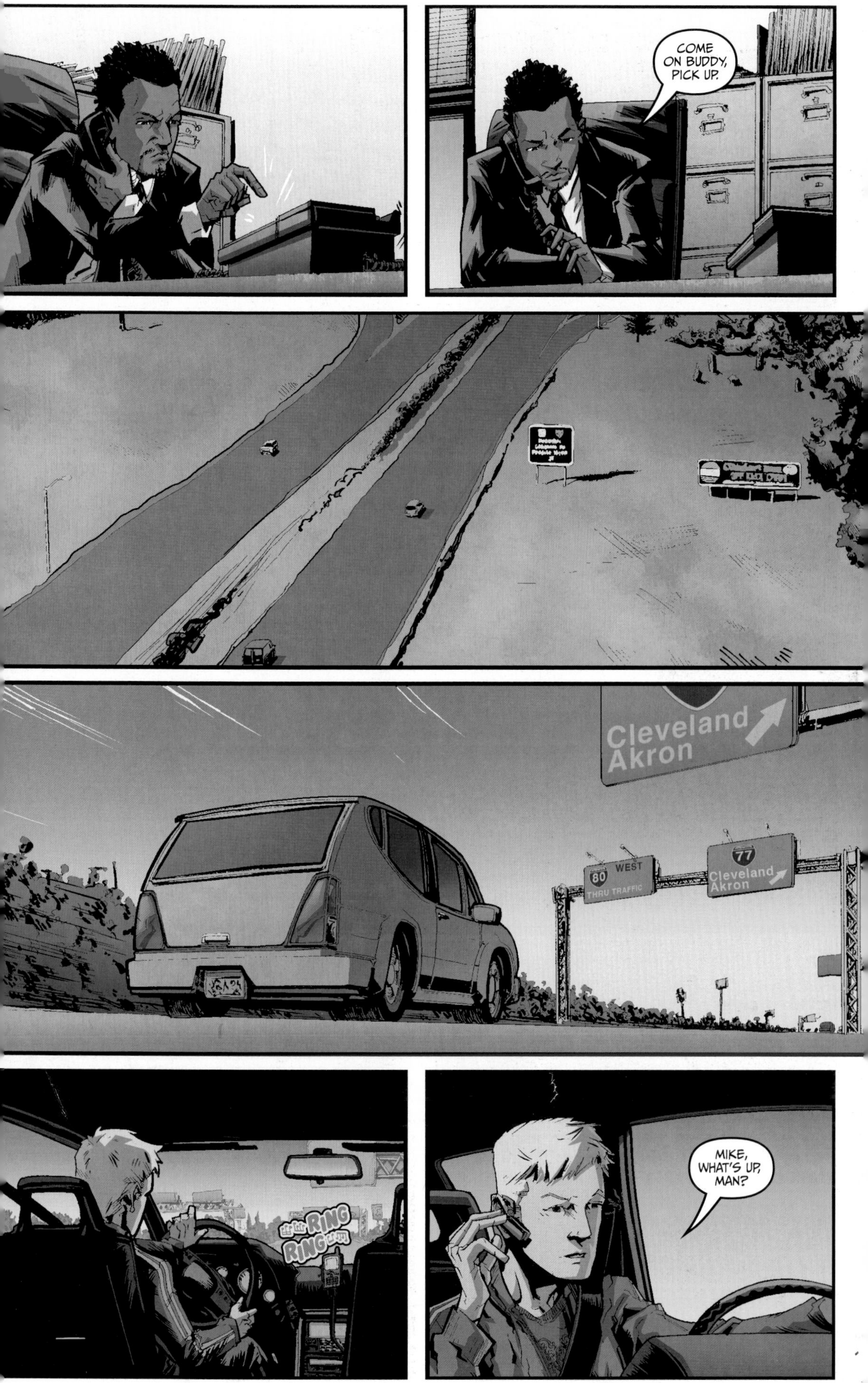
COME ON BUDDY, PICK UP.
Cleveland Akron
80 WEST THRU TRAFFIC
77 Cleveland Akron
RING RING
MIKE, WHAT'S UP, MAN?

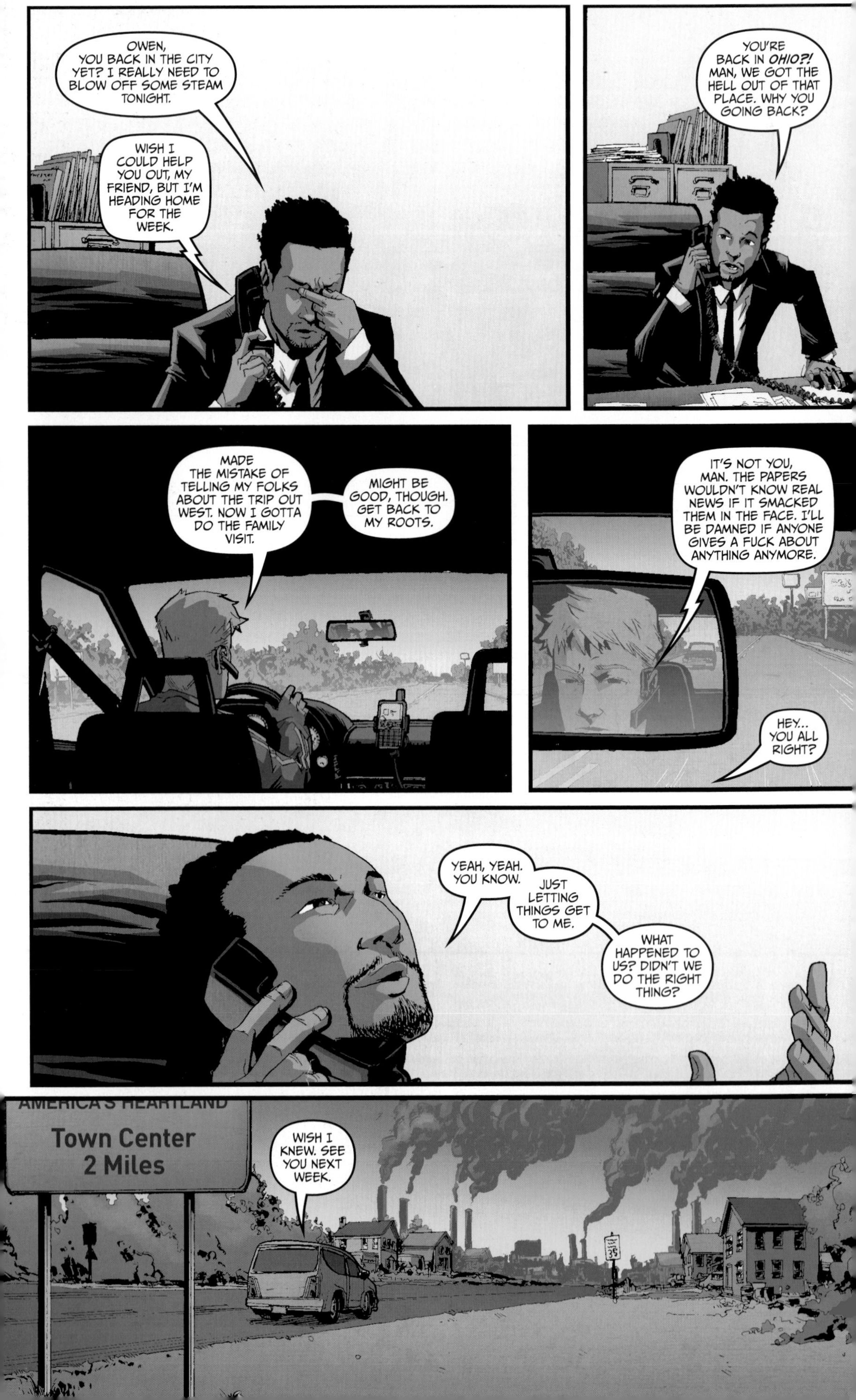
OWEN, YOU BACK IN THE CITY YET? I REALLY NEED TO BLOW OFF SOME STEAM TONIGHT.
WISH I COULD HELP YOU OUT, MY FRIEND, BUT I'M HEADING HOME FOR THE WEEK.
YOU'RE BACK IN OHIO?! MAN, WE GOT THE HELL OUT OF THAT PLACE. WHY YOU GOING BACK?
MADE THE MISTAKE OF TELLING MY FOLKS ABOUT THE TRIP OUT WEST. NOW I GOTTA DO THE FAMILY VISIT.
MIGHT BE GOOD, THOUGH. GET BACK TO MY ROOTS.
IT'S NOT YOU, MAN. THE PAPERS WOULDN'T KNOW REAL NEWS IF IT SMACKED THEM IN THE FACE. I'LL BE DAMNED IF ANYONE GIVES A FUCK ABOUT ANYTHING ANYMORE.
HEY... YOU ALL RIGHT?
YEAH, YEAH. YOU KNOW.
JUST LETTING THINGS GET TO ME.
WHAT HAPPENED TO US? DIDN'T WE DO THE RIGHT THING?
AMERICA'S HEARTLAND
Town Center
2 Miles
WISH I KNEW. SEE YOU NEXT WEEK.

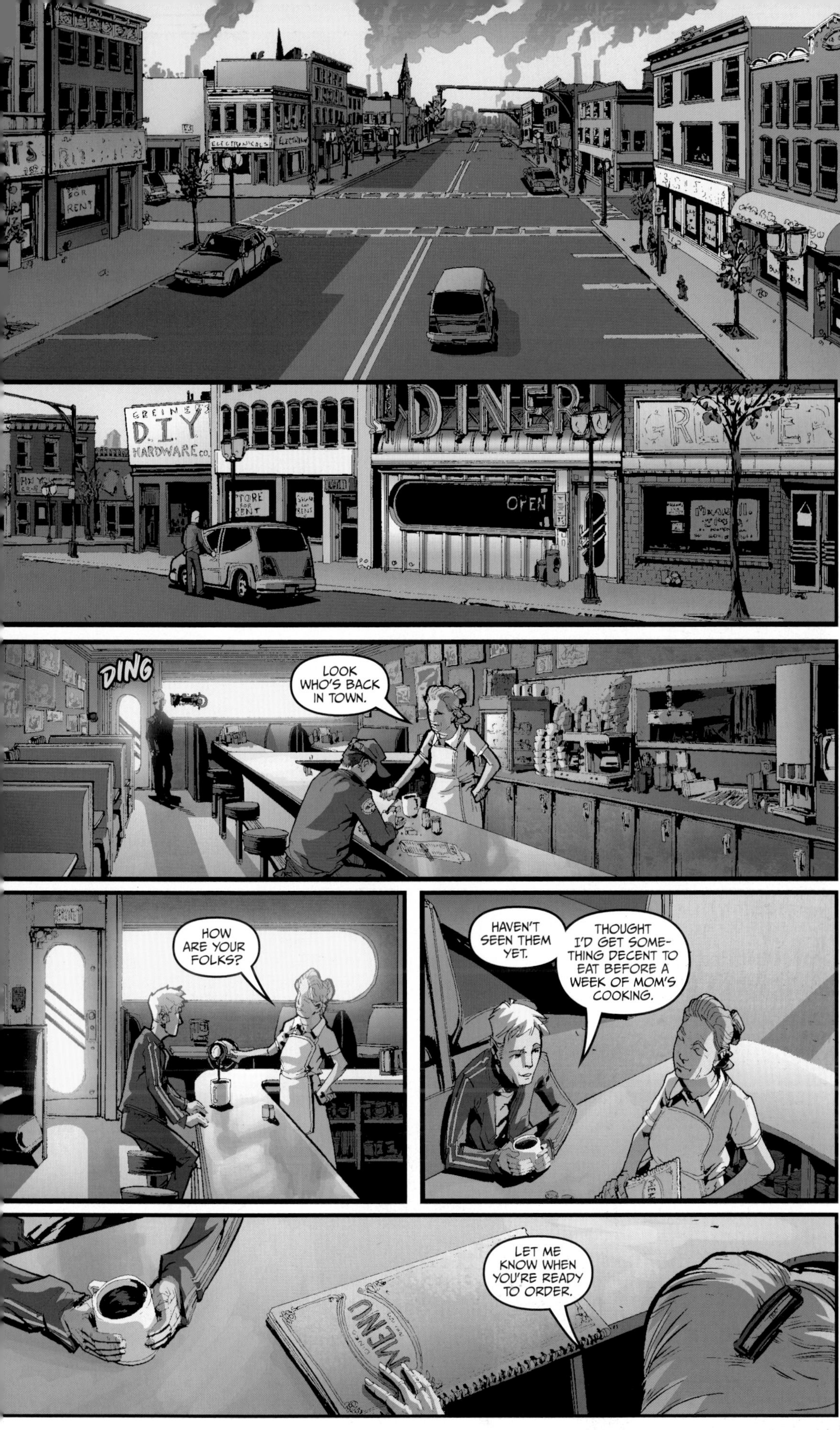
FOR RENT
D.I.Y.
HARDWARE CO.
DINER
OPEN
DING
LOOK WHO'S BACK IN TOWN.
HOW ARE YOUR FOLKS?
HAVEN'T SEEN THEM YET.
THOUGHT I'D GET SOME-THING DECENT TO EAT BEFORE A WEEK OF MOM'S COOKING.
MENU
LET ME KNOW WHEN YOU'RE READY TO ORDER.

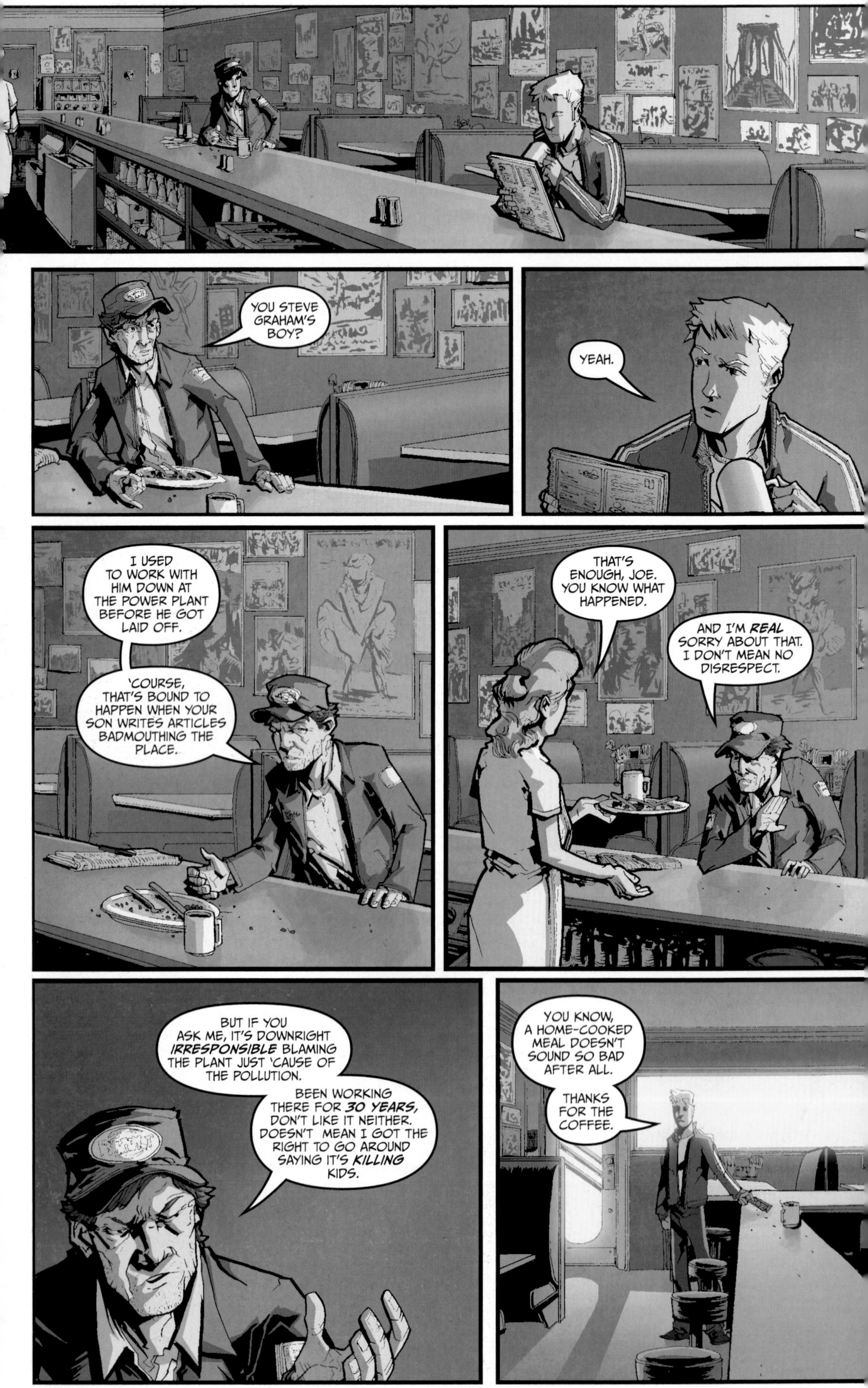
YOU STEVE GRAHAM'S BOY?
YEAH.
I USED TO WORK WITH HIM DOWN AT THE POWER PLANT BEFORE HE GOT LAID OFF.
'COURSE, THAT'S BOUND TO HAPPEN WHEN YOUR SON WRITES ARTICLES BADMOUTHING THE PLACE.
THAT'S ENOUGH, JOE. YOU KNOW WHAT HAPPENED.
AND I'M REAL SORRY ABOUT THAT. I DON'T MEAN NO DISRESPECT.
BUT IF YOU ASK ME, IT'S DOWNRIGHT IRRESPONSIBLE BLAMING THE PLANT JUST 'CAUSE OF THE POLLUTION.
BEEN WORKING THERE FOR 30 YEARS, DON'T LIKE IT NEITHER. DOESN'T MEAN I GOT THE RIGHT TO GO AROUND SAYING IT'S KILLING KIDS.
YOU KNOW, A HOME-COOKED MEAL DOESN'T SOUND SO BAD AFTER ALL.
THANKS FOR THE COFFEE.

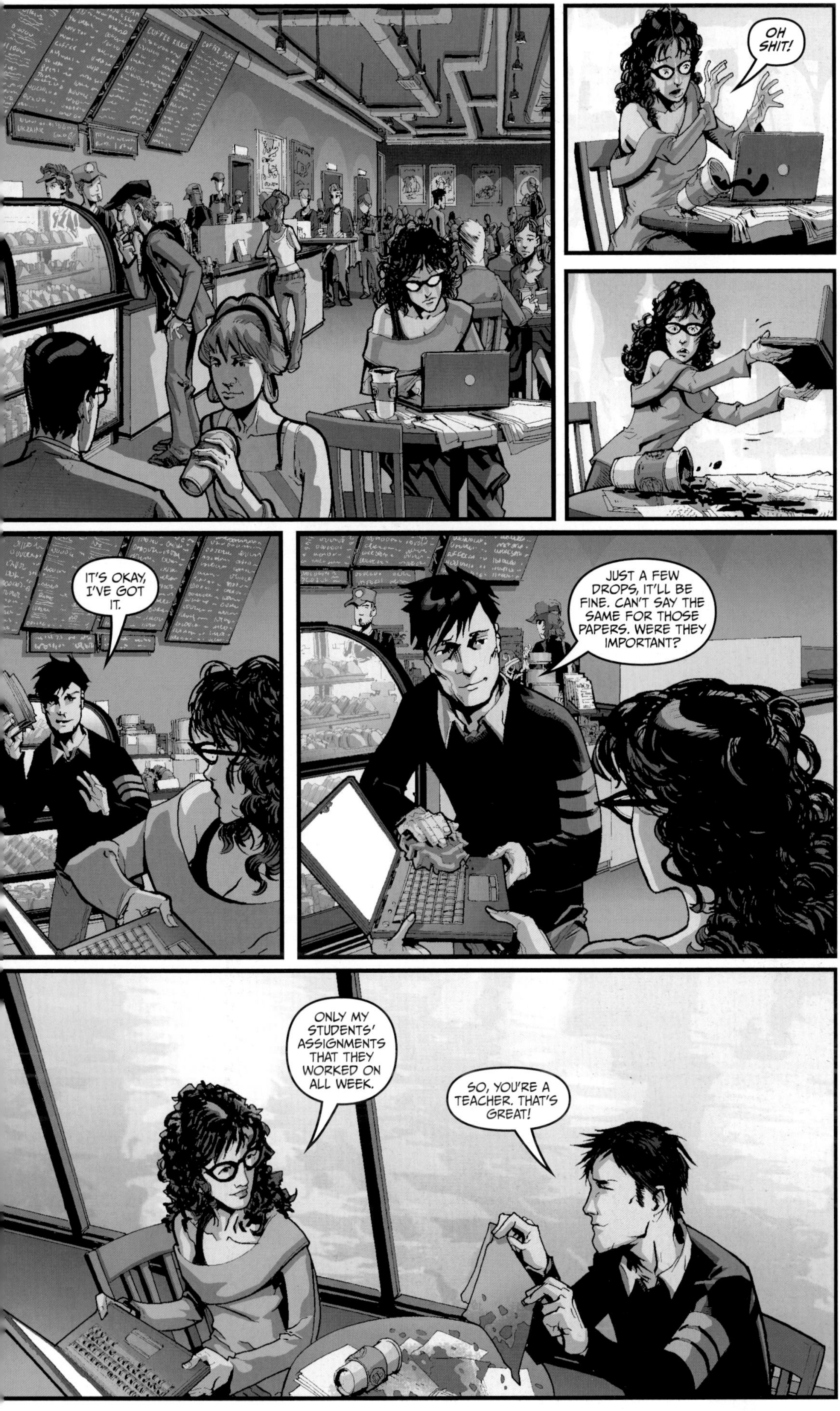
OH SHIT!
IT'S OKAY, I'VE GOT IT.
JUST A FEW DROPS, IT'LL BE FINE. CAN'T SAY THE SAME FOR THOSE PAPERS. WERE THEY IMPORTANT?
ONLY MY STUDENTS' ASSIGNMENTS THAT THEY WORKED ON ALL WEEK.
SO, YOU'RE A TEACHER. THAT'S GREAT!

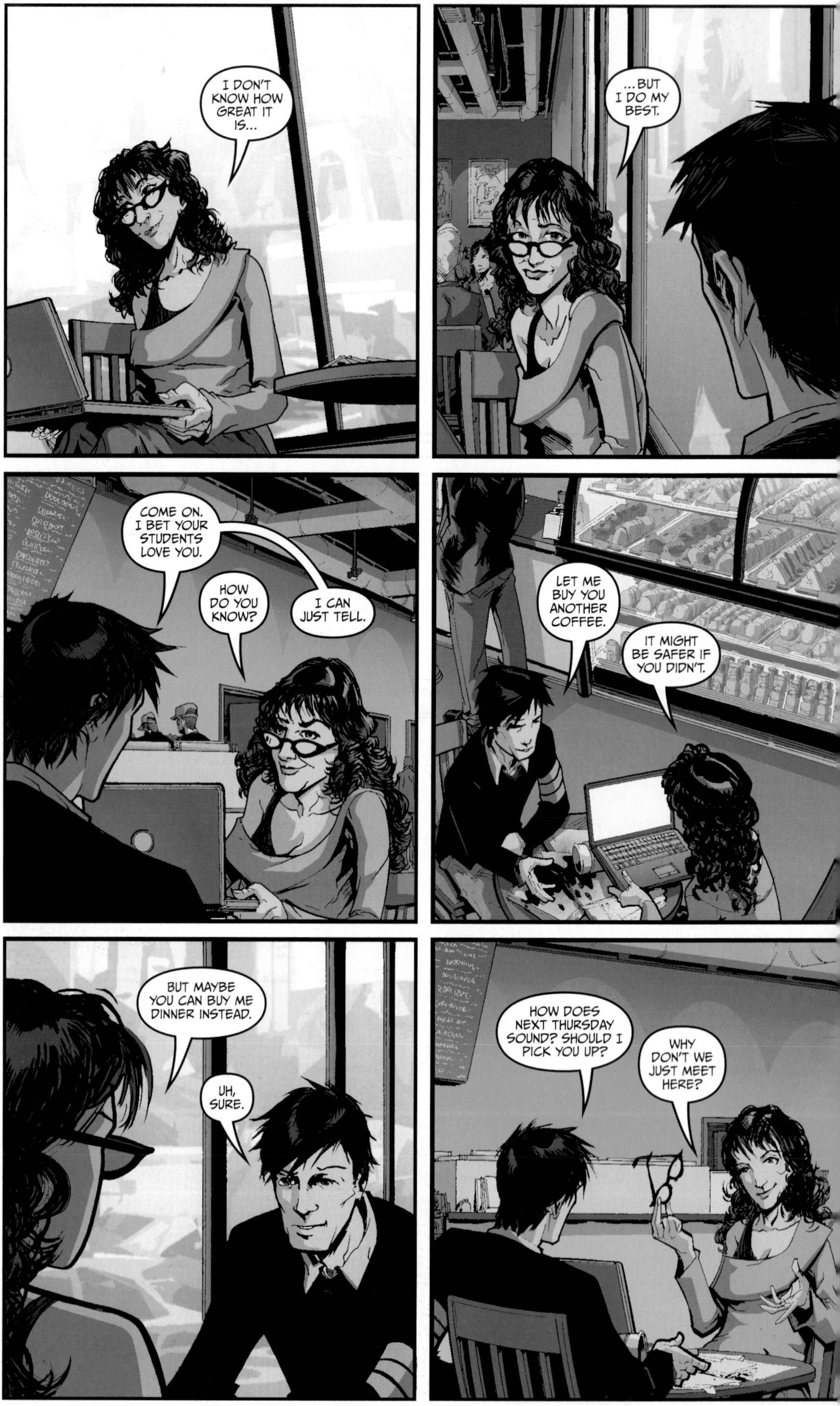
I DON'T KNOW HOW GREAT IT IS...
...BUT I DO MY BEST.
COME ON. I BET YOUR STUDENTS LOVE YOU.
HOW DO YOU KNOW?
I CAN JUST TELL.
LET ME BUY YOU ANOTHER COFFEE.
IT MIGHT BE SAFER IF YOU DIDN'T.
BUT MAYBE YOU CAN BUY ME DINNER INSTEAD.
UH, SURE.
HOW DOES NEXT THURSDAY SOUND? SHOULD I PICK YOU UP?
WHY DON'T WE JUST MEET HERE?

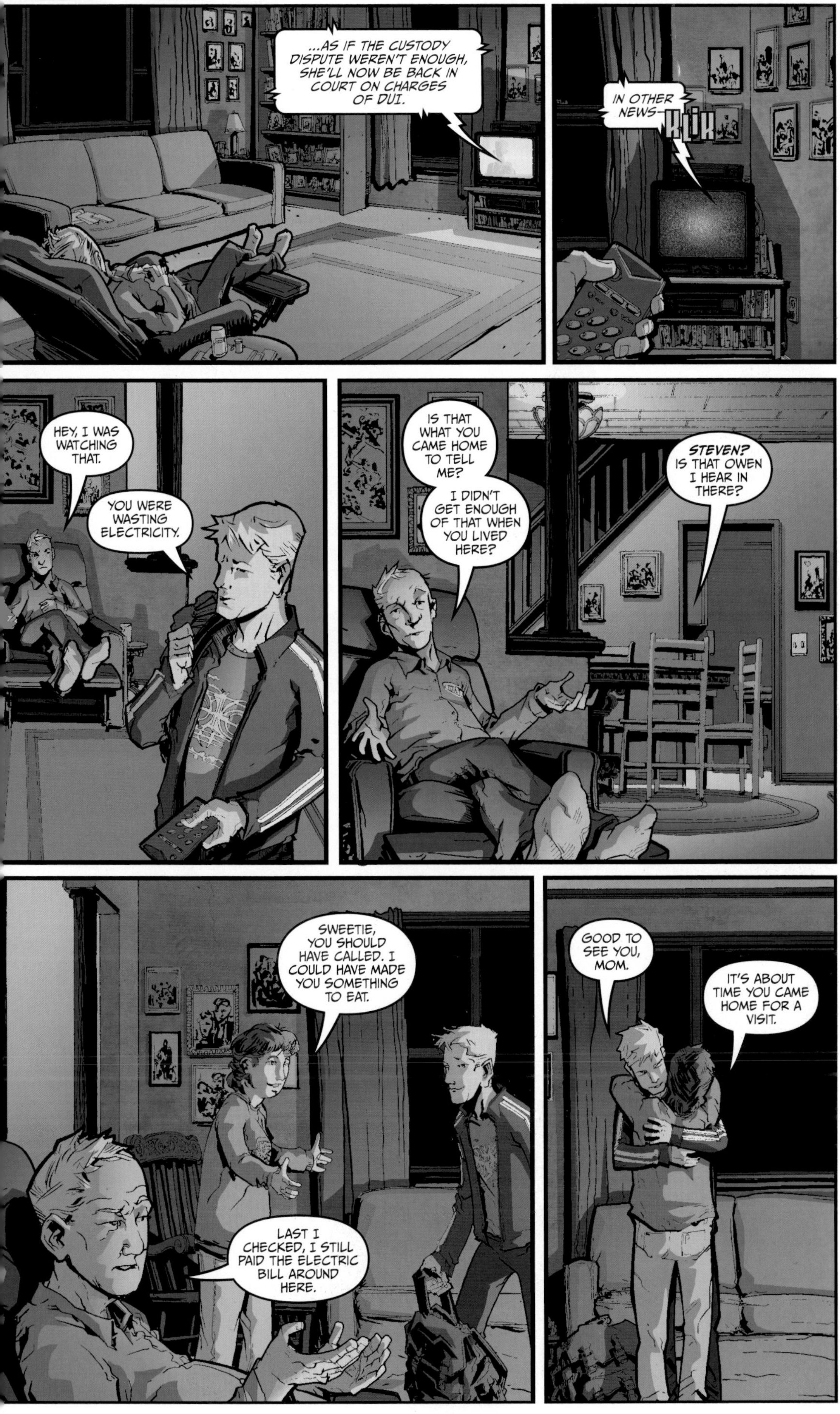
...AS IF THE CUSTODY DISPUTE WEREN'T ENOUGH, SHE'LL NOW BE BACK IN COURT ON CHARGES OF DUI.
IN OTHER NEWS—
KLIK
HEY, I WAS WATCHING THAT.
YOU WERE WASTING ELECTRICITY.
IS THAT WHAT YOU CAME HOME TO TELL ME?
I DIDN'T GET ENOUGH OF THAT WHEN YOU LIVED HERE?
STEVEN? IS THAT OWEN I HEAR IN THERE?
SWEETIE, YOU SHOULD HAVE CALLED. I COULD HAVE MADE YOU SOMETHING TO EAT.
LAST I CHECKED, I STILL PAID THE ELECTRIC BILL AROUND HERE.
GOOD TO SEE YOU, MOM.
IT'S ABOUT TIME YOU CAME HOME FOR A VISIT.

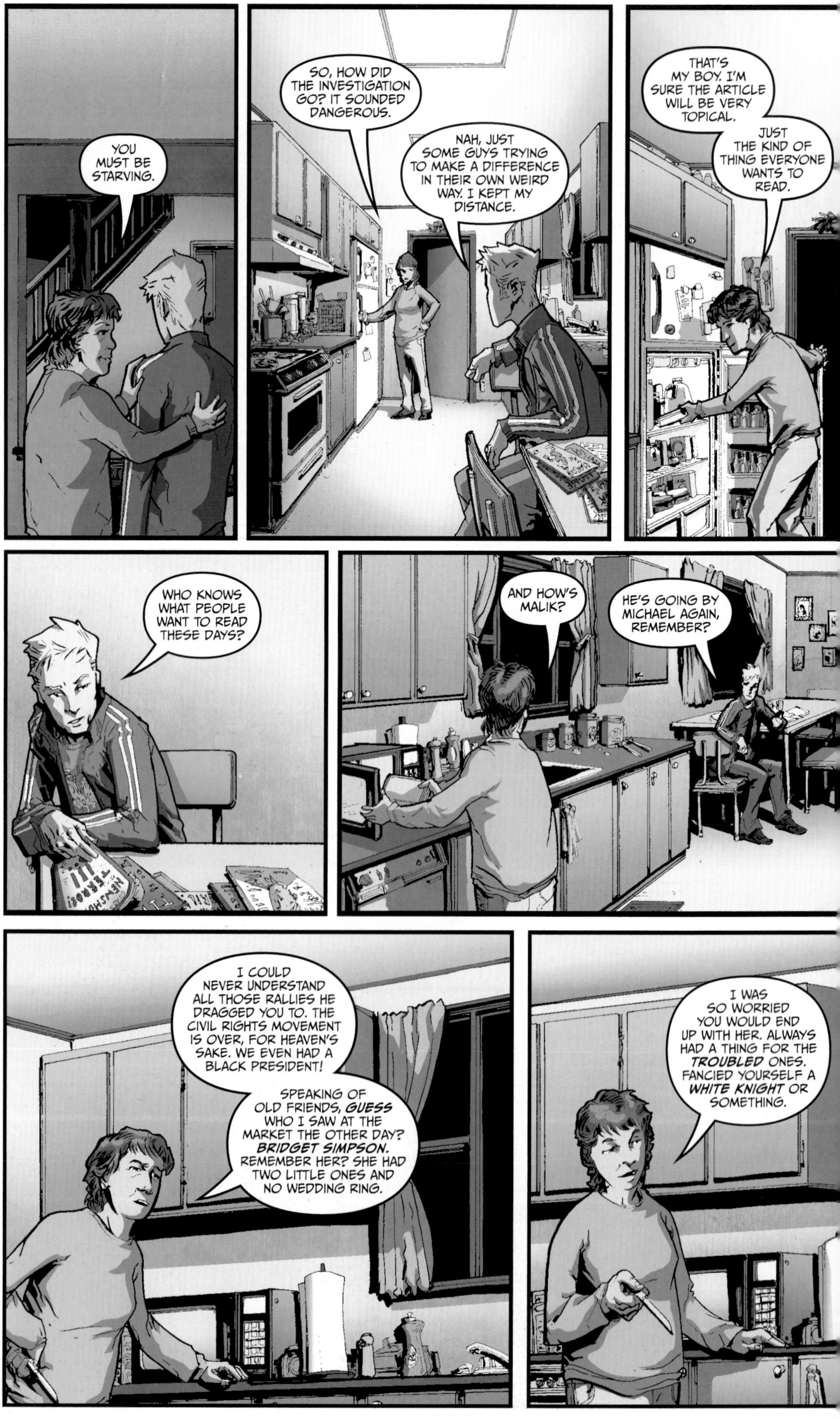
YOU MUST BE STARVING.
SO, HOW DID THE INVESTIGATION GO? IT SOUNDED DANGEROUS.
NAH, JUST SOME GUYS TRYING TO MAKE A DIFFERENCE IN THEIR OWN WEIRD WAY. I KEPT MY DISTANCE.
THAT'S MY BOY. I'M SURE THE ARTICLE WILL BE VERY TOPICAL.
JUST THE KIND OF THING EVERYONE WANTS TO READ.
WHO KNOWS WHAT PEOPLE WANT TO READ THESE DAYS?
AND HOW'S MALIK?
HE'S GOING BY MICHAEL AGAIN, REMEMBER?
I COULD NEVER UNDERSTAND ALL THOSE RALLIES HE DRAGGED YOU TO. THE CIVIL RIGHTS MOVEMENT IS OVER, FOR HEAVEN'S SAKE. WE EVEN HAD A BLACK PRESIDENT!
SPEAKING OF OLD FRIENDS, **GUESS** WHO I SAW AT THE MARKET THE OTHER DAY? ***BRIDGET SIMPSON.*** REMEMBER HER? SHE HAD TWO LITTLE ONES AND NO WEDDING RING.
I WAS SO WORRIED YOU WOULD END UP WITH HER. ALWAYS HAD A THING FOR THE ***TROUBLED*** ONES. FANCIED YOURSELF A ***WHITE KNIGHT*** OR SOMETHING.

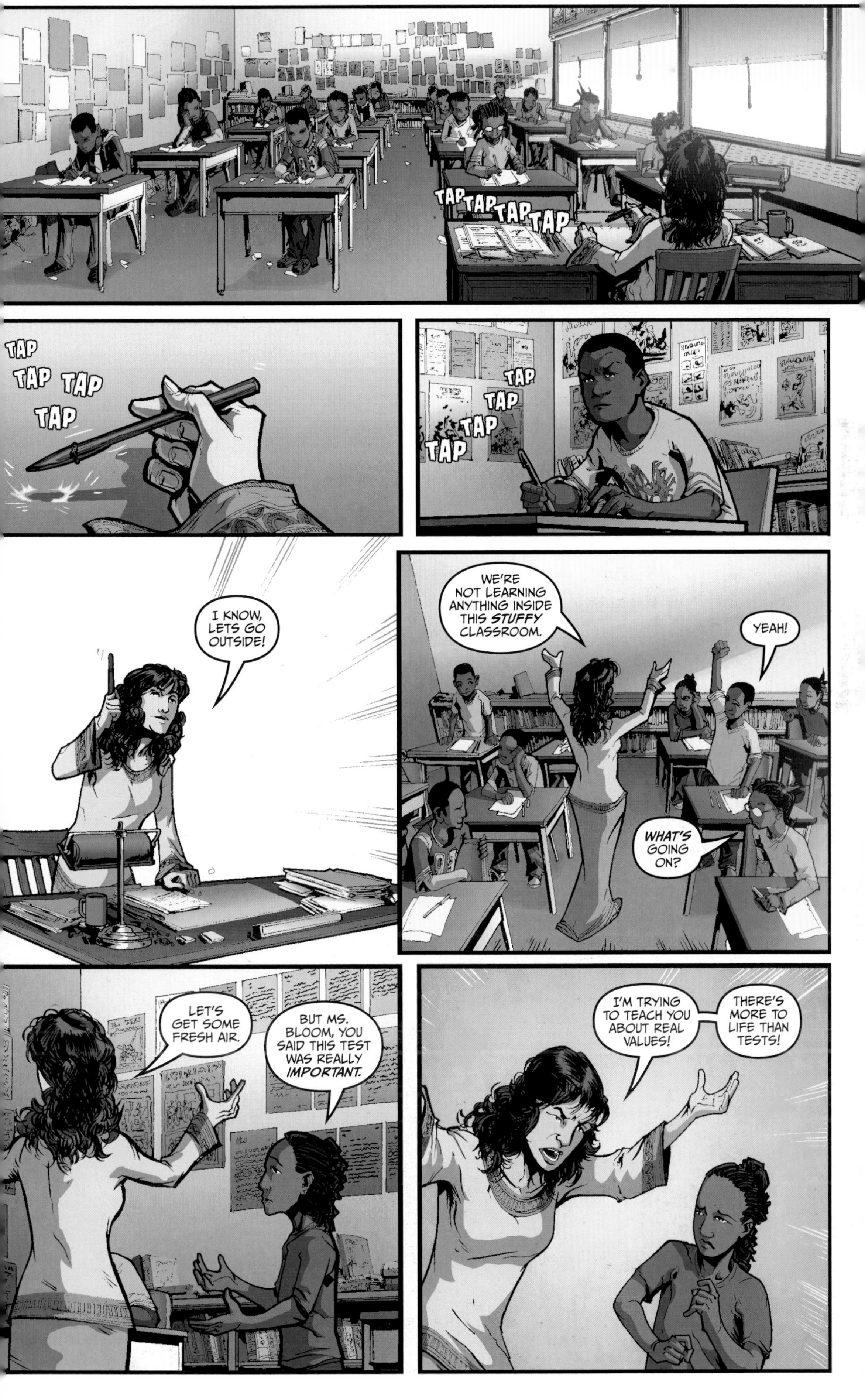
TAP TAP TAP TAP
TAP
TAP TAP
TAP
TAP
TAP
TAP
TAP
I KNOW, LETS GO OUTSIDE!
WE'RE NOT LEARNING ANYTHING INSIDE THIS *STUFFY* CLASSROOM.
YEAH!
WHAT'S GOING ON?
LET'S GET SOME FRESH AIR.
BUT MS. BLOOM, YOU SAID THIS TEST WAS REALLY *IMPORTANT.*
I'M TRYING TO TEACH YOU ABOUT REAL VALUES!
THERE'S MORE TO LIFE THAN TESTS!

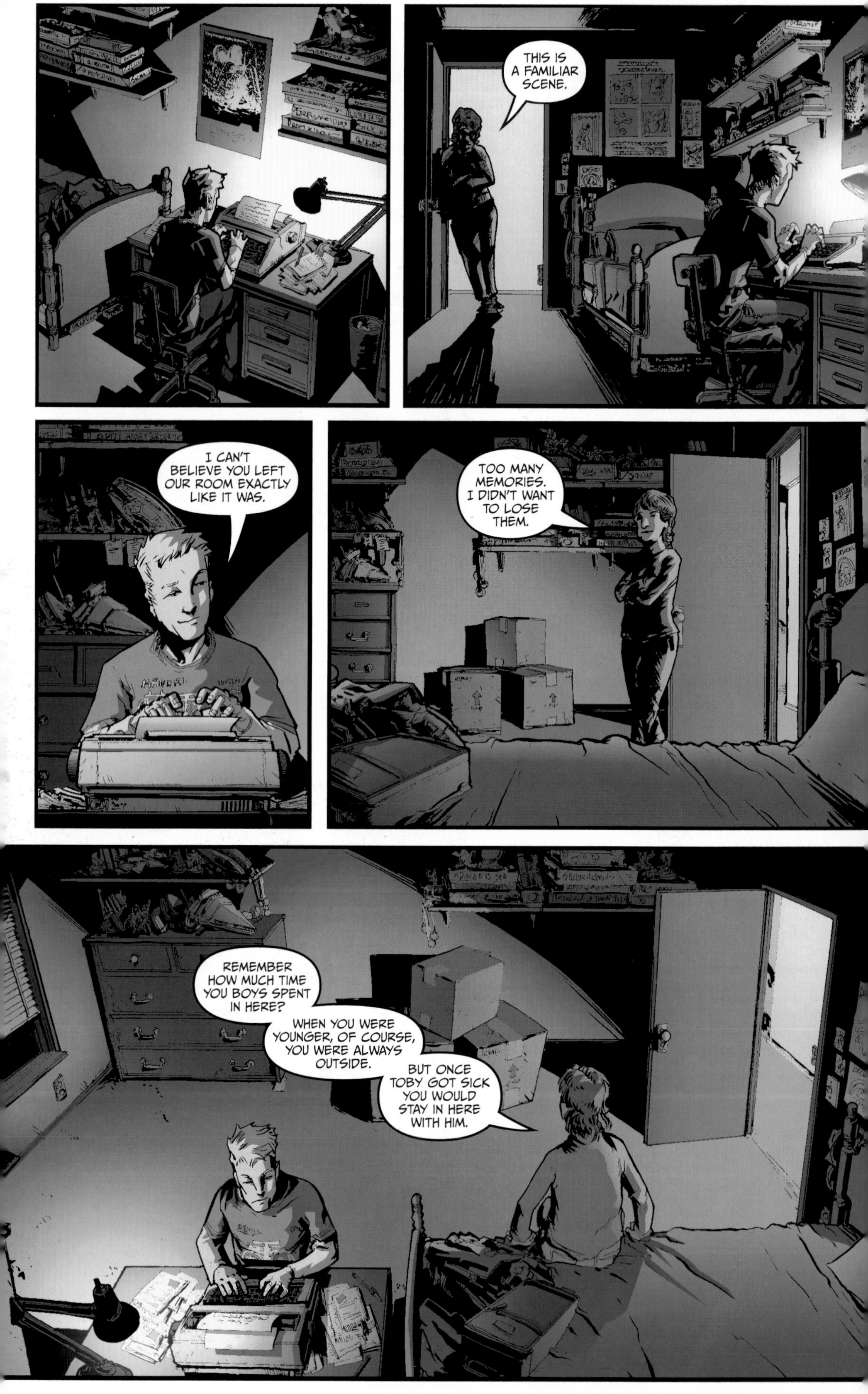
THIS IS A FAMILIAR SCENE.
I CAN'T BELIEVE YOU LEFT OUR ROOM EXACTLY LIKE IT WAS.
TOO MANY MEMORIES. I DIDN'T WANT TO LOSE THEM.
REMEMBER HOW MUCH TIME YOU BOYS SPENT IN HERE?
WHEN YOU WERE YOUNGER, OF COURSE, YOU WERE ALWAYS OUTSIDE.
BUT ONCE TOBY GOT SICK YOU WOULD STAY IN HERE WITH HIM.

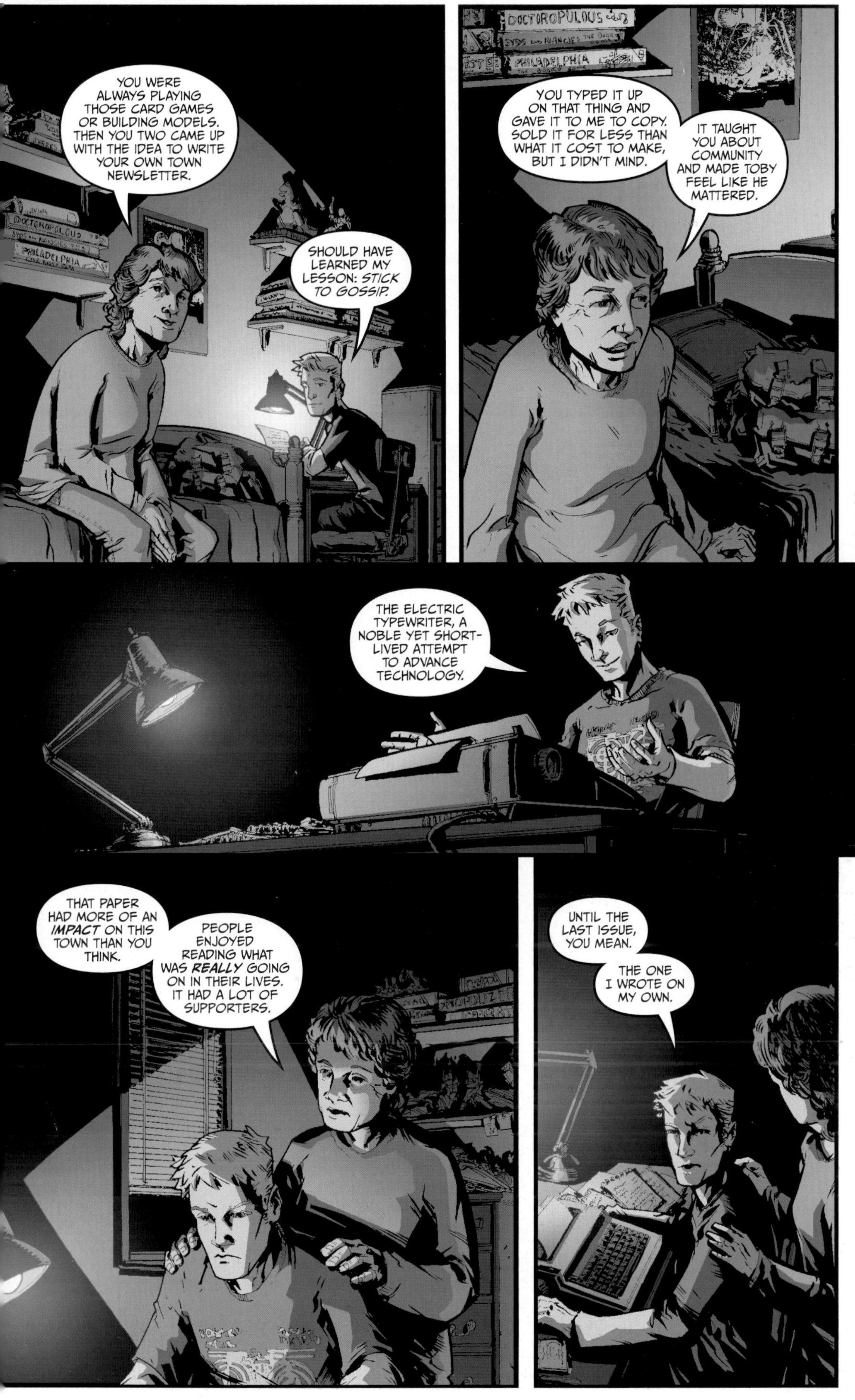

YOU WERE ALWAYS PLAYING THOSE CARD GAMES OR BUILDING MODELS. THEN YOU TWO CAME UP WITH THE IDEA TO WRITE YOUR OWN TOWN NEWSLETTER.
SHOULD HAVE LEARNED MY LESSON: *STICK TO GOSSIP.*
DOCTOROPULOUS
PHILADELPHIA
YOU TYPED IT UP ON THAT THING AND GAVE IT TO ME TO COPY. SOLD IT FOR LESS THAN WHAT IT COST TO MAKE, BUT I DIDN'T MIND.
IT TAUGHT YOU ABOUT COMMUNITY AND MADE TOBY FEEL LIKE HE MATTERED.
THE ELECTRIC TYPEWRITER, A NOBLE YET SHORT-LIVED ATTEMPT TO ADVANCE TECHNOLOGY.
THAT PAPER HAD MORE OF AN ***IMPACT*** ON THIS TOWN THAN YOU THINK.
PEOPLE ENJOYED READING WHAT WAS ***REALLY*** GOING ON IN THEIR LIVES. IT HAD A LOT OF SUPPORTERS.
UNTIL THE LAST ISSUE, YOU MEAN.
THE ONE I WROTE ON MY OWN.

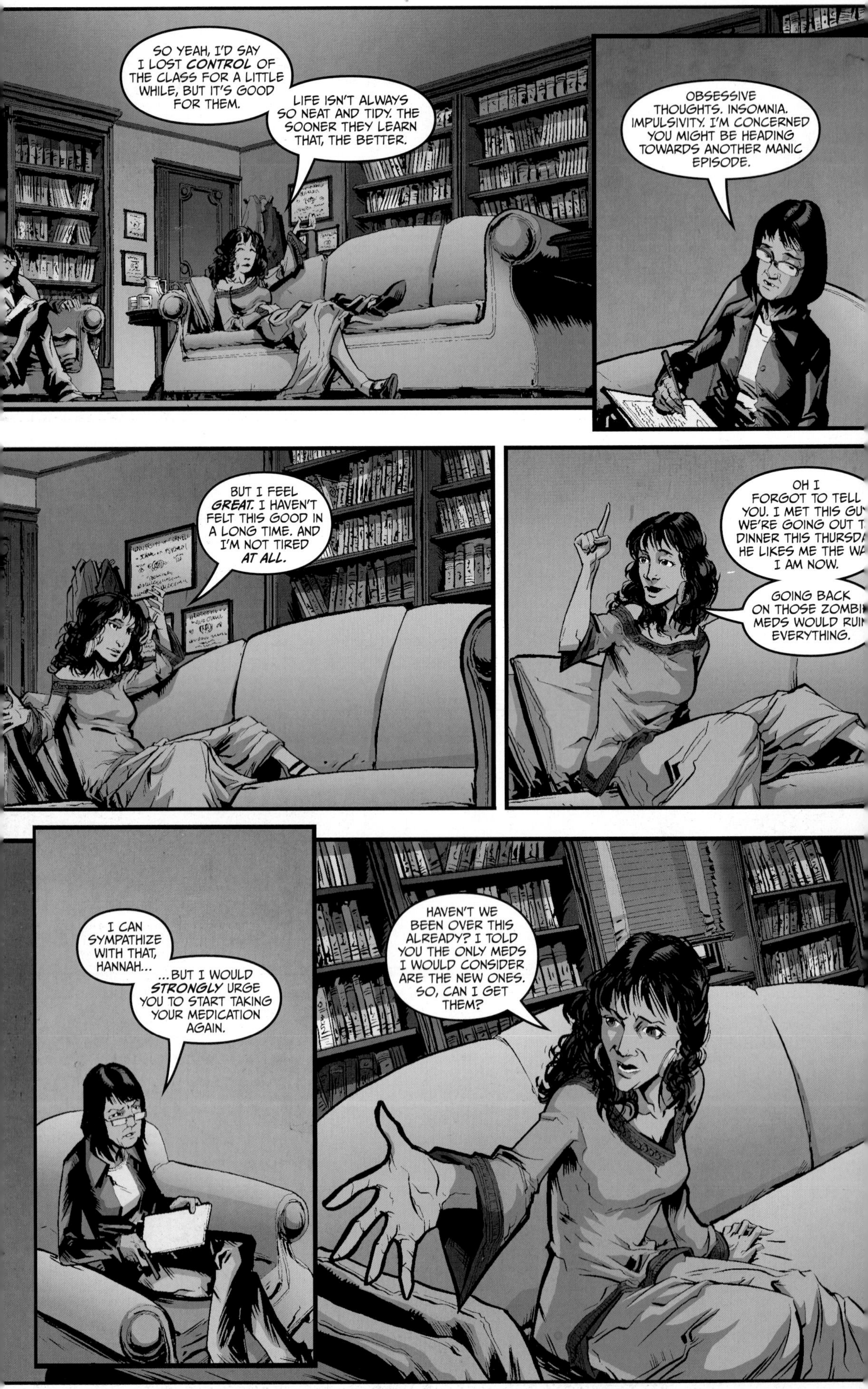
SO YEAH, I'D SAY I LOST CONTROL OF THE CLASS FOR A LITTLE WHILE, BUT IT'S GOOD FOR THEM.
LIFE ISN'T ALWAYS SO NEAT AND TIDY. THE SOONER THEY LEARN THAT, THE BETTER.
OBSESSIVE THOUGHTS. INSOMNIA. IMPULSIVITY. I'M CONCERNED YOU MIGHT BE HEADING TOWARDS ANOTHER MANIC EPISODE.
BUT I FEEL GREAT. I HAVEN'T FELT THIS GOOD IN A LONG TIME. AND I'M NOT TIRED AT ALL.
GOING BACK ON THOSE ZOMBI MEDS WOULD RUI EVERYTHING.
I CAN SYMPATHIZE WITH THAT, HANNAH...
...BUT I WOULD STRONGLY URGE YOU TO START TAKING YOUR MEDICATION AGAIN.
HAVEN'T WE BEEN OVER THIS ALREADY? I TOLD YOU THE ONLY MEDS I WOULD CONSIDER ARE THE NEW ONES. SO, CAN I GET THEM?

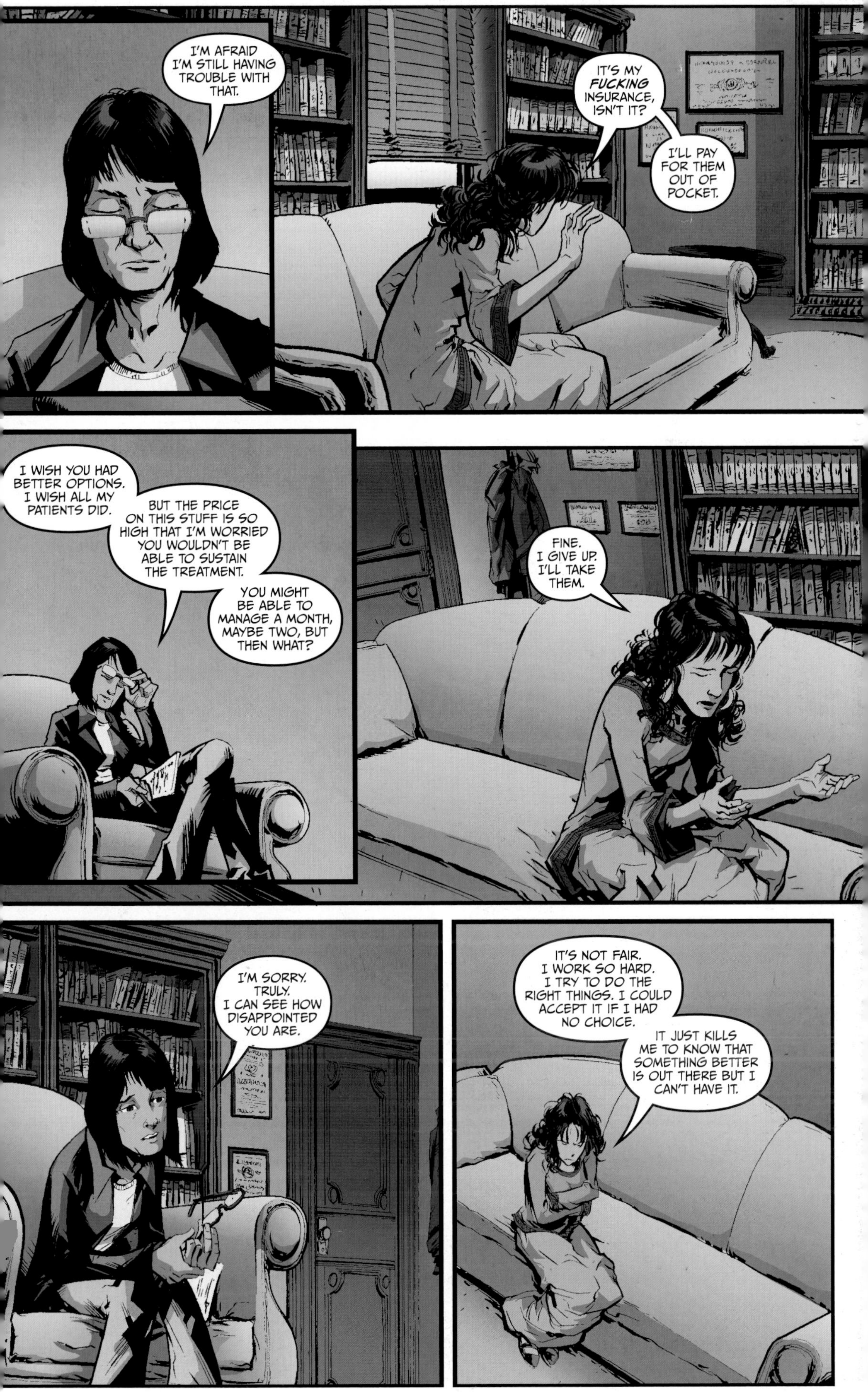

I'M AFRAID I'M STILL HAVING TROUBLE WITH THAT.
IT'S MY *FUCKING* INSURANCE, ISN'T IT?
I'LL PAY FOR THEM OUT OF POCKET.
I WISH YOU HAD BETTER OPTIONS. I WISH ALL MY PATIENTS DID.
BUT THE PRICE ON THIS STUFF IS SO HIGH THAT I'M WORRIED YOU WOULDN'T BE ABLE TO SUSTAIN THE TREATMENT.
YOU MIGHT BE ABLE TO MANAGE A MONTH, MAYBE TWO, BUT THEN WHAT?
FINE. I GIVE UP. I'LL TAKE THEM.
I'M SORRY. TRULY. I CAN SEE HOW DISAPPOINTED YOU ARE.
IT'S NOT FAIR. I WORK SO HARD. I TRY TO DO THE RIGHT THINGS. I COULD ACCEPT IT IF I HAD NO CHOICE.
IT JUST KILLS ME TO KNOW THAT SOMETHING BETTER IS OUT THERE BUT I CAN'T HAVE IT.

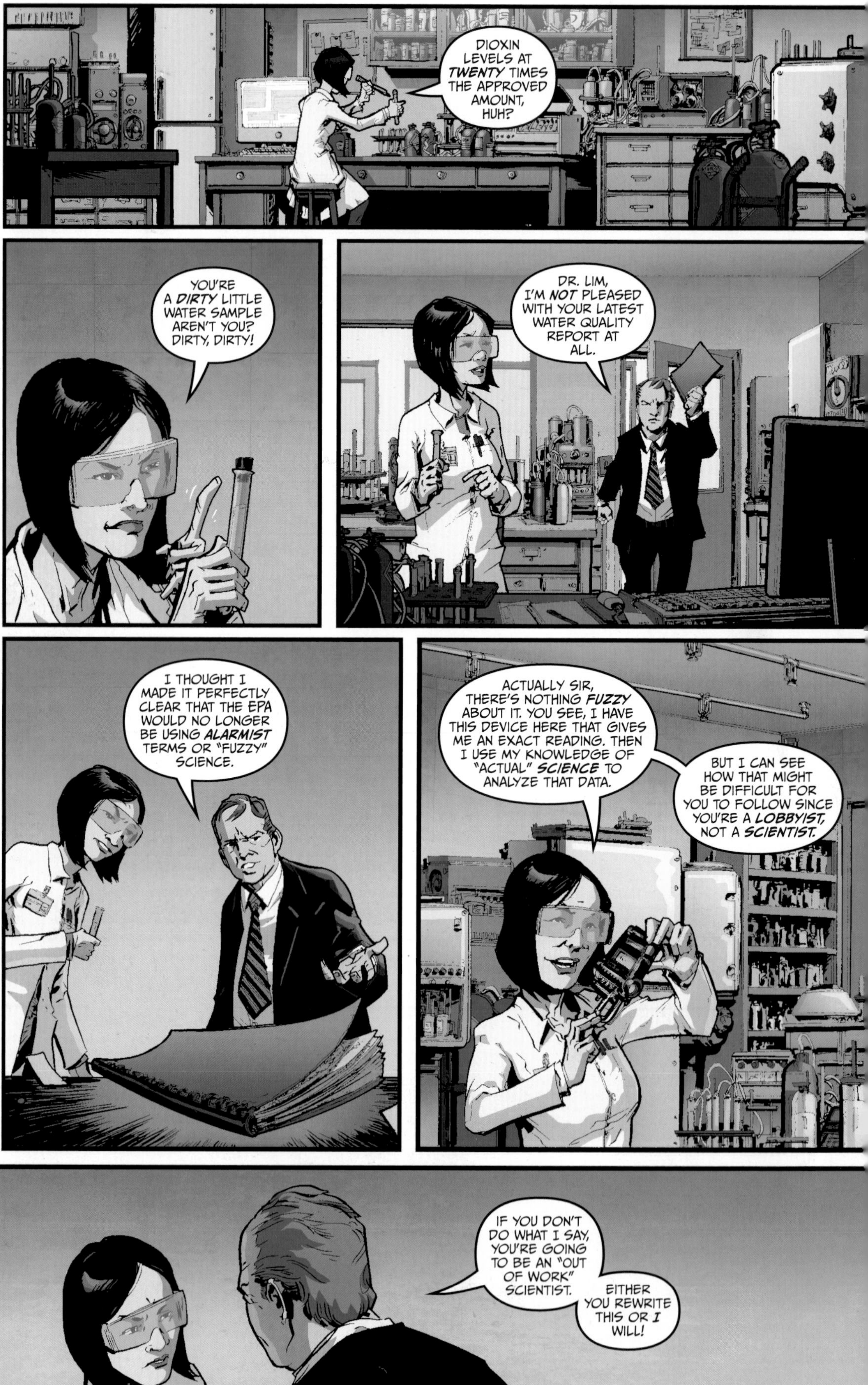
DIOXIN LEVELS AT TWENTY TIMES THE APPROVED AMOUNT, HUH?
YOU'RE A DIRTY LITTLE WATER SAMPLE AREN'T YOU? DIRTY, DIRTY!
DR. LIM, I'M NOT PLEASED WITH YOUR LATEST WATER QUALITY REPORT AT ALL.
I THOUGHT I MADE IT PERFECTLY CLEAR THAT THE EPA WOULD NO LONGER BE USING ALARMIST TERMS OR "FUZZY" SCIENCE.
ACTUALLY SIR, THERE'S NOTHING FUZZY ABOUT IT. YOU SEE, I HAVE THIS DEVICE HERE THAT GIVES ME AN EXACT READING. THEN I USE MY KNOWLEDGE OF "ACTUAL" SCIENCE TO ANALYZE THAT DATA.
BUT I CAN SEE HOW THAT MIGHT BE DIFFICULT FOR YOU TO FOLLOW SINCE YOU'RE A LOBBYIST, NOT A SCIENTIST.
IF YOU DON'T DO WHAT I SAY, YOU'RE GOING TO BE AN "OUT OF WORK" SCIENTIST.
EITHER YOU REWRITE THIS OR I WILL!

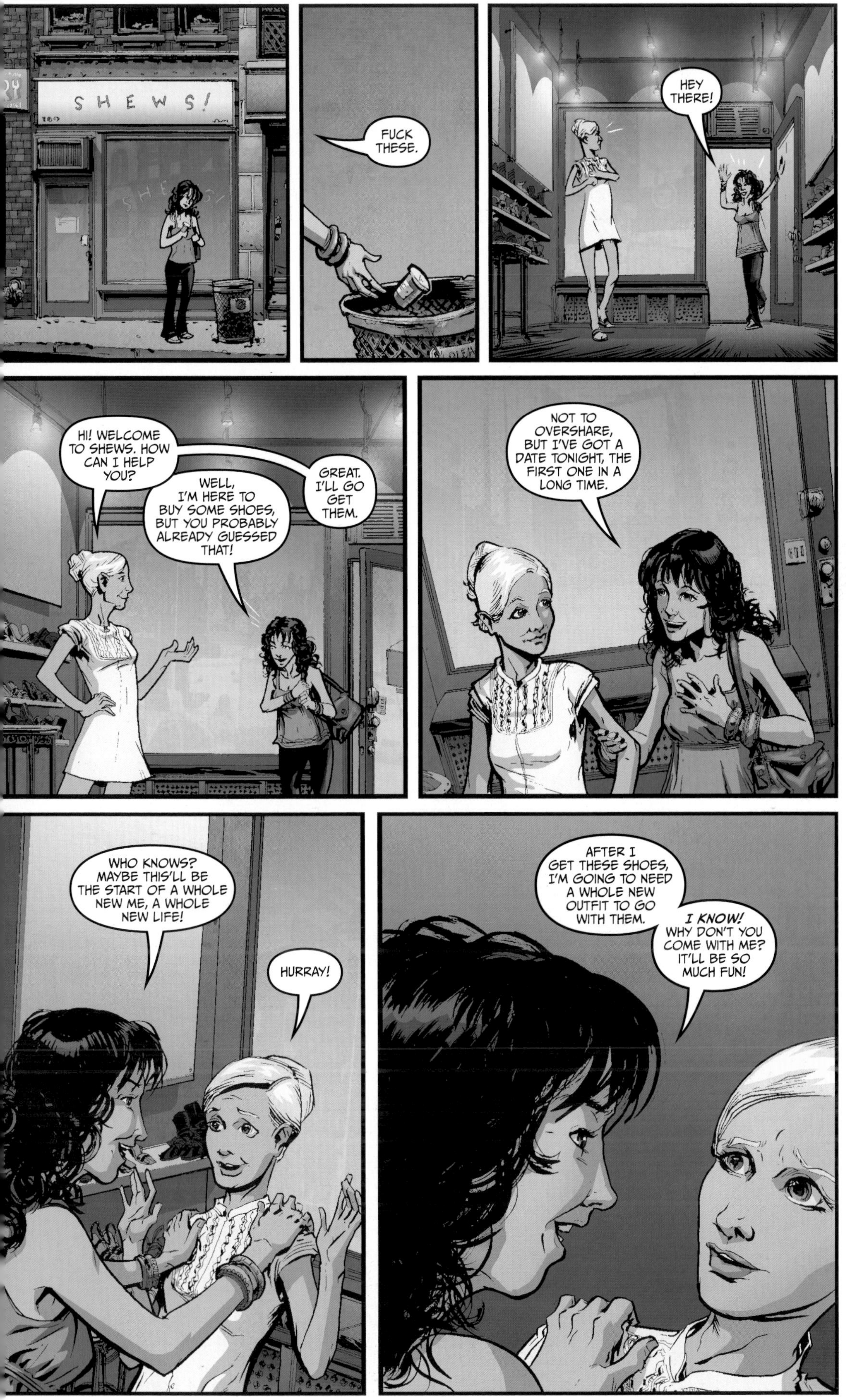
SHEWS!
FUCK THESE.
HEY THERE!
HI! WELCOME TO SHEWS. HOW CAN I HELP YOU?
WELL, I'M HERE TO BUY SOME SHOES, BUT YOU PROBABLY ALREADY GUESSED THAT!
GREAT. I'LL GO GET THEM.
NOT TO OVERSHARE, BUT I'VE GOT A DATE TONIGHT, THE FIRST ONE IN A LONG TIME.
WHO KNOWS? MAYBE THIS'LL BE THE START OF A WHOLE NEW ME, A WHOLE NEW LIFE!
HURRAY!
AFTER I GET THESE SHOES, I'M GOING TO NEED A WHOLE NEW OUTFIT TO GO WITH THEM.
I KNOW! WHY DON'T YOU COME WITH ME? IT'LL BE SO MUCH FUN!

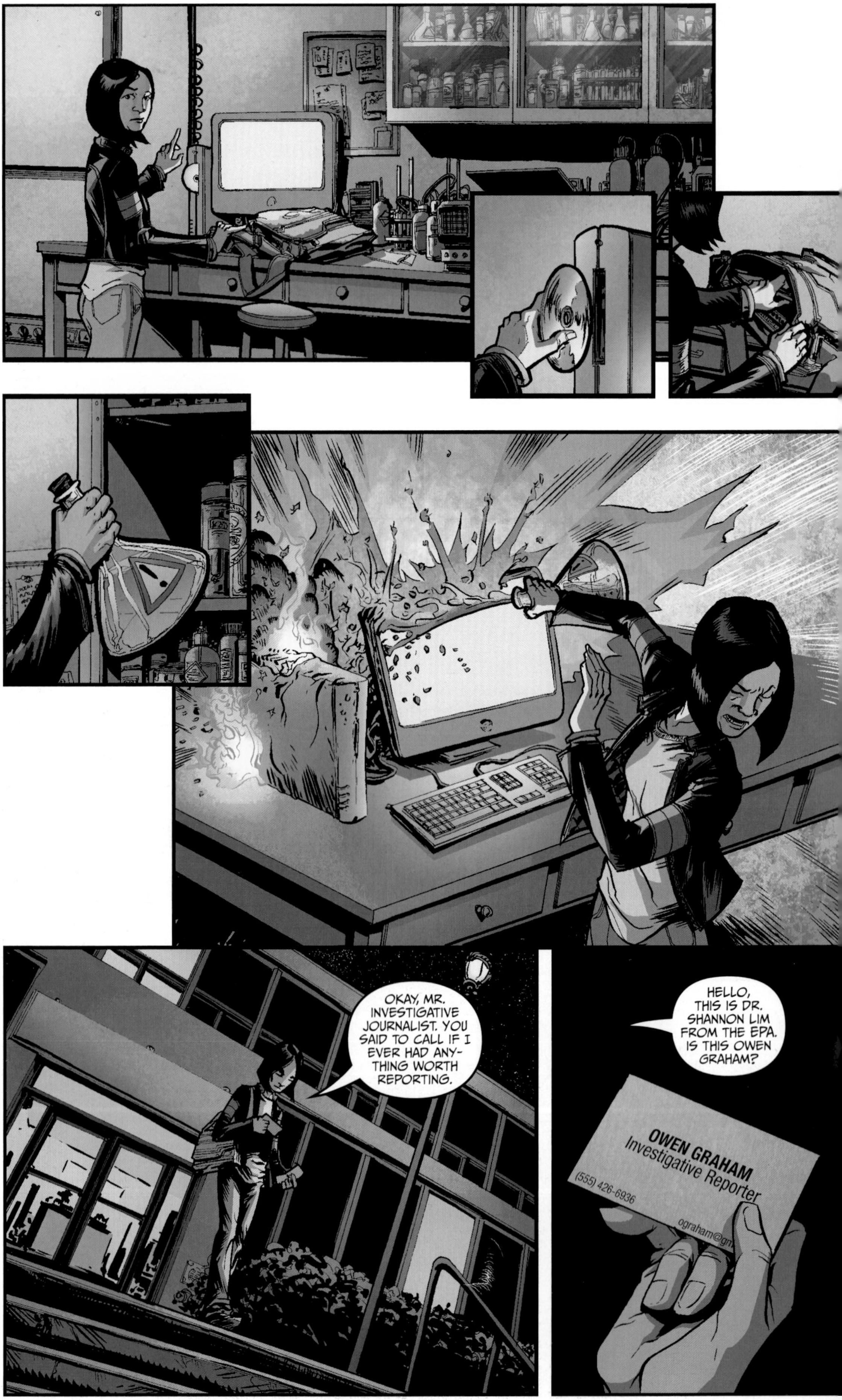
OKAY, MR. INVESTIGATIVE JOURNALIST. YOU SAID TO CALL IF I EVER HAD ANYTHING WORTH REPORTING.
HELLO, THIS IS DR. SHANNON LIM FROM THE EPA. IS THIS OWEN GRAHAM?
OWEN GRAHAM
Investigative Reporter
(555) 426-6936

...THAT'S INTERESTING INFORMATION, DR. LIM, BUT I'M NOT SURE IF MY EDITOR WILL GO FOR THAT KIND OF STORY.

I'M HEADING BACK TO THE CITY TONIGHT. WHY DON'T WE MEET UP IN THE MORNING?

CRAP! YOU'VE GOT TO BE KIDDING ME.

THERE'S THIS COFFEE SHOP ON CARMINE...

JUST WHEN I GET THIS GUY CORNERED, HE'S ON THE MOVE AGAIN. HE'S UP TO SOMETHING ALL RIGHT...

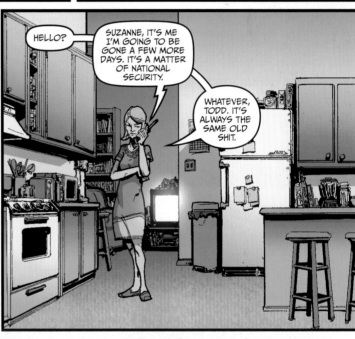

HELLO?

SUZANNE, IT'S ME I'M GOING TO BE GONE A FEW MORE DAYS. IT'S A MATTER OF NATIONAL SECURITY.

WHATEVER, TODD. IT'S ALWAYS THE SAME OLD SHIT.

GIMME A FUCKING BREAK, ALL RIGHT? I'M DOING THIS FOR OUR COUNTRY AND FOR ABBY'S FUTURE.

MAYBE YOU DON'T GIVE A SHIT ABOUT WHAT KIND OF WORLD SHE GROWS UP IN, BUT--

YEAH, YEAH, IT'S ALWAYS FOR THE GREATER GOOD. NEVER MIND THAT YOU'RE MISSING ANOTHER ONE OF HER RECITALS.

YOU KNOW, ABBY'S ALWAYS PUT ON A HAPPY FACE WHEN YOU'VE BEEN GONE, BUT NOW I DON'T EVEN THINK SHE'S FAKING IT ANYMORE.

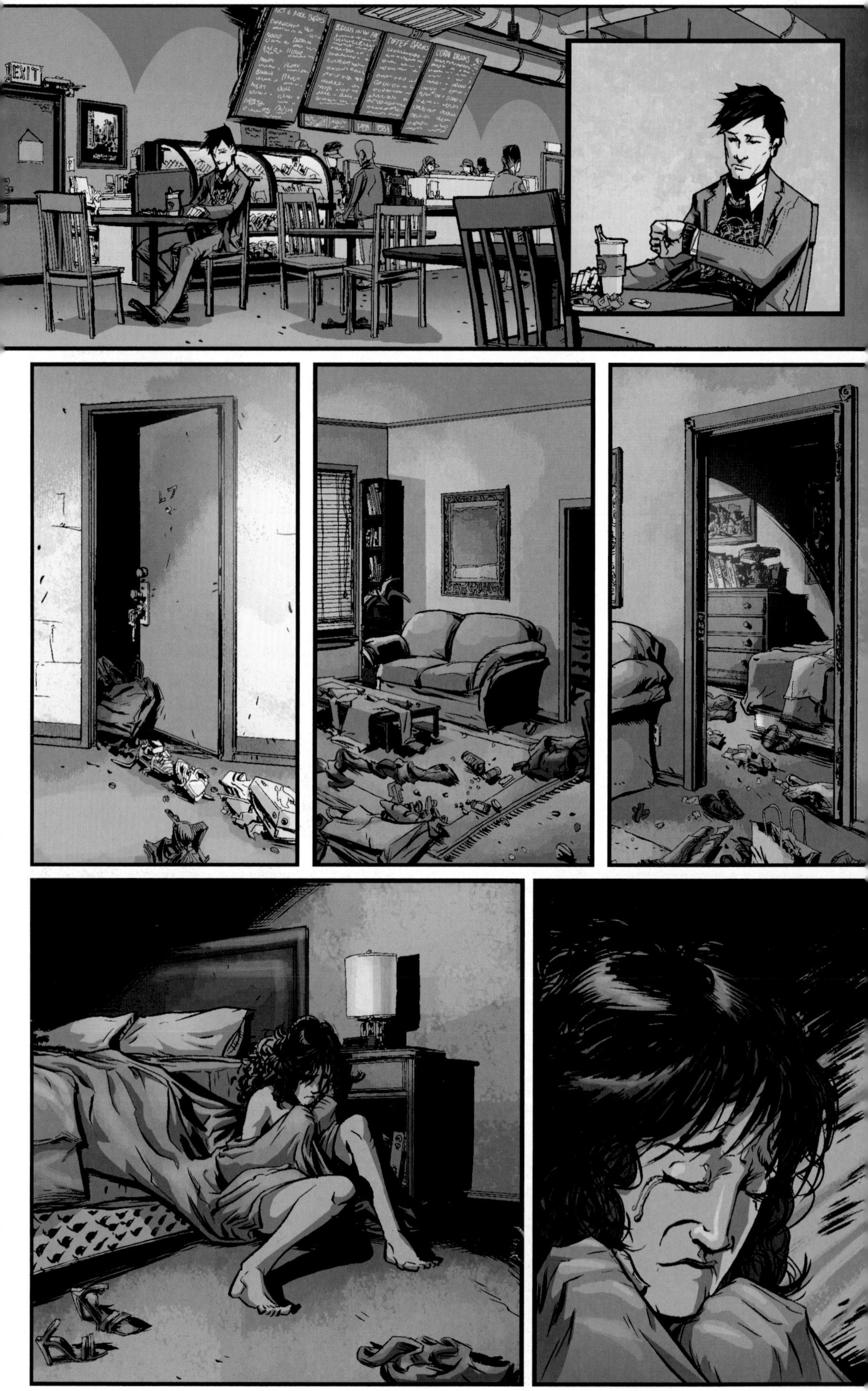
EXIT

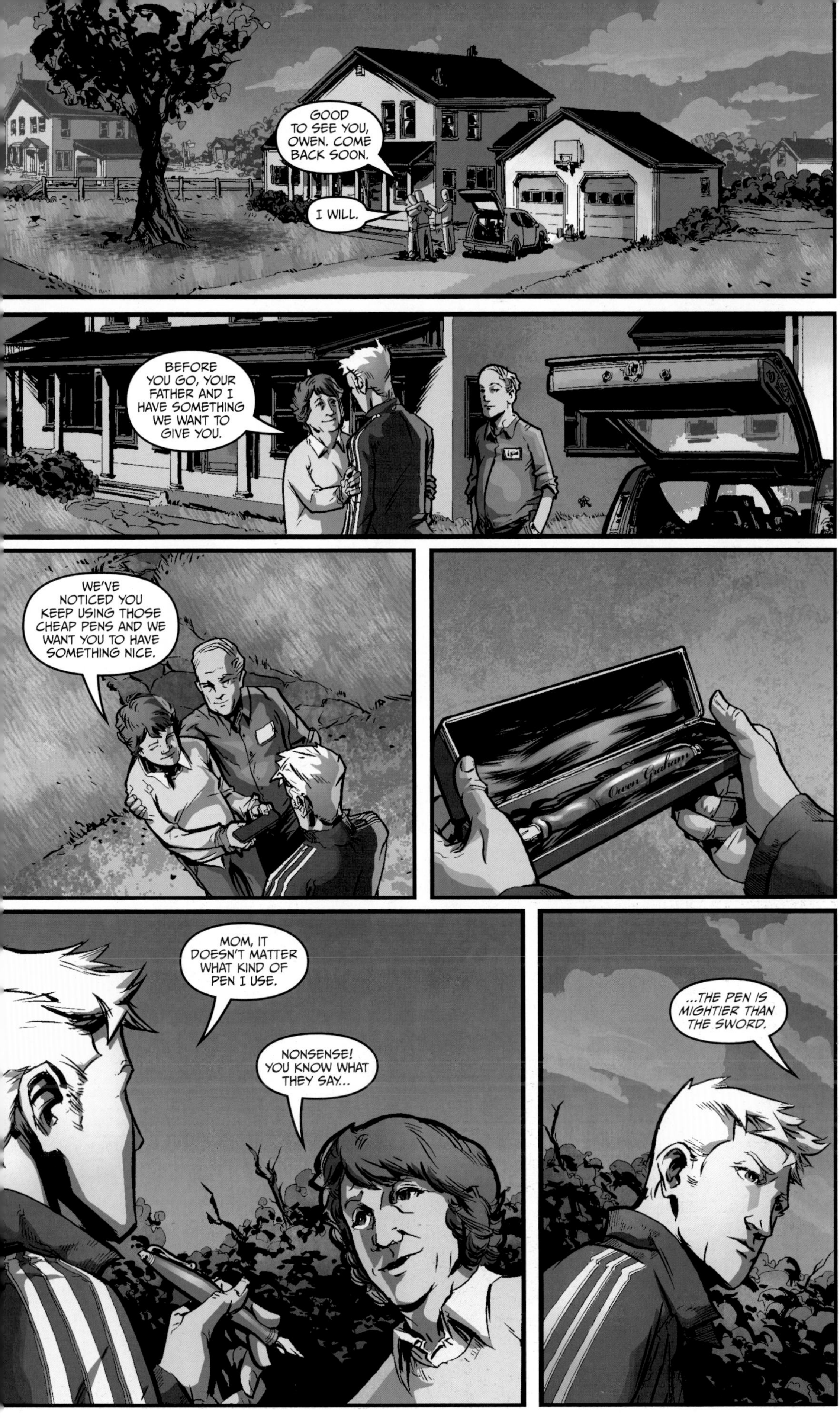
GOOD TO SEE YOU, OWEN. COME BACK SOON.
I WILL.
BEFORE YOU GO, YOUR FATHER AND I HAVE SOMETHING WE WANT TO GIVE YOU.
WE'VE NOTICED YOU KEEP USING THOSE CHEAP PENS AND WE WANT YOU TO HAVE SOMETHING NICE.
Owen Graham
MOM, IT DOESN'T MATTER WHAT KIND OF PEN I USE.
NONSENSE! YOU KNOW WHAT THEY SAY...
...THE PEN IS MIGHTIER THAN THE SWORD.

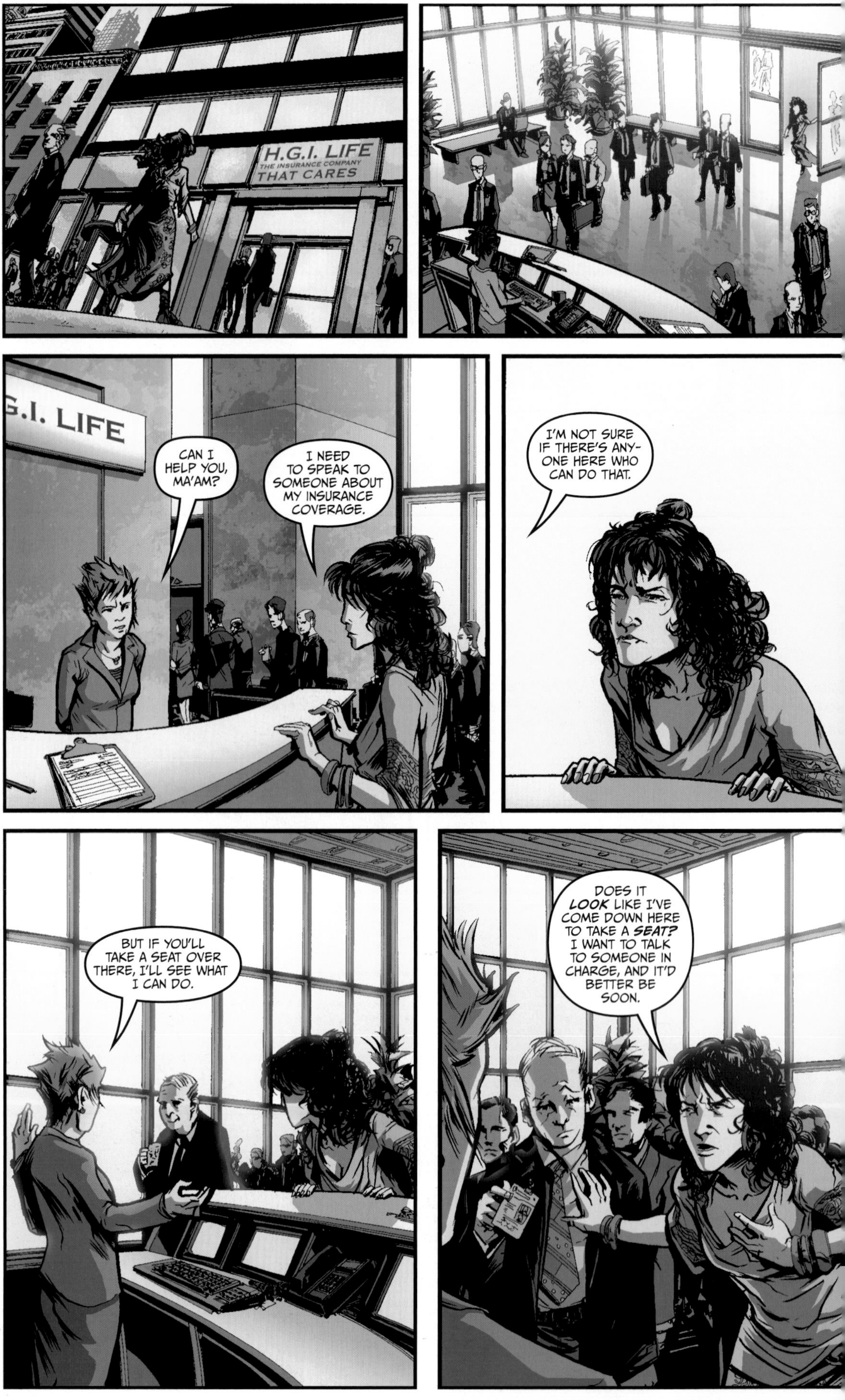
H.G.I. LIFE
THE INSURANCE COMPANY
THAT CARES
G.I. LIFE
CAN I HELP YOU, MA'AM?
I NEED TO SPEAK TO SOMEONE ABOUT MY INSURANCE COVERAGE.
I'M NOT SURE IF THERE'S ANY-ONE HERE WHO CAN DO THAT.
BUT IF YOU'LL TAKE A SEAT OVER THERE, I'LL SEE WHAT I CAN DO.
DOES IT LOOK LIKE I'VE COME DOWN HERE TO TAKE A SEAT? I WANT TO TALK TO SOMEONE IN CHARGE, AND IT'D BETTER BE SOON.

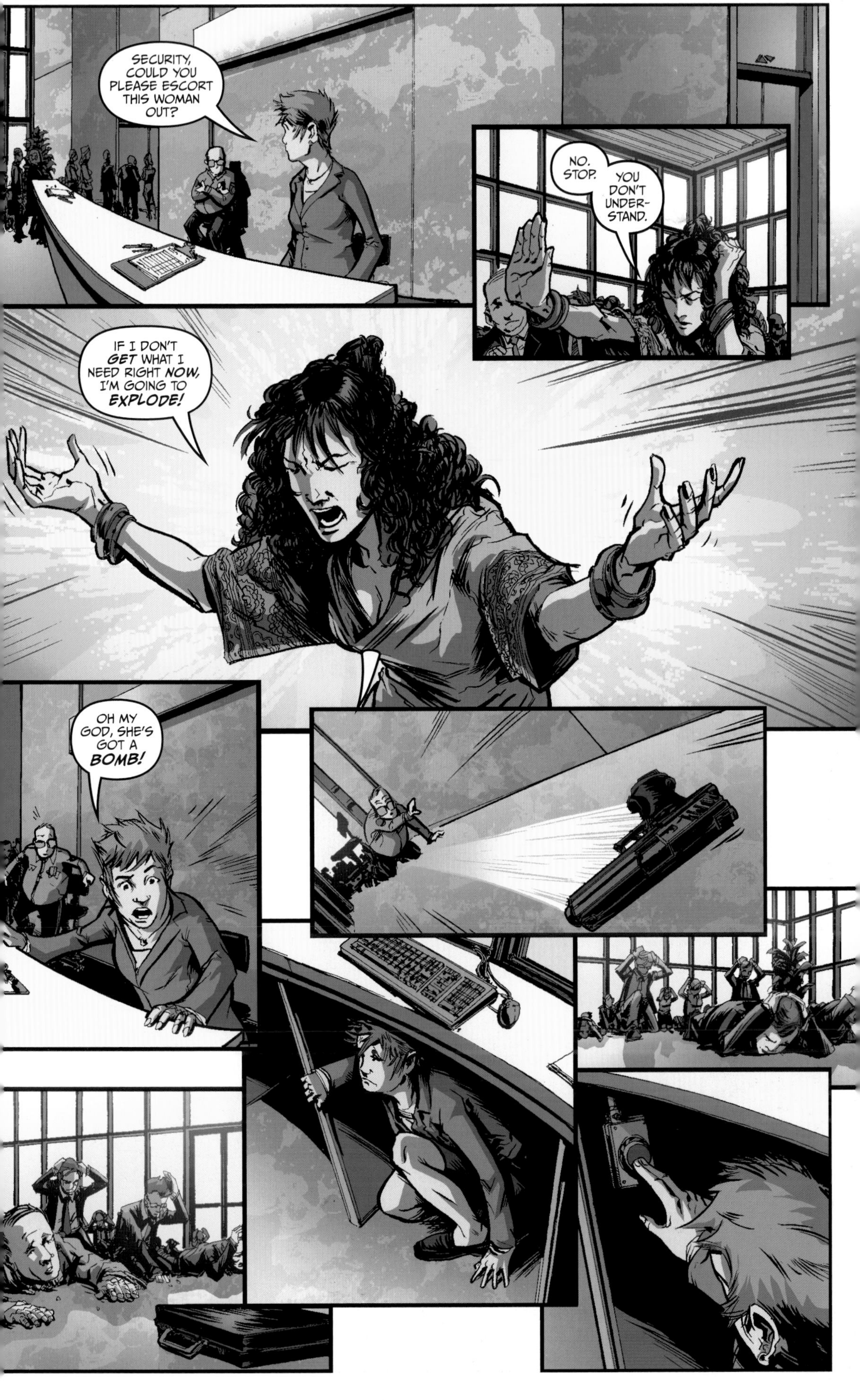
SECURITY, COULD YOU PLEASE ESCORT THIS WOMAN OUT?
NO. STOP.
YOU DON'T UNDER-STAND.
IF I DON'T *GET* WHAT I NEED RIGHT *NOW,* I'M GOING TO *EXPLODE!*
OH MY GOD, SHE'S GOT A *BOMB!*

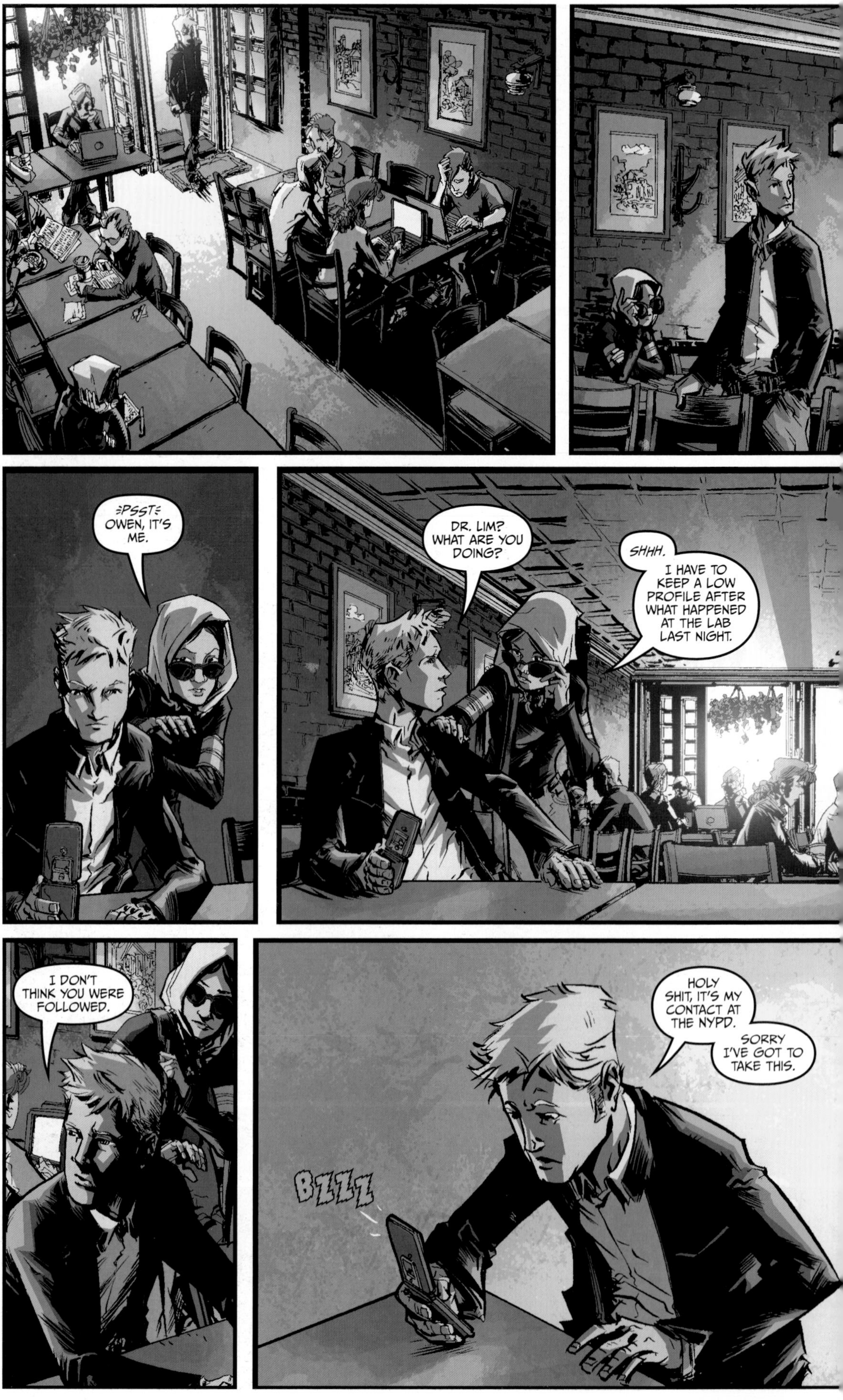
=PSST= OWEN, IT'S ME.
DR. LIM? WHAT ARE YOU DOING?
SHHH.
I HAVE TO KEEP A LOW PROFILE AFTER WHAT HAPPENED AT THE LAB LAST NIGHT.
I DON'T THINK YOU WERE FOLLOWED.
BZZZ
HOLY SHIT, IT'S MY CONTACT AT THE NYPD.
SORRY I'VE GOT TO TAKE THIS.

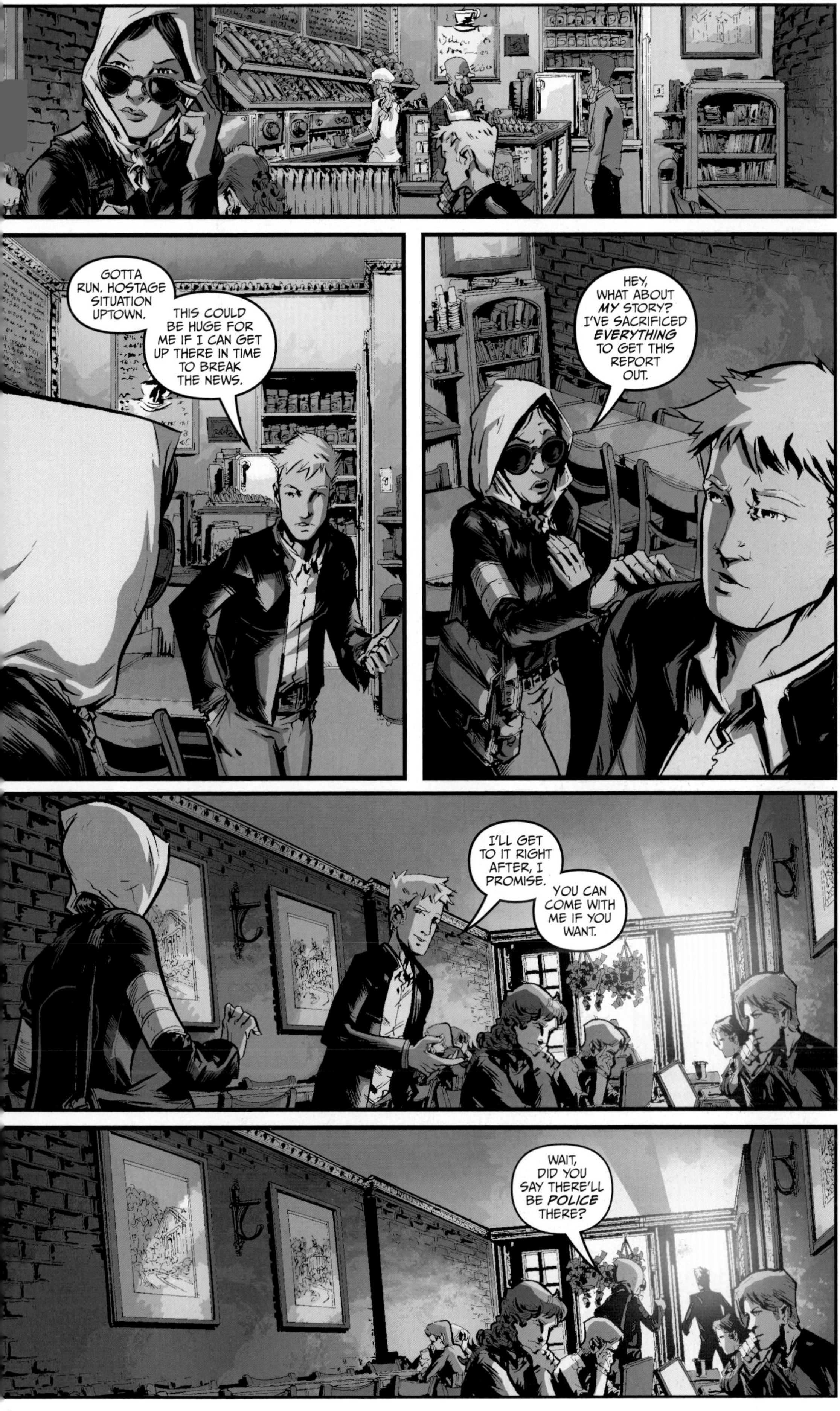
GOTTA RUN. HOSTAGE SITUATION UPTOWN.
THIS COULD BE HUGE FOR ME IF I CAN GET UP THERE IN TIME TO BREAK THE NEWS.
HEY, WHAT ABOUT *MY* STORY? I'VE SACRIFICED *EVERYTHING* TO GET THIS REPORT OUT.
I'LL GET TO IT RIGHT AFTER, I PROMISE.
YOU CAN COME WITH ME IF YOU WANT.
WAIT, DID YOU SAY THERE'LL BE *POLICE* THERE?

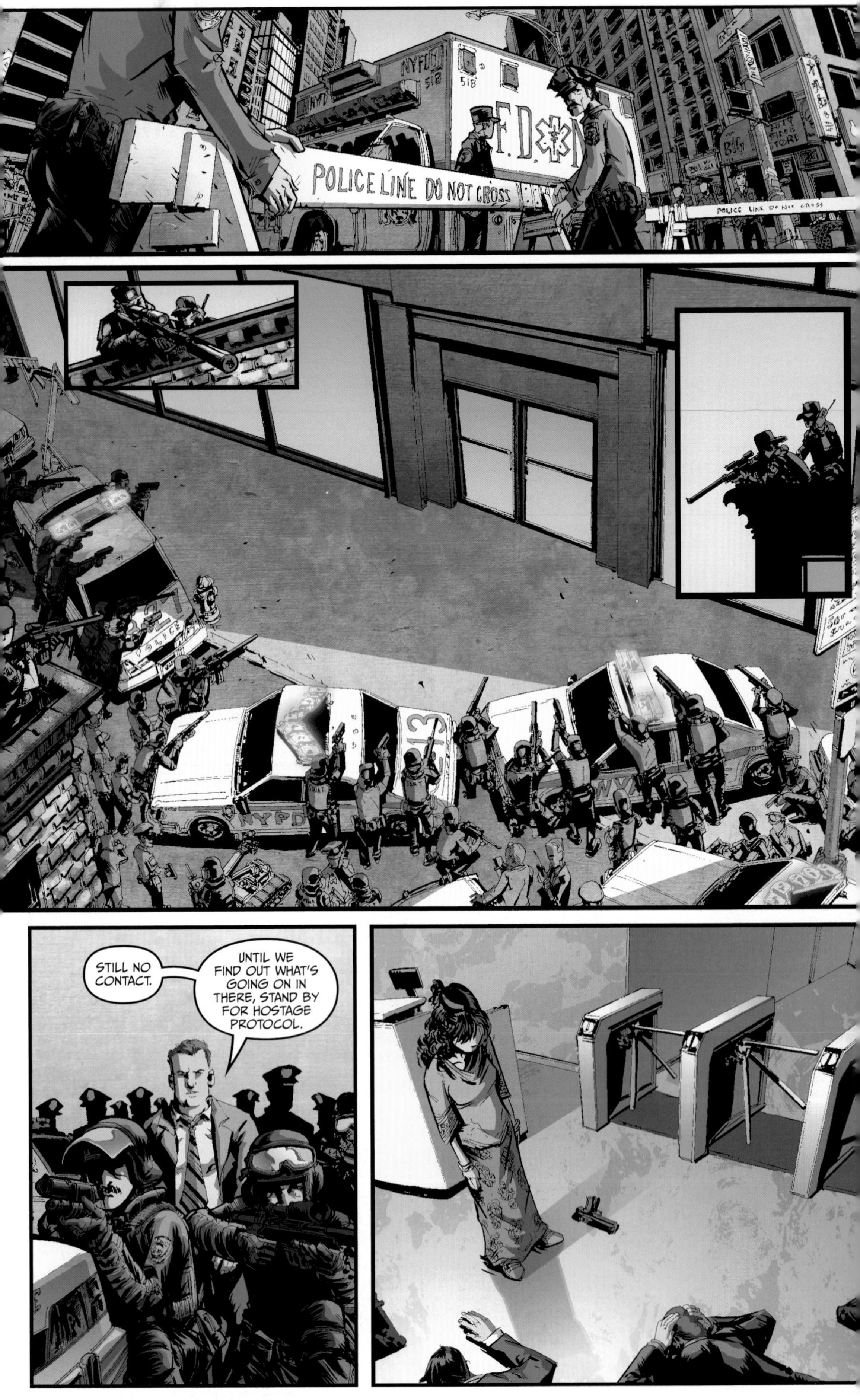
POLICE LINE DO NOT CROSS
POLICE LINE DO NOT CROSS
NYPD
STILL NO CONTACT.
UNTIL WE FIND OUT WHAT'S GOING ON IN THERE, STAND BY FOR HOSTAGE PROTOCOL.

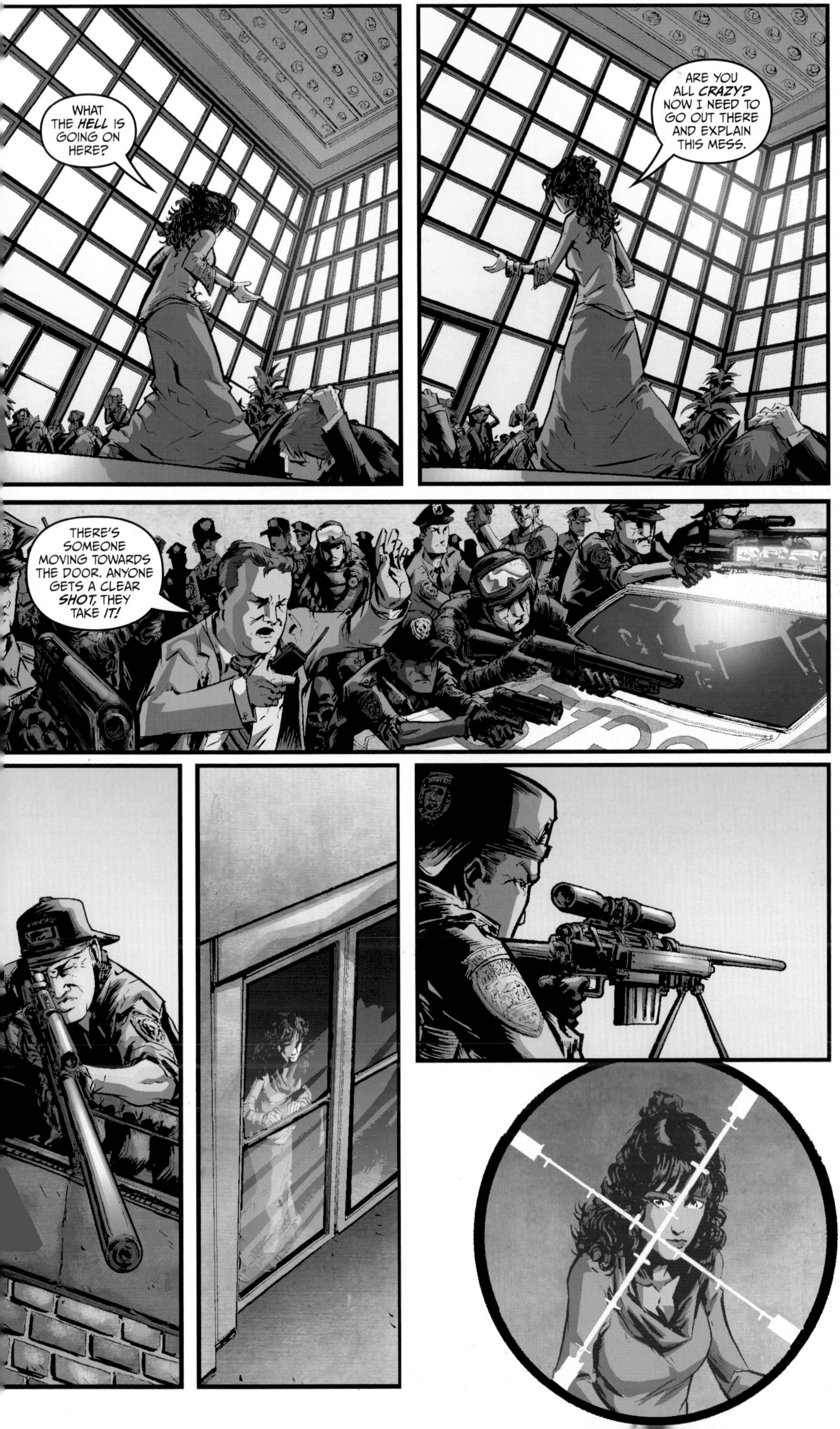
WHAT THE HELL IS GOING ON HERE?
ARE YOU ALL CRAZY? NOW I NEED TO GO OUT THERE AND EXPLAIN THIS MESS.
THERE'S SOMEONE MOVING TOWARDS THE DOOR. ANYONE GETS A CLEAR SHOT, THEY TAKE IT!

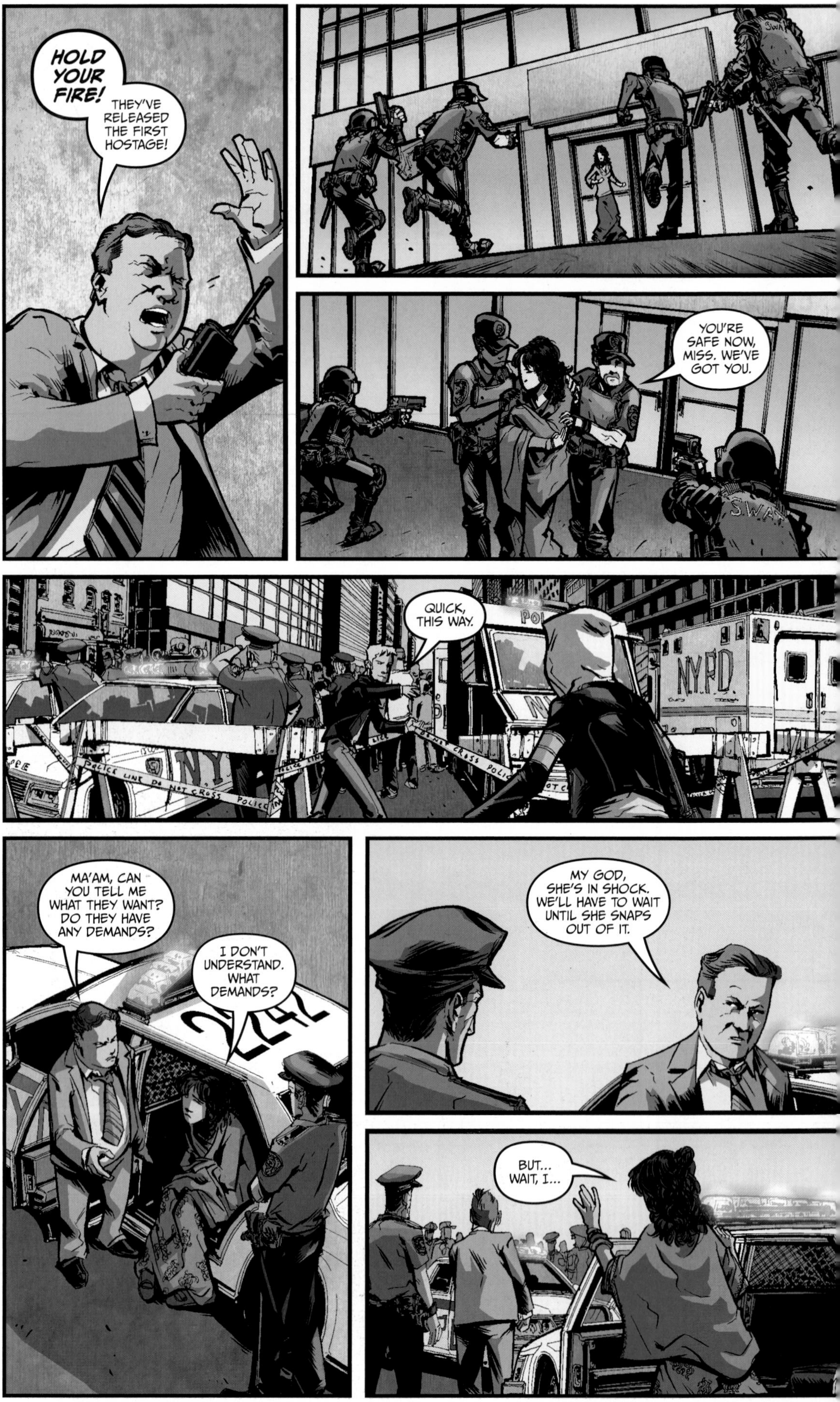
HOLD YOUR FIRE!
THEY'VE RELEASED THE FIRST HOSTAGE!
SWAT
YOU'RE SAFE NOW, MISS. WE'VE GOT YOU.
SWAT
QUICK, THIS WAY.
NYPD
POLICE LINE DO NOT CROSS
MA'AM, CAN YOU TELL ME WHAT THEY WANT? DO THEY HAVE ANY DEMANDS?
I DON'T UNDERSTAND. WHAT DEMANDS?
2242
MY GOD, SHE'S IN SHOCK. WE'LL HAVE TO WAIT UNTIL SHE SNAPS OUT OF IT.
BUT... WAIT, I...

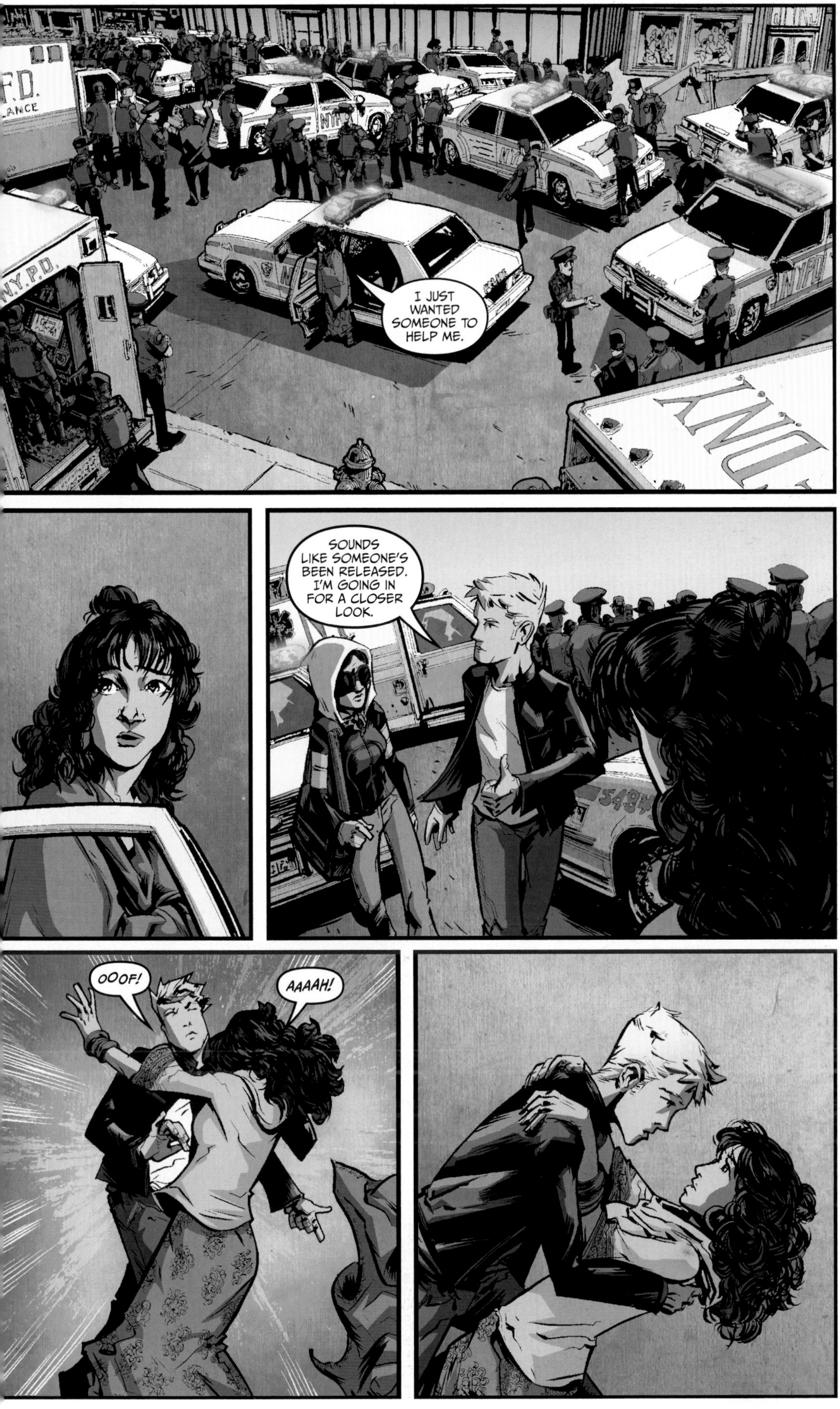

I JUST WANTED SOMEONE TO HELP ME.
SOUNDS LIKE SOMEONE'S BEEN RELEASED. I'M GOING IN FOR A CLOSER LOOK.
OOOF!
AAAAH!

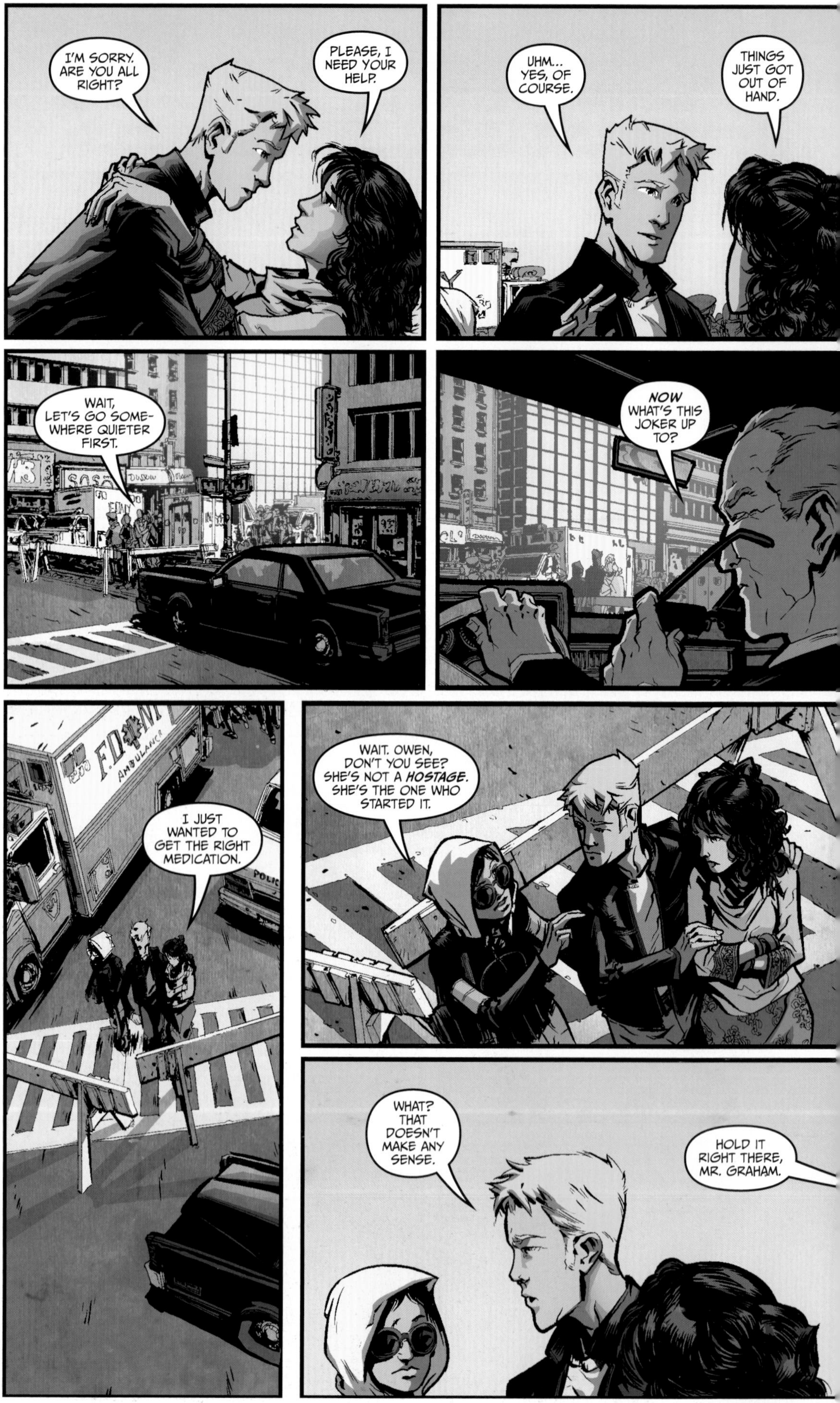
I'M SORRY. ARE YOU ALL RIGHT?
PLEASE, I NEED YOUR HELP.
UHM... YES, OF COURSE.
THINGS JUST GOT OUT OF HAND.
WAIT, LET'S GO SOME-WHERE QUIETER FIRST.
NOW WHAT'S THIS JOKER UP TO?
I JUST WANTED TO GET THE RIGHT MEDICATION.
WAIT. OWEN, DON'T YOU SEE? SHE'S NOT A HOSTAGE. SHE'S THE ONE WHO STARTED IT.
WHAT? THAT DOESN'T MAKE ANY SENSE.
HOLD IT RIGHT THERE, MR. GRAHAM.

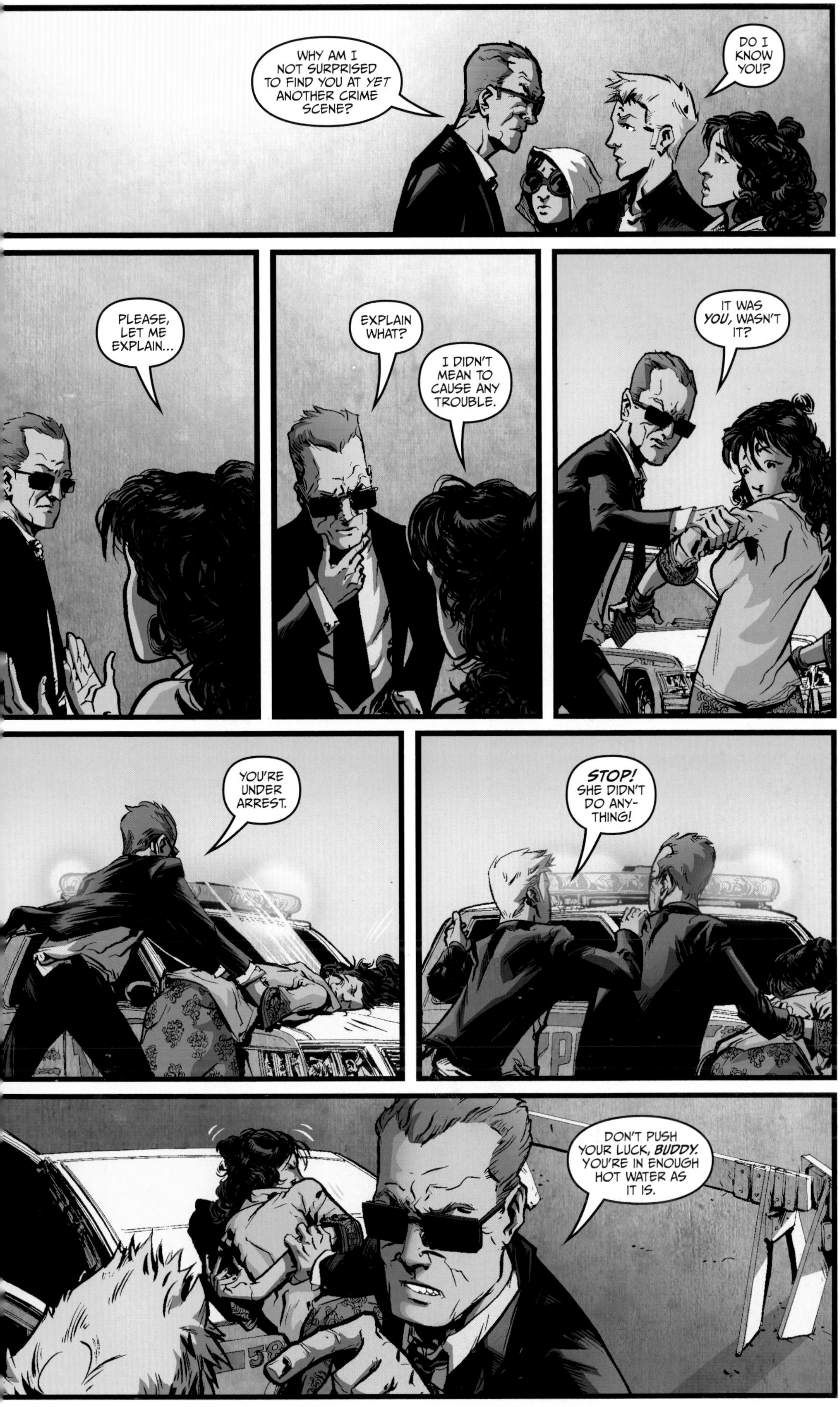
WHY AM I NOT SURPRISED TO FIND YOU AT YET ANOTHER CRIME SCENE?
DO I KNOW YOU?
PLEASE, LET ME EXPLAIN...
EXPLAIN WHAT?
I DIDN'T MEAN TO CAUSE ANY TROUBLE.
IT WAS YOU, WASN'T IT?
YOU'RE UNDER ARREST.
STOP! SHE DIDN'T DO ANY-THING!
DON'T PUSH YOUR LUCK, BUDDY. YOU'RE IN ENOUGH HOT WATER AS IT IS.

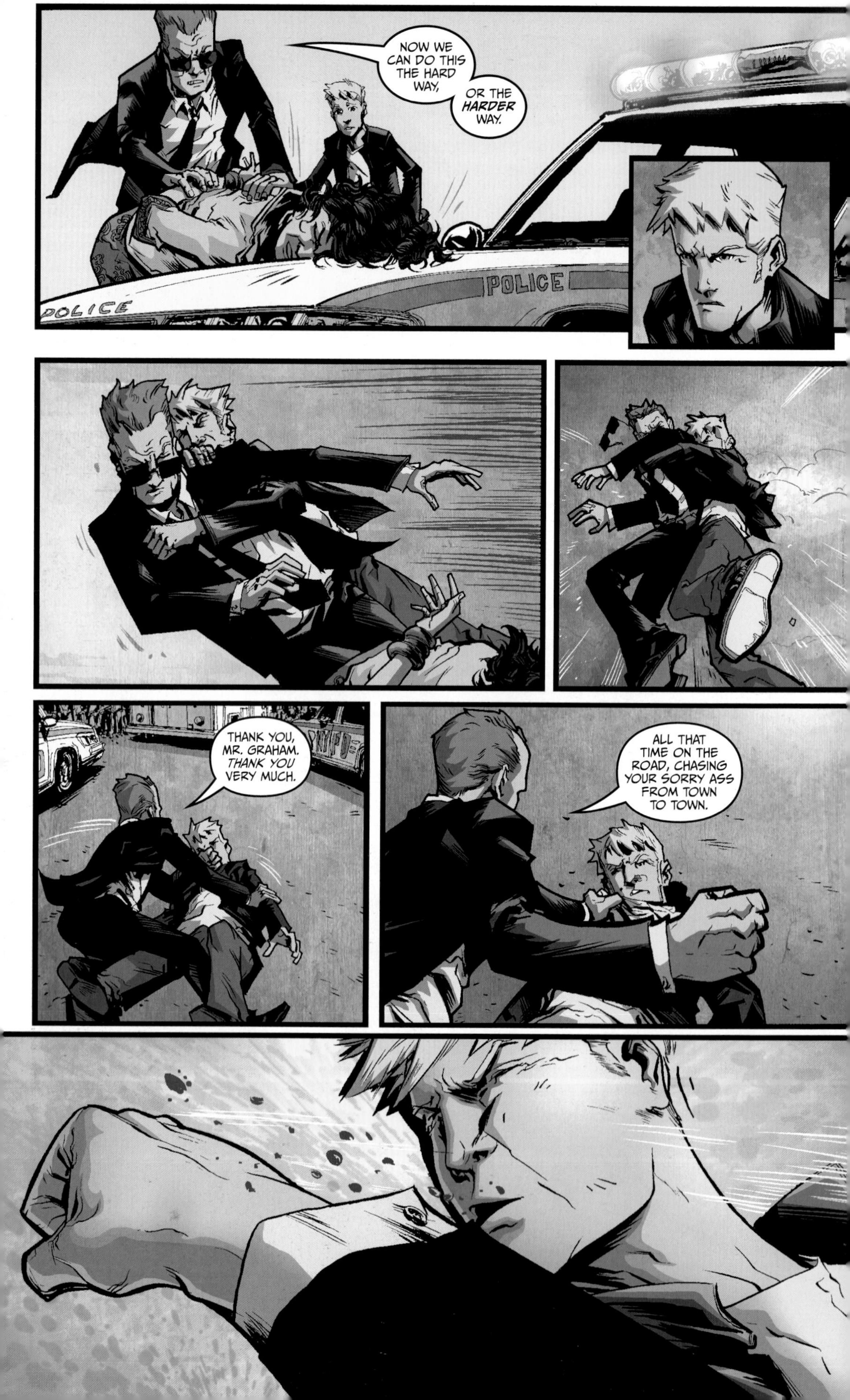
NOW WE CAN DO THIS THE HARD WAY,
OR THE *HARDER* WAY.
POLICE
POLICE
THANK YOU, MR. GRAHAM. *THANK YOU* VERY MUCH.
ALL THAT TIME ON THE ROAD, CHASING YOUR SORRY ASS FROM TOWN TO TOWN.

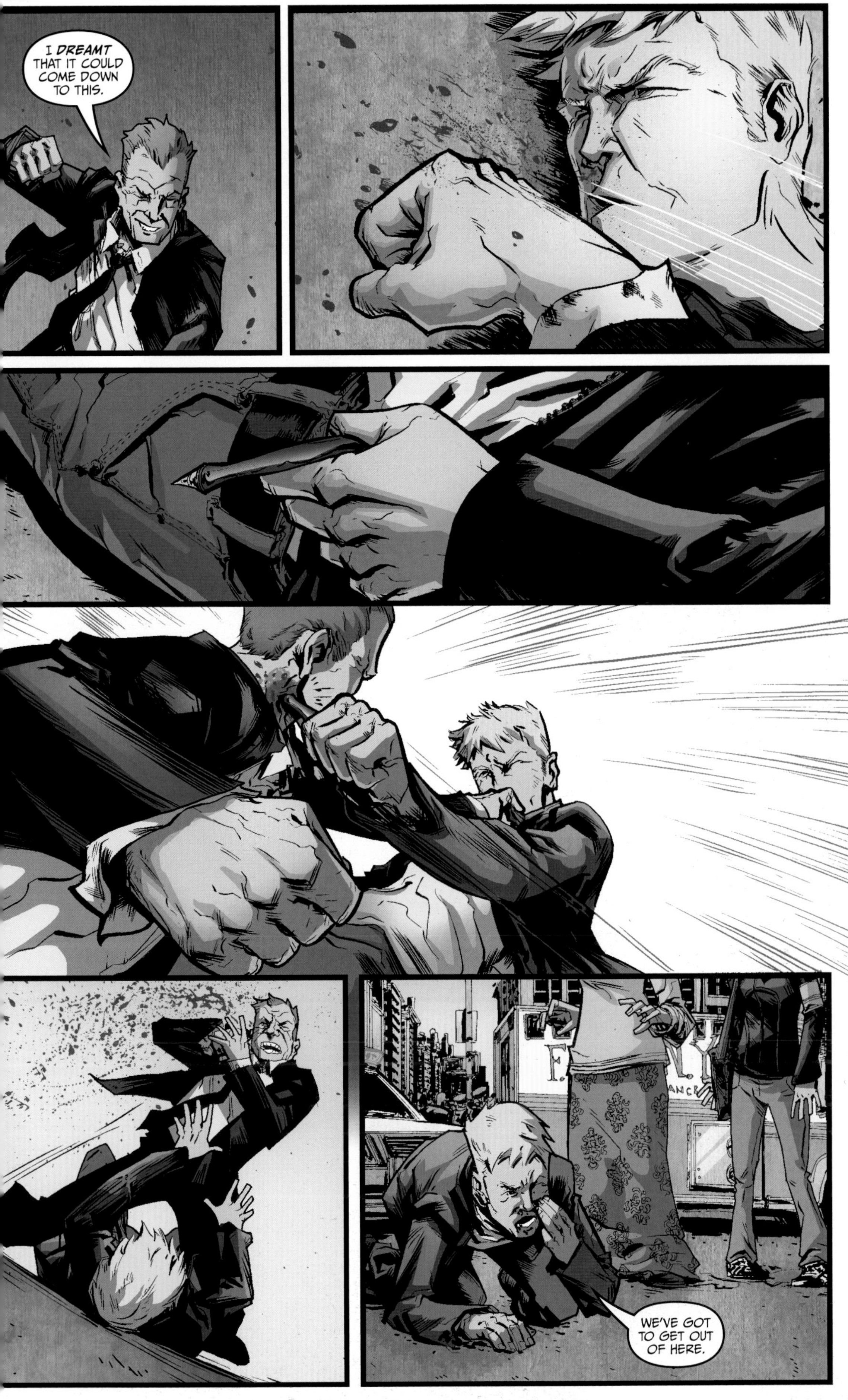
I DREAMT THAT IT COULD COME DOWN TO THIS.
WE'VE GOT TO GET OUT OF HERE.

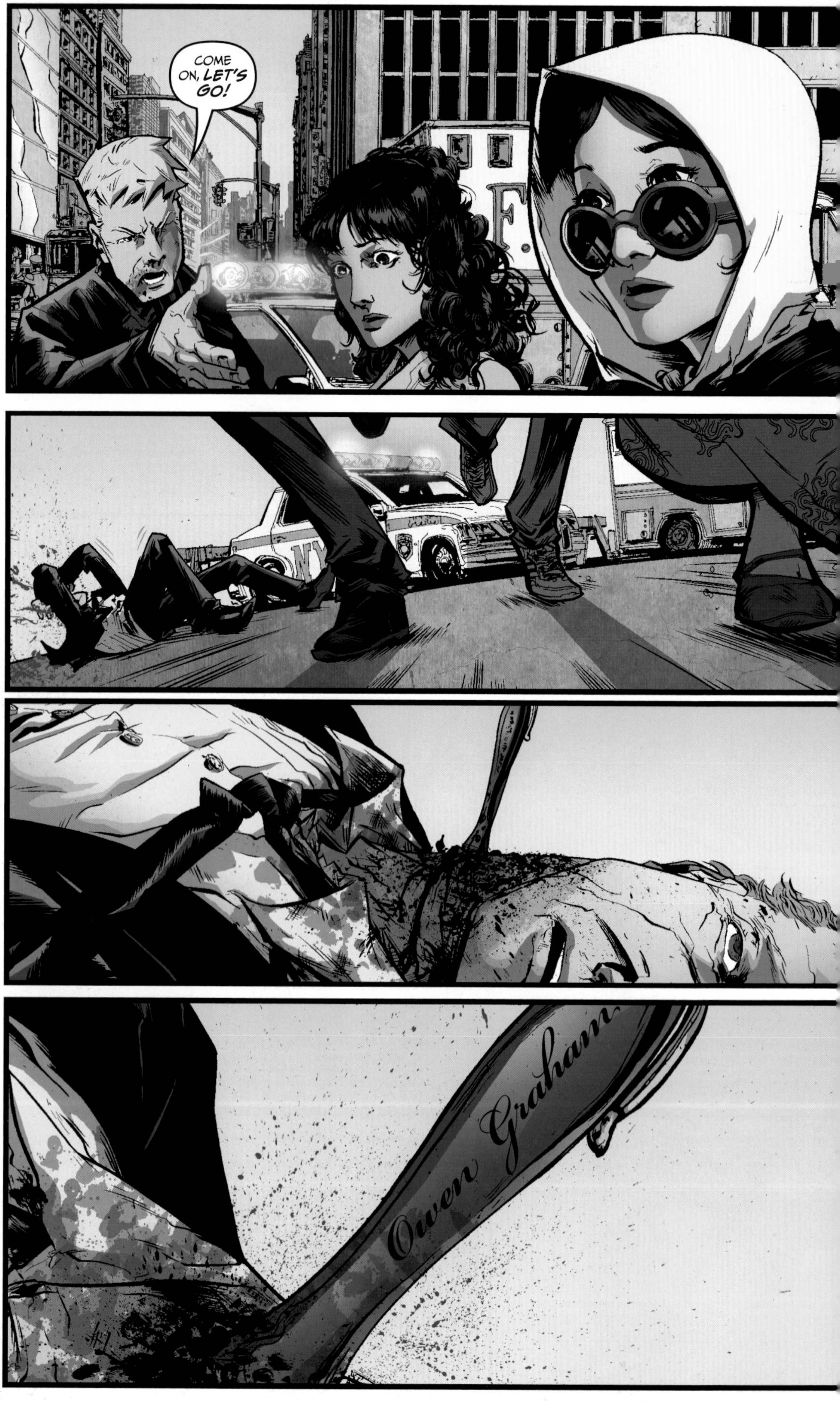
COME ON, LET'S GO!
Owen Graham

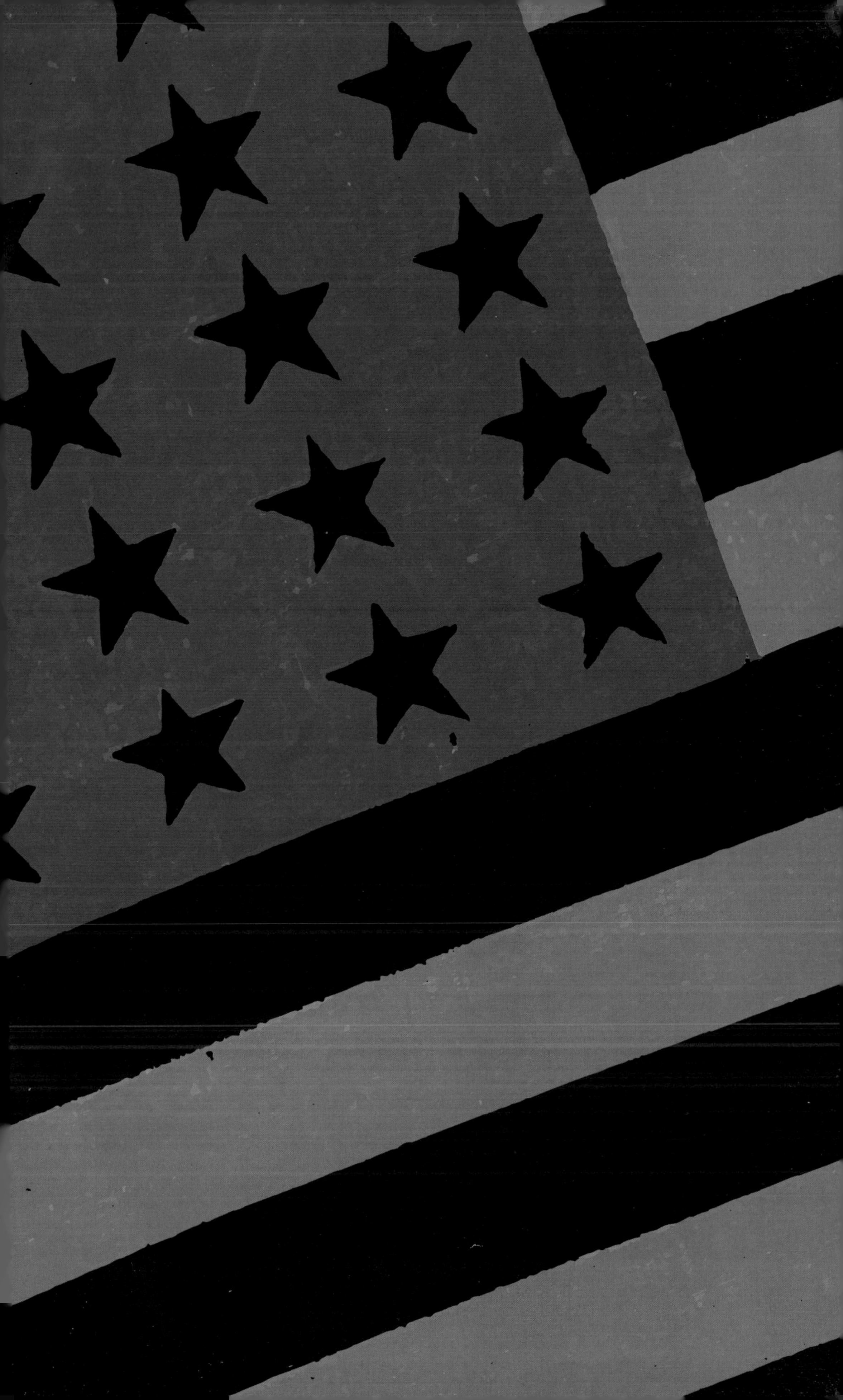

Chapter 2

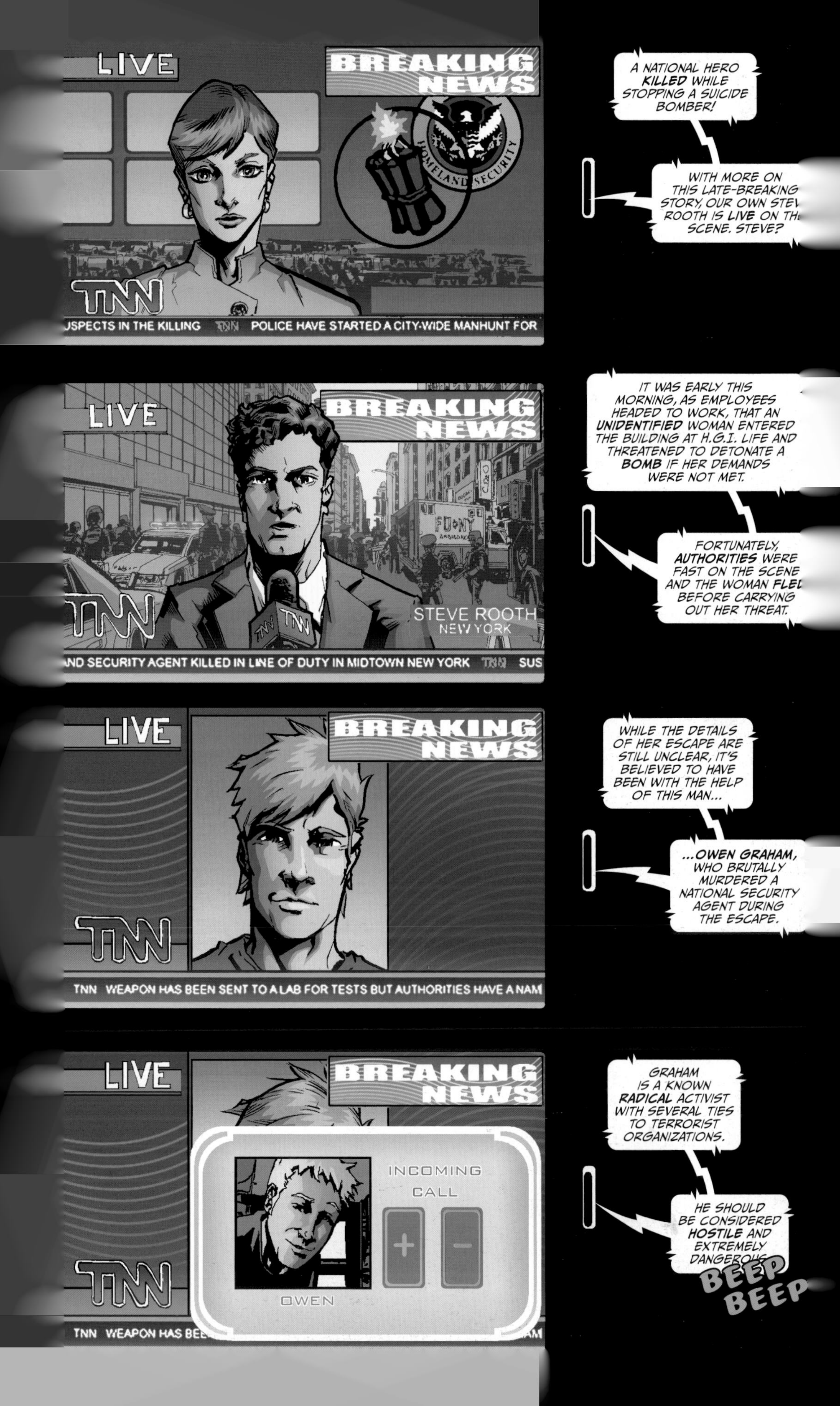

LIVE
BREAKING NEWS
HOMELAND SECURITY
TNN
USPECTS IN THE KILLING TNN POLICE HAVE STARTED A CITY-WIDE MANHUNT FOR
A NATIONAL HERO KILLED WHILE STOPPING A SUICIDE BOMBER!
WITH MORE ON THIS LATE-BREAKING STORY, OUR OWN STEV ROOTH IS LIVE ON TH SCENE. STEVE?
LIVE
BREAKING NEWS
TNN
STEVE ROOTH
NEW YORK
ND SECURITY AGENT KILLED IN LINE OF DUTY IN MIDTOWN NEW YORK TNN SUS
IT WAS EARLY THIS MORNING, AS EMPLOYEES HEADED TO WORK, THAT AN UNIDENTIFIED WOMAN ENTERED THE BUILDING AT H.G.I. LIFE AND THREATENED TO DETONATE A BOMB IF HER DEMANDS WERE NOT MET.
FORTUNATELY, AUTHORITIES WERE FAST ON THE SCENE AND THE WOMAN FLE BEFORE CARRYING OUT HER THREAT.
LIVE
BREAKING NEWS
TNN
TNN WEAPON HAS BEEN SENT TO A LAB FOR TESTS BUT AUTHORITIES HAVE A NAM
WHILE THE DETAILS OF HER ESCAPE ARE STILL UNCLEAR, IT'S BELIEVED TO HAVE BEEN WITH THE HELP OF THIS MAN...
...OWEN GRAHAM, WHO BRUTALLY MURDERED A NATIONAL SECURITY AGENT DURING THE ESCAPE.
LIVE
BREAKING NEWS
TNN
INCOMING CALL
+ −
OWEN
TNN WEAPON HAS BEE
GRAHAM IS A KNOWN RADICAL ACTIVIST WITH SEVERAL TIES TO TERRORIST ORGANIZATIONS.
HE SHOULD BE CONSIDERED HOSTILE AND EXTREMELY DANGEROUS
BEEP BEEP

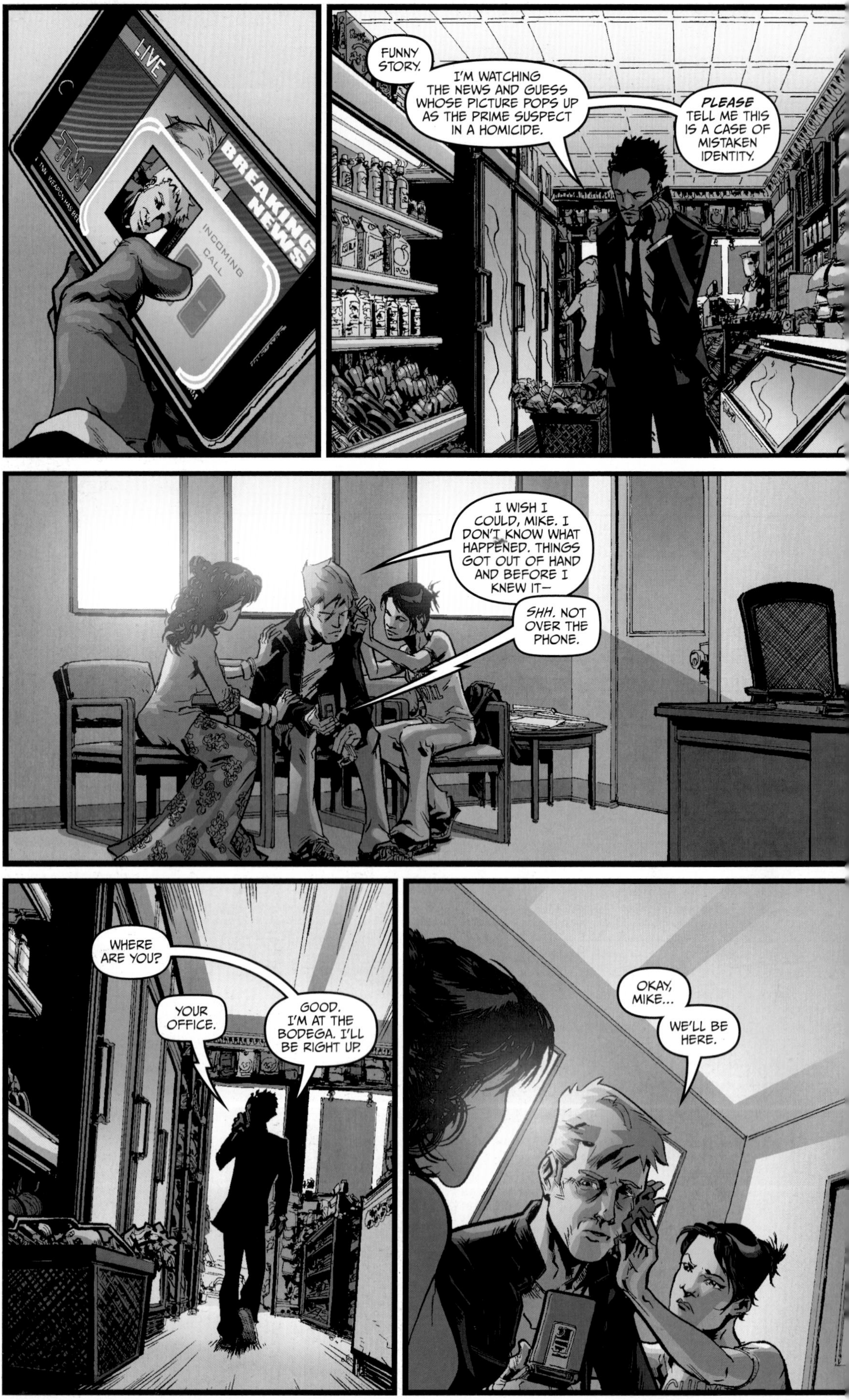
LIVE
BREAKING NEWS
INCOMING CALL
FUNNY STORY.
I'M WATCHING THE NEWS AND GUESS WHOSE PICTURE POPS UP AS THE PRIME SUSPECT IN A HOMICIDE.
PLEASE TELL ME THIS IS A CASE OF MISTAKEN IDENTITY.
I WISH I COULD, MIKE. I DON'T KNOW WHAT HAPPENED. THINGS GOT OUT OF HAND AND BEFORE I KNEW IT—
SHH. NOT OVER THE PHONE.
WHERE ARE YOU?
YOUR OFFICE.
GOOD. I'M AT THE BODEGA. I'LL BE RIGHT UP.
OKAY, MIKE...
WE'LL BE HERE.

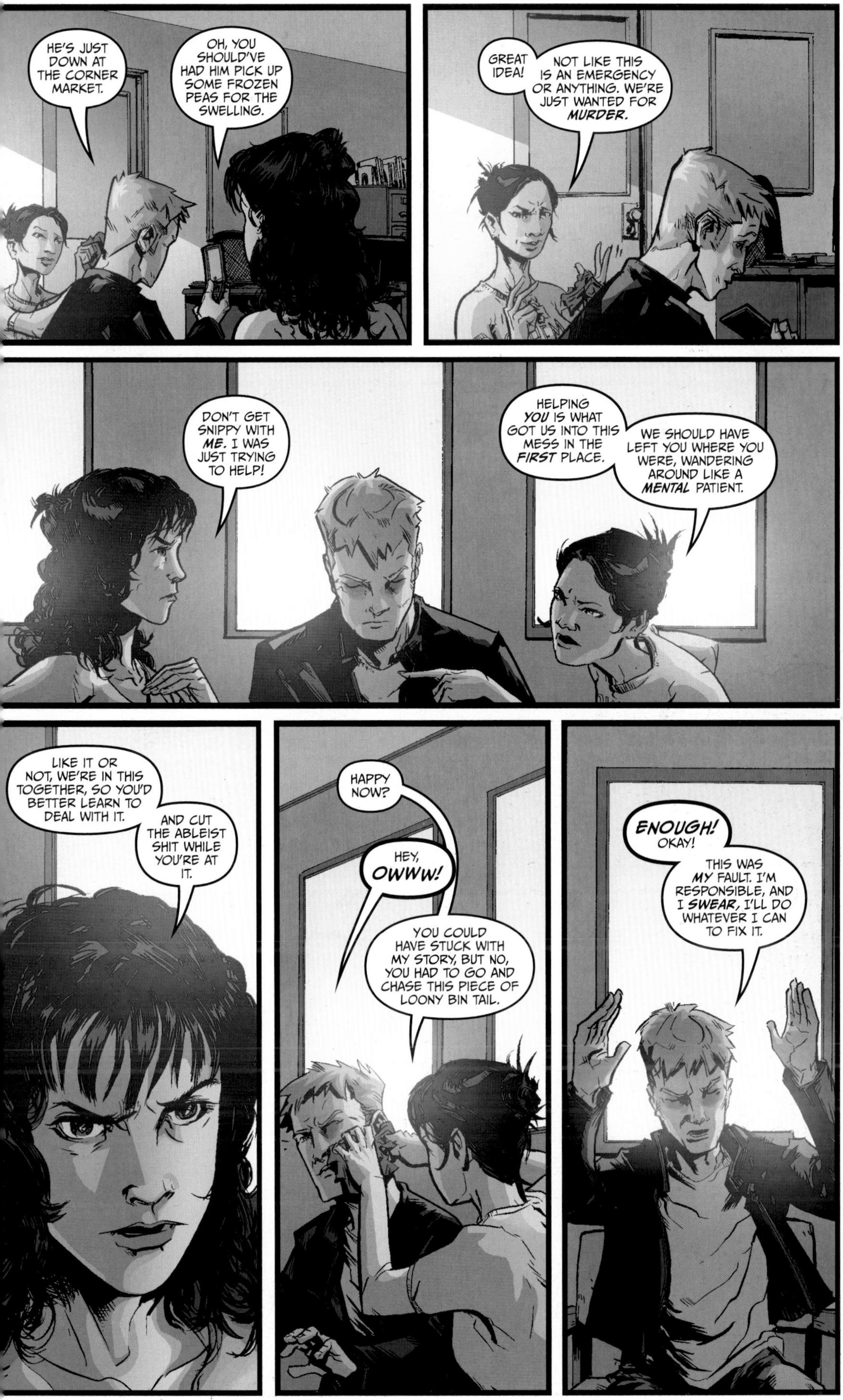
HE'S JUST DOWN AT THE CORNER MARKET.
OH, YOU SHOULD'VE HAD HIM PICK UP SOME FROZEN PEAS FOR THE SWELLING.
GREAT IDEA!
NOT LIKE THIS IS AN EMERGENCY OR ANYTHING. WE'RE JUST WANTED FOR MURDER.
DON'T GET SNIPPY WITH ME. I WAS JUST TRYING TO HELP!
HELPING YOU IS WHAT GOT US INTO THIS MESS IN THE FIRST PLACE.
WE SHOULD HAVE LEFT YOU WHERE YOU WERE, WANDERING AROUND LIKE A MENTAL PATIENT.
LIKE IT OR NOT, WE'RE IN THIS TOGETHER, SO YOU'D BETTER LEARN TO DEAL WITH IT.
AND CUT THE ABLEIST SHIT WHILE YOU'RE AT IT.
HAPPY NOW?
HEY, OWWW!
YOU COULD HAVE STUCK WITH MY STORY, BUT NO, YOU HAD TO GO AND CHASE THIS PIECE OF LOONY BIN TAIL.
ENOUGH! OKAY!
THIS WAS MY FAULT. I'M RESPONSIBLE, AND I SWEAR, I'LL DO WHATEVER I CAN TO FIX IT.

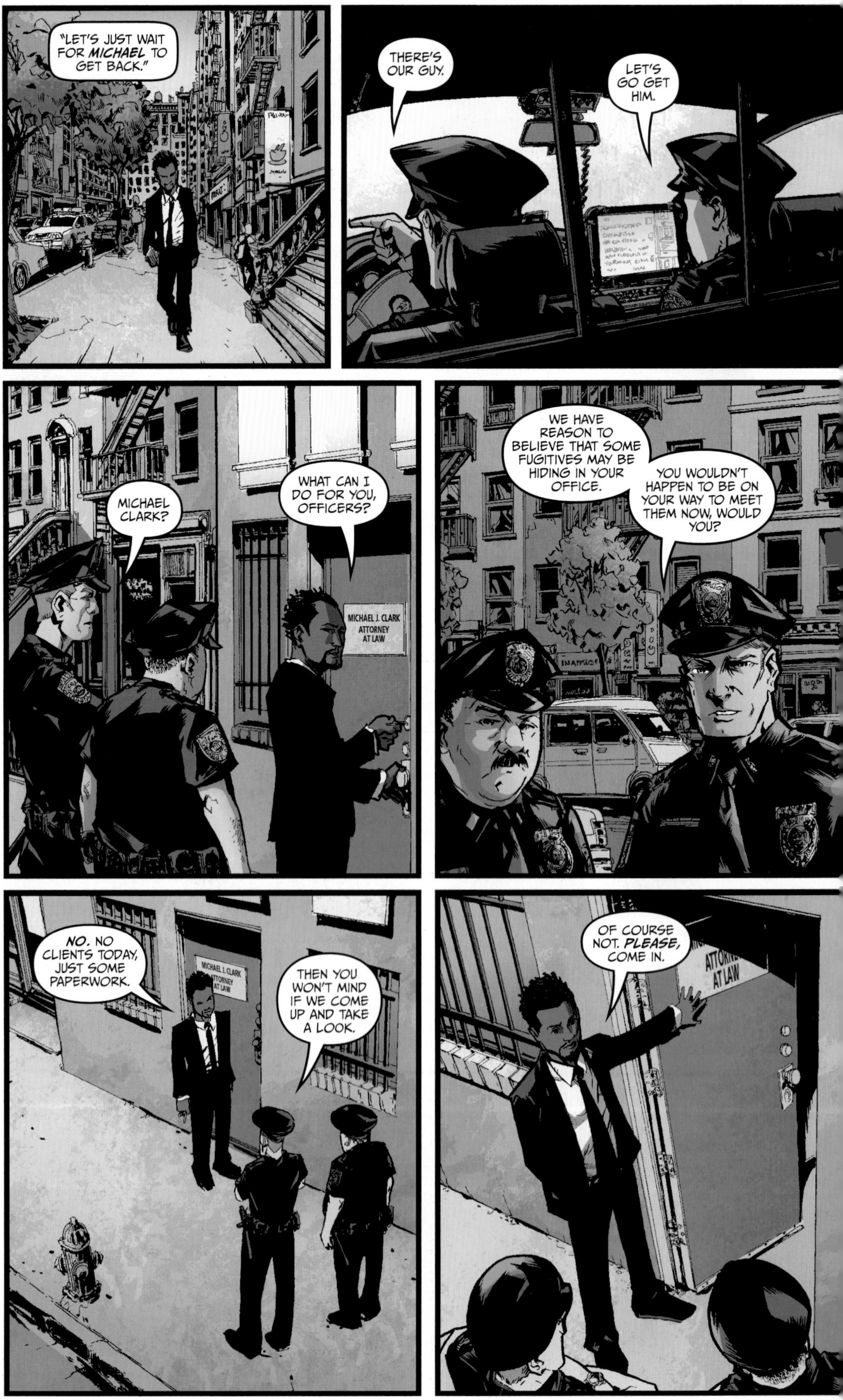
"LET'S JUST WAIT FOR MICHAEL TO GET BACK."
THERE'S OUR GUY.
LET'S GO GET HIM.
MICHAEL CLARK?
WHAT CAN I DO FOR YOU, OFFICERS?
MICHAEL J. CLARK ATTORNEY AT LAW
WE HAVE REASON TO BELIEVE THAT SOME FUGITIVES MAY BE HIDING IN YOUR OFFICE.
YOU WOULDN'T HAPPEN TO BE ON YOUR WAY TO MEET THEM NOW, WOULD YOU?
NO. NO CLIENTS TODAY, JUST SOME PAPERWORK.
MICHAEL J. CLARK ATTORNEY AT LAW
THEN YOU WON'T MIND IF WE COME UP AND TAKE A LOOK.
OF COURSE NOT. PLEASE, COME IN.
ATTORNEY AT LAW

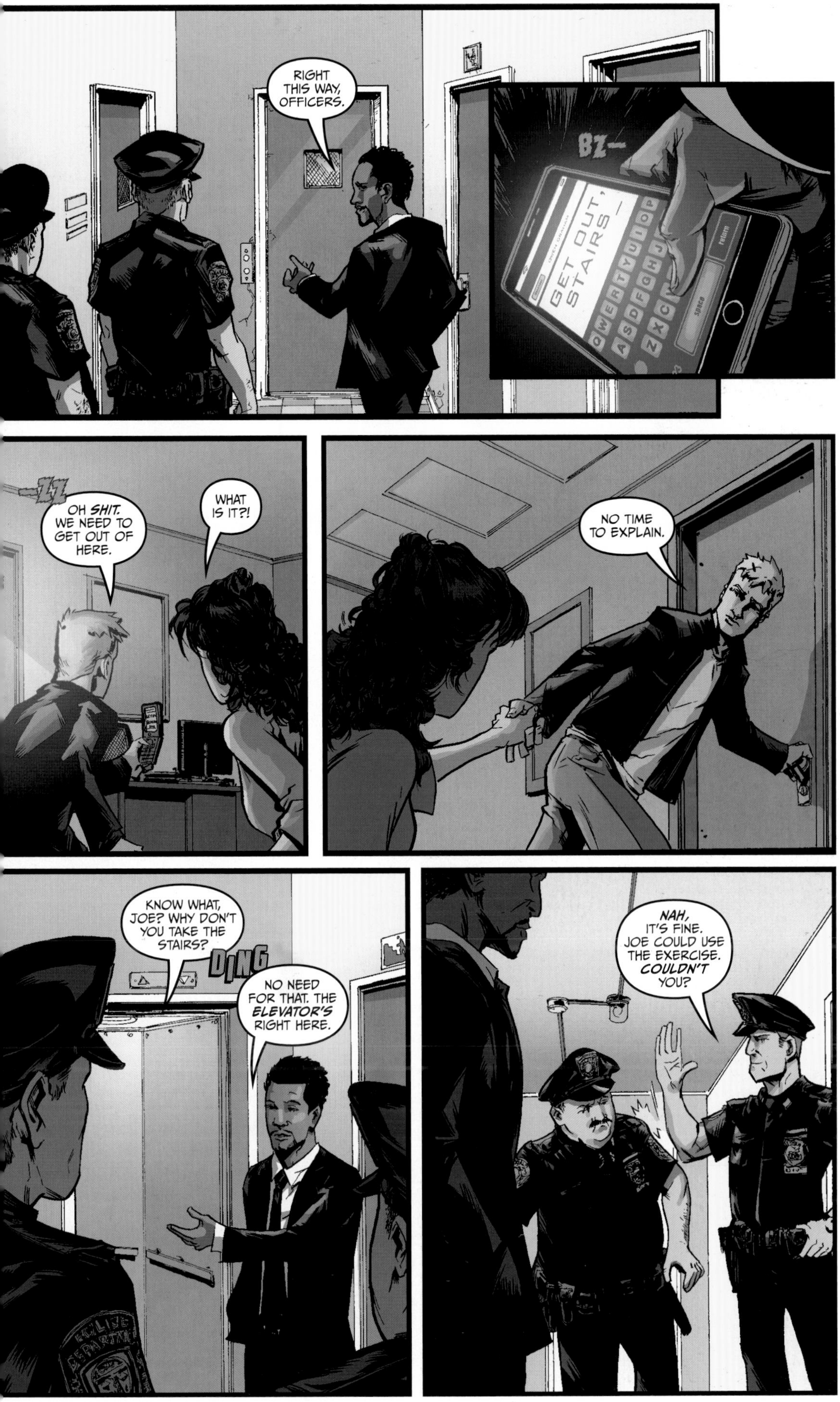
RIGHT THIS WAY, OFFICERS.
BZ--
GET OUT, STAIRS_
OH SHIT. WE NEED TO GET OUT OF HERE.
WHAT IS IT?!
NO TIME TO EXPLAIN.
KNOW WHAT, JOE? WHY DON'T YOU TAKE THE STAIRS?
DING
NO NEED FOR THAT. THE ELEVATOR'S RIGHT HERE.
NAH, IT'S FINE. JOE COULD USE THE EXERCISE. COULDN'T YOU?

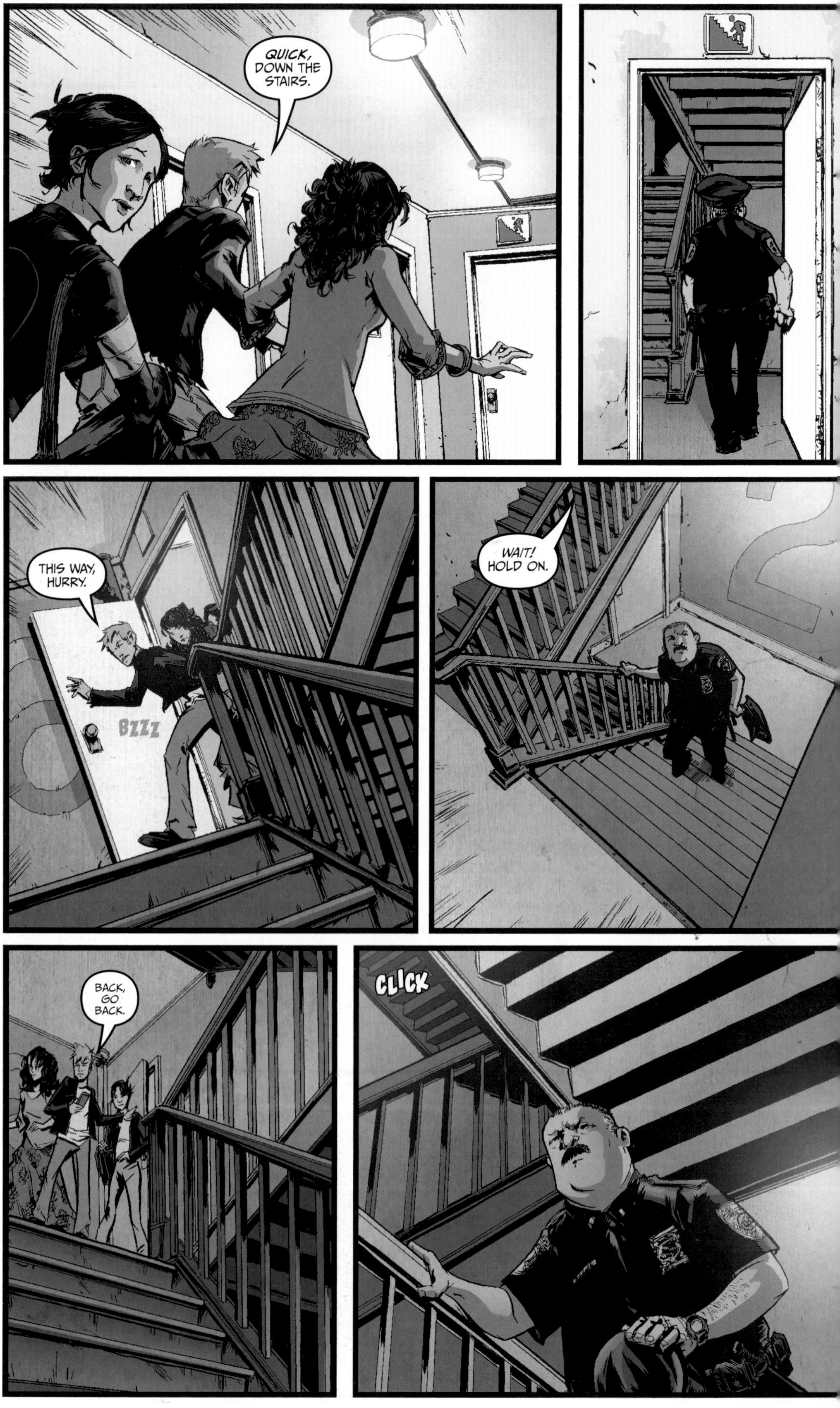
QUICK, DOWN THE STAIRS.
THIS WAY, HURRY.
BZZZ
WAIT! HOLD ON.
BACK, GO BACK.
CLICK

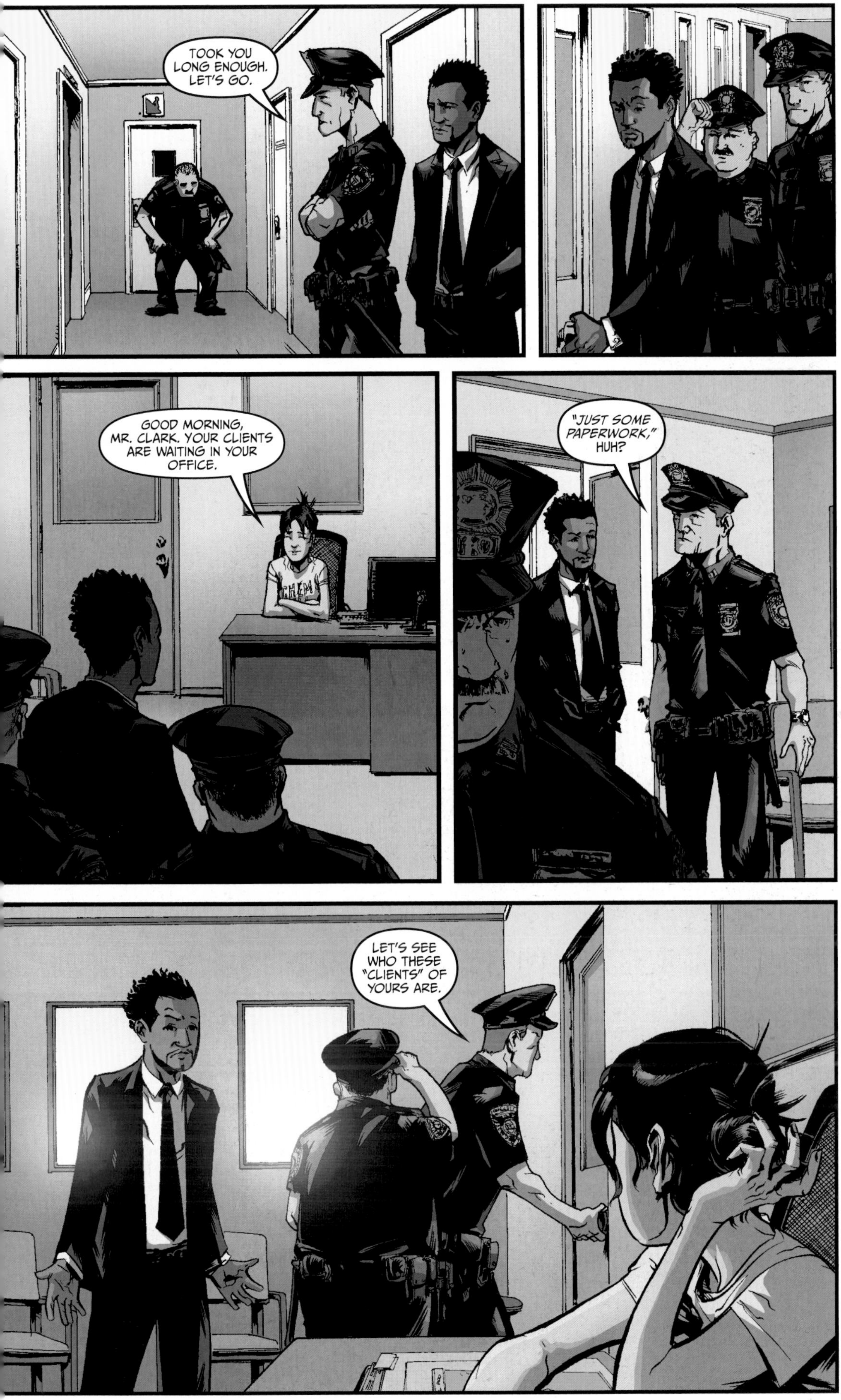
TOOK YOU LONG ENOUGH. LET'S GO.
GOOD MORNING, MR. CLARK. YOUR CLIENTS ARE WAITING IN YOUR OFFICE.
"JUST SOME PAPERWORK," HUH?
LET'S SEE WHO THESE "CLIENTS" OF YOURS ARE.

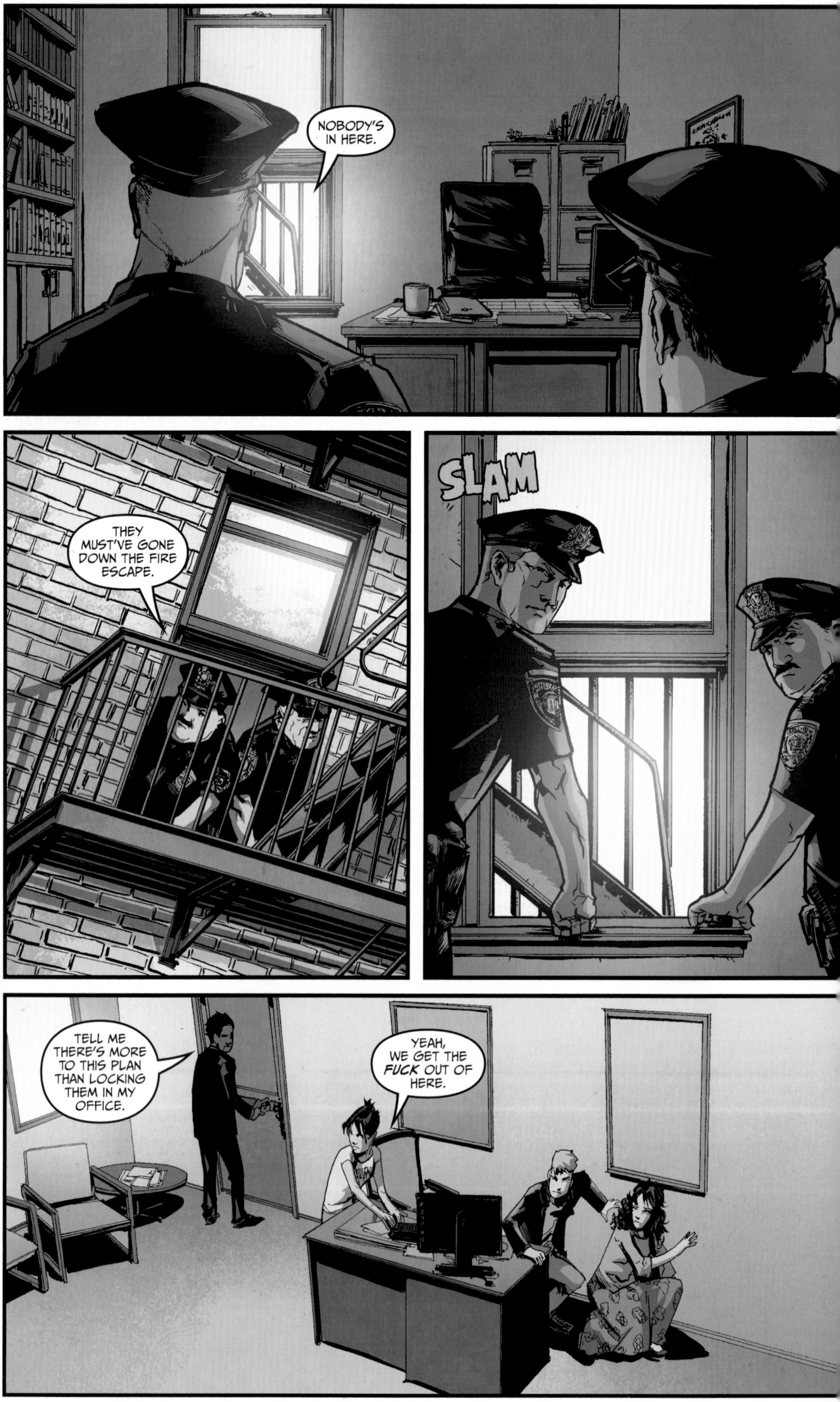
NOBODY'S IN HERE.
THEY MUST'VE GONE DOWN THE FIRE ESCAPE.
SLAM
TELL ME THERE'S MORE TO THIS PLAN THAN LOCKING THEM IN MY OFFICE.
YEAH, WE GET THE *FUCK* OUT OF HERE.

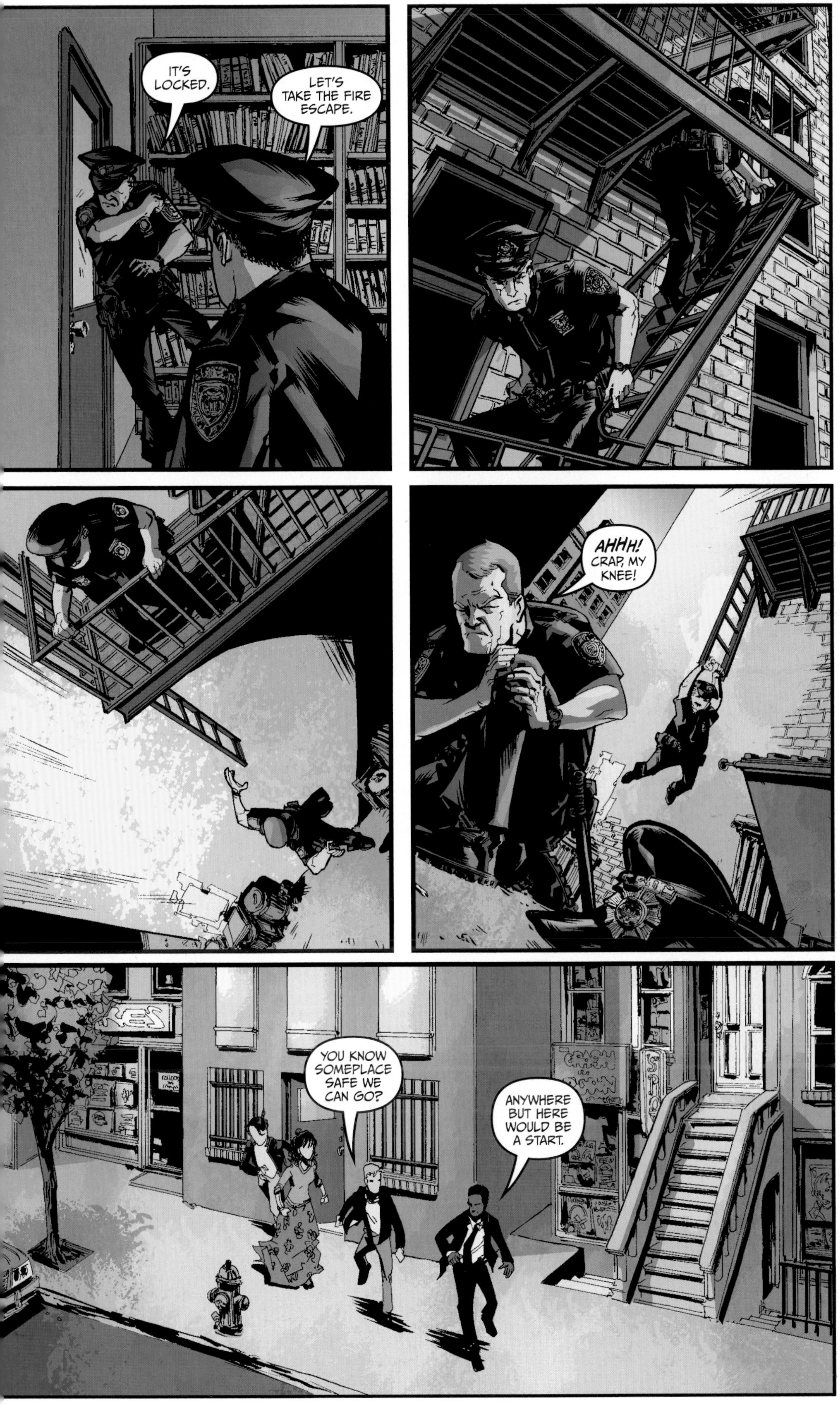
IT'S LOCKED.
LET'S TAKE THE FIRE ESCAPE.
AHHH! CRAP, MY KNEE!
YOU KNOW SOMEPLACE SAFE WE CAN GO?
ANYWHERE BUT HERE WOULD BE A START.

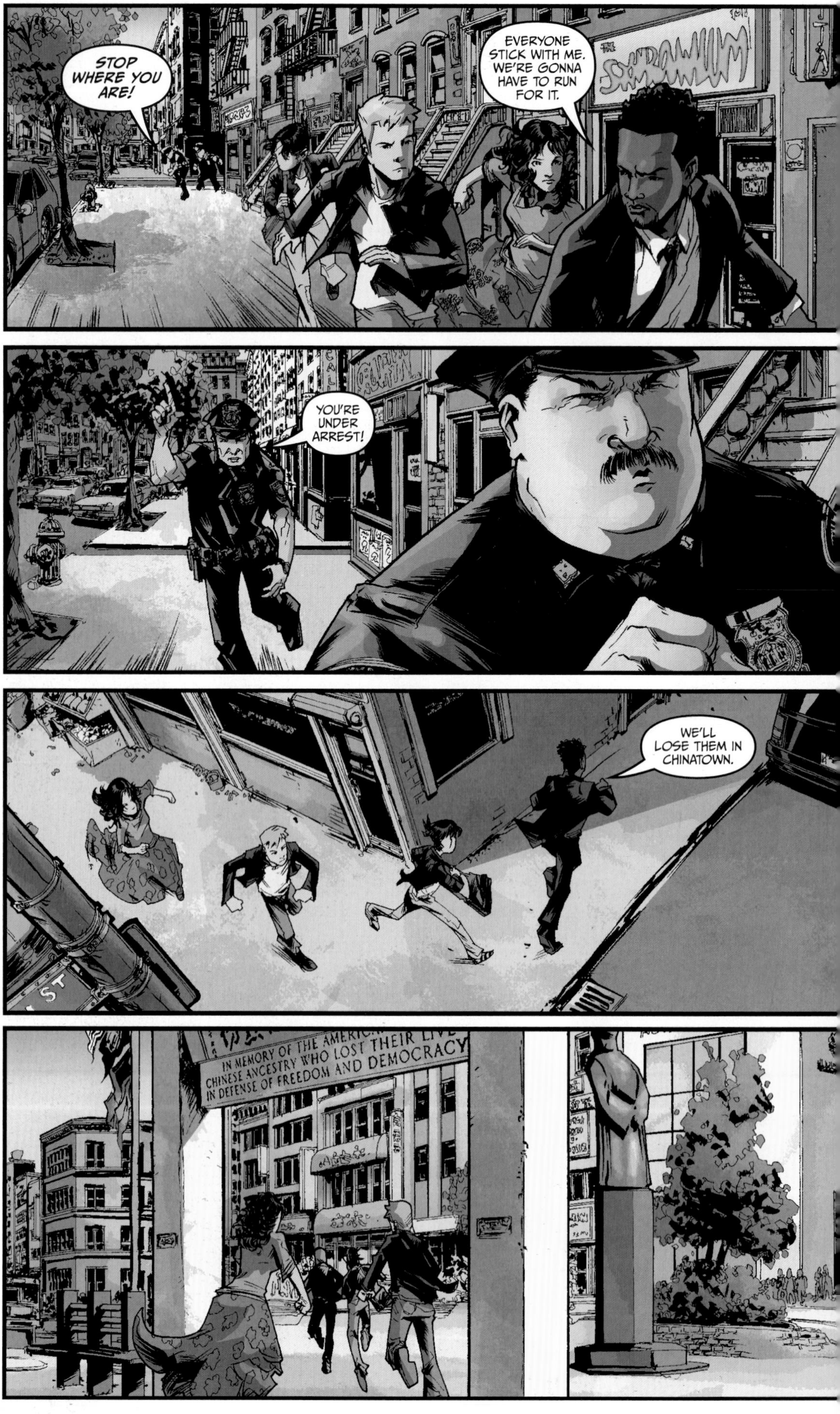
STOP WHERE YOU ARE!
EVERYONE STICK WITH ME. WE'RE GONNA HAVE TO RUN FOR IT.
YOU'RE UNDER ARREST!
WE'LL LOSE THEM IN CHINATOWN.
IN MEMORY OF THE AMERIC
CHINESE ANCESTRY WHO LOST THEIR LIV
IN DEFENSE OF FREEDOM AND DEMOCRACY

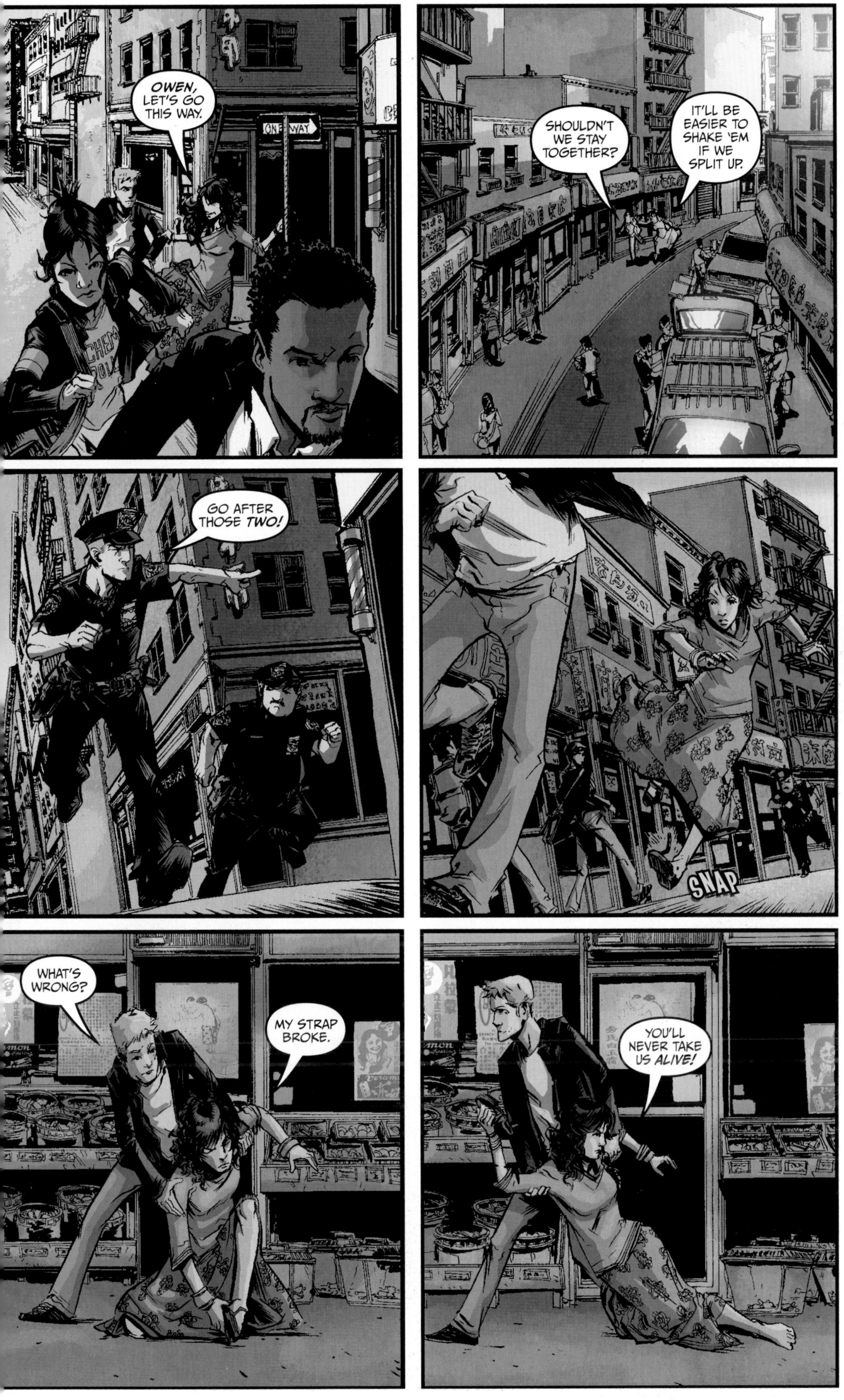

OWEN, LET'S GO THIS WAY.
ONE WAY
SHOULDN'T WE STAY TOGETHER?
IT'LL BE EASIER TO SHAKE 'EM IF WE SPLIT UP.
GO AFTER THOSE TWO!
SNAP
WHAT'S WRONG?
MY STRAP BROKE.
YOU'LL NEVER TAKE US ALIVE!

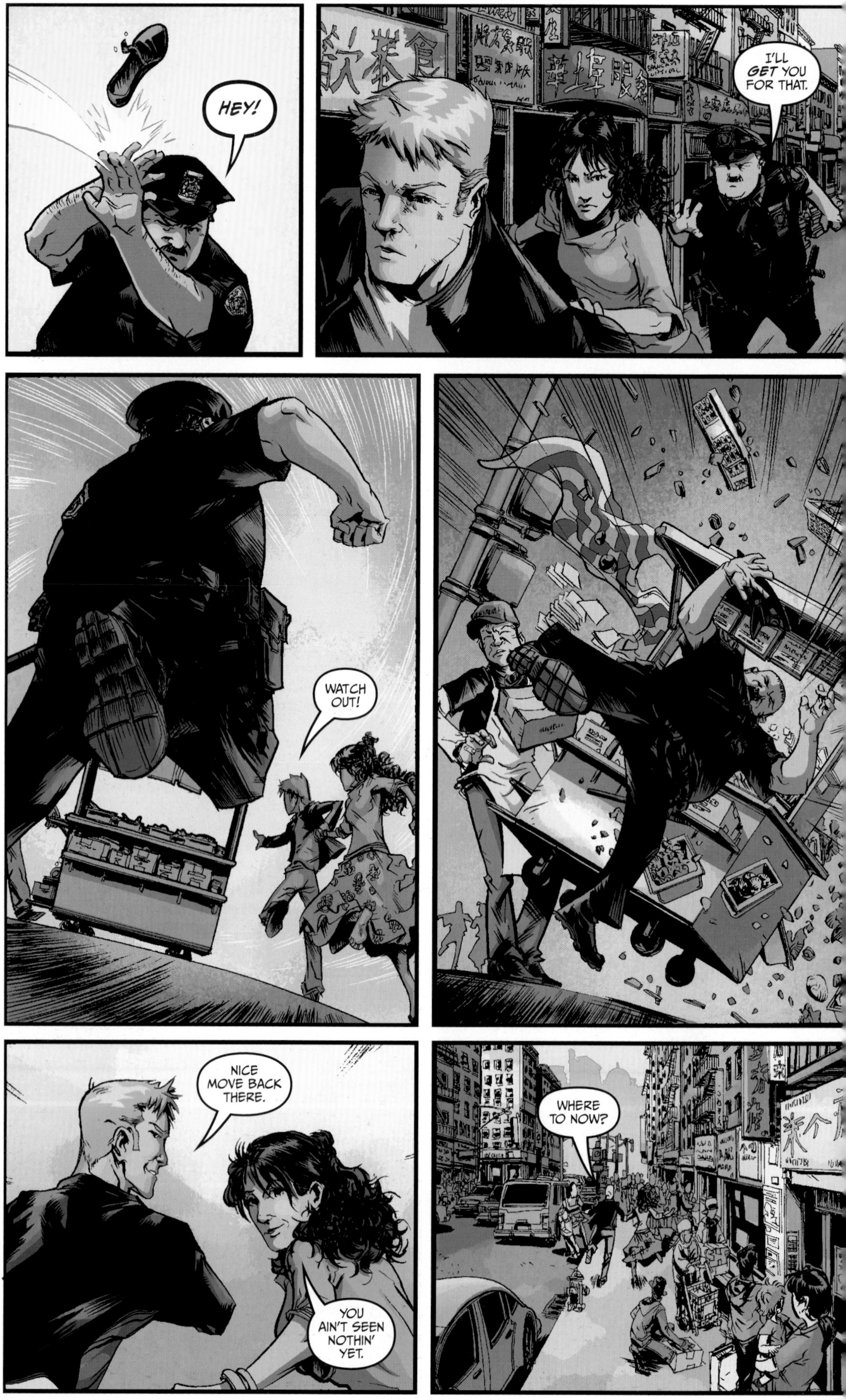
HEY!
I'LL GET YOU FOR THAT.
WATCH OUT!
NICE MOVE BACK THERE.
YOU AIN'T SEEN NOTHIN' YET.
WHERE TO NOW?

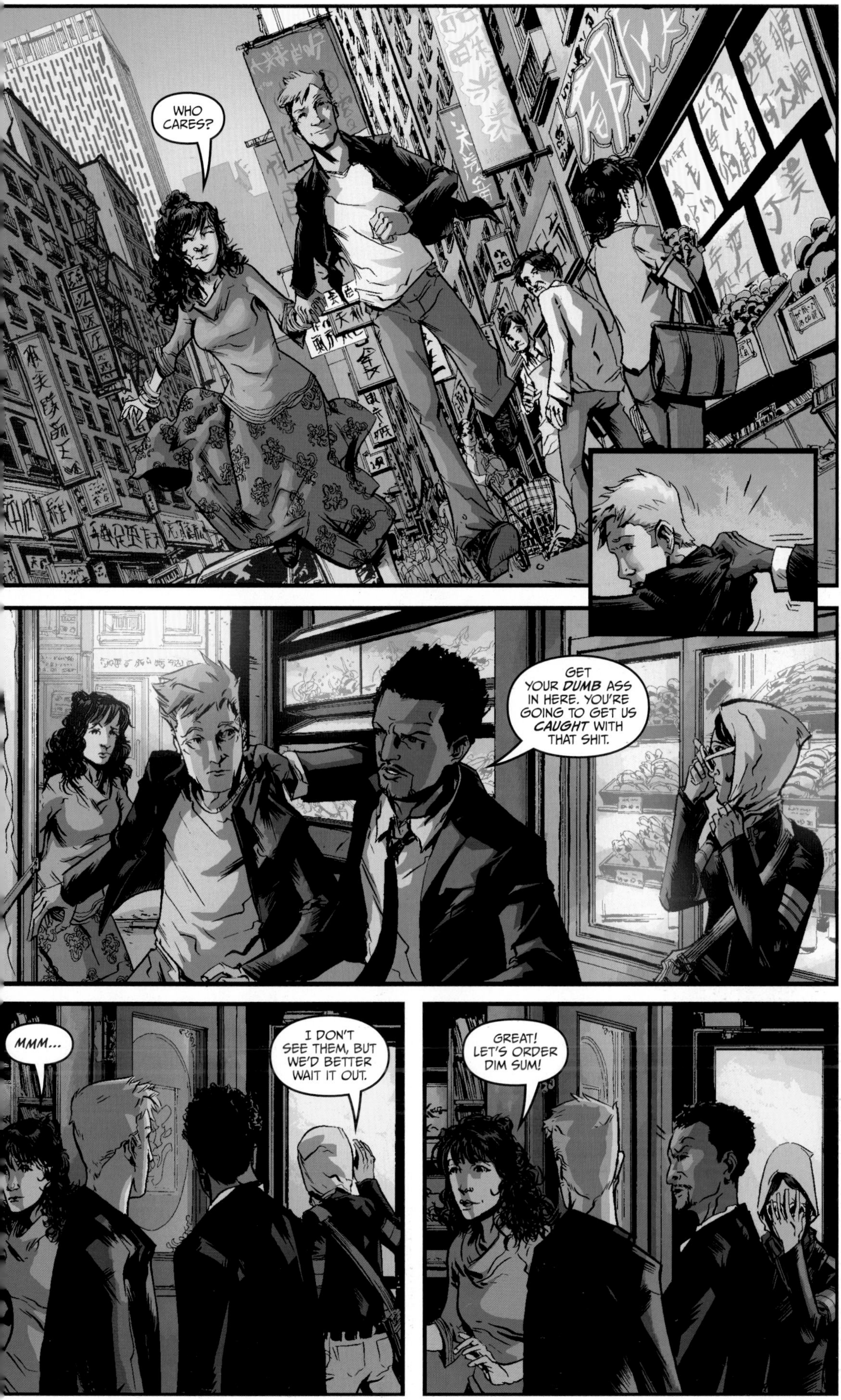
WHO CARES?
GET YOUR DUMB ASS IN HERE. YOU'RE GOING TO GET US CAUGHT WITH THAT SHIT.
MMM...
I DON'T SEE THEM, BUT WE'D BETTER WAIT IT OUT.
GREAT! LET'S ORDER DIM SUM!

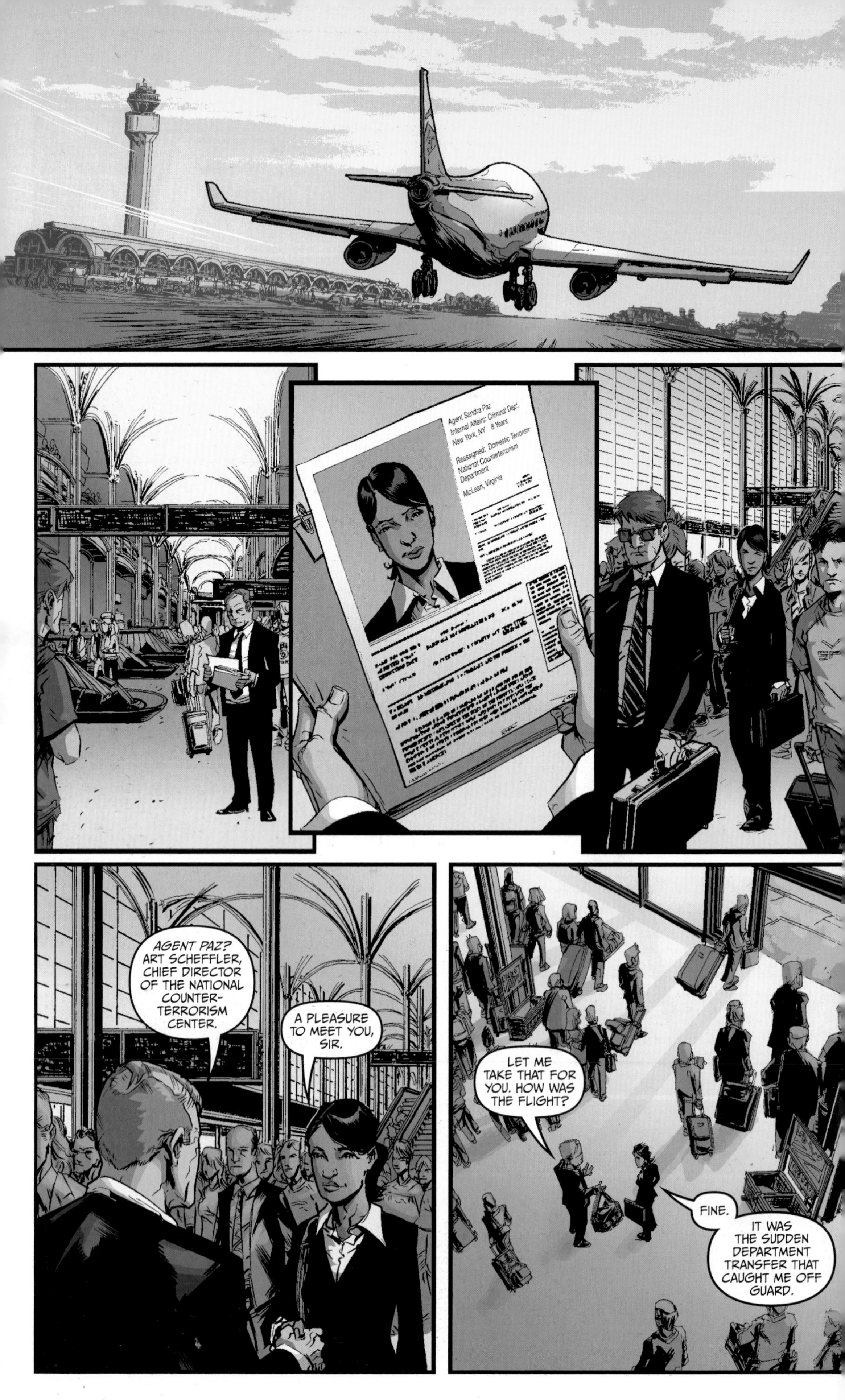
Agent Sandra Paz
Internal Affairs: Criminal Dept.
New York, NY 8 Years
Reassigned: Domestic Terrorism
National Counterterrorism
Department
McLean, Virginia
AGENT PAZ? ART SCHEFFLER, CHIEF DIRECTOR OF THE NATIONAL COUNTER-TERRORISM CENTER.
A PLEASURE TO MEET YOU, SIR.
LET ME TAKE THAT FOR YOU. HOW WAS THE FLIGHT?
FINE.
IT WAS THE SUDDEN DEPARTMENT TRANSFER THAT CAUGHT ME OFF GUARD.

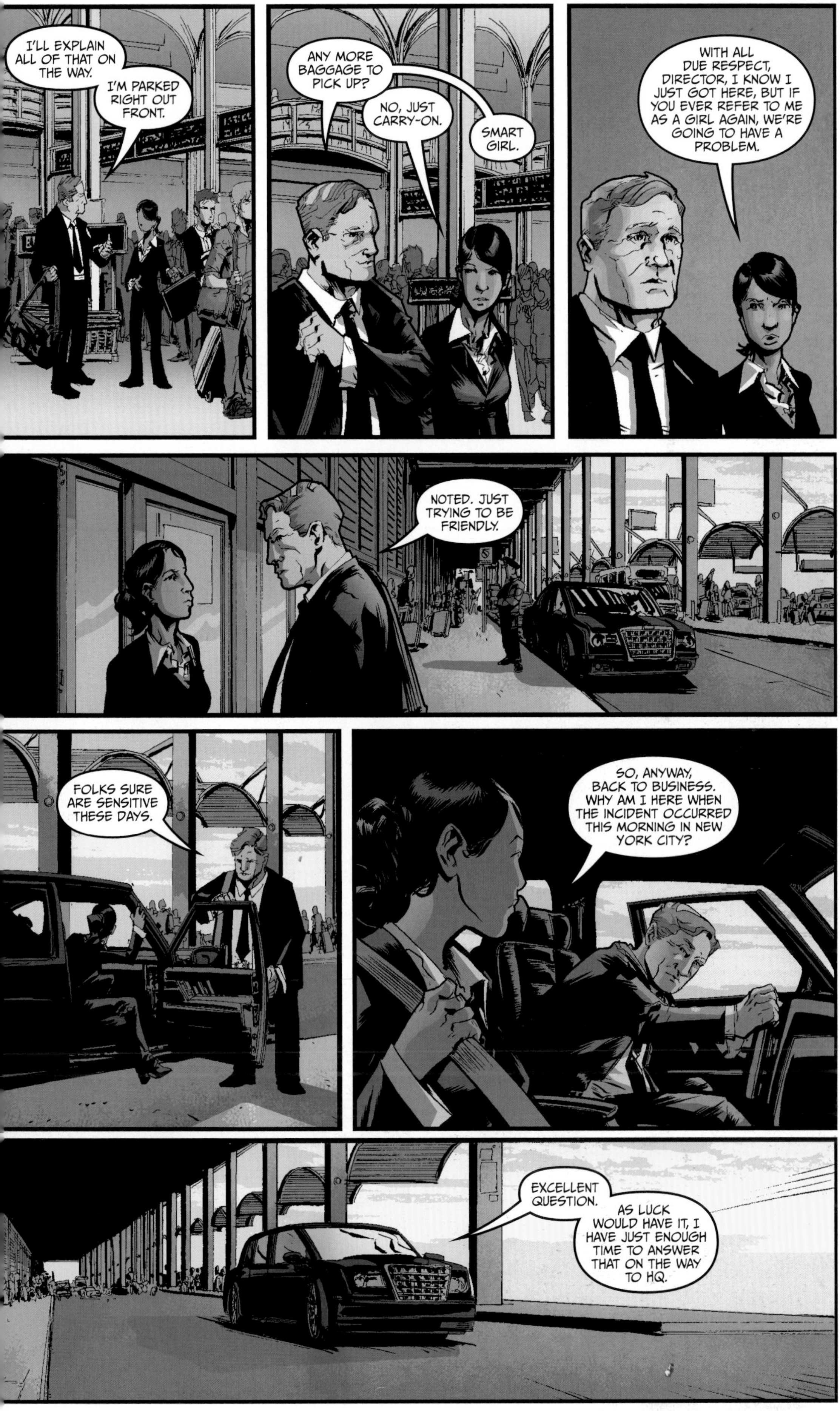
I'LL EXPLAIN ALL OF THAT ON THE WAY.
I'M PARKED RIGHT OUT FRONT.
ANY MORE BAGGAGE TO PICK UP?
NO, JUST CARRY-ON.
SMART GIRL.
WITH ALL DUE RESPECT, DIRECTOR, I KNOW I JUST GOT HERE, BUT IF YOU EVER REFER TO ME AS A GIRL AGAIN, WE'RE GOING TO HAVE A PROBLEM.
NOTED. JUST TRYING TO BE FRIENDLY.
FOLKS SURE ARE SENSITIVE THESE DAYS.
SO, ANYWAY, BACK TO BUSINESS. WHY AM I HERE WHEN THE INCIDENT OCCURRED THIS MORNING IN NEW YORK CITY?
EXCELLENT QUESTION.
AS LUCK WOULD HAVE IT, I HAVE JUST ENOUGH TIME TO ANSWER THAT ON THE WAY TO HQ.

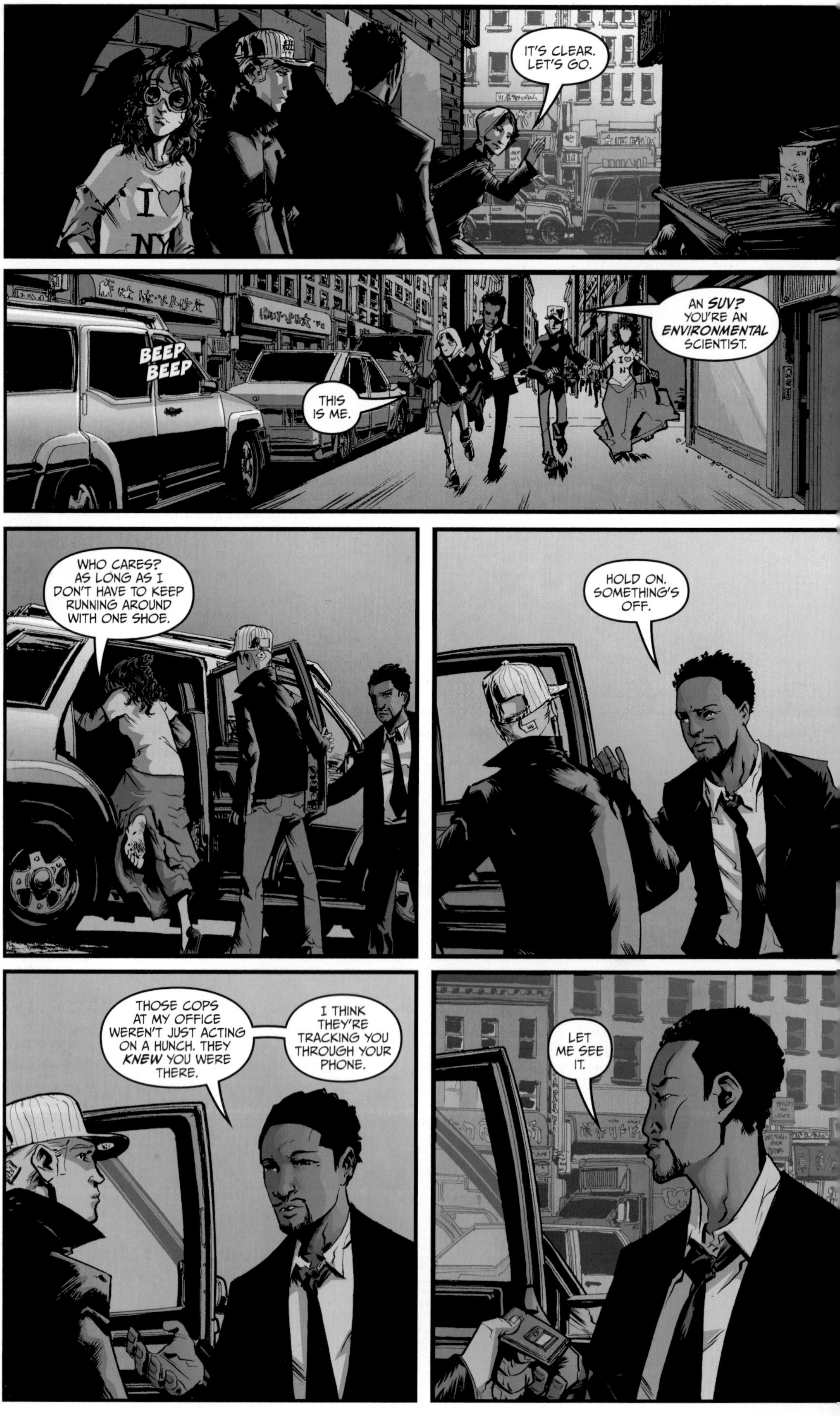
IT'S CLEAR. LET'S GO.
AN SUV? YOU'RE AN ENVIRONMENTAL SCIENTIST.
BEEP BEEP
THIS IS ME.
WHO CARES? AS LONG AS I DON'T HAVE TO KEEP RUNNING AROUND WITH ONE SHOE.
HOLD ON. SOMETHING'S OFF.
THOSE COPS AT MY OFFICE WEREN'T JUST ACTING ON A HUNCH. THEY KNEW YOU WERE THERE.
I THINK THEY'RE TRACKING YOU THROUGH YOUR PHONE.
LET ME SEE IT.

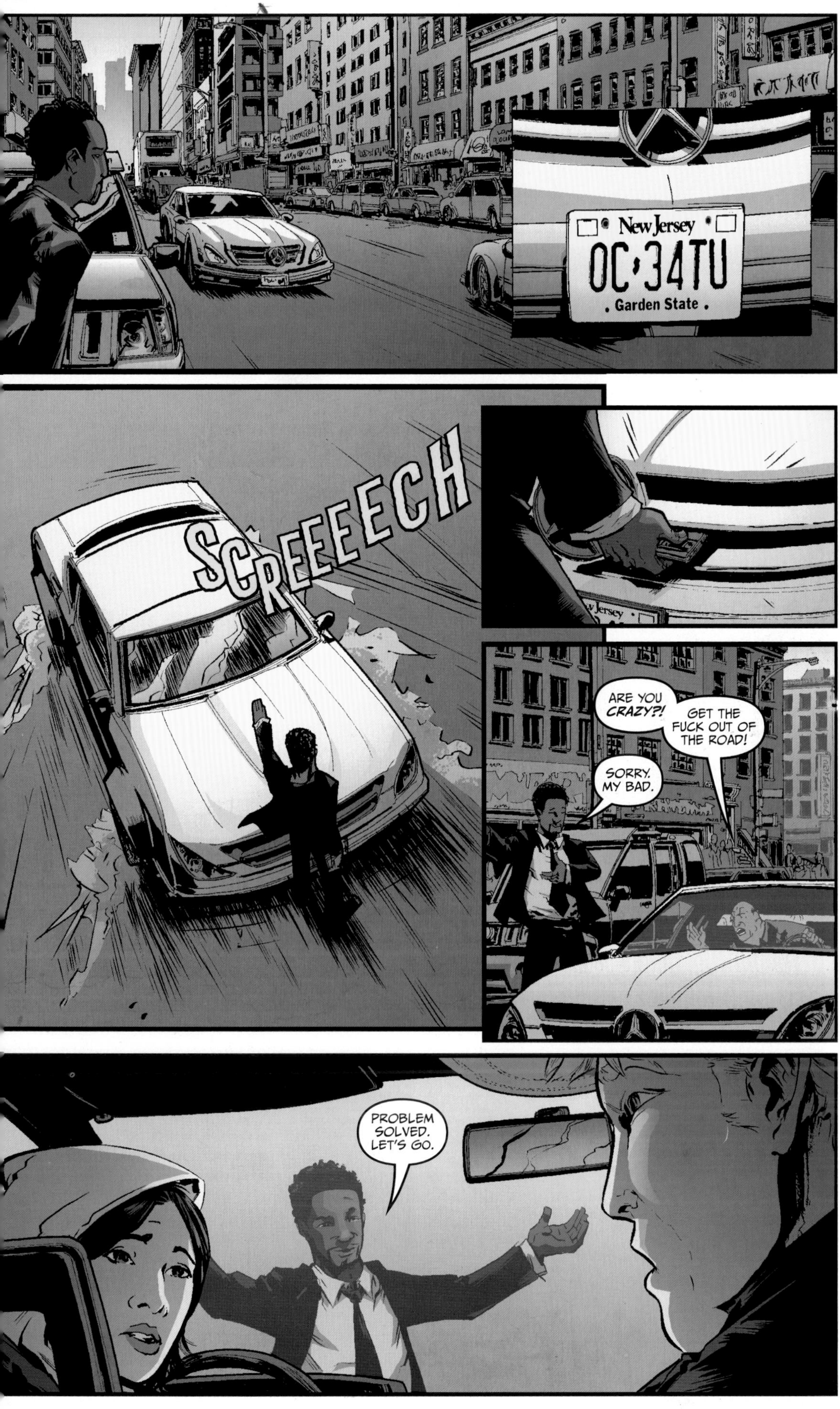

New Jersey
OC 34TU
Garden State
SCREEEECH
New Jersey
ARE YOU CRAZY?!
GET THE FUCK OUT OF THE ROAD!
SORRY. MY BAD.
PROBLEM SOLVED. LET'S GO.

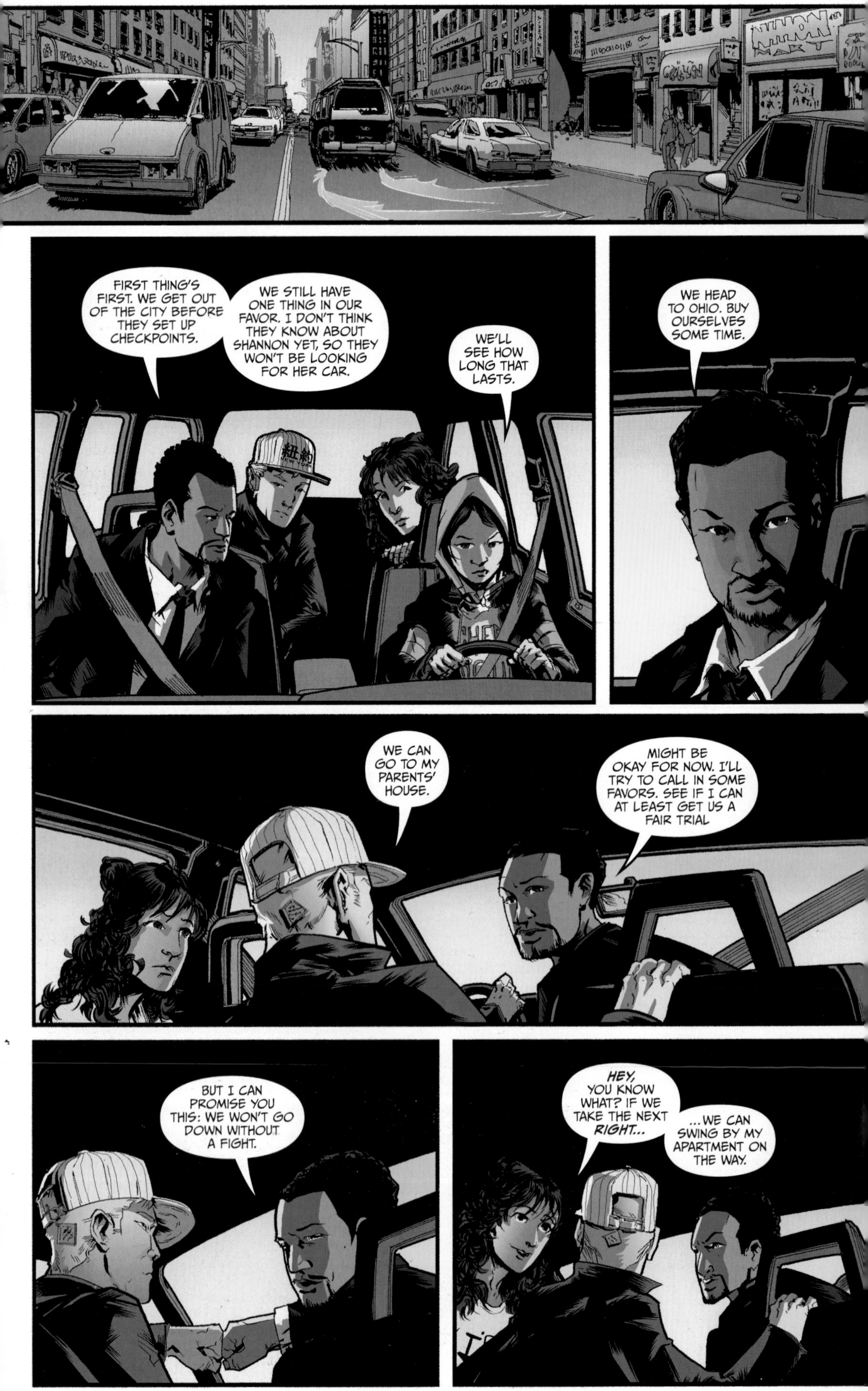
FIRST THING'S FIRST. WE GET OUT OF THE CITY BEFORE THEY SET UP CHECKPOINTS.
WE STILL HAVE ONE THING IN OUR FAVOR. I DON'T THINK THEY KNOW ABOUT SHANNON YET, SO THEY WON'T BE LOOKING FOR HER CAR.
WE'LL SEE HOW LONG THAT LASTS.
WE HEAD TO OHIO. BUY OURSELVES SOME TIME.
WE CAN GO TO MY PARENTS' HOUSE.
MIGHT BE OKAY FOR NOW. I'LL TRY TO CALL IN SOME FAVORS. SEE IF I CAN AT LEAST GET US A FAIR TRIAL
BUT I CAN PROMISE YOU THIS: WE WON'T GO DOWN WITHOUT A FIGHT.
HEY, YOU KNOW WHAT? IF WE TAKE THE NEXT *RIGHT*...
...WE CAN SWING BY MY APARTMENT ON THE WAY.

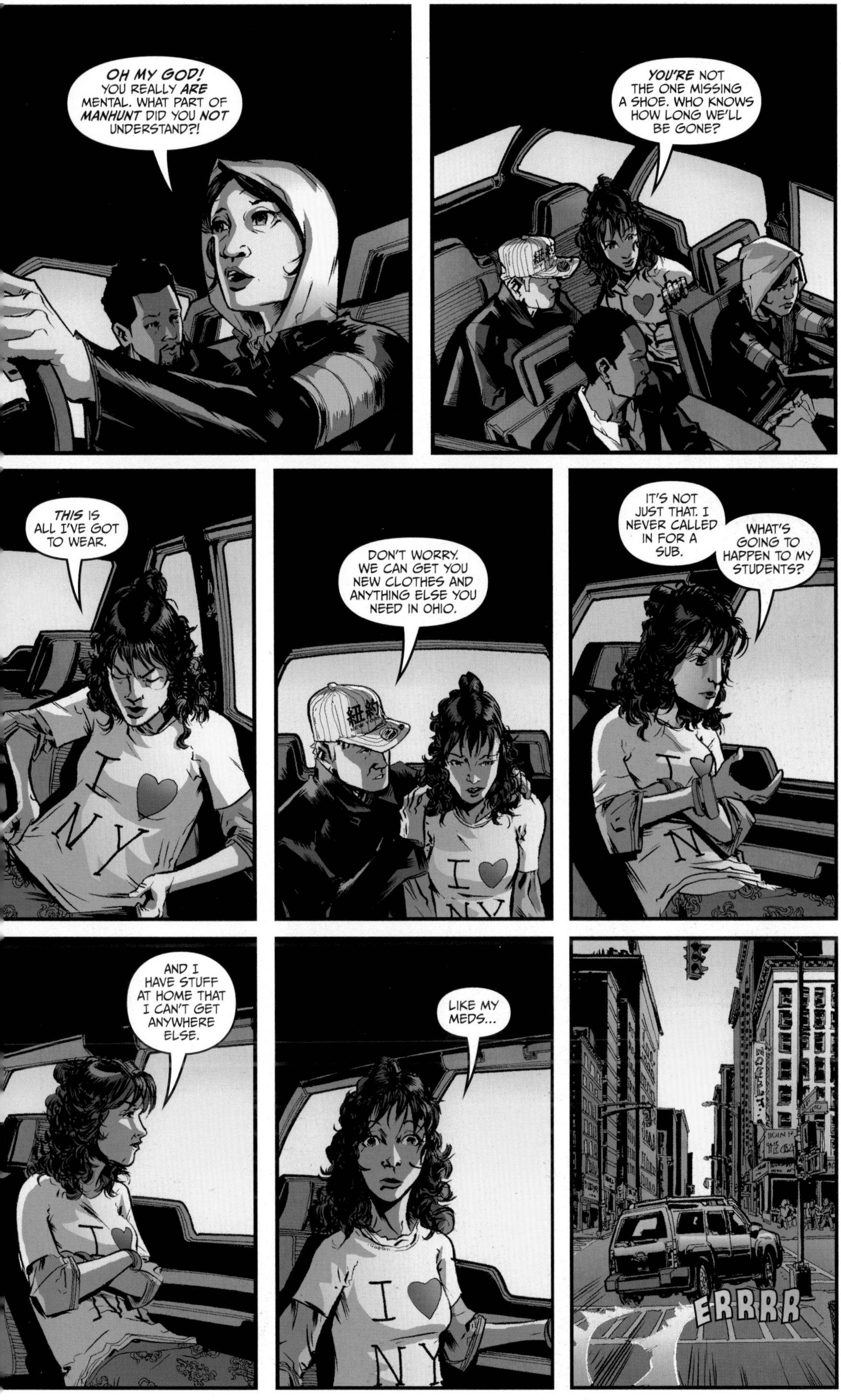

OH MY GOD! YOU REALLY ARE MENTAL. WHAT PART OF MANHUNT DID YOU NOT UNDERSTAND?!
YOU'RE NOT THE ONE MISSING A SHOE. WHO KNOWS HOW LONG WE'LL BE GONE?
THIS IS ALL I'VE GOT TO WEAR.
DON'T WORRY. WE CAN GET YOU NEW CLOTHES AND ANYTHING ELSE YOU NEED IN OHIO.
IT'S NOT JUST THAT. I NEVER CALLED IN FOR A SUB.
WHAT'S GOING TO HAPPEN TO MY STUDENTS?
AND I HAVE STUFF AT HOME THAT I CAN'T GET ANYWHERE ELSE.
LIKE MY MEDS...
ERRRR

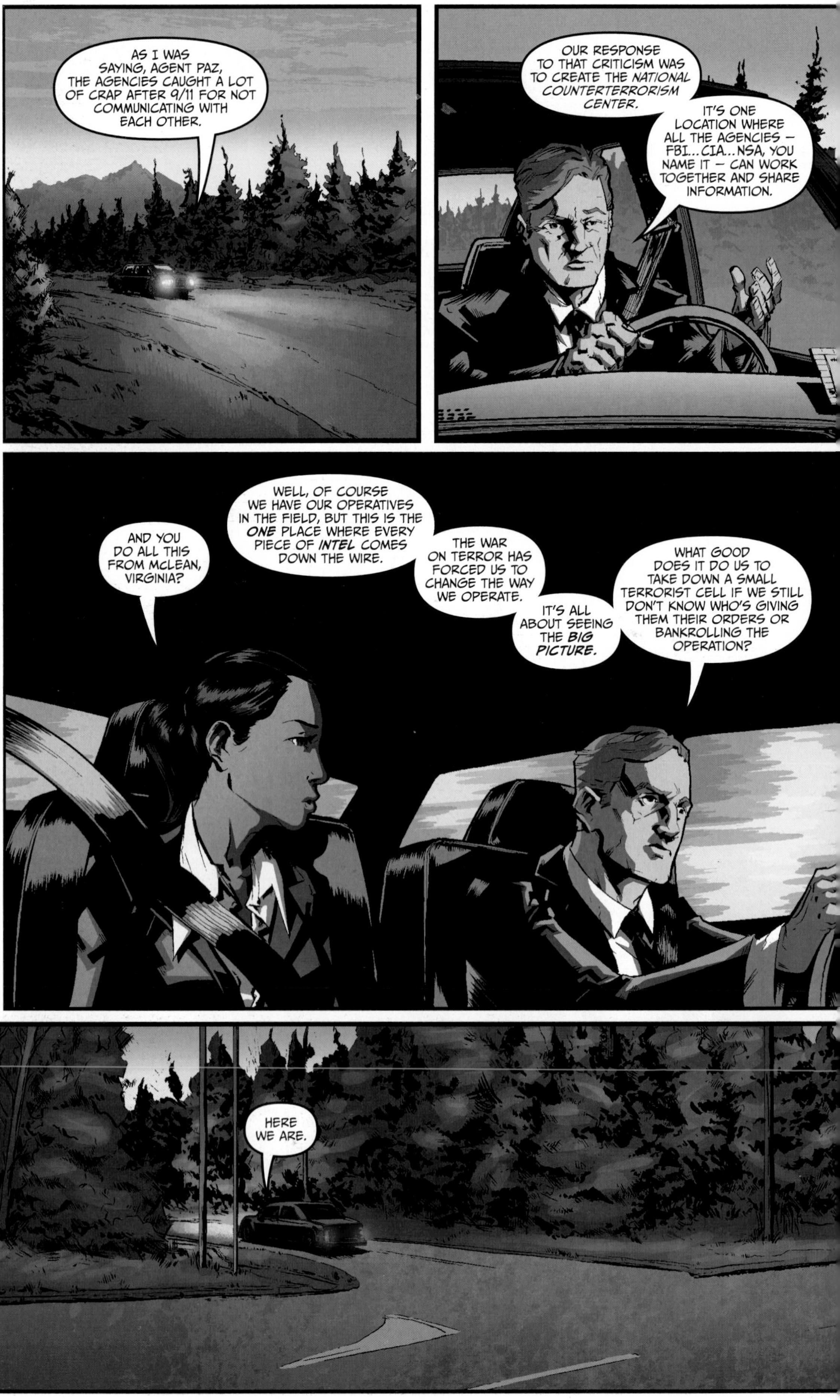
AS I WAS SAYING, AGENT PAZ, THE AGENCIES CAUGHT A LOT OF CRAP AFTER 9/11 FOR NOT COMMUNICATING WITH EACH OTHER.
OUR RESPONSE TO THAT CRITICISM WAS TO CREATE THE *NATIONAL COUNTERTERRORISM CENTER.*
IT'S ONE LOCATION WHERE ALL THE AGENCIES — FBI...CIA...NSA, YOU NAME IT — CAN WORK TOGETHER AND SHARE INFORMATION.
AND YOU DO ALL THIS FROM McLEAN, VIRGINIA?
WELL, OF COURSE WE HAVE OUR OPERATIVES IN THE FIELD, BUT THIS IS THE ***ONE*** PLACE WHERE EVERY PIECE OF ***INTEL*** COMES DOWN THE WIRE.
THE WAR ON TERROR HAS FORCED US TO CHANGE THE WAY WE OPERATE.
IT'S ALL ABOUT SEEING THE ***BIG PICTURE.***
WHAT GOOD DOES IT DO US TO TAKE DOWN A SMALL TERRORIST CELL IF WE STILL DON'T KNOW WHO'S GIVING THEM THEIR ORDERS OR BANKROLLING THE OPERATION?
HERE WE ARE.

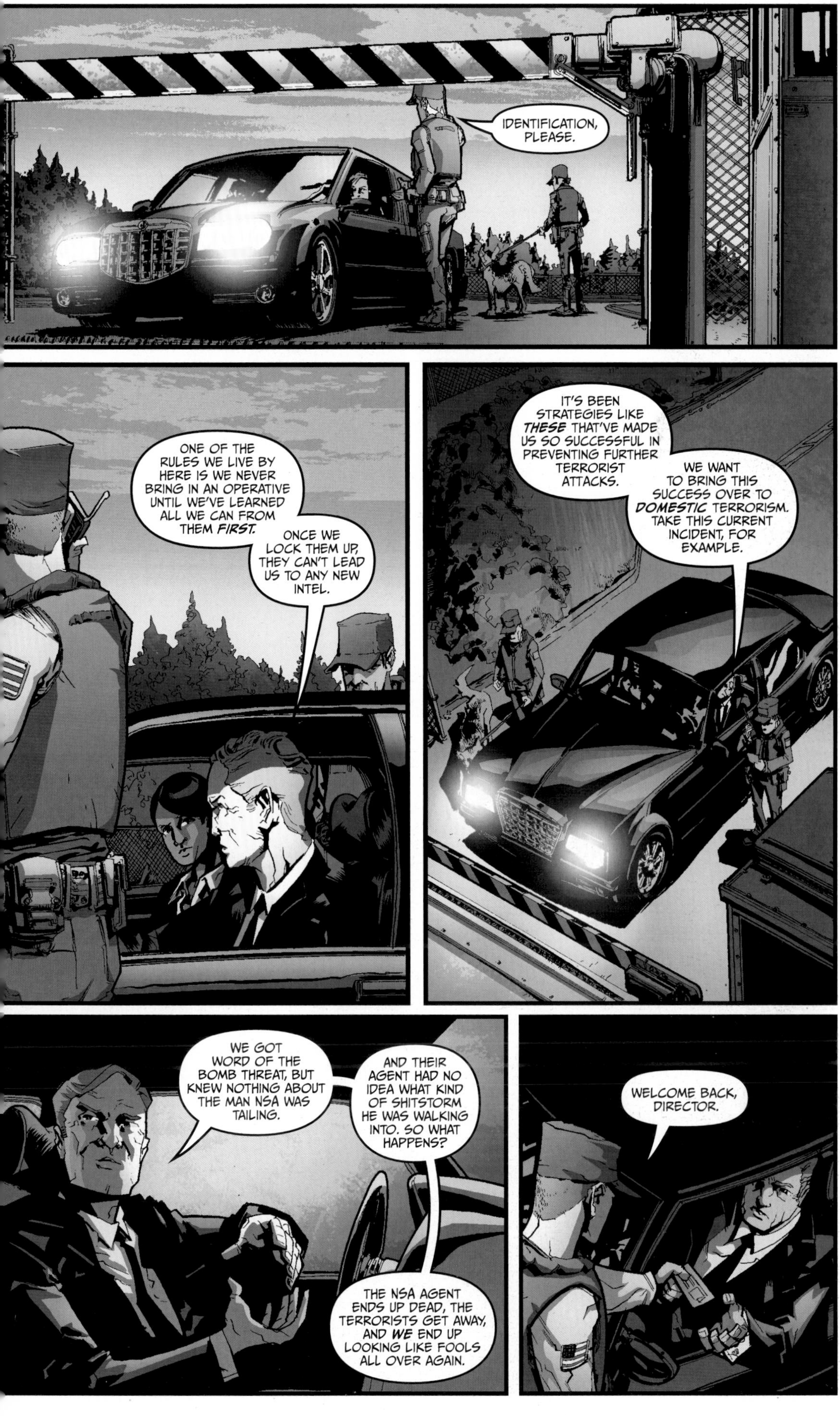
IDENTIFICATION, PLEASE.
ONE OF THE RULES WE LIVE BY HERE IS WE NEVER BRING IN AN OPERATIVE UNTIL WE'VE LEARNED ALL WE CAN FROM THEM *FIRST.*
ONCE WE LOCK THEM UP, THEY CAN'T LEAD US TO ANY NEW INTEL.
IT'S BEEN STRATEGIES LIKE *THESE* THAT'VE MADE US SO SUCCESSFUL IN PREVENTING FURTHER TERRORIST ATTACKS.
WE WANT TO BRING THIS SUCCESS OVER TO *DOMESTIC* TERRORISM. TAKE THIS CURRENT INCIDENT, FOR EXAMPLE.
WE GOT WORD OF THE BOMB THREAT, BUT KNEW NOTHING ABOUT THE MAN NSA WAS TAILING.
AND THEIR AGENT HAD NO IDEA WHAT KIND OF SHITSTORM HE WAS WALKING INTO. SO WHAT HAPPENS?
THE NSA AGENT ENDS UP DEAD, THE TERRORISTS GET AWAY, AND *WE* END UP LOOKING LIKE FOOLS ALL OVER AGAIN.
WELCOME BACK, DIRECTOR.

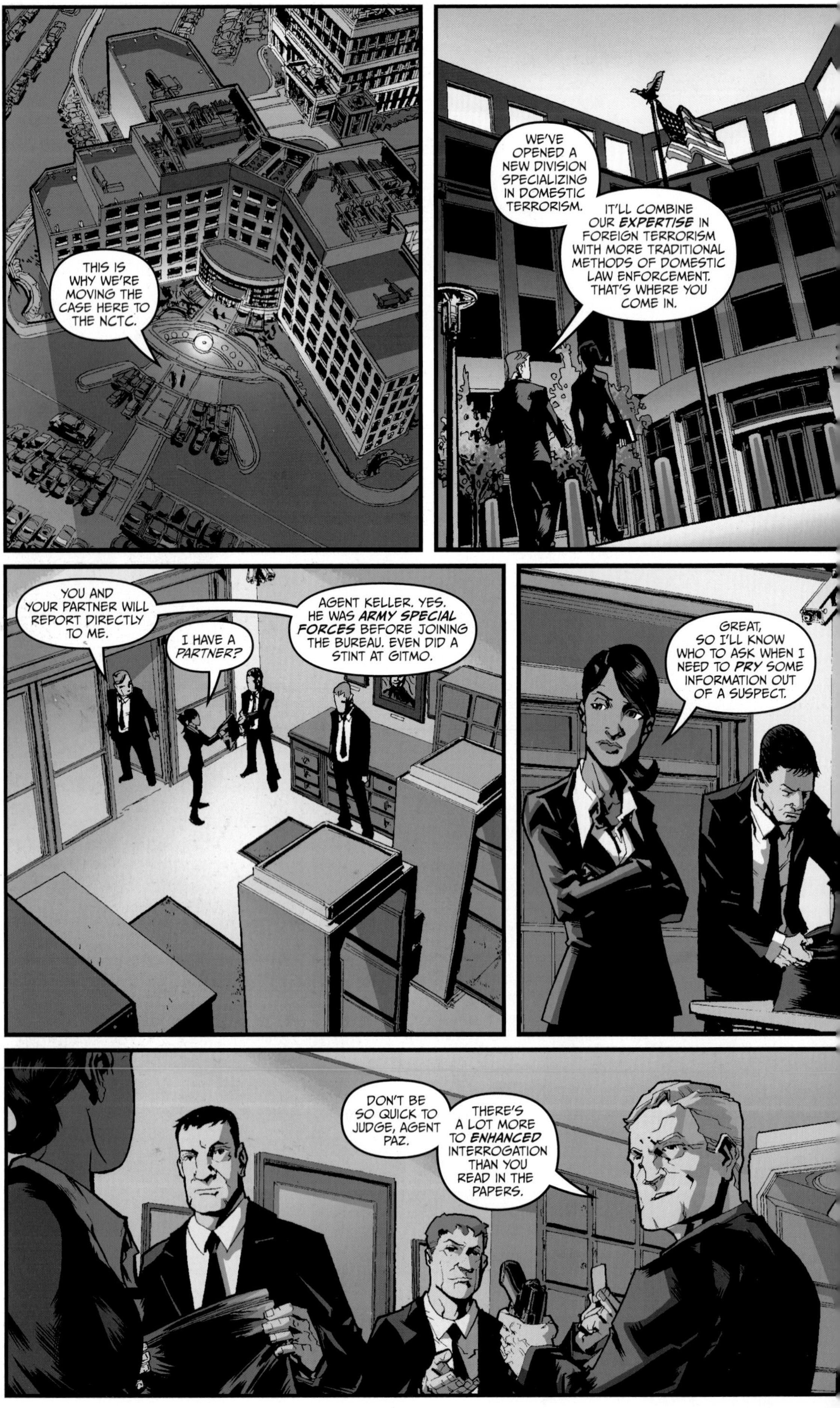
THIS IS WHY WE'RE MOVING THE CASE HERE TO THE NCTC.
WE'VE OPENED A NEW DIVISION SPECIALIZING IN DOMESTIC TERRORISM.
IT'LL COMBINE OUR EXPERTISE IN FOREIGN TERRORISM WITH MORE TRADITIONAL METHODS OF DOMESTIC LAW ENFORCEMENT. THAT'S WHERE YOU COME IN.
YOU AND YOUR PARTNER WILL REPORT DIRECTLY TO ME.
I HAVE A PARTNER?
AGENT KELLER. YES. HE WAS ARMY SPECIAL FORCES BEFORE JOINING THE BUREAU. EVEN DID A STINT AT GITMO.
GREAT, SO I'LL KNOW WHO TO ASK WHEN I NEED TO PRY SOME INFORMATION OUT OF A SUSPECT.
DON'T BE SO QUICK TO JUDGE, AGENT PAZ.
THERE'S A LOT MORE TO ENHANCED INTERROGATION THAN YOU READ IN THE PAPERS.

I'M STILL UNCLEAR ON ONE THING, DIRECTOR. DOESN'T ALL THIS DEPEND ON THERE BEING MORE TO THIS CASE THAN WHAT'S EVIDENT?

ON THE SURFACE THIS CASE MIGHT *APPEAR* TO BE AN ISOLATED ATTACK...

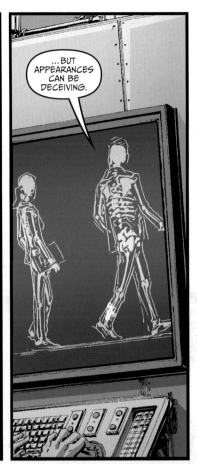

...BUT APPEARANCES CAN BE DECEIVING.

THE TRUTH IS, WE CAN'T AFFORD TO WAIT FOR THE *NEXT* ATTACK.

NOW IS THE TIME FOR US TO IMPLEMENT THE STRATEGIES WE'LL USE NOT JUST FOR THIS SITUATION, BUT FOR ANY FUTURE THREATS.

SMILE.

HUH?

SNAP

Sandra Paz

Domestic Terrorism Department

Employee Id. Number 16

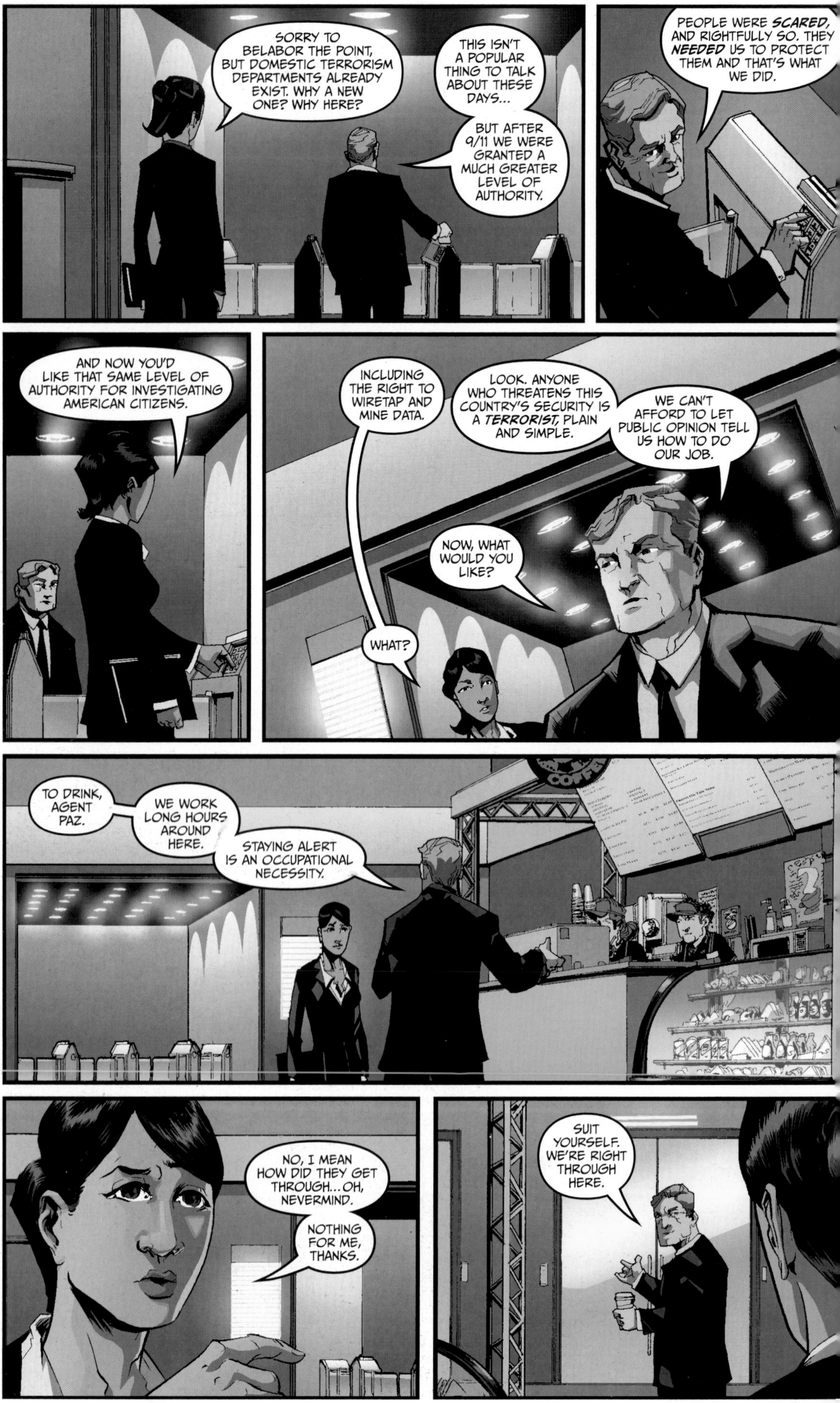
SORRY TO BELABOR THE POINT, BUT DOMESTIC TERRORISM DEPARTMENTS ALREADY EXIST. WHY A NEW ONE? WHY HERE?
THIS ISN'T A POPULAR THING TO TALK ABOUT THESE DAYS...
BUT AFTER 9/11 WE WERE GRANTED A MUCH GREATER LEVEL OF AUTHORITY.
PEOPLE WERE **SCARED**, AND RIGHTFULLY SO. THEY **NEEDED** US TO PROTECT THEM AND THAT'S WHAT WE DID.
AND NOW YOU'D LIKE THAT SAME LEVEL OF AUTHORITY FOR INVESTIGATING AMERICAN CITIZENS.
INCLUDING THE RIGHT TO WIRETAP AND MINE DATA.
LOOK. ANYONE WHO THREATENS THIS COUNTRY'S SECURITY IS A **TERRORIST**, PLAIN AND SIMPLE.
WE CAN'T AFFORD TO LET PUBLIC OPINION TELL US HOW TO DO OUR JOB.
NOW, WHAT WOULD YOU LIKE?
WHAT?
TO DRINK, AGENT PAZ.
WE WORK LONG HOURS AROUND HERE.
STAYING ALERT IS AN OCCUPATIONAL NECESSITY.
NO, I MEAN HOW DID THEY GET THROUGH...OH, NEVERMIND.
NOTHING FOR ME, THANKS.
SUIT YOURSELF. WE'RE RIGHT THROUGH HERE.

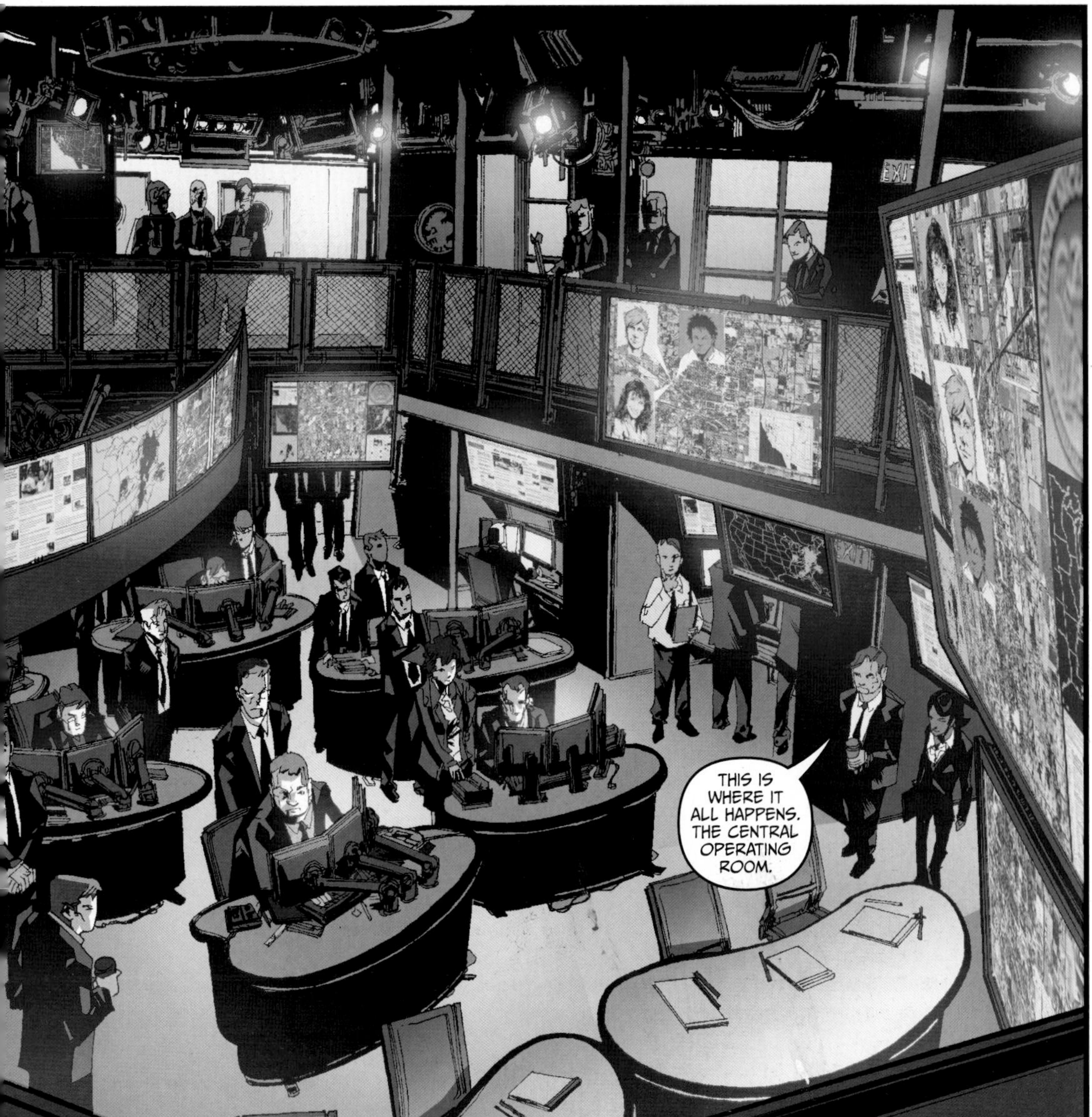
THIS IS WHERE IT ALL HAPPENS. THE CENTRAL OPERATING ROOM.

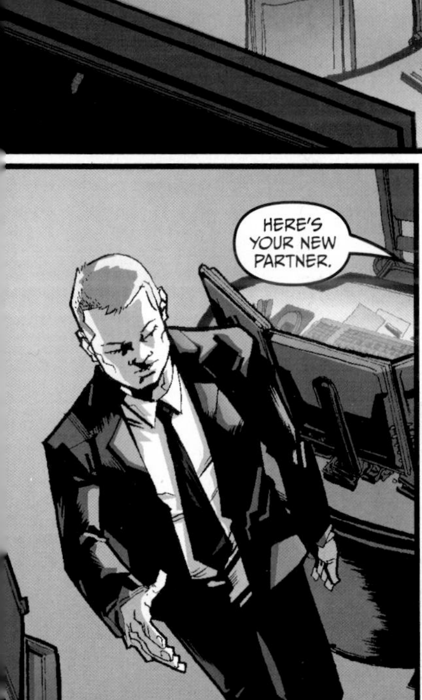
HERE'S YOUR NEW PARTNER.

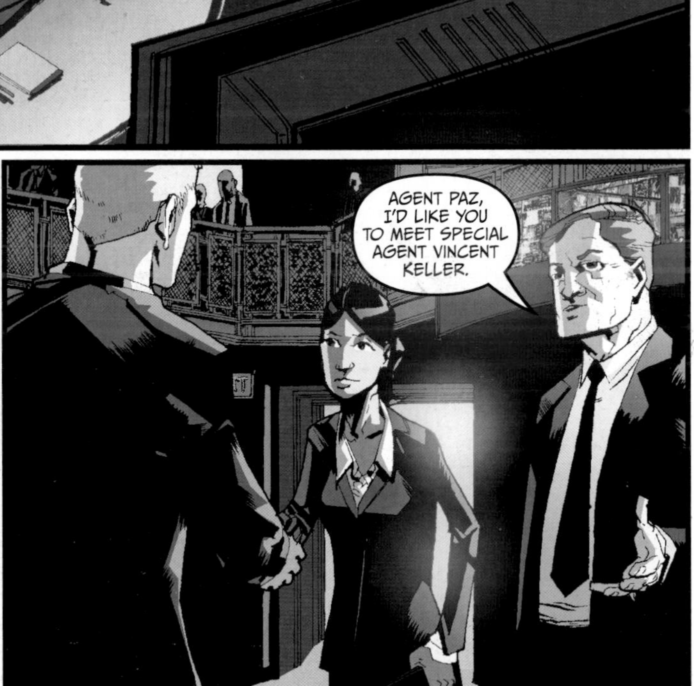
AGENT PAZ, I'D LIKE YOU TO MEET SPECIAL AGENT VINCENT KELLER.

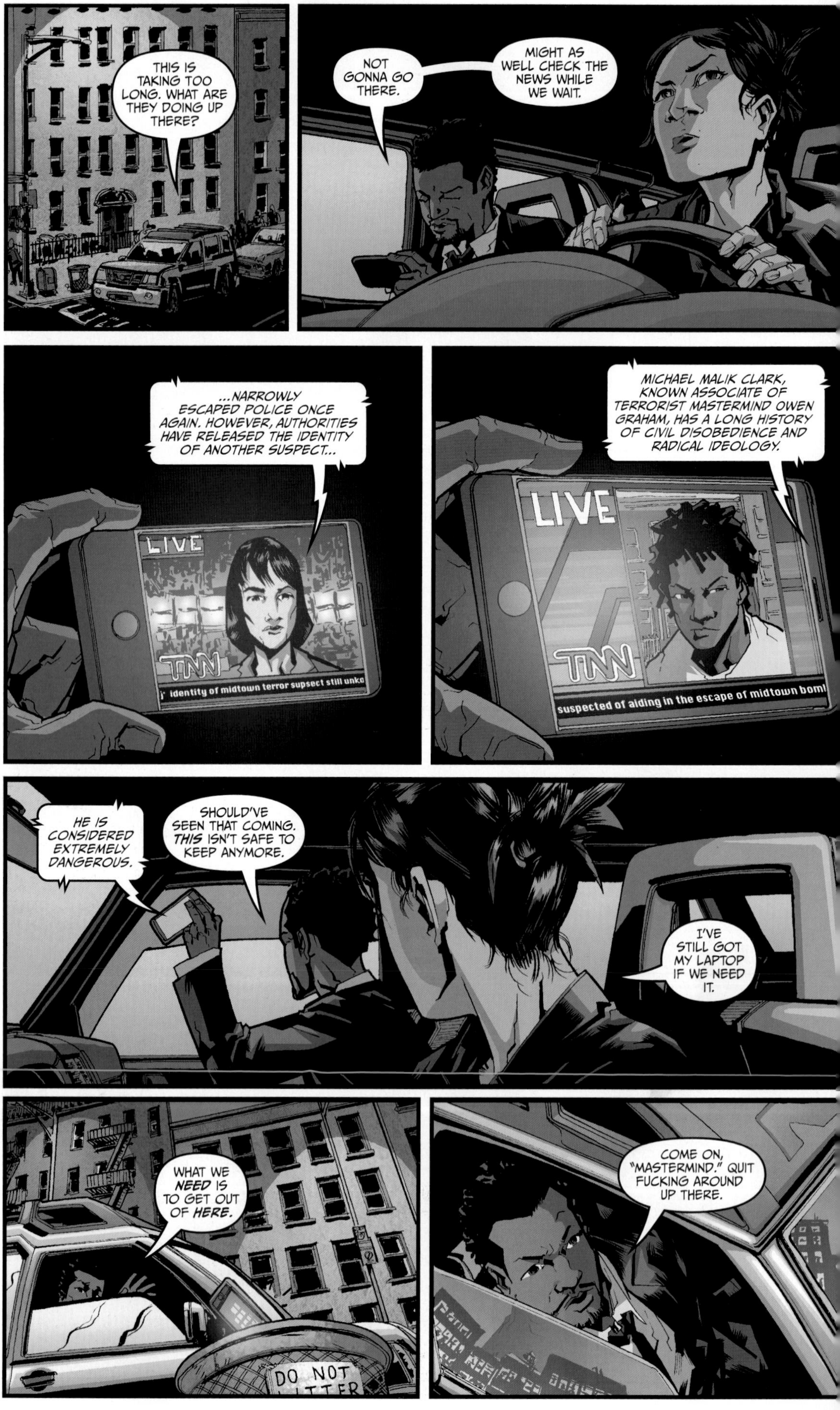
THIS IS TAKING TOO LONG. WHAT ARE THEY DOING UP THERE?
NOT GONNA GO THERE.
MIGHT AS WELL CHECK THE NEWS WHILE WE WAIT.
...NARROWLY ESCAPED POLICE ONCE AGAIN. HOWEVER, AUTHORITIES HAVE RELEASED THE IDENTITY OF ANOTHER SUSPECT...
LIVE
TNN
identity of midtown terror supsect still unkn
MICHAEL MALIK CLARK, KNOWN ASSOCIATE OF TERRORIST MASTERMIND OWEN GRAHAM, HAS A LONG HISTORY OF CIVIL DISOBEDIENCE AND RADICAL IDEOLOGY.
LIVE
TNN
suspected of aiding in the escape of midtown bom
HE IS CONSIDERED EXTREMELY DANGEROUS.
SHOULD'VE SEEN THAT COMING. THIS ISN'T SAFE TO KEEP ANYMORE.
I'VE STILL GOT MY LAPTOP IF WE NEED IT.
WHAT WE NEED IS TO GET OUT OF HERE.
DO NOT
COME ON, "MASTERMIND." QUIT FUCKING AROUND UP THERE.

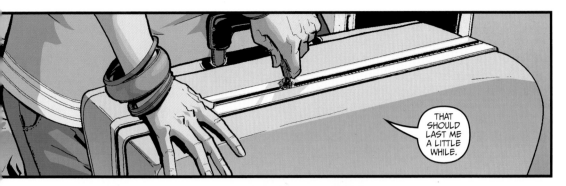

THAT SHOULD LAST ME A LITTLE WHILE.

READY TO GO BE OUTLAWS?

WHEN YOU PUT IT LIKE THAT, IT SOUNDS LIKE AN ADVENTURE, NOT THE END OF LIFE AS WE KNOW IT.

WELCOME TO MY WORLD, ONE CATASTROPHE AFTER ANOTHER.

DOESN'T ANY OF THIS SCARE YOU? WE'RE GOING TO BE FUGITIVES.

OKAY, SURE! YOU CONVINCED ME.

WE COULD JUST STAY HERE UNTIL THEY DRAG US AWAY. HOW ABOUT THAT?

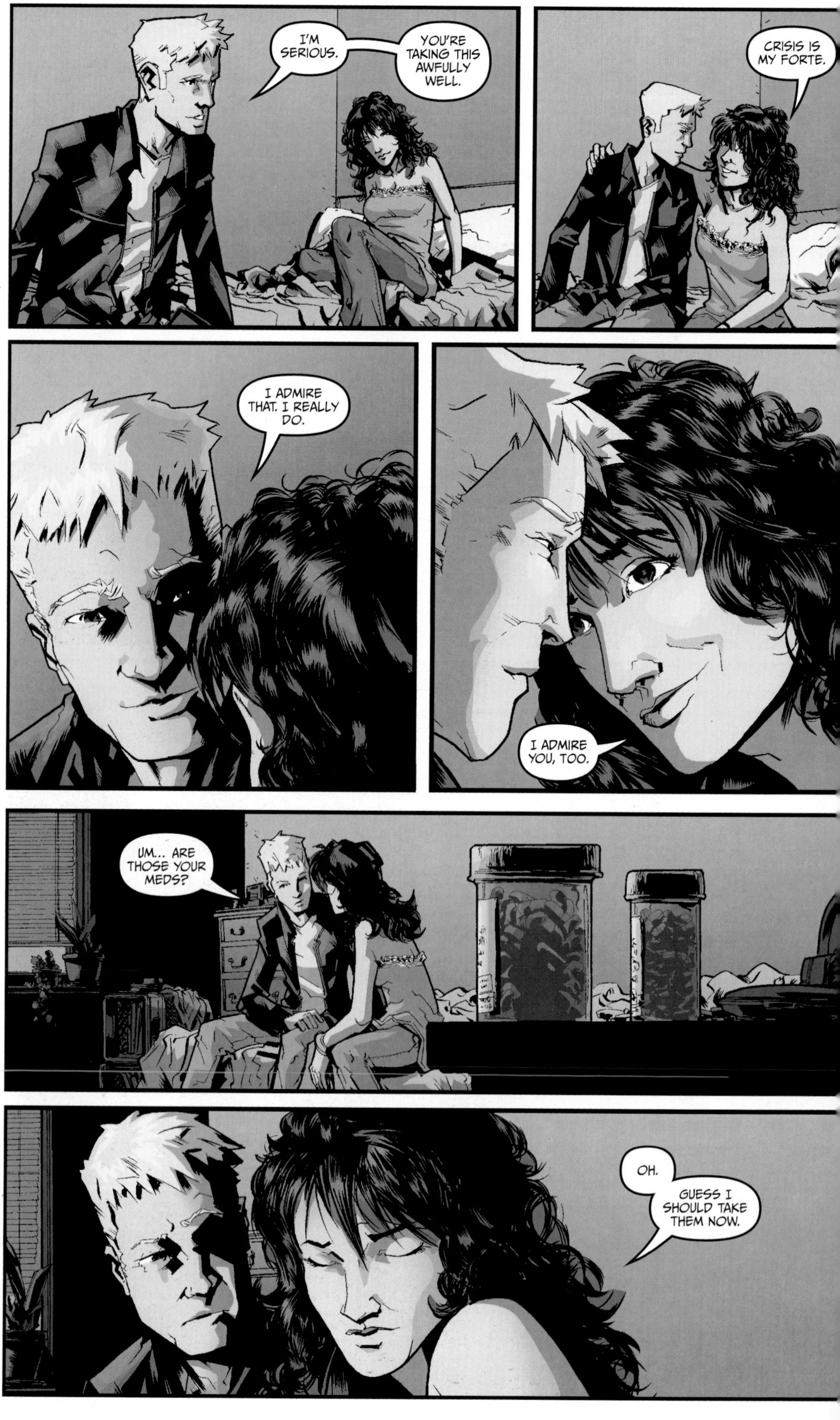
I'M SERIOUS.
YOU'RE TAKING THIS AWFULLY WELL.
CRISIS IS MY FORTE.
I ADMIRE THAT. I REALLY DO.
I ADMIRE YOU, TOO.
UM... ARE THOSE YOUR MEDS?
OH.
GUESS I SHOULD TAKE THEM NOW.

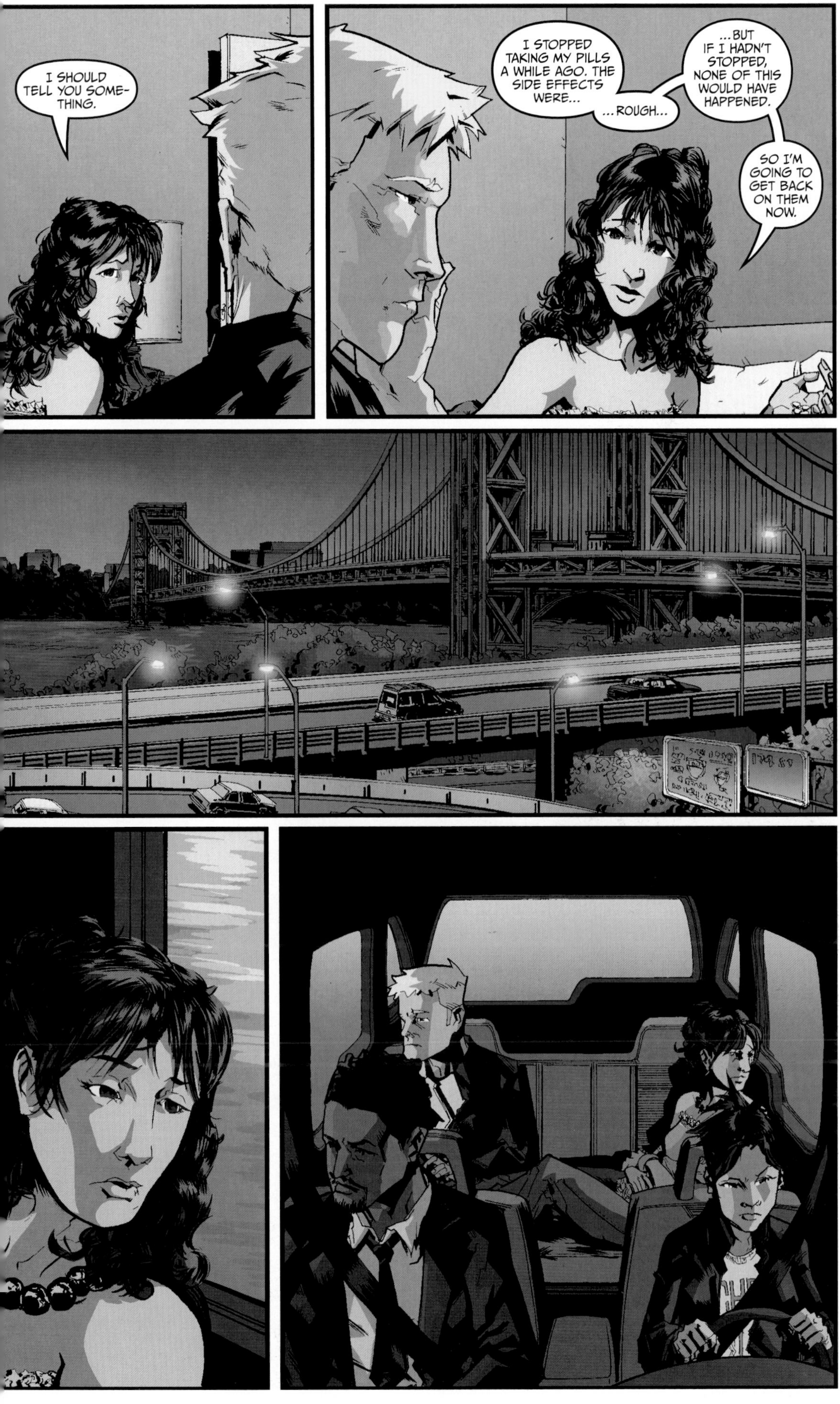
I SHOULD TELL YOU SOME-THING.
I STOPPED TAKING MY PILLS A WHILE AGO. THE SIDE EFFECTS WERE...
...ROUGH...
...BUT IF I HADN'T STOPPED, NONE OF THIS WOULD HAVE HAPPENED.
SO I'M GOING TO GET BACK ON THEM NOW.

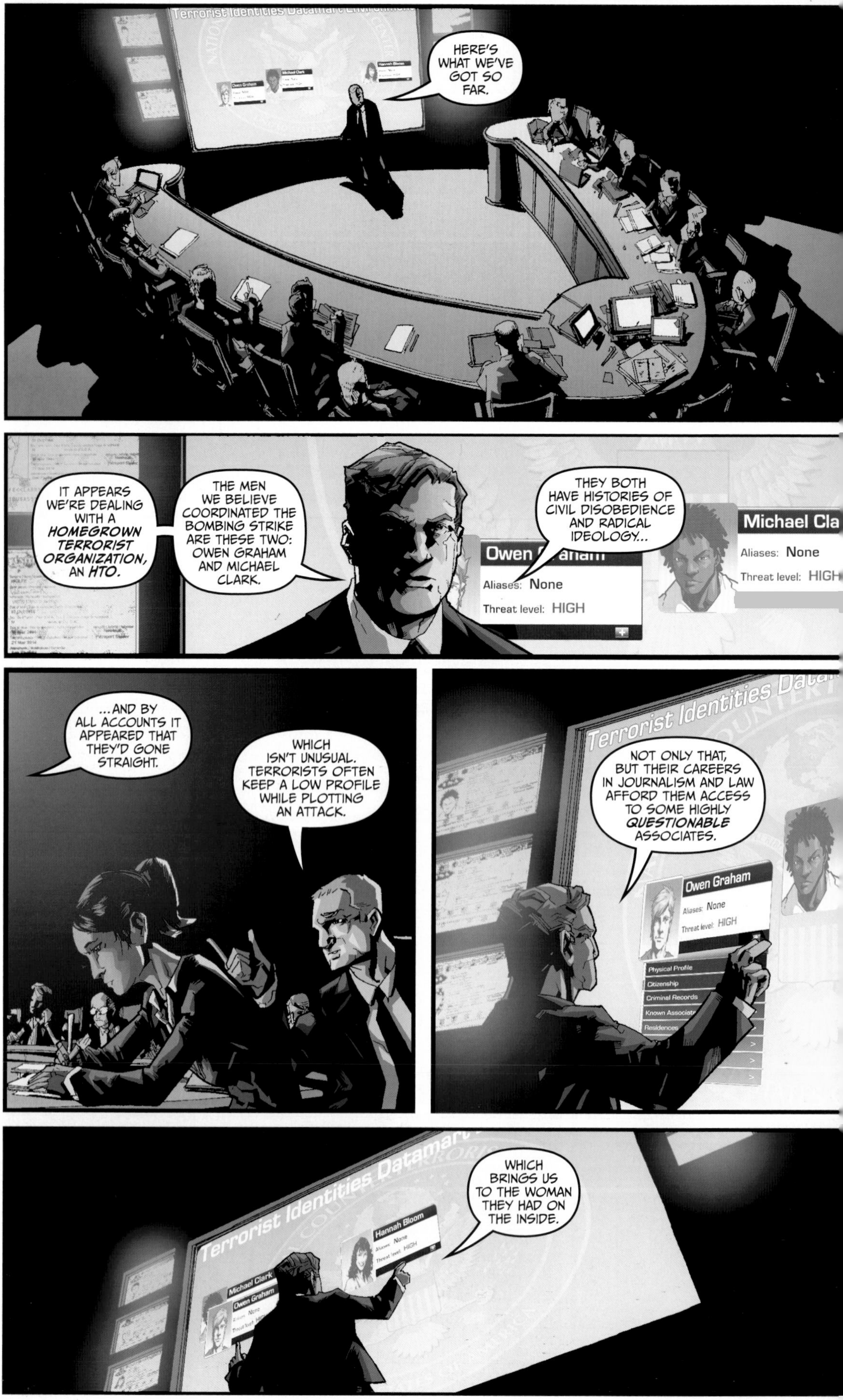

HERE'S WHAT WE'VE GOT SO FAR.

IT APPEARS WE'RE DEALING WITH A *HOMEGROWN TERRORIST ORGANIZATION*, AN *HTO*.

THE MEN WE BELIEVE COORDINATED THE BOMBING STRIKE ARE THESE TWO: OWEN GRAHAM AND MICHAEL CLARK.

THEY BOTH HAVE HISTORIES OF CIVIL DISOBEDIENCE AND RADICAL IDEOLOGY...

Owen Graham
Aliases: None
Threat level: HIGH

Michael Cla
Aliases: None
Threat level: HIGH

...AND BY ALL ACCOUNTS IT APPEARED THAT THEY'D GONE STRAIGHT.

WHICH ISN'T UNUSUAL. TERRORISTS OFTEN KEEP A LOW PROFILE WHILE PLOTTING AN ATTACK.

NOT ONLY THAT, BUT THEIR CAREERS IN JOURNALISM AND LAW AFFORD THEM ACCESS TO SOME HIGHLY *QUESTIONABLE* ASSOCIATES.

Terrorist Identities Data

Owen Graham
Aliases: None
Threat level: HIGH

Physical Profile
Citizenship
Criminal Records
Known Associate
Residences

WHICH BRINGS US TO THE WOMAN THEY HAD ON THE INSIDE.

Terrorist Identities Datamar

Hannah Bloom
Aliases: None
Threat level: HIGH

Michael Clark
Owen Graham

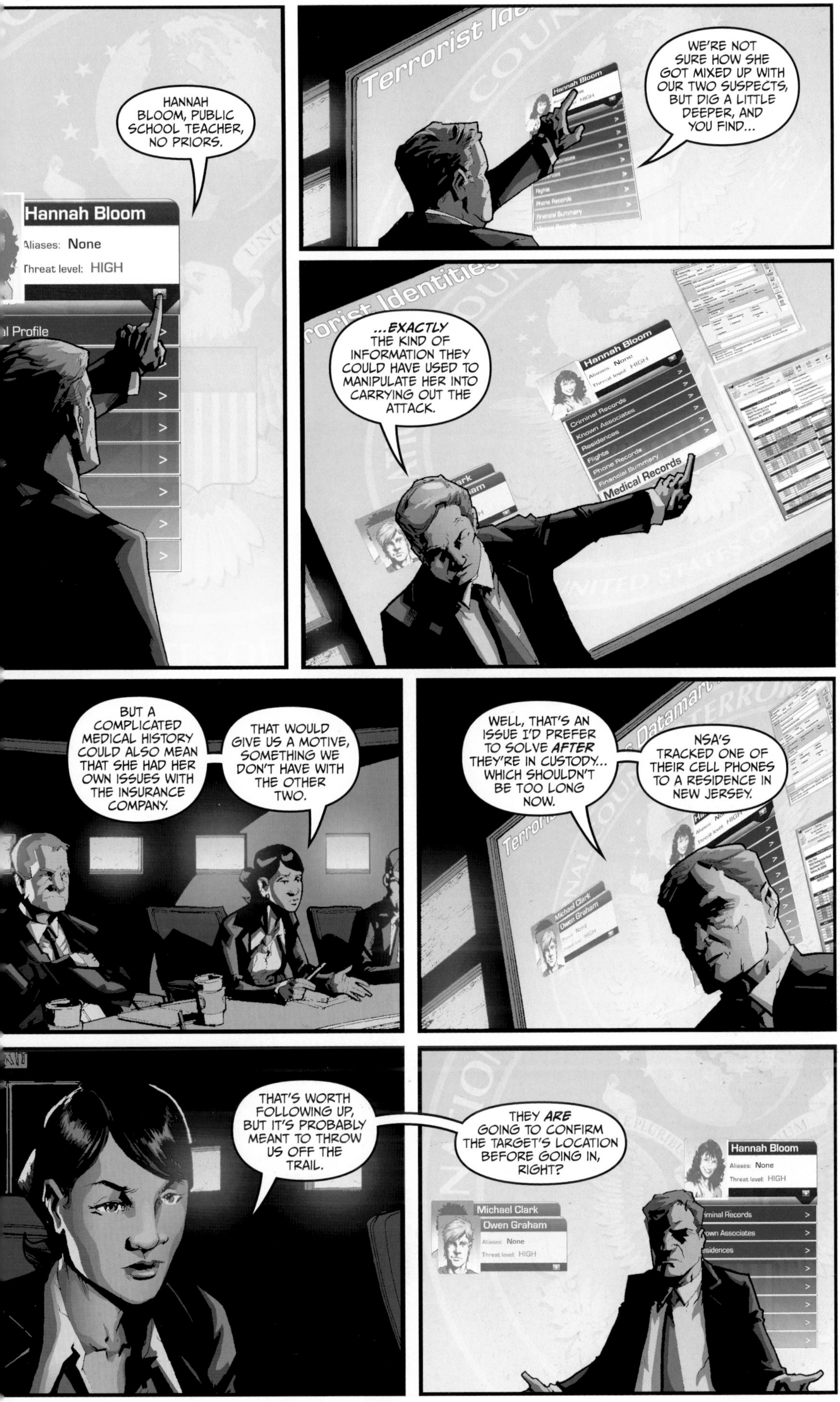
HANNAH BLOOM, PUBLIC SCHOOL TEACHER, NO PRIORS.
Hannah Bloom
Aliases: None
Threat level: HIGH
Terrorist Id
WE'RE NOT SURE HOW SHE GOT MIXED UP WITH OUR TWO SUSPECTS, BUT DIG A LITTLE DEEPER, AND YOU FIND...
Terrorist Identities
...*EXACTLY* THE KIND OF INFORMATION THEY COULD HAVE USED TO MANIPULATE HER INTO CARRYING OUT THE ATTACK.
Hannah Bloom
Criminal Records
Known Associates
Residences
Flights
Phone Records
Financial Summary
Medical Records
UNITED STATES
BUT A COMPLICATED MEDICAL HISTORY COULD ALSO MEAN THAT SHE HAD HER OWN ISSUES WITH THE INSURANCE COMPANY.
THAT WOULD GIVE US A MOTIVE, SOMETHING WE DON'T HAVE WITH THE OTHER TWO.
WELL, THAT'S AN ISSUE I'D PREFER TO SOLVE *AFTER* THEY'RE IN CUSTODY... WHICH SHOULDN'T BE TOO LONG NOW.
NSA'S TRACKED ONE OF THEIR CELL PHONES TO A RESIDENCE IN NEW JERSEY.
Michael Clark
Owen Graham
THAT'S WORTH FOLLOWING UP, BUT IT'S PROBABLY MEANT TO THROW US OFF THE TRAIL.
THEY *ARE* GOING TO CONFIRM THE TARGET'S LOCATION BEFORE GOING IN, RIGHT?
Hannah Bloom
Aliases: None
Threat level: HIGH
Michael Clark
Owen Graham
Aliases: None
Threat level: HIGH

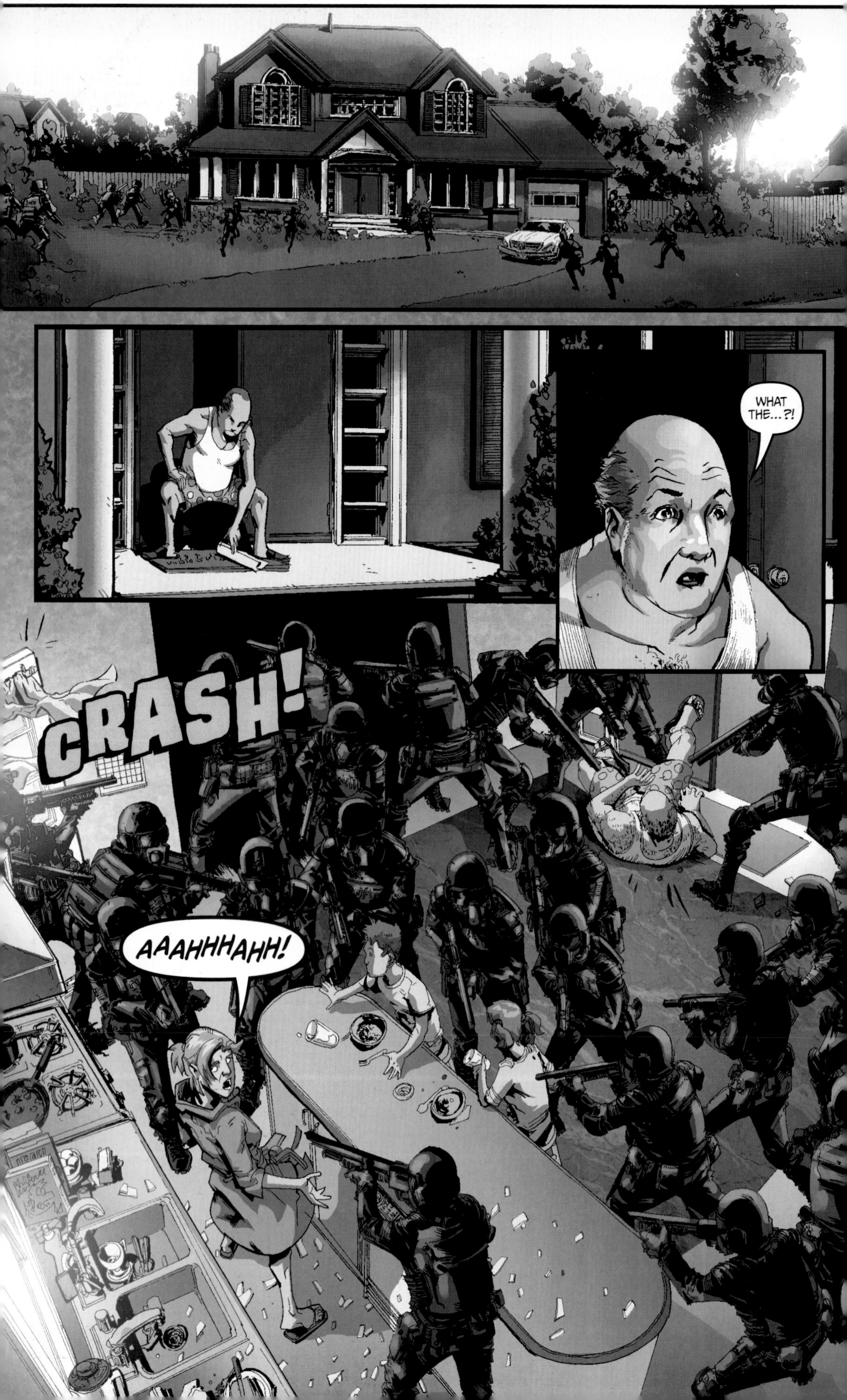
WHAT THE...?!
CRASH!
AAAHHHAHH!

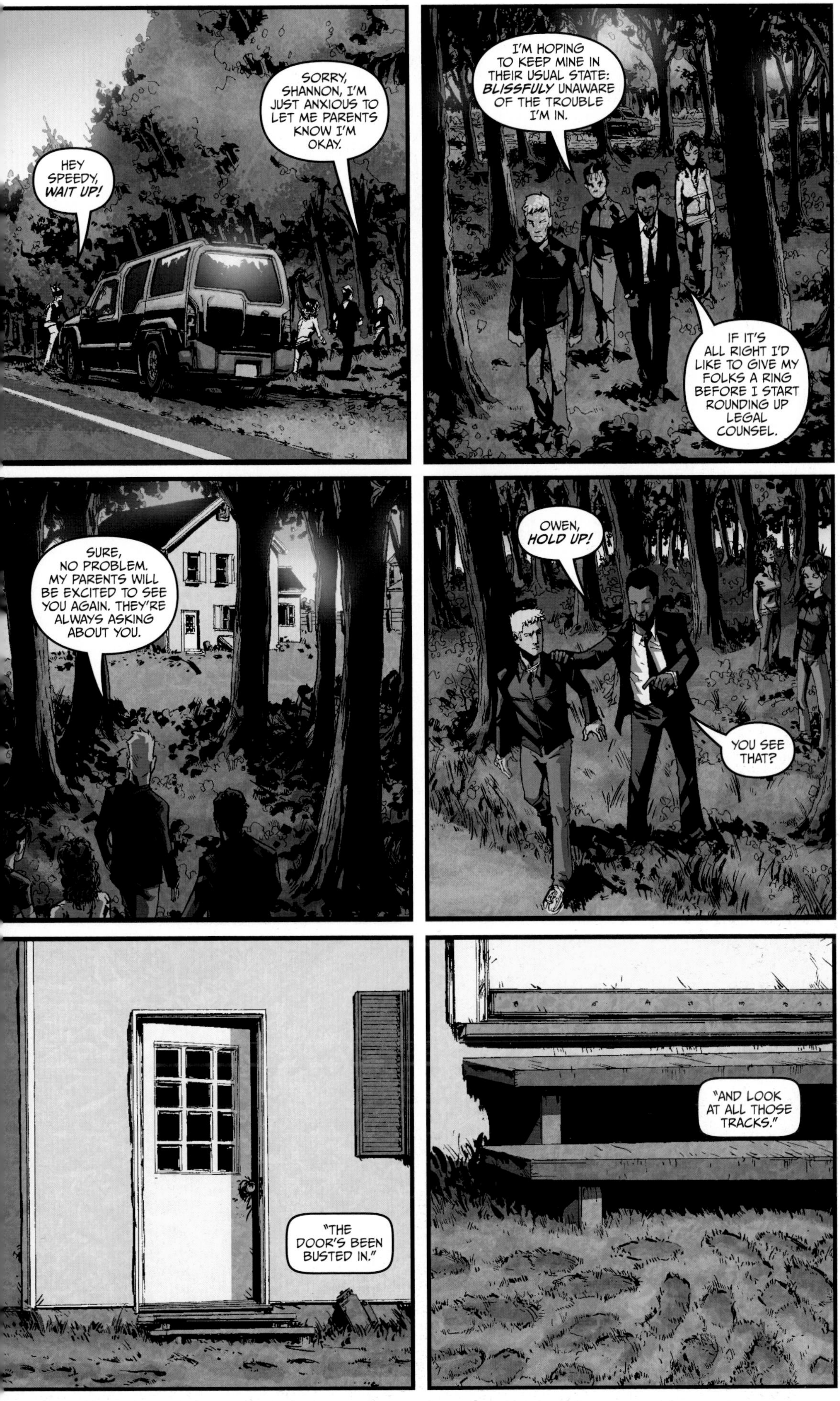
HEY SPEEDY, WAIT UP!
SORRY, SHANNON, I'M JUST ANXIOUS TO LET ME PARENTS KNOW I'M OKAY.
I'M HOPING TO KEEP MINE IN THEIR USUAL STATE: BLISSFULY UNAWARE OF THE TROUBLE I'M IN.
IF IT'S ALL RIGHT I'D LIKE TO GIVE MY FOLKS A RING BEFORE I START ROUNDING UP LEGAL COUNSEL.
SURE, NO PROBLEM. MY PARENTS WILL BE EXCITED TO SEE YOU AGAIN. THEY'RE ALWAYS ASKING ABOUT YOU.
OWEN, HOLD UP!
YOU SEE THAT?
"THE DOOR'S BEEN BUSTED IN."
"AND LOOK AT ALL THOSE TRACKS."

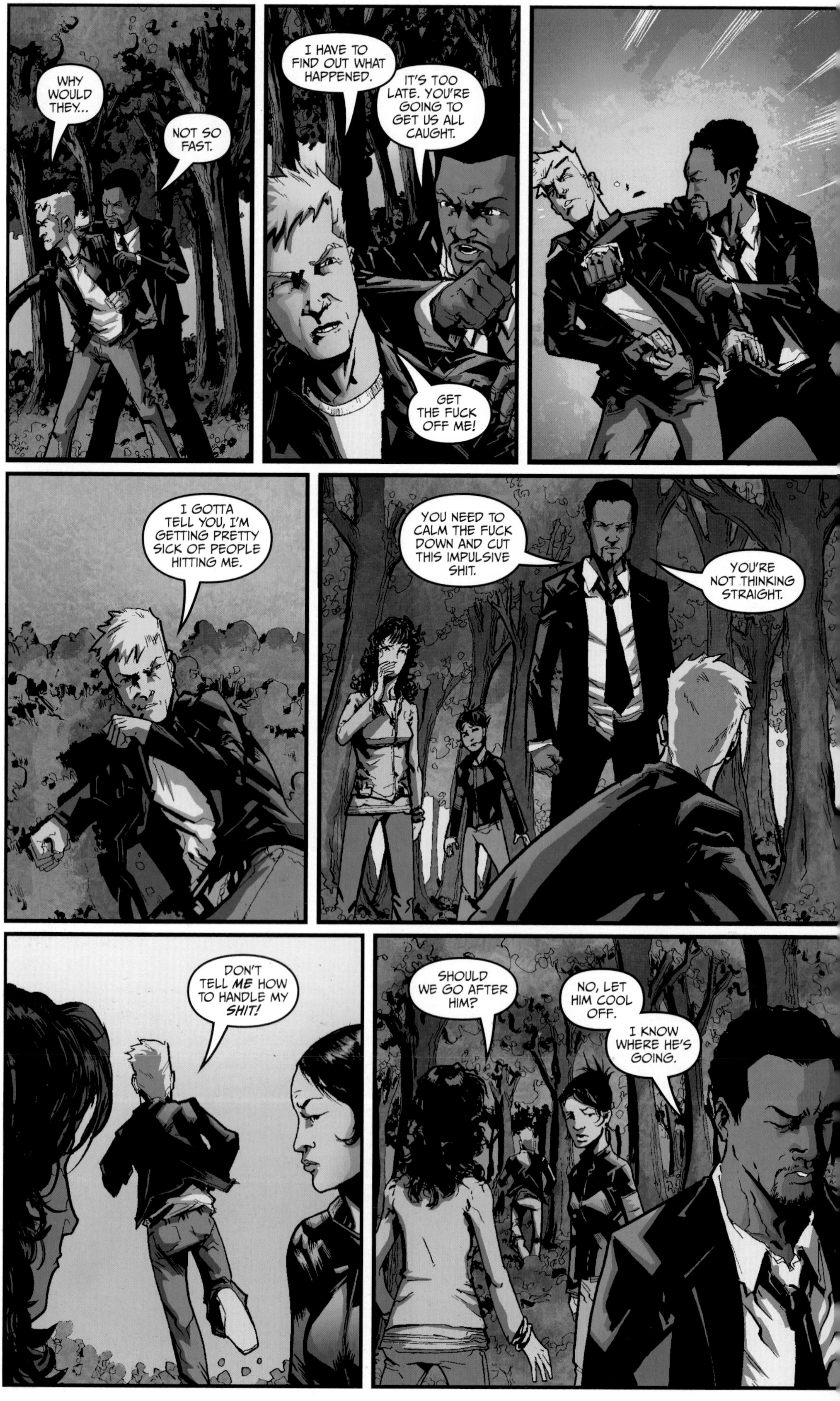

WHY WOULD THEY...
NOT SO FAST.
I HAVE TO FIND OUT WHAT HAPPENED.
IT'S TOO LATE. YOU'RE GOING TO GET US ALL CAUGHT.
GET THE FUCK OFF ME!
I GOTTA TELL YOU, I'M GETTING PRETTY SICK OF PEOPLE HITTING ME.
YOU NEED TO CALM THE FUCK DOWN AND CUT THIS IMPULSIVE SHIT.
YOU'RE NOT THINKING STRAIGHT.
DON'T TELL ME HOW TO HANDLE MY SHIT!
SHOULD WE GO AFTER HIM?
NO, LET HIM COOL OFF.
I KNOW WHERE HE'S GOING.

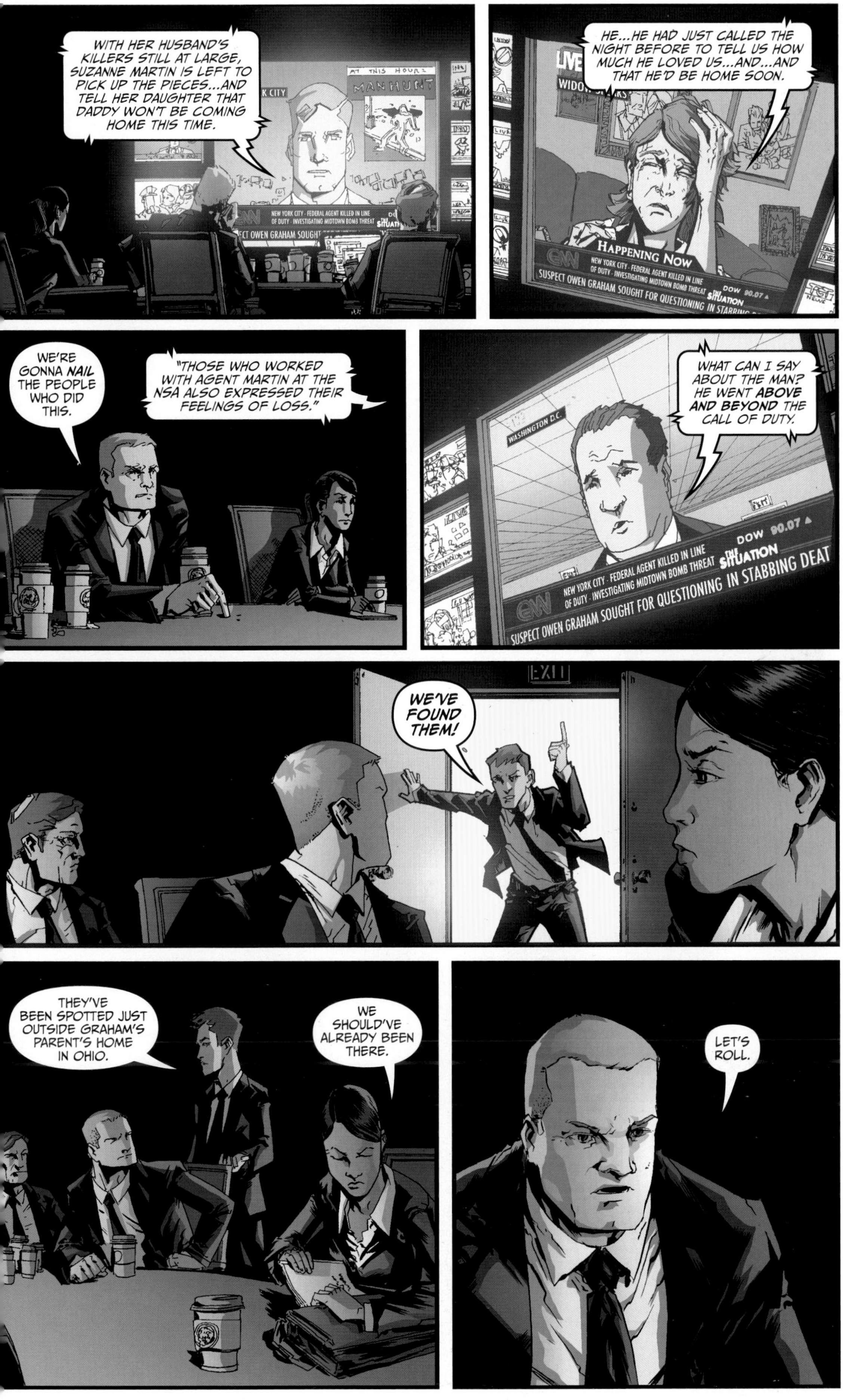
WITH HER HUSBAND'S KILLERS STILL AT LARGE, SUZANNE MARTIN IS LEFT TO PICK UP THE PIECES...AND TELL HER DAUGHTER THAT DADDY WON'T BE COMING HOME THIS TIME.
MANHUNT
NEW YORK CITY - FEDERAL AGENT KILLED IN LINE OF DUTY - INVESTIGATING MIDTOWN BOMB THREAT
HE...HE HAD JUST CALLED THE NIGHT BEFORE TO TELL US HOW MUCH HE LOVED US...AND...AND THAT HE'D BE HOME SOON.
HAPPENING NOW
SUSPECT OWEN GRAHAM SOUGHT FOR QUESTIONING IN STABBING
WE'RE GONNA NAIL THE PEOPLE WHO DID THIS.
"THOSE WHO WORKED WITH AGENT MARTIN AT THE NSA ALSO EXPRESSED THEIR FEELINGS OF LOSS."
WHAT CAN I SAY ABOUT THE MAN? HE WENT ABOVE AND BEYOND THE CALL OF DUTY.
WASHINGTON D.C.
DOW 90.07
THE SITUATION
SUSPECT OWEN GRAHAM SOUGHT FOR QUESTIONING IN STABBING DEAT
EXIT
WE'VE FOUND THEM!
THEY'VE BEEN SPOTTED JUST OUTSIDE GRAHAM'S PARENT'S HOME IN OHIO.
WE SHOULD'VE ALREADY BEEN THERE.
LET'S ROLL.

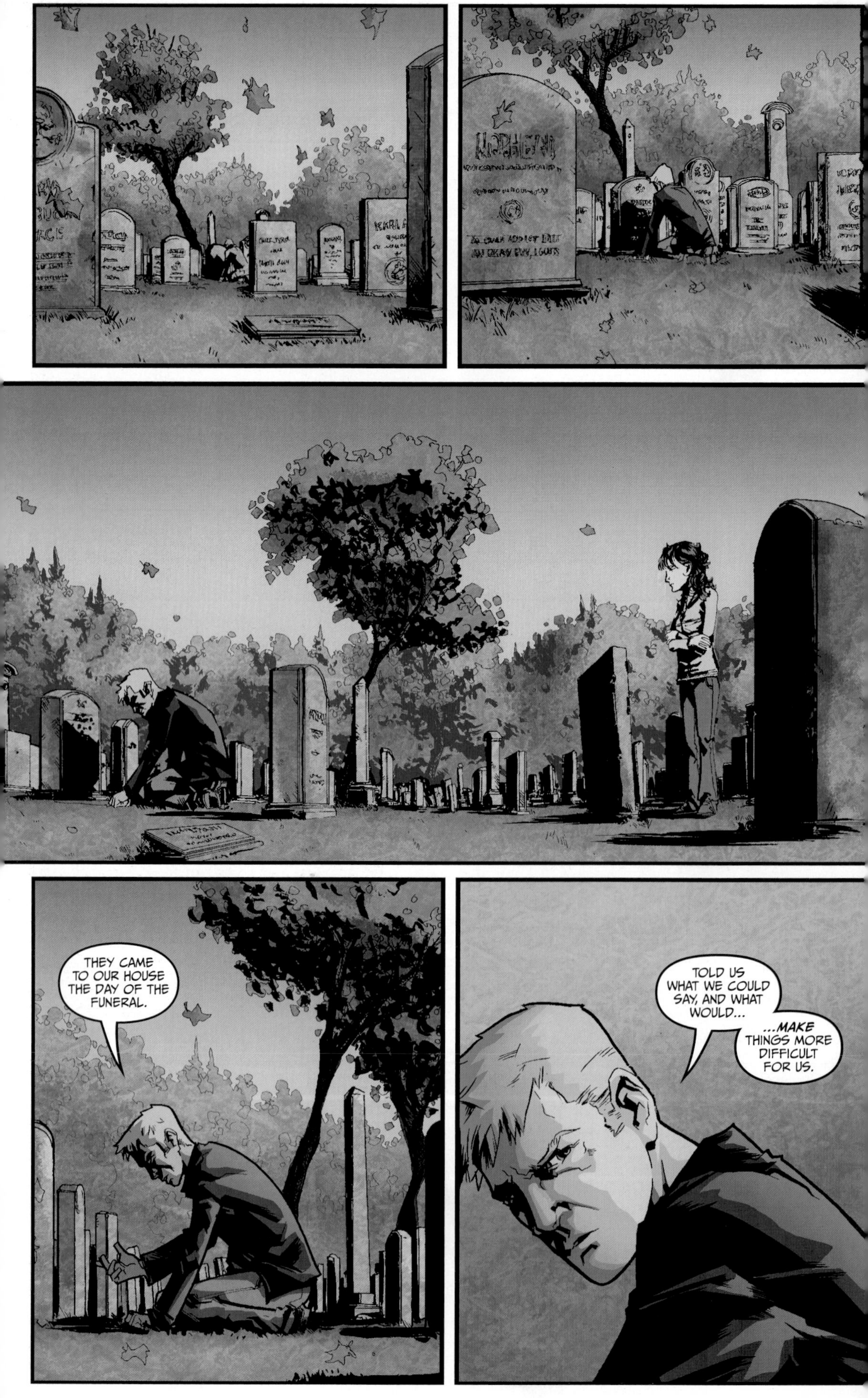
THEY CAME TO OUR HOUSE THE DAY OF THE FUNERAL.
TOLD US WHAT WE COULD SAY, AND WHAT WOULD...
...MAKE THINGS MORE DIFFICULT FOR US.

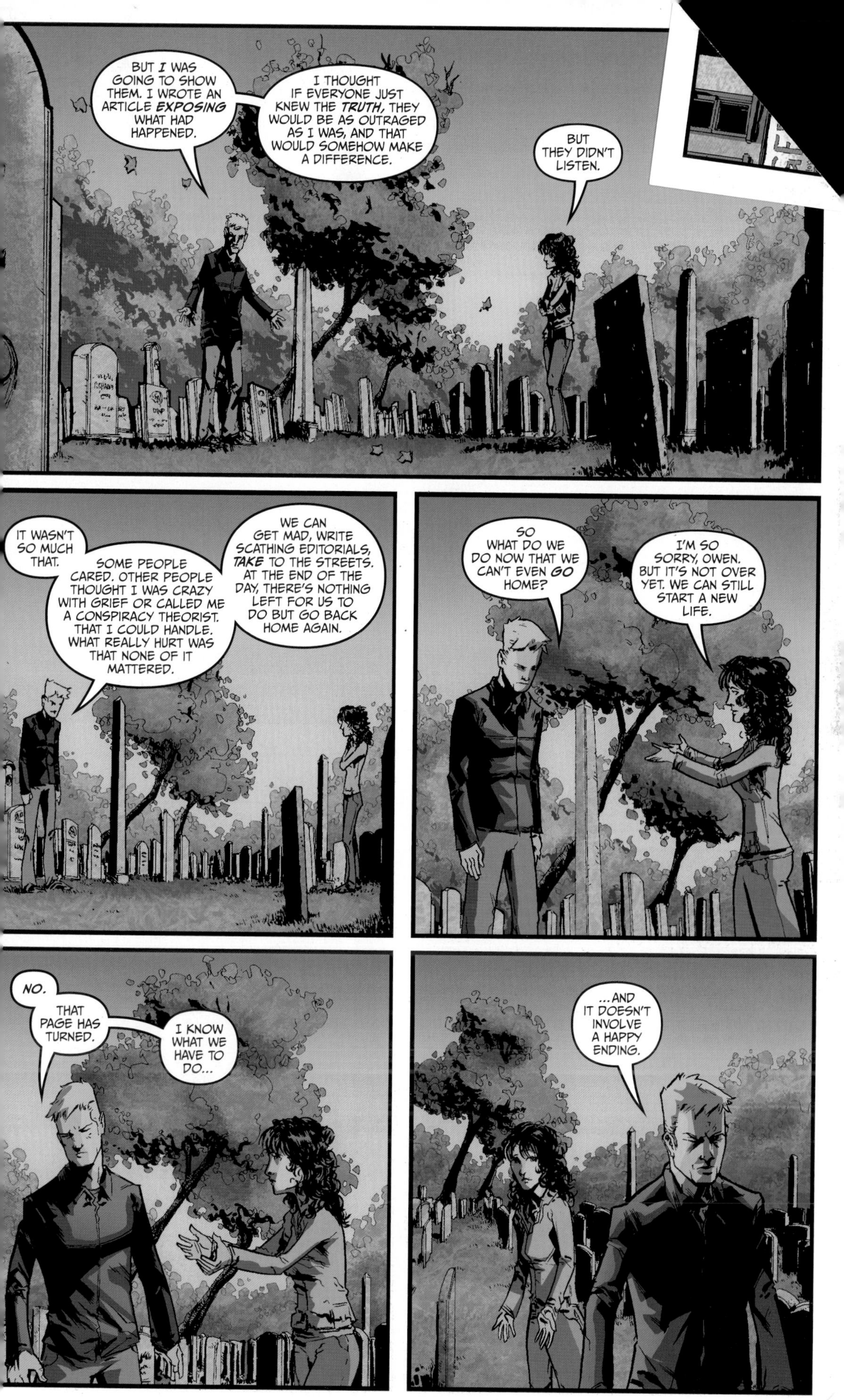

BUT I WAS GOING TO SHOW THEM. I WROTE AN ARTICLE EXPOSING WHAT HAD HAPPENED.
I THOUGHT IF EVERYONE JUST KNEW THE TRUTH, THEY WOULD BE AS OUTRAGED AS I WAS, AND THAT WOULD SOMEHOW MAKE A DIFFERENCE.
BUT THEY DIDN'T LISTEN.
IT WASN'T SO MUCH THAT.
SOME PEOPLE CARED. OTHER PEOPLE THOUGHT I WAS CRAZY WITH GRIEF OR CALLED ME A CONSPIRACY THEORIST. THAT I COULD HANDLE. WHAT REALLY HURT WAS THAT NONE OF IT MATTERED.
WE CAN GET MAD, WRITE SCATHING EDITORIALS, TAKE TO THE STREETS. AT THE END OF THE DAY, THERE'S NOTHING LEFT FOR US TO DO BUT GO BACK HOME AGAIN.
SO WHAT DO WE DO NOW THAT WE CAN'T EVEN GO HOME?
I'M SO SORRY, OWEN. BUT IT'S NOT OVER YET. WE CAN STILL START A NEW LIFE.
NO.
THAT PAGE HAS TURNED.
I KNOW WHAT WE HAVE TO DO...
...AND IT DOESN'T INVOLVE A HAPPY ENDING.

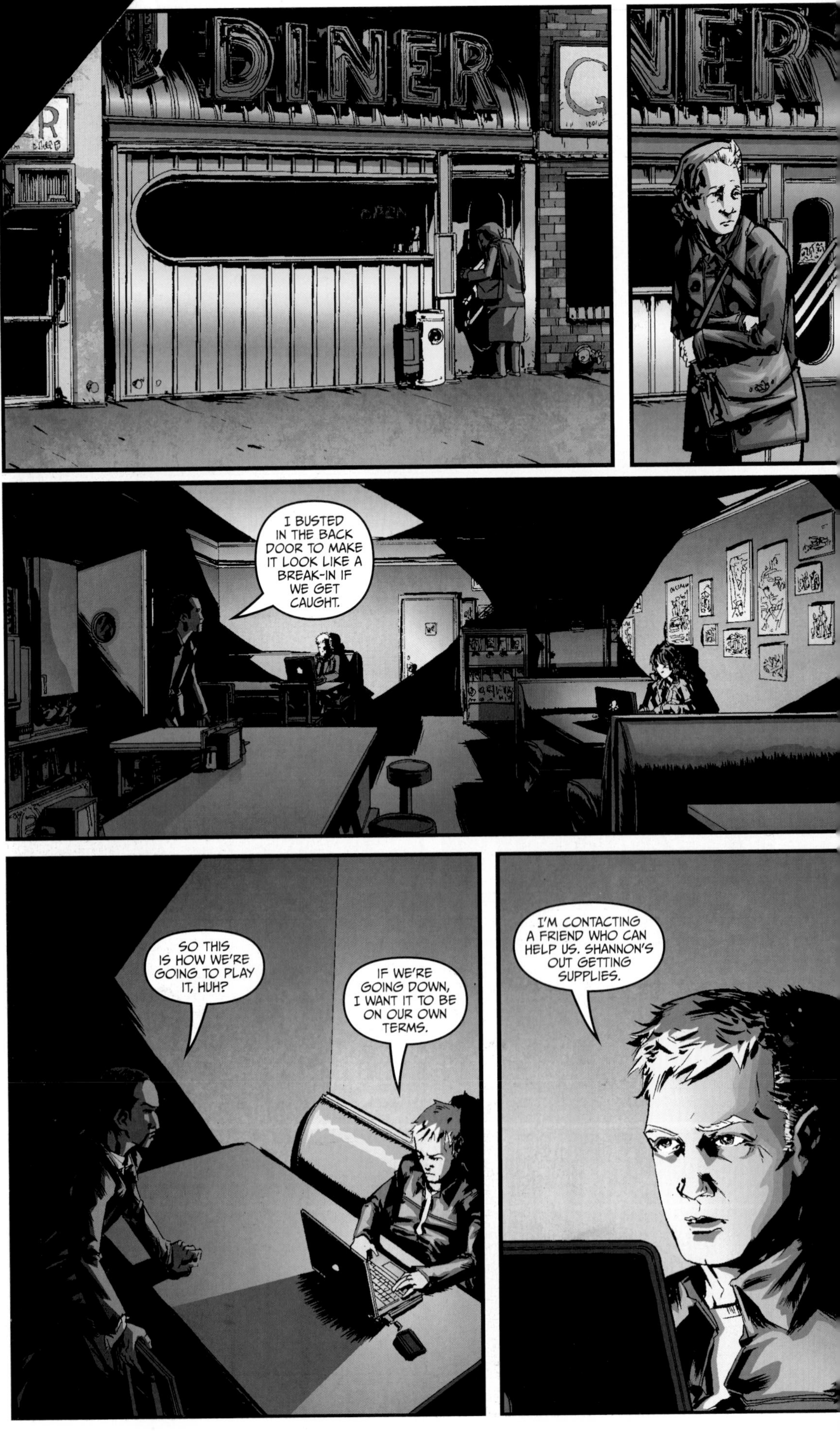
DINER
OPEN
I BUSTED IN THE BACK DOOR TO MAKE IT LOOK LIKE A BREAK-IN IF WE GET CAUGHT.
SO THIS IS HOW WE'RE GOING TO PLAY IT, HUH?
IF WE'RE GOING DOWN, I WANT IT TO BE ON OUR OWN TERMS.
I'M CONTACTING A FRIEND WHO CAN HELP US. SHANNON'S OUT GETTING SUPPLIES.

I NEVER THOUGHT IT WOULD COME TO THIS.

IT'S LIBERATING, I GUESS.

WE TRIED TO DO THINGS THEIR WAY, DIDN'T WE? AND LOOK WHERE THAT GOT US.

WHAT'S WRONG WITH HER?

SHE'LL BE FINE.

SLAM!

THERE MIGHT NOT BE A SHOP LEFT IN THIS TOWN BESIDES THOSE TWO MEGA-STORES, BUT GODDAMN IT IF THEY DON'T HAVE EVERYTHING YOU NEED TO BUILD YOUR OWN BOMB.

HEY, MERRY SUNSHINE, WE ABOUT READY TO DO THIS? 'CAUSE MY SUV'S LOOKING MIGHTY SUSPICIOUS OUT THERE WITH THAT BIG LADDER STRAPPED TO THE ROOF.

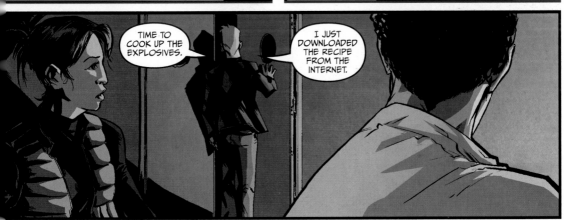

TIME TO COOK UP THE EXPLOSIVES.

I JUST DOWNLOADED THE RECIPE FROM THE INTERNET.

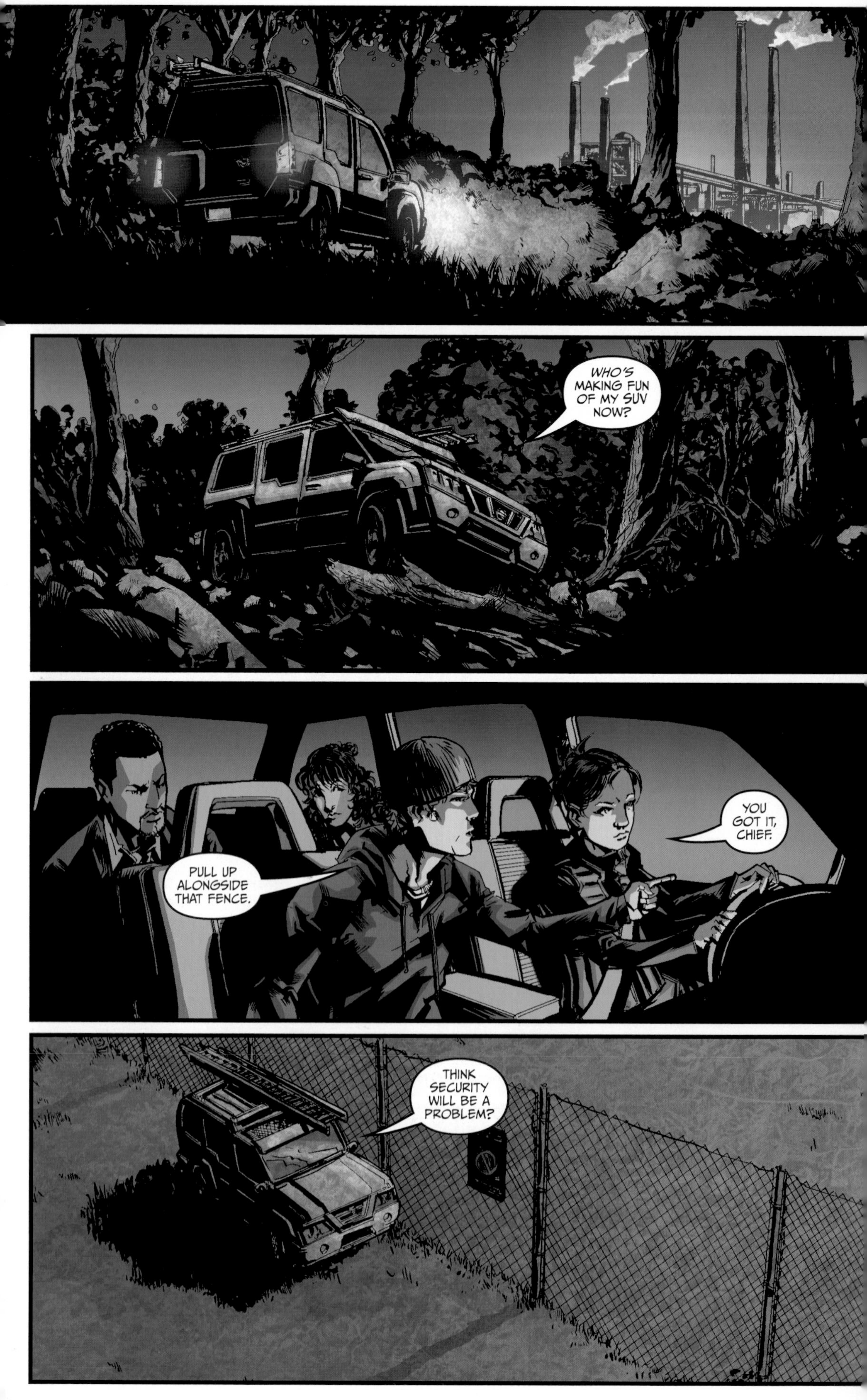
WHO'S MAKING FUN OF MY SUV NOW?
YOU GOT IT, CHIEF.
PULL UP ALONGSIDE THAT FENCE.
THINK SECURITY WILL BE A PROBLEM?

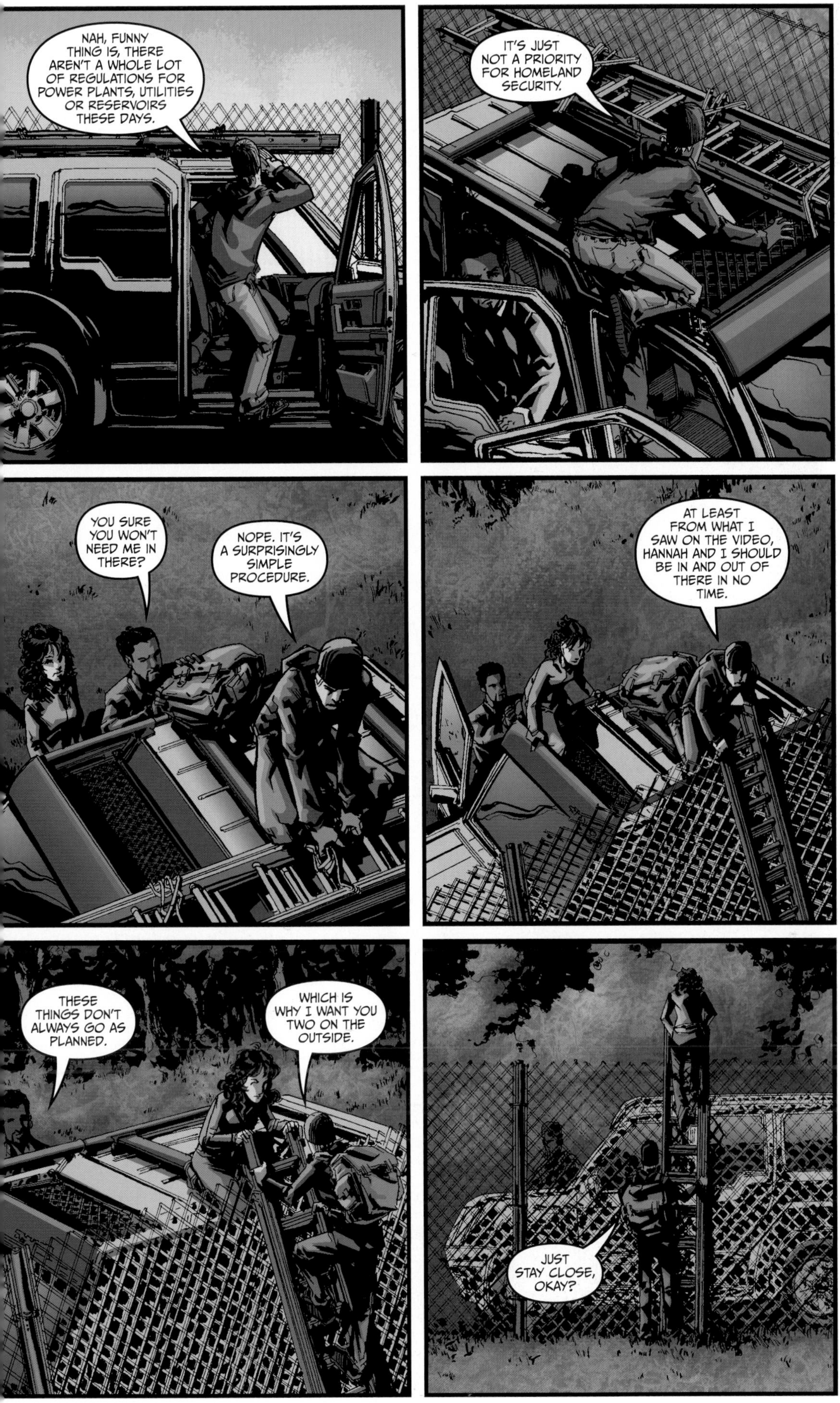
NAH, FUNNY THING IS, THERE AREN'T A WHOLE LOT OF REGULATIONS FOR POWER PLANTS, UTILITIES OR RESERVOIRS THESE DAYS.
IT'S JUST NOT A PRIORITY FOR HOMELAND SECURITY.
YOU SURE YOU WON'T NEED ME IN THERE?
NOPE. IT'S A SURPRISINGLY SIMPLE PROCEDURE.
AT LEAST FROM WHAT I SAW ON THE VIDEO, HANNAH AND I SHOULD BE IN AND OUT OF THERE IN NO TIME.
THESE THINGS DON'T ALWAYS GO AS PLANNED.
WHICH IS WHY I WANT YOU TWO ON THE OUTSIDE.
JUST STAY CLOSE, OKAY?

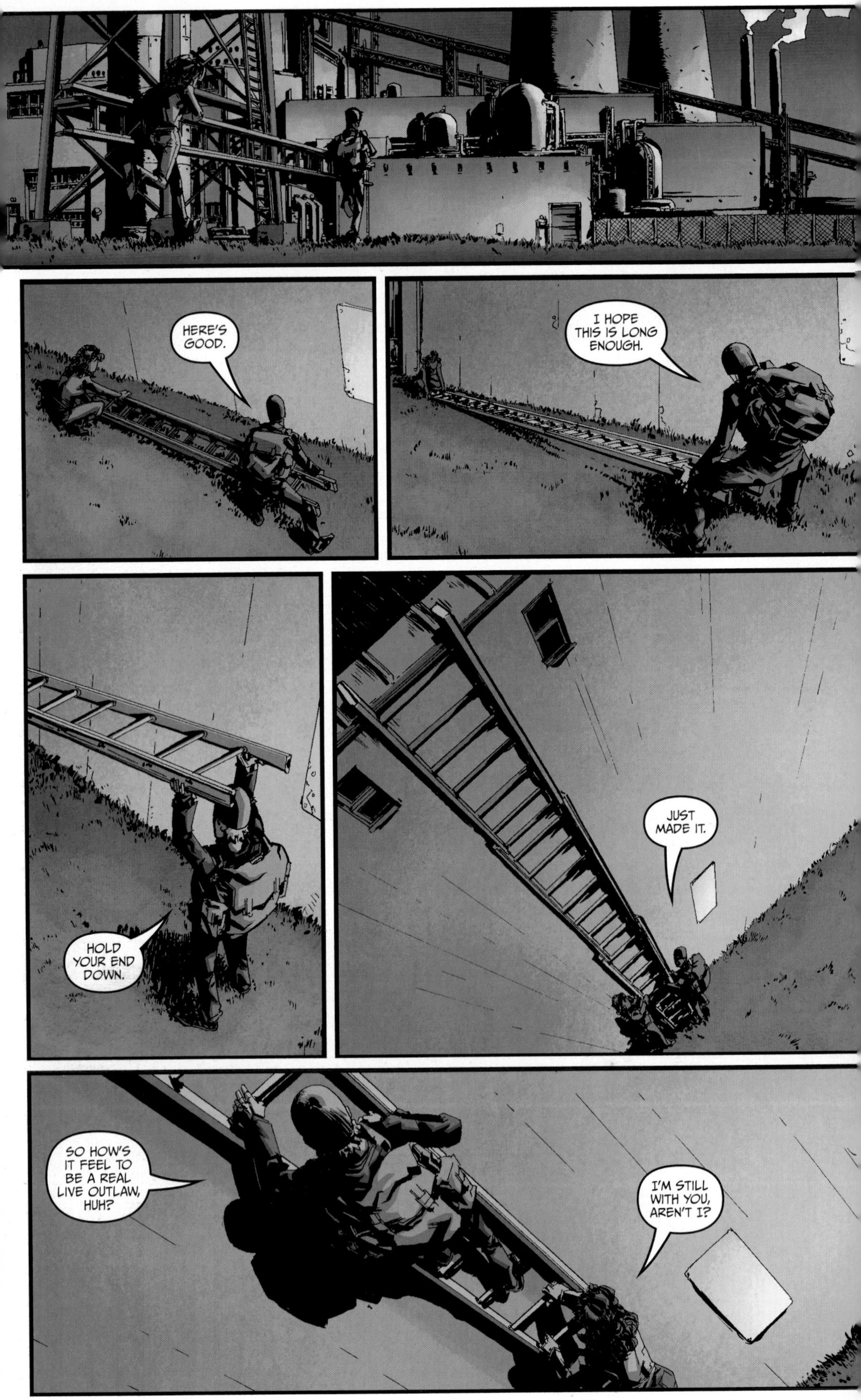
HERE'S GOOD.
I HOPE THIS IS LONG ENOUGH.
HOLD YOUR END DOWN.
JUST MADE IT.
SO HOW'S IT FEEL TO BE A REAL LIVE OUTLAW, HUH?
I'M STILL WITH YOU, AREN'T I?

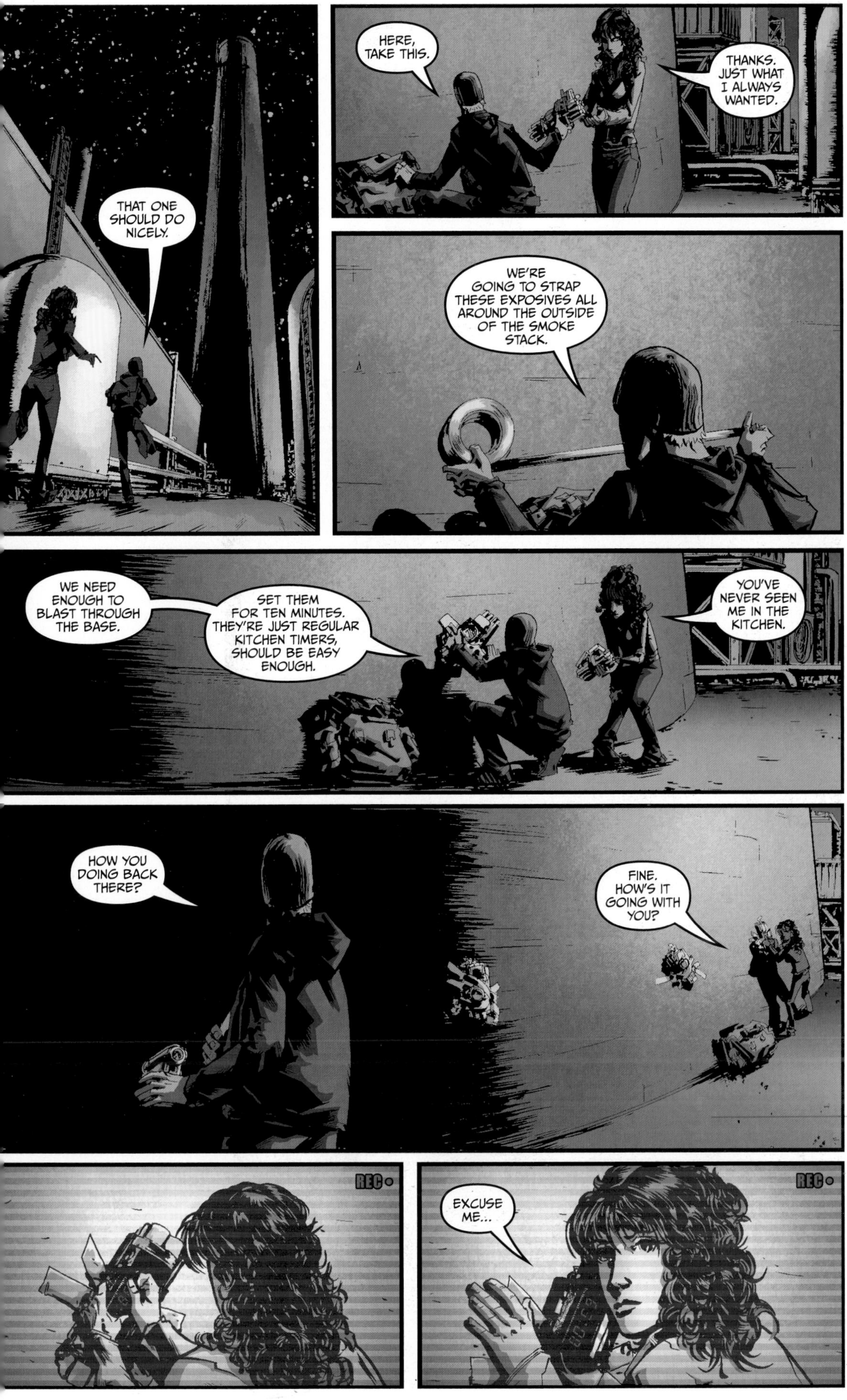
THAT ONE SHOULD DO NICELY.
HERE, TAKE THIS.
THANKS. JUST WHAT I ALWAYS WANTED.
WE'RE GOING TO STRAP THESE EXPOSIVES ALL AROUND THE OUTSIDE OF THE SMOKE STACK.
WE NEED ENOUGH TO BLAST THROUGH THE BASE.
SET THEM FOR TEN MINUTES. THEY'RE JUST REGULAR KITCHEN TIMERS, SHOULD BE EASY ENOUGH.
YOU'VE NEVER SEEN ME IN THE KITCHEN.
HOW YOU DOING BACK THERE?
FINE. HOW'S IT GOING WITH YOU?
REC
REC
EXCUSE ME...

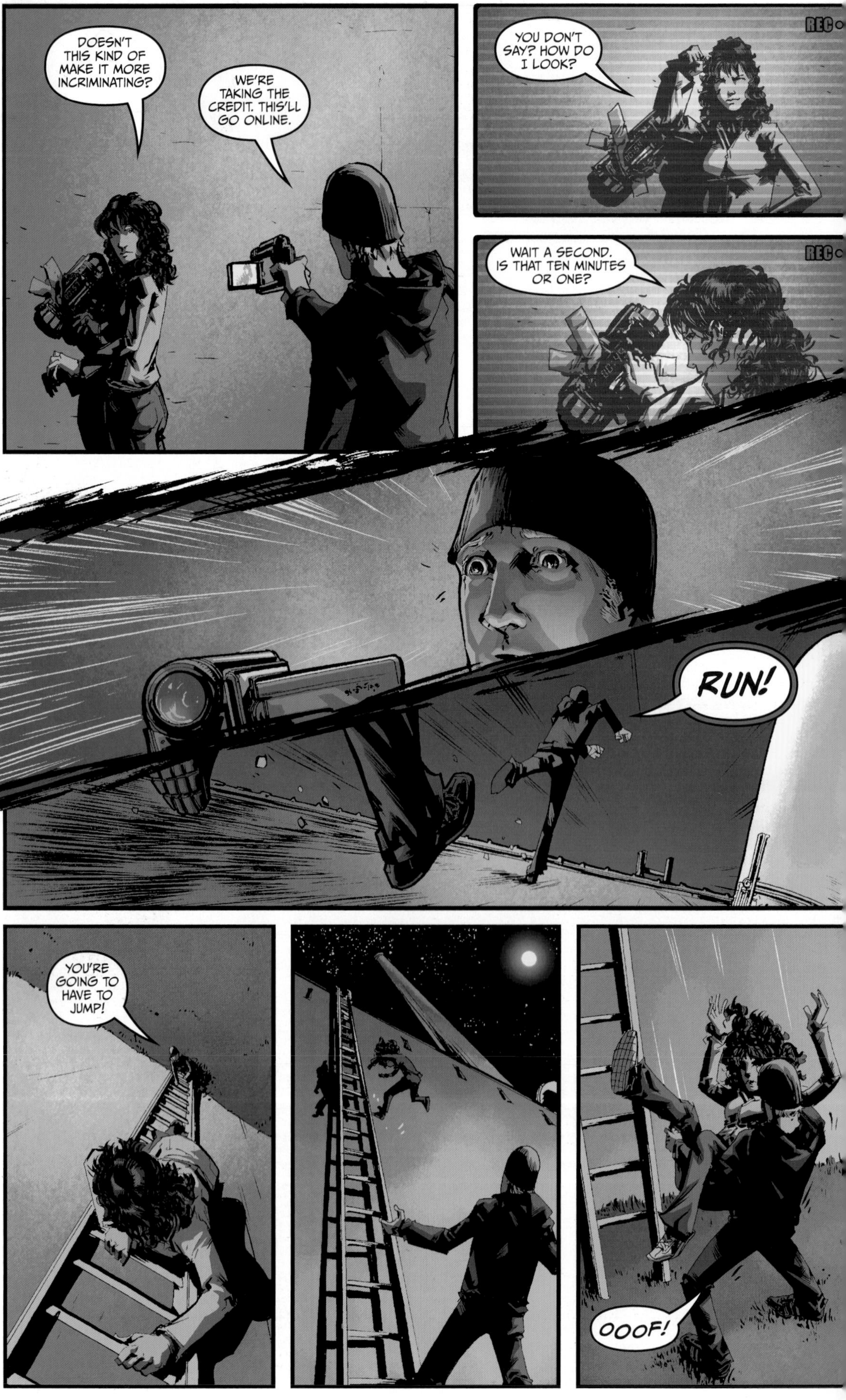
DOESN'T THIS KIND OF MAKE IT MORE INCRIMINATING?
WE'RE TAKING THE CREDIT. THIS'LL GO ONLINE.
REC
YOU DON'T SAY? HOW DO I LOOK?
REC
WAIT A SECOND. IS THAT TEN MINUTES OR ONE?
RUN!
YOU'RE GOING TO HAVE TO JUMP!
OOOF!

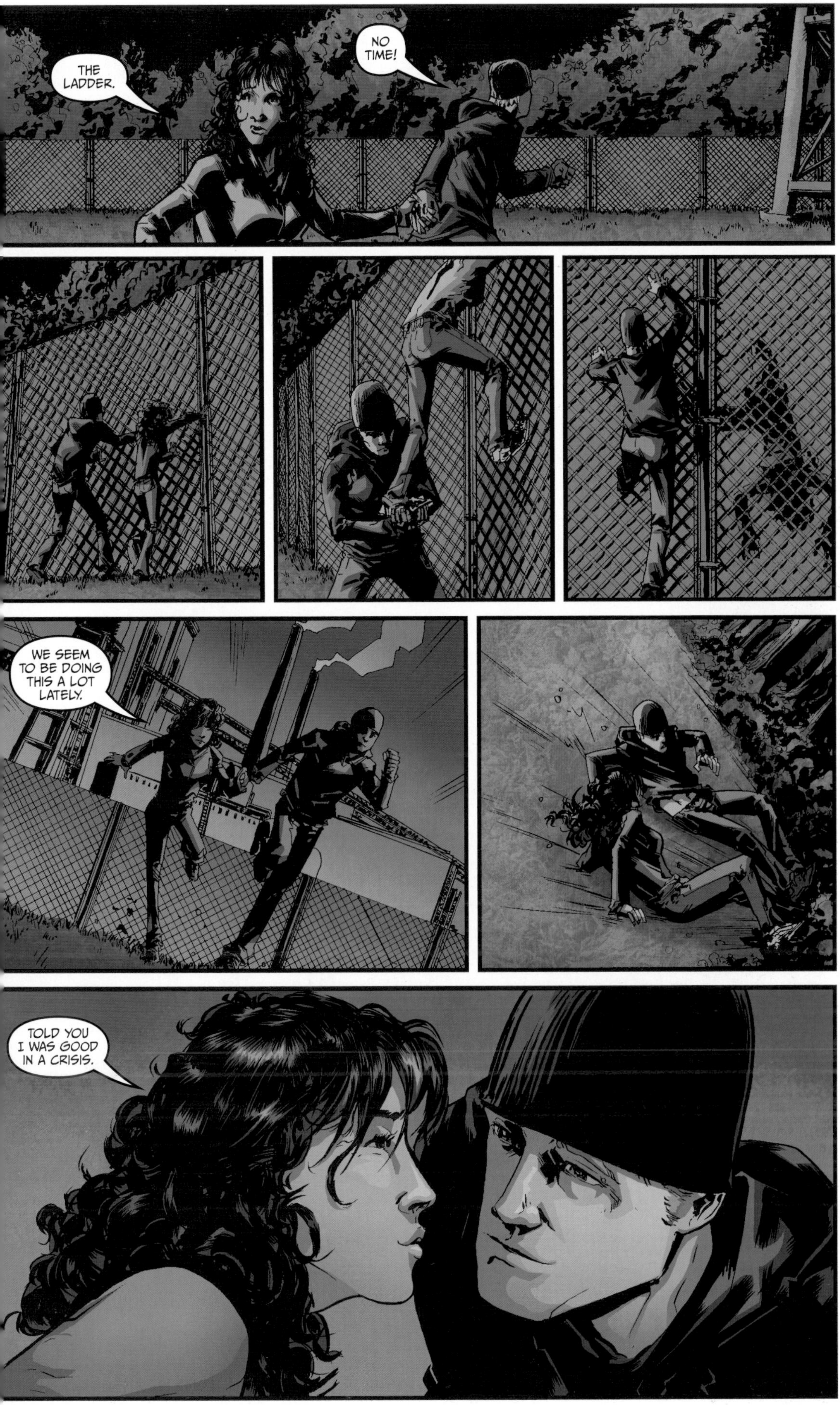
THE LADDER.
NO TIME!
WE SEEM TO BE DOING THIS A LOT LATELY.
TOLD YOU I WAS GOOD IN A CRISIS.

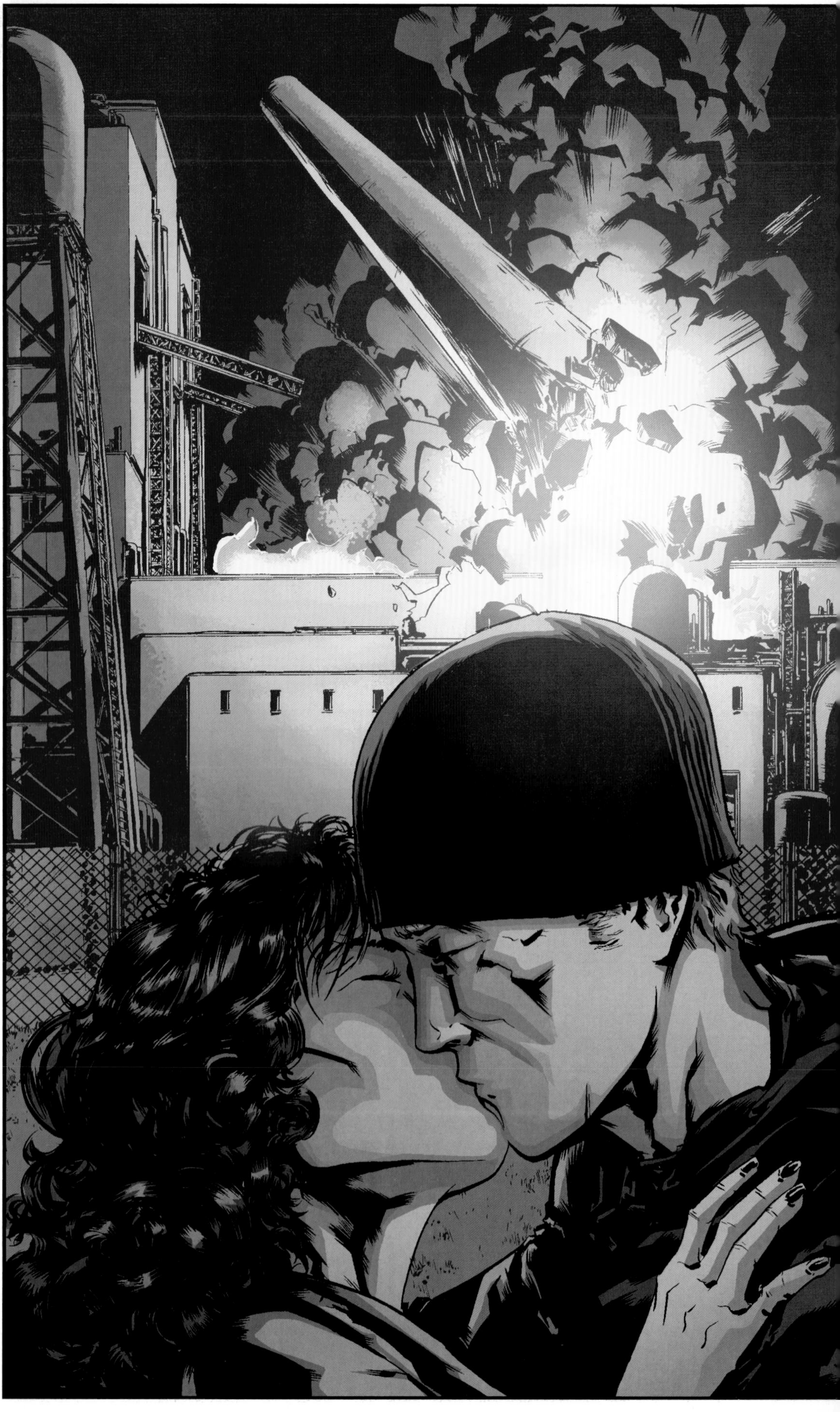

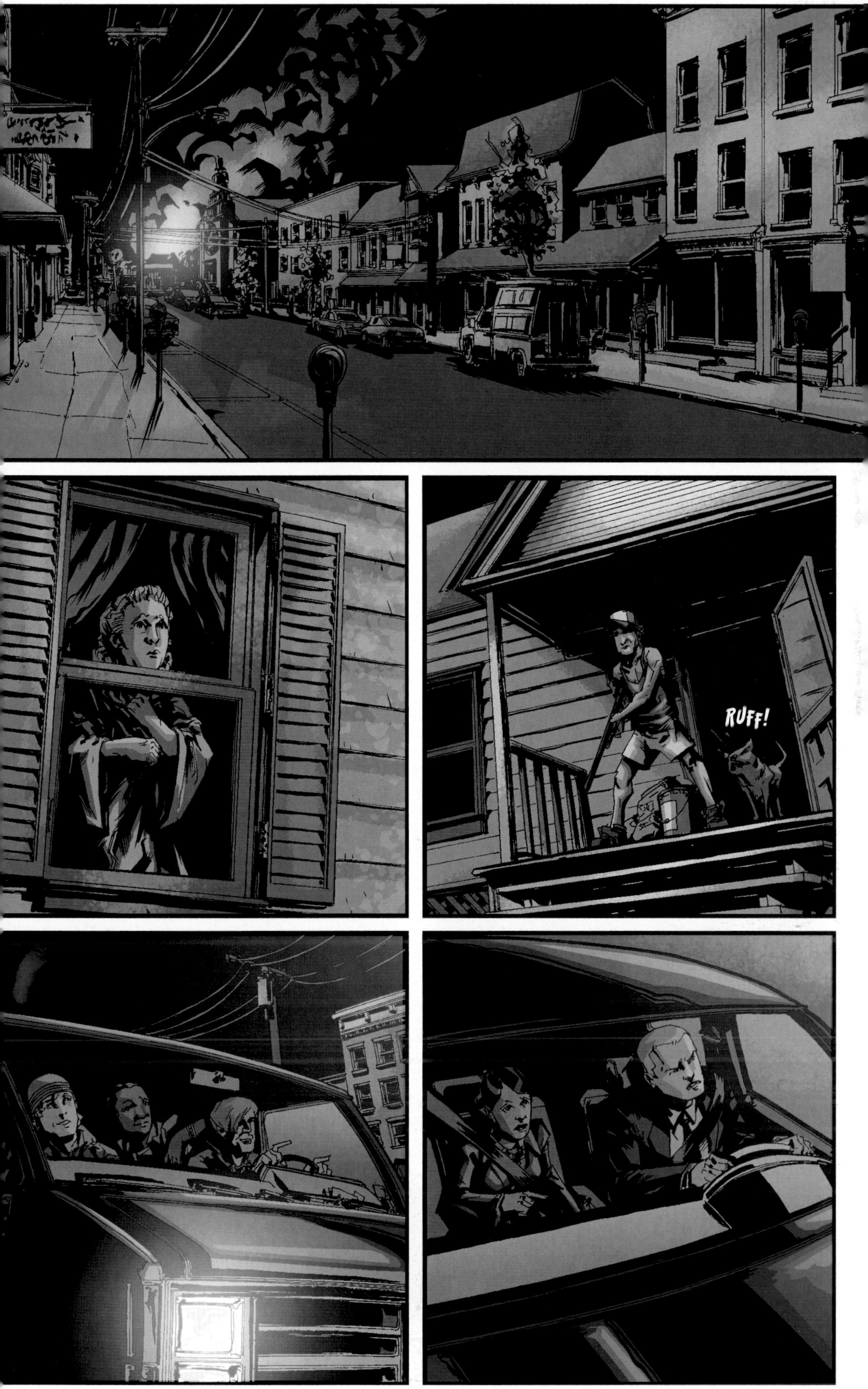
RUFF!

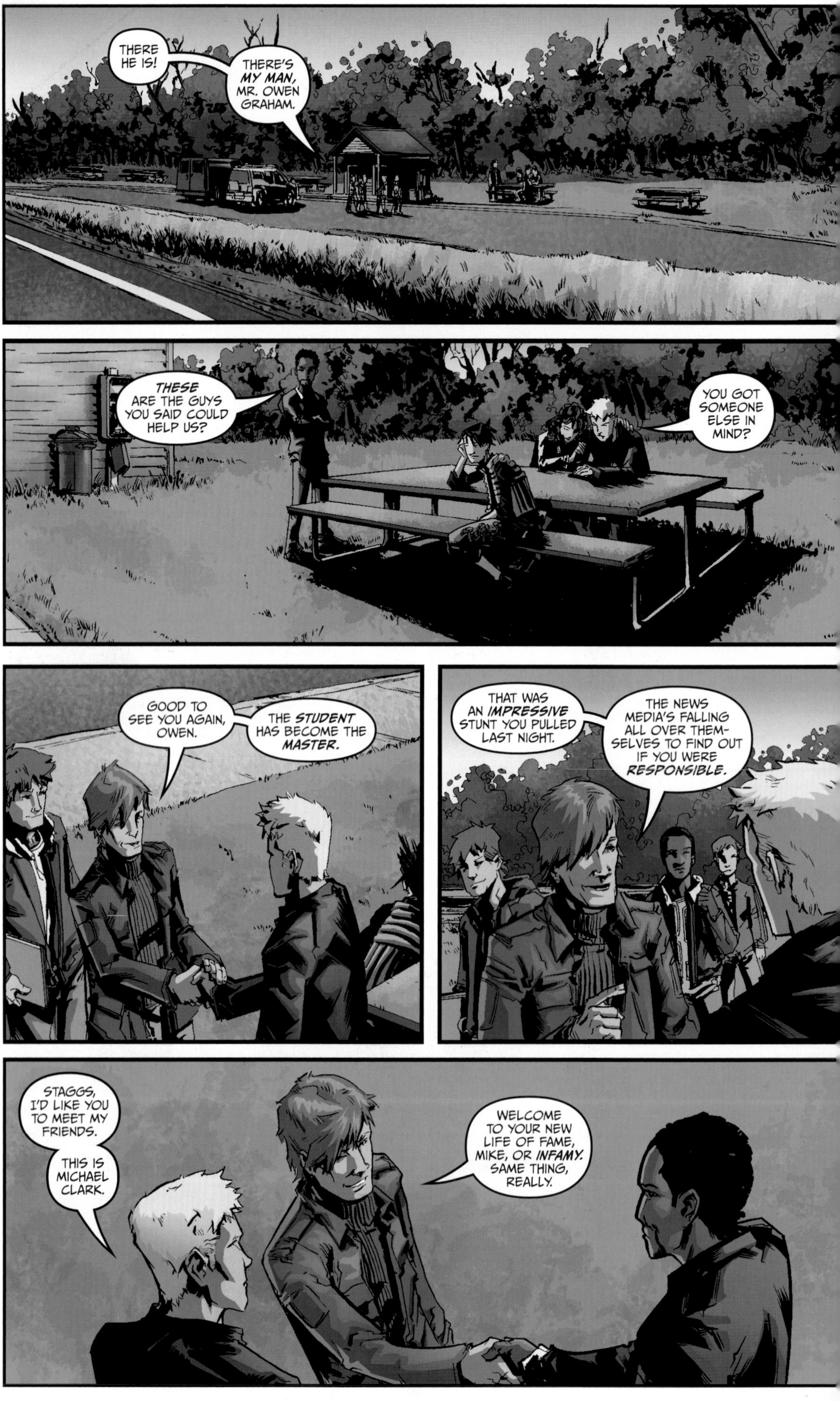
THERE HE IS!
THERE'S *MY MAN,* MR. OWEN GRAHAM.
THESE ARE THE GUYS YOU SAID COULD HELP US?
YOU GOT SOMEONE ELSE IN MIND?
GOOD TO SEE YOU AGAIN, OWEN.
THE *STUDENT* HAS BECOME THE *MASTER.*
THAT WAS AN *IMPRESSIVE* STUNT YOU PULLED LAST NIGHT.
THE NEWS MEDIA'S FALLING ALL OVER THEM-SELVES TO FIND OUT IF YOU WERE *RESPONSIBLE.*
STAGGS, I'D LIKE YOU TO MEET MY FRIENDS.
THIS IS MICHAEL CLARK.
WELCOME TO YOUR NEW LIFE OF FAME, MIKE, OR *INFAMY.* SAME THING, REALLY.

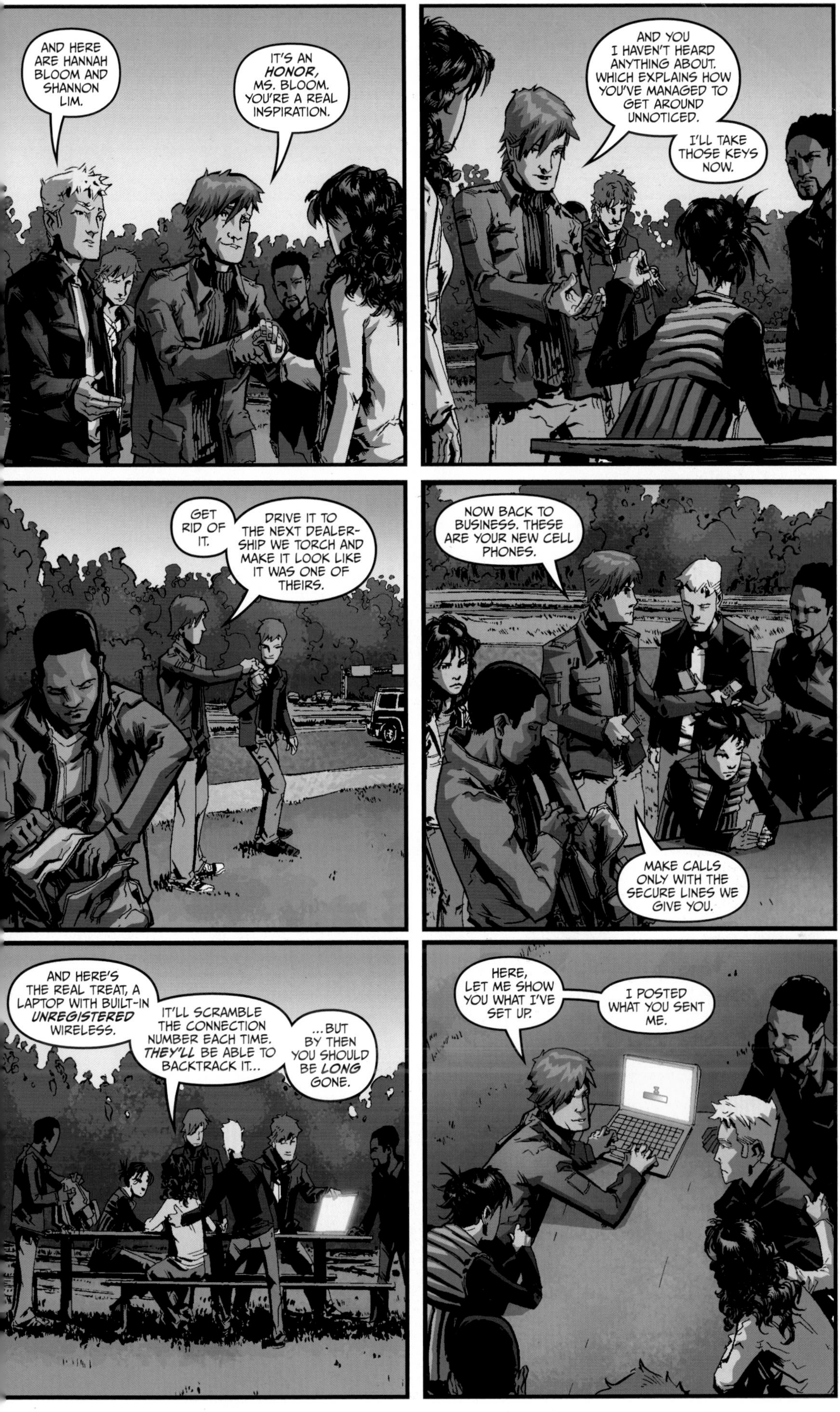
AND HERE ARE HANNAH BLOOM AND SHANNON LIM.
IT'S AN HONOR, MS. BLOOM. YOU'RE A REAL INSPIRATION.
AND YOU I HAVEN'T HEARD ANYTHING ABOUT. WHICH EXPLAINS HOW YOU'VE MANAGED TO GET AROUND UNNOTICED.
I'LL TAKE THOSE KEYS NOW.
GET RID OF IT.
DRIVE IT TO THE NEXT DEALER-SHIP WE TORCH AND MAKE IT LOOK LIKE IT WAS ONE OF THEIRS.
NOW BACK TO BUSINESS. THESE ARE YOUR NEW CELL PHONES.
MAKE CALLS ONLY WITH THE SECURE LINES WE GIVE YOU.
AND HERE'S THE REAL TREAT, A LAPTOP WITH BUILT-IN UNREGISTERED WIRELESS.
IT'LL SCRAMBLE THE CONNECTION NUMBER EACH TIME. THEY'LL BE ABLE TO BACKTRACK IT...
...BUT BY THEN YOU SHOULD BE LONG GONE.
HERE, LET ME SHOW YOU WHAT I'VE SET UP.
I POSTED WHAT YOU SENT ME.

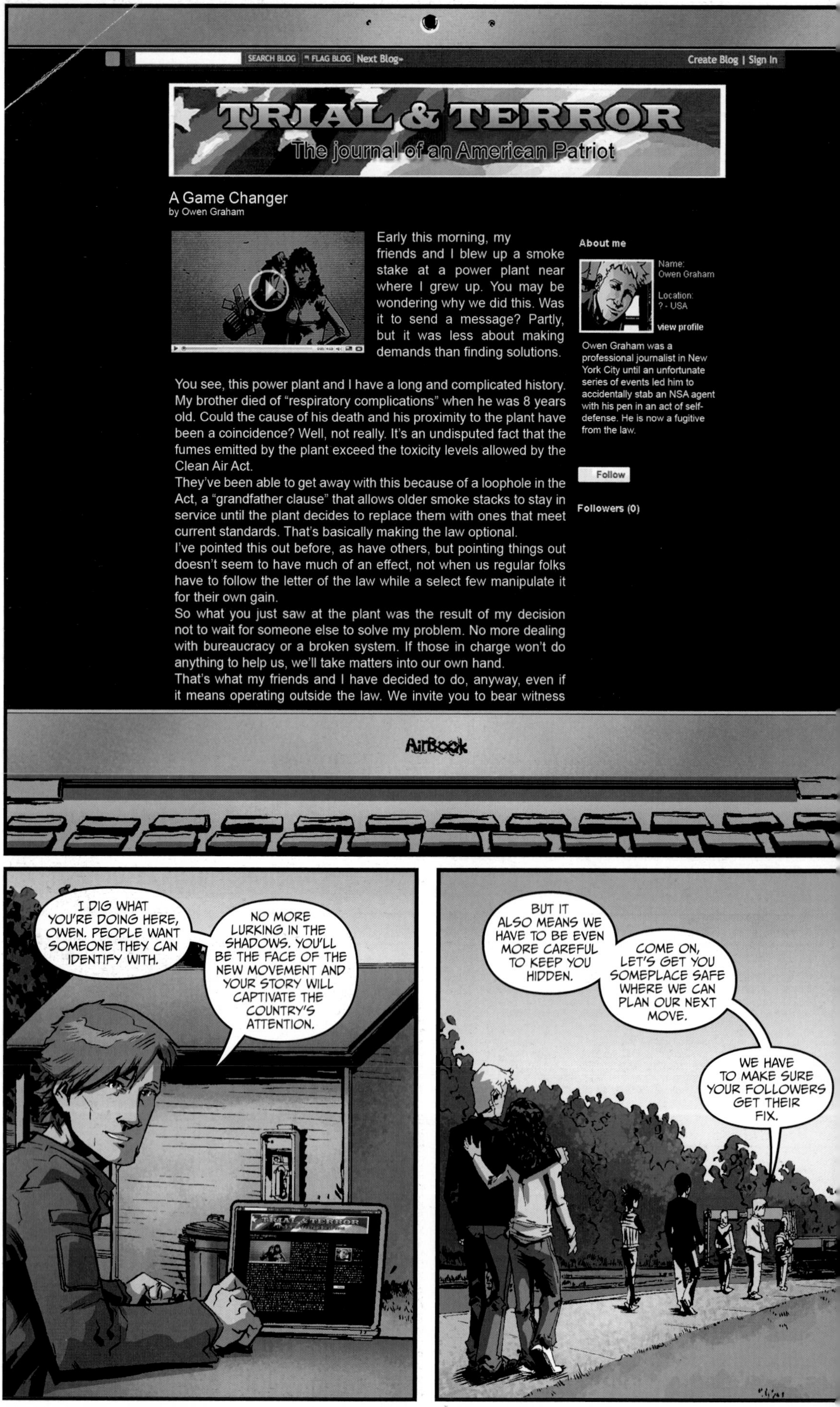
SEARCH BLOG
FLAG BLOG
Next Blog»
Create Blog | Sign In
TRIAL & TERROR
The journal of an American Patriot
A Game Changer
by Owen Graham
Early this morning, my friends and I blew up a smoke stake at a power plant near where I grew up. You may be wondering why we did this. Was it to send a message? Partly, but it was less about making demands than finding solutions.
You see, this power plant and I have a long and complicated history. My brother died of "respiratory complications" when he was 8 years old. Could the cause of his death and his proximity to the plant have been a coincidence? Well, not really. It's an undisputed fact that the fumes emitted by the plant exceed the toxicity levels allowed by the Clean Air Act.
They've been able to get away with this because of a loophole in the Act, a "grandfather clause" that allows older smoke stacks to stay in service until the plant decides to replace them with ones that meet current standards. That's basically making the law optional.
I've pointed this out before, as have others, but pointing things out doesn't seem to have much of an effect, not when us regular folks have to follow the letter of the law while a select few manipulate it for their own gain.
So what you just saw at the plant was the result of my decision not to wait for someone else to solve my problem. No more dealing with bureaucracy or a broken system. If those in charge won't do anything to help us, we'll take matters into our own hand.
That's what my friends and I have decided to do, anyway, even if it means operating outside the law. We invite you to bear witness
About me
Name:
Owen Graham
Location:
? - USA
view profile
Owen Graham was a professional journalist in New York City until an unfortunate series of events led him to accidentally stab an NSA agent with his pen in an act of self-defense. He is now a fugitive from the law.
Follow
Followers (0)
AirBook
I DIG WHAT YOU'RE DOING HERE, OWEN. PEOPLE WANT SOMEONE THEY CAN IDENTIFY WITH.
NO MORE LURKING IN THE SHADOWS. YOU'LL BE THE FACE OF THE NEW MOVEMENT AND YOUR STORY WILL CAPTIVATE THE COUNTRY'S ATTENTION.
BUT IT ALSO MEANS WE HAVE TO BE EVEN MORE CAREFUL TO KEEP YOU HIDDEN.
COME ON, LET'S GET YOU SOMEPLACE SAFE WHERE WE CAN PLAN OUR NEXT MOVE.
WE HAVE TO MAKE SURE YOUR FOLLOWERS GET THEIR FIX.

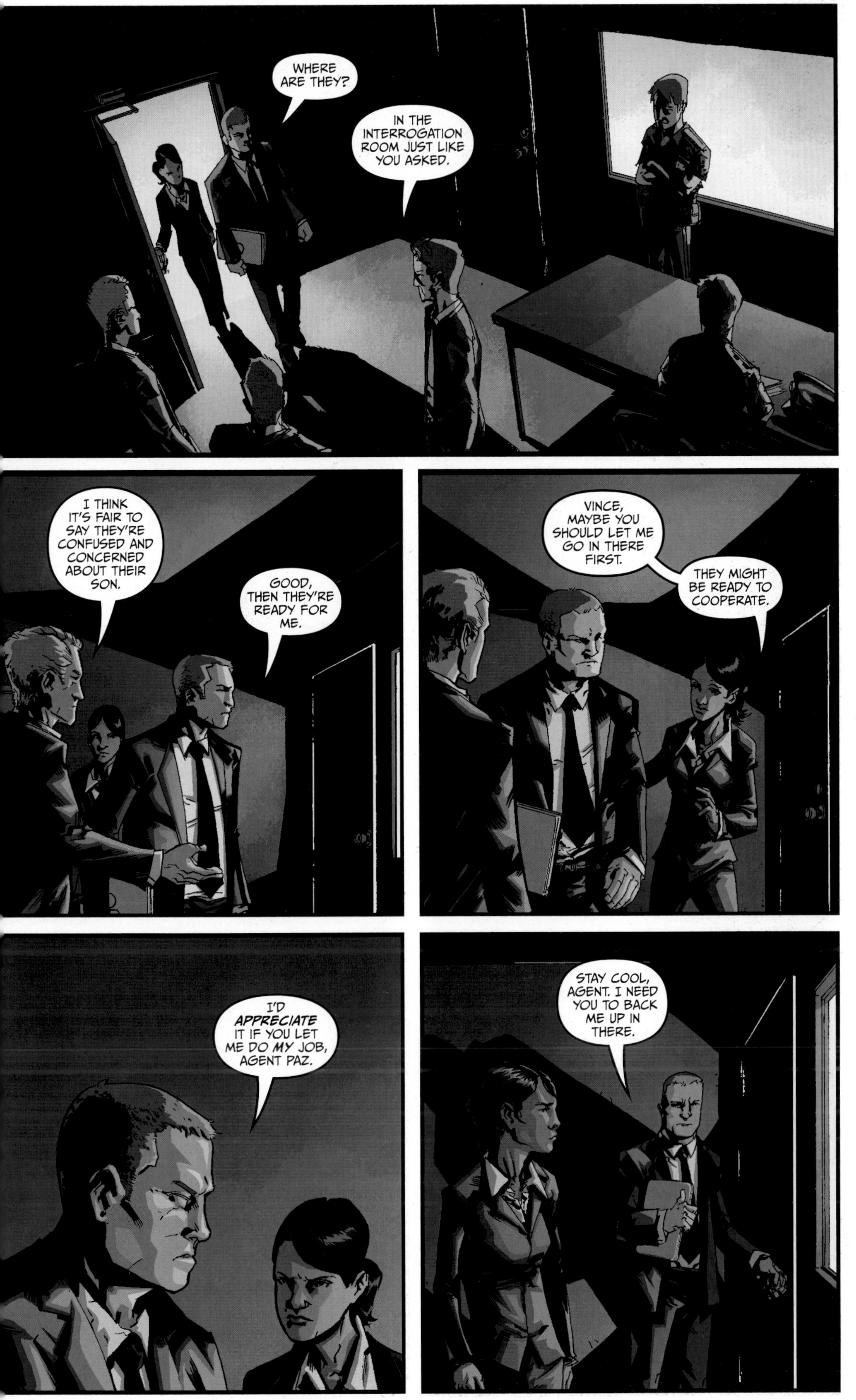
WHERE ARE THEY?
IN THE INTERROGATION ROOM JUST LIKE YOU ASKED.
I THINK IT'S FAIR TO SAY THEY'RE CONFUSED AND CONCERNED ABOUT THEIR SON.
GOOD, THEN THEY'RE READY FOR ME.
VINCE, MAYBE YOU SHOULD LET ME GO IN THERE FIRST.
THEY MIGHT BE READY TO COOPERATE.
I'D *APPRECIATE* IT IF YOU LET ME DO *MY* JOB, AGENT PAZ.
STAY COOL, AGENT. I NEED YOU TO BACK ME UP IN THERE.

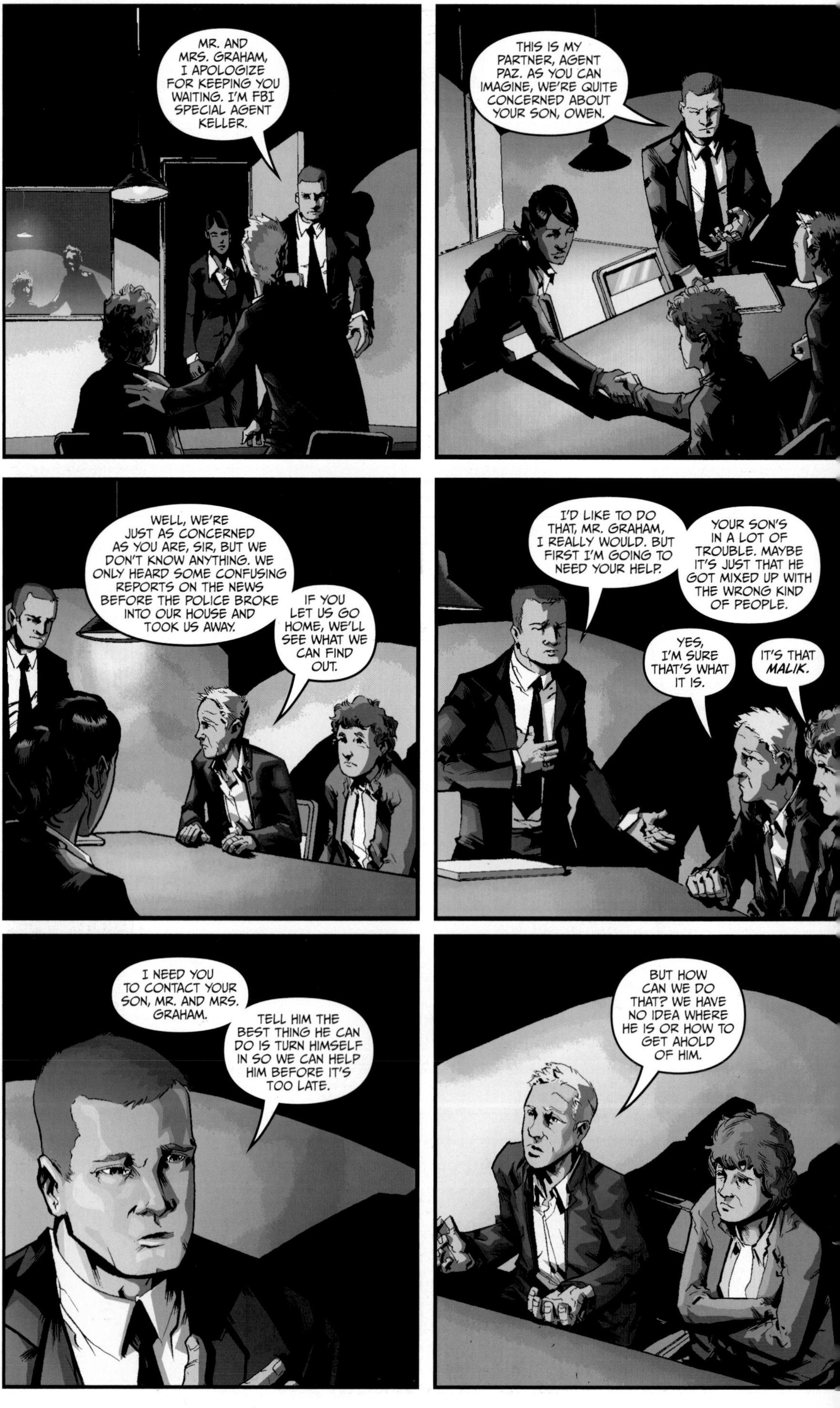
MR. AND MRS. GRAHAM, I APOLOGIZE FOR KEEPING YOU WAITING. I'M FBI SPECIAL AGENT KELLER.
THIS IS MY PARTNER, AGENT PAZ. AS YOU CAN IMAGINE, WE'RE QUITE CONCERNED ABOUT YOUR SON, OWEN.
WELL, WE'RE JUST AS CONCERNED AS YOU ARE, SIR, BUT WE DON'T KNOW ANYTHING. WE ONLY HEARD SOME CONFUSING REPORTS ON THE NEWS BEFORE THE POLICE BROKE INTO OUR HOUSE AND TOOK US AWAY.
IF YOU LET US GO HOME, WE'LL SEE WHAT WE CAN FIND OUT.
I'D LIKE TO DO THAT, MR. GRAHAM, I REALLY WOULD. BUT FIRST I'M GOING TO NEED YOUR HELP.
YOUR SON'S IN A LOT OF TROUBLE. MAYBE IT'S JUST THAT HE GOT MIXED UP WITH THE WRONG KIND OF PEOPLE.
YES, I'M SURE THAT'S WHAT IT IS.
IT'S THAT *MALIK.*
I NEED YOU TO CONTACT YOUR SON, MR. AND MRS. GRAHAM.
TELL HIM THE BEST THING HE CAN DO IS TURN HIMSELF IN SO WE CAN HELP HIM BEFORE IT'S TOO LATE.
BUT HOW CAN WE DO THAT? WE HAVE NO IDEA WHERE HE IS OR HOW TO GET AHOLD OF HIM.

WELL, YOU SEE YOUR SON SET UP A BLOG.

IT'S THIS PAGE ON THE INTERNET WHERE HE PUT UP INFORMATION ON HOW HE HELPED DESTROY A POWER PLANT.

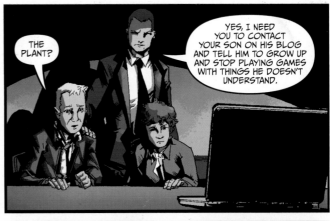

THE PLANT?

YES, I NEED YOU TO CONTACT YOUR SON ON HIS BLOG AND TELL HIM TO GROW UP AND STOP PLAYING GAMES WITH THINGS HE DOESN'T UNDERSTAND.

I...I JUST DON'T KNOW.

WHAT IS IT, STEVEN?

AGENT KELLER, I DON'T KNOW A LOT ABOUT WHAT'S BEEN GOING ON, MOSTLY BECAUSE YOU'VE KEPT US LOCKED UP IN HERE.

BUT I DO KNOW THAT MY SON IS A DECENT MAN AND HE WOULD NEVER DO SOMETHING LIKE THIS WITHOUT GOOD REASON.

WE WON'T HELP YOU GET TO OUR BOY, AGENT KELLER. IF YOU WANT TO CATCH HIM, YOU'RE GOING TO HAVE TO DO IT YOURSELF.

LISTEN TO ME WHEN I TELL YOU THIS.

I'VE HUNTED DOWN EXTREMISTS WHO HAVE NOTHING LEFT BUT THEIR GOD AND THEIR HOLY WAR. THESE ARE PEOPLE WHO'VE LIVED THEIR WHOLE LIVES WITHOUT THE SIMPLE COMFORTS WE TAKE FOR GRANTED EVERY DAY.

THEY HAVE NO PROBLEM SLEEPING IN DITCHES OR GOING DAYS WITHOUT FOOD, AND STILL I'VE FOUND THEM. AND BELIEVE ME, WHEN I DID, IT *WASN'T* VERY PRETTY.

SO YOU TELL ME, MR. AND MRS. GRAHAM, JUST HOW LONG YOU THINK YOUR SPOILED LITTLE SUBURBAN BOY IS GOING TO MAKE IT OUT THERE?

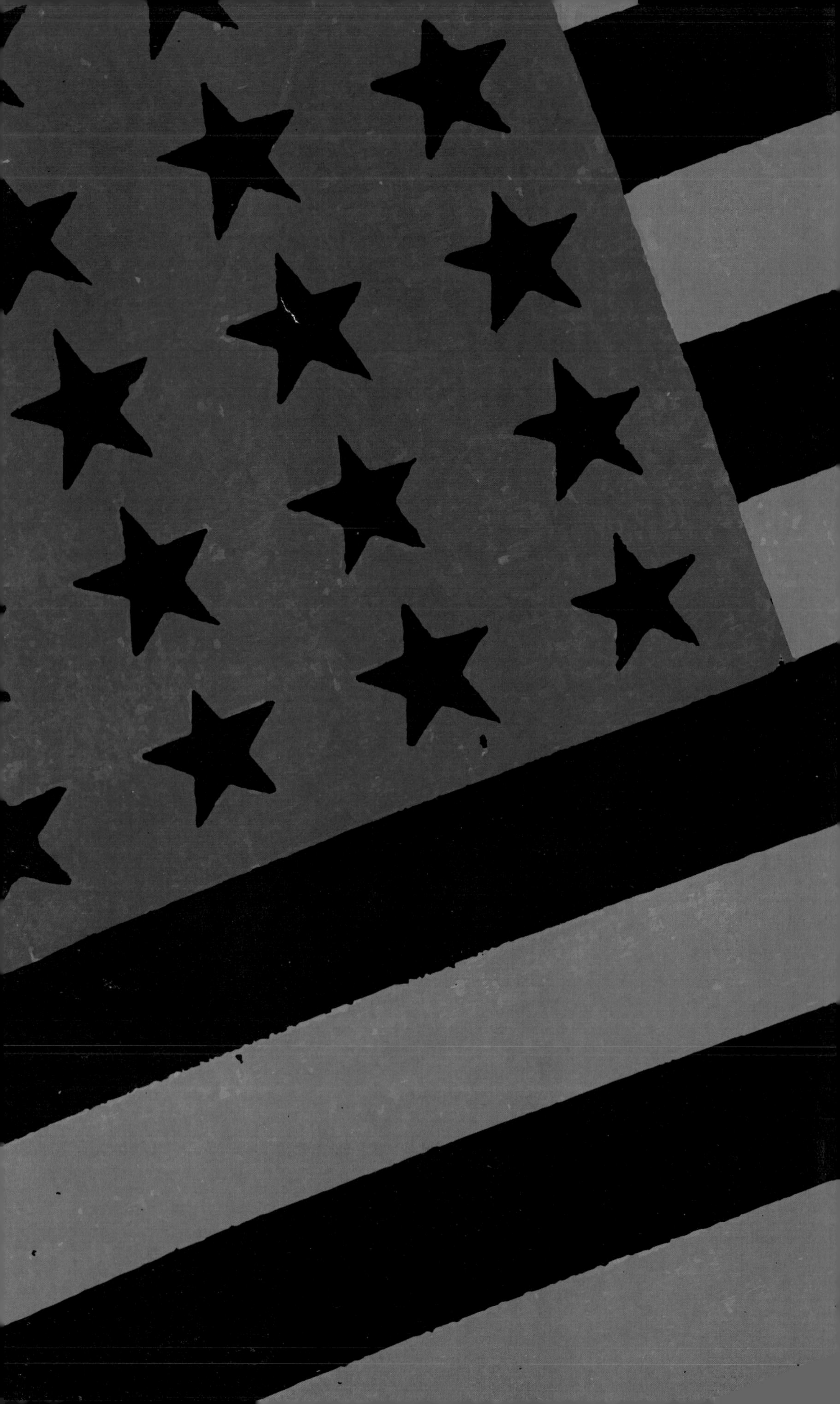

Chapter 3

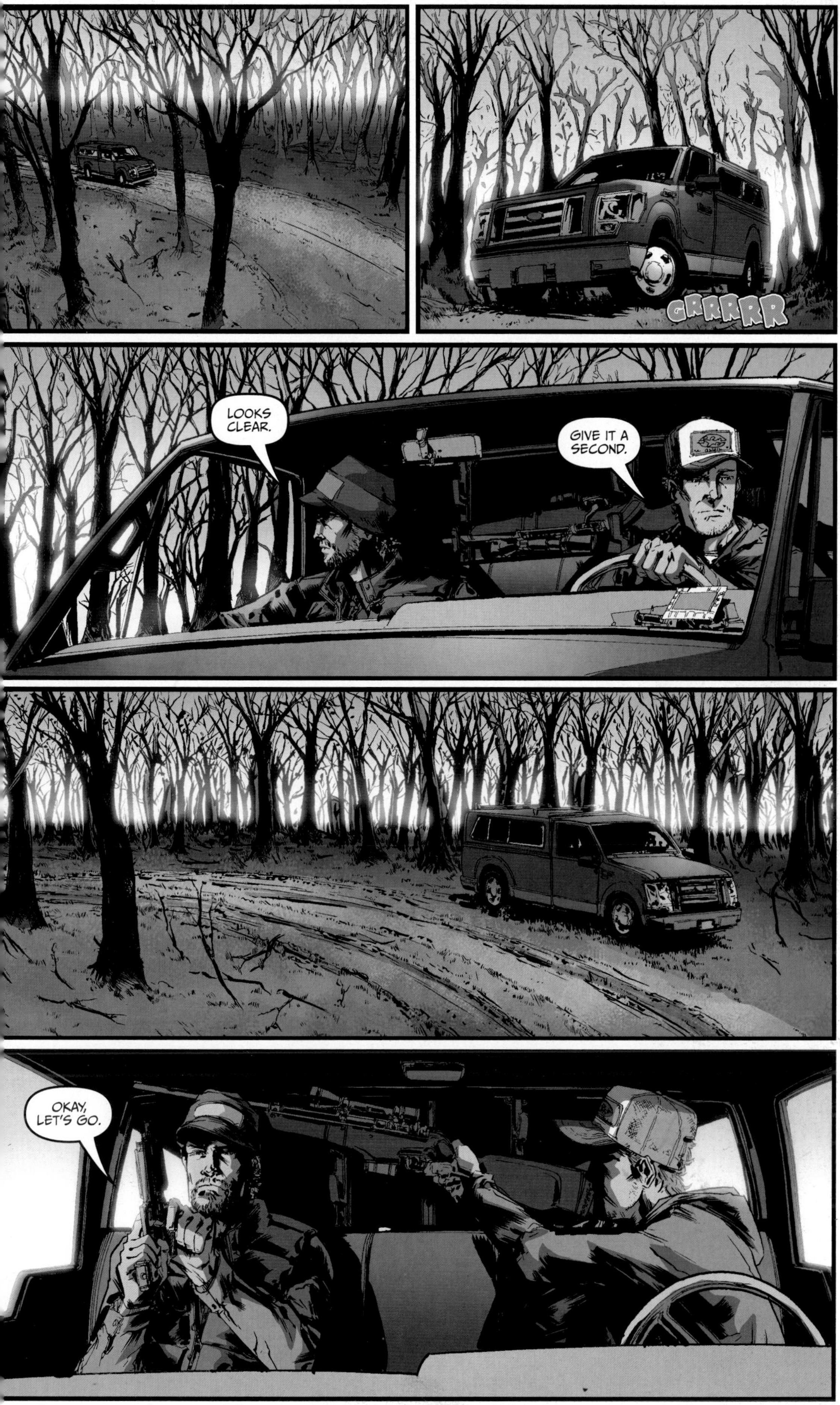
GRRRRR
LOOKS CLEAR.
GIVE IT A SECOND.
OKAY, LET'S GO.

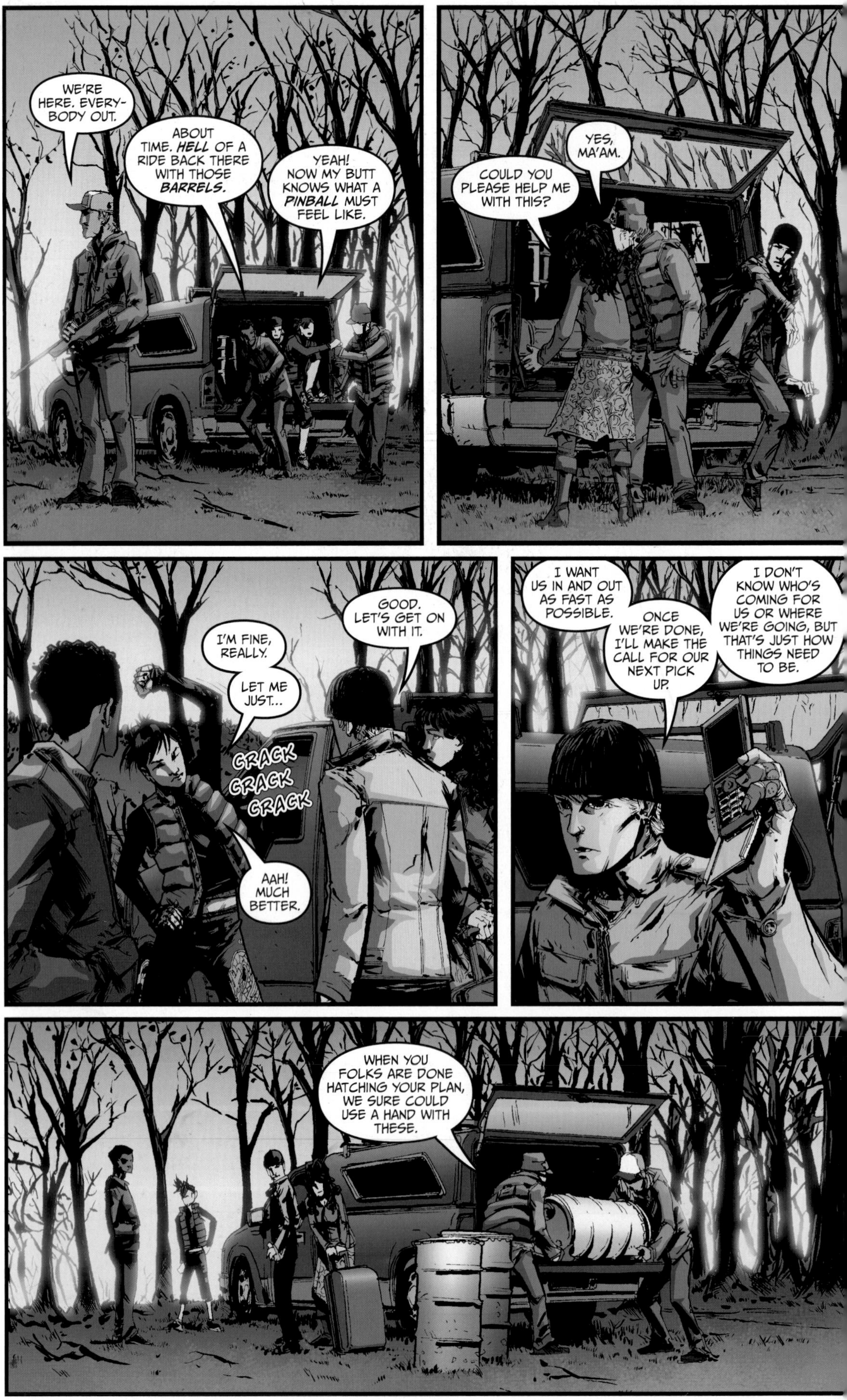

WE'RE HERE. EVERY-BODY OUT.
ABOUT TIME. **HELL** OF A RIDE BACK THERE WITH THOSE **BARRELS.**
YEAH! NOW MY BUTT KNOWS WHAT A **PINBALL** MUST FEEL LIKE.
COULD YOU PLEASE HELP ME WITH THIS?
YES, MA'AM.
I'M FINE, REALLY.
LET ME JUST...
CRACK CRACK CRACK
AAH! MUCH BETTER.
GOOD. LET'S GET ON WITH IT.
I WANT US IN AND OUT AS FAST AS POSSIBLE.
ONCE WE'RE DONE, I'LL MAKE THE CALL FOR OUR NEXT PICK UP.
I DON'T KNOW WHO'S COMING FOR US OR WHERE WE'RE GOING, BUT THAT'S JUST HOW THINGS NEED TO BE.
WHEN YOU FOLKS ARE DONE HATCHING YOUR PLAN, WE SURE COULD USE A HAND WITH THESE.

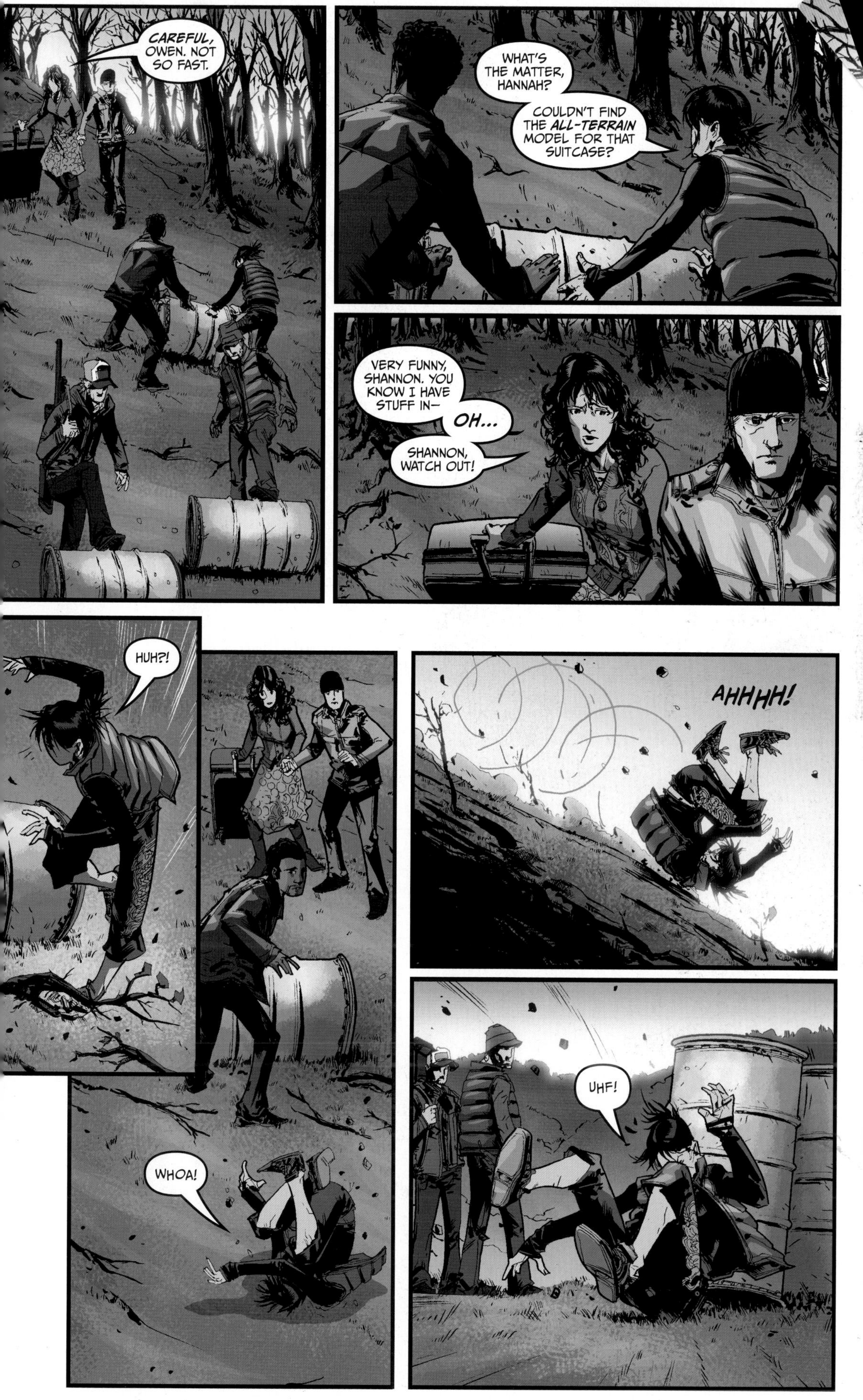
CAREFUL, OWEN. NOT SO FAST.
WHAT'S THE MATTER, HANNAH?
COULDN'T FIND THE ALL-TERRAIN MODEL FOR THAT SUITCASE?
VERY FUNNY, SHANNON. YOU KNOW I HAVE STUFF IN—
OH...
SHANNON, WATCH OUT!
HUH?!
WHOA!
AHHHH!
UHF!

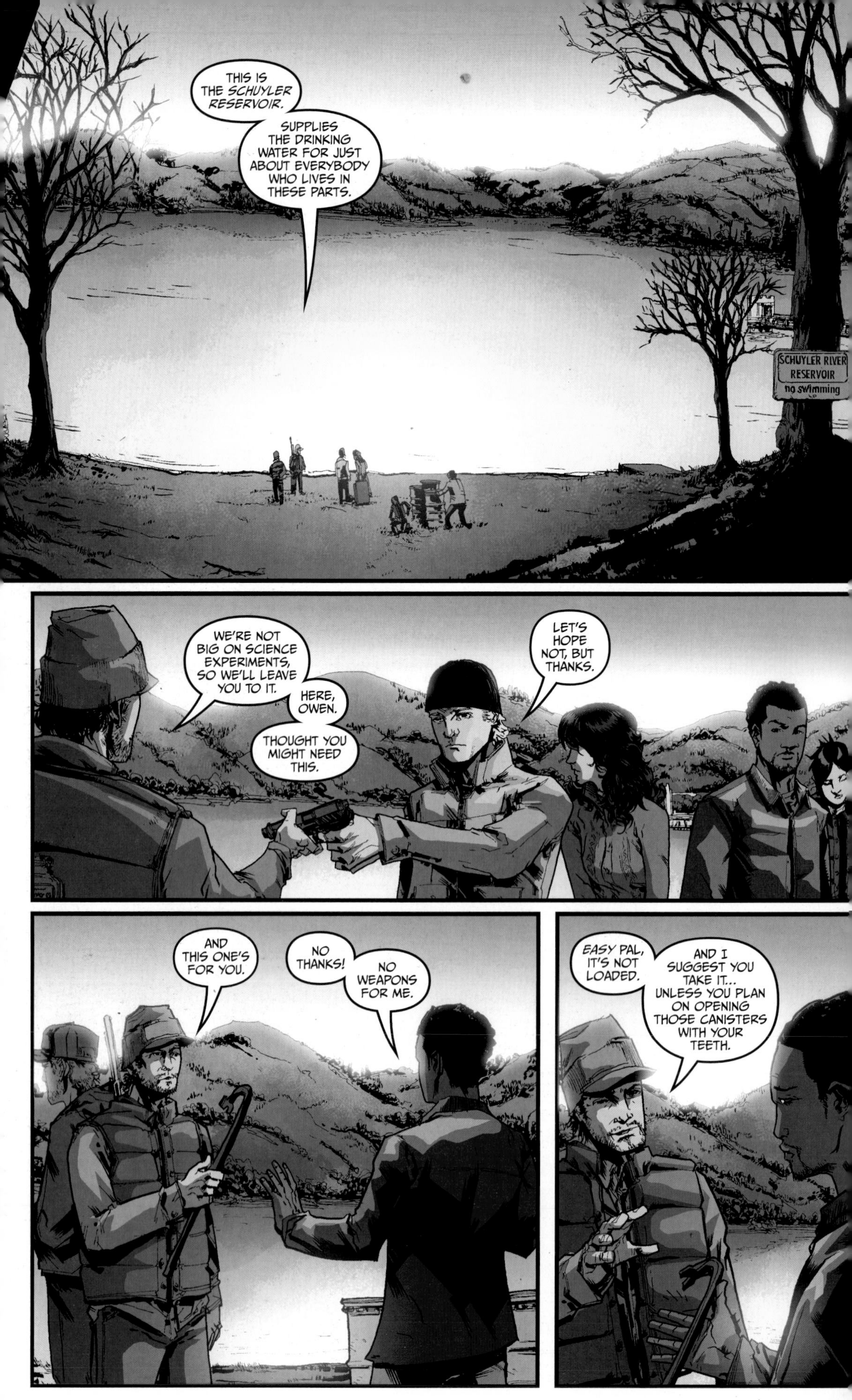
THIS IS THE SCHUYLER RESERVOIR.
SUPPLIES THE DRINKING WATER FOR JUST ABOUT EVERYBODY WHO LIVES IN THESE PARTS.
SCHUYLER RIVER RESERVOIR no swimming
WE'RE NOT BIG ON SCIENCE EXPERIMENTS, SO WE'LL LEAVE YOU TO IT.
HERE, OWEN.
THOUGHT YOU MIGHT NEED THIS.
LET'S HOPE NOT, BUT THANKS.
AND THIS ONE'S FOR YOU.
NO THANKS!
NO WEAPONS FOR ME.
EASY PAL, IT'S NOT LOADED.
AND I SUGGEST YOU TAKE IT... UNLESS YOU PLAN ON OPENING THOSE CANISTERS WITH YOUR TEETH.

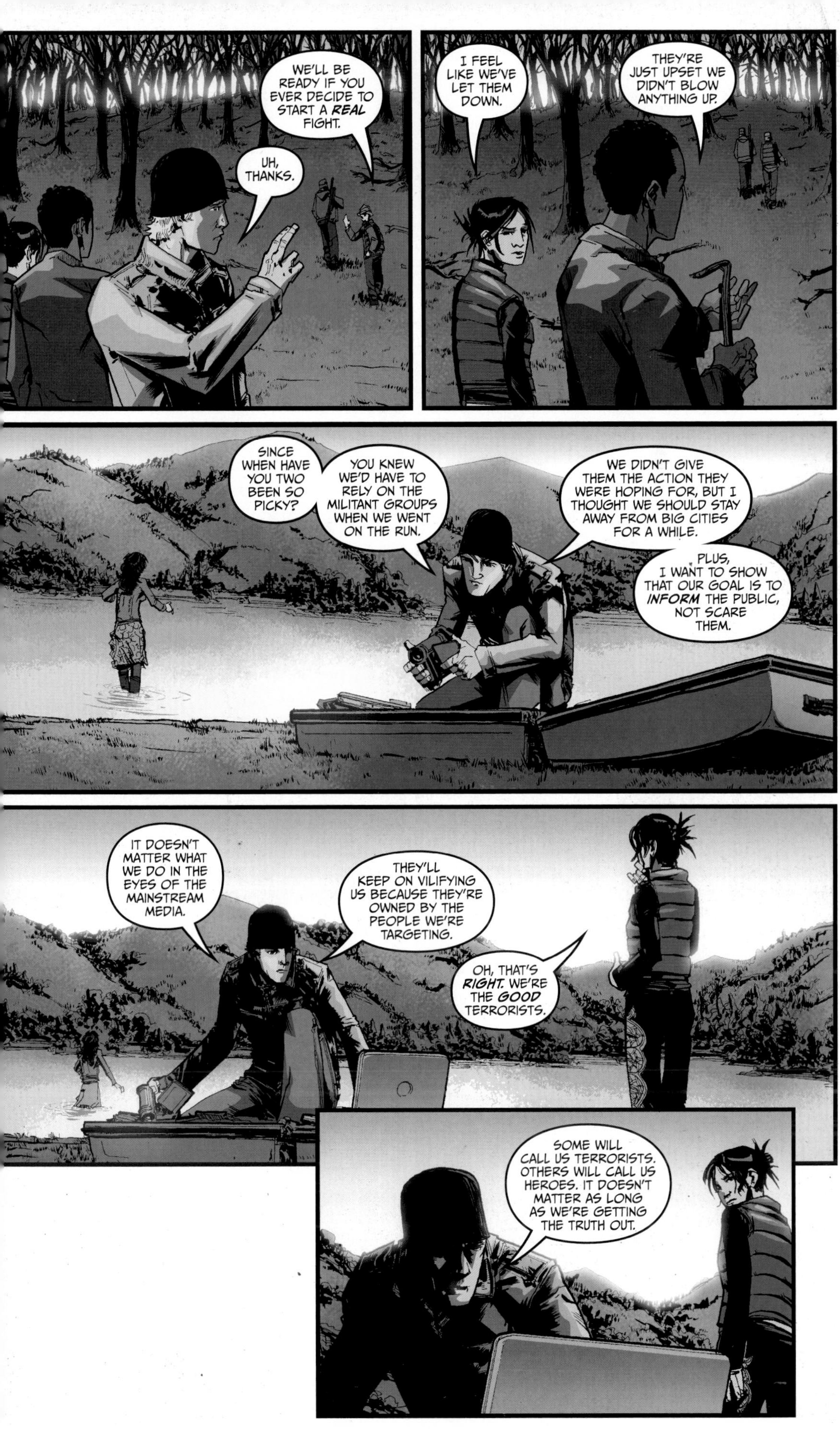
WE'LL BE READY IF YOU EVER DECIDE TO START A *REAL* FIGHT.
UH, THANKS.
I FEEL LIKE WE'VE LET THEM DOWN.
THEY'RE JUST UPSET WE DIDN'T BLOW ANYTHING UP.
SINCE WHEN HAVE YOU TWO BEEN SO PICKY?
YOU KNEW WE'D HAVE TO RELY ON THE MILITANT GROUPS WHEN WE WENT ON THE RUN.
WE DIDN'T GIVE THEM THE ACTION THEY WERE HOPING FOR, BUT I THOUGHT WE SHOULD STAY AWAY FROM BIG CITIES FOR A WHILE.
PLUS, I WANT TO SHOW THAT OUR GOAL IS TO *INFORM* THE PUBLIC, NOT SCARE THEM.
IT DOESN'T MATTER WHAT WE DO IN THE EYES OF THE MAINSTREAM MEDIA.
THEY'LL KEEP ON VILIFYING US BECAUSE THEY'RE OWNED BY THE PEOPLE WE'RE TARGETING.
OH, THAT'S *RIGHT.* WE'RE THE *GOOD* TERRORISTS.
SOME WILL CALL US TERRORISTS. OTHERS WILL CALL US HEROES. IT DOESN'T MATTER AS LONG AS WE'RE GETTING THE TRUTH OUT.

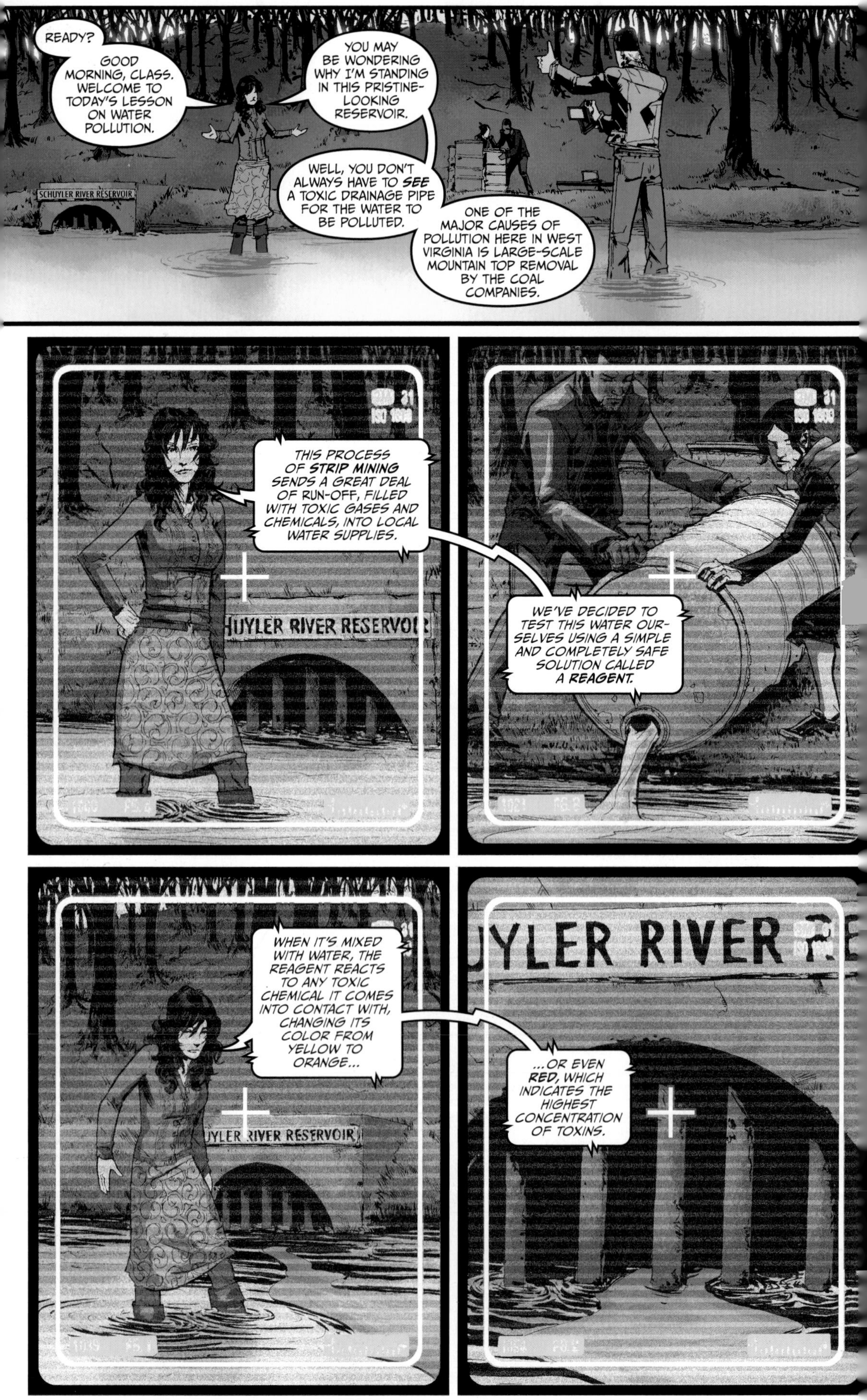

READY?
GOOD MORNING, CLASS. WELCOME TO TODAY'S LESSON ON WATER POLLUTION.
YOU MAY BE WONDERING WHY I'M STANDING IN THIS PRISTINE-LOOKING RESERVOIR.
SCHUYLER RIVER RESERVOIR
WELL, YOU DON'T ALWAYS HAVE TO SEE A TOXIC DRAINAGE PIPE FOR THE WATER TO BE POLLUTED.
ONE OF THE MAJOR CAUSES OF POLLUTION HERE IN WEST VIRGINIA IS LARGE-SCALE MOUNTAIN TOP REMOVAL BY THE COAL COMPANIES.
THIS PROCESS OF STRIP MINING SENDS A GREAT DEAL OF RUN-OFF, FILLED WITH TOXIC GASES AND CHEMICALS, INTO LOCAL WATER SUPPLIES.
HUYLER RIVER RESERVOI
WE'VE DECIDED TO TEST THIS WATER OURSELVES USING A SIMPLE AND COMPLETELY SAFE SOLUTION CALLED A REAGENT.
WHEN IT'S MIXED WITH WATER, THE REAGENT REACTS TO ANY TOXIC CHEMICAL IT COMES INTO CONTACT WITH, CHANGING ITS COLOR FROM YELLOW TO ORANGE...
UYLER RIVER RESERVOIR
UYLER RIVER
...OR EVEN RED, WHICH INDICATES THE HIGHEST CONCENTRATION OF TOXINS.

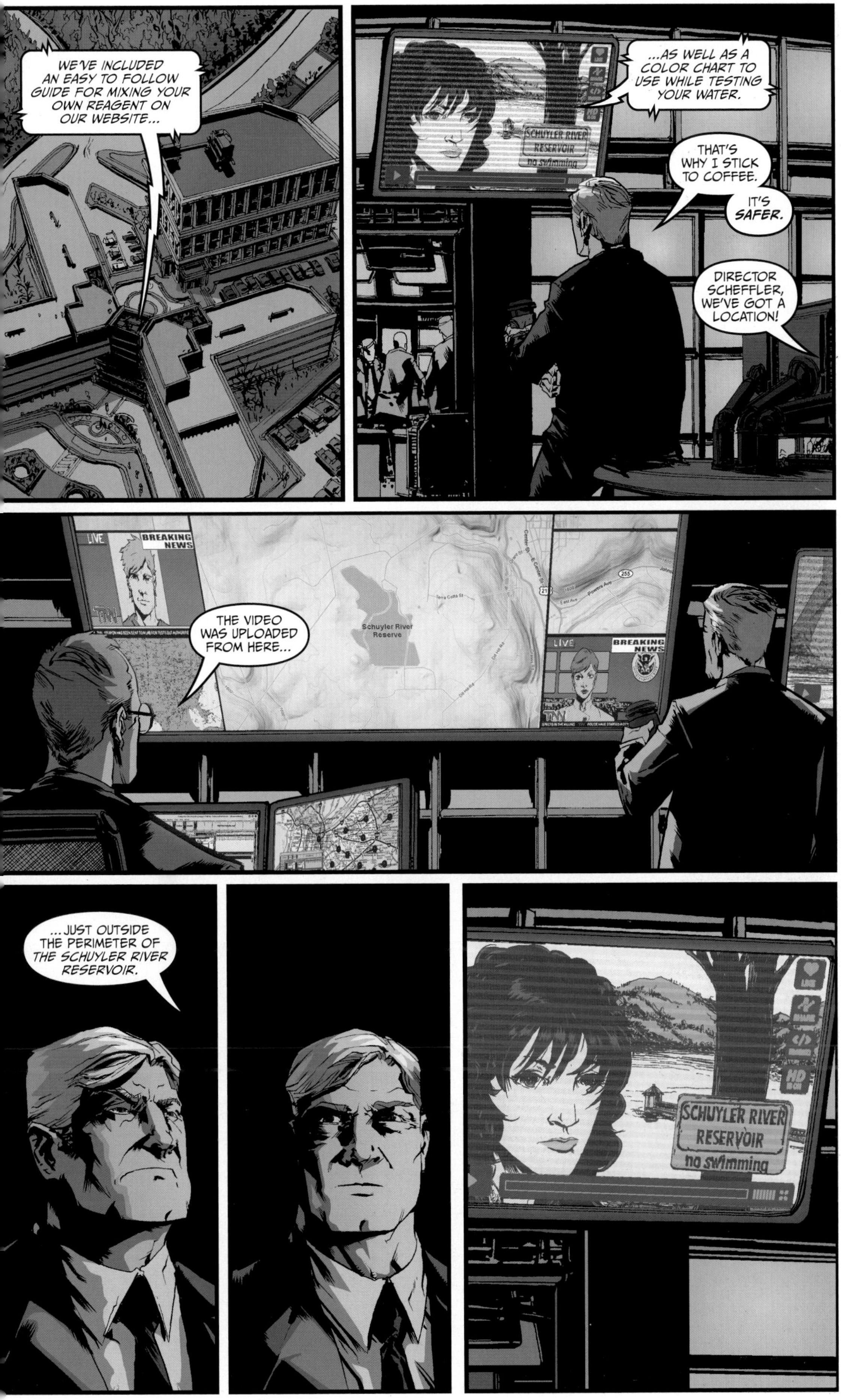
WE'VE INCLUDED AN EASY TO FOLLOW GUIDE FOR MIXING YOUR OWN REAGENT ON OUR WEBSITE...
SCHUYLER RIVER RESERVOIR no swimming
...AS WELL AS A COLOR CHART TO USE WHILE TESTING YOUR WATER.
THAT'S WHY I STICK TO COFFEE.
IT'S SAFER.
DIRECTOR SCHEFFLER, WE'VE GOT A LOCATION!
LIVE
BREAKING NEWS
Schuyler River Reserve
THE VIDEO WAS UPLOADED FROM HERE...
...JUST OUTSIDE THE PERIMETER OF THE SCHUYLER RIVER RESERVOIR.
SCHUYLER RIVER RESERVOIR no swimming

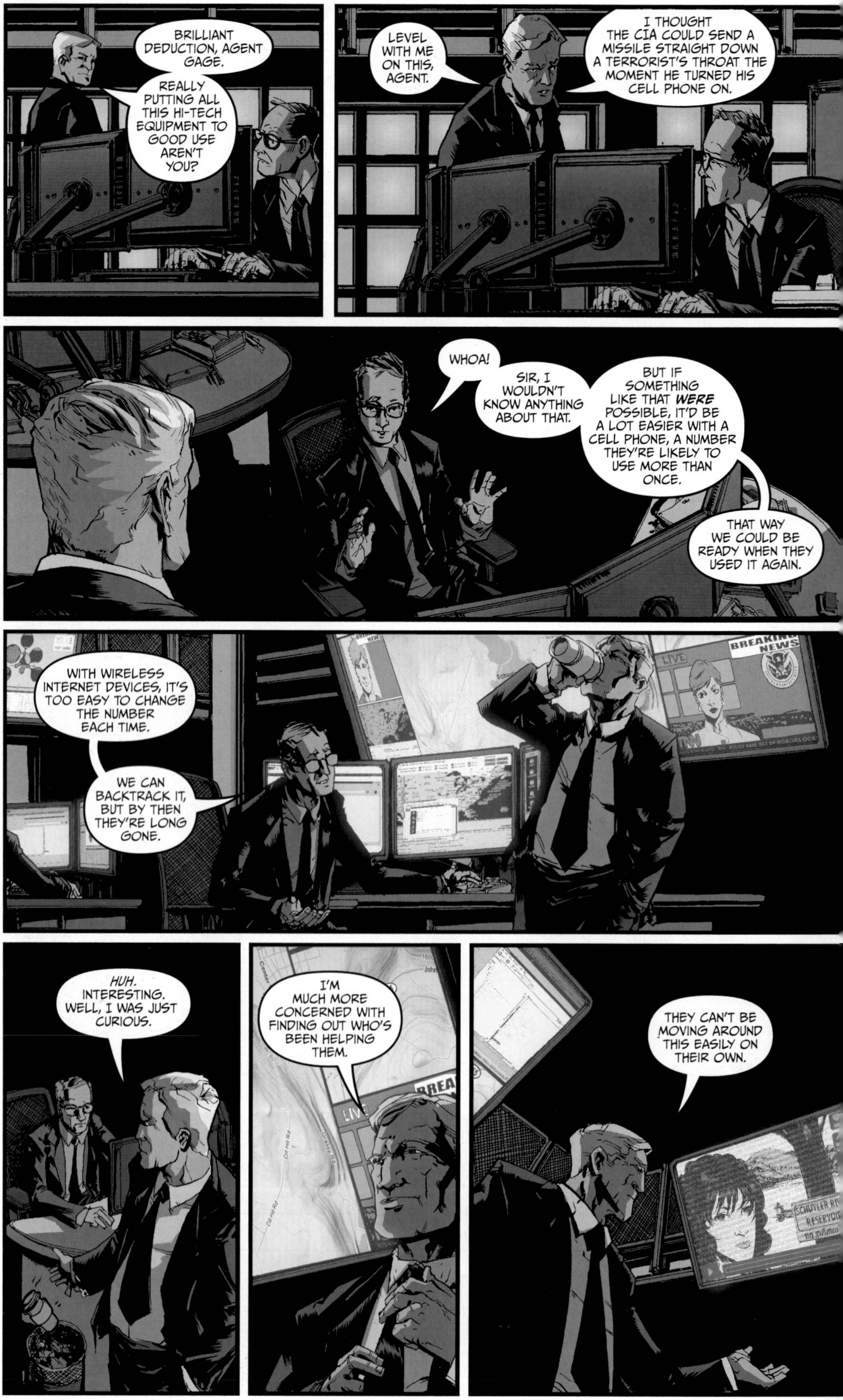
BRILLIANT DEDUCTION, AGENT GAGE.
REALLY PUTTING ALL THIS HI-TECH EQUIPMENT TO GOOD USE AREN'T YOU?
LEVEL WITH ME ON THIS, AGENT.
I THOUGHT THE CIA COULD SEND A MISSILE STRAIGHT DOWN A TERRORIST'S THROAT THE MOMENT HE TURNED HIS CELL PHONE ON.
WHOA!
SIR, I WOULDN'T KNOW ANYTHING ABOUT THAT.
BUT IF SOMETHING LIKE THAT *WERE* POSSIBLE, IT'D BE A LOT EASIER WITH A CELL PHONE, A NUMBER THEY'RE LIKELY TO USE MORE THAN ONCE.
THAT WAY WE COULD BE READY WHEN THEY USED IT AGAIN.
WITH WIRELESS INTERNET DEVICES, IT'S TOO EASY TO CHANGE THE NUMBER EACH TIME.
WE CAN BACKTRACK IT, BUT BY THEN THEY'RE LONG GONE.
BREAKING NEWS
LIVE
HUH. INTERESTING. WELL, I WAS JUST CURIOUS.
I'M MUCH MORE CONCERNED WITH FINDING OUT WHO'S BEEN HELPING THEM.
THEY CAN'T BE MOVING AROUND THIS EASILY ON THEIR OWN.

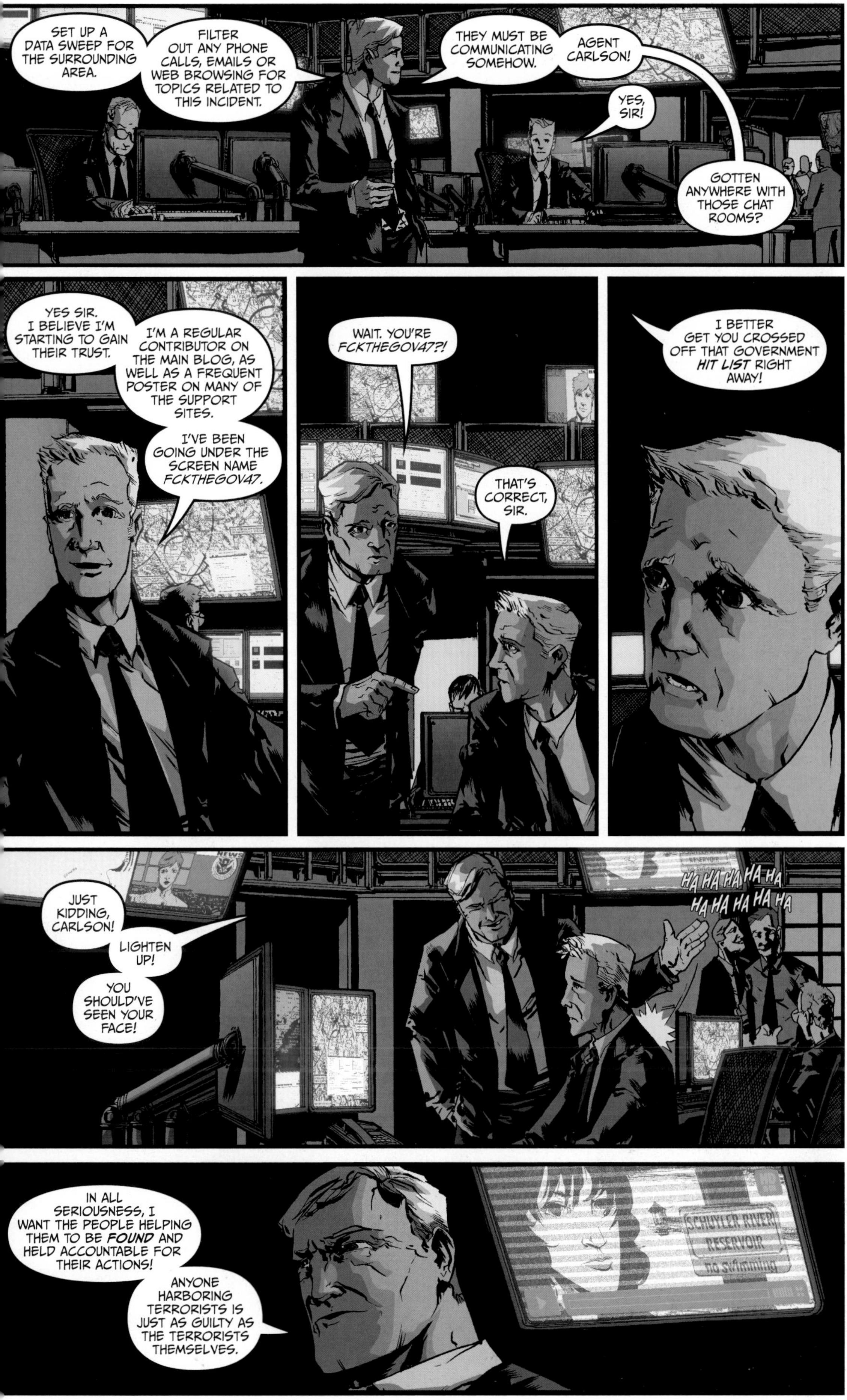
SET UP A DATA SWEEP FOR THE SURROUNDING AREA.
FILTER OUT ANY PHONE CALLS, EMAILS OR WEB BROWSING FOR TOPICS RELATED TO THIS INCIDENT.
THEY MUST BE COMMUNICATING SOMEHOW.
AGENT CARLSON!
YES, SIR!
GOTTEN ANYWHERE WITH THOSE CHAT ROOMS?
YES SIR. I BELIEVE I'M STARTING TO GAIN THEIR TRUST.
I'M A REGULAR CONTRIBUTOR ON THE MAIN BLOG, AS WELL AS A FREQUENT POSTER ON MANY OF THE SUPPORT SITES.
I'VE BEEN GOING UNDER THE SCREEN NAME *FCKTHEGOV47.*
WAIT. YOU'RE *FCKTHEGOV47?!*
THAT'S CORRECT, SIR.
I BETTER GET YOU CROSSED OFF THAT GOVERNMENT ***HIT LIST*** RIGHT AWAY!
JUST KIDDING, CARLSON!
LIGHTEN UP!
YOU SHOULD'VE SEEN YOUR FACE!
HA HA HA HA HA
HA HA HA HA HA
IN ALL SERIOUSNESS, I WANT THE PEOPLE HELPING THEM TO BE ***FOUND*** AND HELD ACCOUNTABLE FOR THEIR ACTIONS!
ANYONE HARBORING TERRORISTS IS JUST AS GUILTY AS THE TERRORISTS THEMSELVES.
SCHUYLER RIVER RESERVOIR
no swimming

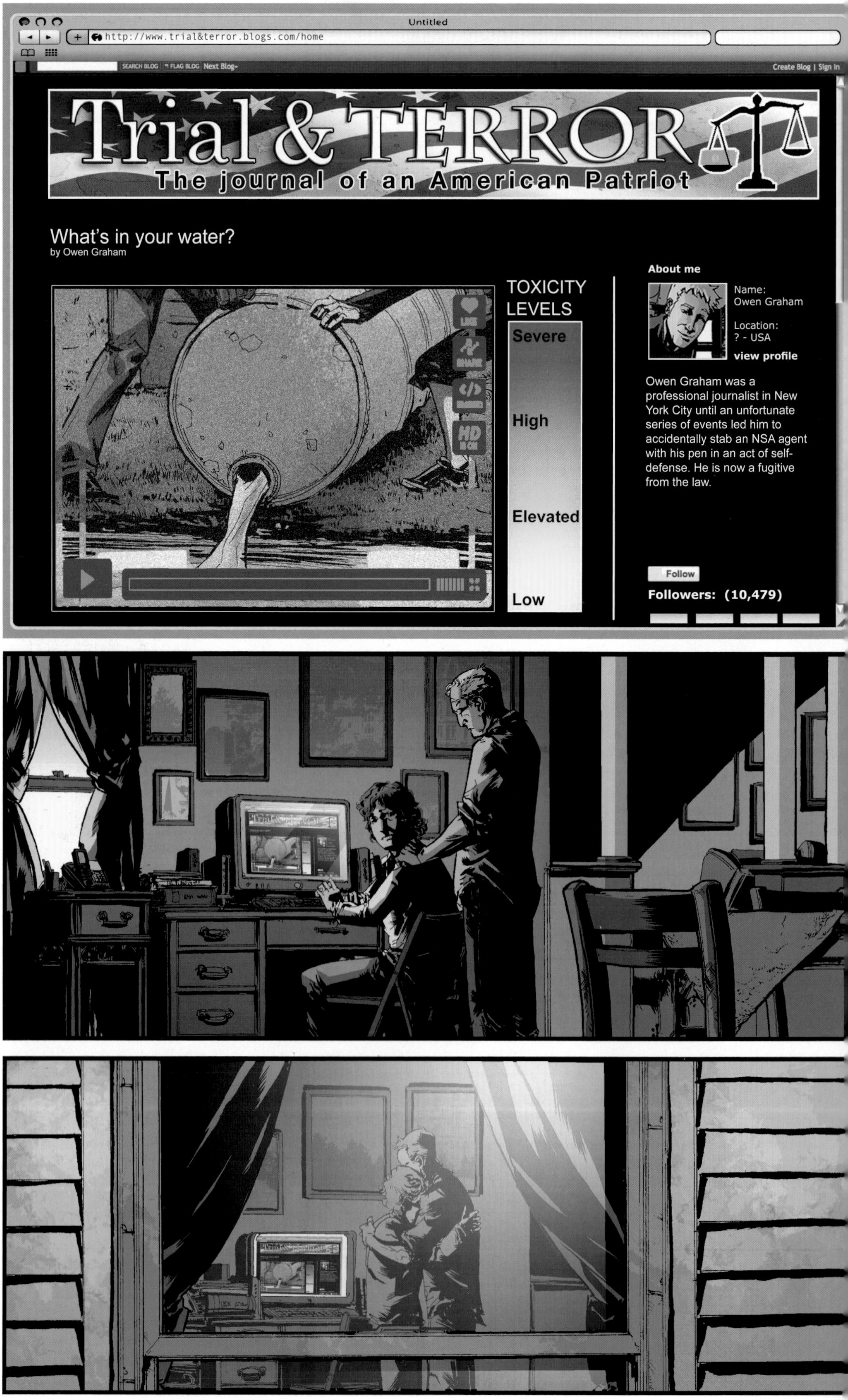
Untitled
http://www.trial&terror.blogs.com/home
SEARCH BLOG
FLAG BLOG
Next Blog
Create Blog | Sign In
Trial & TERROR
The journal of an American Patriot
What's in your water?
by Owen Graham
TOXICITY LEVELS
Severe
High
Elevated
Low
About me
Name:
Owen Graham
Location:
? - USA
view profile
Owen Graham was a professional journalist in New York City until an unfortunate series of events led him to accidentally stab an NSA agent with his pen in an act of self-defense. He is now a fugitive from the law.
Follow
Followers: (10,479)

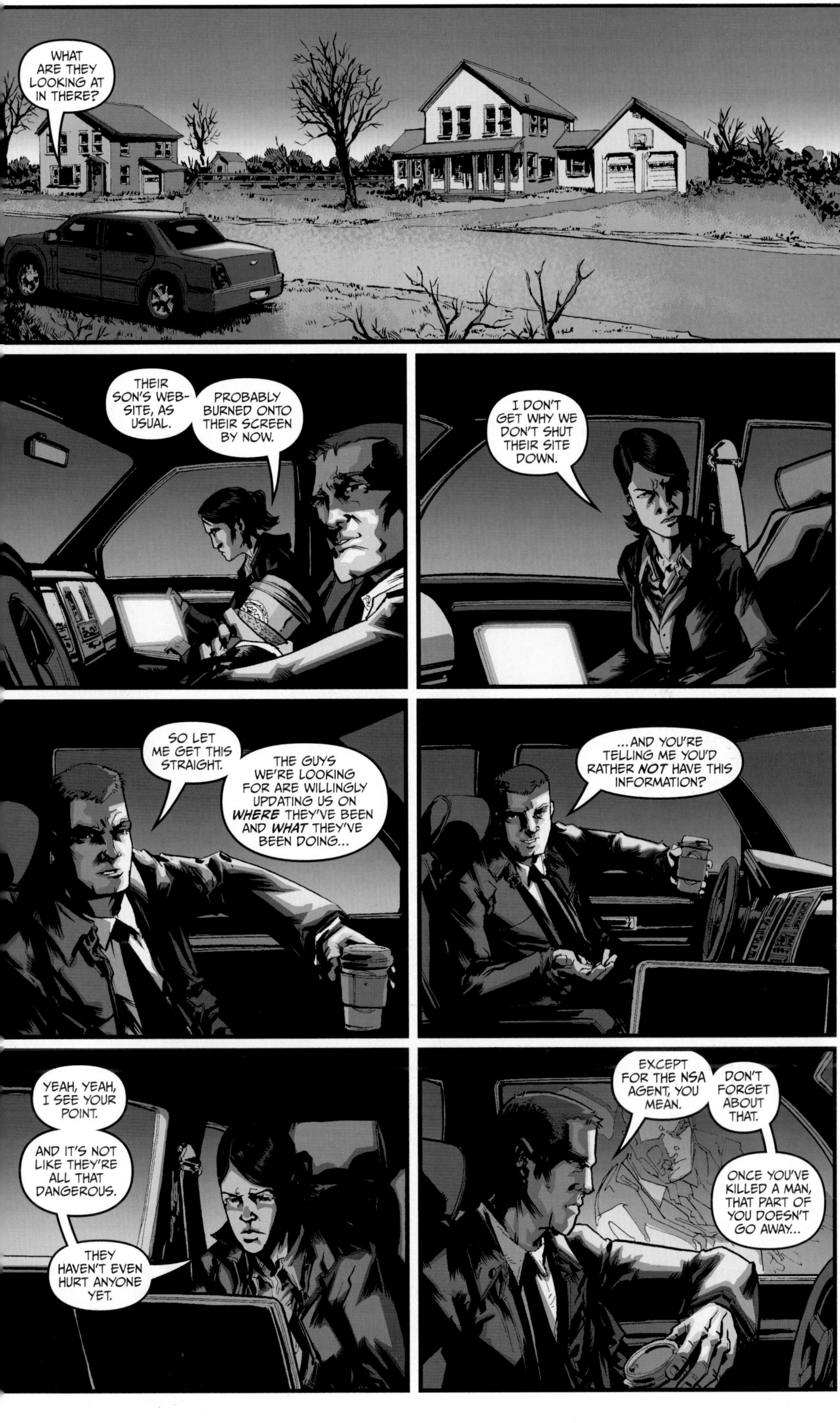
WHAT ARE THEY LOOKING AT IN THERE?
THEIR SON'S WEB-SITE, AS USUAL.
PROBABLY BURNED ONTO THEIR SCREEN BY NOW.
I DON'T GET WHY WE DON'T SHUT THEIR SITE DOWN.
SO LET ME GET THIS STRAIGHT.
THE GUYS WE'RE LOOKING FOR ARE WILLINGLY UPDATING US ON WHERE THEY'VE BEEN AND WHAT THEY'VE BEEN DOING...
...AND YOU'RE TELLING ME YOU'D RATHER NOT HAVE THIS INFORMATION?
YEAH, YEAH, I SEE YOUR POINT.
AND IT'S NOT LIKE THEY'RE ALL THAT DANGEROUS.
THEY HAVEN'T EVEN HURT ANYONE YET.
EXCEPT FOR THE NSA AGENT, YOU MEAN.
DON'T FORGET ABOUT THAT.
ONCE YOU'VE KILLED A MAN, THAT PART OF YOU DOESN'T GO AWAY...

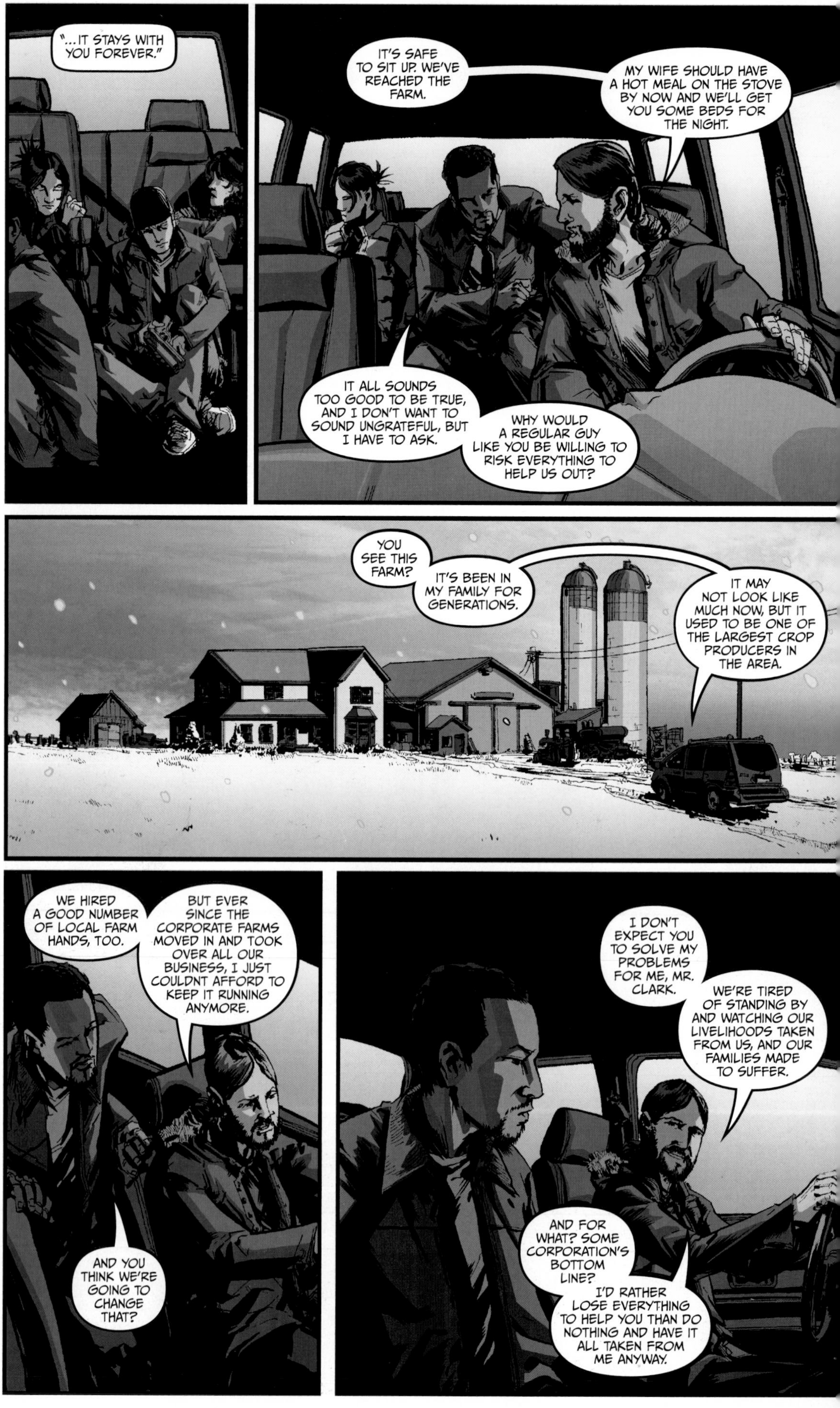
"...IT STAYS WITH YOU FOREVER."
IT'S SAFE TO SIT UP. WE'VE REACHED THE FARM.
MY WIFE SHOULD HAVE A HOT MEAL ON THE STOVE BY NOW AND WE'LL GET YOU SOME BEDS FOR THE NIGHT.
IT ALL SOUNDS TOO GOOD TO BE TRUE, AND I DON'T WANT TO SOUND UNGRATEFUL, BUT I HAVE TO ASK.
WHY WOULD A REGULAR GUY LIKE YOU BE WILLING TO RISK EVERYTHING TO HELP US OUT?
YOU SEE THIS FARM?
IT'S BEEN IN MY FAMILY FOR GENERATIONS.
IT MAY NOT LOOK LIKE MUCH NOW, BUT IT USED TO BE ONE OF THE LARGEST CROP PRODUCERS IN THE AREA.
WE HIRED A GOOD NUMBER OF LOCAL FARM HANDS, TOO.
BUT EVER SINCE THE CORPORATE FARMS MOVED IN AND TOOK OVER ALL OUR BUSINESS, I JUST COULDNT AFFORD TO KEEP IT RUNNING ANYMORE.
AND YOU THINK WE'RE GOING TO CHANGE THAT?
I DON'T EXPECT YOU TO SOLVE MY PROBLEMS FOR ME, MR. CLARK.
WE'RE TIRED OF STANDING BY AND WATCHING OUR LIVELIHOODS TAKEN FROM US, AND OUR FAMILIES MADE TO SUFFER.
AND FOR WHAT? SOME CORPORATION'S BOTTOM LINE?
I'D RATHER LOSE EVERYTHING TO HELP YOU THAN DO NOTHING AND HAVE IT ALL TAKEN FROM ME ANYWAY.

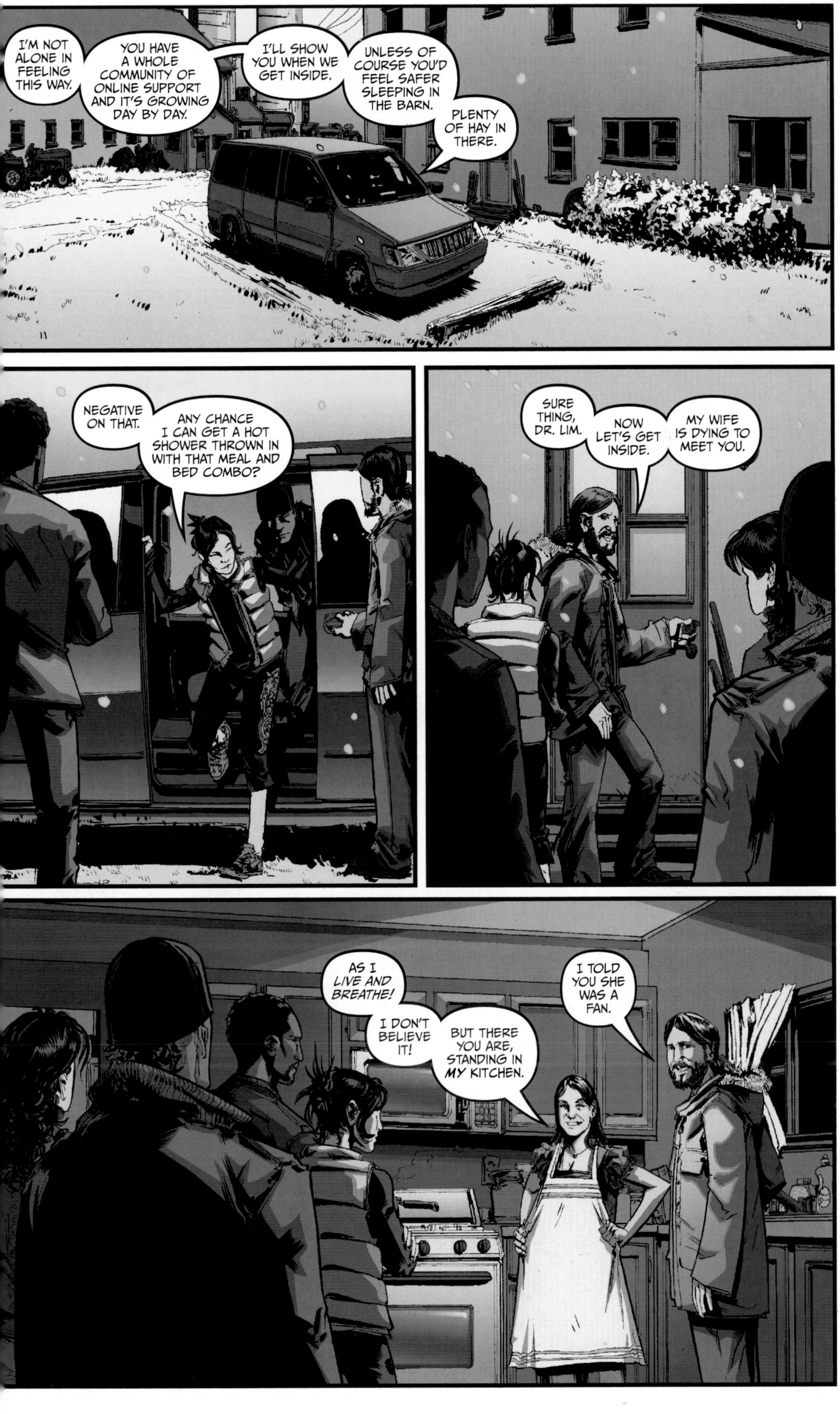

I'M NOT ALONE IN FEELING THIS WAY.
YOU HAVE A WHOLE COMMUNITY OF ONLINE SUPPORT AND IT'S GROWING DAY BY DAY.
I'LL SHOW YOU WHEN WE GET INSIDE.
UNLESS OF COURSE YOU'D FEEL SAFER SLEEPING IN THE BARN.
PLENTY OF HAY IN THERE.
NEGATIVE ON THAT.
ANY CHANCE I CAN GET A HOT SHOWER THROWN IN WITH THAT MEAL AND BED COMBO?
SURE THING, DR. LIM.
NOW LET'S GET INSIDE.
MY WIFE IS DYING TO MEET YOU.
AS I *LIVE AND BREATHE!*
I DON'T BELIEVE IT!
BUT THERE YOU ARE, STANDING IN **MY** KITCHEN.
I TOLD YOU SHE WAS A FAN.

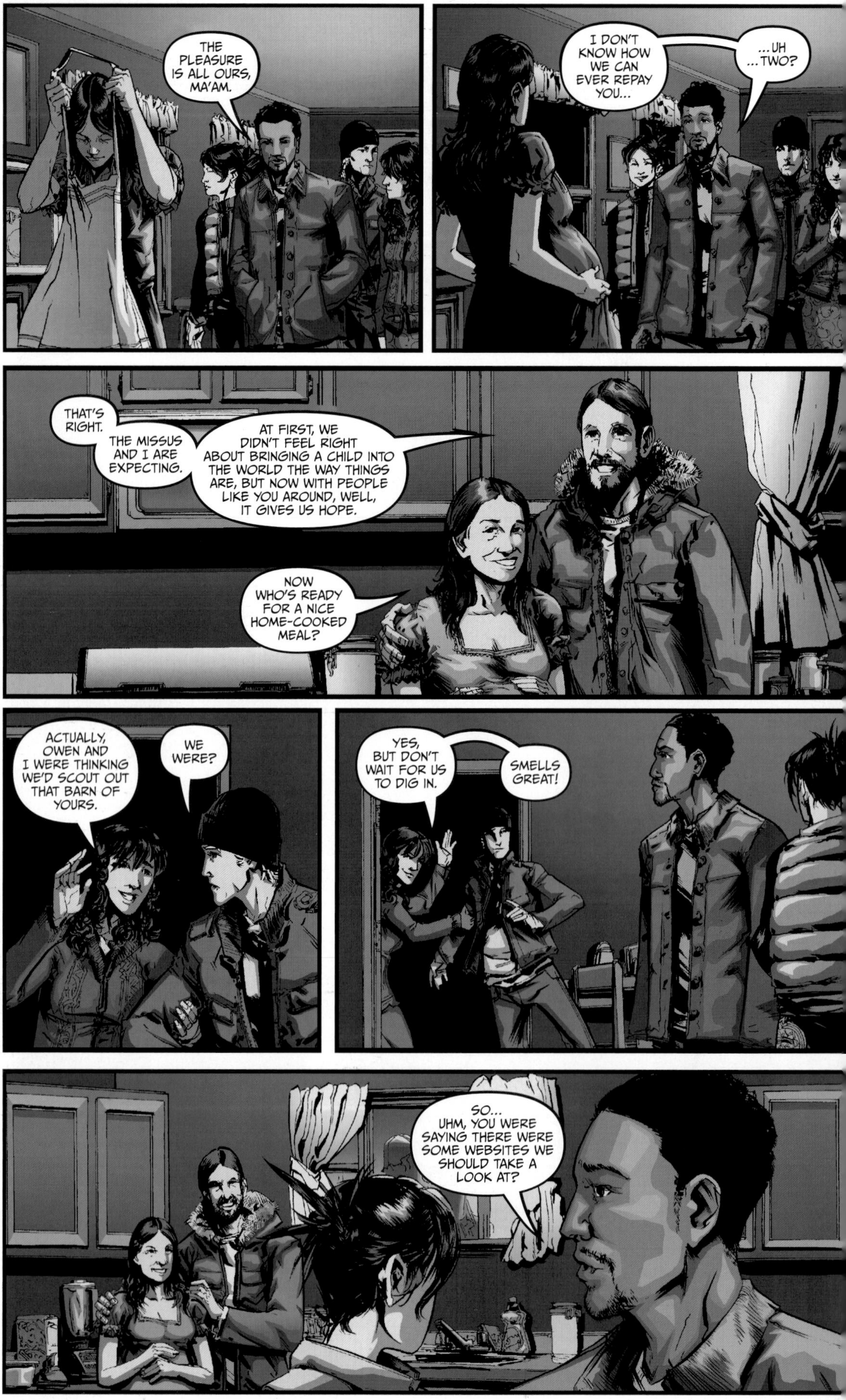
THE PLEASURE IS ALL OURS, MA'AM.
I DON'T KNOW HOW WE CAN EVER REPAY YOU...
...UH ...TWO?
THAT'S RIGHT.
THE MISSUS AND I ARE EXPECTING.
AT FIRST, WE DIDN'T FEEL RIGHT ABOUT BRINGING A CHILD INTO THE WORLD THE WAY THINGS ARE, BUT NOW WITH PEOPLE LIKE YOU AROUND, WELL, IT GIVES US HOPE.
NOW WHO'S READY FOR A NICE HOME-COOKED MEAL?
ACTUALLY, OWEN AND I WERE THINKING WE'D SCOUT OUT THAT BARN OF YOURS.
WE WERE?
YES, BUT DON'T WAIT FOR US TO DIG IN.
SMELLS GREAT!
SO... UHM, YOU WERE SAYING THERE WERE SOME WEBSITES WE SHOULD TAKE A LOOK AT?

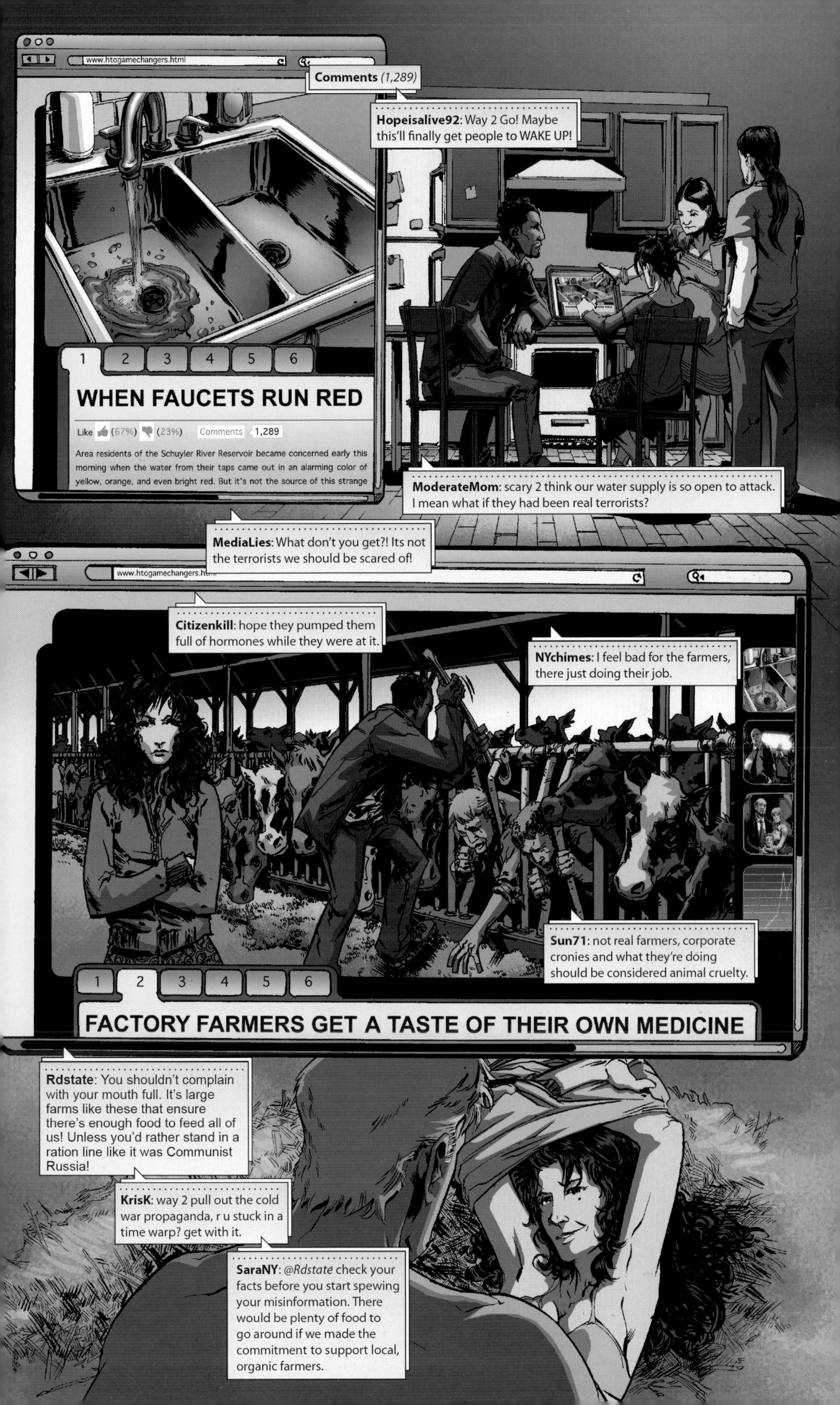

www.htogamechangers.html
Comments (1,289)
Hopeisalive92: Way 2 Go! Maybe this'll finally get people to WAKE UP!
1 2 3 4 5 6
WHEN FAUCETS RUN RED
Like (67%) (23%) Comments 1,289
Area residents of the Schuyler River Reservoir became concerned early this morning when the water from their taps came out in an alarming color of yellow, orange, and even bright red. But it's not the source of this strange
ModerateMom: scary 2 think our water supply is so open to attack. I mean what if they had been real terrorists?
MediaLies: What don't you get?! Its not the terrorists we should be scared of!
www.htogamechangers.html
Citizenkill: hope they pumped them full of hormones while they were at it.
NYchimes: I feel bad for the farmers, there just doing their job.
Sun71: not real farmers, corporate cronies and what they're doing should be considered animal cruelty.
1 2 3 4 5 6
FACTORY FARMERS GET A TASTE OF THEIR OWN MEDICINE
Rdstate: You shouldn't complain with your mouth full. It's large farms like these that ensure there's enough food to feed all of us! Unless you'd rather stand in a ration line like it was Communist Russia!
KrisK: way 2 pull out the cold war propaganda, r u stuck in a time warp? get with it.
SaraNY: @Rdstate check your facts before you start spewing your misinformation. There would be plenty of food to go around if we made the commitment to support local, organic farmers.

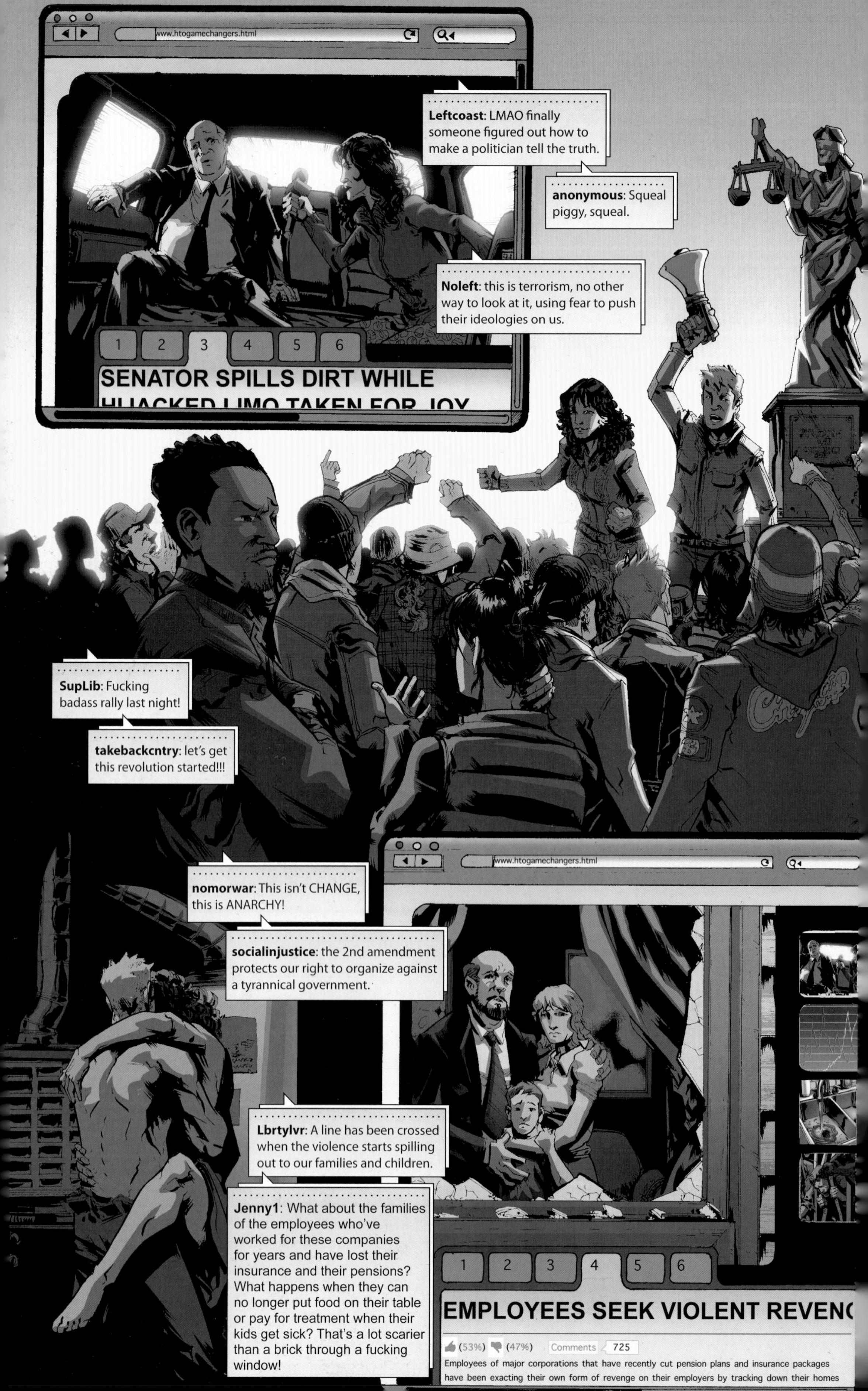
www.htogamechangers.html
Leftcoast: LMAO finally someone figured out how to make a politician tell the truth.
anonymous: Squeal piggy, squeal.
Noleft: this is terrorism, no other way to look at it, using fear to push their ideologies on us.
1 2 3 4 5 6
SENATOR SPILLS DIRT WHILE
SupLib: Fucking badass rally last night!
takebackcntry: let's get this revolution started!!!
www.htogamechangers.html
nomorwar: This isn't CHANGE, this is ANARCHY!
socialinjustice: the 2nd amendment protects our right to organize against a tyrannical government.
Lbrtylvr: A line has been crossed when the violence starts spilling out to our families and children.
Jenny1: What about the families of the employees who've worked for these companies for years and have lost their insurance and their pensions? What happens when they can no longer put food on their table or pay for treatment when their kids get sick? That's a lot scarier than a brick through a fucking window!
1 2 3 4 5 6
EMPLOYEES SEEK VIOLENT REVEN
(53%) (47%) Comments 725
Employees of major corporations that have recently cut pension plans and insurance packages have been exacting their own form of revenge on their employers by tracking down their homes

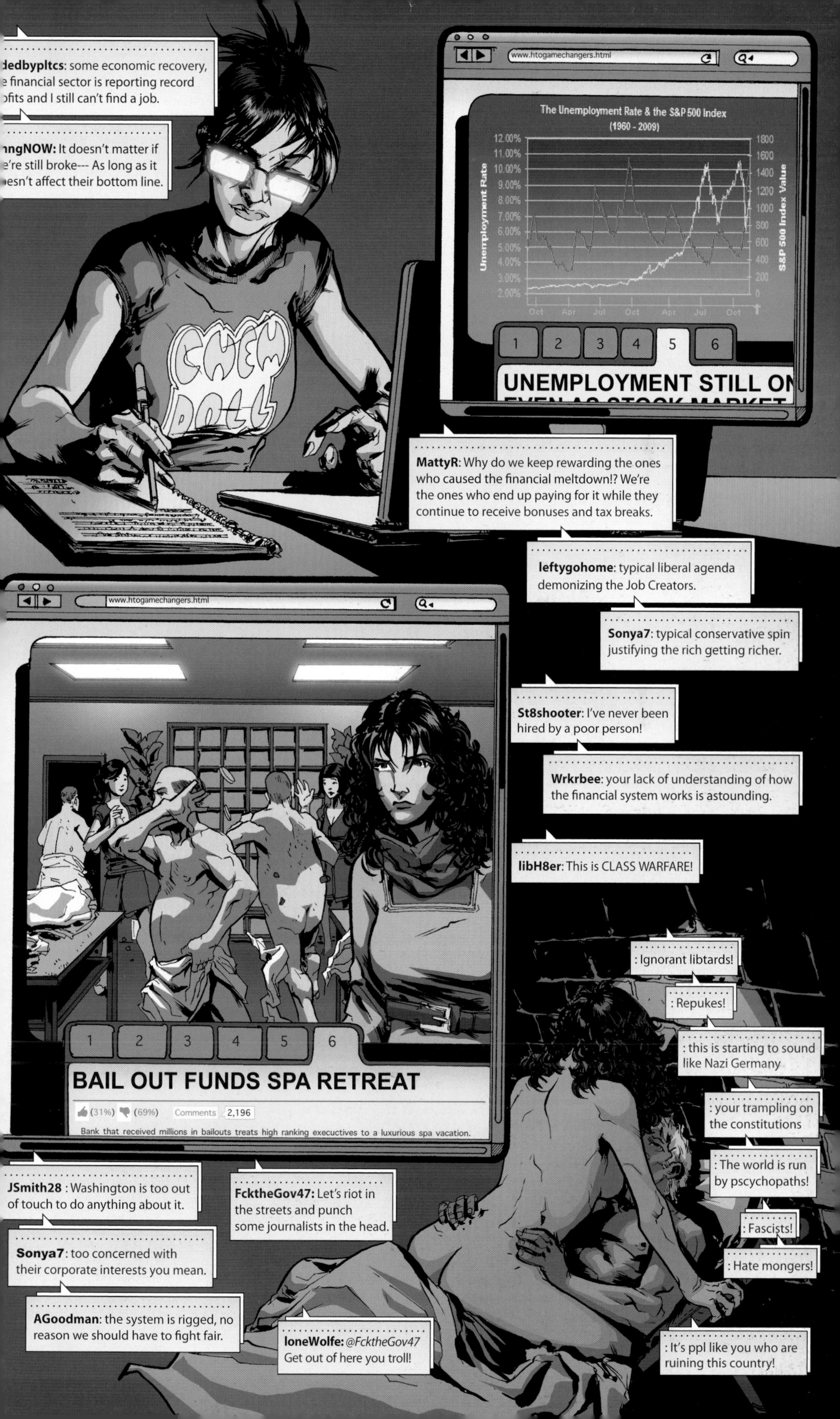
dedbypltcs: some economic recovery,
e financial sector is reporting record
ofits and I still can't find a job.
ngNOW: It doesn't matter if
e're still broke--- As long as it
esn't affect their bottom line.
www.htogamechangers.html
The Unemployment Rate & the S&P 500 Index
(1960 - 2009)
Unemployment Rate
S&P 500 Index Value
12.00% 11.00% 10.00% 9.00% 8.00% 7.00% 6.00% 5.00% 4.00% 3.00% 2.00%
1800 1600 1400 1200 1000 800 600 400 200 0
Oct Apr Jul Oct Apr Jul Oct
1 2 3 4 5 6
UNEMPLOYMENT STILL ON
MattyR: Why do we keep rewarding the ones who caused the financial meltdown!? We're the ones who end up paying for it while they continue to receive bonuses and tax breaks.
leftygohome: typical liberal agenda demonizing the Job Creators.
Sonya7: typical conservative spin justifying the rich getting richer.
St8shooter: I've never been hired by a poor person!
Wrkrbee: your lack of understanding of how the financial system works is astounding.
libH8er: This is CLASS WARFARE!
www.htogamechangers.html
1 2 3 4 5 6
BAIL OUT FUNDS SPA RETREAT
(31%) (69%) Comments 2,196
Bank that received millions in bailouts treats high ranking executives to a luxurious spa vacation.
: Ignorant libtards!
: Repukes!
: this is starting to sound like Nazi Germany
: your trampling on the constitutions
: The world is run by pscychopaths!
: Fascists!
: Hate mongers!
JSmith28 : Washington is too out of touch to do anything about it.
FcktheGov47: Let's riot in the streets and punch some journalists in the head.
Sonya7: too concerned with their corporate interests you mean.
AGoodman: the system is rigged, no reason we should have to fight fair.
loneWolfe: @FcktheGov47 Get out of here you troll!
: It's ppl like you who are ruining this country!

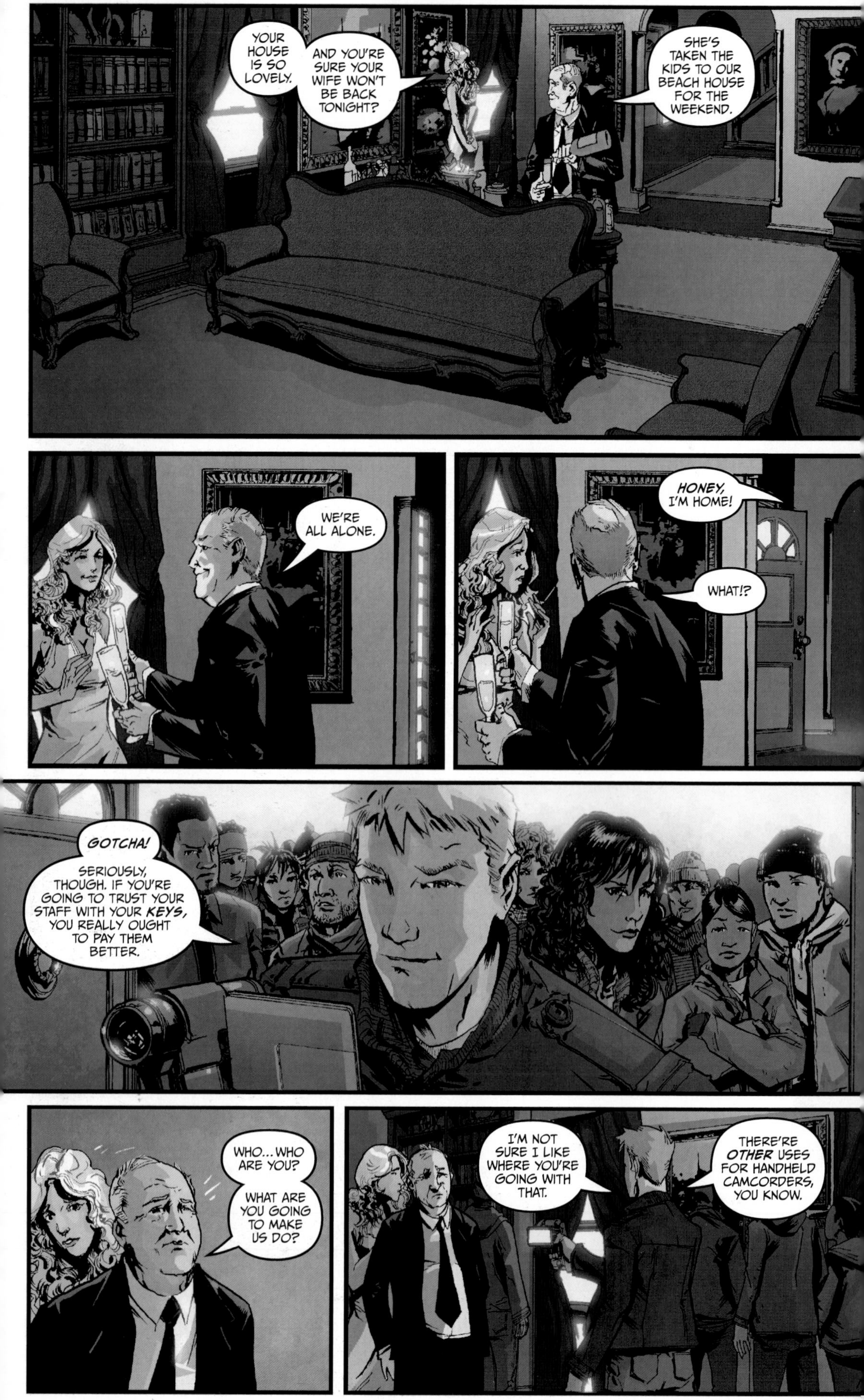
YOUR HOUSE IS SO LOVELY.
AND YOU'RE SURE YOUR WIFE WON'T BE BACK TONIGHT?
SHE'S TAKEN THE KIDS TO OUR BEACH HOUSE FOR THE WEEKEND.
WE'RE ALL ALONE.
HONEY, I'M HOME!
WHAT!?
GOTCHA!
SERIOUSLY, THOUGH. IF YOU'RE GOING TO TRUST YOUR STAFF WITH YOUR *KEYS,* YOU REALLY OUGHT TO PAY THEM BETTER.
WHO...WHO ARE YOU?
WHAT ARE YOU GOING TO MAKE US DO?
I'M NOT SURE I LIKE WHERE YOU'RE GOING WITH THAT.
THERE'RE *OTHER* USES FOR HANDHELD CAMCORDERS, YOU KNOW.

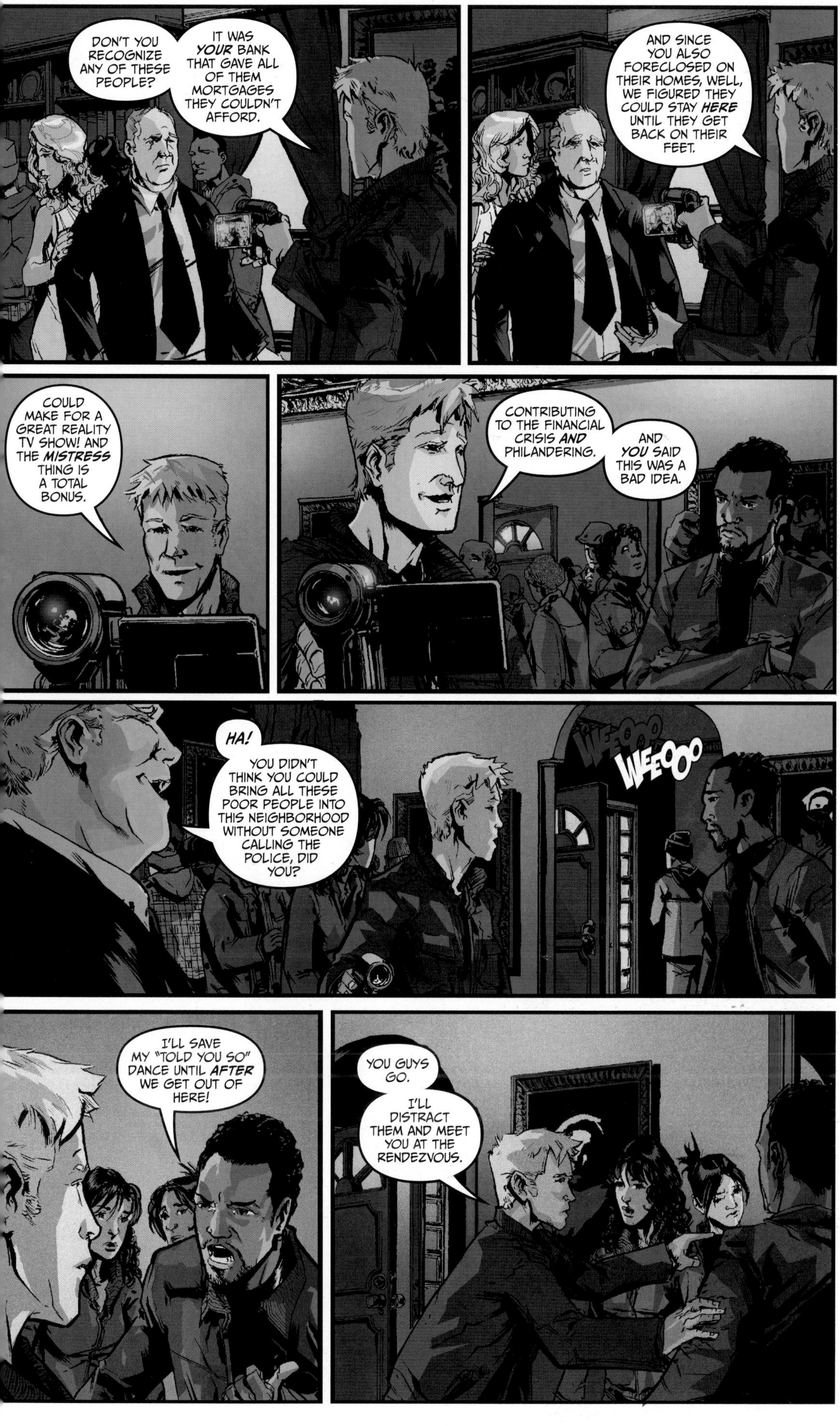
DON'T YOU RECOGNIZE ANY OF THESE PEOPLE?
IT WAS YOUR BANK THAT GAVE ALL OF THEM MORTGAGES THEY COULDN'T AFFORD.
AND SINCE YOU ALSO FORECLOSED ON THEIR HOMES, WELL, WE FIGURED THEY COULD STAY HERE UNTIL THEY GET BACK ON THEIR FEET.
COULD MAKE FOR A GREAT REALITY TV SHOW! AND THE MISTRESS THING IS A TOTAL BONUS.
CONTRIBUTING TO THE FINANCIAL CRISIS AND PHILANDERING.
AND YOU SAID THIS WAS A BAD IDEA.
HA!
YOU DIDN'T THINK YOU COULD BRING ALL THESE POOR PEOPLE INTO THIS NEIGHBORHOOD WITHOUT SOMEONE CALLING THE POLICE, DID YOU?
WEEOOO
WEEOOO
I'LL SAVE MY "TOLD YOU SO" DANCE UNTIL AFTER WE GET OUT OF HERE!
YOU GUYS GO.
I'LL DISTRACT THEM AND MEET YOU AT THE RENDEZVOUS.

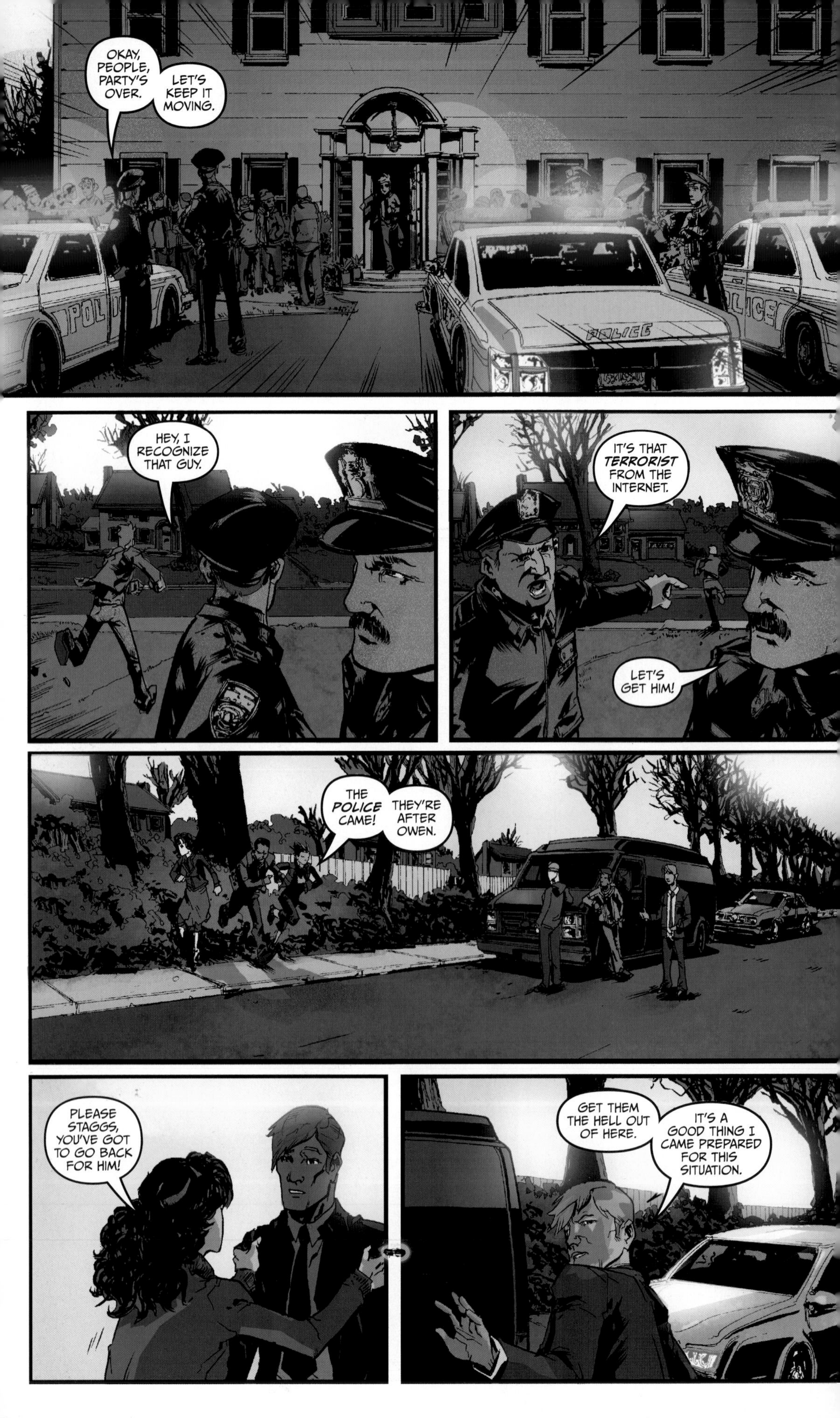
OKAY, PEOPLE, PARTY'S OVER.
LET'S KEEP IT MOVING.
HEY, I RECOGNIZE THAT GUY.
IT'S THAT *TERRORIST* FROM THE INTERNET.
LET'S GET HIM!
THE *POLICE* CAME!
THEY'RE AFTER OWEN.
PLEASE STAGGS, YOU'VE GOT TO GO BACK FOR HIM!
GET THEM THE HELL OUT OF HERE.
IT'S A GOOD THING I CAME PREPARED FOR THIS SITUATION.

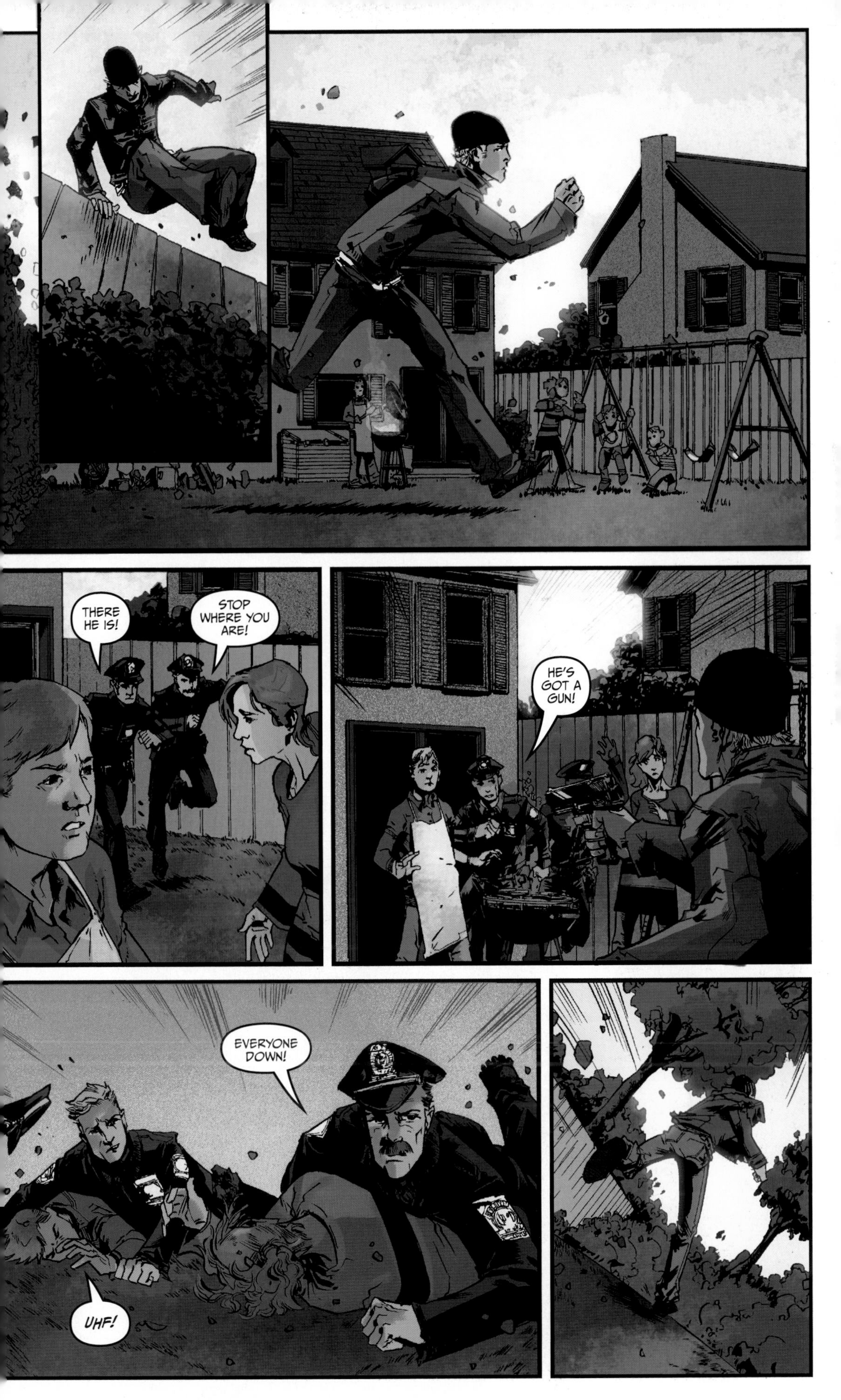
THERE HE IS!
STOP WHERE YOU ARE!
HE'S GOT A GUN!
EVERYONE DOWN!
UHF!

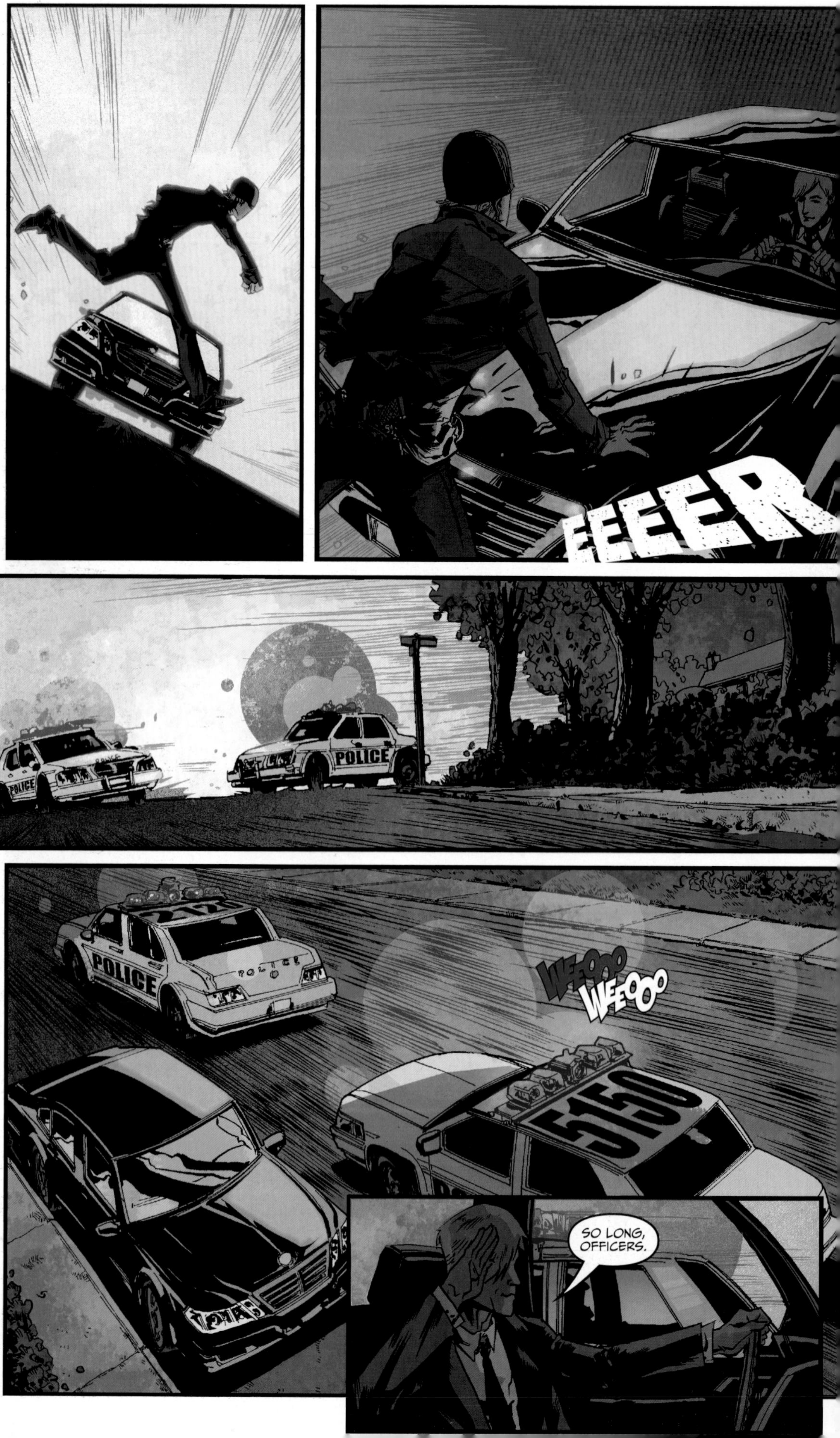

EEEER
POLICE
POLICE
POLICE
WEEOOO
WEEOOO
5150
SO LONG, OFFICERS.

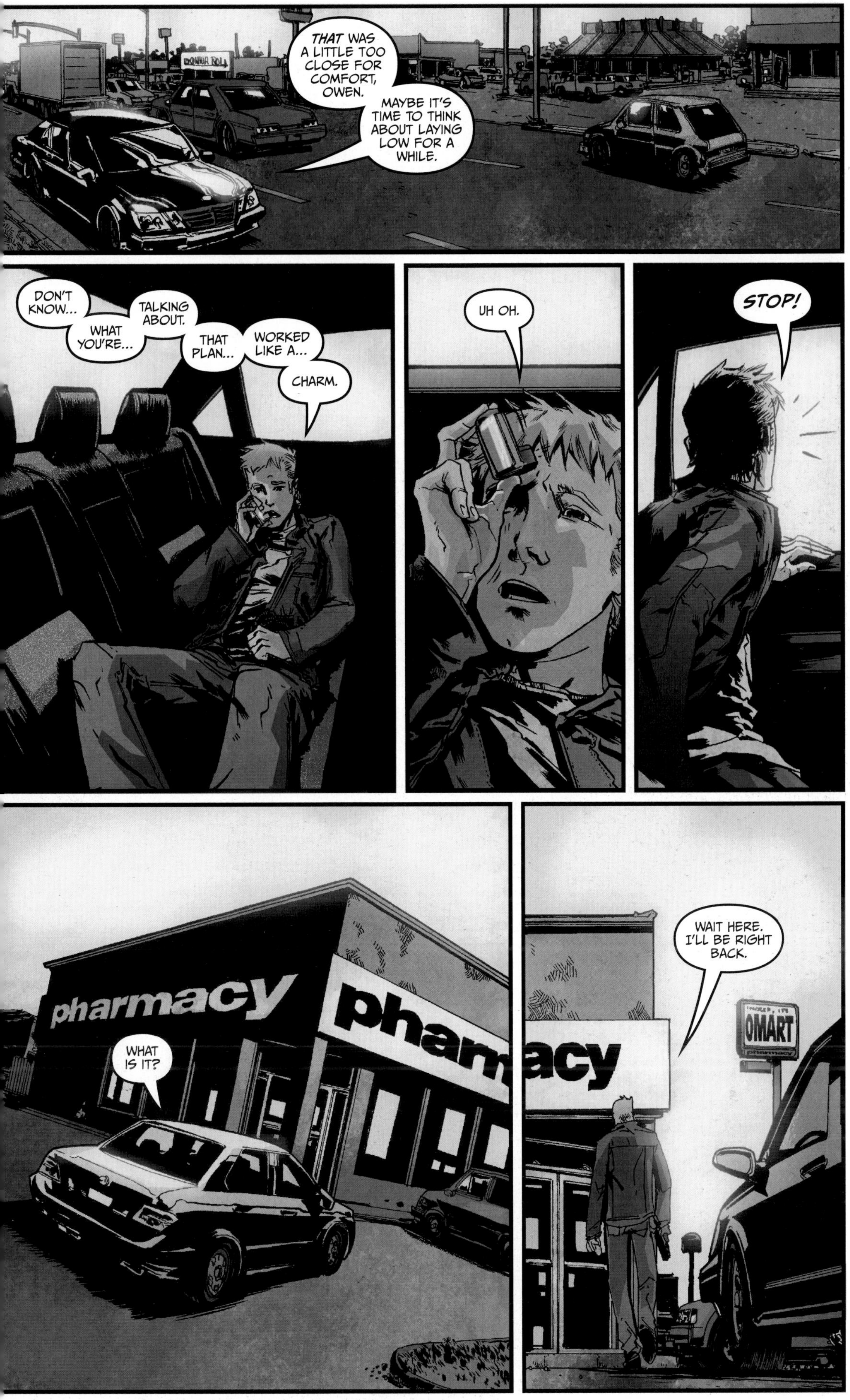
THAT WAS A LITTLE TOO CLOSE FOR COMFORT, OWEN.
MAYBE IT'S TIME TO THINK ABOUT LAYING LOW FOR A WHILE.
DON'T KNOW...
WHAT YOU'RE...
TALKING ABOUT.
THAT PLAN...
WORKED LIKE A...
CHARM.
UH OH.
STOP!
pharmacy
pharmacy
WHAT IS IT?
WAIT HERE. I'LL BE RIGHT BACK.
OMART
pharmacy

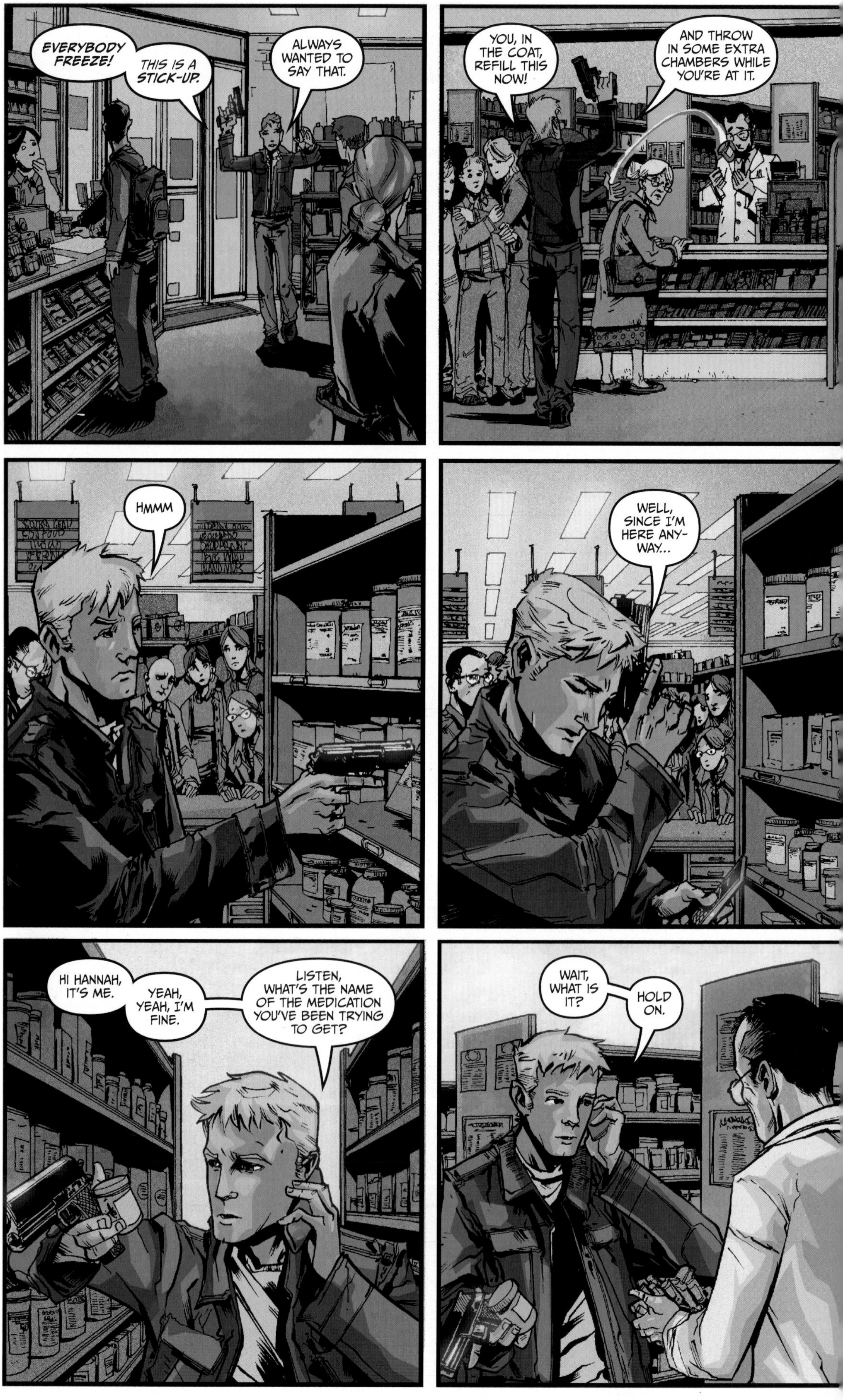
EVERYBODY FREEZE!
THIS IS A STICK-UP.
ALWAYS WANTED TO SAY THAT.
YOU, IN THE COAT, REFILL THIS NOW!
AND THROW IN SOME EXTRA CHAMBERS WHILE YOU'RE AT IT.
HMMM
WELL, SINCE I'M HERE ANY-WAY...
HI HANNAH, IT'S ME.
YEAH, YEAH, I'M FINE.
LISTEN, WHAT'S THE NAME OF THE MEDICATION YOU'VE BEEN TRYING TO GET?
WAIT, WHAT IS IT?
HOLD ON.

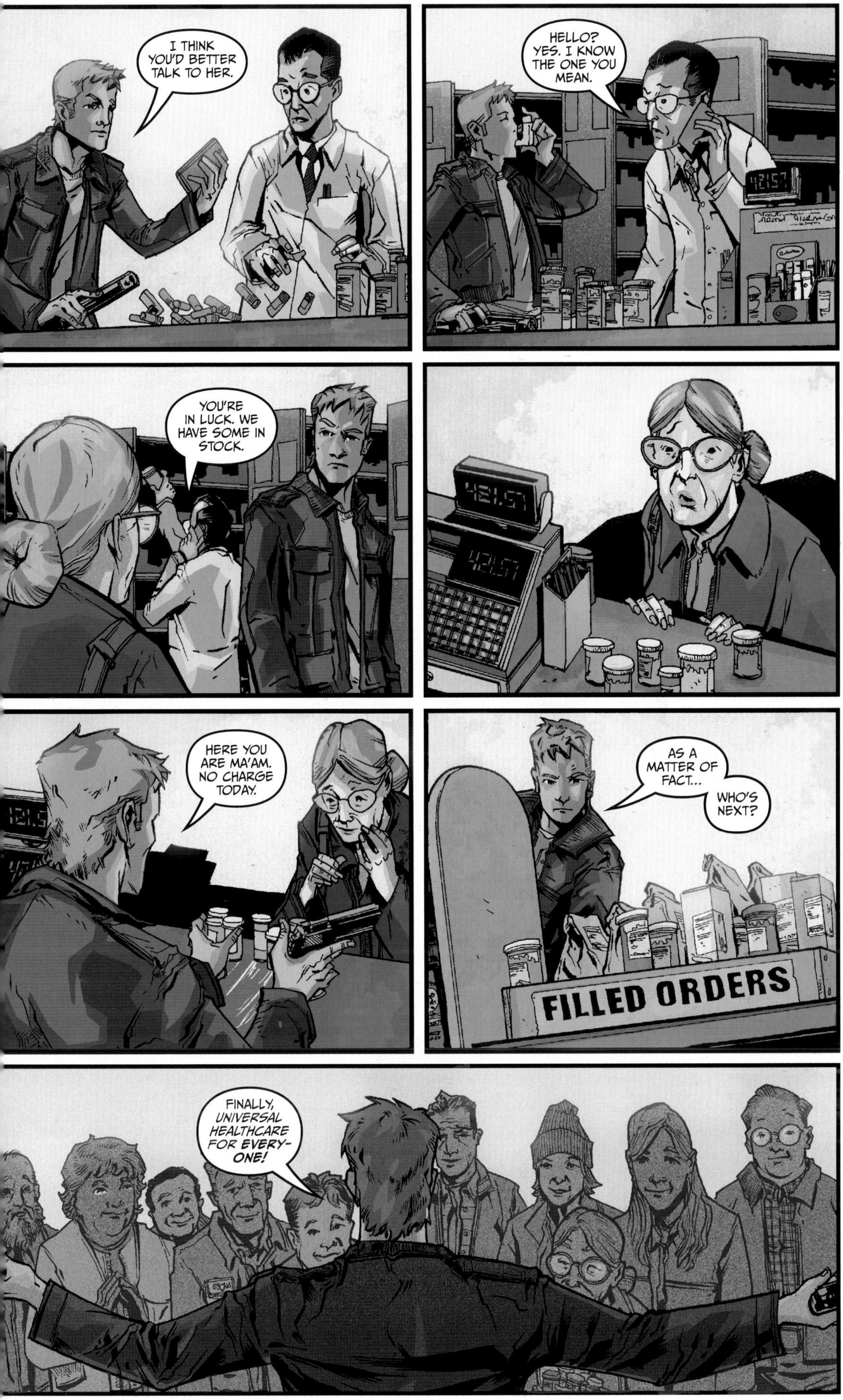
I THINK YOU'D BETTER TALK TO HER.
HELLO? YES. I KNOW THE ONE YOU MEAN.
YOU'RE IN LUCK. WE HAVE SOME IN STOCK.
HERE YOU ARE MA'AM. NO CHARGE TODAY.
AS A MATTER OF FACT...
WHO'S NEXT?
FILLED ORDERS
FINALLY, *UNIVERSAL HEALTHCARE* FOR **EVERY-ONE!**

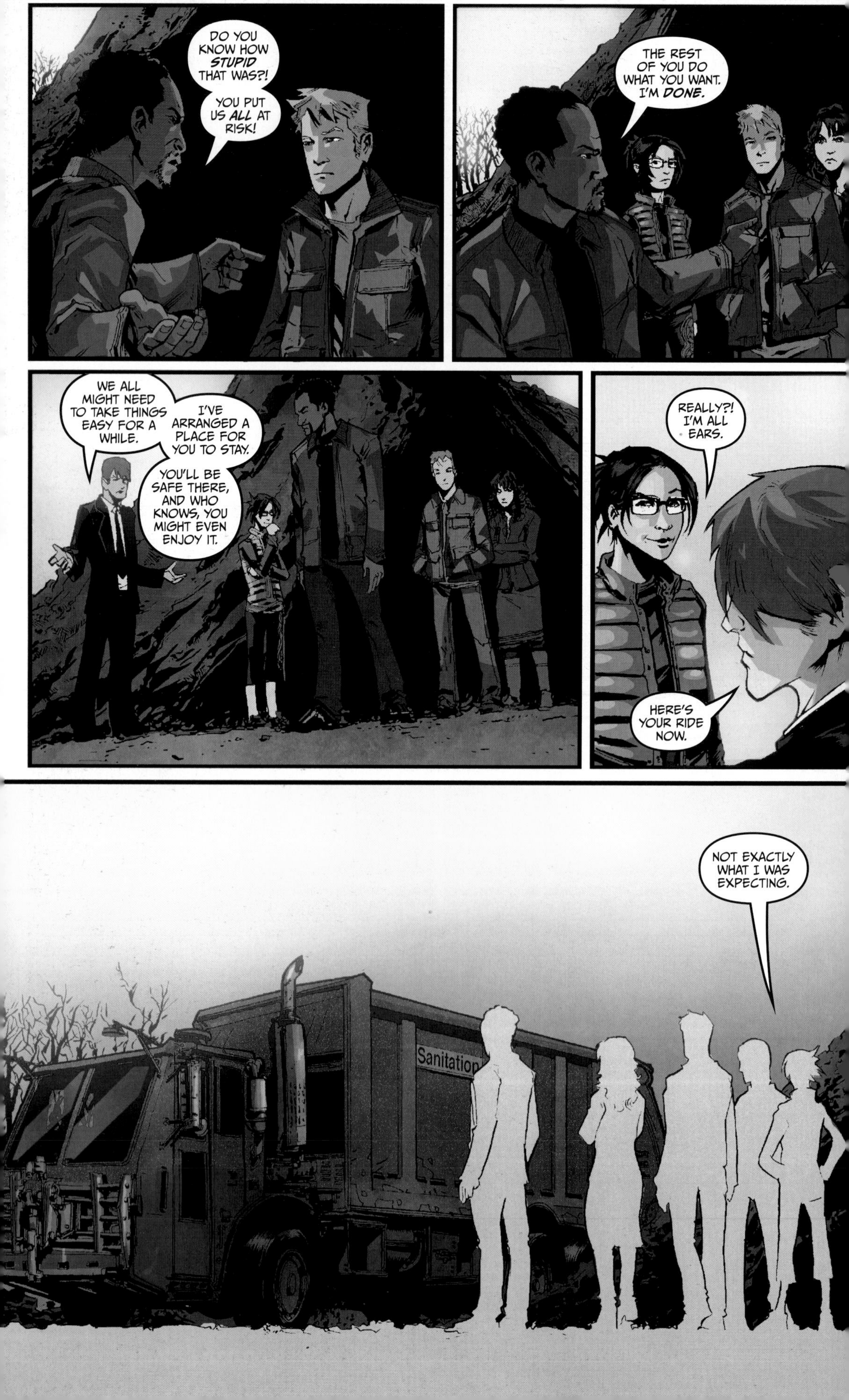
DO YOU KNOW HOW STUPID THAT WAS?!
YOU PUT US ALL AT RISK!
THE REST OF YOU DO WHAT YOU WANT. I'M DONE.
WE ALL MIGHT NEED TO TAKE THINGS EASY FOR A WHILE.
I'VE ARRANGED A PLACE FOR YOU TO STAY.
YOU'LL BE SAFE THERE, AND WHO KNOWS, YOU MIGHT EVEN ENJOY IT.
REALLY?! I'M ALL EARS.
HERE'S YOUR RIDE NOW.
NOT EXACTLY WHAT I WAS EXPECTING.
Sanitation

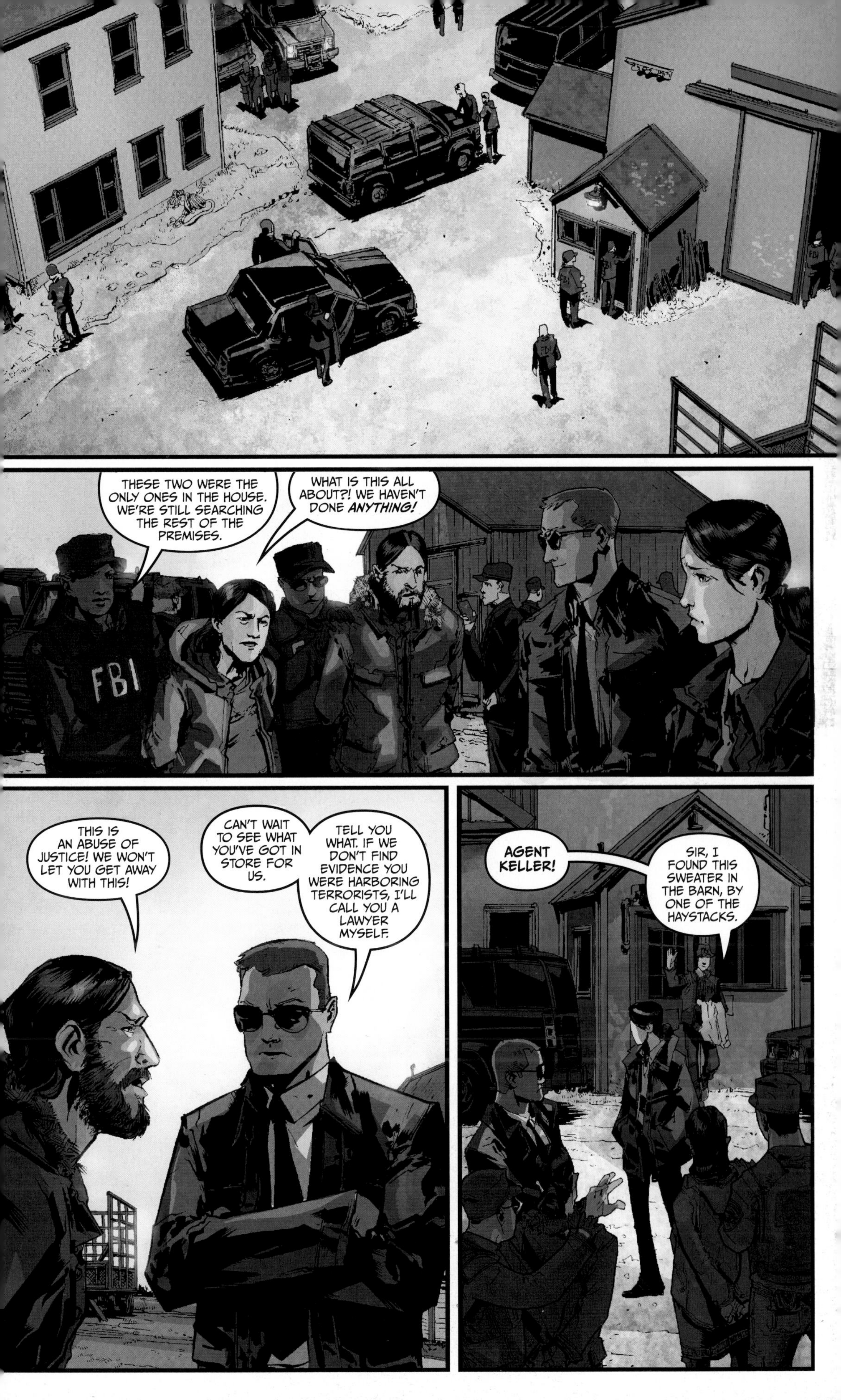
THESE TWO WERE THE ONLY ONES IN THE HOUSE. WE'RE STILL SEARCHING THE REST OF THE PREMISES.
WHAT IS THIS ALL ABOUT?! WE HAVEN'T DONE ANYTHING!
THIS IS AN ABUSE OF JUSTICE! WE WON'T LET YOU GET AWAY WITH THIS!
CAN'T WAIT TO SEE WHAT YOU'VE GOT IN STORE FOR US.
TELL YOU WHAT. IF WE DON'T FIND EVIDENCE YOU WERE HARBORING TERRORISTS, I'LL CALL YOU A LAWYER MYSELF.
AGENT KELLER!
SIR, I FOUND THIS SWEATER IN THE BARN, BY ONE OF THE HAYSTACKS.
FBI

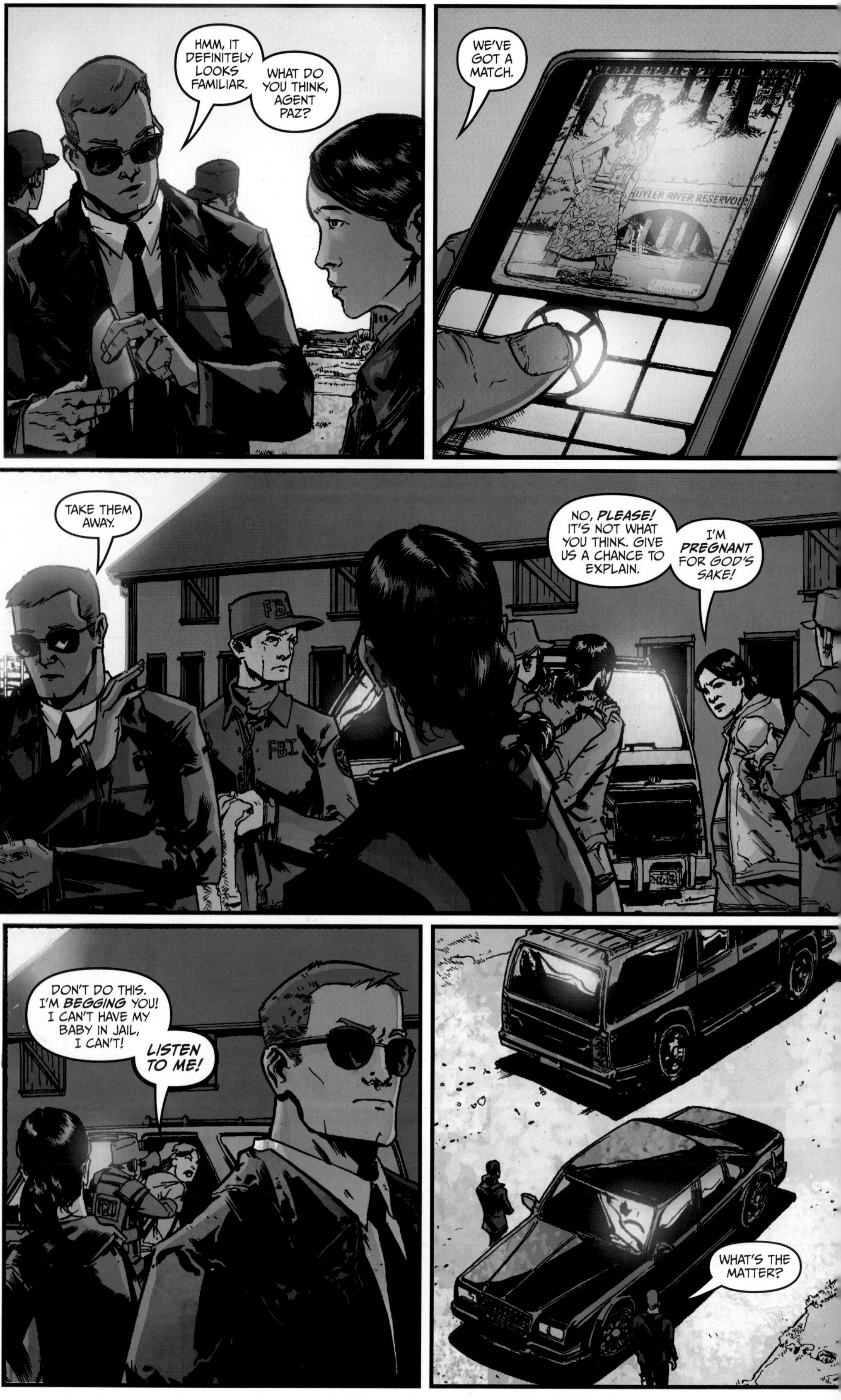
HMM, IT DEFINITELY LOOKS FAMILIAR.
WHAT DO YOU THINK, AGENT PAZ?
WE'VE GOT A MATCH.
HUYLER RIVER RESERVOI
TAKE THEM AWAY.
NO, *PLEASE!* IT'S NOT WHAT YOU THINK. GIVE US A CHANCE TO EXPLAIN.
I'M *PREGNANT* FOR GOD'S SAKE!
FBI
DON'T DO THIS. I'M *BEGGING* YOU! I CAN'T HAVE MY BABY IN JAIL, I CAN'T!
LISTEN TO ME!
WHAT'S THE MATTER?

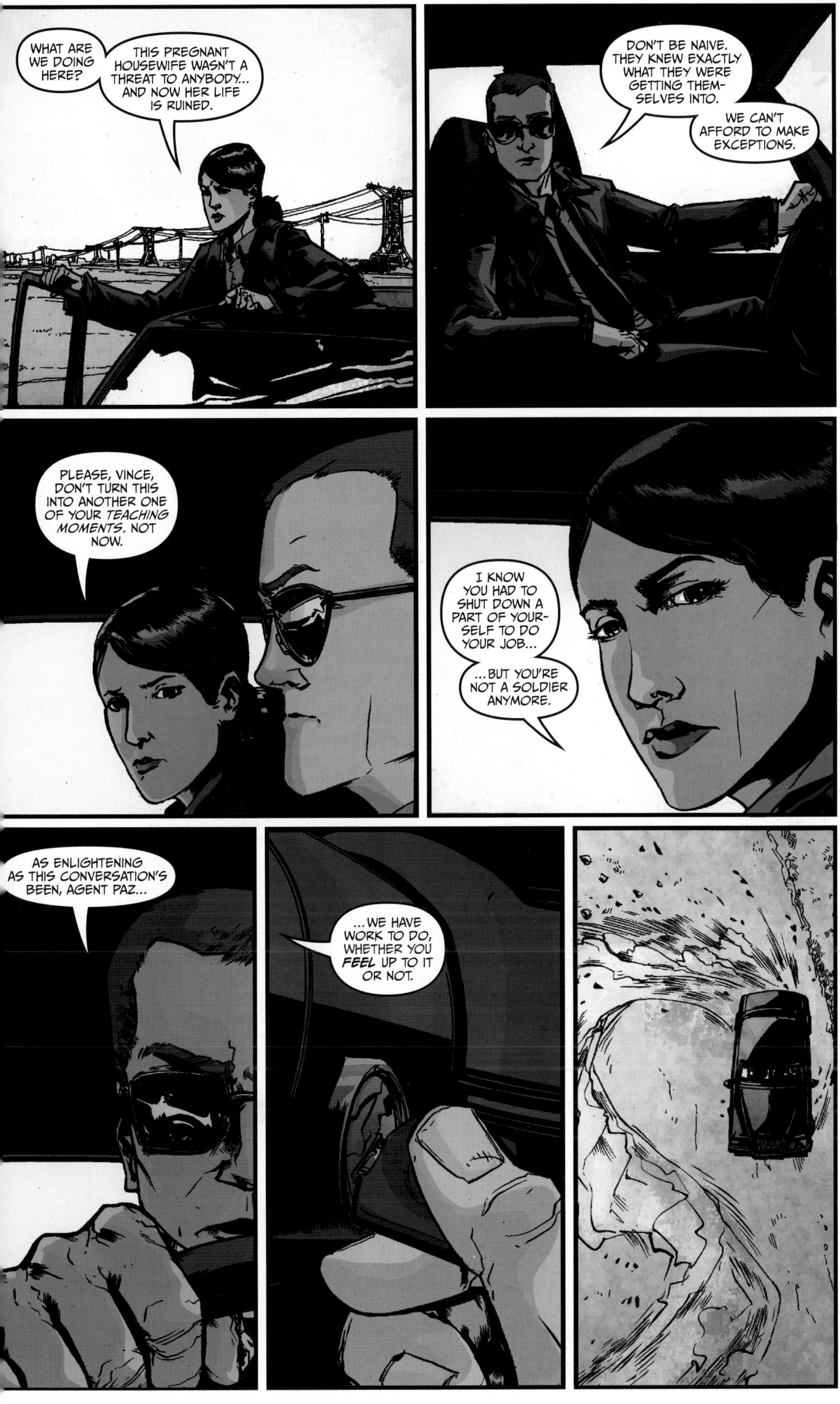

WHAT ARE WE DOING HERE?
THIS PREGNANT HOUSEWIFE WASN'T A THREAT TO ANYBODY... AND NOW HER LIFE IS RUINED.
DON'T BE NAIVE. THEY KNEW EXACTLY WHAT THEY WERE GETTING THEM-SELVES INTO.
WE CAN'T AFFORD TO MAKE EXCEPTIONS.
PLEASE, VINCE, DON'T TURN THIS INTO ANOTHER ONE OF YOUR *TEACHING MOMENTS.* NOT NOW.
I KNOW YOU HAD TO SHUT DOWN A PART OF YOUR-SELF TO DO YOUR JOB...
...BUT YOU'RE NOT A SOLDIER ANYMORE.
AS ENLIGHTENING AS THIS CONVERSATION'S BEEN, AGENT PAZ...
...WE HAVE WORK TO DO, WHETHER YOU ***FEEL*** UP TO IT OR NOT.

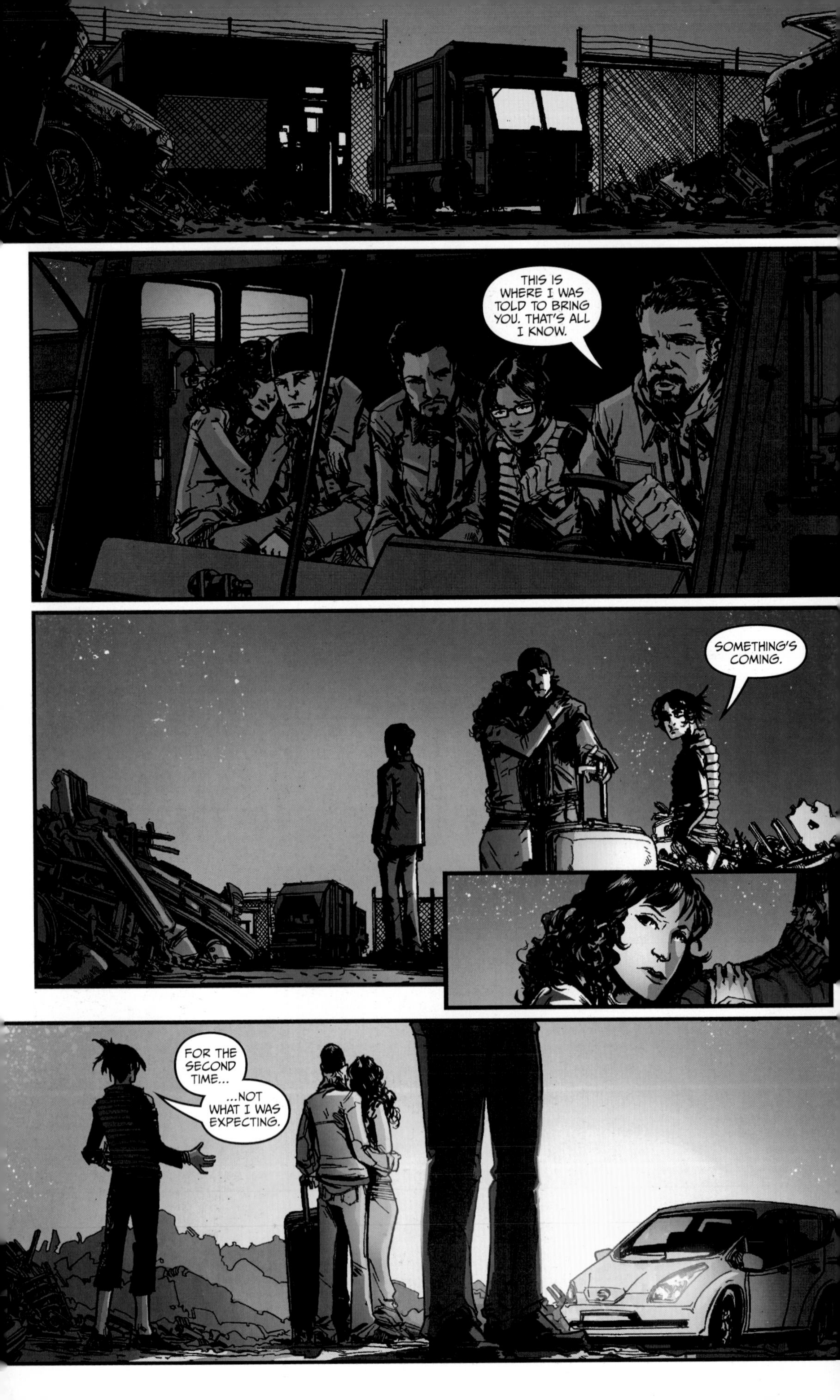
THIS IS WHERE I WAS TOLD TO BRING YOU. THAT'S ALL I KNOW.
SOMETHING'S COMING.
FOR THE SECOND TIME...
...NOT WHAT I WAS EXPECTING.

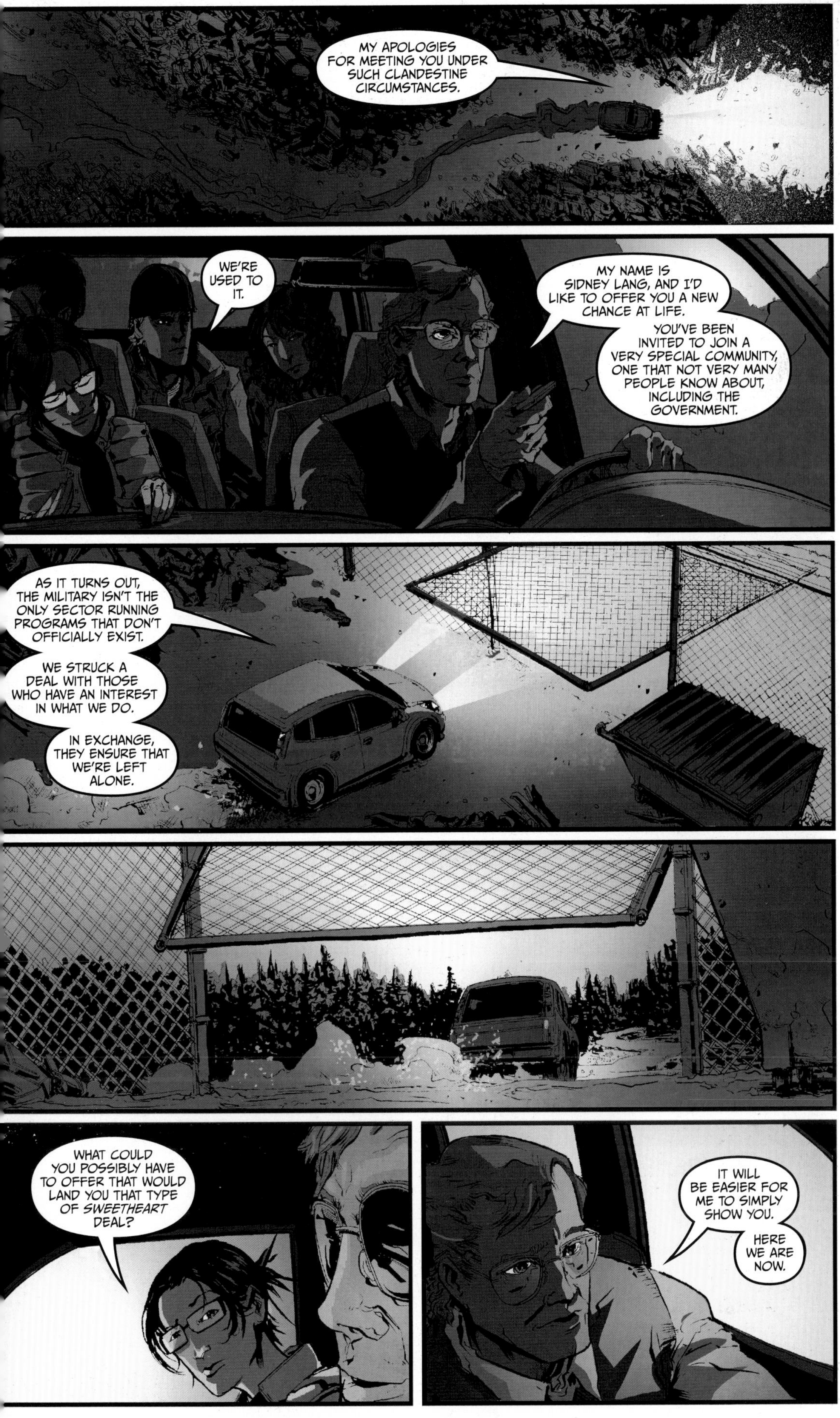
MY APOLOGIES FOR MEETING YOU UNDER SUCH CLANDESTINE CIRCUMSTANCES.
WE'RE USED TO IT.
MY NAME IS SIDNEY LANG, AND I'D LIKE TO OFFER YOU A NEW CHANCE AT LIFE.
YOU'VE BEEN INVITED TO JOIN A VERY SPECIAL COMMUNITY, ONE THAT NOT VERY MANY PEOPLE KNOW ABOUT, INCLUDING THE GOVERNMENT.
AS IT TURNS OUT, THE MILITARY ISN'T THE ONLY SECTOR RUNNING PROGRAMS THAT DON'T OFFICIALLY EXIST.
WE STRUCK A DEAL WITH THOSE WHO HAVE AN INTEREST IN WHAT WE DO.
IN EXCHANGE, THEY ENSURE THAT WE'RE LEFT ALONE.
WHAT COULD YOU POSSIBLY HAVE TO OFFER THAT WOULD LAND YOU THAT TYPE OF *SWEETHEART* DEAL?
IT WILL BE EASIER FOR ME TO SIMPLY SHOW YOU.
HERE WE ARE NOW.

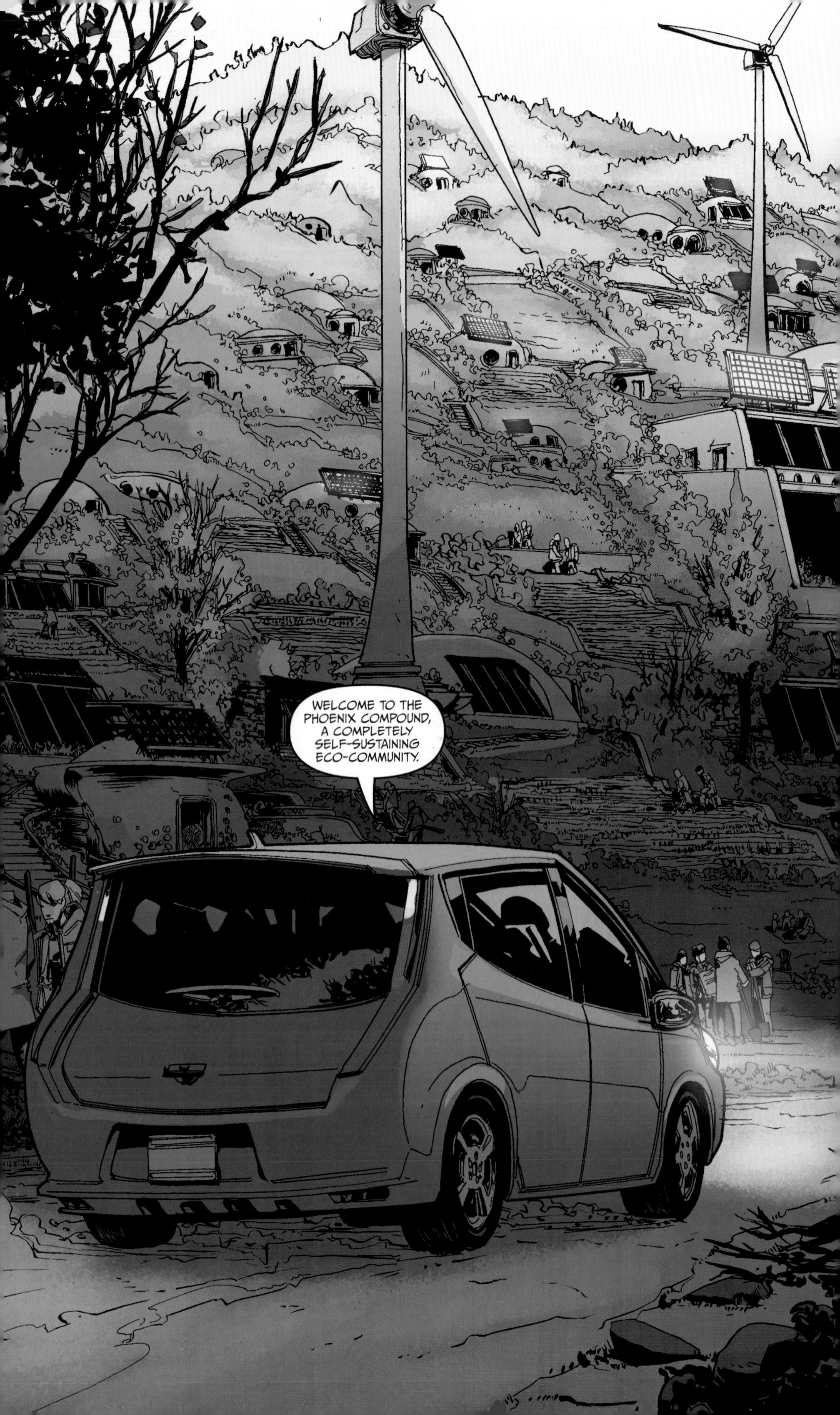
WELCOME TO THE PHOENIX COMPOUND, A COMPLETELY SELF-SUSTAINING ECO-COMMUNITY.

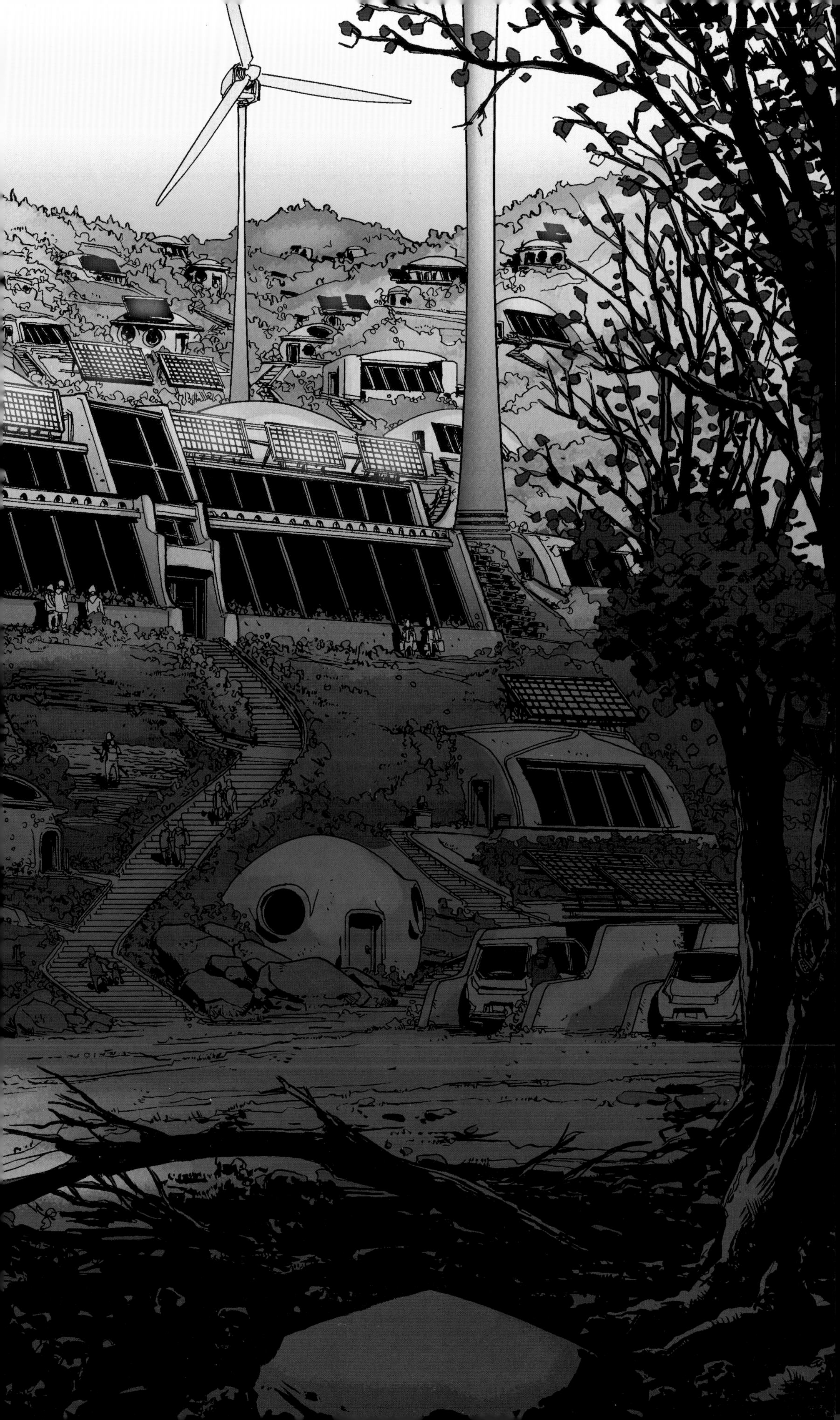

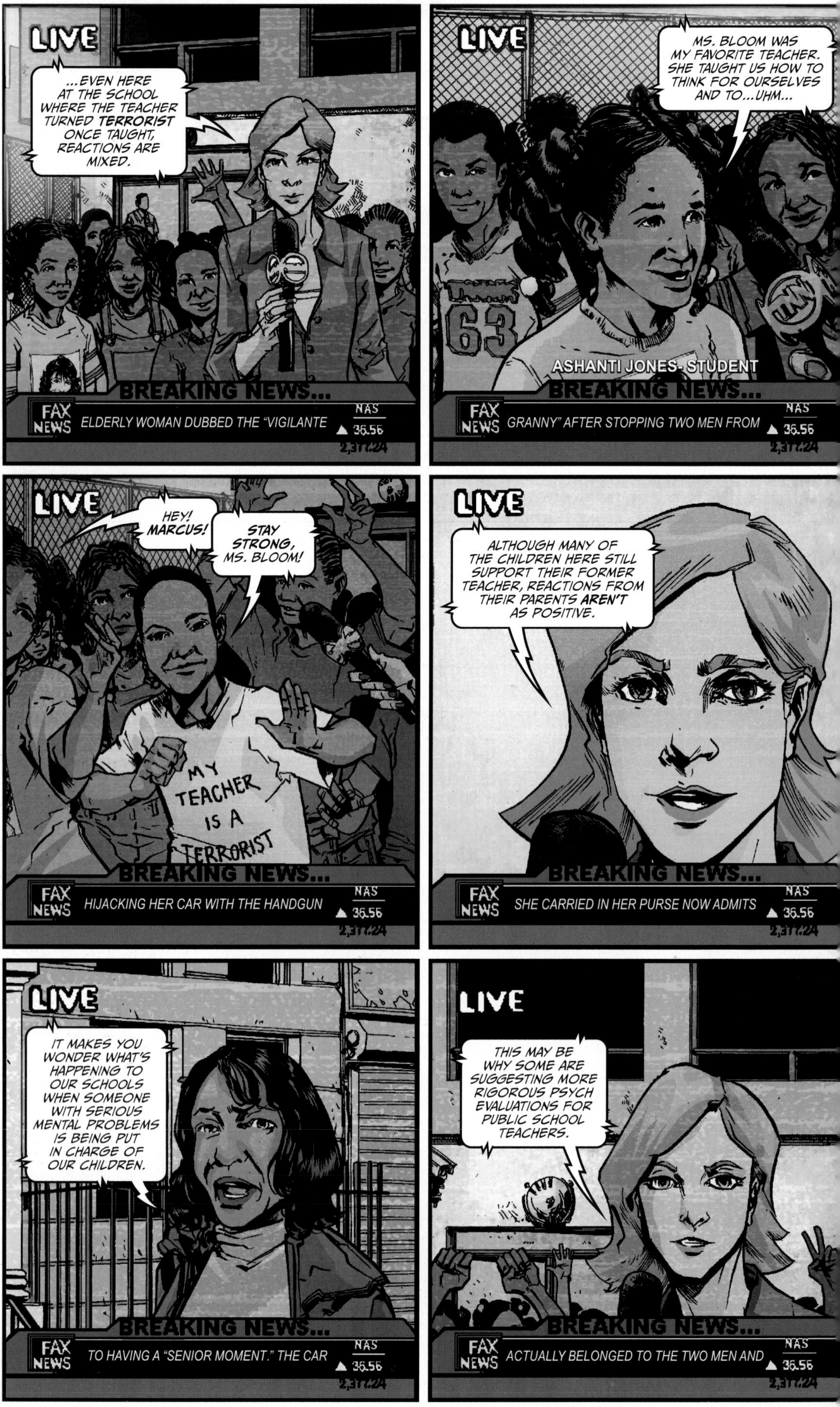
LIVE
...EVEN HERE AT THE SCHOOL WHERE THE TEACHER TURNED TERRORIST ONCE TAUGHT, REACTIONS ARE MIXED.
BREAKING NEWS...
FAX NEWS
ELDERLY WOMAN DUBBED THE "VIGILANTE
NAS
36.56
LIVE
MS. BLOOM WAS MY FAVORITE TEACHER. SHE TAUGHT US HOW TO THINK FOR OURSELVES AND TO...UHM...
63
ASHANTI JONES- STUDENT
BREAKING NEWS...
FAX NEWS
GRANNY" AFTER STOPPING TWO MEN FROM
NAS
36.56
LIVE
HEY! MARCUS!
STAY STRONG, MS. BLOOM!
MY TEACHER IS A TERRORIST
BREAKING NEWS...
FAX NEWS
HIJACKING HER CAR WITH THE HANDGUN
NAS
36.56
LIVE
ALTHOUGH MANY OF THE CHILDREN HERE STILL SUPPORT THEIR FORMER TEACHER, REACTIONS FROM THEIR PARENTS AREN'T AS POSITIVE.
BREAKING NEWS...
FAX NEWS
SHE CARRIED IN HER PURSE NOW ADMITS
NAS
36.56
LIVE
IT MAKES YOU WONDER WHAT'S HAPPENING TO OUR SCHOOLS WHEN SOMEONE WITH SERIOUS MENTAL PROBLEMS IS BEING PUT IN CHARGE OF OUR CHILDREN.
BREAKING NEWS...
FAX NEWS
TO HAVING A "SENIOR MOMENT." THE CAR
NAS
36.56
LIVE
THIS MAY BE WHY SOME ARE SUGGESTING MORE RIGOROUS PSYCH EVALUATIONS FOR PUBLIC SCHOOL TEACHERS.
BREAKING NEWS...
FAX NEWS
ACTUALLY BELONGED TO THE TWO MEN AND
NAS
36.56

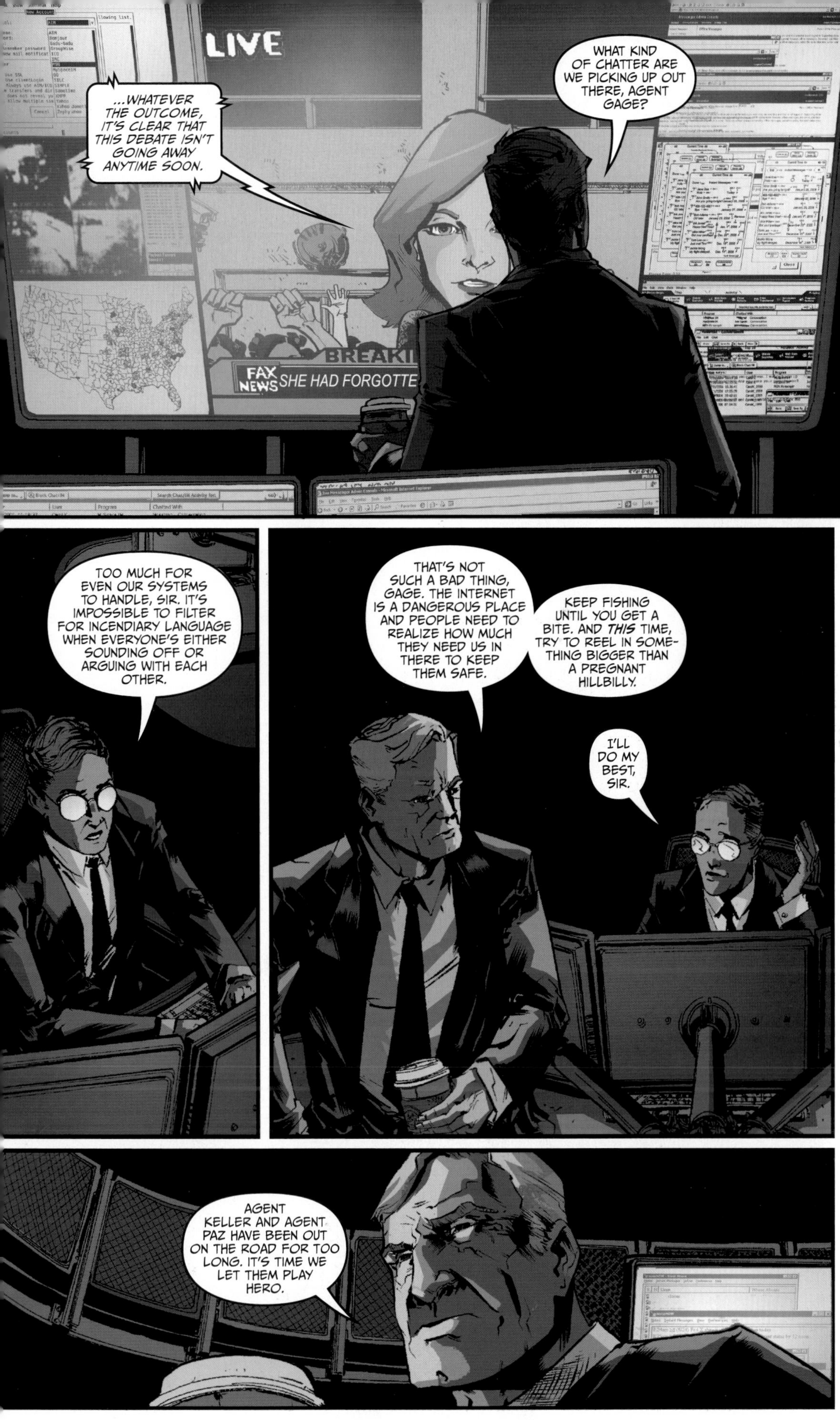
LIVE
...WHATEVER THE OUTCOME, IT'S CLEAR THAT THIS DEBATE ISN'T GOING AWAY ANYTIME SOON.
WHAT KIND OF CHATTER ARE WE PICKING UP OUT THERE, AGENT GAGE?
BREAKI
FAX NEWS
SHE HAD FORGOTTE
TOO MUCH FOR EVEN OUR SYSTEMS TO HANDLE, SIR. IT'S IMPOSSIBLE TO FILTER FOR INCENDIARY LANGUAGE WHEN EVERYONE'S EITHER SOUNDING OFF OR ARGUING WITH EACH OTHER.
THAT'S NOT SUCH A BAD THING, GAGE. THE INTERNET IS A DANGEROUS PLACE AND PEOPLE NEED TO REALIZE HOW MUCH THEY NEED US IN THERE TO KEEP THEM SAFE.
KEEP FISHING UNTIL YOU GET A BITE. AND *THIS* TIME, TRY TO REEL IN SOMETHING BIGGER THAN A PREGNANT HILLBILLY.
I'LL DO MY BEST, SIR.
AGENT KELLER AND AGENT PAZ HAVE BEEN OUT ON THE ROAD FOR TOO LONG. IT'S TIME WE LET THEM PLAY HERO.

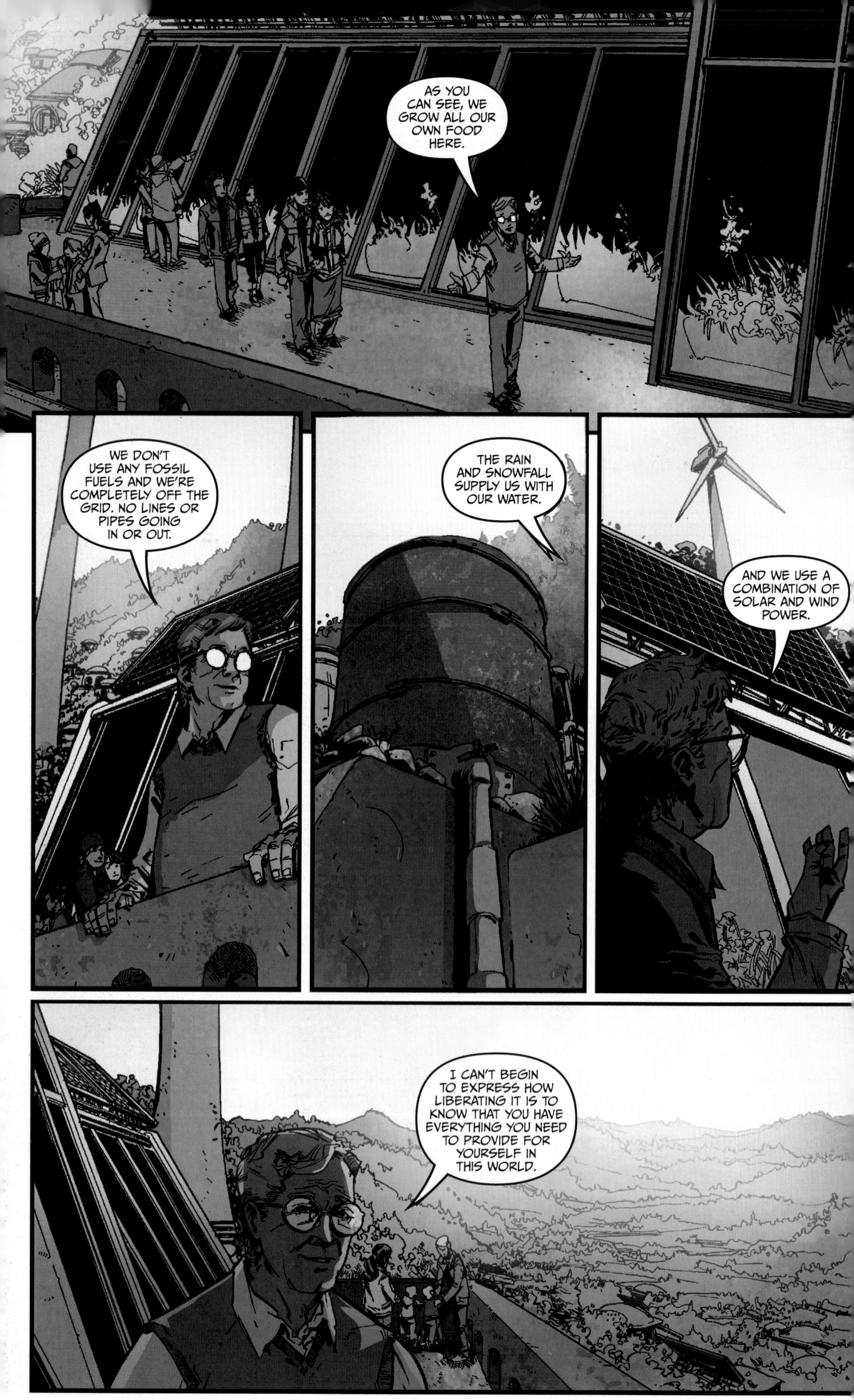
AS YOU CAN SEE, WE GROW ALL OUR OWN FOOD HERE.
WE DON'T USE ANY FOSSIL FUELS AND WE'RE COMPLETELY OFF THE GRID. NO LINES OR PIPES GOING IN OR OUT.
THE RAIN AND SNOWFALL SUPPLY US WITH OUR WATER.
AND WE USE A COMBINATION OF SOLAR AND WIND POWER.
I CAN'T BEGIN TO EXPRESS HOW LIBERATING IT IS TO KNOW THAT YOU HAVE EVERYTHING YOU NEED TO PROVIDE FOR YOURSELF IN THIS WORLD.

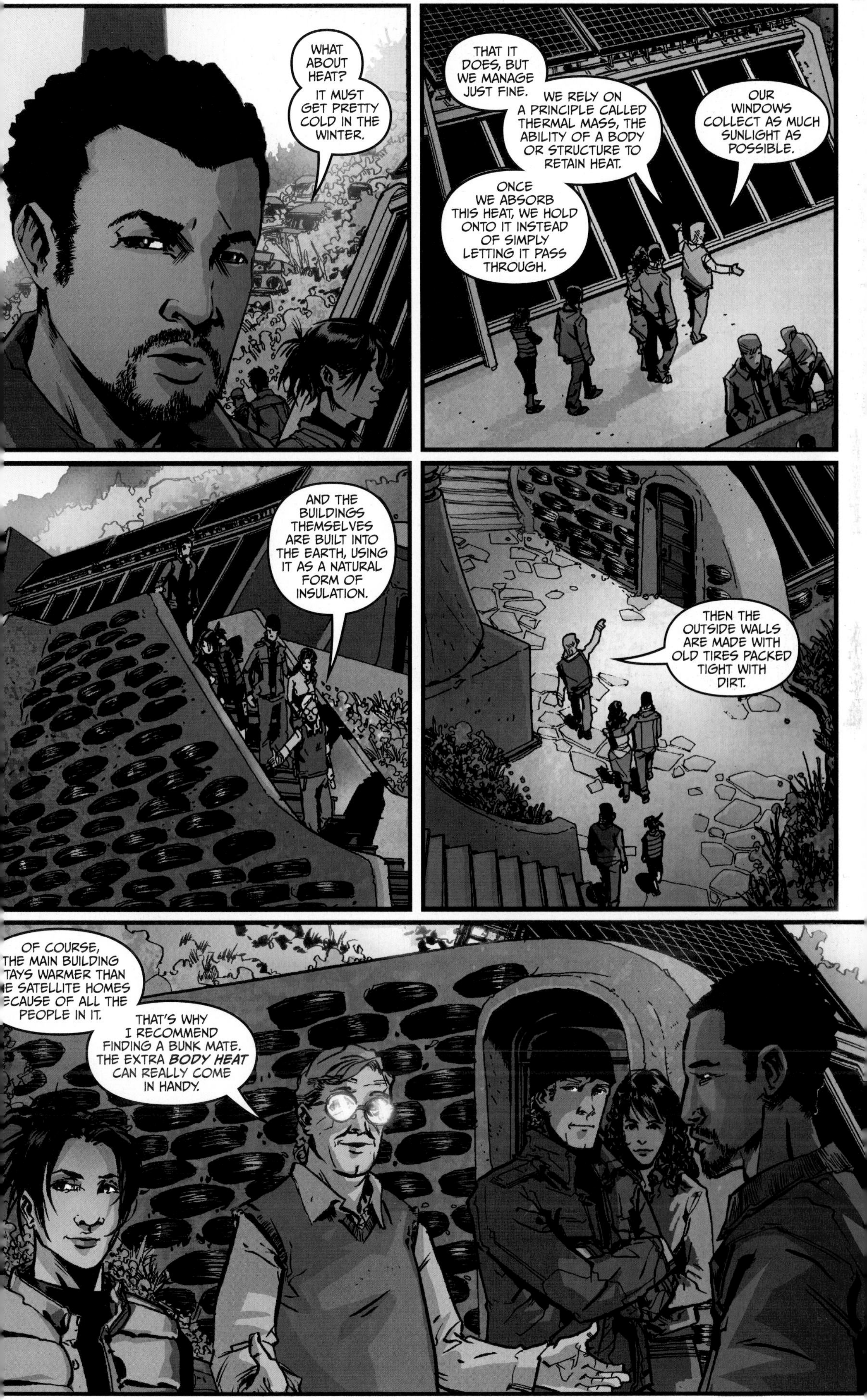
WHAT ABOUT HEAT?
IT MUST GET PRETTY COLD IN THE WINTER.
THAT IT DOES, BUT WE MANAGE JUST FINE.
WE RELY ON A PRINCIPLE CALLED THERMAL MASS, THE ABILITY OF A BODY OR STRUCTURE TO RETAIN HEAT.
ONCE WE ABSORB THIS HEAT, WE HOLD ONTO IT INSTEAD OF SIMPLY LETTING IT PASS THROUGH.
OUR WINDOWS COLLECT AS MUCH SUNLIGHT AS POSSIBLE.
AND THE BUILDINGS THEMSELVES ARE BUILT INTO THE EARTH, USING IT AS A NATURAL FORM OF INSULATION.
THEN THE OUTSIDE WALLS ARE MADE WITH OLD TIRES PACKED TIGHT WITH DIRT.
OF COURSE, THE MAIN BUILDING TAYS WARMER THAN E SATELLITE HOMES ECAUSE OF ALL THE PEOPLE IN IT.
THAT'S WHY I RECOMMEND FINDING A BUNK MATE. THE EXTRA BODY HEAT CAN REALLY COME IN HANDY.

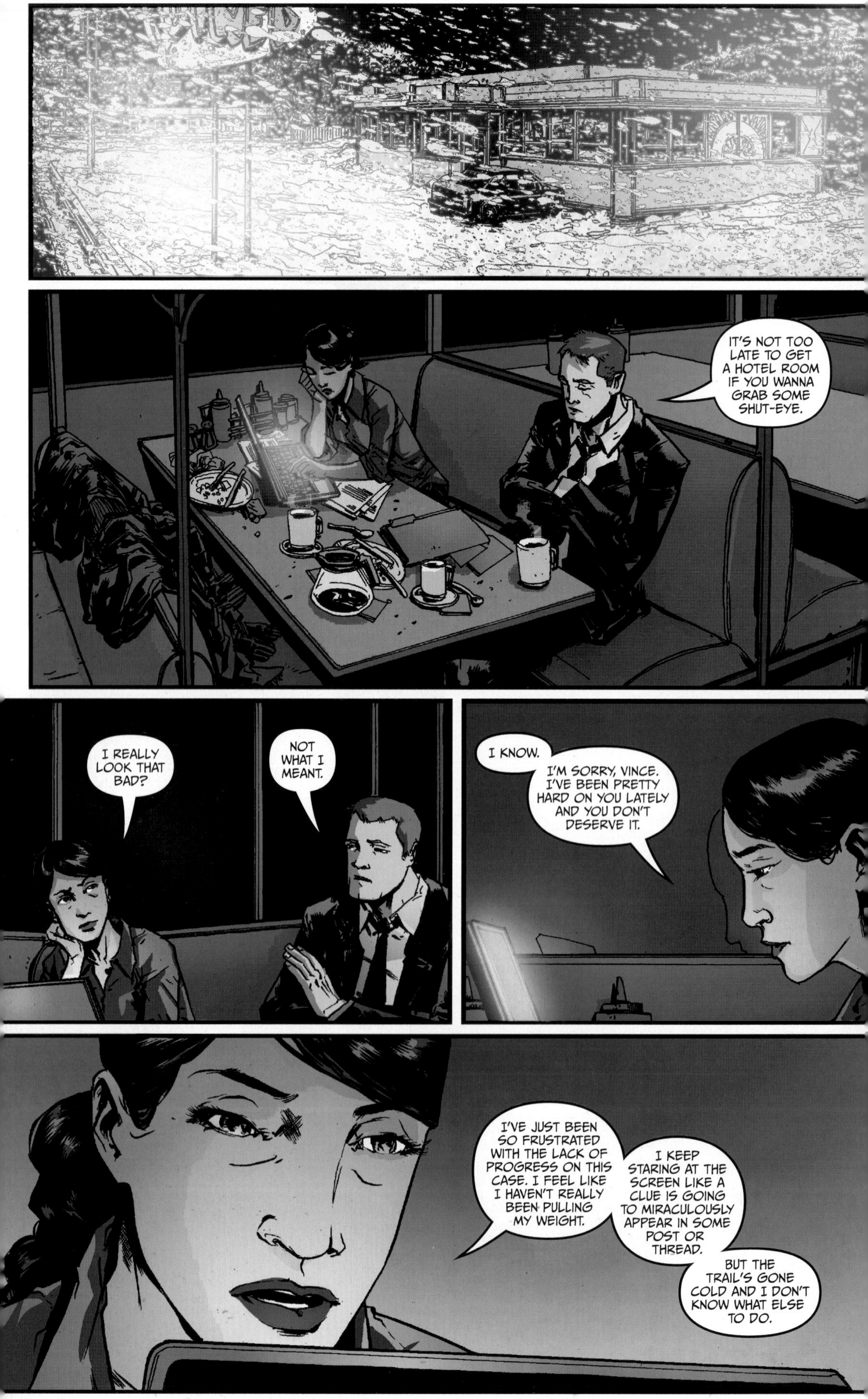
IT'S NOT TOO LATE TO GET A HOTEL ROOM IF YOU WANNA GRAB SOME SHUT-EYE.
I REALLY LOOK THAT BAD?
NOT WHAT I MEANT.
I KNOW.
I'M SORRY, VINCE. I'VE BEEN PRETTY HARD ON YOU LATELY AND YOU DON'T DESERVE IT.
I'VE JUST BEEN SO FRUSTRATED WITH THE LACK OF PROGRESS ON THIS CASE. I FEEL LIKE I HAVEN'T REALLY BEEN PULLING MY WEIGHT.
I KEEP STARING AT THE SCREEN LIKE A CLUE IS GOING TO MIRACULOUSLY APPEAR IN SOME POST OR THREAD.
BUT THE TRAIL'S GONE COLD AND I DON'T KNOW WHAT ELSE TO DO.

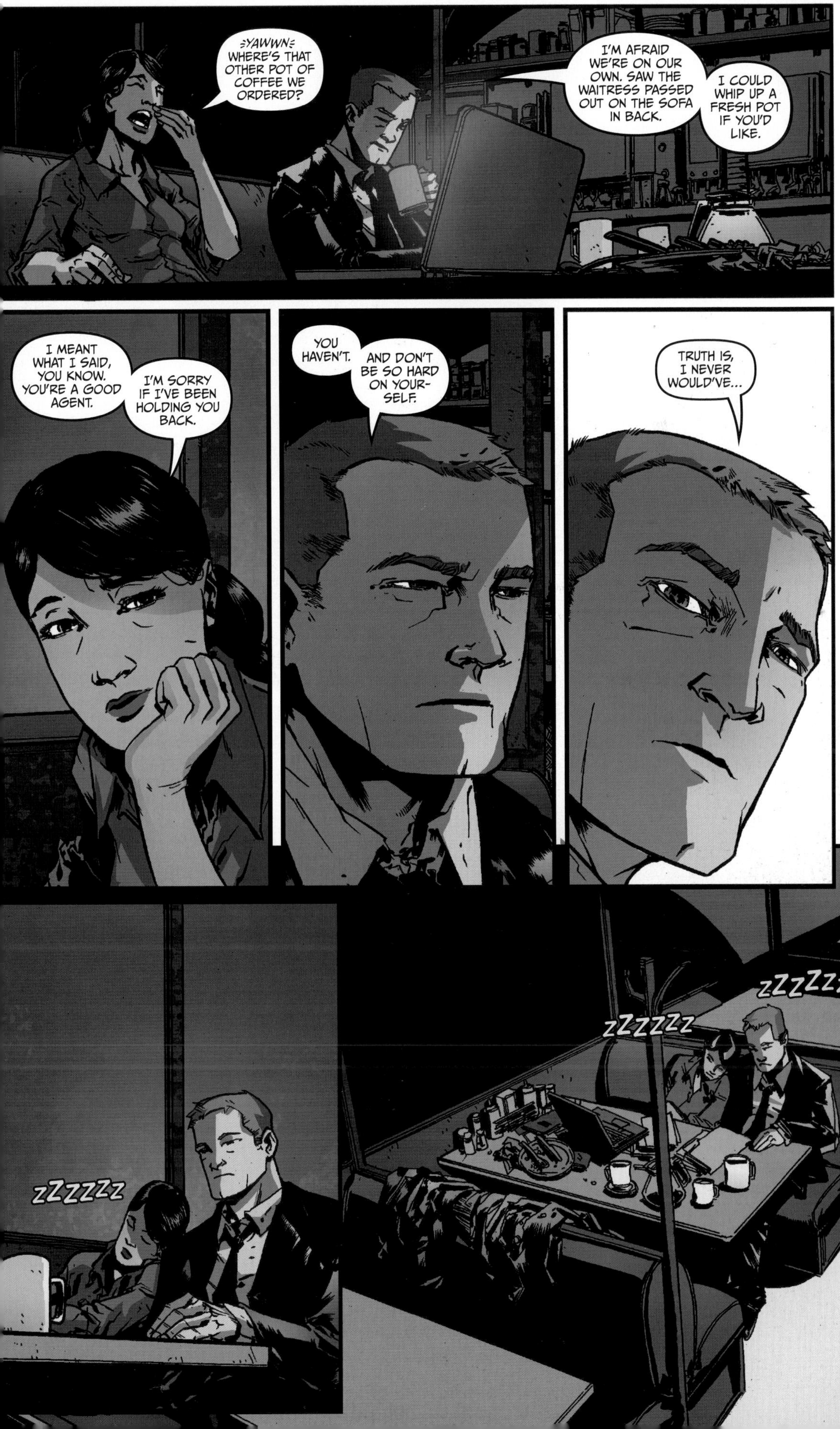

=YAWWN= WHERE'S THAT OTHER POT OF COFFEE WE ORDERED?
I'M AFRAID WE'RE ON OUR OWN. SAW THE WAITRESS PASSED OUT ON THE SOFA IN BACK.
I COULD WHIP UP A FRESH POT IF YOU'D LIKE.
I MEANT WHAT I SAID, YOU KNOW. YOU'RE A GOOD AGENT.
I'M SORRY IF I'VE BEEN HOLDING YOU BACK.
YOU HAVEN'T.
AND DON'T BE SO HARD ON YOUR-SELF.
TRUTH IS, I NEVER WOULD'VE...
zZZZZz
zZZZZZ
zZZZZz

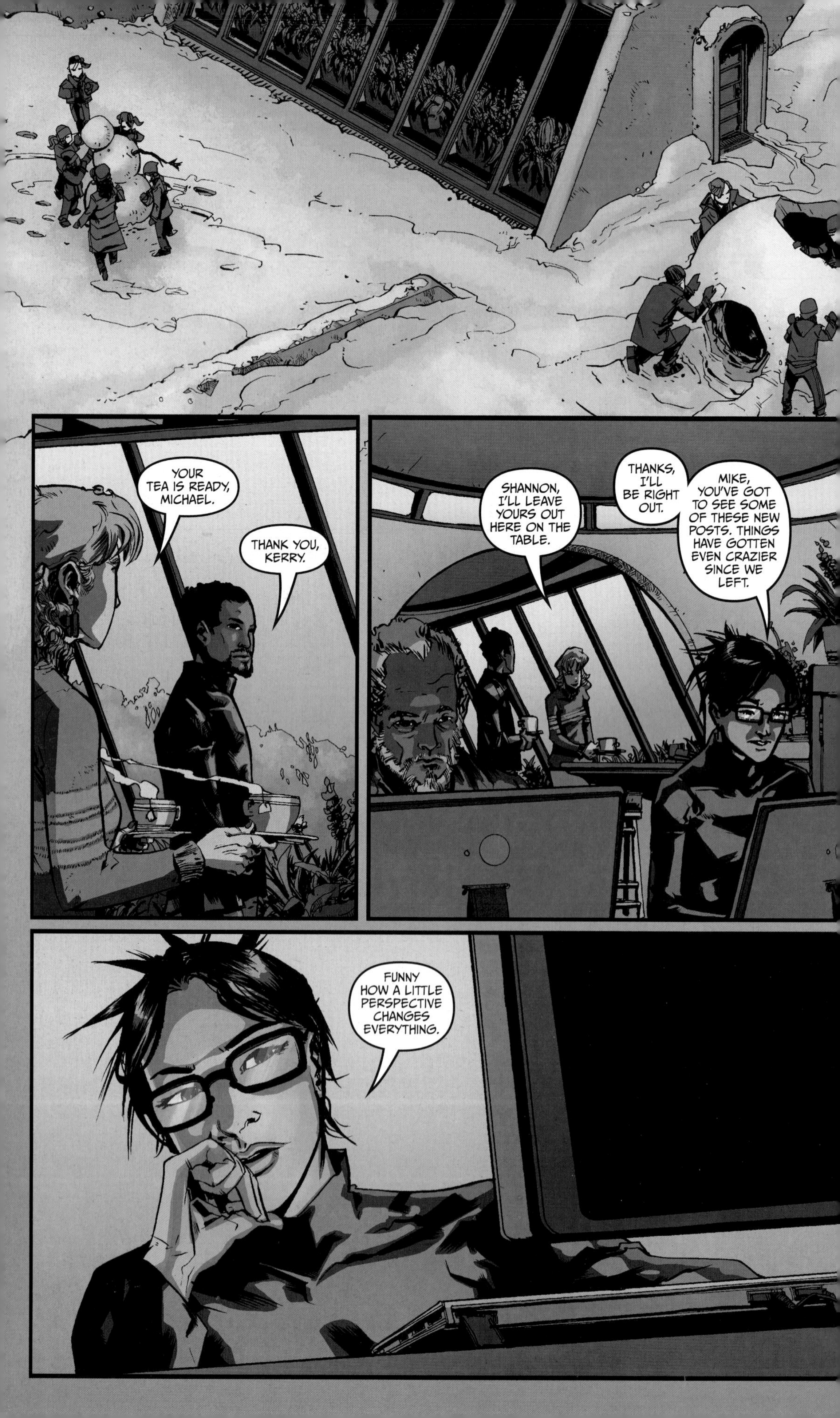
YOUR TEA IS READY, MICHAEL.
THANK YOU, KERRY.
SHANNON, I'LL LEAVE YOURS OUT HERE ON THE TABLE.
THANKS, I'LL BE RIGHT OUT.
MIKE, YOU'VE GOT TO SEE SOME OF THESE NEW POSTS. THINGS HAVE GOTTEN EVEN CRAZIER SINCE WE LEFT.
FUNNY HOW A LITTLE PERSPECTIVE CHANGES EVERYTHING.

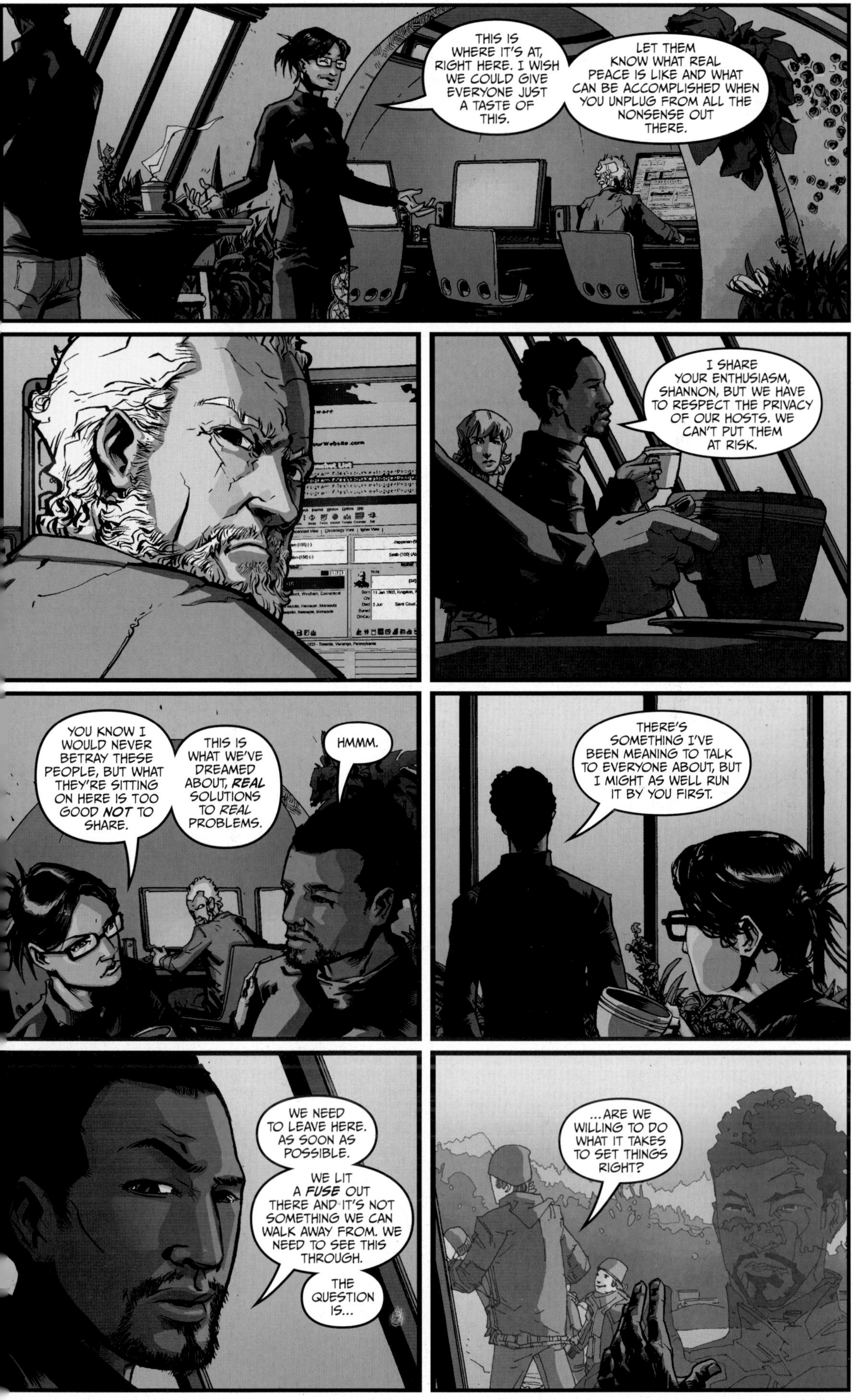
THIS IS WHERE IT'S AT, RIGHT HERE. I WISH WE COULD GIVE EVERYONE JUST A TASTE OF THIS.
LET THEM KNOW WHAT REAL PEACE IS LIKE AND WHAT CAN BE ACCOMPLISHED WHEN YOU UNPLUG FROM ALL THE NONSENSE OUT THERE.
I SHARE YOUR ENTHUSIASM, SHANNON, BUT WE HAVE TO RESPECT THE PRIVACY OF OUR HOSTS. WE CAN'T PUT THEM AT RISK.
YOU KNOW I WOULD NEVER BETRAY THESE PEOPLE, BUT WHAT THEY'RE SITTING ON HERE IS TOO GOOD **NOT** TO SHARE.
THIS IS WHAT WE'VE DREAMED ABOUT, ***REAL*** SOLUTIONS TO *REAL* PROBLEMS.
HMMM.
THERE'S SOMETHING I'VE BEEN MEANING TO TALK TO EVERYONE ABOUT, BUT I MIGHT AS WELL RUN IT BY YOU FIRST.
WE NEED TO LEAVE HERE. AS SOON AS POSSIBLE.
WE LIT A ***FUSE*** OUT THERE AND IT'S NOT SOMETHING WE CAN WALK AWAY FROM. WE NEED TO SEE THIS THROUGH.
THE QUESTION IS...
...ARE WE WILLING TO DO WHAT IT TAKES TO SET THINGS RIGHT?

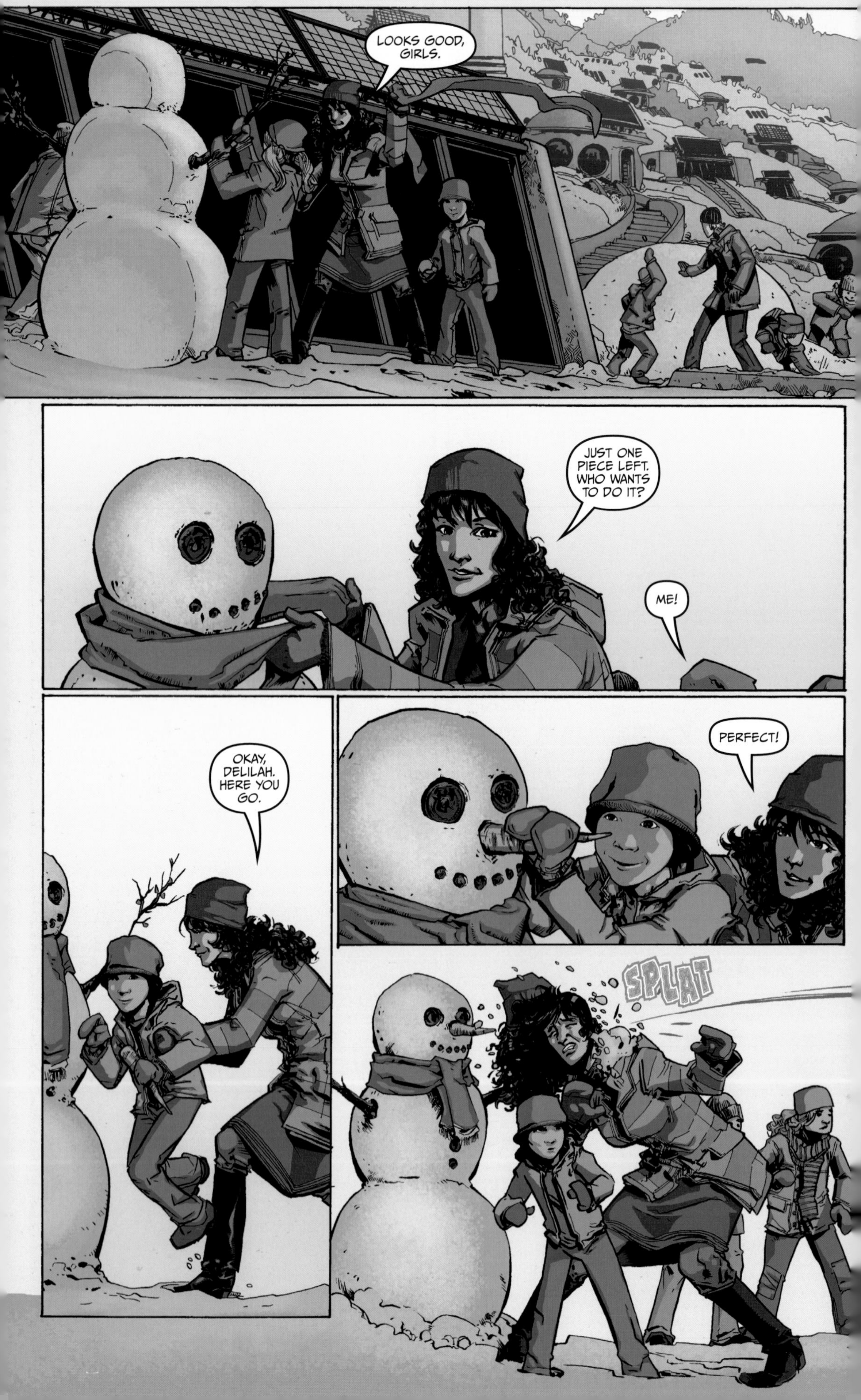
LOOKS GOOD, GIRLS.
JUST ONE PIECE LEFT. WHO WANTS TO DO IT?
ME!
OKAY, DELILAH. HERE YOU GO.
PERFECT!
SPLAT

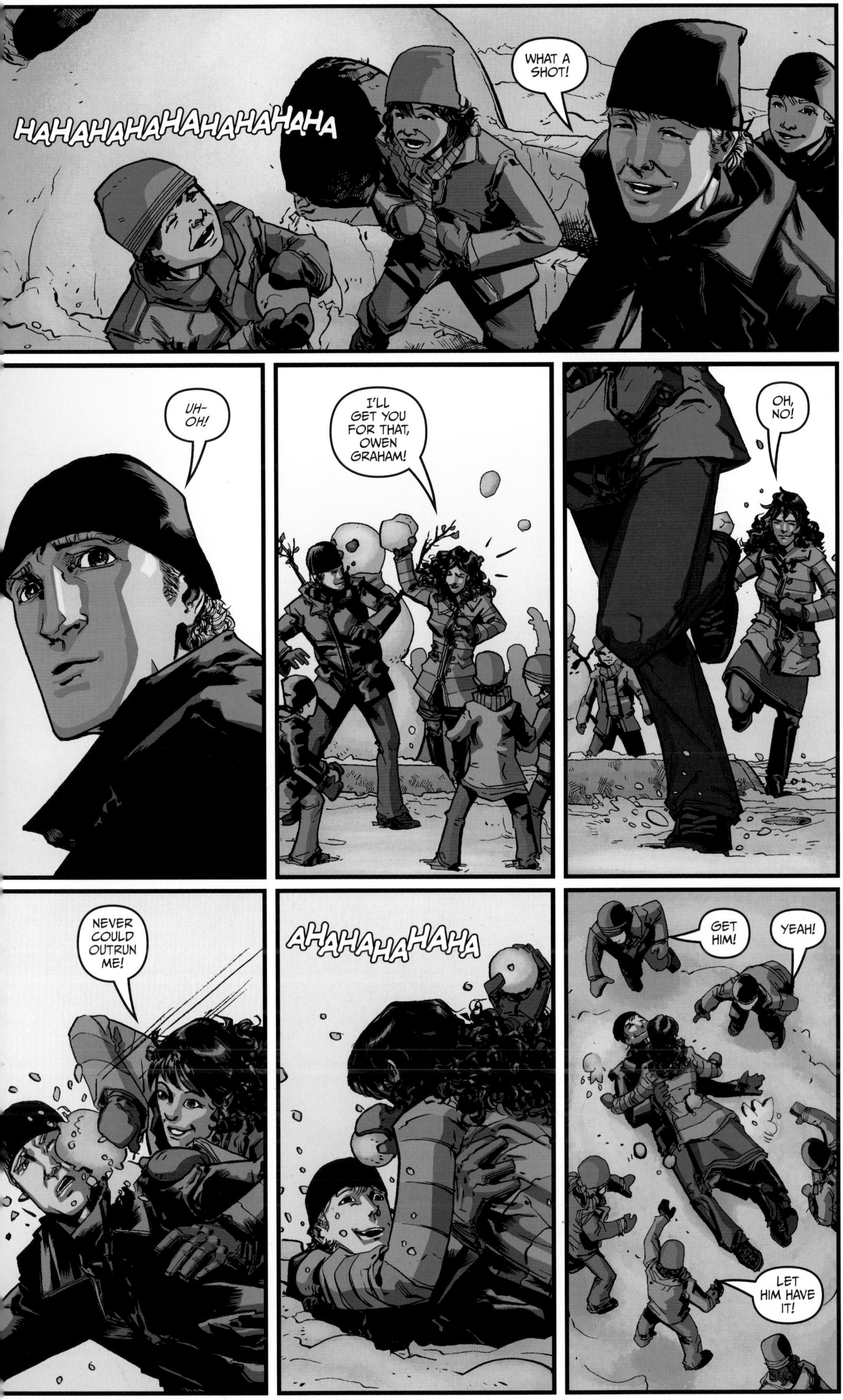
HAHAHAHAHAHAHAHAHAHA
WHAT A SHOT!
UH-OH!
I'LL GET YOU FOR THAT, OWEN GRAHAM!
OH, NO!
NEVER COULD OUTRUN ME!
AHAHAHAHAHAHA
GET HIM!
YEAH!
LET HIM HAVE IT!

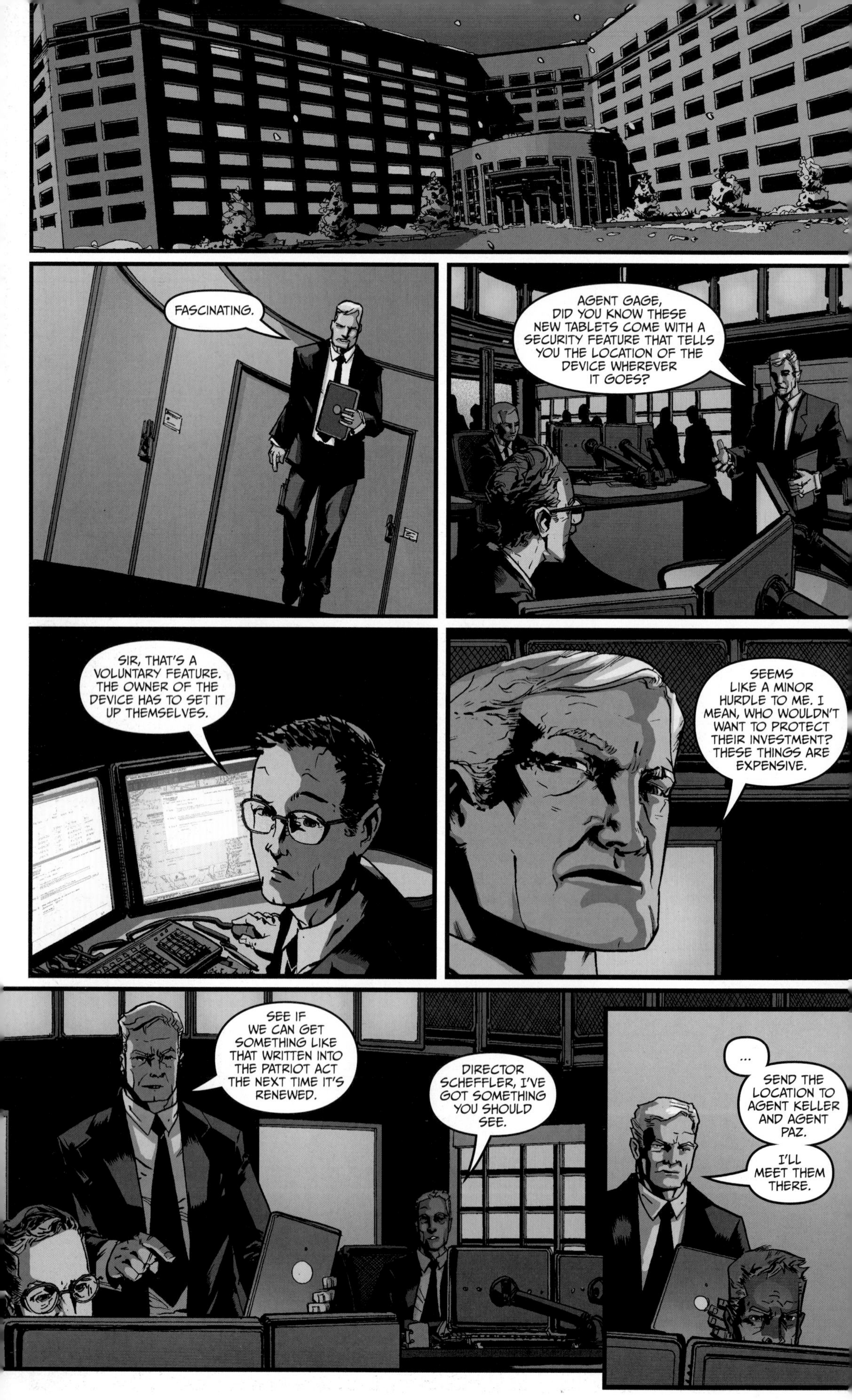
FASCINATING.
AGENT GAGE, DID YOU KNOW THESE NEW TABLETS COME WITH A SECURITY FEATURE THAT TELLS YOU THE LOCATION OF THE DEVICE WHEREVER IT GOES?
SIR, THAT'S A VOLUNTARY FEATURE. THE OWNER OF THE DEVICE HAS TO SET IT UP THEMSELVES.
SEEMS LIKE A MINOR HURDLE TO ME. I MEAN, WHO WOULDN'T WANT TO PROTECT THEIR INVESTMENT? THESE THINGS ARE EXPENSIVE.
SEE IF WE CAN GET SOMETHING LIKE THAT WRITTEN INTO THE PATRIOT ACT THE NEXT TIME IT'S RENEWED.
DIRECTOR SCHEFFLER, I'VE GOT SOMETHING YOU SHOULD SEE.
...
SEND THE LOCATION TO AGENT KELLER AND AGENT PAZ.
I'LL MEET THEM THERE.

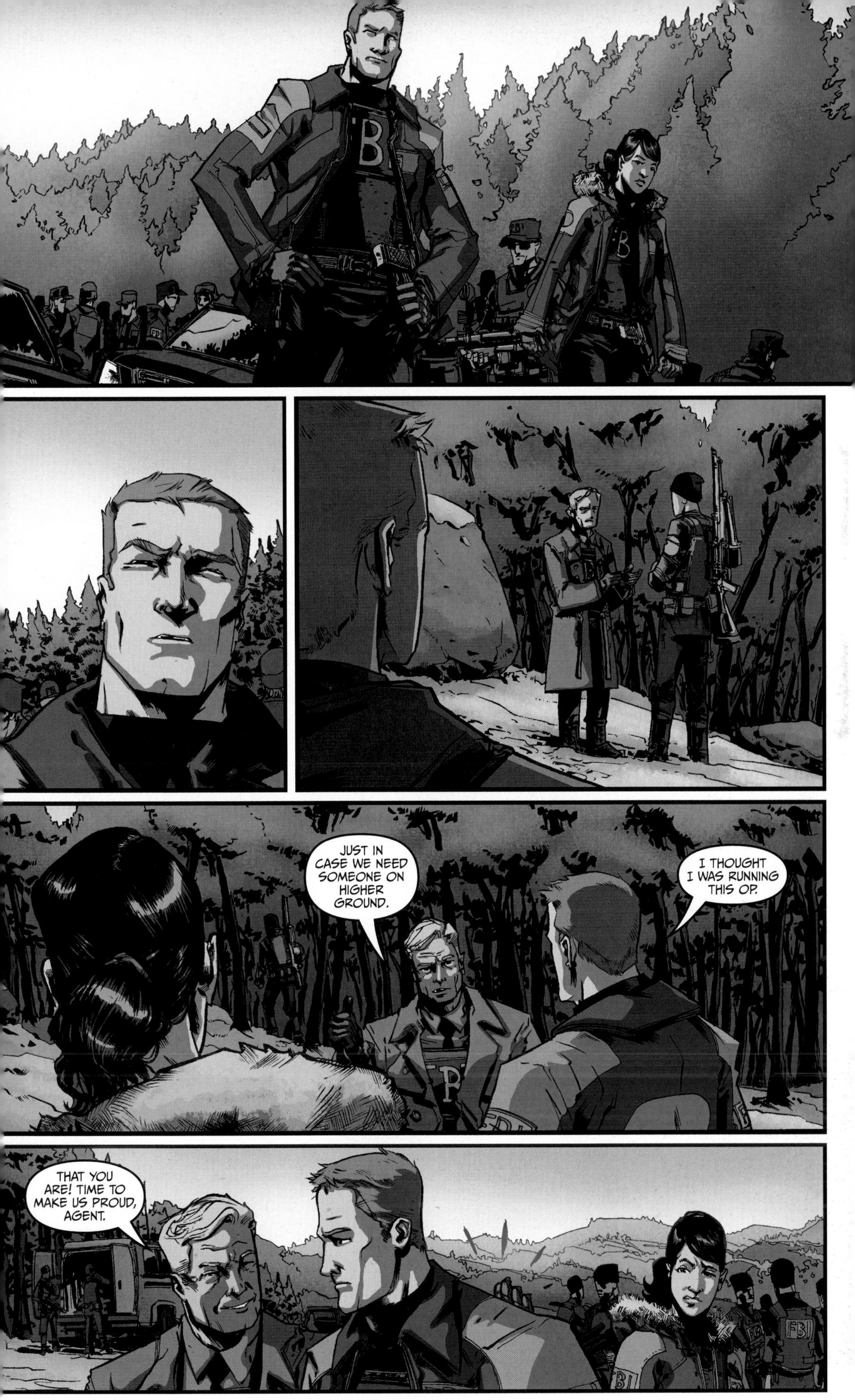
JUST IN CASE WE NEED SOMEONE ON HIGHER GROUND.
I THOUGHT I WAS RUNNING THIS OP.
THAT YOU ARE! TIME TO MAKE US PROUD, AGENT.

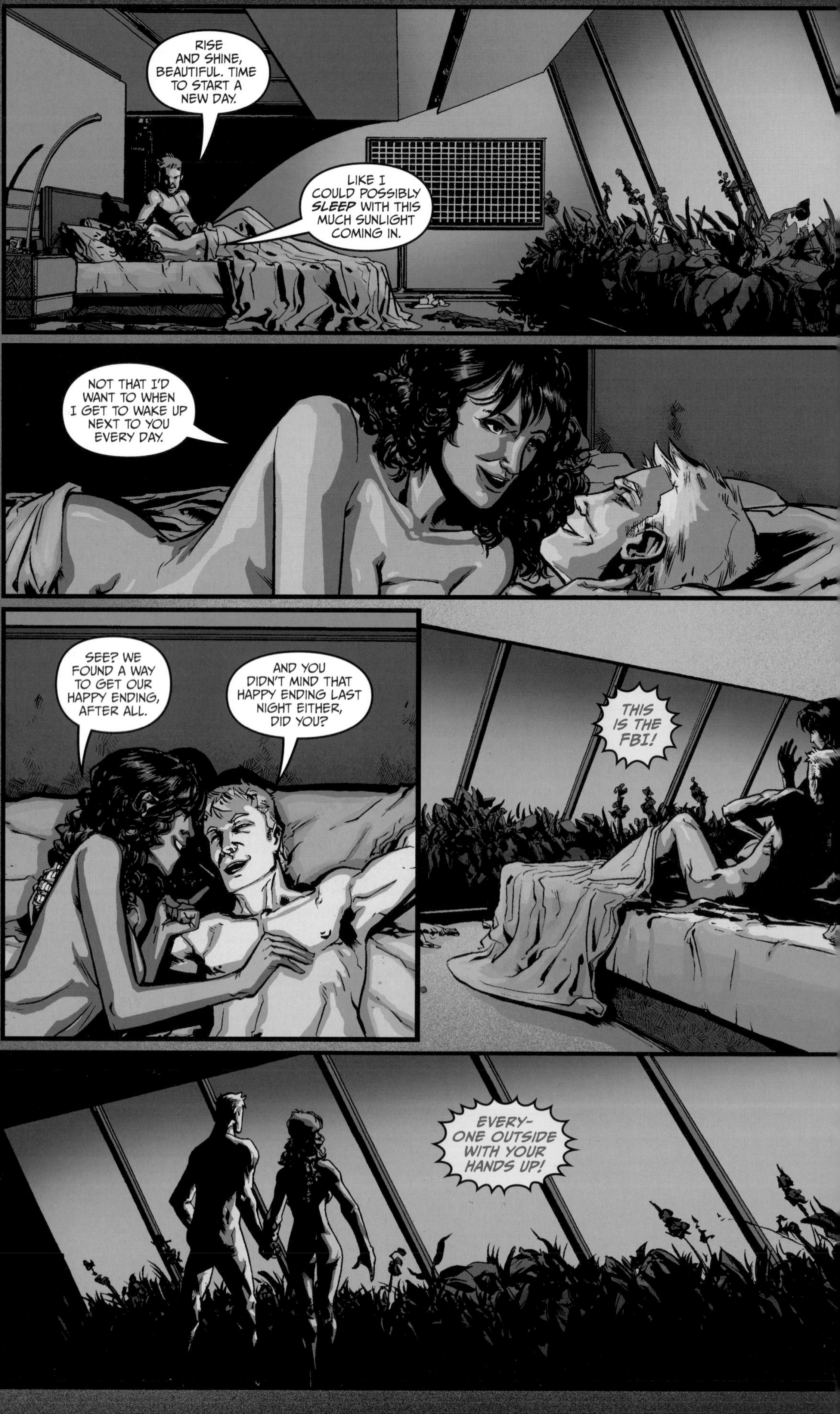
RISE AND SHINE, BEAUTIFUL. TIME TO START A NEW DAY.
LIKE I COULD POSSIBLY SLEEP WITH THIS MUCH SUNLIGHT COMING IN.
NOT THAT I'D WANT TO WHEN I GET TO WAKE UP NEXT TO YOU EVERY DAY.
SEE? WE FOUND A WAY TO GET OUR HAPPY ENDING, AFTER ALL.
AND YOU DIDN'T MIND THAT HAPPY ENDING LAST NIGHT EITHER, DID YOU?
THIS IS THE FBI!
EVERY-ONE OUTSIDE WITH YOUR HANDS UP!

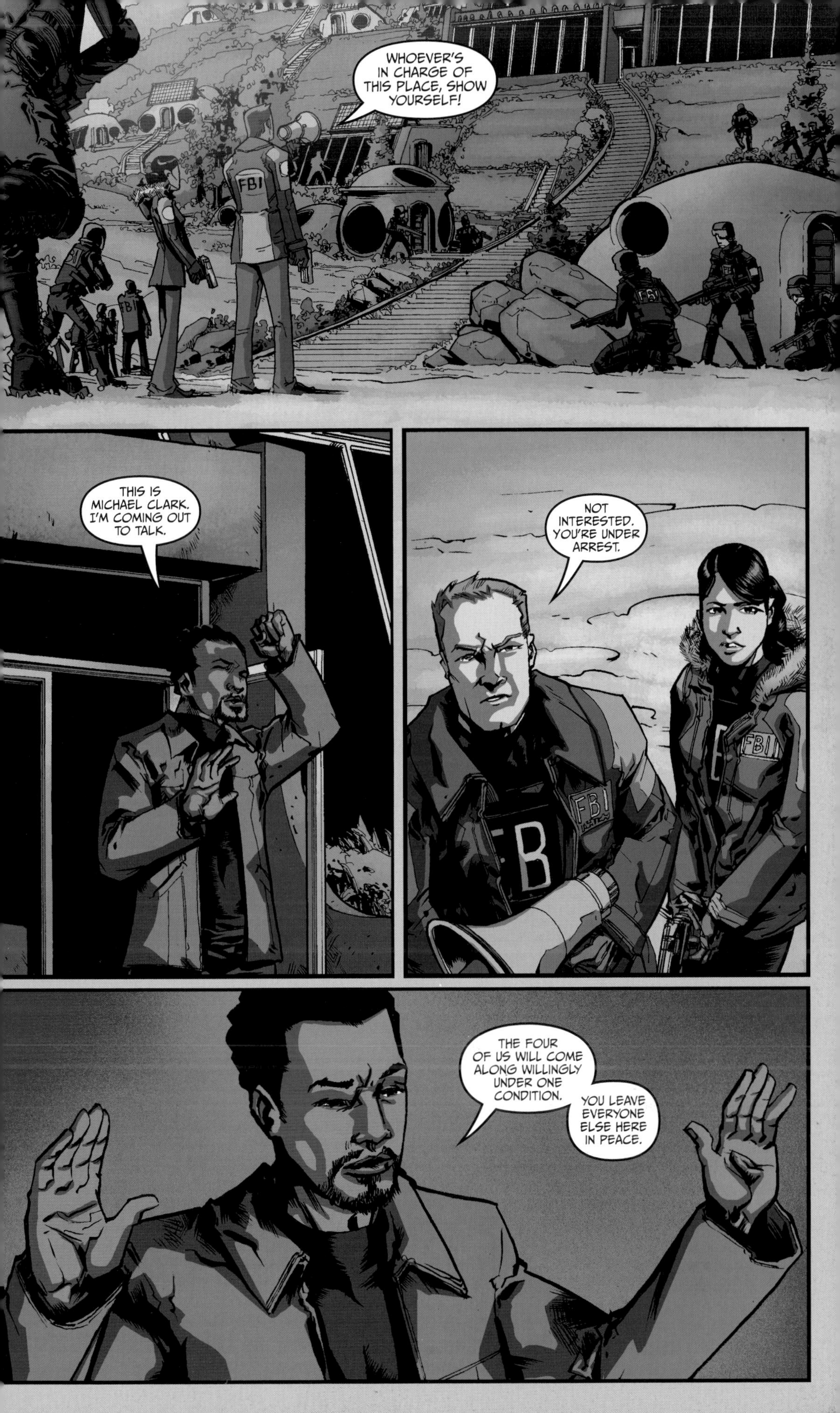
WHOEVER'S IN CHARGE OF THIS PLACE, SHOW YOURSELF!
FBI
THIS IS MICHAEL CLARK. I'M COMING OUT TO TALK.
NOT INTERESTED. YOU'RE UNDER ARREST.
THE FOUR OF US WILL COME ALONG WILLINGLY UNDER ONE CONDITION.
YOU LEAVE EVERYONE ELSE HERE IN PEACE.

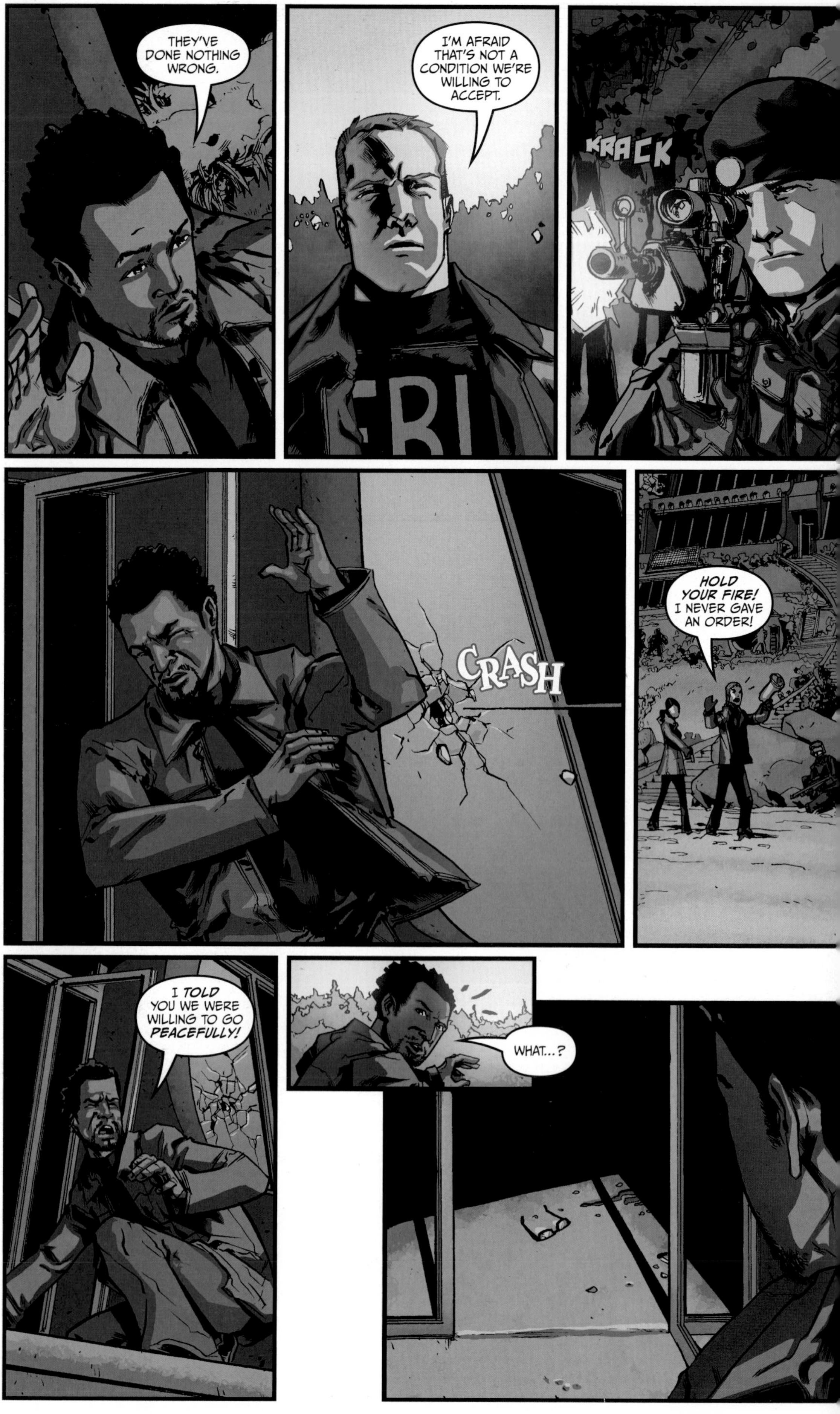
THEY'VE DONE NOTHING WRONG.
I'M AFRAID THAT'S NOT A CONDITION WE'RE WILLING TO ACCEPT.
FBI
KRACK
CRASH
HOLD YOUR FIRE! I NEVER GAVE AN ORDER!
I TOLD YOU WE WERE WILLING TO GO PEACEFULLY!
WHAT...?

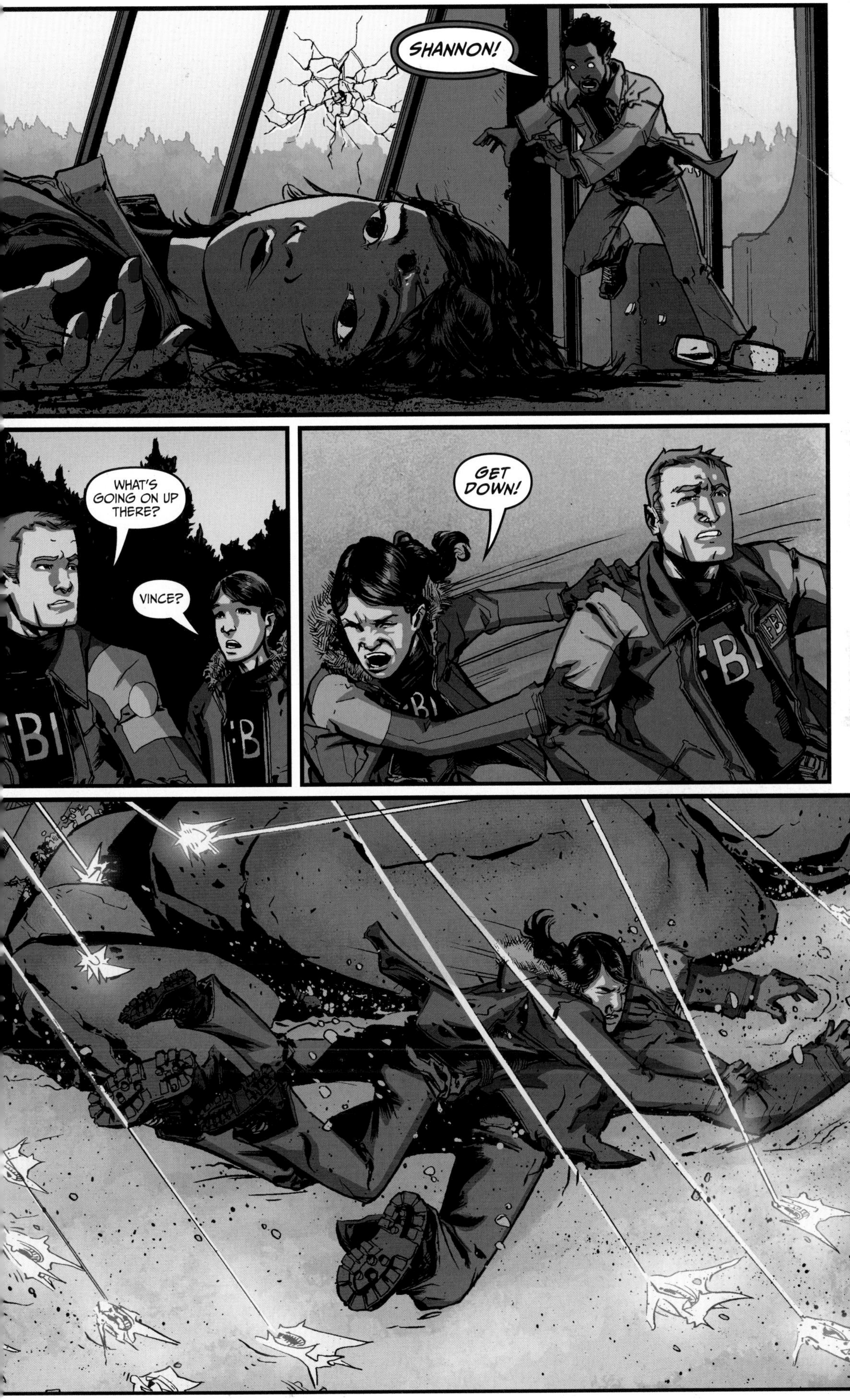
SHANNON!
WHAT'S GOING ON UP THERE?
VINCE?
GET DOWN!

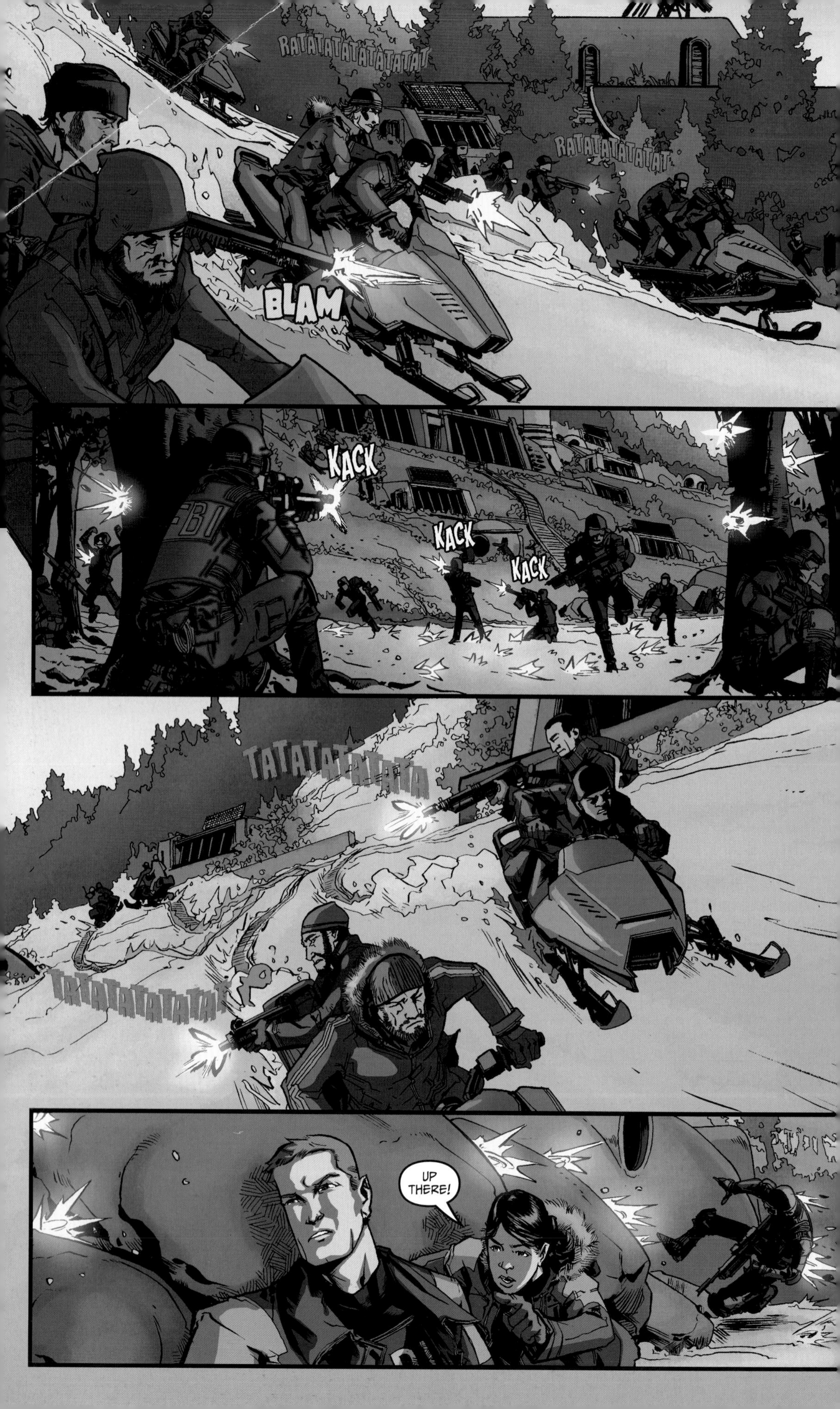
RATATATATATATATAT
RATATATATATAT
BLAM
KACK
FBI
KACK
KACK
TATATATATATATA
TATATATATATAT
UP THERE!

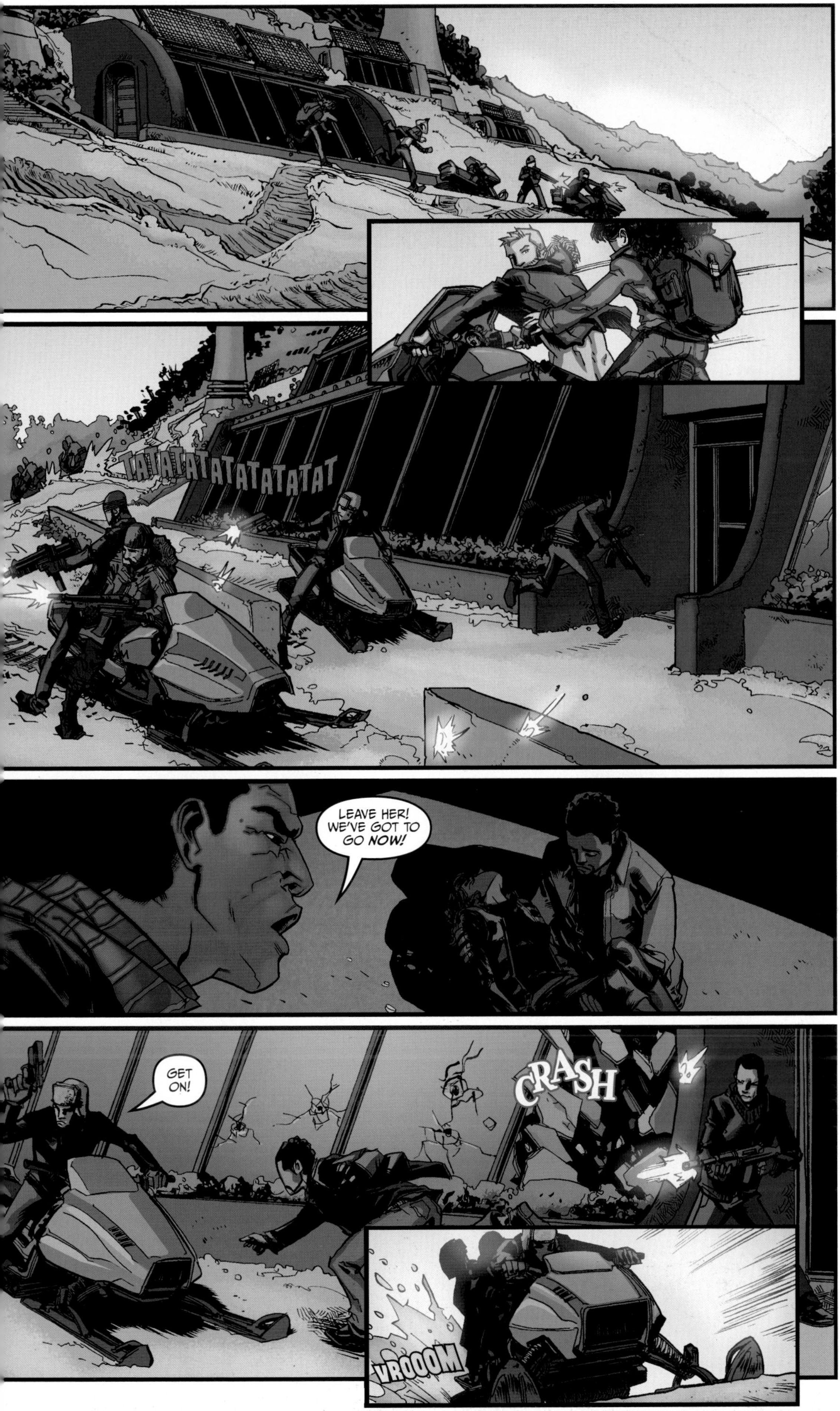
TATATATATATATATAT
LEAVE HER! WE'VE GOT TO GO NOW!
GET ON!
CRASH
VROOOM

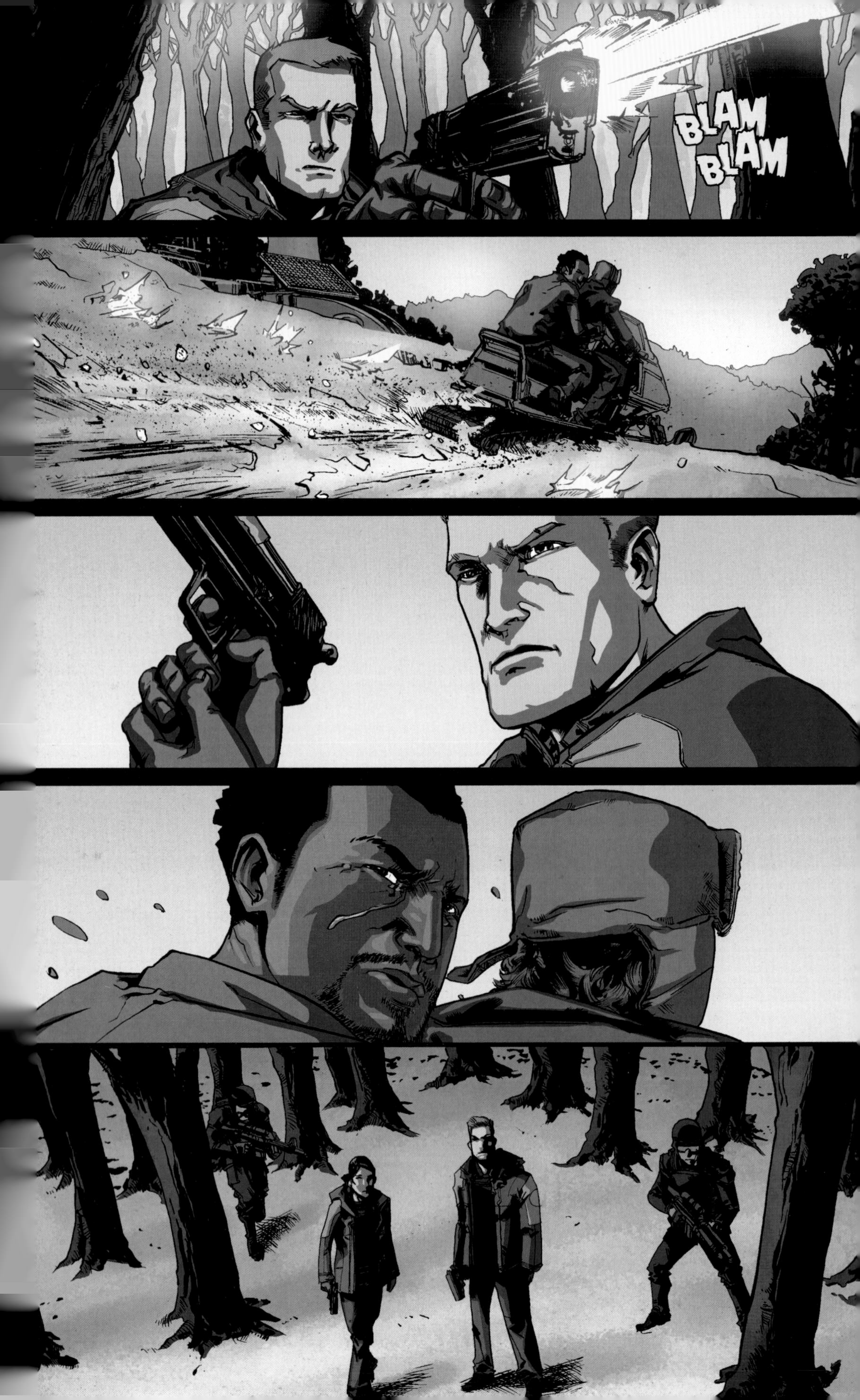
BLAM
BLAM

Chapter 4

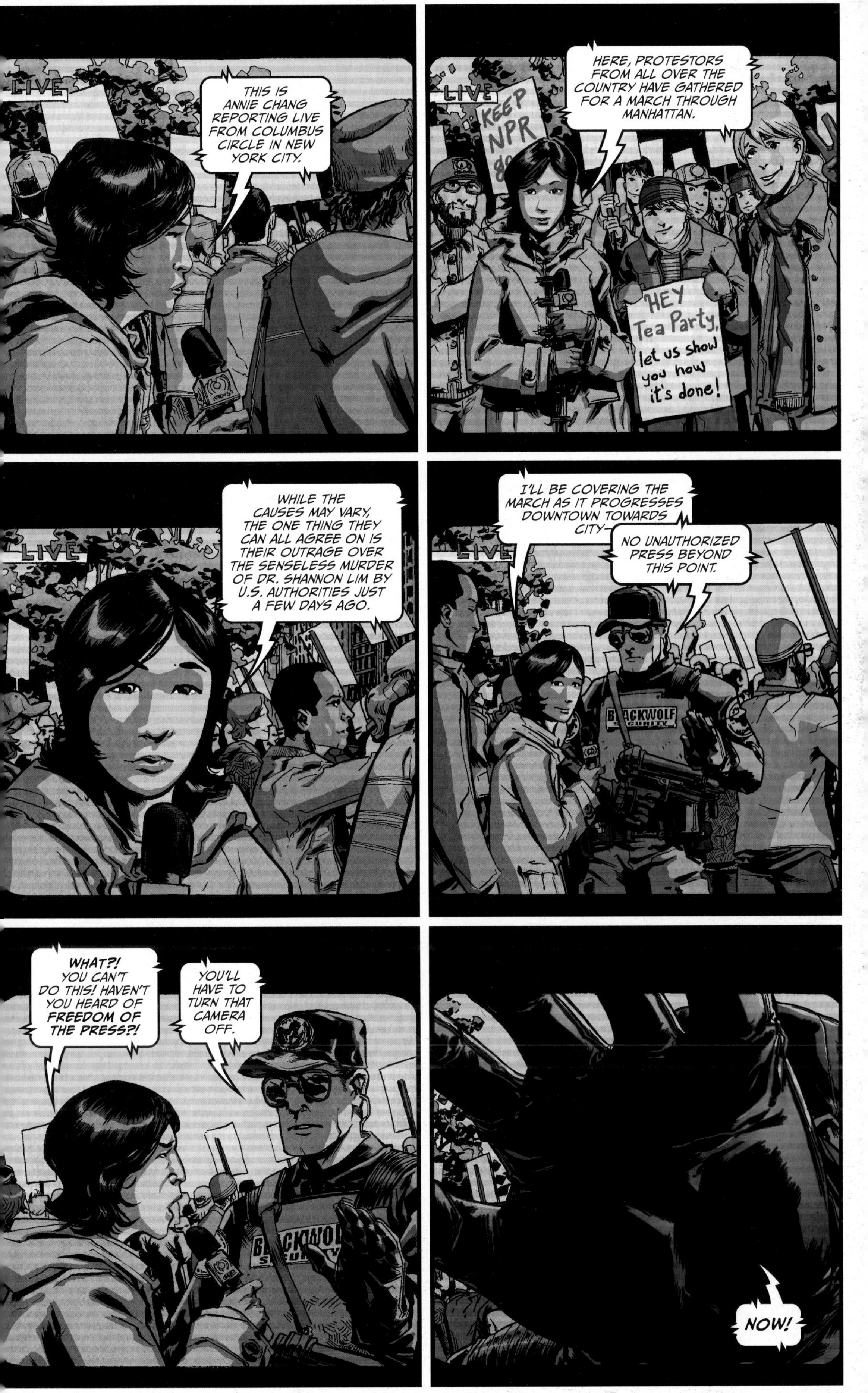

LIVE
THIS IS ANNIE CHANG REPORTING LIVE FROM COLUMBUS CIRCLE IN NEW YORK CITY.
LIVE
KEEP NPR
HERE, PROTESTORS FROM ALL OVER THE COUNTRY HAVE GATHERED FOR A MARCH THROUGH MANHATTAN.
HEY Tea Party, let us show you how it's done!
LIVE
WHILE THE CAUSES MAY VARY, THE ONE THING THEY CAN ALL AGREE ON IS THEIR OUTRAGE OVER THE SENSELESS MURDER OF DR. SHANNON LIM BY U.S. AUTHORITIES JUST A FEW DAYS AGO.
LIVE
I'LL BE COVERING THE MARCH AS IT PROGRESSES DOWNTOWN TOWARDS CITY—
NO UNAUTHORIZED PRESS BEYOND THIS POINT.
WHAT?! YOU CAN'T DO THIS! HAVEN'T YOU HEARD OF FREEDOM OF THE PRESS?!
YOU'LL HAVE TO TURN THAT CAMERA OFF.
NOW!

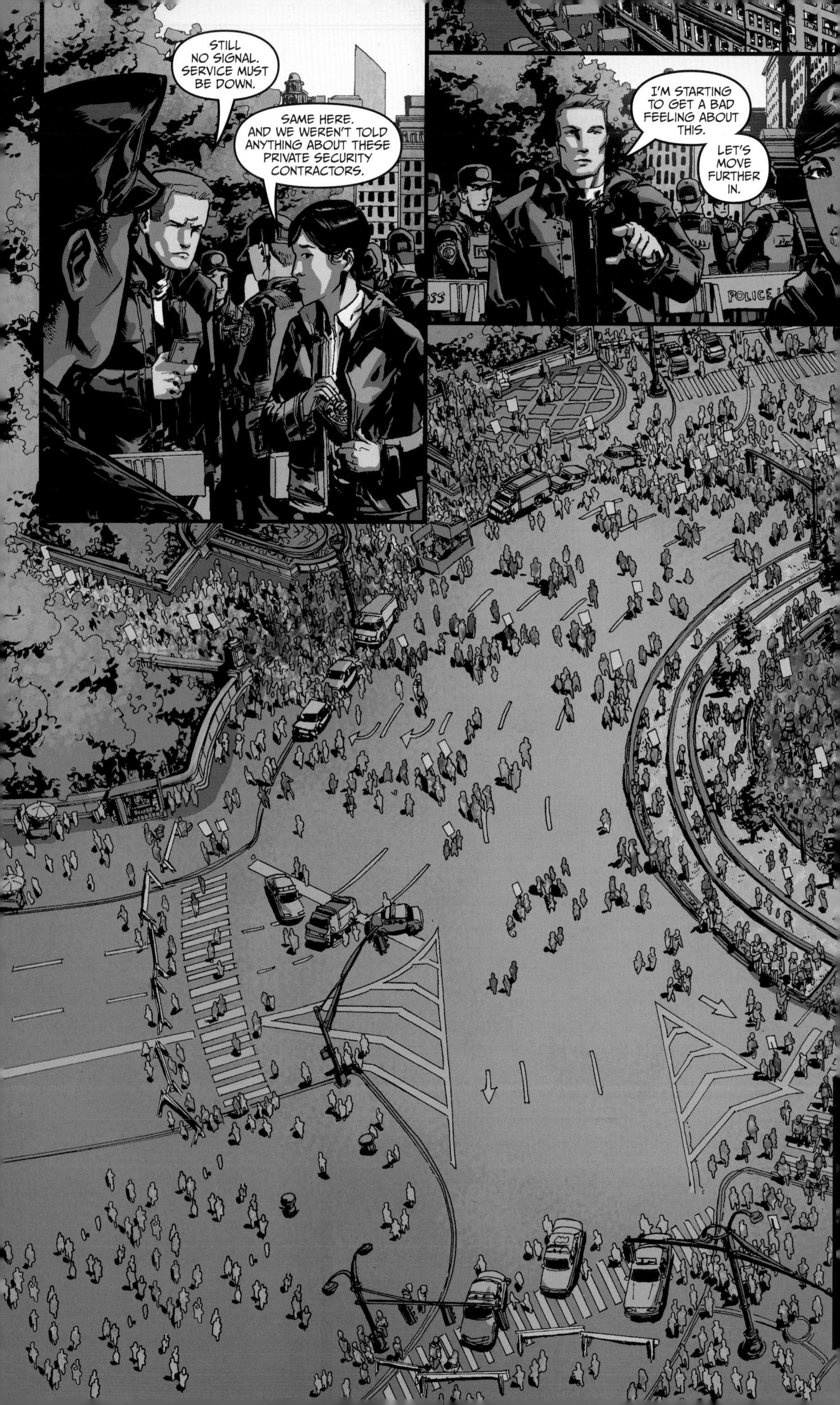
STILL NO SIGNAL. SERVICE MUST BE DOWN.
SAME HERE. AND WE WEREN'T TOLD ANYTHING ABOUT THESE PRIVATE SECURITY CONTRACTORS.
I'M STARTING TO GET A BAD FEELING ABOUT THIS.
LET'S MOVE FURTHER IN.
POLICE

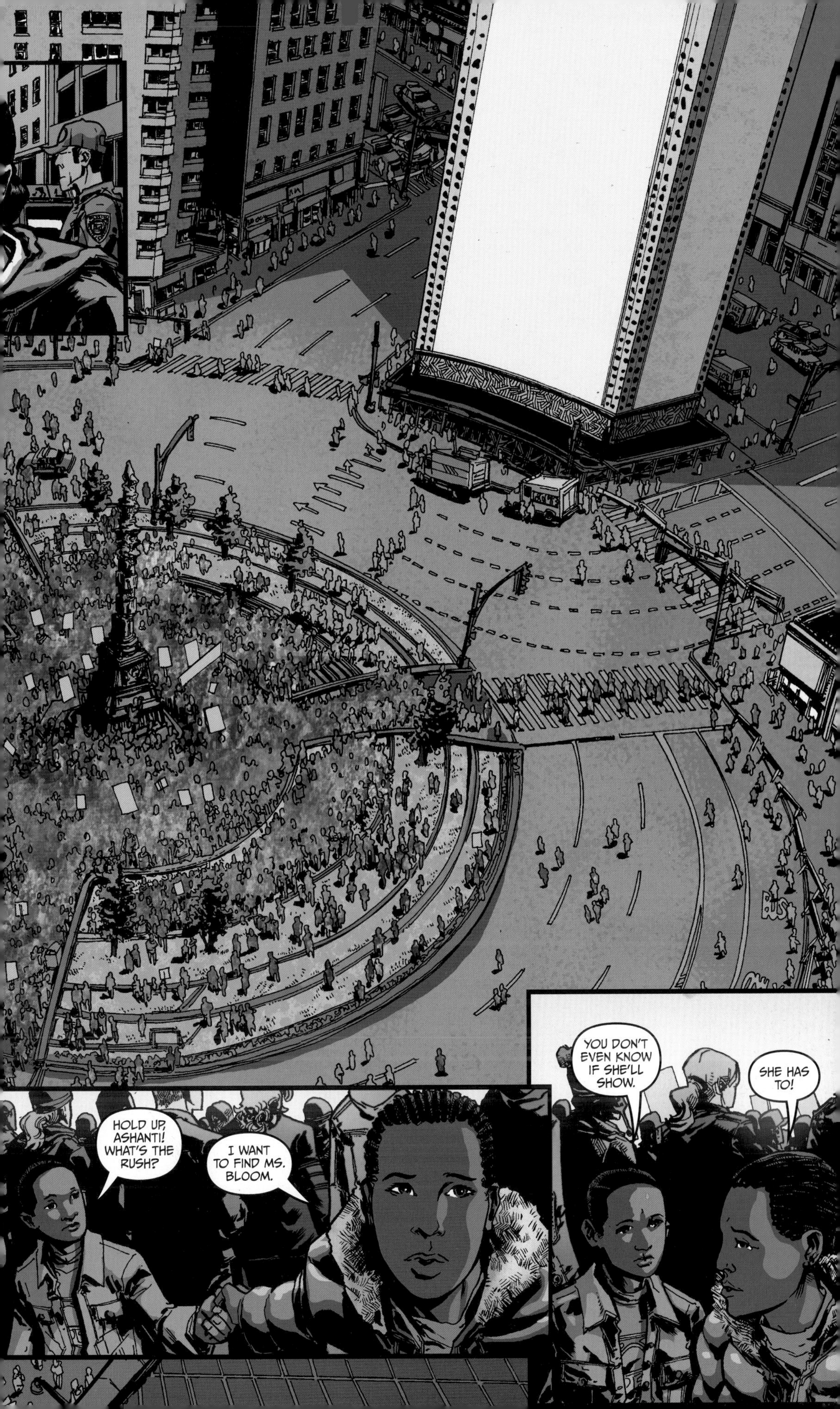

HOLD UP, ASHANTI! WHAT'S THE RUSH?
I WANT TO FIND MS. BLOOM.
YOU DON'T EVEN KNOW IF SHE'LL SHOW.
SHE HAS TO!

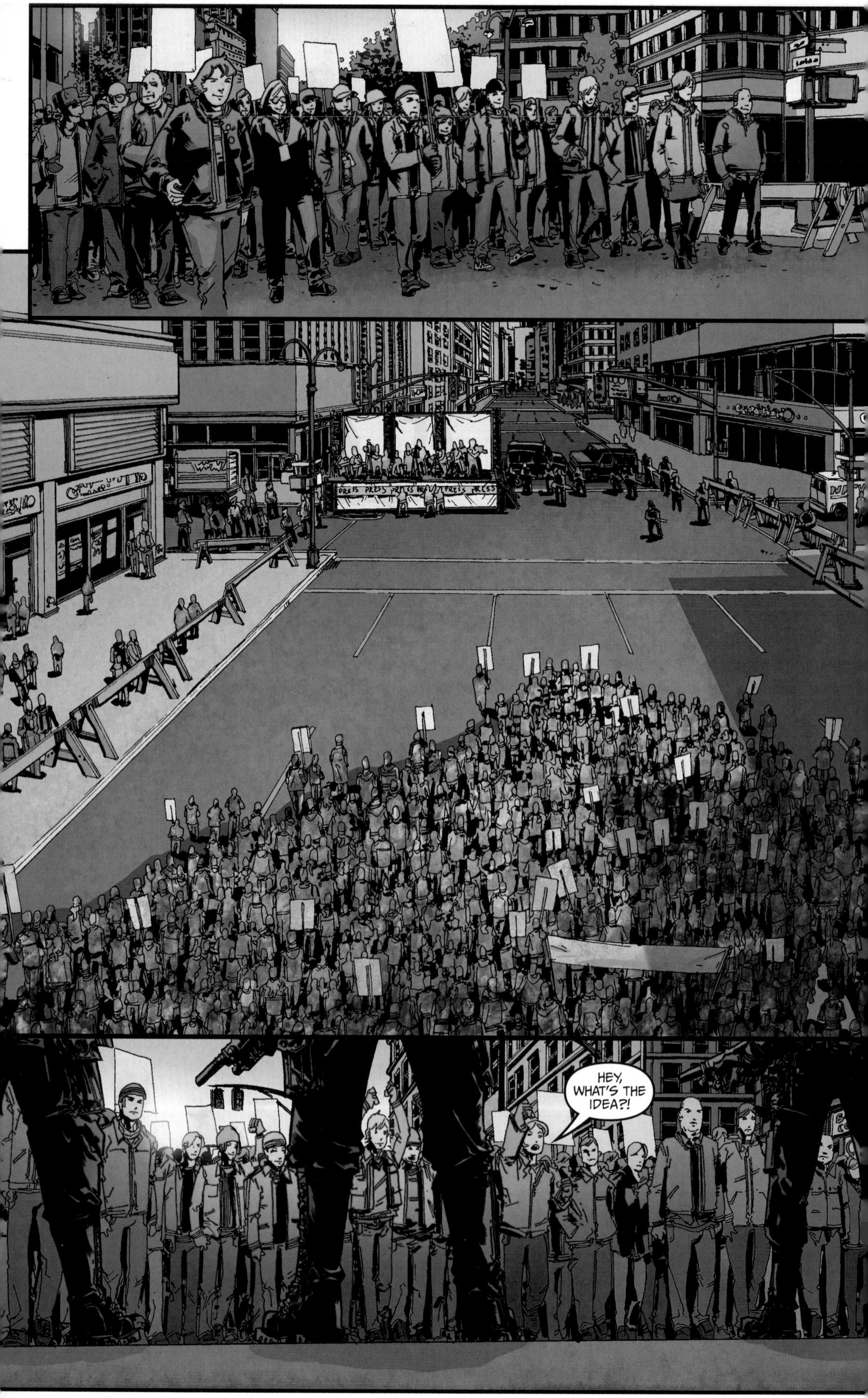

PRESS PRESS PRESS PRESS PRESS PRESS
HEY, WHAT'S THE IDEA?!

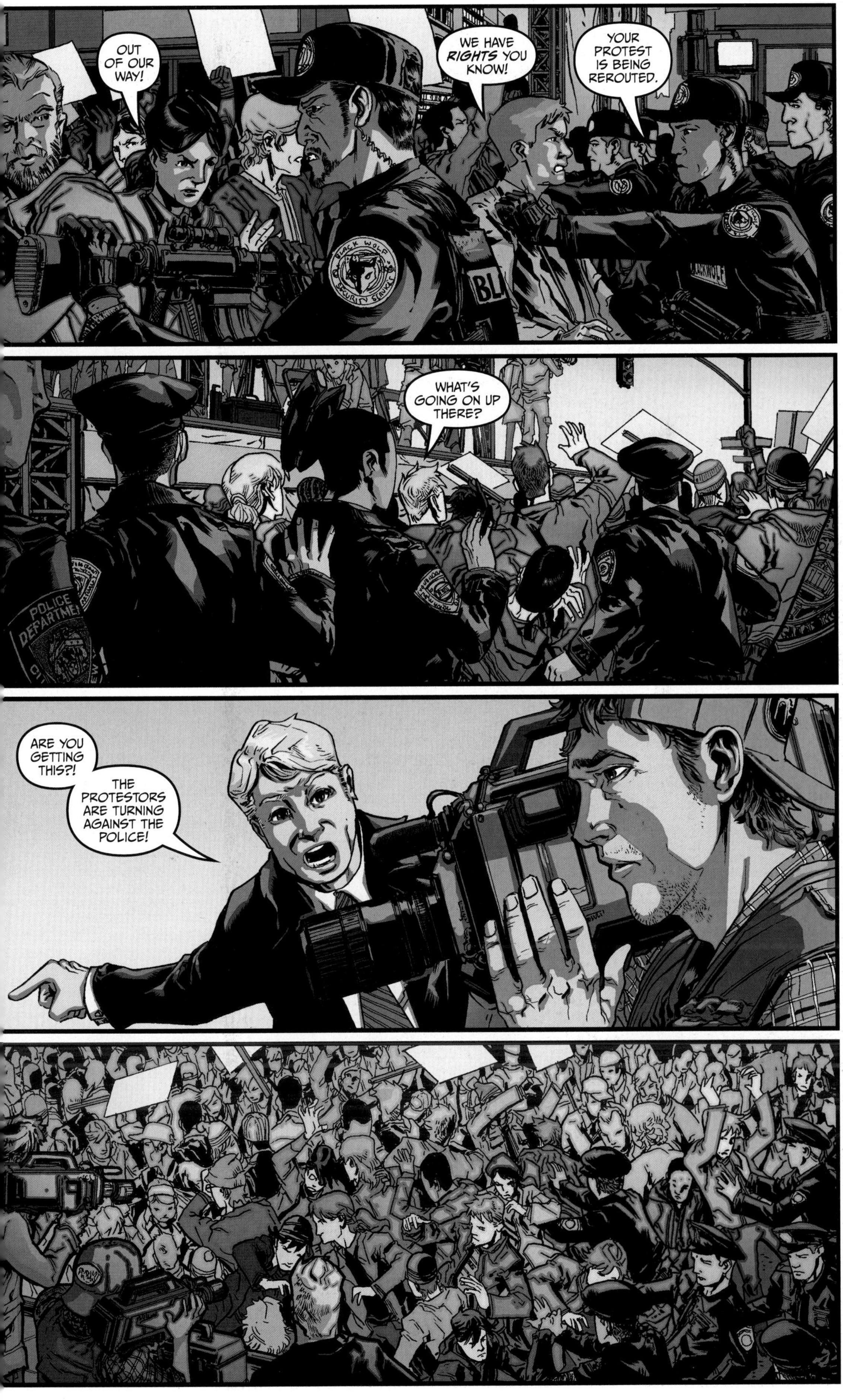
OUT OF OUR WAY!
WE HAVE RIGHTS YOU KNOW!
YOUR PROTEST IS BEING REROUTED.
WHAT'S GOING ON UP THERE?
ARE YOU GETTING THIS?!
THE PROTESTORS ARE TURNING AGAINST THE POLICE!

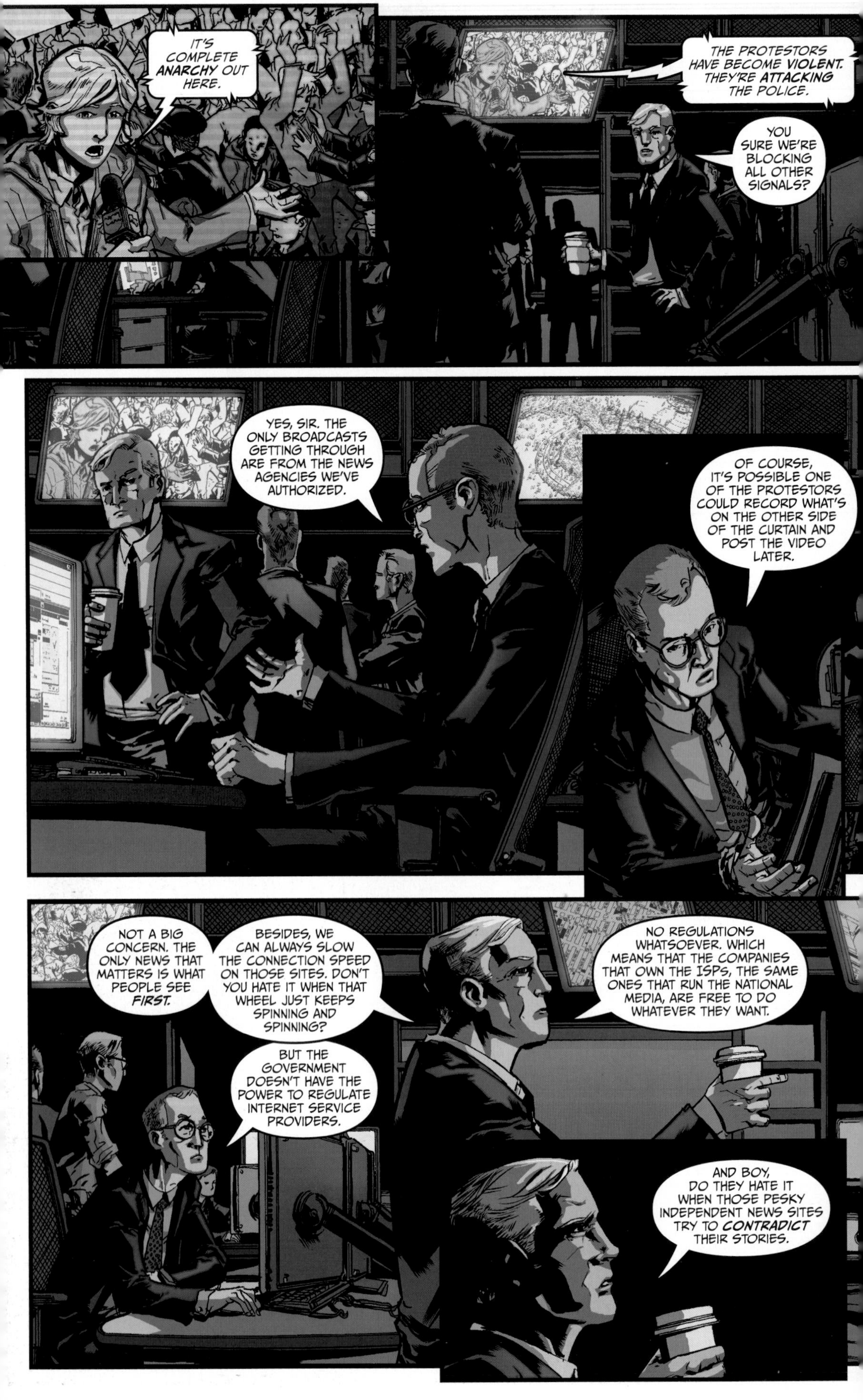

IT'S COMPLETE ANARCHY OUT HERE.
THE PROTESTORS HAVE BECOME VIOLENT. THEY'RE ATTACKING THE POLICE.
YOU SURE WE'RE BLOCKING ALL OTHER SIGNALS?
YES, SIR. THE ONLY BROADCASTS GETTING THROUGH ARE FROM THE NEWS AGENCIES WE'VE AUTHORIZED.
OF COURSE, IT'S POSSIBLE ONE OF THE PROTESTORS COULD RECORD WHAT'S ON THE OTHER SIDE OF THE CURTAIN AND POST THE VIDEO LATER.
NOT A BIG CONCERN. THE ONLY NEWS THAT MATTERS IS WHAT PEOPLE SEE FIRST.
BESIDES, WE CAN ALWAYS SLOW THE CONNECTION SPEED ON THOSE SITES. DON'T YOU HATE IT WHEN THAT WHEEL JUST KEEPS SPINNING AND SPINNING?
BUT THE GOVERNMENT DOESN'T HAVE THE POWER TO REGULATE INTERNET SERVICE PROVIDERS.
NO REGULATIONS WHATSOEVER. WHICH MEANS THAT THE COMPANIES THAT OWN THE ISPS, THE SAME ONES THAT RUN THE NATIONAL MEDIA, ARE FREE TO DO WHATEVER THEY WANT.
AND BOY, DO THEY HATE IT WHEN THOSE PESKY INDEPENDENT NEWS SITES TRY TO CONTRADICT THEIR STORIES.

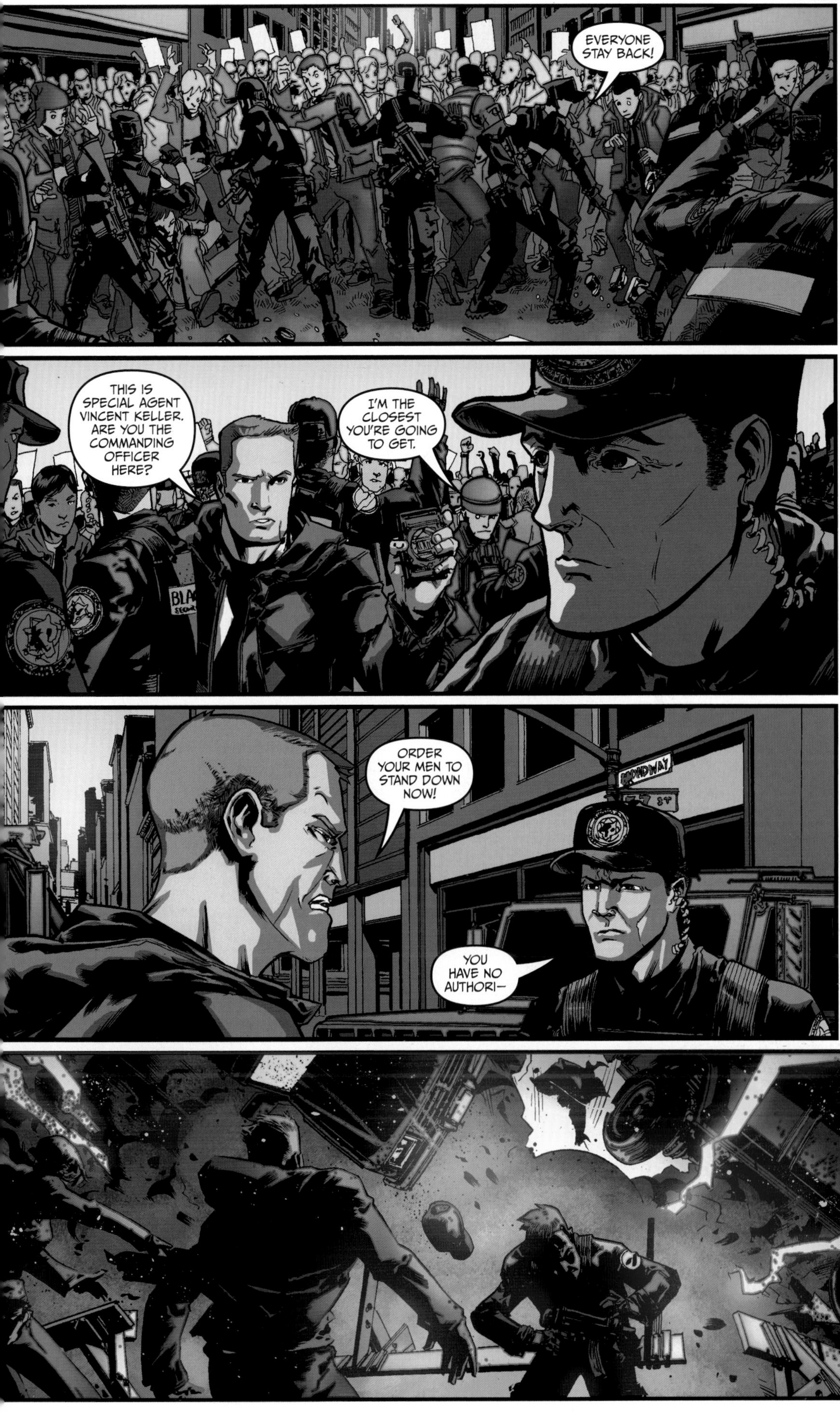
EVERYONE STAY BACK!
THIS IS SPECIAL AGENT VINCENT KELLER. ARE YOU THE COMMANDING OFFICER HERE?
I'M THE CLOSEST YOU'RE GOING TO GET.
ORDER YOUR MEN TO STAND DOWN NOW!
BROADWAY
YOU HAVE NO AUTHORI—

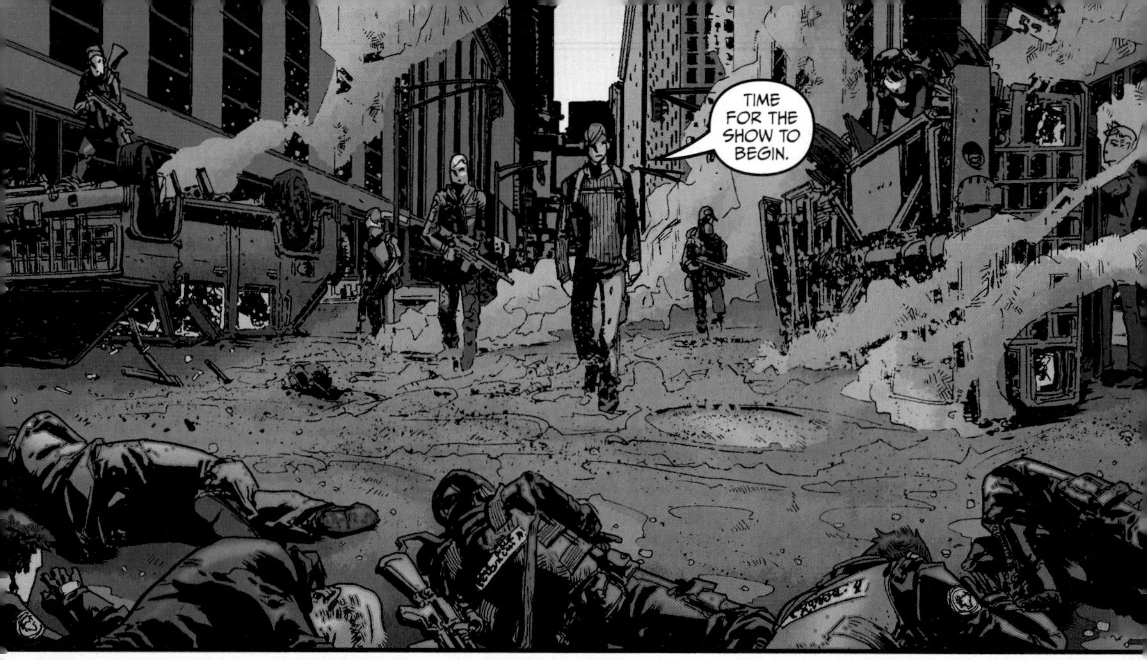
TIME FOR THE SHOW TO BEGIN.

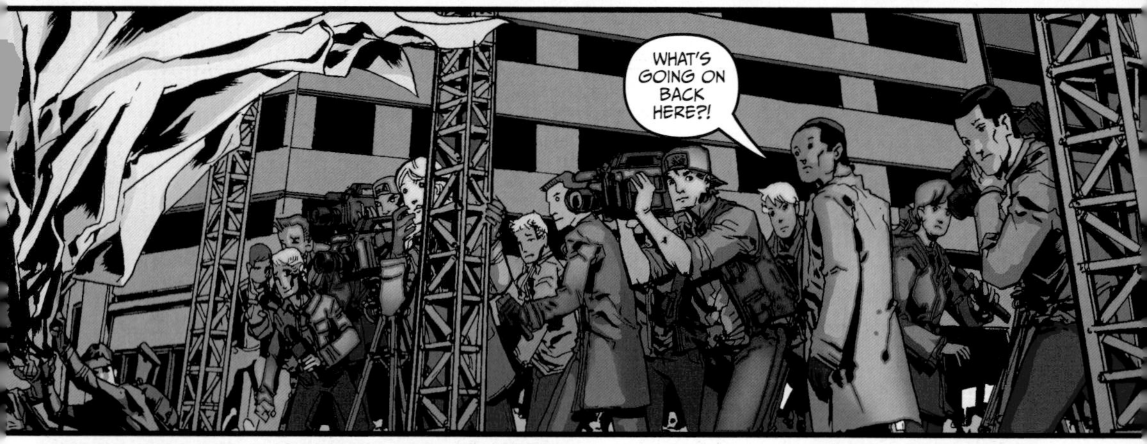
WHAT'S GOING ON BACK HERE?!

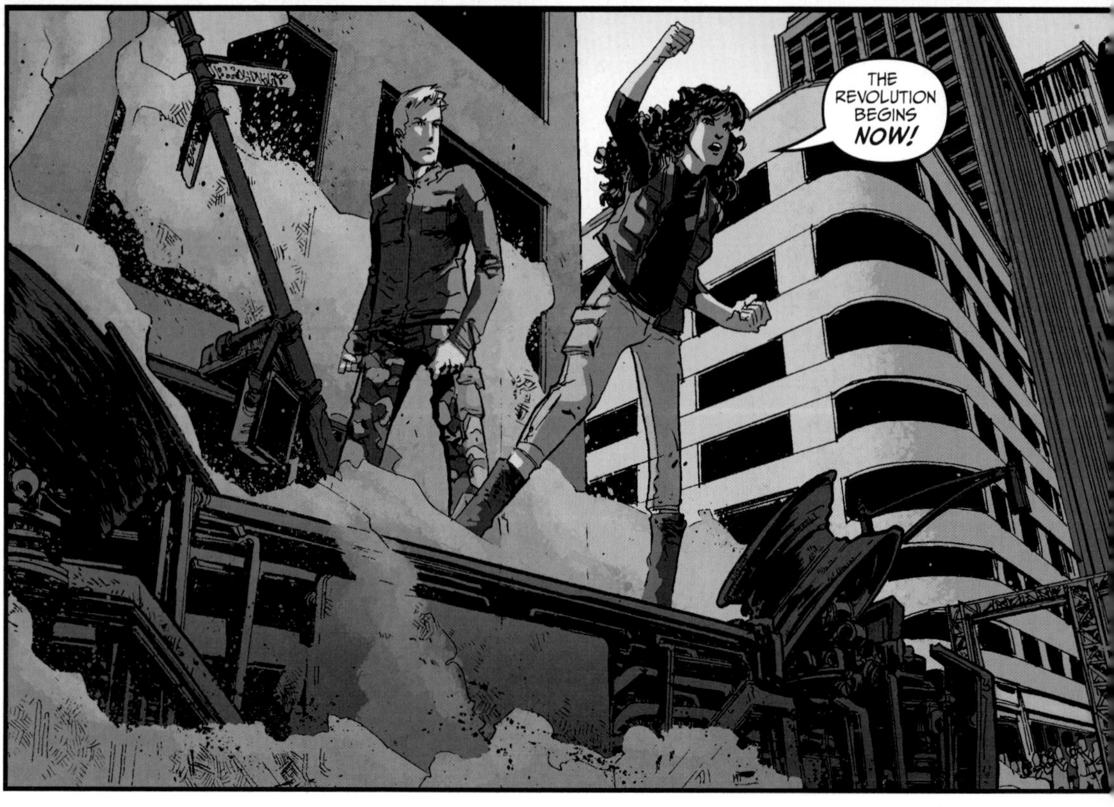
THE REVOLUTION BEGINS *NOW!*

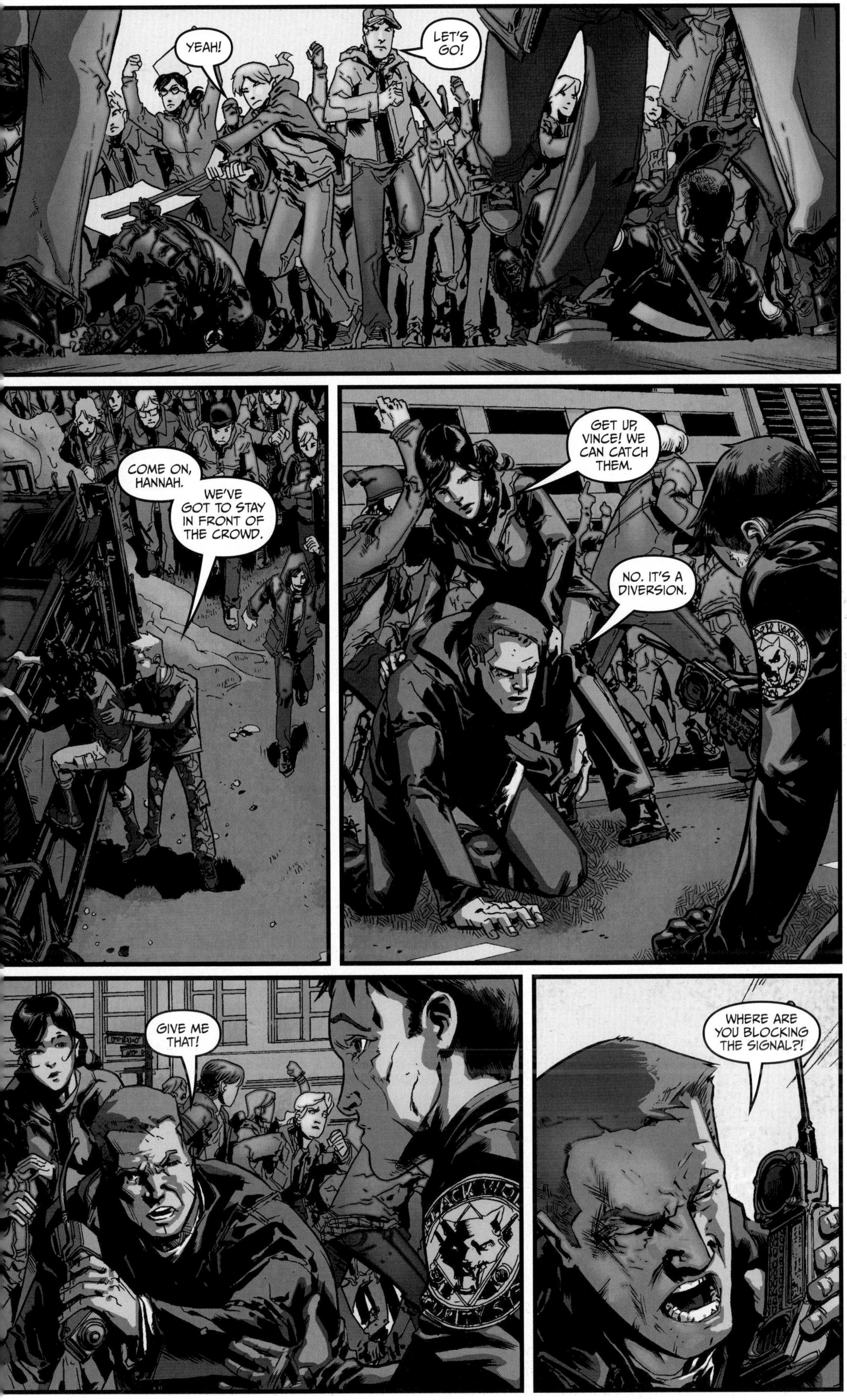

YEAH!
LET'S GO!
COME ON, HANNAH.
WE'VE GOT TO STAY IN FRONT OF THE CROWD.
GET UP, VINCE! WE CAN CATCH THEM.
NO. IT'S A DIVERSION.
GIVE ME THAT!
WHERE ARE YOU BLOCKING THE SIGNAL?!

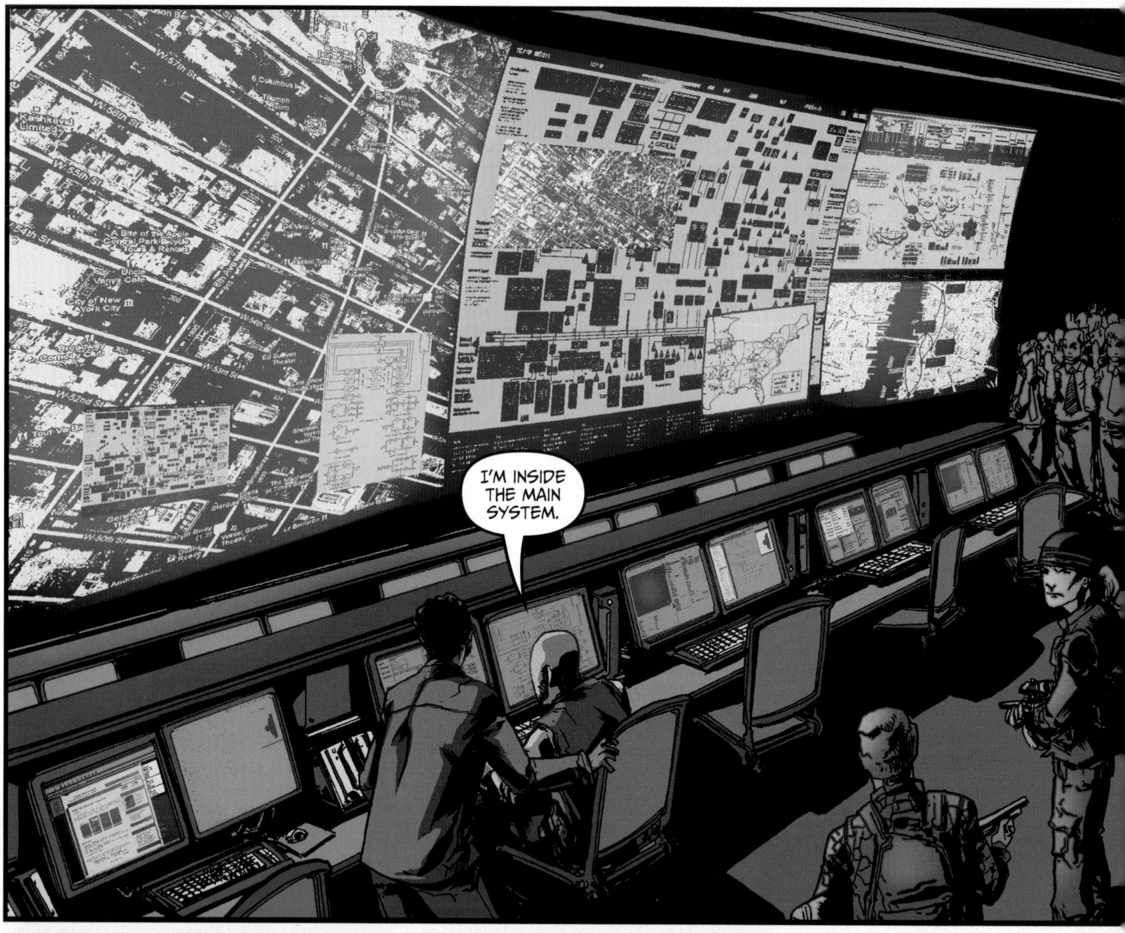

I'M INSIDE THE MAIN SYSTEM.

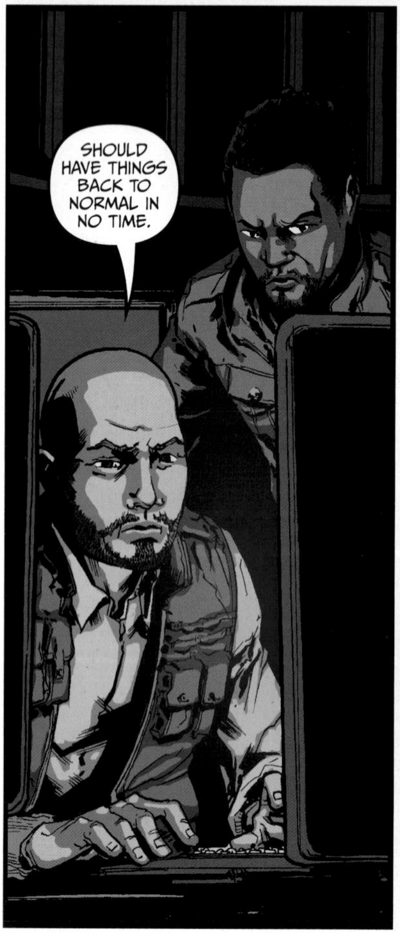

SHOULD HAVE THINGS BACK TO NORMAL IN NO TIME.

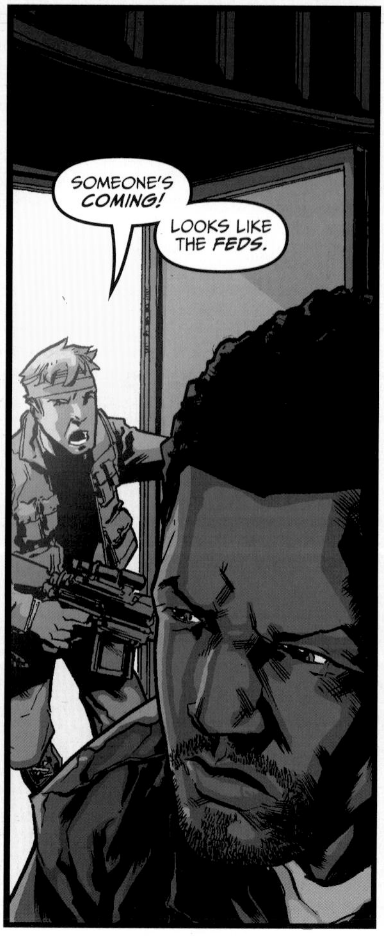

SOMEONE'S *COMING!*
LOOKS LIKE THE *FEDS.*

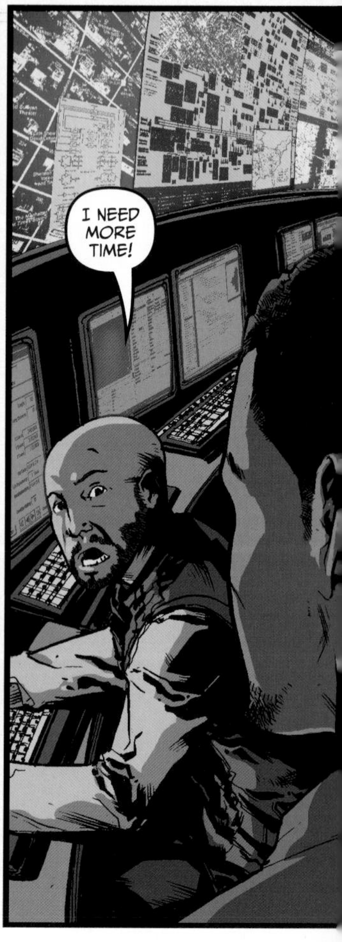

I NEED MORE TIME!

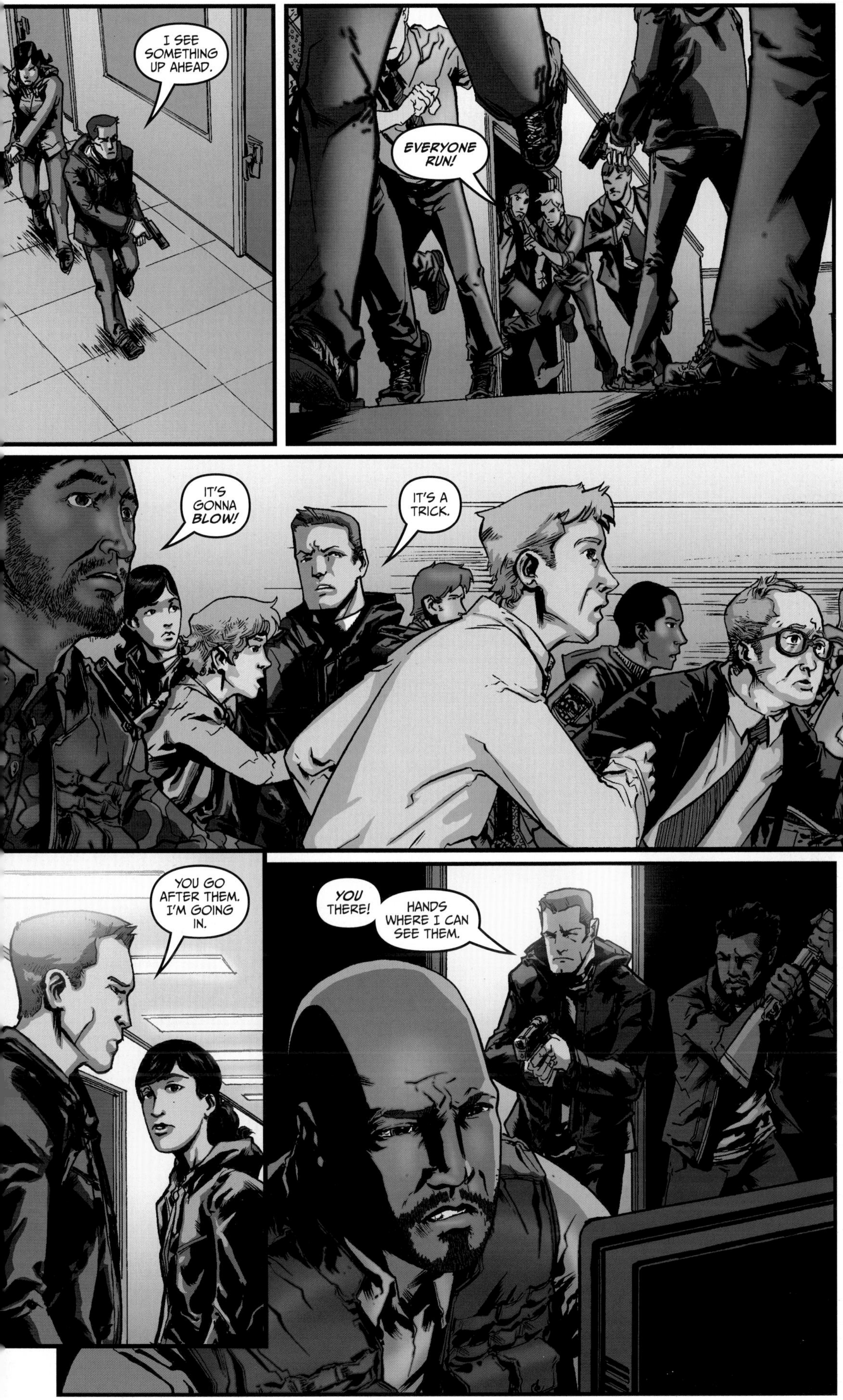

I SEE SOMETHING UP AHEAD.
EVERYONE RUN!
IT'S GONNA BLOW!
IT'S A TRICK.
YOU GO AFTER THEM. I'M GOING IN.
YOU THERE!
HANDS WHERE I CAN SEE THEM.

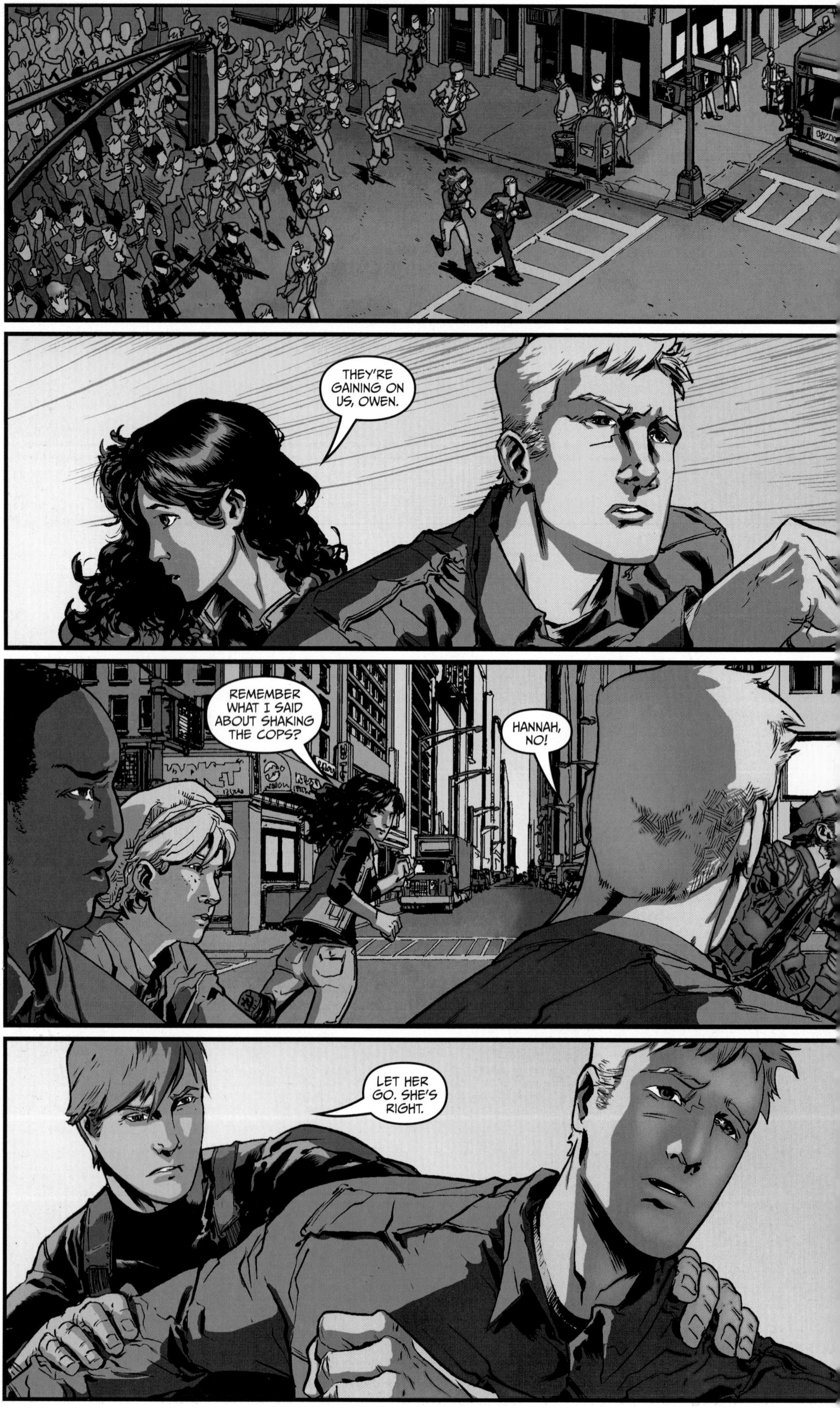
THEY'RE GAINING ON US, OWEN.
REMEMBER WHAT I SAID ABOUT SHAKING THE COPS?
HANNAH, NO!
LET HER GO. SHE'S RIGHT.

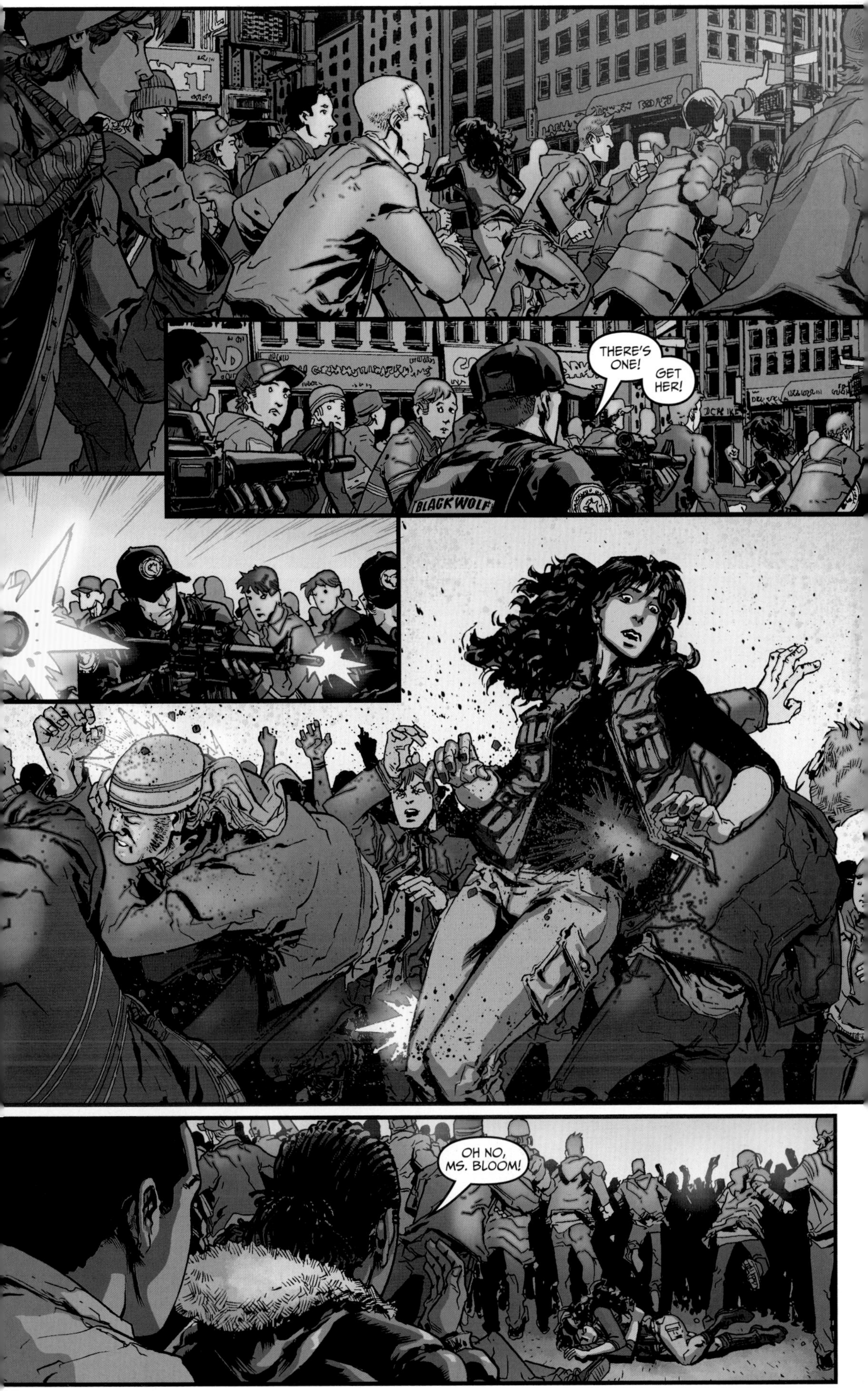
THERE'S ONE!
GET HER!
BLACKWOLF
OH NO, MS. BLOOM!

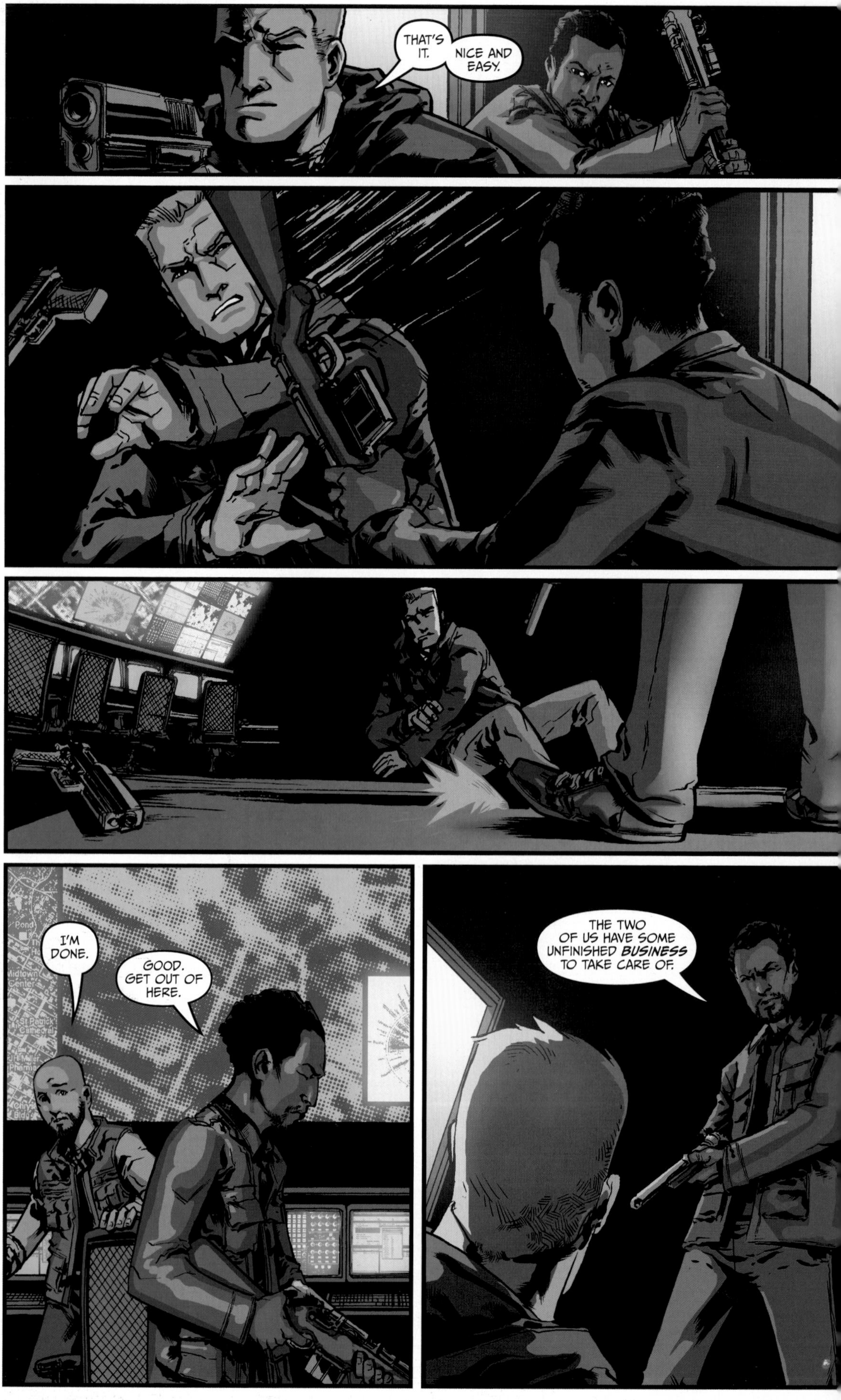
THAT'S IT.
NICE AND EASY.
I'M DONE.
GOOD. GET OUT OF HERE.
THE TWO OF US HAVE SOME UNFINISHED *BUSINESS* TO TAKE CARE OF.

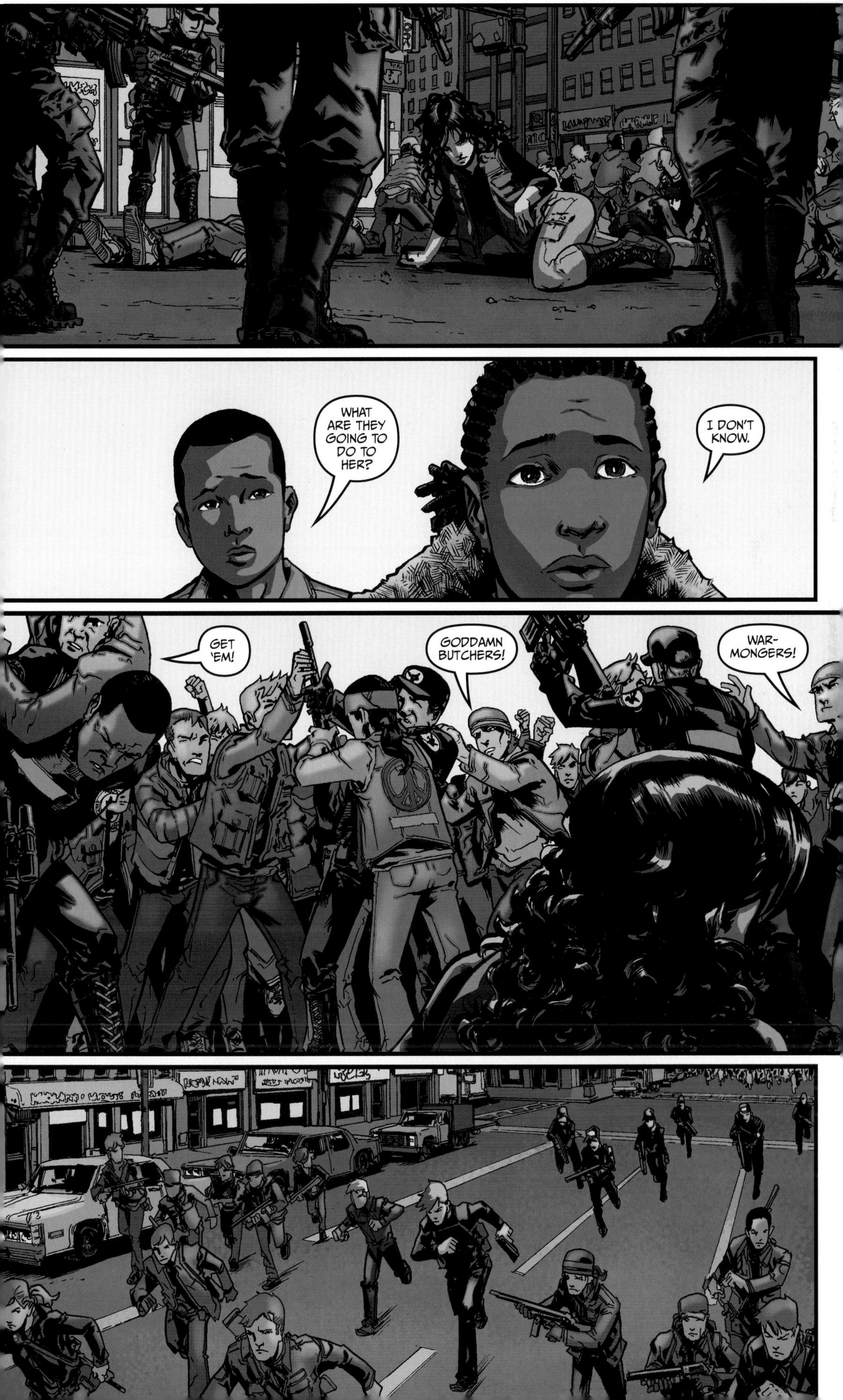

WHAT ARE THEY GOING TO DO TO HER?
I DON'T KNOW.
GET 'EM!
GODDAMN BUTCHERS!
WAR-MONGERS!

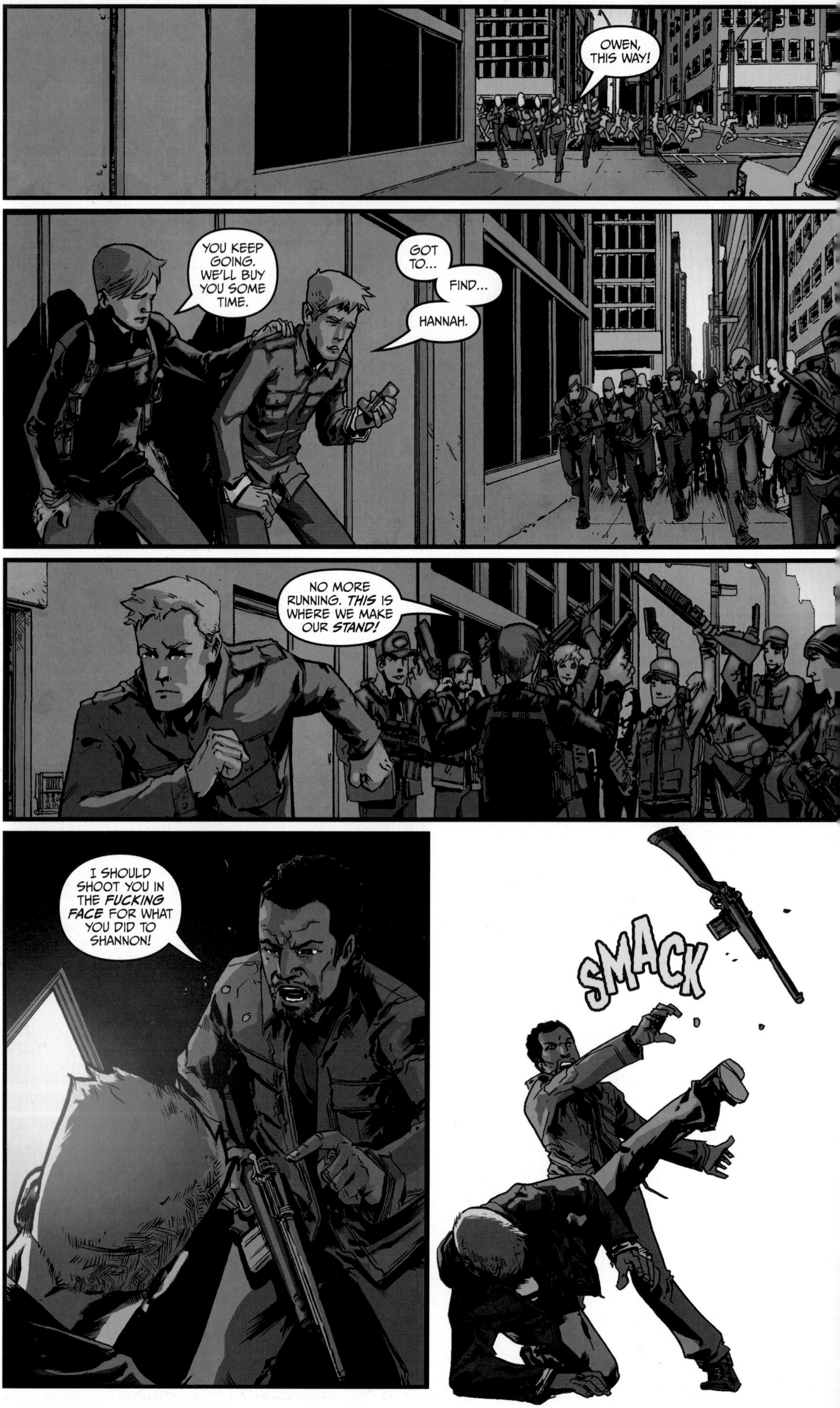
OWEN, THIS WAY!
YOU KEEP GOING. WE'LL BUY YOU SOME TIME.
GOT TO...
FIND...
HANNAH.
NO MORE RUNNING. THIS IS WHERE WE MAKE OUR STAND!
I SHOULD SHOOT YOU IN THE FUCKING FACE FOR WHAT YOU DID TO SHANNON!
SMACK

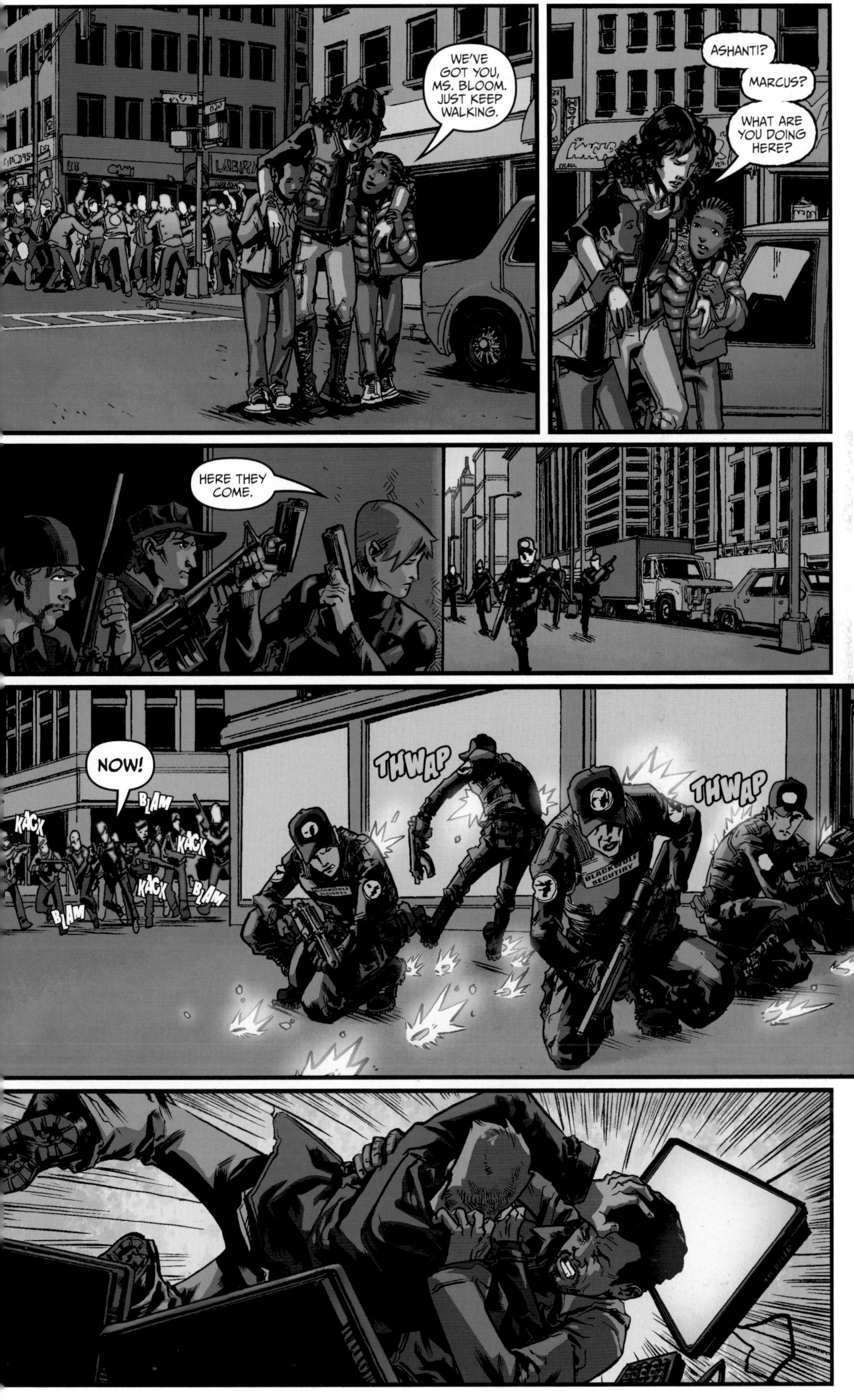
WE'VE GOT YOU, MS. BLOOM. JUST KEEP WALKING.
ASHANTI?
MARCUS?
WHAT ARE YOU DOING HERE?
HERE THEY COME.
NOW!
KACK
BLAM
KACK
KACK
BLAM
BLAM
THWAP
THWAP
BLACKWULF SECUTITY

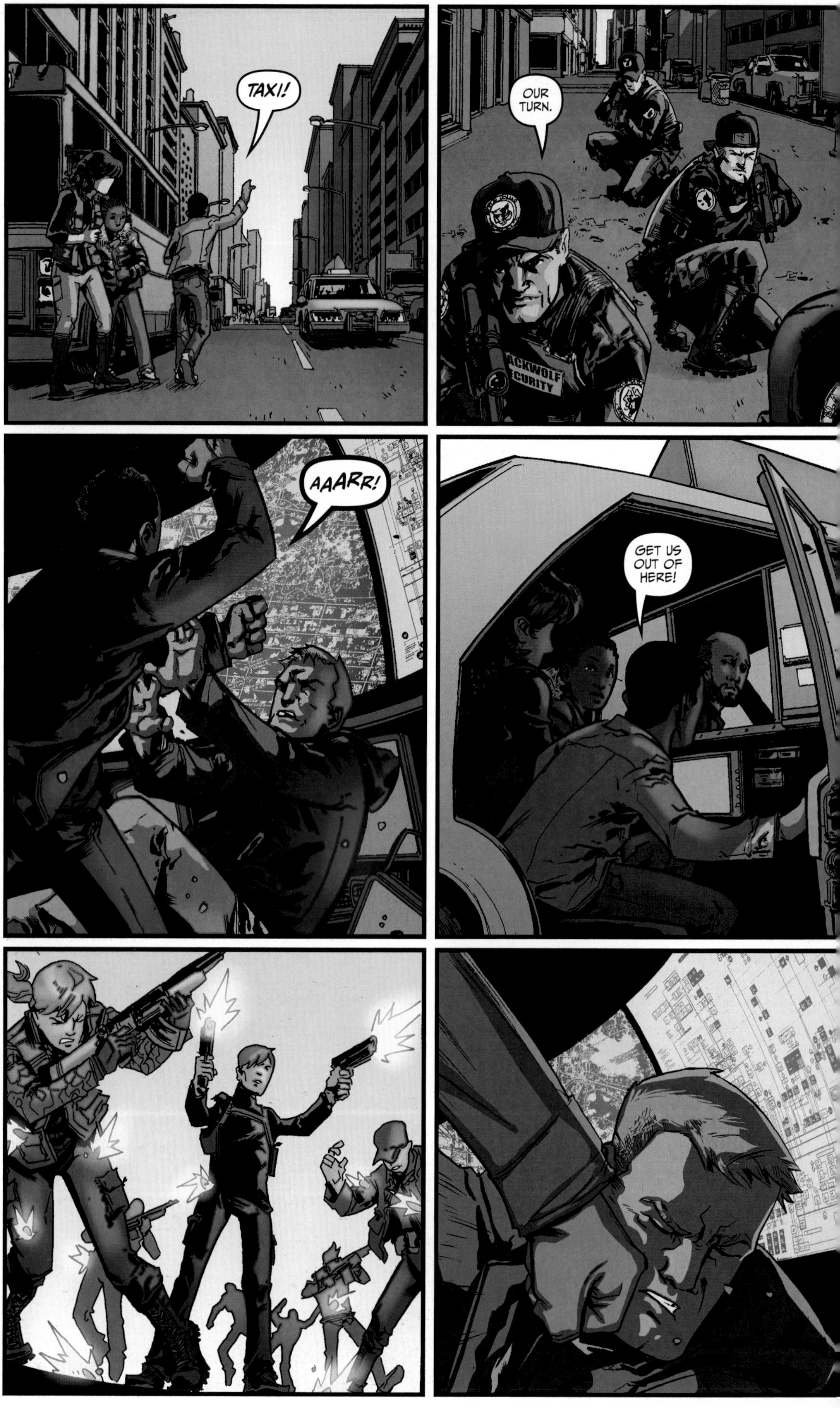
TAXI!
OUR TURN.
ACKWOLF
CURITY
AAARR!
GET US OUT OF HERE!

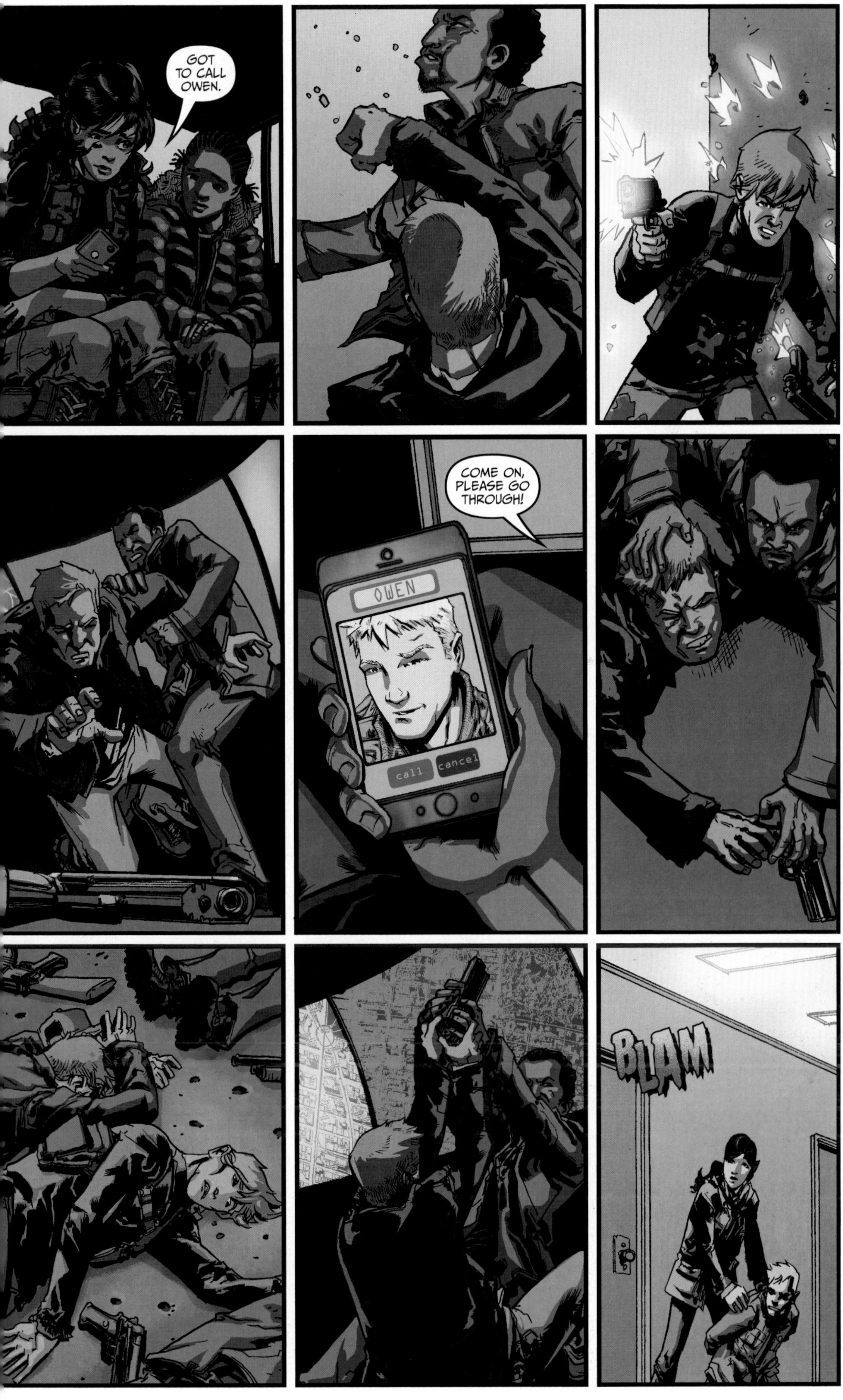
GOT TO CALL OWEN.
COME ON, PLEASE GO THROUGH!
OWEN
call
cancel
BLAM

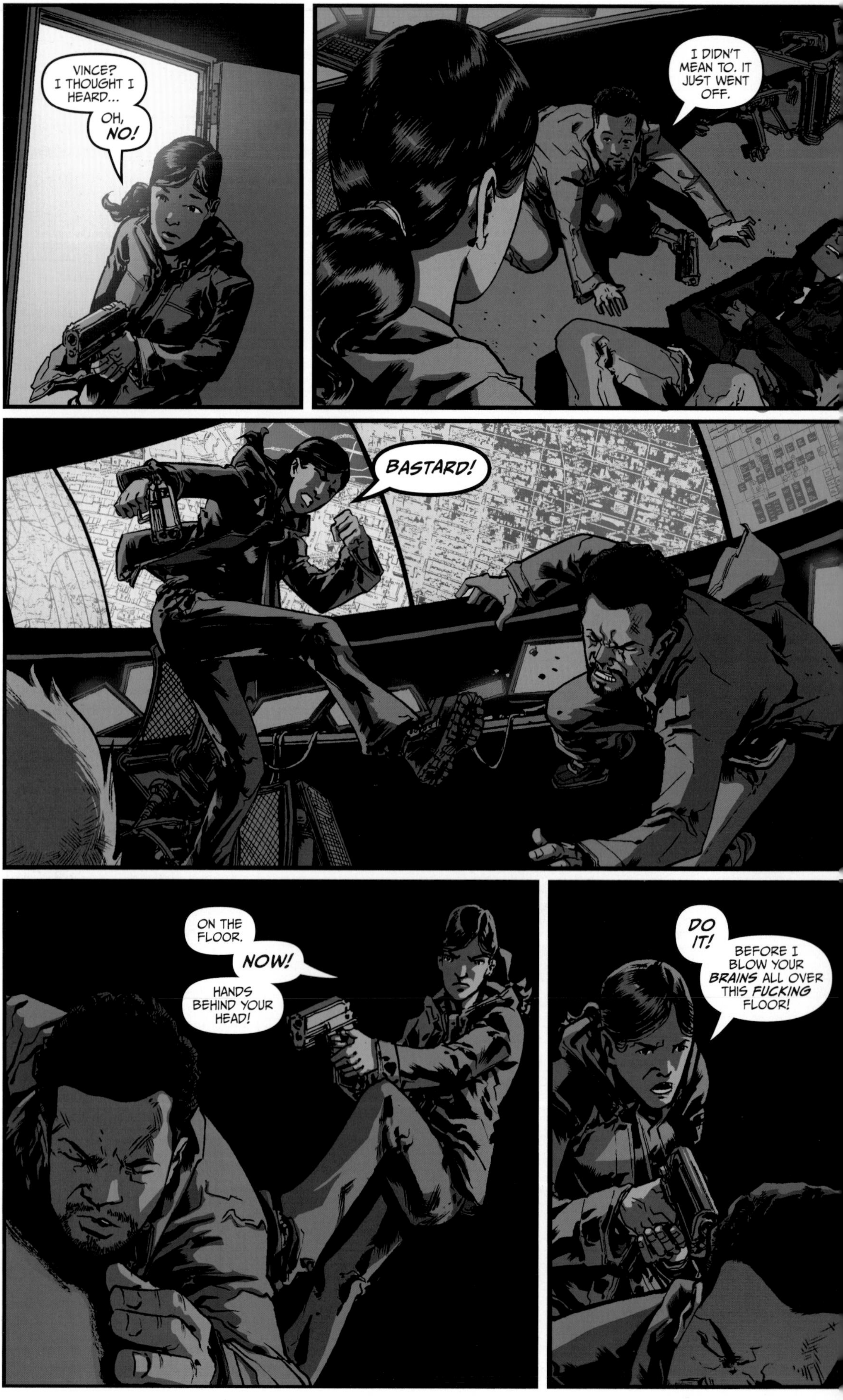

VINCE? I THOUGHT I HEARD...
OH, NO!
I DIDN'T MEAN TO. IT JUST WENT OFF.
BASTARD!
ON THE FLOOR.
NOW!
HANDS BEHIND YOUR HEAD!
DO IT!
BEFORE I BLOW YOUR BRAINS ALL OVER THIS FUCKING FLOOR!

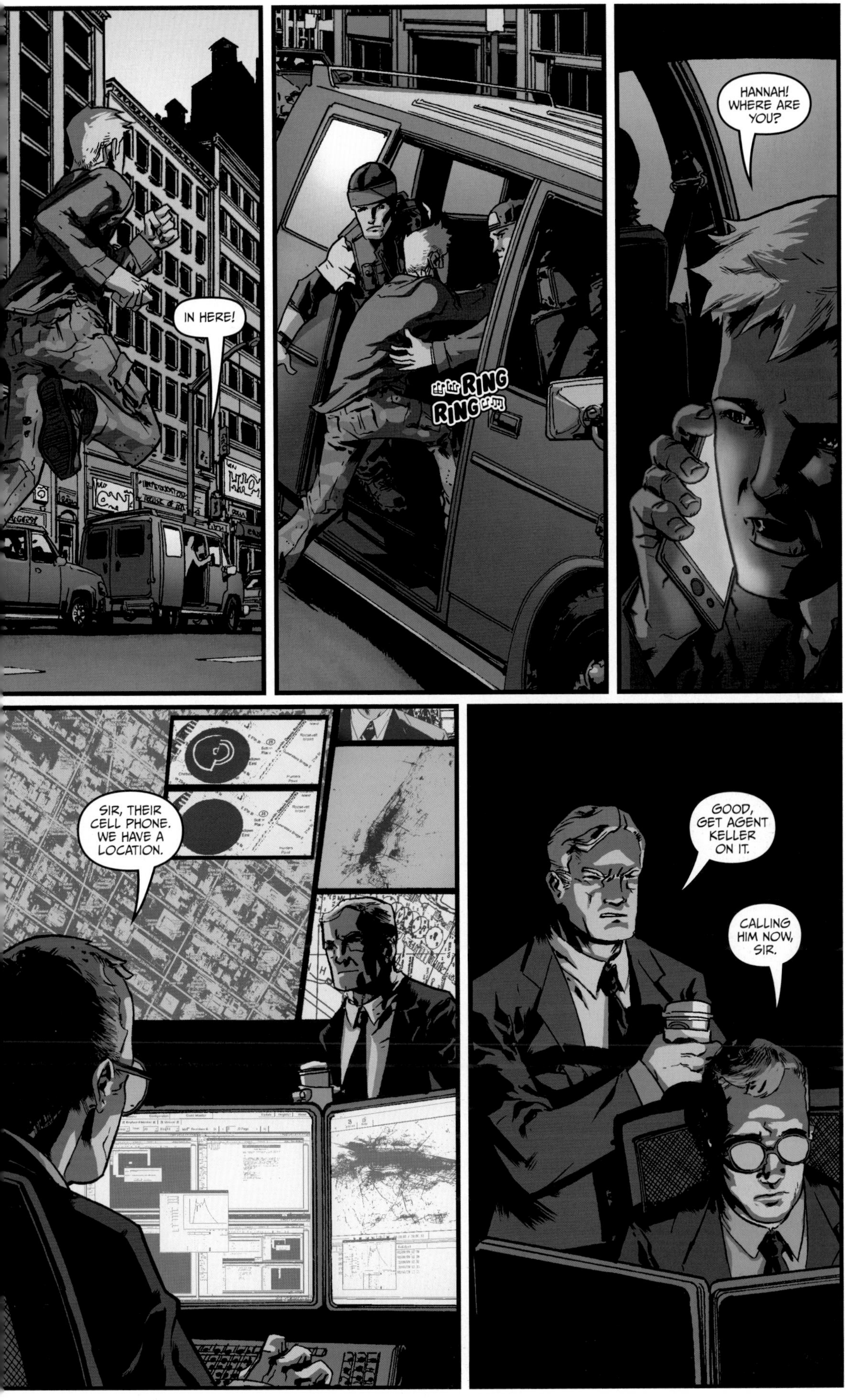
IN HERE!
RING RING
HANNAH! WHERE ARE YOU?
SIR, THEIR CELL PHONE. WE HAVE A LOCATION.
GOOD, GET AGENT KELLER ON IT.
CALLING HIM NOW, SIR.

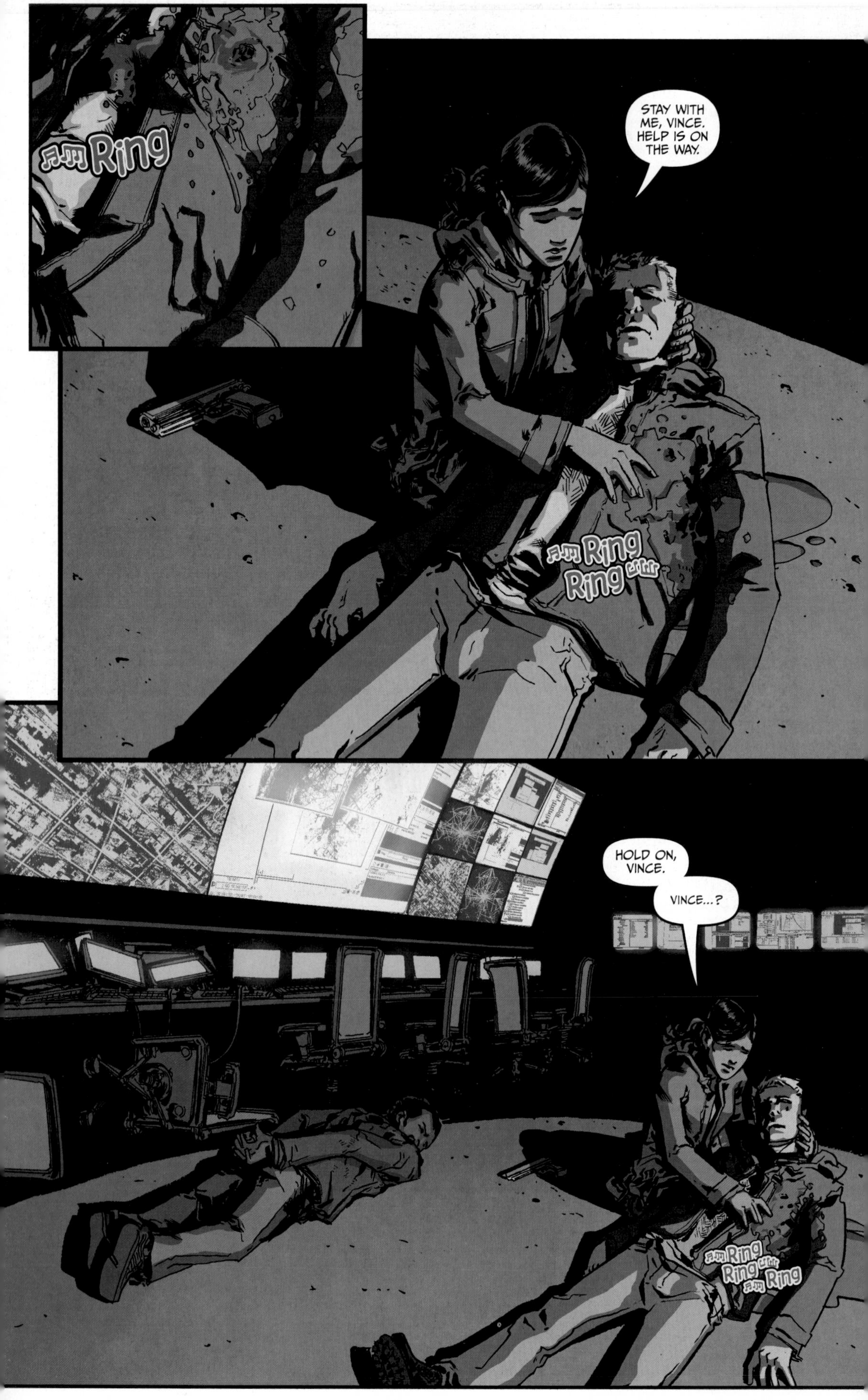
Ring
STAY WITH ME, VINCE. HELP IS ON THE WAY.
Ring
Ring
HOLD ON, VINCE.
VINCE...?
Ring
Ring
Ring

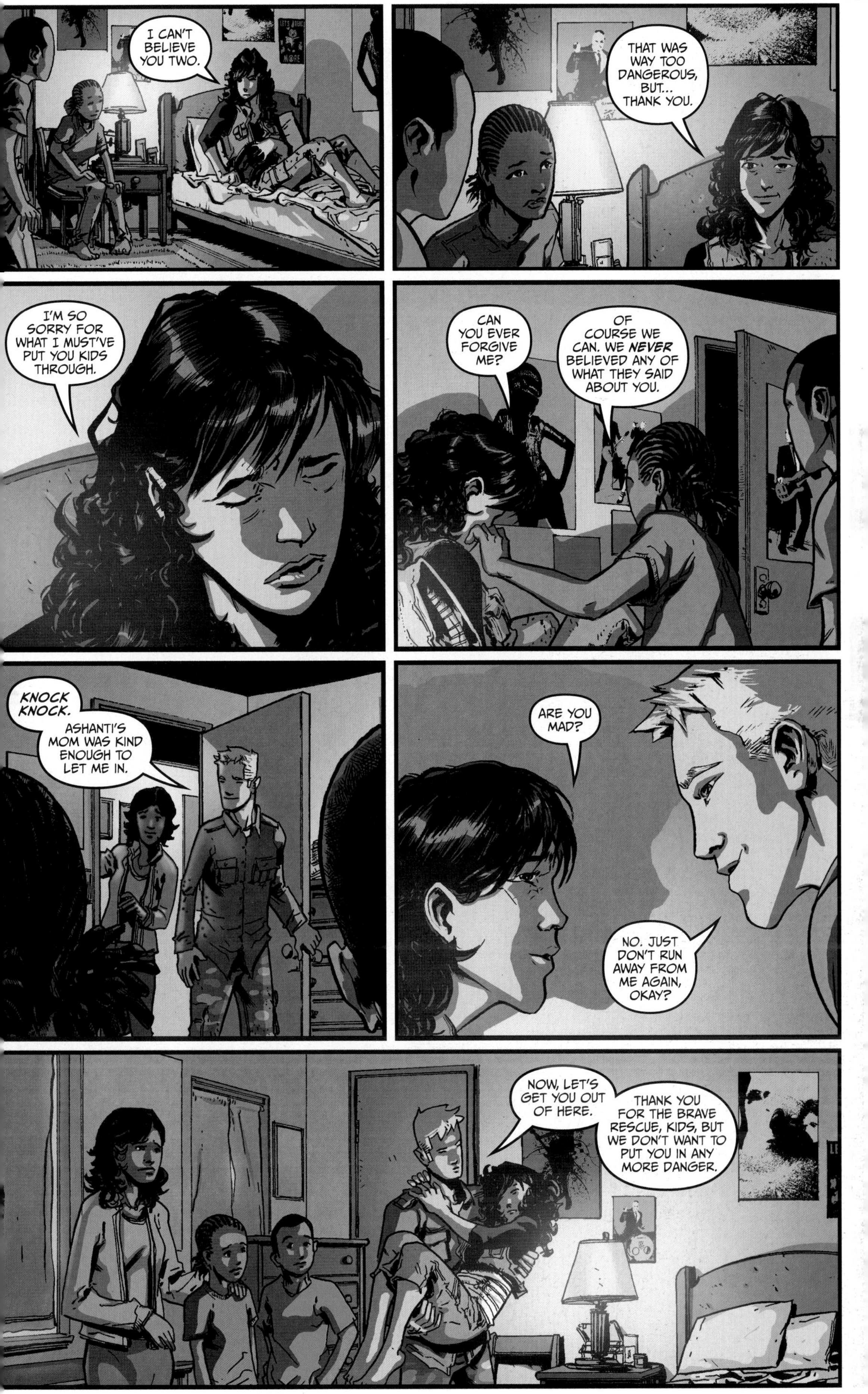
I CAN'T BELIEVE YOU TWO.
THAT WAS WAY TOO DANGEROUS, BUT... THANK YOU.
I'M SO SORRY FOR WHAT I MUST'VE PUT YOU KIDS THROUGH.
CAN YOU EVER FORGIVE ME?
OF COURSE WE CAN. WE *NEVER* BELIEVED ANY OF WHAT THEY SAID ABOUT YOU.
KNOCK KNOCK.
ASHANTI'S MOM WAS KIND ENOUGH TO LET ME IN.
ARE YOU MAD?
NO. JUST DON'T RUN AWAY FROM ME AGAIN, OKAY?
NOW, LET'S GET YOU OUT OF HERE.
THANK YOU FOR THE BRAVE RESCUE, KIDS, BUT WE DON'T WANT TO PUT YOU IN ANY MORE DANGER.

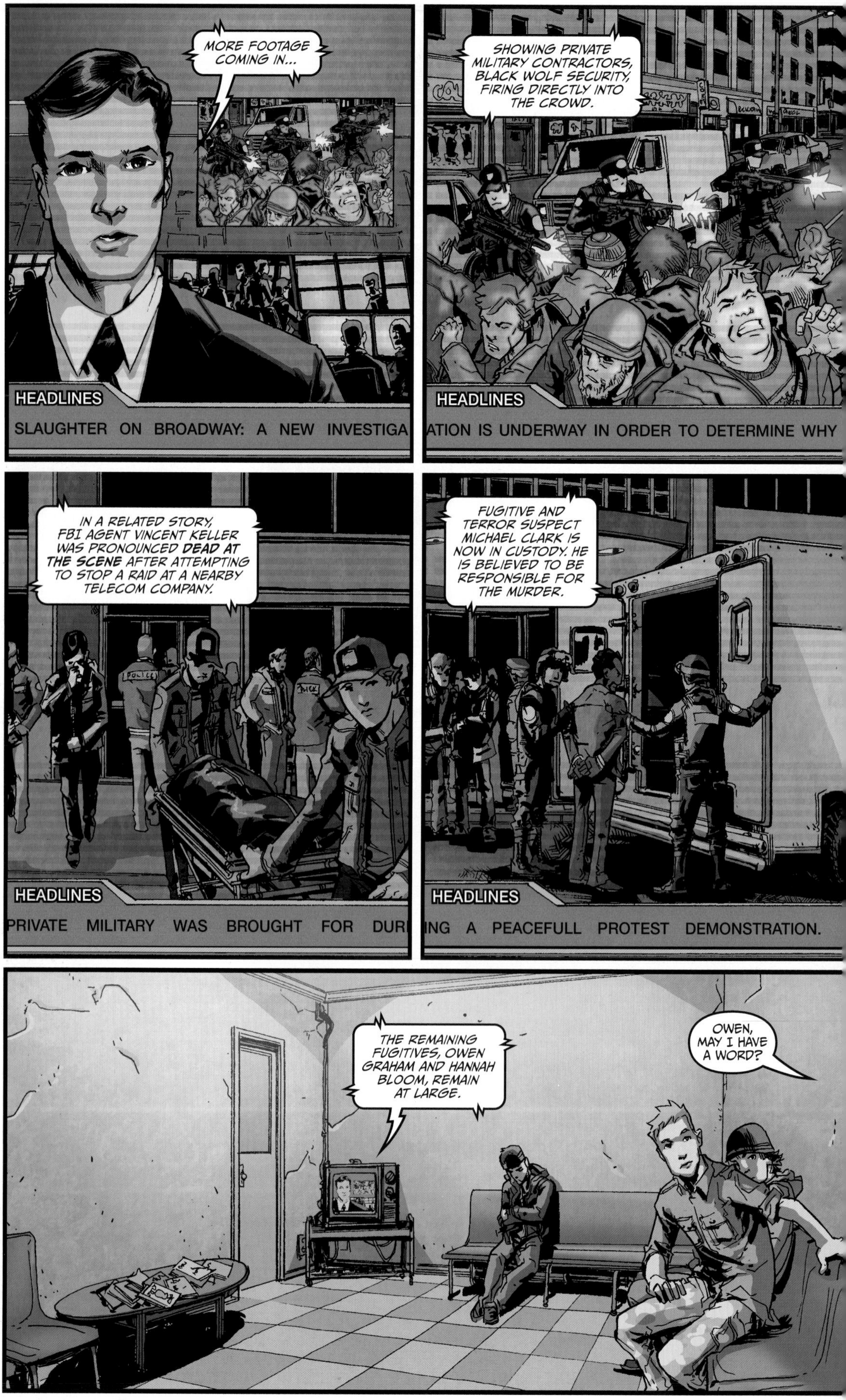

MORE FOOTAGE COMING IN...
HEADLINES
SLAUGHTER ON BROADWAY: A NEW INVESTIGA
SHOWING PRIVATE MILITARY CONTRACTORS, BLACK WOLF SECURITY, FIRING DIRECTLY INTO THE CROWD.
HEADLINES
ATION IS UNDERWAY IN ORDER TO DETERMINE WHY
IN A RELATED STORY, FBI AGENT VINCENT KELLER WAS PRONOUNCED DEAD AT THE SCENE AFTER ATTEMPTING TO STOP A RAID AT A NEARBY TELECOM COMPANY.
HEADLINES
PRIVATE MILITARY WAS BROUGHT FOR DURI
FUGITIVE AND TERROR SUSPECT MICHAEL CLARK IS NOW IN CUSTODY. HE IS BELIEVED TO BE RESPONSIBLE FOR THE MURDER.
HEADLINES
ING A PEACEFULL PROTEST DEMONSTRATION.
THE REMAINING FUGITIVES, OWEN GRAHAM AND HANNAH BLOOM, REMAIN AT LARGE.
OWEN, MAY I HAVE A WORD?

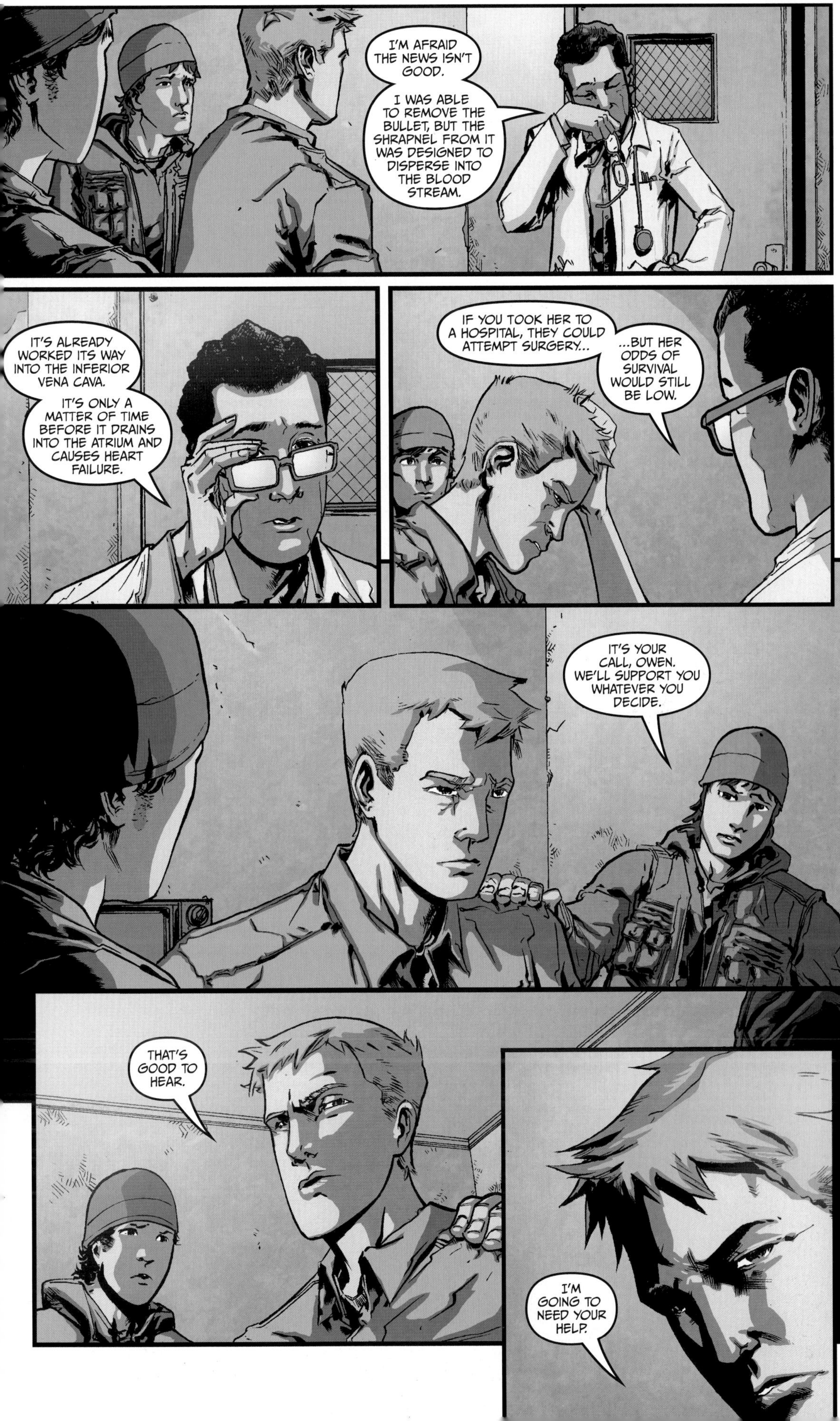
I'M AFRAID THE NEWS ISN'T GOOD.
I WAS ABLE TO REMOVE THE BULLET, BUT THE SHRAPNEL FROM IT WAS DESIGNED TO DISPERSE INTO THE BLOOD STREAM.
IT'S ALREADY WORKED ITS WAY INTO THE INFERIOR VENA CAVA.
IT'S ONLY A MATTER OF TIME BEFORE IT DRAINS INTO THE ATRIUM AND CAUSES HEART FAILURE.
IF YOU TOOK HER TO A HOSPITAL, THEY COULD ATTEMPT SURGERY...
...BUT HER ODDS OF SURVIVAL WOULD STILL BE LOW.
IT'S YOUR CALL, OWEN. WE'LL SUPPORT YOU WHATEVER YOU DECIDE.
THAT'S GOOD TO HEAR.
I'M GOING TO NEED YOUR HELP.

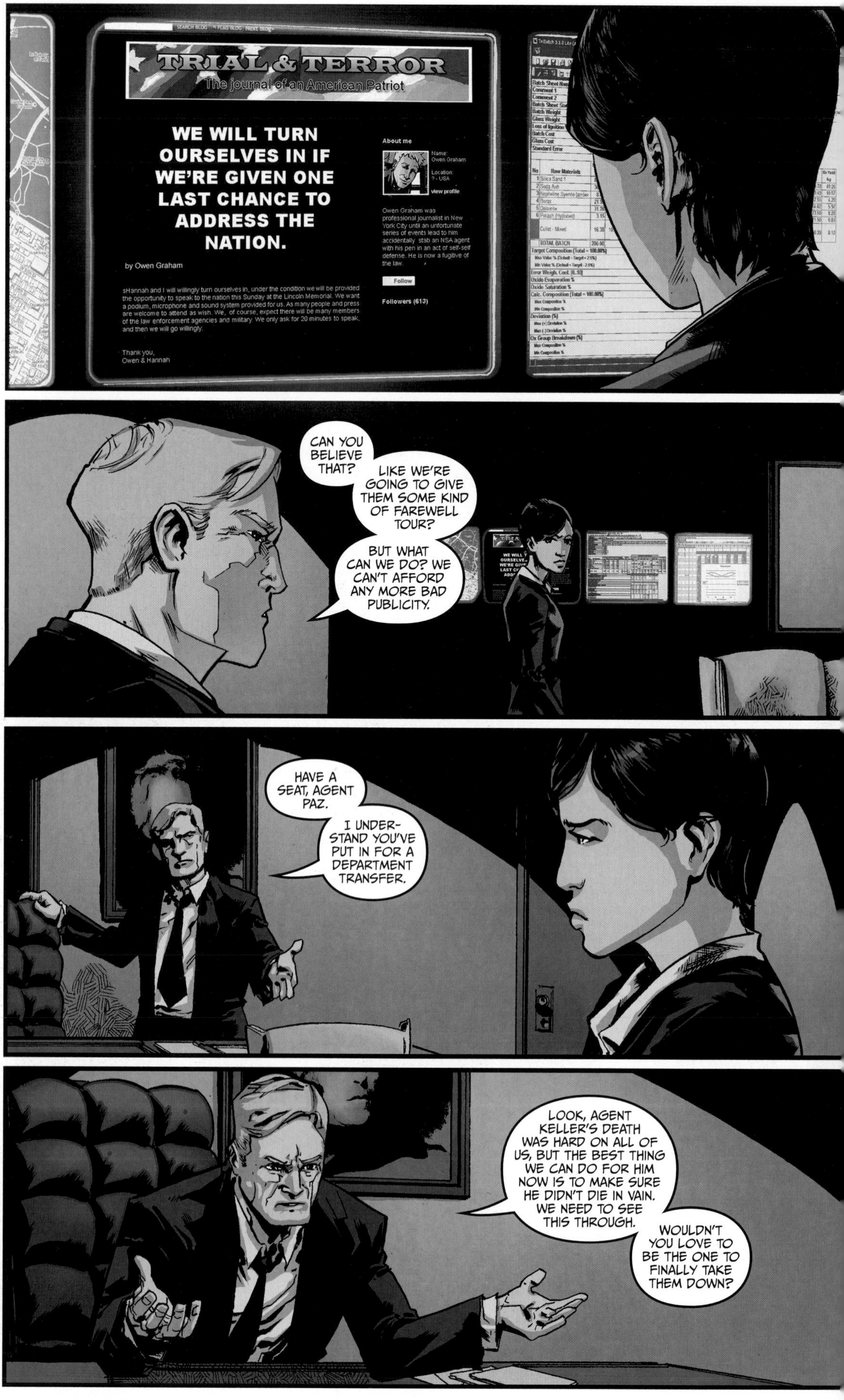
SEARCH BLOG
FLAG BLOG
Next Blog»
TRIAL & TERROR
The journal of an American Patriot
WE WILL TURN OURSELVES IN IF WE'RE GIVEN ONE LAST CHANCE TO ADDRESS THE NATION.
by Owen Graham
sHannah and I will willingly turn ourselves in, under the condition we will be provided the opportunity to speak to the nation this Sunday at the Lincoln Memorial. We want a podium, microphone and sound system provided for us. As many people and press are welcome to attend as wish. We, of course, expect there will be many members of the law enforcement agencies and military. We only ask for 20 minutes to speak, and then we will go willingly.
Thank you,
Owen & Hannah
About me
Name: Owen Graham
Location: ? - USA
view profile
Owen Graham was professional journalist in New York City until an unfortunate series of events lead to him accidentally stab an NSA agent with his pen in an act of self-self defense. He is now a fugitive of the law.
Follow
Followers (613)
CAN YOU BELIEVE THAT?
LIKE WE'RE GOING TO GIVE THEM SOME KIND OF FAREWELL TOUR?
BUT WHAT CAN WE DO? WE CAN'T AFFORD ANY MORE BAD PUBLICITY.
HAVE A SEAT, AGENT PAZ.
I UNDER-STAND YOU'VE PUT IN FOR A DEPARTMENT TRANSFER.
LOOK, AGENT KELLER'S DEATH WAS HARD ON ALL OF US, BUT THE BEST THING WE CAN DO FOR HIM NOW IS TO MAKE SURE HE DIDN'T DIE IN VAIN. WE NEED TO SEE THIS THROUGH.
WOULDN'T YOU LOVE TO BE THE ONE TO FINALLY TAKE THEM DOWN?

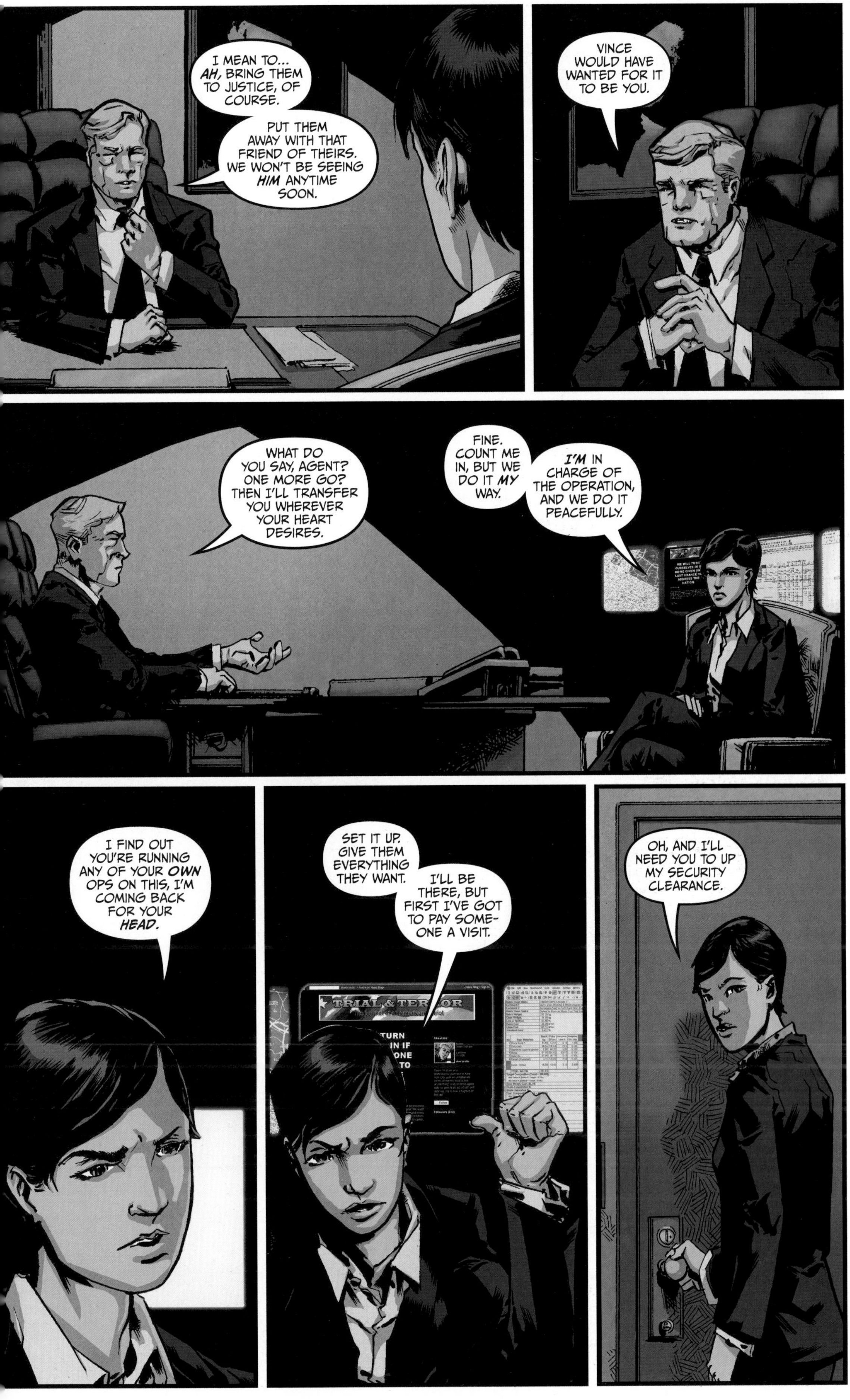
I MEAN TO... AH, BRING THEM TO JUSTICE, OF COURSE.
PUT THEM AWAY WITH THAT FRIEND OF THEIRS. WE WON'T BE SEEING HIM ANYTIME SOON.
VINCE WOULD HAVE WANTED FOR IT TO BE YOU.
WHAT DO YOU SAY, AGENT? ONE MORE GO? THEN I'LL TRANSFER YOU WHEREVER YOUR HEART DESIRES.
FINE. COUNT ME IN, BUT WE DO IT MY WAY.
I'M IN CHARGE OF THE OPERATION, AND WE DO IT PEACEFULLY.
I FIND OUT YOU'RE RUNNING ANY OF YOUR OWN OPS ON THIS, I'M COMING BACK FOR YOUR HEAD.
SET IT UP. GIVE THEM EVERYTHING THEY WANT.
I'LL BE THERE, BUT FIRST I'VE GOT TO PAY SOME-ONE A VISIT.
TRIAL & TERROR
OH, AND I'LL NEED YOU TO UP MY SECURITY CLEARANCE.

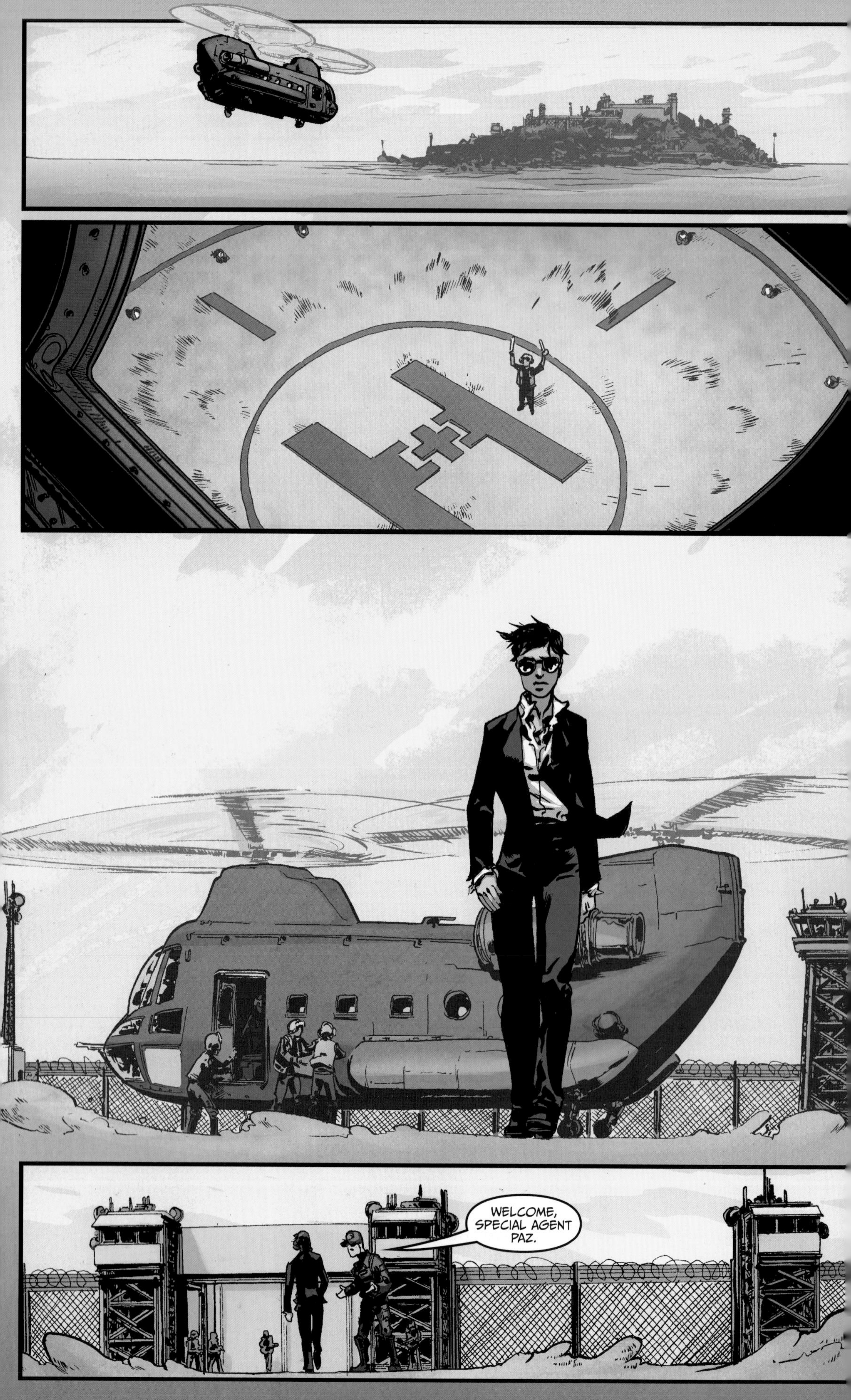
WELCOME, SPECIAL AGENT PAZ.

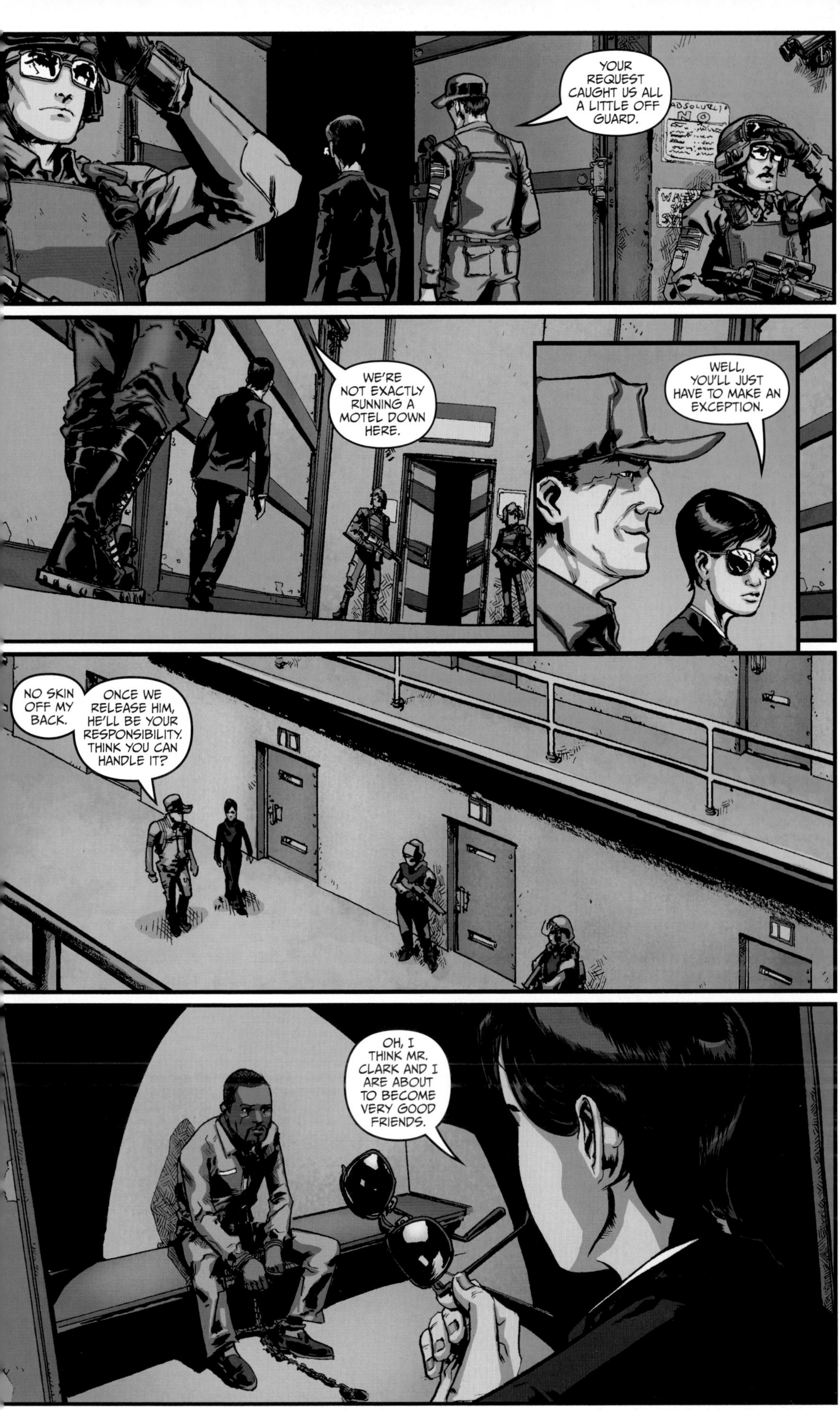
YOUR REQUEST CAUGHT US ALL A LITTLE OFF GUARD.
WE'RE NOT EXACTLY RUNNING A MOTEL DOWN HERE.
WELL, YOU'LL JUST HAVE TO MAKE AN EXCEPTION.
NO SKIN OFF MY BACK.
ONCE WE RELEASE HIM, HE'LL BE YOUR RESPONSIBILITY. THINK YOU CAN HANDLE IT?
OH, I THINK MR. CLARK AND I ARE ABOUT TO BECOME VERY GOOD FRIENDS.

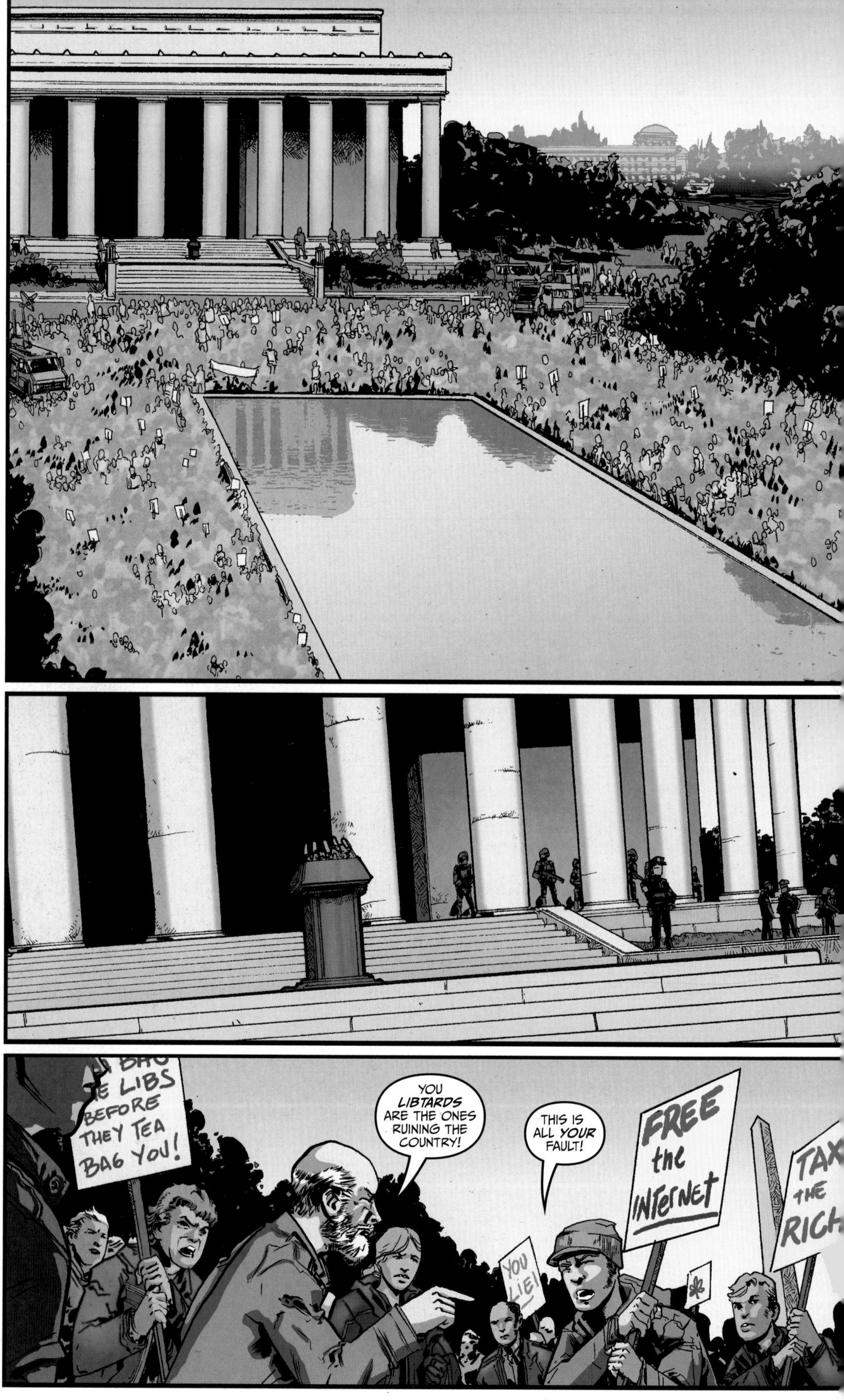
LIBS
BEFORE
THEY TEA
BAG YOU!
YOU
LIBTARDS
ARE THE ONES
RUINING THE
COUNTRY!
THIS IS
ALL *YOUR*
FAULT!
FREE
the
INTERNET
YOU
LIE!
THE

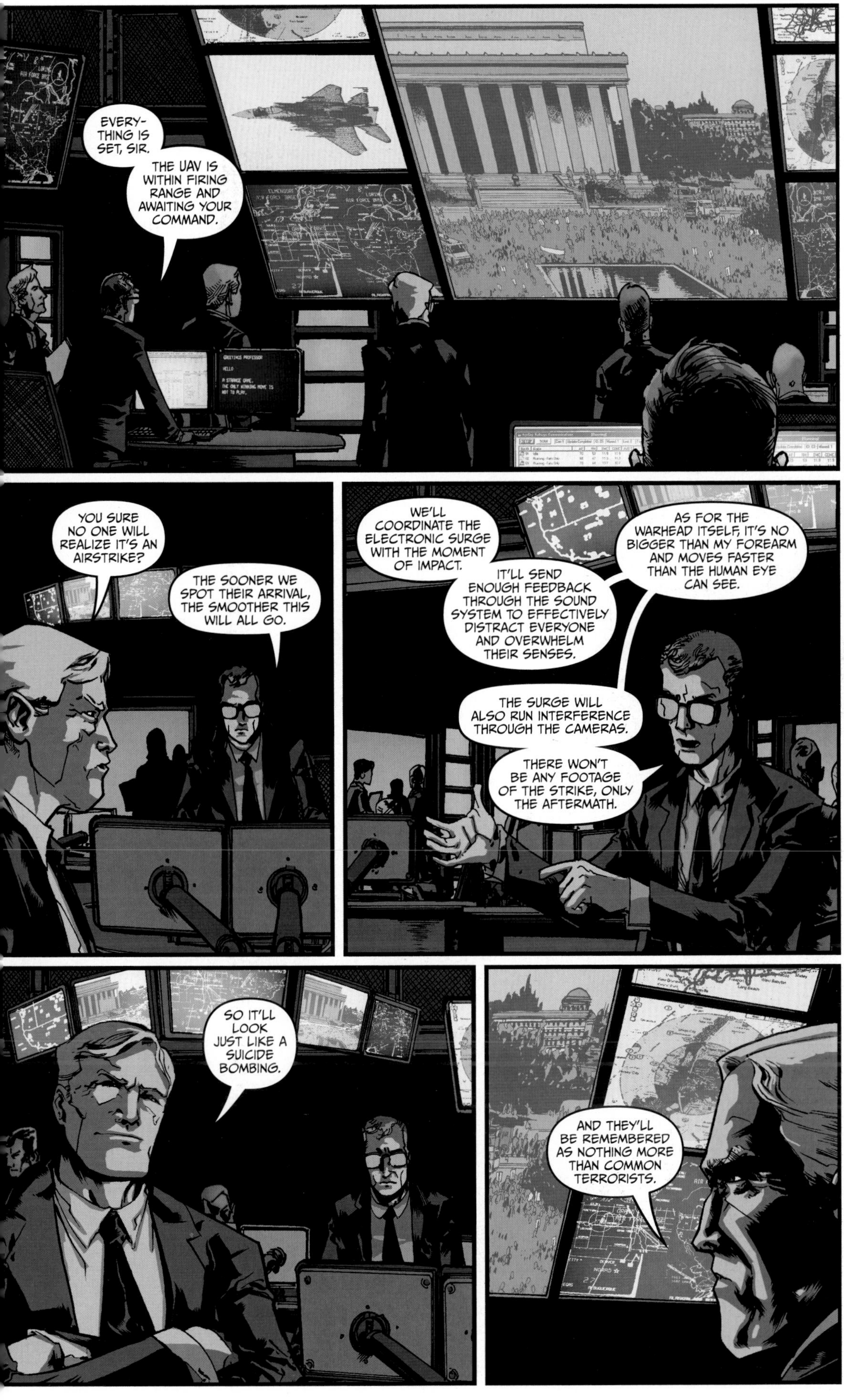
EVERY-THING IS SET, SIR.
THE UAV IS WITHIN FIRING RANGE AND AWAITING YOUR COMMAND.
YOU SURE NO ONE WILL REALIZE IT'S AN AIRSTRIKE?
THE SOONER WE SPOT THEIR ARRIVAL, THE SMOOTHER THIS WILL ALL GO.
WE'LL COORDINATE THE ELECTRONIC SURGE WITH THE MOMENT OF IMPACT.
IT'LL SEND ENOUGH FEEDBACK THROUGH THE SOUND SYSTEM TO EFFECTIVELY DISTRACT EVERYONE AND OVERWHELM THEIR SENSES.
AS FOR THE WARHEAD ITSELF, IT'S NO BIGGER THAN MY FOREARM AND MOVES FASTER THAN THE HUMAN EYE CAN SEE.
THE SURGE WILL ALSO RUN INTERFERENCE THROUGH THE CAMERAS.
THERE WON'T BE ANY FOOTAGE OF THE STRIKE, ONLY THE AFTERMATH.
SO IT'LL LOOK JUST LIKE A SUICIDE BOMBING.
AND THEY'LL BE REMEMBERED AS NOTHING MORE THAN COMMON TERRORISTS.

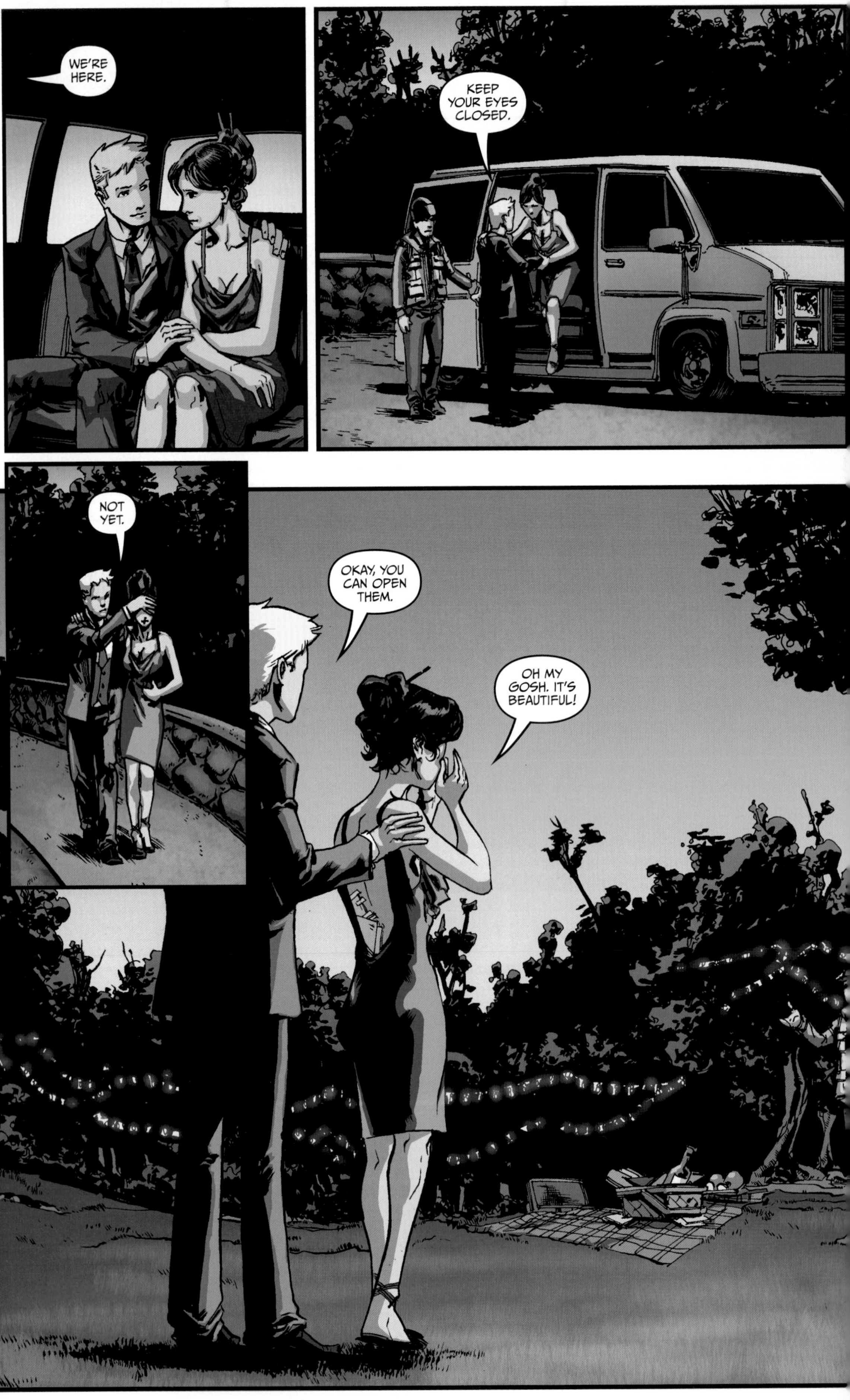
WE'RE HERE.
KEEP YOUR EYES CLOSED.
NOT YET.
OKAY, YOU CAN OPEN THEM.
OH MY GOSH. IT'S BEAUTIFUL!

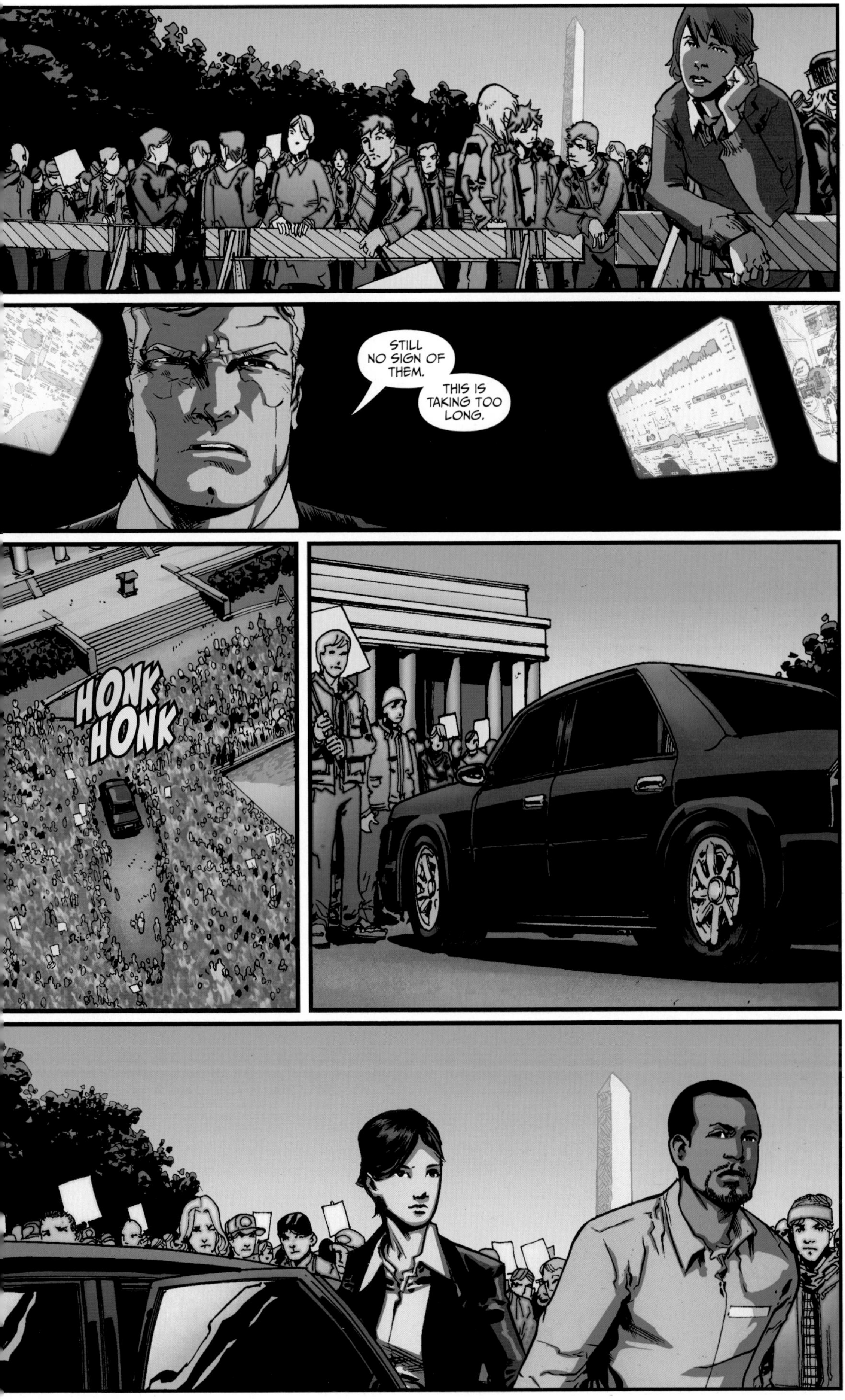
STILL NO SIGN OF THEM.
THIS IS TAKING TOO LONG.
HONK HONK

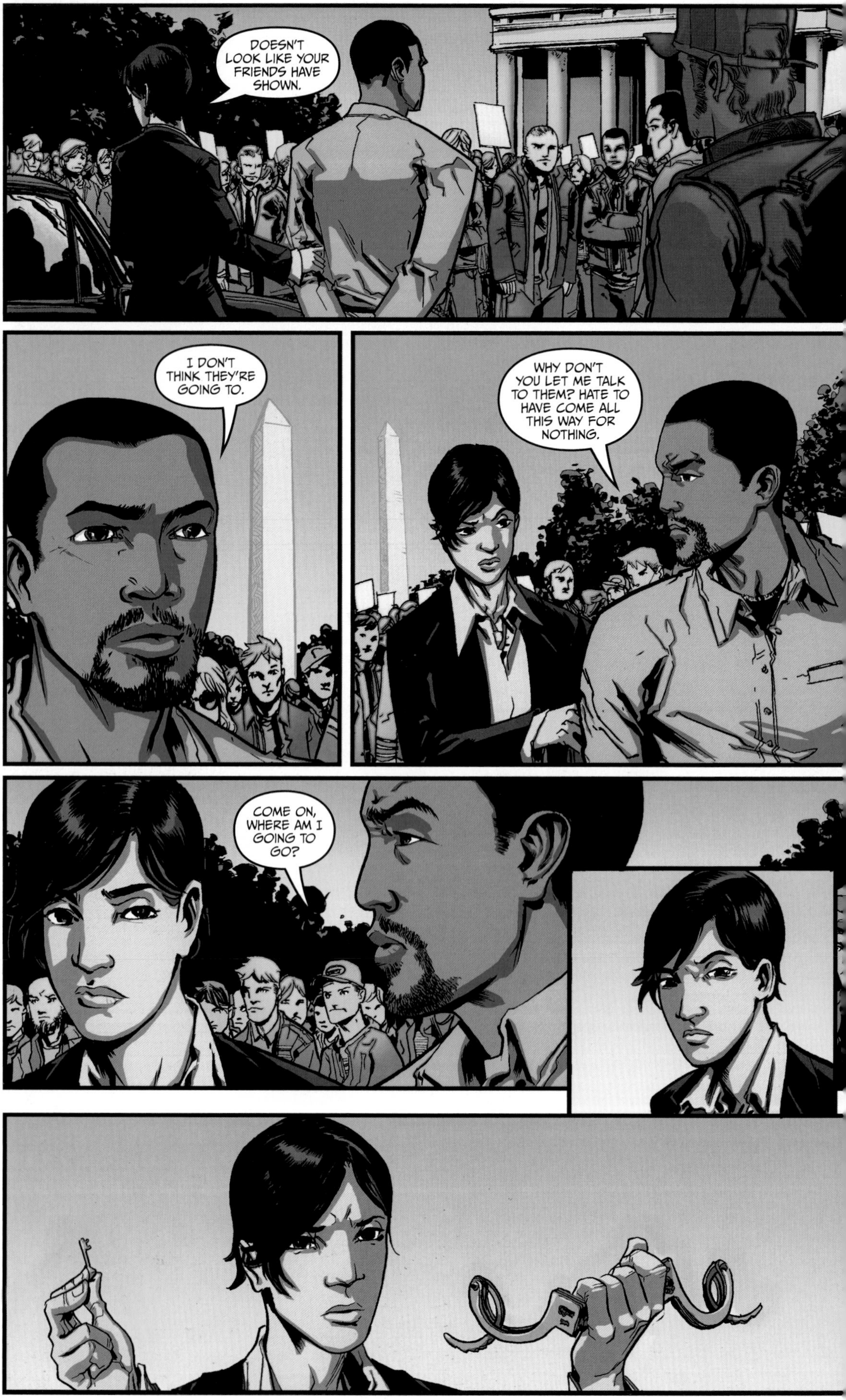

DOESN'T LOOK LIKE YOUR FRIENDS HAVE SHOWN.
I DON'T THINK THEY'RE GOING TO.
WHY DON'T YOU LET ME TALK TO THEM? HATE TO HAVE COME ALL THIS WAY FOR NOTHING.
COME ON, WHERE AM I GOING TO GO?

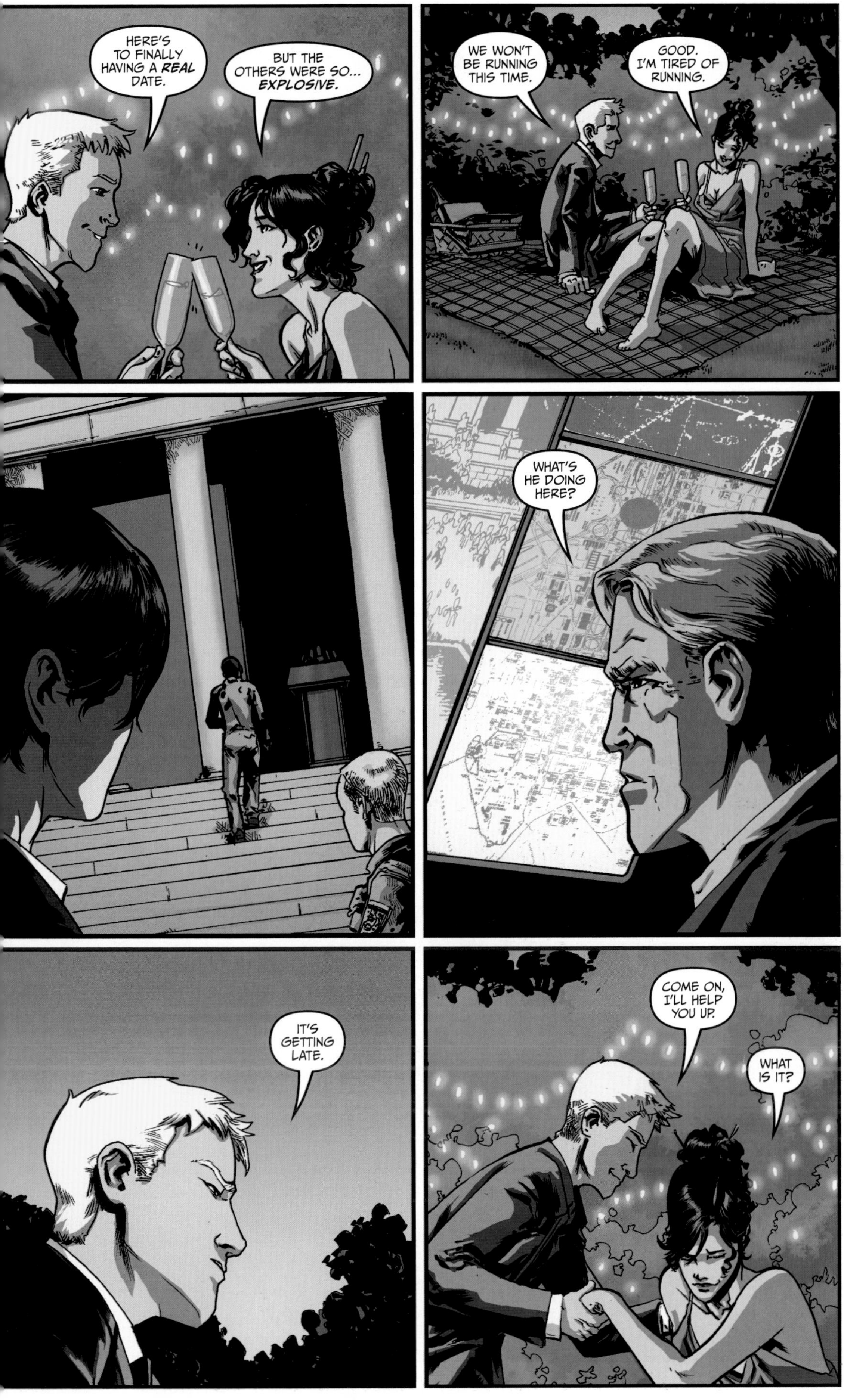
HERE'S TO FINALLY HAVING A *REAL* DATE.
BUT THE OTHERS WERE SO... *EXPLOSIVE.*
WE WON'T BE RUNNING THIS TIME.
GOOD. I'M TIRED OF RUNNING.
WHAT'S HE DOING HERE?
IT'S GETTING LATE.
COME ON, I'LL HELP YOU UP.
WHAT IS IT?

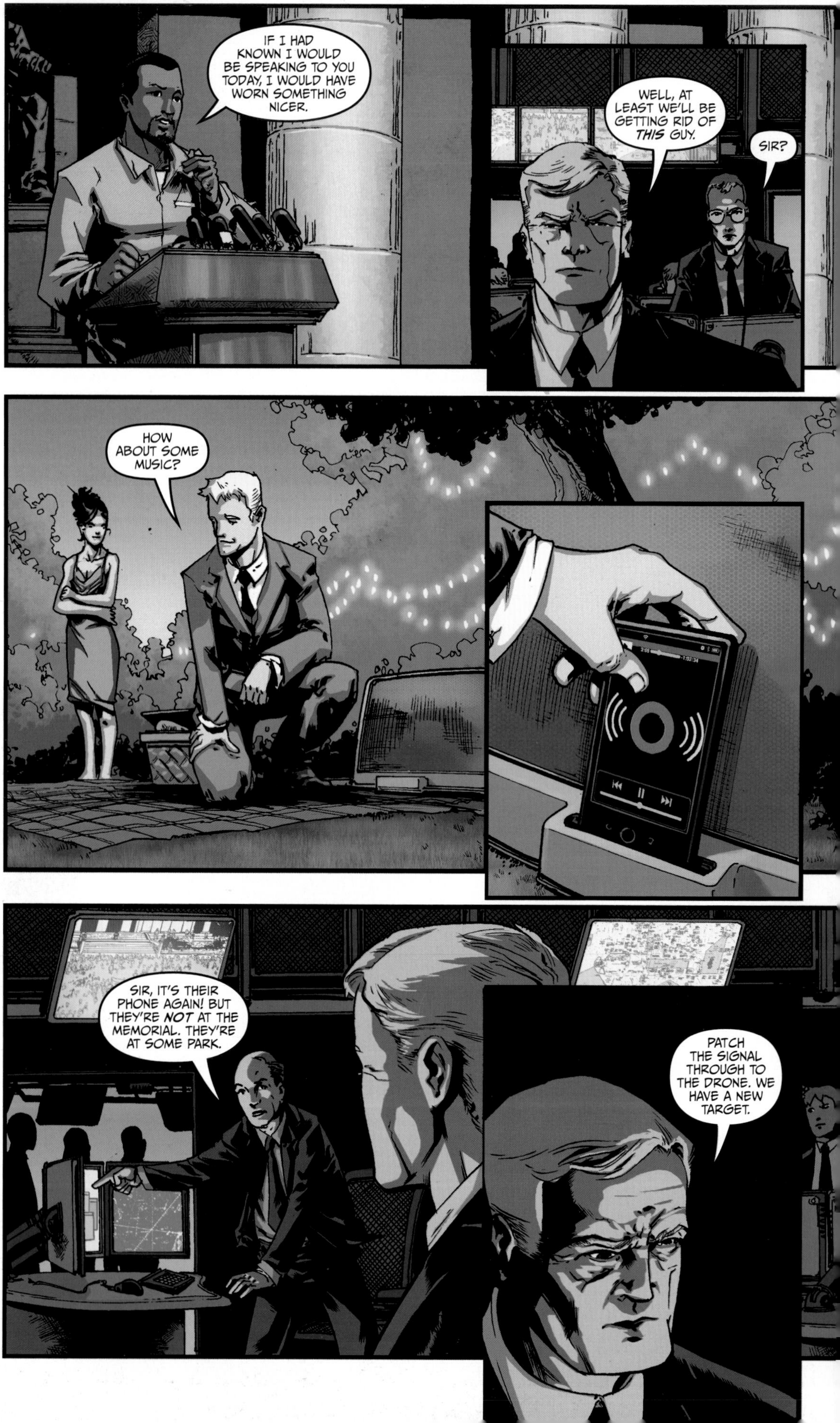
IF I HAD KNOWN I WOULD BE SPEAKING TO YOU TODAY, I WOULD HAVE WORN SOMETHING NICER.
WELL, AT LEAST WE'LL BE GETTING RID OF *THIS* GUY.
SIR?
HOW ABOUT SOME MUSIC?
SIR, IT'S THEIR PHONE AGAIN! BUT THEY'RE *NOT* AT THE MEMORIAL. THEY'RE AT SOME PARK.
PATCH THE SIGNAL THROUGH TO THE DRONE. WE HAVE A NEW TARGET.

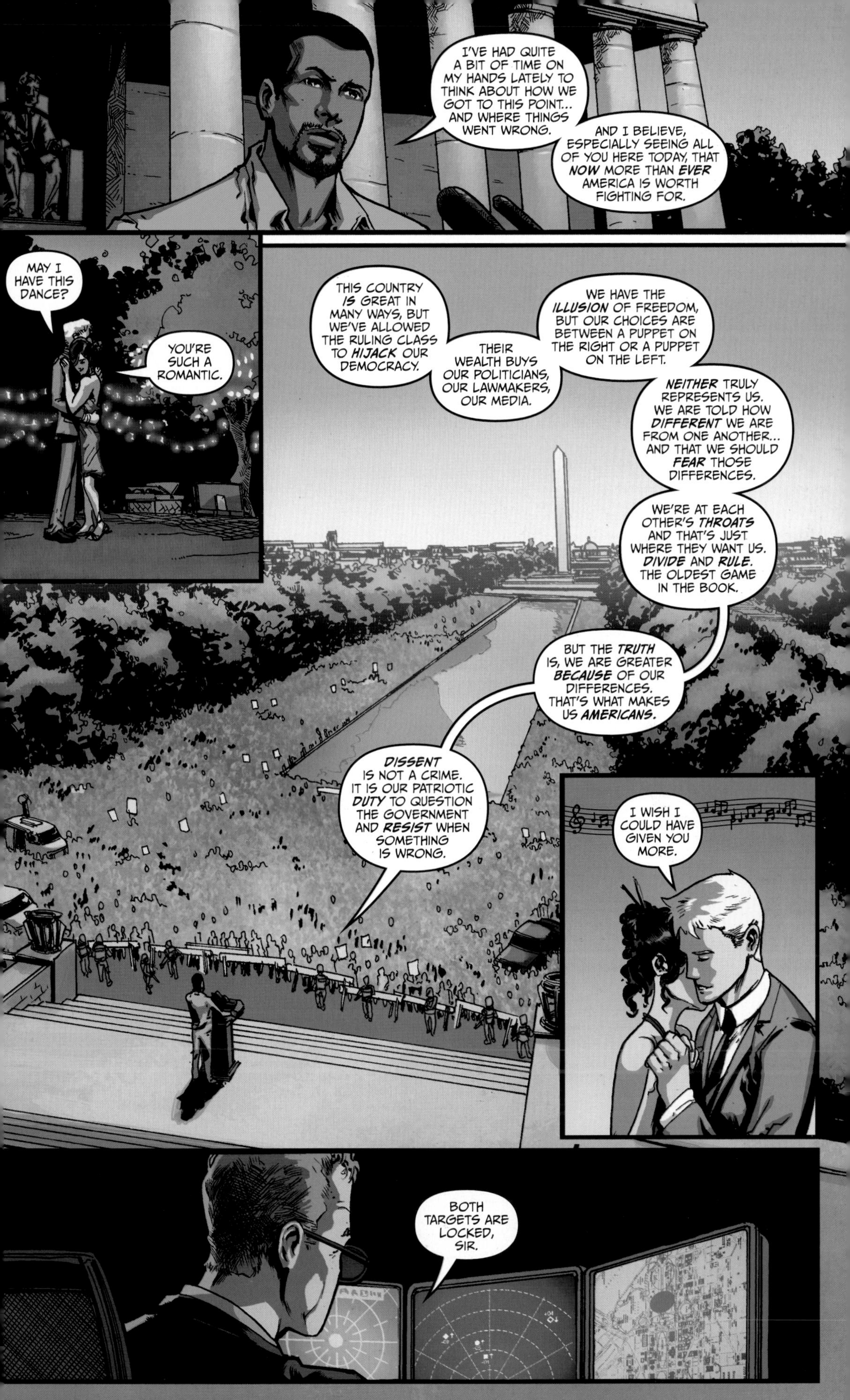

I'VE HAD QUITE A BIT OF TIME ON MY HANDS LATELY TO THINK ABOUT HOW WE GOT TO THIS POINT... AND WHERE THINGS WENT WRONG.
AND I BELIEVE, ESPECIALLY SEEING ALL OF YOU HERE TODAY, THAT *NOW* MORE THAN *EVER* AMERICA IS WORTH FIGHTING FOR.
MAY I HAVE THIS DANCE?
YOU'RE SUCH A ROMANTIC.
THIS COUNTRY *IS* GREAT IN MANY WAYS, BUT WE'VE ALLOWED THE RULING CLASS TO *HIJACK* OUR DEMOCRACY.
THEIR WEALTH BUYS OUR POLITICIANS, OUR LAWMAKERS, OUR MEDIA.
WE HAVE THE *ILLUSION* OF FREEDOM, BUT OUR CHOICES ARE BETWEEN A PUPPET ON THE RIGHT OR A PUPPET ON THE LEFT.
NEITHER TRULY REPRESENTS US. WE ARE TOLD HOW *DIFFERENT* WE ARE FROM ONE ANOTHER... AND THAT WE SHOULD *FEAR* THOSE DIFFERENCES.
WE'RE AT EACH OTHER'S *THROATS* AND THAT'S JUST WHERE THEY WANT US. *DIVIDE* AND *RULE*. THE OLDEST GAME IN THE BOOK.
BUT THE *TRUTH* IS, WE ARE GREATER *BECAUSE* OF OUR DIFFERENCES. THAT'S WHAT MAKES US *AMERICANS*.
DISSENT IS NOT A CRIME. IT IS OUR PATRIOTIC *DUTY* TO QUESTION THE GOVERNMENT AND *RESIST* WHEN SOMETHING IS WRONG.
I WISH I COULD HAVE GIVEN YOU MORE.
BOTH TARGETS ARE LOCKED, SIR.

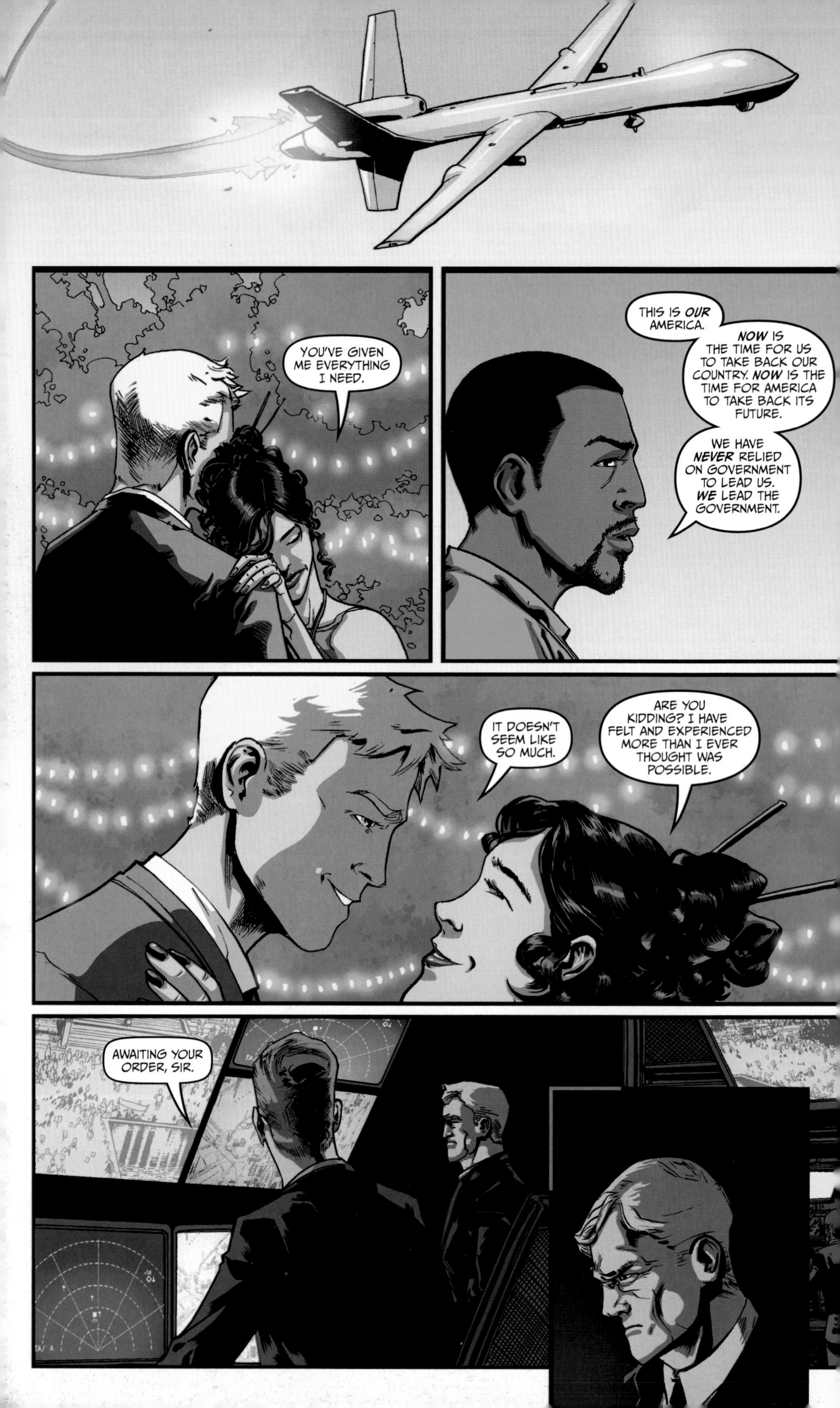
YOU'VE GIVEN ME EVERYTHING I NEED.
THIS IS OUR AMERICA.
NOW IS THE TIME FOR US TO TAKE BACK OUR COUNTRY. NOW IS THE TIME FOR AMERICA TO TAKE BACK ITS FUTURE.
WE HAVE NEVER RELIED ON GOVERNMENT TO LEAD US. WE LEAD THE GOVERNMENT.
IT DOESN'T SEEM LIKE SO MUCH.
ARE YOU KIDDING? I HAVE FELT AND EXPERIENCED MORE THAN I EVER THOUGHT WAS POSSIBLE.
AWAITING YOUR ORDER, SIR.

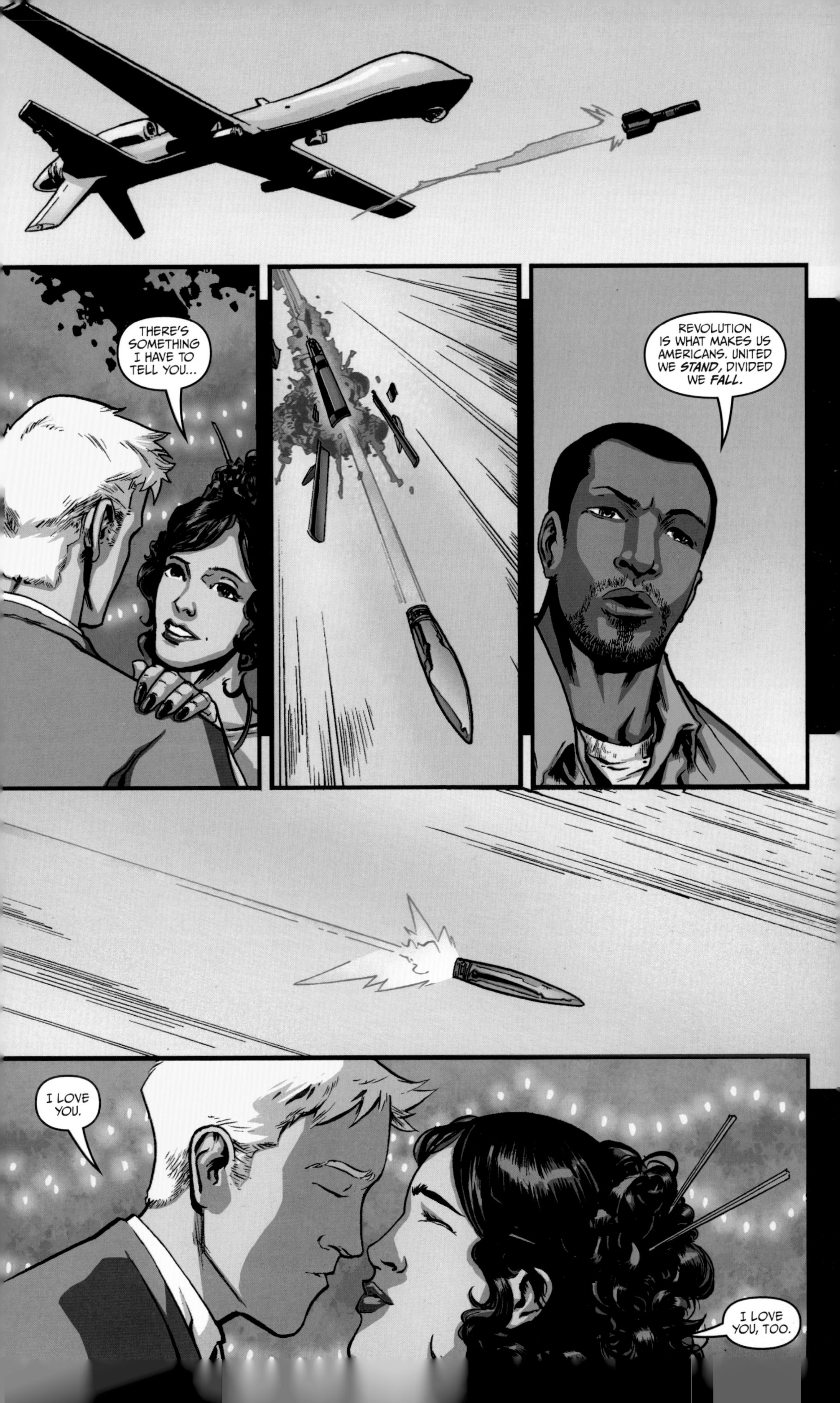
THERE'S SOMETHING I HAVE TO TELL YOU...
REVOLUTION IS WHAT MAKES US AMERICANS. UNITED WE *STAND,* DIVIDED WE *FALL.*
I LOVE YOU.
I LOVE YOU, TOO.

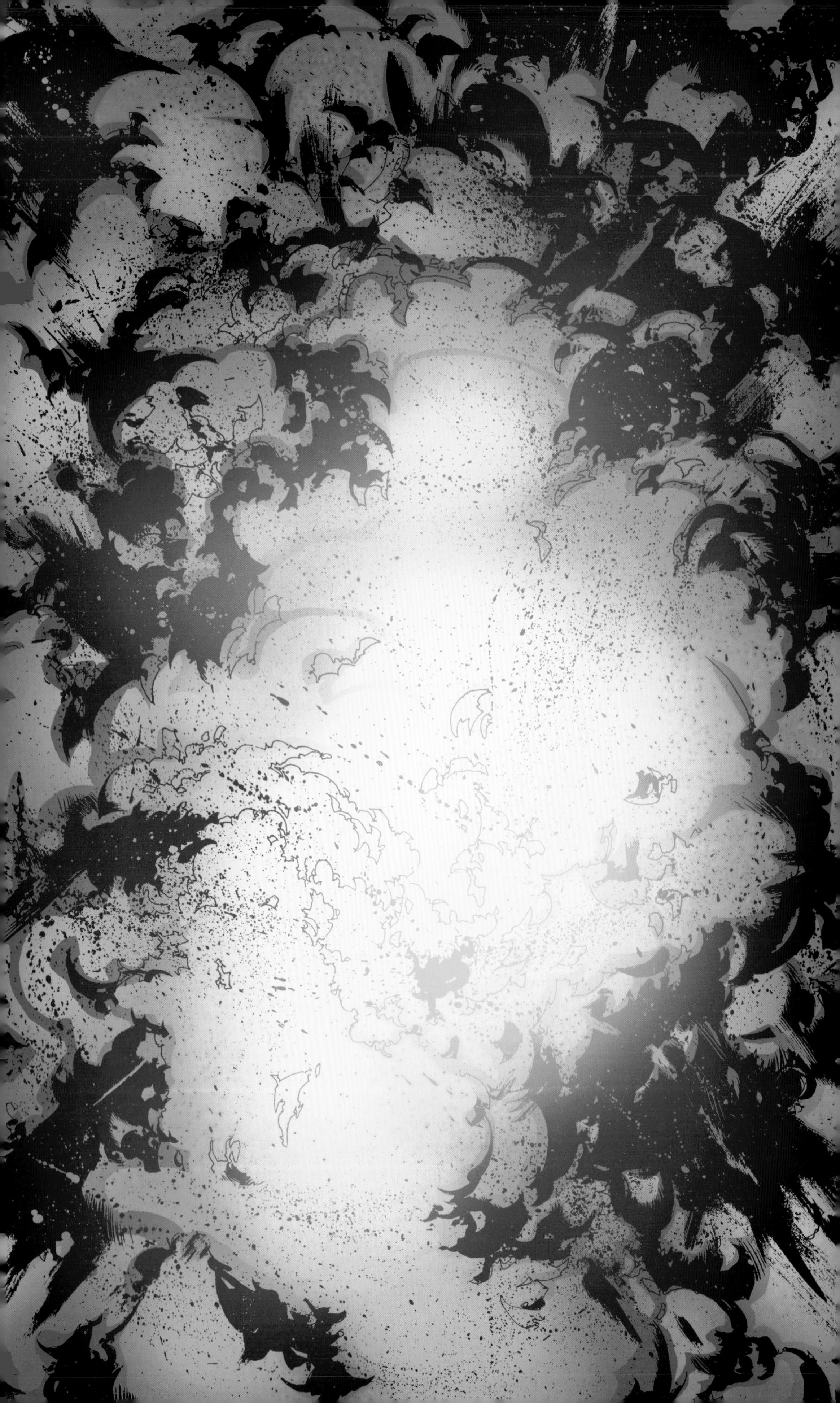

Ten years after his review for the original edition of AMERICAN TERRORIST, Brett Schenker of GraphicPolicy.com interviews writers Tyler & Wendy Chin-Tanner.

It's been ten years since AMERICAN TERRORIST was first released. Can you take us through how the series came about?

TYLER: Comics were born as a response to WWII, so they've always been political. We wanted to draw on that tradition and update it in graphic novel form to tell a politically engaged story set in the real world. We couldn't tell that story with superheroes, so we decided to create heroes who were regular people experiencing the kinds of problems that are reflective of our world and the current historical moment.

WENDY: We began writing AMERICAN TERRORIST during W's second term, but we didn't finish it until after Obama came into office. This made us ask ourselves what actually does and does not change when we elect a different president. As a couple, we were also about to become parents for the first time, so we were thinking very carefully about the kind of world we wanted our child to live in and what our responsibilities were as citizens to give her that world. After our baby was born, having a creative project to work on together in those first dizzying months of parenthood also gave us a space to connect outside of family life. It became an escape, even if it was just in our minds, from the drudgery and domestic intensity of being new parents.

AMERICAN TERRORIST touches on political and social issues we're still dealing with today. How does it feel reflecting on that, especially as it feels we're no closer to solutions?

WENDY: AMERICAN TERRORIST was originally conceived as post-9/11 era narrative. As Americans and as New Yorkers, we couldn't have imagined experiencing an even greater calamity in our lifetime. But here we are, in 2020, in the midst of the Covid-19 pandemic, putting the finishing touches on this new edition quarantined with our family. Like all national emergencies, this one reveals all the leaks in our rapidly sinking ship of state.

TYLER: Going through the book again now, we've been surprised by how persistent the many issues portrayed in it continue to be. In some ways, that's incredibly depressing, but the truth is, these issues are part of the ongoing work of being Americans. Our national values and ideals are rooted in the idea that we the people are responsible for our own government. While we hope as much as anyone else that progress will be made, the questions we grappled with in this book will always be relevant to the inherent struggles of American identity and politics.

How did artist Andy MacDonald come on board the project?

TYLER: We originally reached out to people I knew from the Kubert School and people we met at conventions, but that didn't lead us to the right artist. Finally, I opened up a box of comics and pulled out NYC MECH. Sure, it was robots, but it also featured some beautiful scenes of NYC and the storytelling felt just right for our book.

WENDY: When we reached out to Andy, it wasn't much of a hard sell. We told him the premise and he said, "Count me in."

This is the first time the full color pages by Matt Wilson and Michael Wiggam see print. Was the series always meant to be in color?

TYLER: AMERICAN TERRORIST was always meant to be colored and Matt was on board from the beginning, but then his career really started taking off and he couldn't commit the time to the project. For a while, we couldn't find the right colorist to pick up for him—we couldn't find the right match—and considering that we were going to self-publish the book, it was a lot cheaper for us to put it out in black and white. As it turns out, we discovered Michael shortly after that decision. Thankfully, with the emergence of digital, we were able to put it out in full color without the same financial constraints as print.

The series has so many issues that it discusses or highlights: environmental, civil rights, healthcare, drone strikes. They're all there and each could probably be a story by itself. When developing the story did you debate at all focusing in on fewer issues?

WENDY: Our political environment is a constellation of many different interconnecting issues, so it felt realistic and natural to portray it that way. But we were careful to make sure that everything we wrote about made sense in terms of the interiority and motivations of each of our characters, and those factors dictated their actions and responses to whatever problems we threw their way. We weren't aiming for hyperrealism, but we were trying to strike a balance between an emotional truth and the heightened reality of a political thriller.

The characters in AMERICAN TERRORIST are complicated and diverse. Did you have a favorite to write, and why? And what's your process for writing well-rounded characters with believable dialogue?

WENDY: America is complicated and diverse. Any narrative whose function is to hold up a mirror to America has to reflect its complexity and diversity.

TYLER: Parents shouldn't pick favorites among their children, but Shannon and Michael definitely have fun voices.

WENDY: Our process for writing well-rounded characters is to understand their backstories and motivations to a much larger degree than what's overtly shown on the page. We really get to know them intimately, as people. Then when it comes time for the dialogue, we go back and forth, read it out loud over and over, and rework it until it sounds right. We are willing to go toe to toe over every word.

AMERICAN TERRORIST feels like a call to action, but it allows the reader to decide what exactly that call to action means personally. Was it difficult to find this balance?

TYLER: The idea was not to be prescriptive, but to provoke readers to ask questions and work out the solutions for themselves. We wanted to offer a more in-depth view of issues, their context and their background by portraying people's lived experiences and emotional stakes. Of course, things played out in a hyperbolic way in the book, but the chain of events and consequences are based on how our real world systems and institutions work.

WENDY: We both have backgrounds in teaching, so our tendency is to want to just make people think, not spoon feed them the answers. We identify with Hannah's feeling that critical thinking is one of our most important tools.

AMERICAN TERRORIST feels dangerous, possibly incendiary, in all the right ways. If you were to boil it down into one sentence, or even a word, how would you describe what it means to you?

WENDY: This is why we can't have nice things.

AMERICAN TERRORIST ends on a beat of destruction and loss... right after a beat of hope and promise. How did you decide the ending, and was that an internal discussion, or did you always know?

TYLER: We wanted to end the book without explicitly stating what happened. We wanted to leave the reader on a note of both hope AND destruction, because there always needs to be a level of destruction preceding growth.

WENDY: The question of how much we actually need to burn things down is debatable, but we certainly have to get uncomfortable to get where want to go.

Character designs by Andy MacDonald

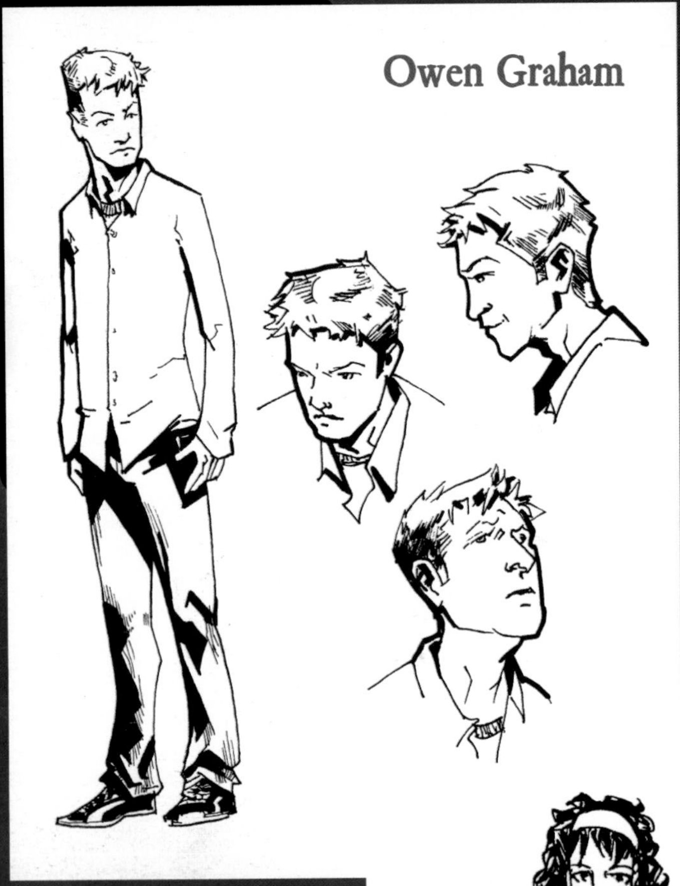

Owen Graham

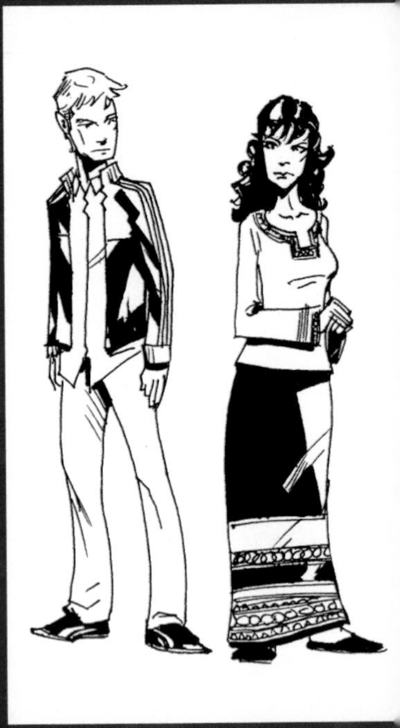

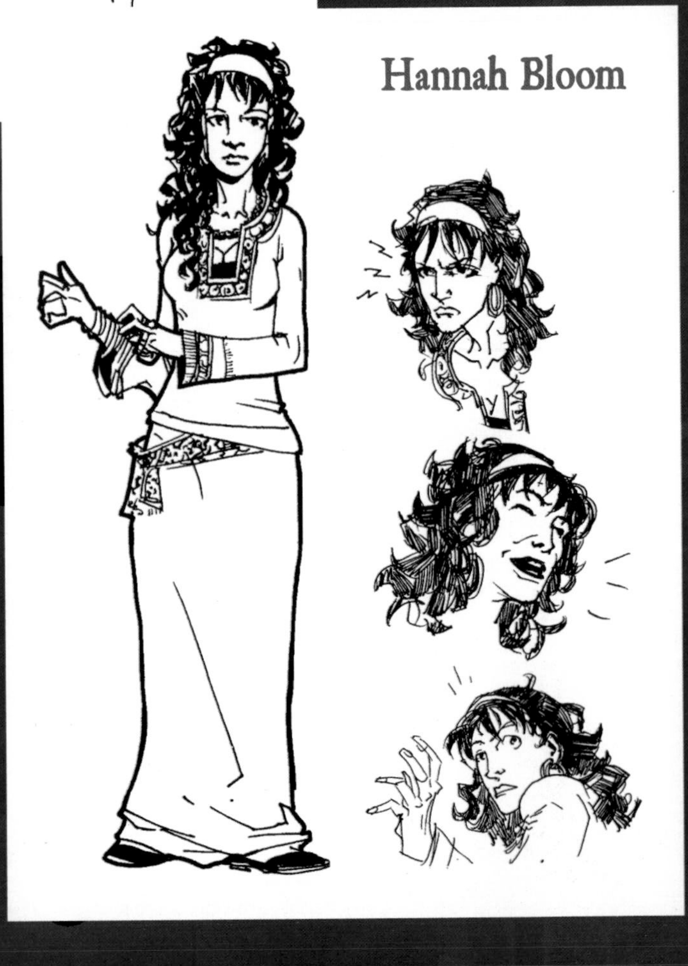

Hannah Bloom

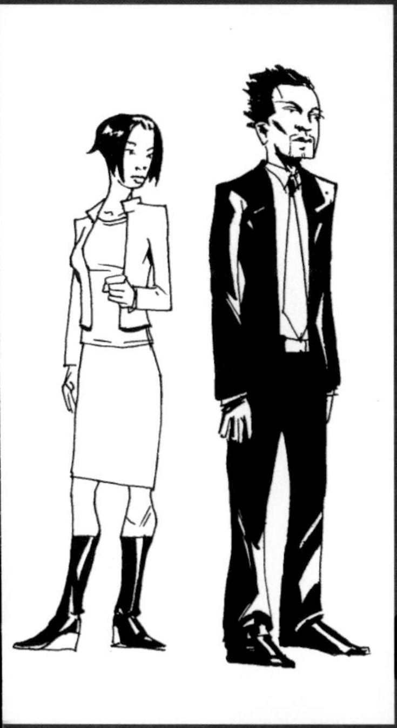

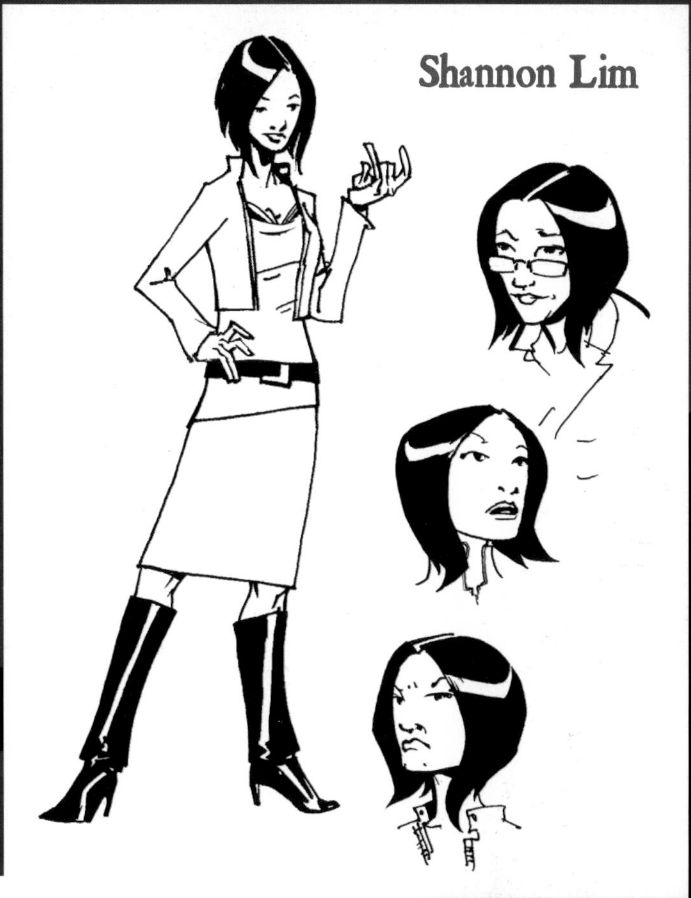
Shannon Lim

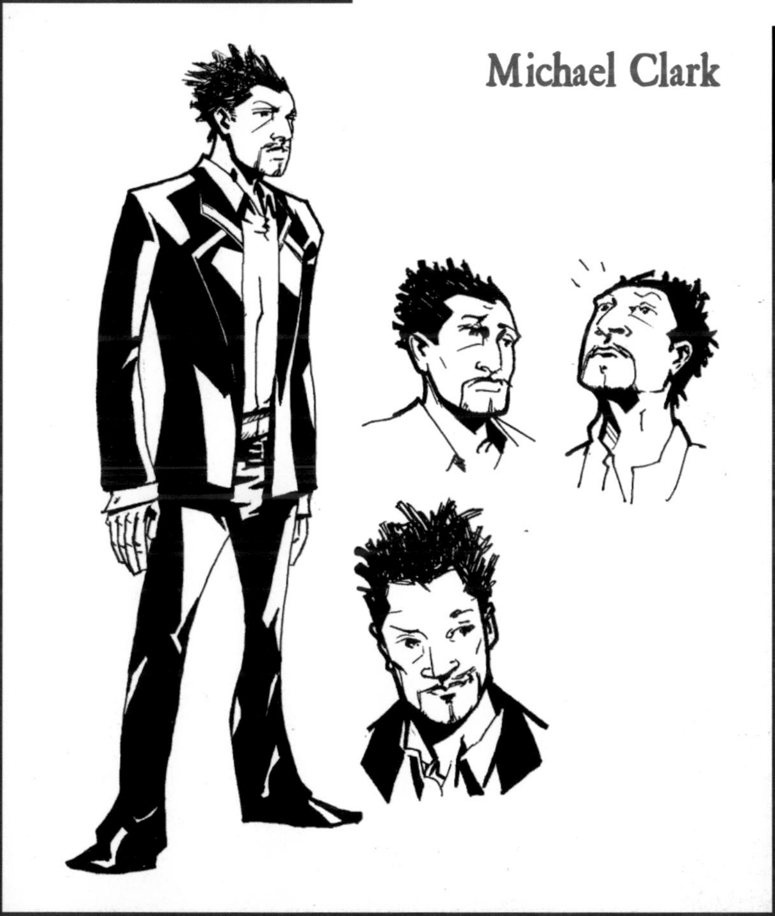
Michael Clark

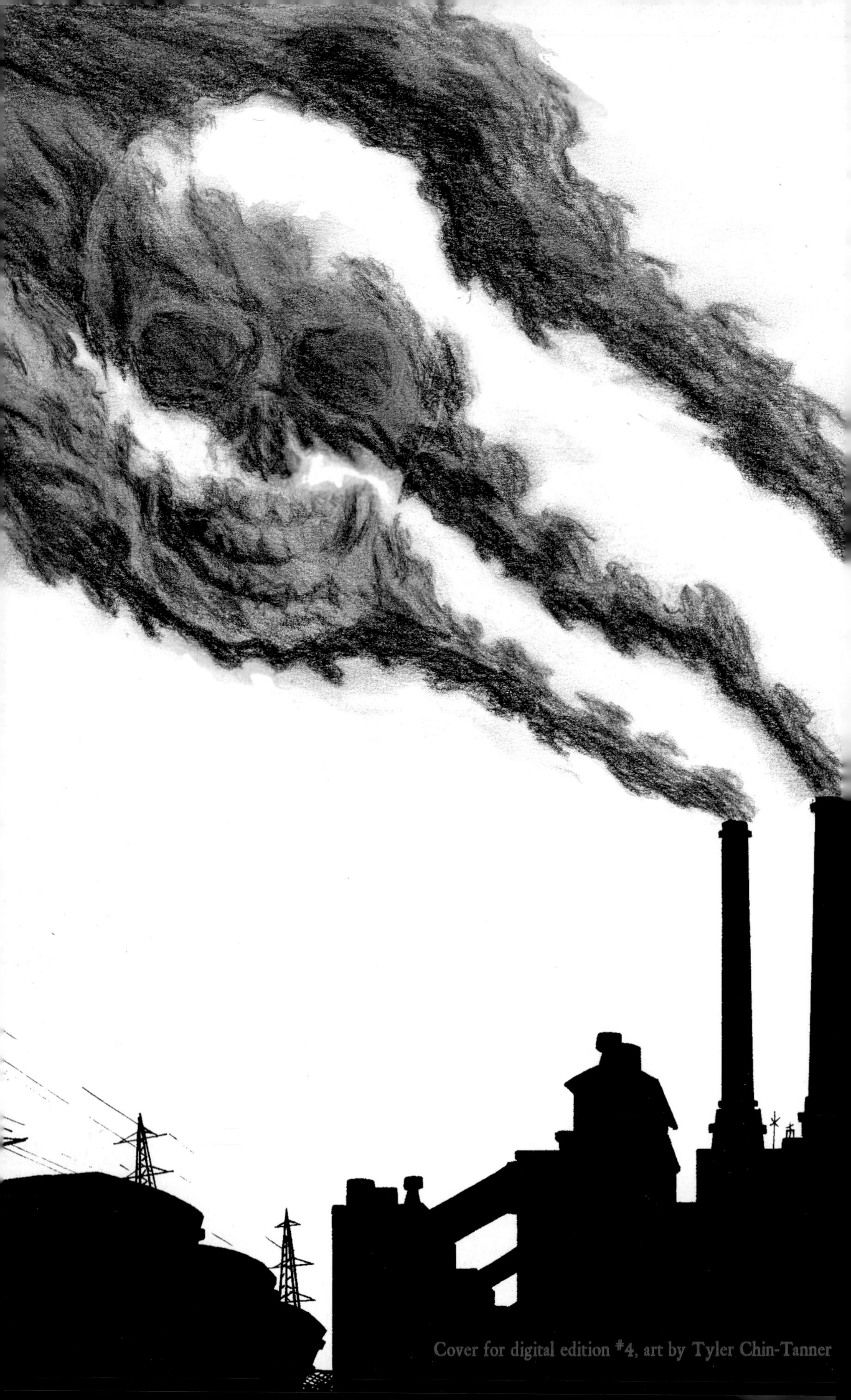

Cover for digital edition #4, art by Tyler Chin-Tanner